TWO VERY DIFFFRENT PEOPLES—
ONE SWORN TO PROTECT THE
GREAT MAMMOTH, THE OTHER
HUNTING IT AS THE ULTIMATE SACRIFICE

**CHA-KWENA**—Born to be shaman, still more boy than man, he is duped by treachery that robs him of the tribe's most precious possession . . . and makes him vow to protect not only his people, but the great beasts of the Earth.

**TA-MAYA**—The headman's sensuously lovely daughter, she is betrothed to her childhood love—until the day the strangers come, and a mysterious warrior awakens her desire . . . but is he monster or man?

**MASAU**—The magnificent mystic warrior of the People of the Watching Star, he believes slaughter and deception can save his tribe—until a woman's love challenges him to choose a different future . . . or face his doom.

**YSUNA**—A beautiful medicine woman driven by visions and lust, she slakes her madness only by blood sacrifice, and lives only to destroy the People of the Red World—and seize incomparable power.

**KOSAR-EH**—Gentle clown and storyteller, left unable to hunt by a childhood injury—but not unwilling to fight when the woman he secretly loves is lured away from her people to her ruin . . . or her murder.

**BANTAM BOOKS BY WILLIAM SARABANDE**

**WOLVES OF THE DAWN**

THE
FIRST
AMERICANS

# THE SACRED STONES

WILLIAM
SARABANDE

Created by the producers of
**The Holts: An American Dynasty**
and **The Children of the Lion.**

*Book Creations Inc., Canaan, NY • Lyle Kenyon Engel, Founder*

DOMAIN™

BANTAM BOOKS
NEW YORK • TORONTO • LONDON • SYDNEY • AUCKLAND

THE SACRED STONES

A Bantam Domain Book / published by arrangement with
Book Creations, Inc.

Bantam edition / November 1991

Produced by Book Creations, Inc.
Lyle Kenyon Engel, Founder

DOMAIN and the portrayal of a boxed "d" are trademarks of
Bantam Books, a division of Bantam Doubleday Dell
Publishing Group, Inc.

ISBN 0-553-29105-X

Published simultaneously in the United States and Canada

Bantam Books are published by Bantam Books, a division of Bantam Doubleday Dell Publishing Group, Inc. Its trademark, consist-
ing of the words "Bantam Books" and the portrayal of a rooster, is
Registered in U.S. Patent and Trademark Office and in other
countries. Marca Registrada. Bantam Books, 666 Fifth Avenue,
New York, New York 10103.

PRINTED IN THE UNITED STATES OF AMERICA

OPM     0 9 8 7 6 5 4 3

*To Karen Nelson, librarian, Big Bear Lake, California, with thanks for all the unsolicited sleuthing on behalf of Torka's band and this new generation of the First Americans!*

THE RED WORLD

NORTH

EAST

LAND OF PEOPLE OF
THE WATCHING STAR

LAND OF GRASS

BLUE MESAS

PROMONTORY

PASS THROUGH MESAS
TO SHI-WANA'S VILLAGE

MASAU'S PASS

RED HILLS

ISH-IWI'S VILLAGE

LAKE

PINYON GROVES

GREAT GATHERING PLACE

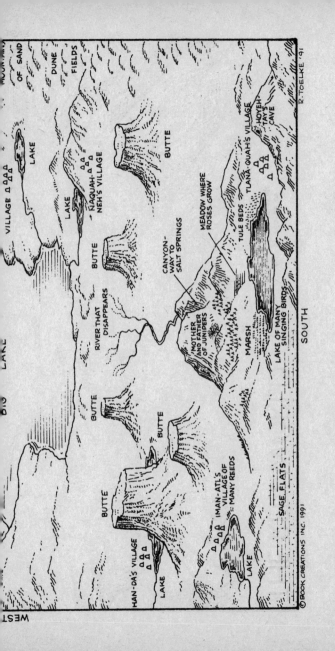

# THE SACRED STONES

# PROLOGUE

# THUNDER IN THE SKY

"Great Spirit . . . Grandfather of the People . . . White Giant of Many Names . . . hear me. I call to you, I raise my arms, I turn. I set my face toward the four corners of the world, where the spirits of the wind are born and where you, Thunder in the Sky, walk in the flesh of clouds and in the shadowing power of eagles. Behold me: I am Ysuna, Daughter of the Sun, wisewoman of the People of the Watching Star. On this dawn I bring you a gift of life. On this dawn I bring you a bride. May the blood of this people and of Thunder in the Sky be one!"

A shiver of delight ran beneath Ah-nee's skin as she listened to the wisewoman's words. Ah-nee was twelve years old and far from home. But she had been a woman for eighteen moons, and when the sun rose above the curve of the western hills and the daybreak star faded from the sky, she would become a bride.

Naked and glistening from head to toe with oil that had been rendered from mammoth fat and colored with powdered red hematite and ground willow buds, she stood trembling with excitement outside the ceremonial sweat lodge from which she had just emerged. Nai, the young woman who had been her attendant during the past four days and nights of ritual purification, emerged from the sweat lodge to stand close at her back.

"Remember, do not turn around!"

Ah-nee heard Nai's warning clearly even though drums were sounding so loudly that they shook the world.

Nai's command continued in an imperative whisper. "Do not speak! No matter what you see or hear from this moment on, obey in all things. And above all else, you must not be afraid!"

*Afraid?* Ah-nee found the advice preposterous. Her

1

head went high. This was the predawn of her wedding morning. Why should she be afraid?

The drumbeat was growing even louder. She stood as tall as her meager height would allow, thinking of Nai's words and remembering that the old women of the Red World had warned her that Spirit Rat, Eater of Courage, Father of Fear, would come to her this day. But they had been wrong, completely and absolutely wrong! The sweet sadness that was homesickness touched her. If only the old women of the Red World were with her now! She had not expected to miss them so much or to long for their loving counsel.

She sighed. There was no use mourning for that which could not be. The old women of the Red World were far away to the southwest, asleep in the reed-covered lakeside lodges of her people. For love of a wandering stranger she had spurned their advice, disdained the misgivings of old Ish-iwi, shaman of her band, and resolutely turned her back upon them and their ways. It would be many moons before she would see any of them again.

She took a deep, deliberate breath and succeeded in driving away her recollections of home and loved ones. In time they would realize that she had made the right decision. In time they would nod and smile and admit that she had not been wrong to leave them. In time . . . but now the moment was as sweet as a freshly dug camas root. She savored it as she stared straight ahead, across the Village of the People of the Watching Star. The vast, circular sprawl of tall, cone-shaped, garishly painted hide-covered lodges still looked strange to her. She reminded herself that she had chosen to be there, that she was about to become the woman of the man of her choice, and that for want of him, she had voluntarily traveled north into a strange land. She had lived among his people for a moon now. As he had promised, they had treated her better than she had ever been treated in her life.

Expectation stirred within her. Lest her feet touch the earth on this sacred occasion, a rare carpet of long-haired mammoth hide had been rolled out before her. Overlaid with freshly cut boughs of artemesia, the finely combed pelage, gray leaves, and tender new stalks tickled the soles of her feet. A fragrant crown of silver-leafed purple sage circled her brow; its rich, herbaceous scent was heady. She inhaled hungrily, not only because it was sacred to the People of the Watching Star but because the smell of sage was reminiscent of home—of broad, arid plains to the west of the distant lake country where her father, brothers, and the other men of her band hunted rabbits and antelope at this time of year.

Clutched in her small right hand was a blue-berried juniper branch. It, too, was sacred to the People of the Watching Star and also carried the scent of home—of autumn treks into red-earthed highlands, where juniper woods yielded to pinyon forests. Her people gathered pine nuts there until the first snows of winter sent them following deer and small, striped horses to shelter beside ice-free springs within the foothills.

She sighed again. Her memories were as heady as the evening air; but the night was nearly over, and this was not a time for thoughts of the past. In her left hand was a gift for the man who would soon become her husband. It was a timeworn dagger, which appeared to be made of bone but possessed the weight and texture of polished stone. The medicine woman, Ysuna, had brought it to her on the morning of her first day within the sweat lodge.

"For the bride," the wisewoman had explained. "Bathe it in the sweat of your body. Polish it with your hair. Keep it close to your flesh in these hours of purification. Then bring it forth to him."

"I thank you, Ysuna, but I have made gifts for him in the manner of my people: a new sleeping robe of twisted rabbit fur, sandals of brushwood, and—"

"No. Nothing from the Red World. You must give him this sacred stone dagger, my child. It has been with my people since time beyond beginning. Can you make out the carvings on the blade? It is said that they were incised by magic in days when the White Giant roared, the mountains walked, and all the people of this world were one. The stone is old, so very old. Touch it, Little Sister. It is a portion of the scattered bones of First Man and First Woman. When all the bones are found, mammoth will return to the world in great numbers, and all the people of the Four Winds will be one again as they feast upon the sacred meat that once sustained their ancestors."

Ah-nee remembered running a finger down the strangely textured blade and informing Ysuna softly: "In the Red World, whence I came, the meat of the mammoth is forbidden. Such stones as these are sacred relics. Old Ish-iwi, shaman of my band, possesses one that is no bigger than an acorn. It has these same marks. The wise man has said that they are the marks of Life Giver. Ish-iwi has told my people that it is our link with the past and with our ancestors. Without it our band would lose its strength and hope."

The expression upon Ysuna's ageless, extraordinarily beautiful face had gone as blank and smooth as an unused drumskin. "Life Giver?"

"Yes. Great Ghost Spirit. Grandfather of All."

"Ah, yes, of course. Life Giver. Great Ghost Spirit. Thunder in the Sky. It *is* the same then. Are there sacred stones to be found among other bands than yours in the Red World?"

"Oh, yes. As many stones as there are tribes. What do the marks on the blade mean, Ysuna?"

"That is not for you to know, Little Sister. The meaning is best left in the care of wise ones. When the time comes, bring the dagger forth to the one you have chosen. He will understand its significance even if you do not."

Ah-nee's heartbeat quickened now as her memories faded. She could see him—Maliwal, the one they called Wolf. How she loved him! He was clad in a grotesque hooded leather cape that made his head look like a tuskless mammoth's, complete with elephantine ears and a trunk. The well-preserved mammoth's trunk flopped in front of his face. His body was painted gray, and his arms and limbs were resplendent with the colors and patterns that symbolized life to his people. He ascended the broad stone steps of the enormous platformed dais before which the wisewoman stood with her arms raised skyward and her head thrown back.

*How beautiful she looks,* thought Ah-nee, distracted from the sight of Maliwal's bizarre raiment. Even with her back turned, Ysuna commanded attention. Among the People of the Red World it was unheard of for a woman to be one with the spirits. But Ysuna was not of the Red World; she was a daughter of the People of the Watching Star and no ordinary woman. It was rumored that she had borne witness to the beginning of the world. Yet, despite her years, Ysuna's hair was as black as the wings of a raven and so long that had she stepped backward, her bare, tattooed heels could have trod upon its feather-tasseled ends. Now, as always, the wisewoman was clothed in her astounding robe of skins taken from the small, yellow-backed brown birds that always rode high upon the head and shoulders of the mammoth.

Taller than most men and as straight backed as a fire-hardened spear shaft, Ysuna was the focus of her people's lives. Men worshiped her, women feared her, and children were forbidden to walk within the fall of her shadow. Dogs that crossed it were clubbed to death. Nevertheless, from Ah-nee's first tremulous moments in this great camp of strangers, Ysuna had taken her under her wing, calling her Little Sister and doting upon her with a tenderness that could only be described as motherly. Ah-nee's heart swelled with love for the wisewoman. Ah-nee's own mother was long dead, and she had found in Ysuna a cherished replacement.

The girl smiled. The crinkling of her eyes caused mammoth oil to seep into the corners of her lids. Remembering Nai's warning not to move, Ah-nee tried to blink it away, but it was no use. Through a filmy red haze she continued to stare ahead, past Ysuna to the dais.

It was the largest, most amazing, and completely terrifying structure that Ah-nee had ever seen, and it had taken the People of the Watching Star four days to construct. Bonefires burned on either side of two huge, four-man drums, which flanked the stairway. The dais was framed entirely by mammoth bones and elaborately adorned with long strands of eagle feathers, multicolored tubular beads, and disks of bone. It towered above the ground, a monstrous replication of a living mammoth.

Maliwal was standing on a raftlike platform of mammoth ribs positioned between two halves of a severed mammoth skull. On either side of him, the skull's hollow eyes stared sightlessly ahead while its massive tusks extended forward like two polished white tree trunks.

Every man, woman, and child of the People of the
Watching Star assembled in two long columns on either
side of the dais. Even their mangy, quarrelsome dogs
were with them as, in ceremonial paint, feathers, and
garments of pigmented skins, they stared at her and shouted
her name.

"Ah-nee!"

She flinched, startled. Maliwal did not call her name;
he trumpeted it in as good an imitation of a mammoth as
any man could hope to make.

"Ah-nee!" The people echoed him in unison, chanting
her name, trilling their tongues, shaking animal-scrotum
rattles, and whistling fiercely through hollow bones as the
dogs barked and howled and the beat of the drums
intensified.

Overwhelmed, Ah-nee stared at the drums, unlike
any she had seen in the land of her own people. They
were suspended above the earth from upright posts of
concentrically arranged mammoth femurs. Nai had called
them thunder drums. Six feet in circumference, they were
great circles of bent willow wood, over which mammoth
skin had been stretched taut, then warmed over sacred
fires until all moisture had been removed. Each was struck
by four men who wailed in cadence with the pounding of
their fur-padded bone beaters, but Ah-nee barely heard
them.

Ysuna had turned toward her. The wisewoman was no
longer alone before the dais. *He*—Masau, mystic warrior
of the People of the Watching Star and younger brother of
Maliwal—had joined her.

Ah-nee's body sang whenever she looked at him. Her
mouth went dry. She swallowed; it did not help. Masau
looked at her, his dark eyes narrowed with speculation
within the black mask of tattooing. He had recently returned to his people from a hunting trek to the west.

Without doubt, he was the most magnificent man she
had ever seen. Did Maliwal suspect how attracted she was
to Mystic Warrior? she wondered. And if he did, what
must he think?

In the glow of the ceremonial fires that had been
heaped high with dried bones, precious wood, and baskets

full of sagebrush, Ah-nee looked guiltily away from Masau and focused her attention upon Maliwal.

Her man-to-be stood tall, a solitary figure against the fading night. Maliwal was strong and clever and exceedingly good to look upon—even when he was dressed as a mammoth! Not one man among his own people came close to equaling him in stature, wisdom, or consideration of her every whim. Despite her attraction to his younger brother, she had no regrets about becoming Maliwal's woman. Soon she would make a gift of herself to him. The thought made her shiver with pride and anticipation.

"Come!" With outstretched arms Maliwal was gesturing her forward. His teeth showed white in his gray-painted face as he held up the trunk of the mammoth so that she could see his wide and winning smile—a smile just for her. She nearly swooned with pleasure and was sorry when he allowed the trunk of his mammoth mask to fall before his face.

Now he began to dance. He swayed, he beckoned, he trumpeted. He turned his buttocks toward her, shaking them as he flicked the tufted mammoth tail that was attached to the back of his loincloth; then he turned again, leaped high in the air, and faced her. Working his hips, he jerked up on a cord that erected the ankle-length front half of his loincloth. It was no ordinary groin cover; long and pendulous, it was a remnant of a male mammoth, which could never serve a human female, except in her nightmares.

The people roared with laughter, and Ah-nee felt her face flush. For all her eagerness to become the woman of this handsome big-game hunter of the north, she was still a virgin.

"Come!" Maliwal trumpeted again, hoisting his loin cover high to reveal his fully erect and engorged tattooed penis beneath it. "Come, Daughter of the People of the Watching Star! Come, Ah-nee! Come to Thunder in the Sky! It is time!"

Maliwal's mammoth dance had gone beyond the subtlety of symbolism. His male part was big, very big, and Ah-nee's thighs tightened defensively. And yet, deep within her loins, the fire of receptiveness was ignited by the sight of him. She was moist, throbbing, and eager to receive that for which she had longed since the first moment she had set eyes upon him.

"You must go to him," Nai whispered at her back. "*Now!*"

"Come!" he called again. "As the mammoth has at last returned to feed in the marshes of Eagle Lake, so now must Ah-nee come to Thunder in the Sky!"

She wished that Maliwal would use his own name. She wished that he would speak of the joining of man to woman, not of woman to mammoth. She could not understand his preoccupation with the animals. Everything his people did was associated with the great tuskers. Mammoth were totem to her people, too, and rare in the lakelands to the south. In these hard grasslands of the north, where mammoth were more scarce than even giant sloths, saber-toothed cats, and long-horned bison, Ah-nee could not understand why Maliwal's people hunted them. Even now, in this sacred ritual of marriage, her man-to-be was acting out some strange display on behalf of the great mammoth spirit, Thunder in the Sky—as though Maliwal and the spirit were one. It was a disturbing thought. What would the old women of the Red World say if they could see and hear him now? Ah-nee wondered.

*I told you so.*

The girl gritted her teeth. She would not let her memories of the well-meaning but easily frightened old women ruin the most wonderful night of her life. When the ceremony was over and Maliwal and she were alone in each other's arms at last, he would know soon enough that it was far more enjoyable to be a man than a mammoth.

Nai was twisting the knuckles of her fist in the small of Ah-nee's back, urging her on. It was time to ascend the dais, to take the husband of her choice. Ah-nee began to walk forward. She moved slowly, as though in a dream. The faces of the People of the Watching Star seemed to float by . . . such serious faces, mouths set, eyes full of secrets. Why were they no longer smiling?

"Behold!" they cried as one.

The beat of the drums quickened, pounding in her head and heart.

"Behold the bride!" the men shouted in unison, extending their hands and shaking their scrotum rattles close to her face so their fingers touched her as she passed.

The beat of drums grew louder.

"She is beautiful! She is perfect! A worthy bride!" proclaimed the women, trilling their tongues as they reached to touch her.

And still the beat of drums grew faster, louder.

"She comes!" echoed the children as they, too, reached out.

It seemed as though not a portion of her skin had not been host to questing fingertips. Then the drums abruptly stopped. Startled by the sudden silence, Ah-nee stopped, too, at the base of the dais.

High above her on the platform, Maliwal was standing still now, arms out, loincloth down, his face freed of the mammoth mask, which he had flung over his back. How handsome he was. How welcoming as he smiled and spoke her name with infinite love and admiration.

Ysuna stood before her. Masau, the mystic warrior, magnificent in a robe of eagle feathers and a plumed headdress such as Ah-nee had never seen, was at the wisewoman's side. One of his spears was in his hand. Briefly she wondered why, and then pondered the meaning of his name. Mystic Warrior. The word *mystic* was familiar enough, but the term *warrior* was alien to her. It did not matter, not now. His cold, dark eyes, like obsidian in moonlight, were on her. She flinched as though cut by them. She did not like the look in his eyes. She caught her breath and averted her gaze, grateful now that she was to be for Maliwal and not for his younger brother.

"Little Sister! At last the moment comes!" Ysuna was radiant.

Ah-nee sighed with pleasure as the wisewoman swept her into a loving embrace. She could have stayed close to Ysuna forever, but the moment passed, and Ysuna stepped back.

"How young and perfect you are, Little Sister. Will you name me Sister as well?"

"Yes, and gladly, for truly you are the sister and the mother that I have sorely missed."

Ysuna's chin went up. Her nostrils expanded, and her long eyes narrowed. A pale blue vein pulsed in the ex-

posed length of her throat. "And will you now call yourself
forevermore a daughter of the People of the Watching Star
and come consenting to this moment of union with us?"

Ah-nee hesitated. It had occurred to her that even
though marriage would make her a woman of Maliwal and
Ysuna's tribe, she would nevertheless always be a daughter of her own band, a child of the People of the Red
World. But if she spoke her thoughts aloud, Ysuna would
certainly be offended. Ah-nee wished only to please the
wisewoman in all things. And so she said openly and
without regret, certain that Ysuna had never honored anyone as she was being honored now, "Yes, my sister. I *will*
call myself a daughter of the People of the Watching Star.
Yes! I *do* come consenting to this moment of union with
Maliwal and with your people!"

Ysuna lowered her head. Her eyes were very wide
now, her features composed. Her skin appeared translucent in the light of flames and fading stars. "And with the
Great Ghost Spirit? With Thunder in the Sky?"

Ah-nee was keenly aware of every eye in the band
upon her. Even the dogs were staring, waiting breathlessly. Masau's eyes were half-closed with speculation. A
muscle worked high at his jawline, but he did not speak.
Ah-nee was glad; the man put her on edge, and it was
obvious that her response would be of great importance.
She wanted to say the right thing. The People of the
Watching Star were her people now, and she wanted to
make them happy with her. She wanted the moment and
the night to be perfect so that her marriage to Maliwal
would be flawless, too. She swallowed. "Yes. I come consenting to Thunder in the Sky."

The sigh of relief that went out of every mouth was
obliterated by the sudden frenzied beating of the drums.
Ysuna's features expanded into a mask of triumph as she
flung up her arms. But it was Masau who spoke clearly
and coldly and loudly enough for all to hear:

"So be it! Ah-nee comes consenting to Thunder in the
Sky! Let no man or woman or child ever say otherwise!"

Ah-nee almost laughed with pleasure as Ysuna cried
out in joyous ecstasy, "Go then, my little sister! Go to that
which you seek of your own will! Thunder in the Sky
awaits his bride!"

As the People of the Watching Star cheered she obeyed eagerly. The daybreak star was fading in the west. Soon the night would die, and the sun would be born again. Ah-nee held the juniper bough in one hand and the dagger in the other as her small, bare feet carried her quickly up the steps to her waiting man-to-be. Breathless, she stood before him at last.

Maliwal grinned when he took the bough in his left hand and accepted the dagger with his right. Ah-nee smiled when she passed the gifts to him. He traced the contours of her body with the juniper branch, forcing Ah-nee to suppress a giggle. Ultimately she failed; the bough tickled her skin. She was relieved when he tucked the branch into the waistband that supported his loincloth. His strong arm suddenly drew her close, and she gasped with pleasure. The dagger was in his right hand, and the girl could feel its blade pressed flat beneath her breasts.

Maliwal bent close and spoke in a low, rattling purr. "I saw the way you have looked at him ever since he came back to the village. Four days and nights of purification have not wiped the wanting of my brother from your heart."

The words struck her dumb, as did the dark glint of murderous intent within his eyes. She tried to twist away, but it was no use. His lips twitched as he snarled and drove the dagger deep.

She screamed, not loudly. It was a soft cry of incredulity. As she stiffened in his arms he twisted the knife, then pulled it out and jabbed deep again, searching for her heart.

"No . . . don't . . . noooo . . ." The protest bled out of her as she went lax in his arms.

At last he let her fall. Confused, unable to speak, she lay on her back, staring up at him. The knife was in his hand. The sun was rising behind him, but the world was growing dark.

Ysuna appeared above her, and hope flared bright and real. Ah-nee stared upward. Ysuna leaned over her and smiled. Now, for the first time, Ah-nee noticed that beneath the shaman's feathered cloak was a heavy gorget woven of sinew and tufts of human hair. Small, irregularly shaped bones dangled from the collar and clicked in the wind. No! Not bones! *Stones*—sacred stones—one of which was the size of an acorn. Although Ah-nee's vision was failing, the little stone somehow loomed large in her misted eyes. She had seen it before, in the Red World, around the neck of old Ish-iwi, shaman of her band.

Ah-nee reached up with one small hand. "Sister . . . Ysuna . . . Mother . . ." Ah-nee was not certain if she spoke the words or thought them.

Ysuna did not move. She stood tall as the dawn wind lifted her hair. Her smile lengthened into the long, sinuous smile of a sun-warmed serpent. "Yes, Little Sister. It *is* Ish-iwi's sacred stone. I will have them all in time." Her brows expanded across her unlined forehead, and she said in a low, throaty voice to the brothers, "All is not lost. Did you hear her words? She still names us as her own. Finish her quickly, Masau, before she speaks again and offends the god. Thunder in the Sky is awaiting his bride."

The shadow of death fell upon Ah-nee. She saw its face as the mystic warrior ascended to the platform, hesitated for a moment, then raised his spear. Weak from shock and loss of blood, Ah-nee felt no pain when the lanceolate spearhead sliced through her breastbone and found her heart. There was only light—a bright, explosive light followed by a cold, terrible pressure, which suddenly expanded, then collapsed inward into darkness.

Ah-nee could no longer see the wisewoman. Her spirit was leaving her body. She could feel herself drifting away. "Why?" The question sighed out of the dying girl with her last breath.

Ysuna made no attempt to answer. She knelt and checked for a pulse at Ah-nee's throat. Finding none, she nodded, pleased. "Good. She is dead. Thunder in the Sky will be pleased by this sacrifice, as he has been pleased by all the others, as he will be pleased by all those that will follow."

"What about the captive old wise man who followed her here from the place where the two flat-topped mountains meet?"

"Is Ish-iwi still alive? You fool, Maliwal! He knows too much. Go! Kill him. Your brother will stand with me now to do what must be done."

\*   \*   \*

From his vantage point atop a high hill, Ish-iwi, the old wise man, looked down upon the village of the People of the Watching Star. Gagged and bound by his wrists to a stake of mammoth bone, he had witnessed it all: the construction of the dais, the girl's ascent to the platform, and then her death. He had not expected that. Nor could he understand what he was seeing now: They were butchering her—*skinning* her—and singing while they did it!

Sickened with horror, he averted his eyes. His breath came in ragged gasps that scraped his parched throat; it had been three days since he had partaken of water or food. When ants had begun to explore his body, when the first small, questing insect pincers had closed upon his flesh to draw blood and pain, he had winced and shaken himself, raging against his gag and thongs. It had done no good. Stimulated by his movement, the ants, resting by night and feeding by day, continued to make short work of him. Now, as the morning sun warmed the grasses of the hilltop, they were coming once again for their daily feeding. He was beyond caring. Swollen and bleeding, his wrists burned and oozed serum from bone-deep wounds that he had inflicted upon himself while desperately struggling to be free.

"Have you enjoyed the entertainment?"

Startled, the old man looked up, and a low moan of hatred went out of him. Maliwal, spear in hand, a wolfish grin on his broad, handsome face, was standing over him. The hunter had removed the grotesque cape, and blood splotched his bare, painted chest and his right hand and forearm. Ish-iwi raised his head defiantly. His loathing for the hunter was so intense, it was almost sweet to him. The blood that spattered Maliwal's flesh was Ah-nee's, the poor, foolish child. He had warned her against leaving her people, and the old women had counseled her not to go. But she had refused to listen. Ah-nee had never been one for listening.

"What is it, old man? Are you not glad to see me?" Maliwal laughed as he hunkered down and, with his spear resting across his thighs, balanced on the balls of his moccasined feet. "You do not look well. I was not certain if you would still be alive. It is good that you have lasted long enough to observe the ceremony. It is a ritual not to be forgotten, don't you agree?"

The old man growled and glared.

Maliwal laughed again. "What? Can't speak with a gag in your mouth? And you a magic man! What would your people think of your power if they could see you now, eh?" He clucked his tongue in admonishment, then leaned close to speak in the tone of a conspirator. "No one from your Red World has ever witnessed what your old eyes have seen. It's an honor, you know. Had my brother been the one to have found you stalking about at the edges of our encampment, he would have killed you immediately. But I have always been one to take my time about such things. Why rush that which brings pleasure, eh? Besides, I thought that you would be grateful to be allowed to see *real* magic before you die! What's that you say? Oh, the gag . . ."

Ish-iwi winced despite himself as Maliwal suddenly jabbed forward with his stone-headed spear to slice through the gag. The long, exquisitely sharp, leaf-shaped projectile point opened a five-inch gash in his cheek. Maliwal's smile became a smirk when he saw the blood.

The old man would not give his tormentor satisfaction by reacting to his torment. He was already half-dead from thirst, hunger, and exposure, not to mention from the slow poisoning of the ants. What was a little more pain? Nothing.

He spat out the wad of nettles that had been jammed into his mouth and held in place by the buckskin gag. The nettles had done their work; his tongue was numb and swollen to three times its normal size. His jaw ached horribly as he worked it from side to side. He wished that he could massage it, but his hands were still bound, and he would die before he would show weakness by asking Maliwal to untie them.

"Well?" Maliwal prodded with the word as well as with the tip of his spear. "What did you think? She died well, eh?"

The question nearly undid the old man's resolve. "She *died*." The affirmation stung his spirit more cruelly than the acidic bites of the ants had stung his flesh.

Maliwal shrugged. "It had to be."

"Why? She trusted you. She loved you."

"They all trust me. They all love me. Right to the end." Maliwal's brow came down. Worry replaced amusement in his eyes. "This one . . . she should not have screamed."

Incredulous, the old man's mind focused upon only one word: "*All?*"

"Did you think that Ah-nee was the first?" He laughed. "No. Since Thunder in the Sky first spoke his will to Ysuna, there have been many—daughters from the People of the Grass, daughters from the People of the Mountains . . . Now that no more mammoth are to be found to the east and west, we go south and take the daughters of the People of the Red World."

"Why?"

"Ysuna has told us how it must be. At first there were those who doubted her, but no more. Each time a bride has been sacrificed, the Great Spirit has sent mammoth to feed his People of the Watching Star." Maliwal's manner became relaxed, open, friendly. "So few mammoth can be found in the world these days. Have you noticed this, old man? And yet the number of the People of the Watching Star increases. Our tribe is great, and we must have mammoth meat if it is to remain so. When the cow mammoth that comes to drink at Eagle Lake has been slaughtered and consumed, we will break camp and move farther south. There are still mammoth to be hunted on the shores of the many lakes of the Red World. But do not worry, Ish-iwi—we will not tell the people of your little band how your magic powers failed you at the end of your days." He smiled. "You should not have followed the girl."

"I did not. I followed one whom I suspected of being a thief. I followed *you*. You betrayed my trust and stole the sacred stone that has been entrusted to the wise men of my band since time beyond beginning. I should never have shown you where I kept it."

"Do not feel too badly. They all have shown me what I have asked to see. All the old men, the 'wise' men, the age-addled fools who have been trusted to guard that which they are unworthy of possessing. When you first discovered that the sacred stone was missing, you no doubt wondered if you had misplaced it. You looked! You worried! You tried not to think that old men always forget where they put things. But you are no ordinary old man. No, you are a wise man! And even though you have lived longer than any man among my people is allowed to live, you must have begun to remember little by little the interest that I, a stranger, took in a relic that should have been of little import to me!"

The old man's mouth had gone dry. He stared, shamed by the truth. "I . . . no . . . it was not like that."

"Of course it was! It was exactly like that! How long did it take you to work up the fortitude to admit to your people that the sacred stone was gone, much less voice your suspicion that I had stolen it? What happened then? I will tell you: Because you are an old man who has been misplacing things for a very long time, no one believed your accusation. I, Maliwal, a stranger from a distant land, had won their confidence, while you, Ish-iwi, had lost it . . . most likely long before I ever arrived. And so, when no one was looking, you came alone after me in the hope of winning back your pride. Yes. I see the truth in your eyes.

"But cheer up! Soon my people will be moving south to hunt the mammoth of the Red World. When we come to your village, your people will pay for their disrespect and disbelief. We will kill them, you see. If we don't, they will alert others of your tribe to our ways, and soon there will not be a band in the Red World that will not hide its sacred relics and refuse to yield its daughters to us. Don't look at me like that, you old fool. Your village won't be the first to be burned, nor will it be the last."

Hot blood was still gushing from the gash in Ish-iwi's cheek. The wound was starting to throb, and the ants were mounting their first invasion of the day. He barely felt the sting. He was cold, colder than he had ever been in his life. "Why would you do this when the land is rich in game? In buffalo and horse, in antelope and—"

"Since time beyond beginning the meat of mammoth has been sacred to the People of the Watching Star. No other will do for us. Thunder in the Sky has spoken in the dreams of our wisewoman. Its word has shown us our path. Thunder in the Sky will continue to nourish the People of the Watching Star with the flesh of the mammoth only if we make blood sacrifices of the daughters of those who eat the flesh of his children."

"But none among the People of Grass, the People of the Mountains, or the People of the Red World are mammoth hunters! And Ah-nee never ate the flesh of a tusker in her life!"

Belligerence narrowed Maliwal's dark eyes into slits. "Better your daughters than ours. It is a good arrangement. Your women, your girls, they mean nothing to us. They do not understand our intentions until it is too late. When they come to me, I make certain that they eat the flesh of mammoth soon enough. Once they name Ysuna their sister and freely call themselves the daughters of the Watching Star, they choose the way in which it must end for them. In that moment they turn their backs upon their people and become ours to do with as we must."

The old man was almost too appalled to speak. "Do you imagine that your god of the mammoth does not know that what you offer to him is false? Do you believe that Thunder in the Sky did not hear poor Ah-nee scream? You are a such a brave man, Maliwal—a thief, a slayer of young women and—"

"Of old men!" As Maliwal leaped to his feet his spear struck downward with all his strength behind it. It drove straight through the old man's gut. Maliwal smiled, satisfied. "When words are all a man has with which to defend himself, he should choose them with more care, Ish-iwi. You have lived too long. I will leave you now so you may die alone . . . and contemplate the fate of your people, who will soon join you in the world beyond this world."

# PART I

---

# THE RED WORLD

# 1

"Cha-kwena!" the old man called. "Cha-kwena! Where are you, boy?"

*I am here.*

The Moon of Grass was rising over the Red World as the youth answered not with words but with thoughts. He lay motionless in the darkness of the treetop, sprawled belly down like a young lynx on the massive, outreaching shaggy red branch of the ancient juniper. *You are a shaman, my grandfather. Hear me. Find me. If you can.*

Some twenty feet below, Hoyeh-tay stopped dead. He was small but straight backed and light on his feet despite his many years. His sudden stop caused the great horned owl that perched on his shoulder to fly skyward, *oo-oo*ing in distress. The shaman took no note of the bird; he was too preoccupied circling and sniffing the night air.

Cha-kwena held his breath. The old man, wearing sandals of woven sagebrush, a loin cover of antelope hide, and a short cape of twisted rabbit fur, looked like a hunting animal closing on its prey. Was it by magic or by exquisitely honed skill that his grandfather had unerringly followed him out of the Village by the Lake of Many Singing Birds, across the wetlands, into the hills, and high into this deep, thickly forested canyon? The boy's brow furrowed. He had been so careful to depart from the village without being seen, to leave no sign, to walk in stealth so that no one would be able to follow him to this secret place, which he had made his own so many moons before. He should have known that his precautions would create no obstacle to his grandfather. Named for his helping animal spirit, Wise and Watchful Owl, old Hoyeh-tay was a shaman of many gifts and undisputed magical power.

"Ah, Cha-kwena, there you are! You have smoothed

the dust of the earth and the oil of the juniper onto your skin to mask your scent, but it is no use. I can still catch the smell of you and feel your eyes upon me. Are you dream-seeking *again?*"

The boy's wide, sunbrowned face expanded with annoyance and shame. Most boys began at twelve to dream the visions that shaped their lives. But Cha-kwena, thirteen and nearly a man, was still seeking the dream that would identify his helping animal spirit, explain the purpose of his life to him, and ultimately lead him to discover the name that would be his throughout his adulthood.

"I know you are here, Cha-kwena! It will do you no good to keep silent!"

The boy sighed, rolled his eyes in exasperation, and sat upright. There was no use trying to hide from Old Owl. Straddling the branch, Cha-kwena dangled his bare legs and sandaled feet as he stared down at his grandfather. The old man had been forgetful of late, but he always knew his grandson's thoughts and whereabouts. "You *are* Shaman," the boy conceded.

Hoyeh-tay's small round eyes were as bright and quick as tadpoles darting in the shallows of a moonlit stream. "Of course I am Shaman! As you will be someday. Now come down from that tree."

Anger pricked Cha-kwena. "It isn't fair. Sooner or later my helping animal spirit will make itself known to me in my dreams. It *will!* And then you will know that I am no different from any other youth in the Red World. I want to be a hunter, like Dakan-eh, and continue my training with the other boys. I have *not* been called to be a shaman, my grandfather!"

"Bah! You must stop trying to be like the others, Cha-kwena. Like it or not, since the death of your father, you are my only surviving male descendant and have been called to walk the shaman's path. Ever since you were the littlest boy, the spirits of all the animals have come to speak within your dreams. Always it is you who finds and heals the injured bird or the abandoned fawn or cub. There is a powerful and unique magic in this. Stop trying to ignore it."

The boy felt sick. How many creatures had he taken into his care over the years? Perhaps too many. He thought

of the one-eyed hawk that he had found in the tule marsh
to the west of the village. When he had brought it home,
it had been so near to death that his mother had urged
him to let her cook it in the family boiling bag. He had
refused. Its convalescence had taken Cha-kwena's time
and patience, but the bird had responded and had been
released to the wild only days before.

"No!" He glared down at the old man. "It was Nar-eh
who was to follow the shaman's way, not me! Never me!"

He roared the declaration, but it sounded hollow. His
father had been dead for less than a moon. It still seemed
impossible. Nar-eh's life spirit had been strong in him one
day and gone from him the next. Who would have thought
that a mushroom could have possessed enough power to
kill him . . . and change his only son's life forever. Cha-
kwena sighed. Nar-eh had never been able to resist
mushrooms. He had plucked them whenever he found
them and had eaten them on the spot. U-wa had often
warned her man to be more careful with them. But Nar-eh
had never been one to listen to his woman. He had been
strong, in his prime, and arrogantly confident that someday
he would be shaman.

A wave of frustration swept through Cha-kwena. "My
mother, U-wa, is still young. She will have to take another
man. The headman has been looking at her with interest,
and she has been looking back. She may yet bear another
son! Your magic could make it so. Then *he* will be the
shaman, and I will be a hunter like Dakan-eh. And until
you tell me that I may, I will not come down from my
tree!"

"What do you mean when you call this great juniper
'my tree'? Has its spirit spoken to name you its master?
Surely then, Cha-kwena, this is a great affirmation that
you have been called to walk the shaman's path, for the
juniper is sacred to our kind."

*Our kind.* Again the boy felt sick. "No! I have not
seen into the future! This tree has *not* spoken to me!"

The old man raised his eyebrows. "No?"

"No!" Cha-kwena wondered if all lies snagged in the
throat and weighted the heart as this one did. He swallowed
hard, for the spirit of this tree *had* spoken to him out of
the darkness. It had summoned him from the village and

deep into this canyon. With the wind to speak for it, it had invited him to ascend its heights. No lions, pumas, or rare, mysterious jaguars had ever climbed as high as he. And when he had stretched out upon the massive musculature of its branches, the great tree had sighed with pleasure, as though welcoming a friend.

But now there was a tension in the branches that he had never felt before. High above, the moon glared down at him with disapproval. Her crooked mouth was frowning, and her gray eyes were wide in the white circle of her pockmarked face. Owl was sailing directly overhead, a broad-winged silhouette.

"Moon, mother of the stars, do not be angry with Cha-kwena!" He winced, startled. His cry had come unbidden from his mouth, and it had been less a plea than a command. "Moon, mother of the stars, I did not mean to shout. Great tree, your kind has been sacred to my people since first we came into the Red World. Cha-kwena has meant no disrespect."

"*Hmm* . . ." The old man shook his head as he raised an arm in welcoming invitation to Owl; the bird swooped down to alight on his forearm. "Did you hear my grandson, old friend? Cha-kwena says that he has not been called to be a shaman, and yet he commands the moon and speaks to the great tree in the manner of one who has already set himself upon the path of the shaman's way."

The owl shifted its weight from one horny foot to another, then hopped up on the old man's shoulder, all the while making low, chortling sounds. It either understood the shaman's words . . . or was digesting a mouse.

Cha-kwena felt the need to be brazen. "You are wrong about me, my grandfather."

"Bah! You cannot fool me, Cha-kwena! The spirit of this great tree has called you into this canyon, just as it once called to me when I was a skinny boy. I, too, came alone into the night to ask the spirits to grant me the dream visions of a hunter . . . but was granted instead the dreams of a shaman."

Cha-kwena was amazed. "You did not *want* to be a shaman?"

"A man must be what he is called to be."

"But I have dreamed no vision! Any of the other boys

at an age to seek his dream time might have come across this place and—"

"Yes. But it was *you* who found it. I brought your father here once, when he was much older than you are now. Together we stood beneath this tree. But if the spirits spoke, Nar-eh did not hear them. I should have known then that he would not follow me in the shaman's way."

Far away within the night, a mammoth trumpeted. It was a rare sound these days, deep and imperative. Cha-kwena listened, transfixed, as Hoyeh-tay stiffened and spoke with awe and reverence. "He has returned. Life Giver . . . Great Ghost Spirit . . . Grandfather of All . . . he has come again from the sky. In the flesh of the great white mammoth he will walk among the People of the Red World and feed once more with the mammoth kind beside the spring of salt."

"Spring of salt? I know of no such place."

"It is sacred, known only to the mammoth kind and to this shaman, who was shown the way by Great Ghost Spirit himself. Ah, Cha-kwena, that he calls to us now, on this night, in this place . . . there could be no sign of greater portent to confirm your calling to the shaman's path."

Cha-kwena shivered against a sudden, inner cold as he looked down at his grandfather. Hoyeh-tay stood motionless while the wind combed through the fur of his cape and the unplaited lengths of his hair. In the moonlit darkness, the shaman's hair was the color of ashes—gray, black, and white. Each long strand was dry and brittle from hours spent bending over the embers of his fire pit, in search of omens.

The boy cringed. *If I become a shaman, then someday I will have hair like that and live alone in a cave, with only spirits and animals to talk to.*

On old Hoyeh-tay's shoulder, Owl stretched, extended a long, gray wing, and, looking straight up at Cha-kwena, *ooo-ooo*ed as though in mockery of the boy's concerns.

Cha-kwena scowled. Had the bird read his thoughts? He could not tell; Owl was his grandfather's helping spirit, not his.

"Come now, Cha-kwena," urged the old man. "It will

not be as bad a life as you think. Come down. I have walked far to spend this night with you. We will raise a fire, and I will tell you stories of the ancient ones so that you will be strong in the wisdom of your ancestors. And I have brought the sacred stone. It is time for you to begin to understand the meaning of its power."

"But I do not want to understand."

"No? That is regrettable. My dreams have told me that this year the pine nuts will be plentiful under the Pinyon Moon in the highland forests, where the two flat-topped mountains meet. If my vision proves correct, the Great Gathering of the People of the Red World will take place this summer."

"Every year you dream that dream. Every year you journey west to the distant mountains to see if your vision is true. Sooner or later, the pine nuts are bound to be plentiful."

The old man's brow arched defensively at the lack of respect in the boy's voice. "This year the dream was very strong. Because I am not as young as I once was, Tlana-quah has frowned on the idea of my going alone. I have decided that—"

"Do not look at me! You need a man at your side, not a boy!"

"Yes. So it is that Dakan-eh has volunteered to escort me. I had thought that you would wish to go along as my apprentice. But since you disdain the shaman's path, perhaps it is best that you remain behind and—"

A wave of excitement flooded through Cha-kwena. "If Dakan-eh is going, I will gladly go, too."

"I thought you might. Your mother has prepared traveling packs for us both. Now come down from that tree. I want to go to the overlook and watch the Great One as he feeds beside the salt spring. Then we will come back here and spend the night. In the shadow of father and mother of all junipers, you will listen and learn from this old man about that to which you have been called."

Owl led the way across a world that gleamed silver and black in the light of Moon. Night Wind followed until Owl, beckoning, disappeared into thick woodlands. Hoyeh-tay walked into the foliage without hesitation. Cha-kwena, surrounded by shrubs and swallowed by the darkness, protested.

"Slow down, Grandfather. I do not know these woods. It is too dark to go on."

"Nonsense. Owl and I know the way. It is not far."

They threaded their way through scrubwood and around boulders. Owl called them on. Now and then Cha-kwena caught a glimpse of the bird's gray shadow passing through the dark, tangled scrubwood.

"Come, boy," urged Hoyeh-tay without looking back. "Do not lag behind, or Great Ghost Spirit may not be at the salt spring when we arrive!"

Shrubs brushed against Cha-kwena's limbs and arms, and several times he had to make a quick grab for his cape lest some branch snatch it away. Hoyeh-tay was well ahead of him in the pine trees now, his small, agile form lost to view.

Cha-kwena's sandaled heels dug for purchase on a needle-covered incline. The scrubwood had thinned considerably; now the pines crowded together, their branches cutting off the light of Moon and her star children. The air within the grove was close and resinous with the strong scent of duff and sap and fallen cones.

Suddenly Cha-kwena cried out. He had walked straight into a tree and bruised his nose and chin. He staggered and nearly fell. When his balance was caught, he bawled in frustration, "Wait, my grandfather! The trees grow too thick!"

"Bah!" old Hoyeh-tay called back through the darkness. "I am not waiting. Use your third eye to find your way!"

"My *what*?"

"Your third eye! You must begin to use your gifts, boy! Let your invisible eye guide you."

Reminding himself that he would have to humor his grandfather if he was going to be allowed to accompany Dakan-eh to the land of the distant pinyon groves, Cha-kwena continued on, hands open and up, arms out and waving at the air lest any other tree impede his progress.

He walked more carefully than before, guided by Hoyeh-tay's steady footfall and the flap of Owl's wings. A few moments later, he broke out of the pines and scrubwood. He stared up. Moon's white face was deathly pale, and her fixed smile seemed full of secrets. Somewhere up ahead a nighthawk shrilled—or was it a flying squirrel or a bat? Cha-kwena was not sure.

Directly ahead, Hoyeh-tay stopped and turned his face up to the night. "Ah, Cousin Bat, I thank you for your greeting!" he said, then added as Cha-kwena came to stand beside him: "Did you see our leather-winged friend, Cha-kwena? He has surely seen both you and me with his invisible eye, the sixth sense that is a gift to all who must move and hunt within the dark."

"I am not a bat. I am a man of the People of the Red World," replied Cha-kwena loftily. "Men hunt by day, not by night."

The old man's face bore the raptorial look of his namesake, Owl, as, with sharp and measuring eyes, he appraised his grandson. "You are a boy, not a man at all. And I agree you are no bat." He clucked his tongue. "No bat would be so inept as to walk into a tree. Nor, I think, would a man and hunter of the People. But do not worry. Owl's eyes will lead us both. We are almost to the salt spring."

Cha-kwena gritted his teeth and considered staying where he was as his grandfather walked on. Then, suddenly, a coyote let off a string of ear-piercing, bloodcurdling yaps and howls. Hackles rose on Cha-kwena's back. He knew that he had no cause to be afraid unless the coyote was inordinately hungry. But in this unfamiliar forest, his imagination was savaged by the creature's howls. He broke and ran, his mind aflame with images of blood and death and ripping teeth.

"Wait for me!" Cha-kwena's command was half-choked by breathless terror. He sped through the darkness, leaped over shrubs, darted around trees, and caught up with his grandfather just as the old man was about to disappear into a dark wall of the forest.

Hoyeh-tay stopped and smiled. "So you *can* fly like a bat and see with an owl's eyes when fear nips at your heels! I thought as much." He laughed, then opened his mouth and howled.

Cha-kwena stared, incredulous. "How do you do that?" he demanded, shamefacedly realizing that it had been

Hoyeh-tay, not a coyote, who had set the fire of panic to his heart and feet.

"I am Shaman!" proclaimed the old man as, with a chuckle, he turned and entered the darkness of the trees.

There are places in the world that speak of magic, places that touch and fill the heart until it aches with longing for all that is rare and wondrous and intangible to all but the spirit. This great moonlit chasm was such a place. Cha-kwena was stunned.

The old man saw the boy's reaction and nodded, gratified. "No one comes to this sacred place," he informed in a reverent whisper. "No one knows of it except the mammoth kind and the shaman. Now that you are to be a shaman, you may come alone to seek the dream visions of a man."

Awed, Cha-kwena squinted down into the dark vastness of the west-facing canyon. It was a huge, darkly vaginal cleft in the earth, as though the skin of Mother Below had been peeled back and laid bare. To Cha-kwena's right, half a mile away, a narrow waterfall plunged into the abyss from the heights—a slender river of liquid moonlight, falling, falling, then disappearing into the blackness of the thickly forested canyon floor. Where the floor widened and the trees thinned, the river pooled, then narrowed and slumped into a deep embankment before it began a multiveined westward run and vanished into a broad plain that shone blue beneath the stars.

Cha-kwena's eyes were drawn back to the depths of the canyon. Something was moving in the darkness far below. He could just make out the shapes of large, rounded boulders swaying amid the trees. "Look, my grandfather! They move! Truly, this place *is* magic!"

"Yes, it is. But look again: Those are mammoth, come to the spring that scabs the lower canyon walls with salt. Like deer, their kind has need of salt."

Cha-kwena could just make out the forms of several mammoth cows and adolescents before he noticed a single calf so light of color that it seemed to glow in the dark. He caught his breath. "The calf is white!"

"As is its father," said Hoyeh-tay.

And in that moment, from out of the deep darkness at

the base of the canyon, another form emerged: white, monolithic, eighteen feet tall, and weighing some fifteen thousand pounds. The white bull mammoth extended its long, inwardly curling tusks, raised its trunk, looked straight up the canyon wall, and trumpeted at the shaman and his apprentice.

Hoyeh-tay leaped to his feet and raised his arms in recognition of his totem, while Cha-kwena covered his ears and cowered, for the shrieking cry of the mammoth had seemed capable of cracking the sky in two.

"Life Giver. Great Ghost Spirit." Hoyeh-tay trembled as he spoke the name of the greatest mammoth of them all. "Cha-kwena, behold the totem of the People of the Red World!"

Cha-kwena was numbed by its immensity. "How can an animal grow to be so big?"

"Life Giver is not an animal, Cha-kwena! His flesh is of the spirit world. It is said that he was born with the earth in the time beyond beginning, that he was already old when First Man and First Woman were young. It is said that his strength gave life to our ancestors as he led them across endless ice and mist and fire on their journey to the Red World. As long as he lives among the People, we will be strong. But when he dies, the People will die with him."

"But how can a totem die, my grandfather?"

For a long time the old man stood unmoving. The wind combed through his hair and ruffled the fur of his cape. Then, as if in a trance, he curled his right hand around the small medicine pouch that he wore around his neck. When Owl swooped down out of the stars to alight upon his head, he seemed not to notice as he said, "As long as a single sacred stone remains in the keeping of the shamans of the Red World, Life Giver cannot die. Our power comes from the stones, Cha-kwena. They are all that is left of the bones of First Man and First Woman. Those who possess them are direct inheritors of a mystic force that has been with the People since time beyond beginning. You must never forget this. You must never doubt that the words and the magic of the shamans of the Red World are what keep Life Giver forever strong and alive. We are the guardians of the sacred stones and of Great Ghost Spirit, just as he is guardian of the People."

Cha-kwena frowned. "You say this only because you think that your words will make me want to be a shaman instead of a hunter."

"I say this because it is the truth! The omens have been strong for you, Cha-kwena, stronger than they ever were for your father. I have many more words to share with you before the dawn and tomorrow's trek to the country of the Blue Mesas. The wind is cold here. Let us return to the sheltering shadow of the giant juniper and allow Life Giver to feed with his little family in peace."

With Owl and Night Wind to keep them company, the old man and the boy passed the night together at the base of the father and mother of all junipers. They raised a small fire, and Cha-kwena fed the flames with deadfall. Hoyeh-tay took the sacred stone from the medicine bag and told the tales of the ancient ones. He spoke in great detail of mammoth and magic things, and of the life to which his grandson had been called by the spirits of their ancestors.

The tales went on and on. Hoyeh-tay recounted epic wanderings across the savage world, where mountains walked and rivers rose to consume the land, where the sky rained fire upon monstrous beings who fed upon the children of men and mated with them, and where the twin sons of First Man and First Woman rose up to make war upon the forces of Creation, subdue the beasts, and set enmity between them and mankind forever.

Cha-kwena listened dutifully, pretending to be interested in stories that he had heard a thousand times before. When the old man spoke of Great Ghost Spirit, however, Cha-kwena's recent sighting of the white mammoth shed a new and intriguing light on a very old and worn story.

The wild creatures of the woods ventured close to listen. Cha-kwena could feel their eyes watching through the darkness. He drew his stone hunting dagger from its sheath of woven bark, but with the fire burning high, no animal threatened. After a while, the old man smiled and told him to put his weapon away.

"The animals of this world are the brothers and sisters of our kind, Cha-kwena. You, who have nurtured and healed so many of them, need have no fear of them."

"But for every animal that I have healed, my grandfather, I have eaten a hundred times its number. They are meat to us, as we are to them. We must be wary—"

"Not in this place. I have told you: The spirits of our ancestors—and theirs—are with us here."

"Then it should be safe to sleep," said Cha-kwena, yawning.

"Not yet. There is plenty of time to sleep. Now there are more tales to be told."

The boy sighed. The stories went on and on, until at last Moon disappeared beyond the western rim of the canyon.

Old Hoyeh-tay pulled his cape around his narrow shoulders and shivered violently.

"I will find more wood to feed the fire," Cha-kwena offered, starting to rise, eager to be away from the old man's endless words.

"No! Wait!"

Cha-kwena obeyed. The old man's tone and manner put the boy on edge. Hoyeh-tay was sitting so stiffly, clutching the sacred stone to his breast. His breathing came quickly and shallowly, as if he had just run a race. "Grandfather, are you all right?"

"I . . . yes." The old man drew in a deep breath and held it. Seconds passed. When he exhaled at last, he clearly was not all right. He shook his head. "How strange. I just had the oddest feeling." He was obviously so unsettled by his thoughts that he could not bring himself to speak them aloud.

"What, my grandfather?"

Hoyeh-tay scowled. "Nothing. Nothing at all." He folded his arms and assumed the cross-legged position of a man who intends to sleep while sitting upright. Owl made sounds of annoyance and flew upward from Hoyeh-tay's shoulder to a more stable perch high amid the branches of the juniper. The shaman, meanwhile, stared into the fire and mumbled.

"Grandfather?"

The old man looked up with a start. "It is late," he

said. "Tomorrow will see the beginning of a long journey for us. When we reach the place where the two mountains meet, perhaps other shamans will have shared my vision and be there to greet us. It will be a good thing to confer with old friends again. Too many moons have passed since I last saw Ish-iwi, shaman of the People of the Red Hills." Pleased by a sudden memory, he smiled and sighed wistfully—an old man's expression of longing for things that can never be again. "Ah, the times Ish-iwi and I enjoyed as boys, when our people came together to pick pine nuts under the Pinyon Moon!" His smile vanished. "It will be good to know that he is well."

"Do you fear otherwise, my grandfather?"

The question obviously disturbed the old man. "What I fear or do not fear may not be revealed lest it come to pass!" he said defensively. "I am Shaman! Remember that. Sleep now, Cha-kwena. I told Dakan-eh that we would meet him at the edge of the village just after dawn."

Cha-kwena tried to sleep, but excitement kept the boy awake. He visualized the many days and nights that lay ahead. To travel with Dakan-eh was every boy's dream! And the place where the two flat-topped mountains met was very far. They would be on the trail for a long time. Dakan-eh would hunt for food and for pleasure, and Cha-kwena would find a way to display his own skill with a spear and throwing stick.

Cha-kwena trembled as he stared across the dying flames at his sleeping grandfather. *You will see*, he thought ferociously. *Dakan-eh and I will work together to make you see. I may be your grandson and I may have seen Great Ghost Spirit, but I was not born to be a shaman!*

He closed his eyes, and at last he slept. He dreamed a comforting dream of the boys' lodge, of his friends, of his snares and spear and spear hurler, and of Dakan-eh, Bold Man, teacher and guide and inspiration. . . .

# 2

In the village beside the Lake of Many Singing Birds, dawn washed the reed-covered lodges with the first soft colors of morning. Mah-ree, younger daughter of Tlanaquah, the headman, and his woman, Ha-xa, was awakened by the silence of the frogs.

Mah-ree was small for an eleven-year-old. When she sat up beside her older sister, the tule reeds of their shared hide-covered mattress barely made a sound. Naked beneath blankets of rabbit fur and beaver skins, Mah-ree shivered when the chill, damp air of morning touched her back.

"Go back to sleep, my sister," Ta-maya mumbled sleepily. She yawned, reached for the covers, and, rolling onto her side, drew them possessively around herself and over her head.

Mah-ree ignored Ta-maya. Urgency swept her to her feet. The gray light of morning illuminated the interior of the snug little lodge. Her eyes swept over familiar surroundings: The vaulted roof supports of bent willow were overlaid with a thatching of woven reeds, which had been bound tightly to the wood with thongs of cordage. The earthen floor was covered with thick mats of tule rushes and cattail leaves, and by the fire pit, her mother's cooking and gathering baskets were neatly stacked. The meticulously rolled bed furs of her parents and the long-unused cradleboard of chokecherry twigs and beautifully painted antelope hide sat upright beside them. Mah-ree wondered if the cradle's presence so near the bed furs might inspire the forces of Creation to set the spark of life once again within Ha-xa's belly.

Mah-ree's heart pounded as her eyes focused on her parents' smoothed and ordered bedding. How had they managed to leave the lodge without waking her? When had they left? Tlana-quah, as headman, had planned to rise early, to offer official words of leave-taking to those who would be traveling from the village this day. Duty and tradition demanded that Ha-xa, as his woman, be at his side. Mah-ree had wanted to be there, too.

She gave her sister's backside an impatient nudge with her toes. "Get up, Ta-maya! If we hurry we may yet have a chance to say good-bye to Dakan-eh before he leaves the village."

Ta-maya groaned in protest. "I said good-bye to him last night."

"But he will be gone for a long time, Ta-maya. Have you made a food gift for him to pack?"

Ta-maya sighed in the way of one who cannot believe the ignorance of another. "That would be an open sign of my consent to become his woman."

Mah-ree frowned. Her sister perplexed her these days. Ta-maya had just turned fifteen. She had been a woman for two moons now and was getting old and mysterious in her ways. "But I thought you wanted to be Dakan-eh's woman."

"I do." Ta-maya yawned again, more prodigiously than before. "There is nothing that I want more. Everyone knows that. But it is not good for a female to be too eager."

Mah-ree pursed her lips thoughtfully. "I will wager you my white bead necklace that Ban-ya has gone to say good-bye to Dakan-eh and has made something for him to take on his journey. If he accepts it . . ."

"He will not. Dakan-eh wants me, *only* me. He has said so, and last night, before the entire band, his eyes repeated his words, and my eyes told him that I will be his. But not yet, and certainly not this morning."

"Ban-ya has big breasts! Bigger than yours! I have heard the old women say that men prefer women with big breasts."

Still in a half-dream state, Ta-maya chuckled deep in her throat at her little sister's somber reminder. She raised her head and peeked up at the girl from under the furs, smiling a sweet, sleepy smile that warmed her lovely face with a sister's deep and sincere affection. "Poor Mah-ree.

Look at you. So solemn! Do you fear that your own breasts will not grow? Stop worrying about them. Who knows? Maybe they will end up as big as Ban-ya's."

Mah-ree's expression grew more solemn as she shook her head. "Dakan-eh looks at her. I have seen him."

Ta-maya was fully awake now. "All the men look at her—all the women and children, too. She is a curiosity, and I do not envy her. Anyway, you do not fool me for a moment, Mah-ree. You want me to go out to Dakan-eh so that you can come along and have an excuse to say your own good-byes to Cha-kwena."

Mah-ree, feeling her face flush, was grateful for the morning gloom.

Ta-maya clucked her tongue. "You should not pester him, Mah-ree. Cha-kwena has much to learn before he can become the shaman. He needs no distractions."

"I will be his woman someday," informed Mah-ree, wishing that she felt as confident as she sounded.

"Perhaps, but not for a long time. Now that he has been chosen to walk in the way of a shaman, things have changed for him. He has more important things on his mind."

"But he does not *want* to be shaman!" protested Mah-ree, and then, unthinking, she blurted out the deepest longing of her heart. "*I* do!"

Ta-maya's eyes went round. "Females cannot be shaman!"

The girl sighed. "I know," she said, and suddenly weary of conversation, stalked naked into the chill light of the morning.

A disturbed Ta-maya sat up and watched her sister go. Mah-ree was such a perplexing child. Where did she get her ideas? No matter. The chill of morning nipped at Ta-maya's face as she bundled the sleeping furs around herself and stared thoughtfully into the gloom; it was not Mah-ree whom she worried about now.

"Ban-ya." She said the name of her childhood friend aloud, tested it on her tongue, and found it inexplicably bitter. Ban-ya was bright. Ban-ya was pretty. Now that the days were warm and everyone went nearly naked, Mah-ree did not have to tell Ta-maya that Dakan-eh was looking at Ban-ya. How could he help himself?

Suddenly restless, Ta-maya rose and, holding her sleeping furs apart, stood looking down at herself. She knew that her body was good to look upon. Everyone said so, especially Dakan-eh. She was just the right height and weight, with a slender waist, flat belly, concave navel, tapering hips, and strong, shapely limbs. But her breasts, although round and high, were nothing when compared to Ban-ya's.

A small sound of dismay escaped her lips. What if Mah-ree was right? What if men did prefer women with big breasts? Was Dakan-eh not a man? Was he, at eighteen, not the best-looking and the boldest man of all?

"Yes!" Ta-maya answered her own question and recalled with a rush of pride how he had singled her out when she had not yet been Mah-ree's age. She could still remember the way her heart had leaped when he declared before the entire band that she would be his first all-the-time woman. He had not asked her; he had *told* her. It was Bold Man's way to take the lead. And although her father's eyes had narrowed dangerously and her mother had reminded the brash young hunter that her elder daughter was not yet a woman to be bartered for, Ta-maya had sensed that they had approved of Dakan-eh's manner when he had not backed down to them.

"I will have her!" he had declared again.

Bedazzled, she had accepted the first of many gifts from him as her parents and the entire band had sucked in a communal breath of amusement. She could still remember speaking out loudly enough for all to hear, "Yes . . . Dakan-eh will be Ta-maya's first man . . . *maybe.*"

*Maybe!* Had she really said maybe? Of course he would be her first man—her *only* man! No one could equal him. And yet until she reciprocated his gift giving with presents of her own, no official commitment existed between them. Both were free to choose others.

"Oh!" she cried out, and was startled by the vehemence of the exclamation. "What a foolish girl you are! Why have you put him off? *Why?*"

Flushed and perplexed, Ta-maya shook her head; she did not know the answer. She was by nature a quiet and gentle young woman. Now, however, as she stood tense and miserable within her sleeping furs, her man-to-be was preparing to go off on a long journey—without a gift to assure him that she would be waiting when he returned.

"Oh!" she exclaimed again, supremely annoyed with herself as she realized that if Mah-ree was right—and she very often was—Ban-ya was probably taking advantage of the situation.

Ta-maya's small hands curled into fists. If Ban-ya were with Dakan-eh now, strutting before him, throwing out her chest and offering herself through words and gifts and wonderful swayings of her ample hips and meaty buttocks, there was nothing to stop Dakan-eh from changing his mind and asking Ban-ya to become his woman.

"No!" Ta-maya dropped to her knees and reached for the carrying case of antelope hide that lay at the side of her mattress. Rummaging through the contents, she took out her best necklace, anklet, wristband, nose ring, and comb of antler that Kosar-eh, the village clown, had carved for her so many years before. "We have been friends forever, Ban-ya, but I will not let you lure my man from me!"

She hurriedly donned her finery, combed her nearly shoulder-length hair, and, taking up the top bed fur, ran from the lodge. The chilly morning air was thick with the damp, lingering scent of night. Ta-maya slung the bed fur around her shoulders. It felt soft and warm against her bare skin as she ran through the still-sleeping village. It would make a fine gift for Dakan-eh to take with him upon his journey, and surely no offering could be more symbolic of the union to which she was now ready to consent with all of her heart.

She ran on, so preoccupied with her thoughts that she failed to make a wide enough turn around the lodge of Kosar-eh the clown. Ta-maya tripped over a scattering of sticks and painted stones that were the playthings of Kosar-eh's four young children, and she might well have plunged straight through the curving, feather-festooned thatching of the capacious lodge had she not put up her hands and twisted sideways in time. With a subdued cry of surprise she skidded along the exterior wall and landed with a thud on her side.

A woman's sharp exclamation came from the interior. "Who's out there, eh? *Eh?*"

Ta-maya knew with a sinking heart that she had awakened the wife of Kosar-eh. Siwi-ni was the last person she wanted to confront this early in the morning. The clown's woman was small and nervous, the complete opposite of her big, good-natured, and much-younger husband. Siwi-ni was near to term with their fifth child, and her pregnancy was making her irritable. She was always angry at someone, and for reasons that Ta-maya could not comprehend, of late Siwi-ni had developed a particular dislike for the headman's elder daughter.

*Poor Kosar-eh*, thought Ta-maya. *To have to live with Siwi-ni every day! No wonder he is often away from his lodge, entertaining the children with his funny games and silly antics.*

"Who's out there, I say? Who disturbs the sleep of the woman and children of Kosar-eh?"

Gathering up her rabbit-skin bed fur, Ta-maya rose hastily to her feet and, without offering a reply, hurried away before the feisty little woman came out scolding and demanding an apology. There was no time to waste; Ta-maya had to reach Dakan-eh before he left for the distant Blue Mesas with a gift from Ban-ya in his hands!

Still slightly disoriented from her fall, rubbing an abraded elbow as she ran, Ta-maya turned right instead of left as she sped past the last few lodges and inadvertently found herself passing too close to the communal lodge of the widow women.

"Oh, no!" Ta-maya tucked her chin in the hope that if she did not look at the old women they would not notice her.

It was no use. She could see the widows, already up and fussing over the makings of their morning cooking fire. Naked save for their capes of bark and furs and feathers, they were three nut-brown, gray-haired, sag-teated sacks of skin bending their twisted bones to the task of the new day and muttering in their eternal argument with one another. They caught sight of her and called her name. With an exhalation of despair, Ta-maya stopped and looked at them—Kahm-ree, Zar-ah, and Xi-ahtli . . . Little May Flower, Pretty Cloud, and Purple Elderberry. Such pretty, youthful names, and yet it was difficult for Ta-maya to imagine that the widows had ever been deserving of them.

"Good morning to you, Ta-maya. What is your hurry?" Kahm-ree, Little May Flower, was the eldest widow. She was also the fattest. Her ancient cape of faded red squirrel fur strained against the girth of her back and shoulders. Although her twisted fingers pinched the garment closed across her chest, the tips of her long, flaccid, enormously brown-nippled breasts could be seen peeking out from below the cape at her hipline.

Ta-maya stared. Kahm-ree's nipples looked like huge, flat, lusterless eyes. She cocked her head and thought of Ban-ya, who was Kahm-ree's granddaughter. She could not help but wonder if her friend's glorious bosom would someday hang loose like Kahm-ree's.

"Good morning, I say!" old Kahm-ree repeated.

Ta-maya bowed her head in respectful acknowledgment; to have done otherwise would have been an unthinkable breach of tribal etiquette. Habit—and hope—prompted her to look up to seek one more old woman among the widows.

*Grandmother!* If Neechee-la were up and about, she would understand Ta-maya's need to hurry on. But Neechee-la was nowhere to be seen.

Sadness struck Ta-maya a hard blow as she remembered that during the depth of the last winter, Neechee-la, Walnut Daughter, mother of Tlana-quah, had abandoned her body and left the widows' lodge to walk the wind forever. The old woman's sweet spirit lingered in Ta-maya's heart and mind. Neechee-la had been so kind and thoughtful, it had always been a pleasure to seek out her company and to help her with the basic tasks in life.

"Good morning to you, Mothers of Many!" After Ta-maya offered the traditional salutation she would have scurried away, but old Zar-ah called her to a stop.

"Wait now a moment!" The old woman's voice crackled with phlegm. She hacked it up and spat, and the glob landed in the fire pit with a splat and a hiss that ended in a considerable puff of steam. "Where are your manners, Ta-maya? Your own grandmother may no longer reside with us, but there is work to do. Lend a young woman's hand to this old woman's fire making!"

Ta-maya drew in a deep and steadying breath. It was all she could do to keep herself from informing Zar-ah that if she would refrain from spitting into the fire, it might not go out; but among the people of the Red World, the young were deferent to the elderly and infirm. Generations of tradition and the good manners that had been instilled within her since her earliest days would not allow her to speak against Zar-ah's bad habits.

"Grandmothers of Many, please let me go my way," she implored. "I will come back to help you with whatever else you may wish, but if I linger here now I will not have a chance to offer my proper good-bye to those who are leaving the village and—"

"Leaving?" Xi-ahtli, as thin and gray and long legged as a heron—and as knobby kneed—interrupted with a merry guffaw. "Why, they have already left. Your mother and father went out to the place of boulders above the lakeshore tule beds to wait with Dakan-eh for the shaman and Cha-kwena. It was not quite dawn when I saw them. I had just come out of the lodge to relieve myself again. The old bladder's not what it used to be, you know! But that has its advantages—it gets one up and started on the day. Doesn't do to sleep too much at my age! Ha! Never know if you'll wake up again!"

Ta-maya eyed the sun. It was not so long past dawn. If she hurried she could catch up with the others. "Respectfully, Grandmothers of Many, I must go now. There is something that I must say to Dakan-eh!"

The old women exchanged knowing looks.

"You should have said your words to Dakan-eh last night," said Kahm-ree, then her mouth pursed into a smug toothless smile. "No doubt Ban-ya has said them for you by now! I sent my granddaughter after Dakan-eh, with Kosar-eh as an escort, keeping her safe. Dakan-eh has looked with a man's eyes at my Ban-ya. You are foolish to keep such a fine man dangling as though he were of no importance. But, then, maybe he is not for you, after all?"

Ta-maya caught her breath. Tears stung beneath her lids as Mah-ree's warning rose to haunt her: *Dakan-eh looks at her. I have seen him.*

"Oh!" cried Ta-maya, and, heedless of manners or traditions, ran on without another moment's hesitation.

"Wait, Ta-maya!" Xi-ahtli sounded worried. "It is not safe for you to go alone from the village! Predators are bound to be lurking around. We will come with you! Come, girls! Grab up your throwing sticks, and let us protect our headman's daughter!"

*Girls?* Ta-maya wondered if it was possible for the old widows still to think of themselves as girls. She did not look back to see if they were following. They were right to be concerned for her, of course. There might well be predators in the vicinity. But in this moment Ta-maya could think of nothing that was more threatening to her than Ban-ya.

Halfway to the place of the boulders, Ta-maya stopped. Mah-ree and her parents were walking toward her, Ha-xa in her winter robe of lynx fur, and Tlana-quah looking every inch the headman in his cape of jaguar skin. Kosar-eh was with them. He had given Mah-ree his beautiful cloak of blue heron feathers to wear against the nip of the morning. Nevertheless, Mah-ree looked sullen and unhappy. No doubt she had been scolded for leaving the village alone. Ta-maya felt sorry for her. Had she failed to reach her destination in time to say good-bye to Cha-kwena? Or, having found him, had she been red-faced and tongue-tied in his presence?

"Ta-maya!"

The greeting came from Kosar-eh. Ta-maya could see that the clown was holding his shriveled right arm bent upward against his broad chest. Her mouth went tight against her teeth. She did not like to look at Kosar-eh's ruined arm. The many old white scars, atrophied muscles, and the way he held the misshapen bones made her think of the folded wing of the injured hawk that Cha-kwena had recently released to the wild. But unlike the hawk, poor Kosar-eh's "wing" would never heal.

Ten long years had passed since that sunny winter day when a camel, which everyone had thought dead, suddenly rose to the attack. The camel had been very old and even larger and more belligerent than most of its kind. When it had ventured close to the village, fearful mothers had called in their children, and the men and youths had hurried out to kill it. With spears and spear hurlers, the task had, everyone thought, been quickly and safely accomplished. No one had gone anywhere near the creature until it was down, with spears protruding everywhere from its shaggy high-humped body. The women and children had cheered and, after gathering up their knives and fleshers, had eagerly run to help with the butchering. But it was not the camel that was to be butchered.

Ta-maya had only been four years old at the time, but she would never forget how, in one moment, the animal had been on its side, wheezing and slobbering and twitching in its death throes—and then, suddenly, it had lumbered up onto huge, splayed feet. Swaying and growling, braying, hissing, and spitting blood, the camel lowered its neck, then extended its massive head and vented its rage upon the closest member of the hunting party. That had been Kosar-eh.

It had all happened so fast, no one had had a chance to react, least of all Kosar-eh. Lifted, chewed, shaken, then hurled thirty feet into a stony embankment, he had been knocked unconscious. The camel, with a sudden whoof and a startled bellow, had rolled its eyes and dropped dead.

Ta-maya shuddered at the memory. Of course the young hunter had not been called Kosar-eh then. That name meant Funny Man and was given to all clowns of the many bands of the Red World. Ta-maya could not remember what his name had been in those long-gone days, but she could recall that he had been a strong, good-looking youth. Then, as now, he had been especially kind to children. At the end of his thirteenth year—a year that he now jestingly referred to as the Year of the Camel—he had excelled at the hunt and had flashed a fine white smile at any number of young girls who would have been proud to make his fire, cook his meat, grind his meal, and lie with him beneath his sleeping furs.

In seconds the camel had destroyed all that—his looks, his hopes, his dreams. No young woman wanted him after that, so the old women of the Red World had nursed him.

He had healed slowly, and then he had been sent away to stay for a long while with the People of the Blue Mesas. There he had learned to live again—not as a hunter but as a clown, a shaman in his own right, for it was said that a cripple such as Kosar-eh was a blessing to his people. When times were bad or food was scarce and old Hoyeh-tay was moved to invoke the sacred stone and make his magic smokes on behalf of the band, Kosar-eh's games and merry antics gave heart to the community and made even the most discouraged member smile with renewed hope.

But although Funny Man was smiling at her now, Ta-maya was not happy. Nor did she smile back as he raised his one good arm in enthusiastic greeting and lengthened his stride as he came toward her. She bit her lower lip and tried to avert her gaze, but she could not. The old widow Kahm-ree, who now arrived to stand breathily at her right, along with Zar-ah and Xi-ahtli—must have asked Kosar-eh to accompany Ban-ya from the village just as he was coming out of his lodge, for the man was without the paint that usually covered the deformities of his face and body and set him apart as a clown. His broken, crooked nose, the scars along the right side of his face, and his misshapen arm were all too evident. Because of her genuine affection for him, Ta-maya could find nothing amusing about his appearance.

Nevertheless, she would have forced a smile had Ban-ya not suddenly emerged from where she had been lagging unseen behind Tlana-quah and Ha-xa. Her short, muscular, sun-reddened legs reached and fell aggressively. Her strong, square feet struck the earth like sandaled hammerstones. She wore a knee-length summer skirt of multicolored bone-beaded strands of twisted fiber. With her shining, freshly greased black hair plaited at the sides and falling loosely down her back, she had obviously prepared herself to entice a man.

*My man!* Anger sparked within Ta-maya, only to be overwhelmed by deeper, much more upsetting emotions as she remembered that Dakan-eh was not her man yet and that Ban-ya had every right to flirt with him. Jealousy, frustration, and regret came together at the back of her throat, choking her like some sort of unpalatable and undigestible pudding. She nearly burst into tears.

Kosar-eh and Tlana-quah were staring after Ban-ya as though they had never seen her before. With one brow arching toward his hairline, the clown appeared to be both intrigued and amused, while the headman's long thoughtful face was furrowed with purely sexual speculation. Ta-maya blushed at the sight of her father's openly lustful expression. She saw her mother scowl with jealous disapproval, and Ta-maya could not restrain herself from doing the same.

What had come over Ban-ya? She was acting like a complete stranger. Although her wide, pretty face was expressionless and unreadable, she held her head defiantly as she swayed her broad hips, deliberately causing the milkweed fibers of her skirt to swing and separate. She wore nothing beneath the garment—nothing!

Ta-maya's heart sank. If Ban-ya had come close to Dakan-eh in that outfit—or lack of one—swinging her hips, flaunting her bosoms, and offering even the most insignificant gift as a sign of her willingness to become Dakan-eh's woman, how could he possibly have refused her . . . as Ta-maya had so foolishly refused him?

"Good morning to you, Ta-maya," said Ban-ya, sauntering smugly toward her. "You have slept much too late!"

Her implication and the little laugh that followed her words were too much for Ta-maya. She reached out and grasped Ban-ya by the wrist, forcing the girl to halt. "Dakan-eh has spoken for me. You know this, Ban-ya! How could you have gone out to him?"

"How could she not? You have not accepted him!" reminded Kahm-ree, springing to Ban-ya's defense. Then, tittering nervously and smiling at the headman, she added: "It is her right. No offense is intended to the headman or his daughter. And what kind of a grandmother would I be if I did not look after my granddaughter's interests?"

"Unusual," replied Tlana-quah tersely, his eyes turning up in his head as he strained to maintain his composure.

Ban-ya smirked. "How could I not have obeyed my grandmother? My mother was too long a widow before going to her new man. There is not much welcome for me in her new lodge. But spirits have favored me. Why should I not let Dakan-eh see what a fine big woman I have become? I want him. But you do not seem to know what you want." This said, she jerked her wrist free of Ta-maya's grasp and, linking her arm in with Kahm-ree's, walked back toward camp.

Ta-maya felt sick as she called, "Did you bring him a gift? Did he accept it?"

Ban-ya did not slow her step or look back, yet her voice rang out, "Of course! Unlike you, he knows a good thing when he sees it!"

# 3

Old Hoyeh-tay shook his head in disbelief. "Truly you are well named, Bold Man! To have asked for Ta-maya and then to have accepted the gift of another woman—and this in front of the headman and his woman!—Tlana-quah will not forget the insult to his favorite daughter. Yes, you do have courage, Dakan-eh. But what of wisdom?"

The elderly shaman's question was the same one that Dakan-eh had been asking himself a thousand times since Hoyeh-tay, the boy Cha-kwena, and he had turned away from the village beside the Lake of Many Singing Birds and headed west toward the distant country of the Blue Mesas.

In her provocative little see-through skirt of cording, with her head politely downturned and her amazing bosom hanging heavy and bare, Ban-ya had looked good to him. Very good.

Dakan-eh gritted his teeth. His emotions were in turmoil. If only it were winter! Ban-ya would not have come bare breasted to him in winter. It would have been easier to refuse her in winter.

He swallowed. His mouth was dry. The early summer sun was warm on his back, but it might as well have been snowing; his spirit was so cold. Ban-ya had roused man need in him, but all women did that. It was Ta-maya he *wanted*. Union with the headman's elder daughter would bring great status to him. Besides, she was a beauty, and she possessed a quality that was elusive and lovely and

rare. He had to have her as his own. Surely the headman
would understand that Bold Man had accepted Ban-ya's
gift only in hope that Ta-maya might be inspired to say yes
to him at last.

"I gave nothing in return," he said defensively to
Hoyeh-tay. "By the traditions of the People I am bound by
no commitment to Ban-ya! Tlana-quah knows this and will
understand what I have done."

Dakan-eh wished that he were more comfortable with
the assertion. Ban-ya's gift had consisted of a small, neatly
assembled traveling pack filled with jerked antelope meat
and cakes of acorn meal. Meat and meal were symbols of
life. When she had offered these, she had also offered
herself. To refuse her now would be allowable; but it
would not be easy, nor would it be taken lightly by her or
any member of her family.

"She had the scent of wanting on her. That's more
than I can say about Ta-maya. Ban-ya knows what she
wants. She'd make you a good wife, Bold Man. Perhaps
the spirits have directed her actions. And have you ever
seen such breasts?"

Feigning a shudder, young Cha-kwena made a face of
revulsion. "Ban-ya could suckle a mammoth!"

The old man laughed. "In time, when you are older,
Cha-kwena, you will come to appreciate such feminine
attributes."

"Never!" the boy insisted. "She could beat a man to
death with her breasts if she had a mind to."

Hoyeh-tay laughed again.

Dakan-eh was not amused. "It is Ta-maya I want as
my all-the-time woman."

"But does she want *you*?" With Owl perching on his
shoulder, Hoyeh-tay looked sideways at Dakan-eh out of a
rheumy eye.

Dakan-eh glowered. Hoyeh-tay was wise and respected,
but he could be as sharp and irritating as a stone lodged in
the fiber sole of a sandal. "I am Bold Man! I need no
one—not even you, Old Owl—to tell me when a woman
wants me!" This said, he glared down as he walked. The
ground beneath his feet was a combination of decomposing
granite and red clay interspersed with broad areas pebbled
with white quartz. Now and then a flake of mica, a grain of

sand, or a yellow nugget that had been washed across the land by some recent rain-induced outflow from the nearby hills caught the light of the sun, sparked bright, and flashed gold.

With the flash came inspiration. Dakan-eh stopped and knelt. Balancing his stone-headed, wood-shafted spear across his thighs, he pinched up three small nuggets and held them lightly in his palm. The largest was no larger than a wood-rat dropping, but all three possessed a characteristic dull gleam. The yellow stone was rare but not unfamiliar; he knew that it was as malleable as bone taken from a fresh kill. Pleased by his discovery, he remembered how, as a peace offering after a heated argument, his father had made beads of such nuggets for his mother. He had pounded them into tiny disks, then polished them until they had shimmered like chips of sunlight. He had pierced them with the point of his flint graver, then strung them upon a twist of sinew. His mother had been so delighted with the present that she had forgotten all about the argument.

Dakan-eh's smile broadened. Perhaps if he were to fashion golden beads for Ta-maya, she would consent to become his woman. She had always seemed to like his presents, but perhaps they had been too practical: a quill carrying case for her sewing needles, tools to lessen the drudgery of food and hide preparation, a cylindrical quail-catching basket that had taken him three entire moons to weave, prime cuts of antelope meat, and a freshly killed hare or fish now and then. Was it time for rare and totally useless things? When it came to gifts, who could say what moved a female's mind? Women had always been an enigma to him.

His fingers curled tightly around the yellow stones. And if he were to give one to Ban-ya along with his apology, she might not be too angry with him for using her so thoughtlessly to further his own aims.

Old Hoyeh-tay cleared his throat. Cha-kwena and he had paused beside Dakan-eh. Now, with a twinkle in his eyes, the old man indicated Bold Man as he said, "The first lesson a future wise man must learn, my grandson, is not to let females wheedle their way into your head."

Dakan-eh glared up at him defensively. "I have done no such thing! The two most desirable young women in the band are mine for the taking! It is I who have turned *their* heads!"

"Is it so?" The old man did not even try to sound convinced. "I wonder. Come now, Bold Man, it is a long way to the pinyon groves in the Land of the Blue Mesas, and the omens as well as my dreams urge me to hurry. How quickly will we be able to make the journey if the one who has been sent along to guard me intends to travel the entire distance on his knees?"

Embarrassed, Dakan-eh rose and, still holding the nuggets, stood tall. "We will go on," he said, and strode out. "And when we return to the village, the headman's daughter will accept me."

"Will she?"

Dakan-eh stopped and turned. When he replied, anger blazed in his voice and from his eyes. "If you know something that I do not, spit it out, Shaman! Or have you forgotten—as you forget so much these days—that telling the future is one of your main callings in life!"

Cha-kwena was visibly startled by the unexpected hostility in Dakan-eh's voice.

Old Hoyeh-tay stood as tall as his meager frame would allow. "Your tone is too sharp, Bold Man. Remember to whom you speak, or when we return to the village I might inform the headman that his elder daughter may have good reason when she hesitates to accept you as her man."

Dakan-eh snorted with undisguised annoyance and disrespect. "You would not do that. I will have the best because I *am* the best. I will have the headman's firstborn daughter. No other woman will do for me. And no other man is good enough for her!"

Hoyeh-tay stiffened. As he squinted up at Dakan-eh it was obvious that he did not like what he saw. "Be careful, Bold Man. With a head so big, you might trip and never see the ground before it rises to meet you as you fall."

The ground did not rise. But a moment later Dakan-eh fell in Cha-kwena's esteem. They had not gone another quarter of a mile before the voice of Tlana-quah called them to pause. Cha-kwena was surprised to see the headman loping toward them from the direction of the village. And Ta-maya, flushed and gasping for breath, was jogging at

his side. Mah-ree ran beside her, holding her sister's hand
while a huffing, furious Ban-ya trailed behind.

*Trouble.* Cha-kwena did not speak the word aloud. If
his instinct proved true, he had no intention of giving old
Hoyeh-tay another excuse to point at him and name him
Shaman. Frowning, he wondered what the runners wanted.
Whatever it was, this was the second time in one morning
that he had seen little Mah-ree trotting breathlessly after
him. His mouth drew into a knot of annoyance as he shook
his head. The girl was turning into a mosquito; everywhere
he went she found ways to buzz around him. Was not one
red-cheeked, stammer-tongued, fawn-eyed good-bye from
her enough for one morning? What was the matter with
her? She used to be such a pleasant little girl.

Tlana-quah and Ta-maya came to a stop before Dakan-
eh and Hoyeh-tay. Mah-ree stood behind her father.

Tlana-quah looked angry; the controlled set of his
mouth and brow revealed the strained tolerance of an
infinitely annoyed parent. Ta-maya's eyes were downcast;
the long, upswept lids were puffed and very red. Mah-ree
looked worried, and neither the headman nor his daughters
turned to acknowledge Ban-ya's presence when she came
to a wheezing, growling halt just to one side of them.

*Definitely trouble,* thought Cha-kwena.

"My daughter would speak to Bold Man." Tlana-quah's
eyes were sharp as they fixed Dakan-eh with open hostility.
"It is her right."

"Speak," Dakan-eh invited Ta-maya. His voice was
flat, his face hard and wary.

Slowly, fearfully, she raised her lovely head and looked
at Dakan-eh out of a face that was radiant with both hope and
contrition. Her voice was soft and tremulous, her manner
wary. "Dakan-eh has accepted a gift from Ban-ya." She paused.
Her face had gone very pale. There were tears in her eyes.

Dakan-eh's head went high.

"I have accepted a gift from Ban-ya," he conceded
coolly.

When Ban-ya's growl became a purring gloat, Ta-
maya hung her head and looked miserable.

Dakan-eh did not flinch. "This is my right," he added.

"Yes! It is his right." Ban-ya's echoing affirmation was
prideful and defiant.

Cha-kwena decided that he did not like Ban-ya. Girls too often tried to maneuver him into situations that he did not like, just as Ta-maya and Ban-ya were now trying to maneuver Bold Man. But Dakan-eh would show them. In a moment he would have both women bowing in submission to him.

Cha-kwena could not keep from smiling. His pride in Dakan-eh could not have been greater had they been brothers. How tall and resolute and implacable was Bold Man.

*When I am a man, I will treat the women in my life firmly, just as Dakan-eh does,* Cha-kwena promised himself. *And when they fail to please me, I will deal with them as Dakan-eh deals with them now, with all of the chilling assurance of a north wind that warns them to know their place lest the storm of his anger fall upon them.*

His thoughts made him feel big and bold; he liked the feeling. He watched Dakan-eh and waited for him to put the women in their place with all of the declarative power of a bull elk in rut. But the seconds became minutes, and still he did not speak.

Old Hoyeh-tay exhaled quietly, thoughtfully, in the manner of one who is trying to solve a troublesome problem. Perched atop the old man's head, Owl's head swiveled as the bird stared around in obvious irritation.

Cha-kwena frowned, distracted when Owl's eyes met his, and the bird chortled irascibly. "It is daylight!" protested Owl to the boy. "Can no one see that I am trying to sleep?"

Cha-kwena gulped and turned his attention back to Dakan-eh. Bold Man's eyes had not left Ta-maya's face since he had first seen her running toward him. His breathing was as ragged as Ta-maya's, and his handsome face was every bit as flushed.

*How strange,* thought Cha-kwena. *Dakan-eh does not look like Bold Man now.* He looked lost, confused, and miserable.

When the hunter spoke, his voice was a whisper of abject apology. "I have accepted the gift . . . but not the giver."

"What?" Ban-ya's question was an explosion of anger.

Color flooded into Ta-maya's face. She looked so truly and perfectly beautiful that Cha-kwena's heart went *thunk* in his chest.

Her eyes were brimming, but not once did they stray from Dakan-eh's face. "Then you may accept this gift from the daughter of Tlana-quah to warm you upon your journey, and may you know that her spirit will travel with you and that her heart will be waiting for your return."

"No!" Ban-ya screeched like an angry leaping cat.

Startled, Cha-kwena jumped a good foot off the ground. He half expected Ban-ya to make a dive at Ta-maya.

"Where is this gift?" Ban-ya demanded.

Cha-kwena stared. They all stared. Dakan-eh, meanwhile, waited, with the silliest, sloppiest look on his face that the boy had ever seen. Cha-kwena scowled with disappointment. Bold Man was behaving like a soft-bellied, squirming grub. What was the matter with him? And what was Ta-maya talking about when she spoke of gifts? Aside from her jewelry, she was as bare of hand as she was of body.

"Oh!" she cried as her hands flew to her face. "I . . . I must have dropped it!"

From behind Tlana-quah, Mah-ree shook her head. "You did," she whispered. "I tried to tell you, but you wouldn't listen."

Ta-maya was stunned. "Why didn't you pick it up for me?"

The girl bit her lower lip. "Because you would not let go of my hand!"

A derisive guffaw exploded out of Ban-ya.

"I *have* brought you a gift, Dakan-eh!" Ta-maya was flustered. "I will go back now and—"

"Enough!" Hoyeh-tay raised his hands high. He looked very annoyed, but not nearly so much as did Owl. The bird flew skyward, screeching belligerently as the old man cried: "I have dreamed the dreams of a shaman! My visions are troubled. The spirits put themselves between Dakan-eh and Ta-maya, at least for now. Although the great white mammoth has returned to the Red World, my dreams call upon me to journey to the Blue Mesas, and so I must—"

Astounded, Tlana-quah caught his breath. "Great Ghost Spirit has returned?"

Hoyeh-tay appeared momentarily disconcerted. "I . . . yes. Life Giver walks once more among the People, as I have said."

"You have not said!" countered Tlana-quah. "Not until this moment."

Cha-kwena felt a coldness stir within his gut. The headman was right; this was the first time that Hoyeh-tay had mentioned the great white mammoth. Cha-kwena had waited this morning for him to speak of their sighting to the headman, but when he had not done so, the boy had assumed that the shaman was keeping it a secret. But now Cha-kwena knew that his grandfather had been caught once more in the snare of his own forgetfulness. The boy felt sorry for him.

Hoyeh-tay was bristling. "Too much time has been given to the good-byes between men and women. But if, at the end of our journey to the two flat-topped mountains, I see that the pinyon harvest will justify a Great Gathering of all the tribes of the Red World and future signs are good, then Ta-maya and Dakan-eh can exchange gifts and be married under the Pinyon Moon in the Land of the Blue Mesas. Let there be no more talk. I must go."

Ban-ya scowled, and Ta-maya blushed pink again, but Dakan-eh was beaming. He looked like Bold Man again, and Cha-kwena was glad for him. The spirits of the ancestors smiled most upon marriage ceremonies held in the Land of the Blue Mesas when the tribes came together under the fertile light of the Pinyon Moon.

Tlana-quah, however, was openly disconcerted. "If Great Ghost Spirit has returned from the sky, you cannot leave the village, Hoyeh-tay. You must sing songs in honor of our totem and officiate at ceremonies and—"

"Bah!" The old man looked disgruntled. "Last night I welcomed our totem. Now the spirits call me to the Land of the Blue Mesas. Come, Cha-kwena."

Cha-kwena blinked in amazement as the old man turned and walked away to the west. When Owl dropped from the sky to land upon Hoyeh-tay's head, he paid the bird no heed. He walked boldly, arrogantly, with his back stubborn, straight, and his skinny legs pounding the earth as though he were angry with it. Tlana-quah called out, demanding that he return, but the shaman only walked faster.

Cha-kwena frowned. No one ignored the headman. It was simply not done. But Hoyeh-tay showed no sign of slowing down.

The headman made a rude snort through his wide nostrils. "I, too, have had enough!" he declared. "I will take Ban-ya and my daughters back to the village. As for you, Dakan-eh, go, I say! Protect our shaman from danger as he follows his visions to the west. Perhaps you will learn something about wisdom as well as patience on the journey! And you, Cha-kwena, remember that you are to be a shaman. Your grandfather is very old, and I fear that there may not be as much time as you think to learn from him all that will be necessary before you take his place in the band. Learn quickly and well from him, Cha-kwena. And be a gentle and understanding guide when his spirit wanders."

"But I . . ." Cha-kwena stopped himself from reminding the headman that he had no wish to be shaman. He had done so before, but his words had fallen upon unreceptive ears. There was no reason to imagine that things would be different now. Besides, the Land of the Blue Mesas beckoned, and he had no desire to be left behind.

A small girl's voice piped up from behind the headman. "May I go with them, my father? I, too, would learn from our shaman."

Cha-kwena grimaced.

Tlana-quah silenced his younger daughter with a bellow that sent her shrinking back. "You? Do not be foolish—your mother will need you now. If Great Ghost Spirit walks once more in the country of this band, there will be much to do. In the absence of their shaman, the People must sing the sacred songs that are pleasing to our totem, gather sweet grass and summer fruit, and bring this food to the places where the mammoth kind are known to feed. Life Giver must be honored and made welcome. The People must walk wisely. They must not raise their voices in anger. As long as the great white mammoth and any of his kind dwell in the land surrounding the Lake of Many Singing Birds, the omens will be good for this people, and the spirits will smile . . . even if the visions of our shaman do not."

# PART II

---

# DAUGHTER OF THE SUN

# 1

Long before ants had taken their fill of Ish-iwi, the old shaman who had been left to die by Maliwal, carrion eaters had come to feed upon his flesh. Even if he had possessed the strength to do so, the holy man would not have screamed in fear or tried to shout them away lest his voice be heard in the village and Maliwal be given further satisfaction.

Although Ish-iwi had failed to retrieve the sacred stone of his band and to rescue young Ah-nee, his rank as a wise man obliged him to die well. And so he watched the hungry-eyed predators come, following the smell of blood, salivating, circling, growling warnings to one another: first Raven, then Rat, then Coyote, then Wolf and Badger. He asked them to go away. He explained to them that they were welcome to his flesh and marrow once he was dead, but if they ate him before his life left his body, they would also eat his spirit and prevent him from joining his ancestors in the world beyond this world. They listened but could not understand.

The smell of the old man's fear and pain, coupled with the sweet stink of his massive gut wound, told the hungry ones that they had found food for the taking. Emboldened by his weakness, the predators ignored his pathetic attempts to shake himself free as they feinted in and back, nipping and tearing away at his tough skin and stringy flesh even as instinct drove them to fight savagely against one another. Fur flew. Teeth flashed. When Wolf made his move to dominate, even Coyote retreated, slathering.

Ish-iwi cried out then, briefly. Wolf was at his throat, and as his head was forced back Raven took his eyes. In the end, however, it was a sag-bellied old, black-maned lion who drove off all lesser comers. He dragged the old man away by the head, uprooting the mammoth-bone stake to which Ish-iwi had been bound. He carried the shaman off while his pride watched hungrily. Later, when the old male was sated, he shared what was left of this meat with many.

Ish-iwi was dead by then, but if his ravaged life spirit had still been lingering anywhere near, his mutilated ghost would have smiled. Blind and dismembered, he could never hope to walk with his ancestors in the spirit world, but the largest portion of his corpse—including his heart, brains, and kidneys, from which the spirit of a man drew its life—had been ingested by a lion. And so it was that Ish-iwi's ghost would have raised its voice in joyous song because now—according to the teaching of the People— his spirit was no longer dishonored. He would live forever as a lion. When they roared, he would roar with them, and as long as a single member of this pride survived, Ish-iwi, wise man of the People of the Red Hills, would live and hunt with them forever.

Ysuna, high priestess of the People of the Watching Star, awoke with a start. Sweating, she sat up and wrapped her long arms around her folded knees. It had come to her again—the dream, the hated and beloved dream of the past, of winters without end, of cold and hunger, of a young girl shivering in a dark mountain cave while her elders despaired and moaned and begged the wind to take their life spirits to the world beyond this world.

The sound of her own voice came to her out of time. It was so young and yet so strong: "How can you want to die? I am young. I have yet to take my first man! I have yet to bear a child! I will not let you make me die! I am not ready!"

"You should never have been allowed to live, left-handed child. I should have strangled you before allowing your mother to weaken my resolve. I should have acted upon a father's right to deny life to a child who displeases him . . . and the spirits!"

Then, as now, she had shamed him and them all: the proud, right-handed women, the courageous right-handed men, the young boys and girls sitting blank eyed and right-handed as they listened to the aching death song of their empty bellies. Although it was forbidden, she had taken up her father's spear and, grasping it in her spirit-cursed left hand, had gone out alone into the wind and storm to hunt. He had followed with the intent to strike his daughter dead for her audacity, but the force of the wind had dropped them both to their knees as, through driving mists of snow, she had seen her first vision, of the white mammoth . . . Great Ghost Spirit . . . Thunder in the Sky.

In that moment the wind had turned and the vision disappeared. In that moment the sun had shown its face for the first time in weeks, and her father had cried out in joy and disbelief. His despised child had led him through the storm to the brink of a defile in which a young bull mammoth had fallen and lay dying. His people were saved. And from that moment on, Ysuna had been called Daughter of the Sun, One Who Brings Life to the People. Her life had never been the same, and no one ever again cared with which hand she ate her meat.

Now the village dogs were barking. A lion roared. The beast was close, too close. Ysuna stiffened, listening. It was not one lion, there were several. This was not the first time they had come to circle the village, to claim her hunting territory and to ruin her peace of mind.

Her hands flexed upon her knees as she regretted having sent Maliwal out from the village with a large party of hunters. They had been gone for two days, searching for fresh signs of mammoth in the broad, open hill country to the south. Although a good number of men remained behind, the women were keeping the children close and complaining every time there was cause to venture to the river for water.

Annoyed, Ysuna rose and shook back the floor-length masses of her hair as she cursed Maliwal for killing the old shaman so close to the village. "Arrogant, stupid, dangerous fool! You, Maliwal, have drawn the lions to us!"

Her words stung the darkness. Somewhere high in the slender, cross-braced pines that extended upward through the open smoke flaps of the hide-covered lodge, a family of mice scurried for cover. Ysuna looked up just as

Nai, the attendant who slept at the foot of her bed, awoke and immediately knelt in absolute deference.

Nai bent low as she cast an expectant gaze upward at her mistress. She knew better than to speak.

Somewhere beyond the lodge, a man shouted the dogs to silence as other voices spoke nervously about the closeness of the lions.

Ysuna's mouth turned down. "Bring me my cloak and my sacred collar, then light the outside torch. There will be no more sleep this night!"

The moon was down and the stars were very bright when the high priestess emerged from her lodge. Nai had ignited the exterior torch, which stood to the left of the entryway. Kindling and fat-impregnated strips of leather spat and smoked and gave offerings of sparks to the night.

Ysuna's head went high. The wind, from the east, blew warmly against her face, rich with the scent of distant grasslands and sage barrens. She liked the way it felt against her skin and the sound it made as it stirred through the many scalps and finger bones that festooned the skull-topped medicine pole that stood to the right of her lodge.

Her eyes narrowed. Most of her people were awake and gathered in small family groups before their individual lodges. As the lions sounded she sensed fear in the way the men, women, and children clustered and whispered.

*Like herd animals*, she thought, and felt contempt for them as well as a deep maternal love. *My people, what would you do without me?*

Her answer came in the form of Masau. She did not like it. With spear in hand and Blood, his shaggy, blue-eyed, wolflike red hunting dog loping beside him, Mystic Warrior strode toward her with an easy, natural authority. *You are the lion that troubles me most*, she thought.

What a sight he was—as stern as the night and as beautiful. His older brother, Maliwal, had never been so handsome or commanding, even though there had been a time—and not so very long ago—when she would have sworn that Maliwal was the finest example of a man that she had ever seen. But that was before Masau had reached his prime.

She swallowed, looked straight into his eyes, and

allowed him to see her displeasure. When he did not flinch or look away, anger touched her. How dare he be so self-assured? Her heartbeat quickened. *Because he is Masau, unlike any man I have ever known. Because, like me, he has always dared to test what he fears most. And because, like me, he favors the use of his left hand. His spirit sees into the world beyond this world to affirm my power and the visions of my dreams. Does he see my weakness?*

A cold and terrible sense of certainty stirred within her breast. *Without me, my people would turn to him, and perhaps it would be as though I had never existed.*

The thought disturbed her deeply. She dismissed it as impossible, yet she continued to appraise him. With his hair blowing in the wind and his torchlit face masked by the intricate pattern of tattooing that he had worn since puberty, his features were set, hard. It was difficult to remember that Masau was the little five-year-old whom she had found abandoned with his older brother so many years before.

Now, as their eyes held, her throat tightened hurtfully. The spirits had seen fit to deny her children. She had raised Maliwal and Masau as her own sons. She had taken them to her sleeping furs and held them to her breast and suckled them even though they were too old and she had no milk. It had pleased her to hold them and to have them suck warmth and motherly love from her; if nothing else, they had drawn the power of life from her flesh, and her touch had brought such pleasure to them that they had no desire to be away from her. She had taught them to be obedient to her will, to be strong and bold and compassionless when they dealt with others, to take pleasure in the hunt, and to revel in the ultimate power of the kill. No natural mother could have felt more love or pride in her sons. When they had felt the first stirrings of manhood, she had offered her breasts again and eagerly opened herself to them, making lovers of them both, assuring them that no other woman was worthy of them and that they would be chiefs at her side when she was old.

*Old.* The word rankled. With Masau standing before her, she had no wish to be old. Nor did she wish to be Mother. Nor would she be bested by one of her own cubs.

"Come, Mystic Warrior," she commanded, and ordered

Nai to bring her spear and traveling pouch of extra spearheads. "Together we will drive away these lions that your brother has so unwisely brought upon us."

With spears in hand and torches held high, the hunters of the People of the Watching Star summoned their dogs and followed their high priestess and Mystic Warrior into the night, fanning out behind their leaders through the darkness, chanting and howling as they warned the lions that they must run away or die.

Confused by the firelit din, the great cats roared as they fled. Now and then a leonine form could be seen leaping and racing gracefully ahead through the darkness. Ysuna was not sure just when the old lame male turned and—in a valiant effort to divert the hunters from his pride—began to charge.

Ysuna stopped dead. The lion was well ahead in the moonlit grass but pounding rapidly toward her. Masau walked a foot ahead of her, and the priestess was outraged. How dare he take the lead! His spear was already up and leveled back across his shoulder, the butt of the shaft braced against the barbed end of his spear hurler, the tip facing forward.

Her mouth went dry. Had he noticed the lion before she had? What was the matter with her? This was no time for taking or giving insult. She had taught Masau everything he knew. *Everything!* She willed herself to stand bravely, to arm her spear hurler with steady hands, and to position herself for a throw.

"Come!" she challenged the charging beast. "Ysuna waits! Come to Daughter of the Sun, Lion, if you would die!"

Beside her, Masau stood poised, unflinching. Ysuna's spear hurtled forward in a hissing arc of death, with Masau's flying right behind.

The lion was dead almost before it hit the ground. Both spears had struck true, but there was no question the kill was Ysuna's. She stepped forward to examine the wounds, then smiled when the hunters gathered to bathe her in the light of their torches and praise. Her blood was singing. With her bare hands she took the heart of the lion. As the others watched she ate of it until she could eat no more. Death, when summoned by her will and steeped in blood, never failed to make her feel strong.

"Here, all of you, eat. Let the power of this lion be ours," she commanded. When all had obeyed, she reminded them that the night was not yet old and that there were more lions to kill.

The spear shafts were withdrawn, and new projectile points were taken from the leather sacks that each hunter carried. It took only a few minutes to fit a new point into the precarved socket at the killing end of each spear shaft. Once secured with a new strip of thong, the refitted shaft was ready for the next throw. Rearmed, Ysuna led Masau and the other hunters onward. A single man was left behind to guard her kill lest carrion eaters come and ruin the skin.

They saw no more lions. The death of the old male and the eating of its heart had allowed the rest of the pride time to outdistance the hunters. With the wind still hard out of the east, the priestess stopped at last in open, rolling grassland. Masau paused beside her, his spear in his left hand and Ysuna's nearly lifeless torch held aloft in the other.

In the guttering light, she saw that the dog Blood stood panting at his master's side. The animal looked tired. She frowned when she realized that she, too, was breathing hard. Masau was not even winded. She had not, however, allowed Mystic Warrior to take the lead again. She had matched him step for step, stride for stride. And while his spear had failed to strike a killing blow, hers had slain a lion! She was *not* old—not yet, perhaps not ever!

The thought pleased and excited her. She felt almost unbearably young and strong and beautiful. She looked at Masau, and her loins warmed, throbbed. Had he seen the youth in her . . . and the beauty . . . and the power? Somehow, as his eyes held upon her face, she knew that he had.

A smile expanded upon her mouth. She could taste the blood of a lion at the back of her throat. It was as sweet as the blood of all the young girls who had died so that their hearts might nourish her with their youth and beauty. Thus they gave her pleasure and assured that forevermore she would be able to win the favor of Thunder in the Sky. Only he could summon his mammoth children to be food for the People of the Watching Star.

A vague mist of worry clouded the moment. She thought of the mammoth cow that had been driven into the algae-thick shallows of Eagle Lake. Hopelessly mired, the animal had been skinned and butchered before she was completely dead. Now the meat of the mammoth cow was nearly gone. Worse, no new sign of mammoth had been found in the land.

The priestess's eyes half closed. Memories of the last sacrificial victim bruised her mind. Ah-nee had not died well; she had screamed and at the last moment had begged for her life. Surely her protest had displeased the god. Ysuna's brow came down. What had Maliwal said to the girl to make her scream? No matter. What was done was done. But Ysuna knew that Maliwal would have to travel far before he found fresh mammoth sign; there were so few mammoth in the world these days, especially for those not in favor with their totem.

Ysuna shifted her spear to her right hand. Her left hand rose; her fingers curled around her gorget of human hair and sacred stones. As always, the touch of the stones soothed her. With the sacred stones gripped in her fist, Ysuna found herself smiling again as she heard her own voice probing gently across time:

"And you say that there are sacred stones to be found among other bands to the south?"

"Oh, yes," the dead Ah-nee had replied. "As many stones as there are tribes."

Ysuna was filled with a sudden wave of near euphoria. *Foolish child. Stupid, guileless, witless girl. There is life in the sacred stones! And power! Wherever they are found, there, too, are found mammoth. And in the flesh and blood of the mammoth children of Thunder in the Sky lies the strength of Ysuna and of the People of the Watching Star!*

Within the curl of her fist, the stones were hot, throbbing in cadence with the beating of her own pulse. With the acquisition of each new stone, she felt younger, stronger, more beautiful, and more alive. How would she feel when all the sacred stones were in her possession? The premise was almost too heady to consider.

It was time to move her people farther south again, to seek out more sacred stones of power. It was time to offer a new bride to Thunder in the Sky. And this time the Daughter of the Sun would see to it that the sacrifice did not scream.

Once again Ysuna tasted the blood in her mouth. Her smile was one of transcendent radiance. She snatched the torch from Masau's hand.

"Behold the power of Ysuna!" she exulted, waving the ebbing brand. "Let lions run in terror from fire for having brought fear to the People of the Watching Star! Because they have offended Ysuna, this night their lives are mine!"

"No!" Neewalatli, one of the hunters, cried out. Small and slim and very young, he was more boy than man. With the exception of a younger sister, Neewalatli was the youngest of the hunter Yatli's brood. He had always been nervous and given to fits of worry. "What if the wind takes the fire south and blows it to Maliwal and the others?"

The warning came too late. Ysuna had already dipped the torch's burning head deep into the grass. "Fire, eat! Grass, burn!" she commanded. And although the torch was guttering, the fire ate, and the grass burned.

"But if the wind turns to the west, the village will burn!" The protest came from the same young hunter who had spoken against Ysuna's actions only a moment before.

Standing next to his son, Yatli's face went tight with dread. Even in the light of a torch, the father's face looked gray, and he elbowed the impertinent boy with such vehemence that Neewalatli staggered.

Ysuna turned and slowly handed the torch to Masau. As Mystic Warrior accepted the brand, his dog, Blood, lowered his shaggy head and growled. Had the priestess heard it, it might have been the last sound the animal ever made. But behind Ysuna the grass was blazing, crackling loudly, and flaming high as the wind drove it eastward.

Silhouetted against the light, the high priestess seemed unreal—a woman born of dreams or nightmares—as she hefted her spear. "Spear, silence the one who has twice dared to speak against the will of Ysuna!"

"No!" cried Neewalatli, but even as the word left his

mouth, the weapon struck him through the throat with
such force that he was propelled backward and pinned to
the earth.

No one moved—not the boy's father, brothers, or
friends. Only his dog responded to his thrashings and
hideous garbled choking. Whining pathetically, the dog
circled him, wagging its tail and licking its master's face
and the fingers and hands that were trying desperately to
pull the spear from his bloodied throat.

"Strangle the dog," Ysuna ordered Yatli with no more
emotion than if she had asked the man to hand her a flask
of water. "Like your youngest son, it knows no honor.
Neither are of use to the People of the Watching Star."

If Yatli flinched, no one saw it. He obeyed Ysuna
without hesitation. The high priestess smiled and nodded,
gratified by his loyalty and pleased by the death of the
dog. But then she saw that Yatli was so shaken, his two
older sons had to assist him to his feet.

Displeased, Ysuna stood erect, observing the father of
the slain boy. "For more years than any of you have lived,
I have been high priestess of the People of the Watching
Star. Those who have chosen to follow me have always
prospered. Those who have stood against me have always
died."

Masau tensed. One dark brow ached speculatively
toward his temple, and a muscle throbbed high at his
jawline. Ysuna did not notice as she strode forward. Placing
one moccasined foot hard on the belly of the dead youth,
she took hold of her spear shaft and pulled back, leaving
the detachable stone head embedded in the torn flesh and
shattered bone of the youngest son of Yatli.

"Now," she challenged. "Are there any others among
you who would question me?"

# 2

For the remainder of the night the grass fire could be seen burning on the eastern horizon, and for all that time Masau, with the dog Blood at his side, stood in silence at the edge of the village.

The wind did not turn, nor did lions return to prowl close to the village.

"Have I not said that it would be so?"

Masau turned. He was not startled by the high priestess's voice. He had known that Ysuna would come to him when she had finished skinning and butchering her kill. She had wrapped herself in the bloody pelt of the lion. It was a magnificent skin, black maned with tawny stripes running laterally across the golden pelage. The scent of the raw, uncured hide was strong and good to him, but the scent of the woman who wore it was better, and the sight of her was even more magnificent.

"Come, Mystic Warrior," she invited, placing a cool, steady hand upon his shoulder. The palm was as wide as a man's, and there were power and command in her touch. "Behold, the night is dying, and the air grows cold. My lodge is warm, Masau . . . as am I. Come. We who have eaten of the lion's heart will lie together in its skin and allow its spirit to roar out of our mouths as we become one."

He did not move. Strange and disconcerting spirits were on him this night. Did she not know that the kill would have been his had he chosen to take it? There was pride in Ysuna's voice and on her extraordinary face. How unchanged she was from that bitterly cold, sunstruck day when he had first set eyes upon her. Maliwal and he had been boys then, weak, sickly striplings abandoned by the starving Bison People in the depth of a winter that had

refused to end. How old had they been? Six? Seven? He
could not remember. They were men now, but only because
Ysuna had chosen to gather them into her long, strong
arms, to share her food and her life and her love with
them. He knew that it had not been an easy choice for
her; he had heard others in the band whisper against her
decision to take in such useless children.

He had grown to manhood, and although he was still
young, he had seen rivers change course, great trees fall,
and lakes disappear under the parching summer sun. He
had walked through mountain passes that had been blocked
by glaciers when he had been a boy, and he had watched
strong men and women age and weaken until, for the good
of all, Ysuna drove them from the band to die.

But still she remained young.

*The day will come when she, too, will grow old.* The
vision flared bright, cold, and unwelcome within his mind.

"Masau, where are your thoughts?"

"They take me as they will," he replied obliquely.

Her eyes were steady and unblinking. The long, angular
lids were half-lowered, holding black pools of starlight
captive as though somehow the night itself were trapped
within her body and she was allowing him to glimpse it
through her eyes . . . as he had glimpsed it when she had
speared Neewalatli . . . as he had seen it in the moment
when she had commanded him to kill the captive girl upon
the dais, and to his shame, he had hesitated.

The memory jabbed sharply. He had killed many a
captive without a moment's hesitation. When Ysuna
commanded, he always obeyed. He owed her his life. Her
dreams told her that Thunder in the Sky demanded brides
in return for mammoth meat, and Masau would fulfill
those dreams as long as Ysuna and the god saw fit.

Restlessness touched him. Why had he hesitated?
The ritual killings had always pleased him as much as
luring the brides to their death brought pleasure to Maliwal.
He had lost count of the number of girls that he and his
brother had assisted into the world beyond this world. It
was beyond his powers of reasoning to understand why
Great Spirit would desire the childish, stupid, ineffectual
creatures. They had never touched the soul of Mystic

Warrior with desire or even with pity. The girls were no more than meat for Thunder in the Sky.

But when the last sacrifice had screamed in protest, Masau had looked up into Ysuna's eyes. Never had he noticed the malevolence there before. Was this what struck fear into others and sent them cowering back from her when they incurred her wrath? And had the look of darkness been for him or for Maliwal, who had caused the girl to scream?

Whatever the answer, the look was gone from Ysuna's eyes now. She was smiling at him, opening the lion skin, holding it wide, and inviting him to take the naked woman within.

"Come." Her voice was as low and resonant as the throaty purr of a great cat when it stretches itself in languor and licks its paws clean of blood and flesh after a kill. "Come, Masau. Be a man with me this night."

He stared. When he looked at Ysuna's perfect body, he could think of nothing else. The spirits of discontent had left him.

The woman closed the lion skin. Then, as if in triumph, she turned and looked back at him over her shoulder. "Come now, Mystic Warrior, before your brother returns to share in a pleasure that will be best if we indulge in it alone."

The statement was unexpected, as was his reaction to it. The spirits that had been haunting him for hours returned to speak through his mouth. "The boy Neewalatli was right. Had the wind turned, it might have driven the flames to the village or toward Maliwal and his hunting party. How could you have taken such a risk, Ysuna? Would you have done the same had I been out from the village?"

She whirled around and stood glaring. "How dare you question me? Without me you would be nothing! Maliwal would be nothing! Your lives are mine! Your power is mine! I know all! I take no 'risk.' The future is known to me before it happens!"

He was stunned. Never before had she directed her wrath toward him. And never before had she looked her age. In anger her features contorted, twisting into the mask of an extraordinarily beautiful but aging stranger. For the first time Masau saw vulnerability in her.

*The day has come upon which she has begun to grow old. Someday she will die. Someday you will live in the world without her.* His love for her struck him like a bolt of thunder. "Ysuna . . ."

She lowered her head, her fury spent. "After all these years, Masau, can you doubt the one who has given you life? the one who loves you above all others? the one who would share her youth and life with you forever?"

He stepped forward and drew her into an embrace. "Ah, Daughter of the Sun, I would do anything to make it so."

# 3

It was late when Maliwal, sweated and blackened with ash, stalked into the village with his dogs and his men. The village dogs, having recognized his scent, looked up from their resting places, yawned, and went back to sleep.

Maliwal frowned as he looked around for Ysuna. Why had she not prepared a greeting for him? Daughter of the Sun anticipated everything; she had known that he was coming back since the very moment he had commanded the others to return. Because she also knew that he was bringing no word of mammoth, she was showing him her disfavor. But what did she expect him to do? He was not blessed by the gift of Seeing. When he had noticed smoke on the horizon, he had rushed home, fearing the worst. How was he to know that the village was not in flames?

Only Nai was coming toward him. A slave! Surely Ysuna must be upset with him to send him such an unworthy welcome. He cursed the fire that had driven him to abandon prematurely the search for mammoth.

"Shh, Maliwal," cautioned Nai, her hand before her

mouth, her posture deferent as she revealed in a whisper: "It was Ysuna herself who set the blaze."

The other hunters murmured in disbelief.

Incredulous, Maliwal glared at the girl. "Why would she do that when she knew that I had a hunting party out from the village?"

"Ysuna does as she will. The fire was meant to drive away lions."

Maliwal did not comment when he heard the explanation. He had been a fool to have left the old wise man to die so close to the village. Nor did he speak when she told of the death of Neewalatli. No one challenged Ysuna's motives. The youngest son of Yatli had always been a fool and deserved to die.

He scowled. Women were coming silently from the lodges of his fellow hunters now, welcoming their returning men in loving, respectful whispers. Expectantly they looked to him for word of mammoth; when he gave none, they bowed their heads, accepting the news with grace but obvious disappointment.

With low grunts that passed for "good night," his fellow hunters left him. With dogs and women at their sides, they shuffled tiredly to their respective lodges. The women would care for the other hunters now; strong, sure feminine hands with oiled fingers would massage their trail-weary muscles until they relaxed into sleep or drew the women down to enjoy other pleasures. Maliwal's loins stirred as he stared off toward the lodge of the high priestess.

"She sleeps with your brother," revealed Nai, coming closer until his paired hunting dogs warned her away with low, menacing growls.

Maliwal's knuckles turned white as his fingers curled around his spears. "I will join them." He would have walked past her had she not risked the ire of the dogs by reaching out to stay him.

"Maliwal, listen. Please!"

Her tone was too imperative to ignore. He ordered the dogs to heel.

She swallowed, took a breath, then went on quickly. "They say that Masau was at her side last night when she made her kill. She gave him first taste of the lion's heart after she had eaten her fill. And later, she cast off her clothes and, wrapped only in the pelt, went to him. Together they went into her lodge. Together—after they sent me away—they roared like the lion on whose skin they lay, although they must have known that you would return. Oh, Maliwal, I would roar for you. Often I dream of how it could be between us. If only you were not hers and I were not her slave."

He stared. Her revelation had not surprised him. Of course she would want him; he was magnificent. Nevertheless, although he eyed her with sexual speculation, he said, "Why would I want you? I *am* Ysuna's. No woman can equal her. You are her *slave*."

"I . . ."

He silenced her with a snarl of impatience. Even in the darkness he could see that her face had paled with fear. Pleased, he reached out with his free arm and jerked her close. The sound of her gasp roused a chuckle from him. He tightened his grip, deliberately hurting her as he admonished, "Do you imagine that you are woman enough to make this man of Ysuna's roar?"

Fear and courage flashed in her eyes. "She blames you for bringing the lions too close to the village. She called you stupid and arrogant. She sent you off to find mammoth while, behind your back, she seeks her pleasure in the arms of Masau. She does not want you anymore, Maliwal. But *I* do!"

Now his eyes were bulging. He released the girl with a shove that was intended to knock her down, but Nai caught her balance and leaped lightly away as the momentum of his blow took him clumsily around in a half circle. The dogs looked to him for an attack command, but he wanted the pleasure of killing her for himself. His face was livid, his spear poised.

"I will not hear your lies! I, Maliwal, am First Man to Ysuna. With her own mouth she has said this to me. It is I whom she sends to seek the mammoth! It is I who secures the sacrifices that are the lifeblood of the People. Always it has been so! Always it *will* be so!"

Nai was shaking. She knew that she had gone too far. "What has made you assume that Ysuna, who knows all, does not also *hear* all? What must she think of her servant now? Perhaps the People of the Watching Star will not have to steal the daughter of another band when it comes time for the next sacrifice."

Nai's legs buckled; she rocked on her feet and nearly fell. She was suddenly and violently sick.

He laughed at her miserable retching and, without another word, headed for the lodge of Ysuna.

Eyes closed, Ysuna lay partially awake in Masau's arms, awash in the warm, familiar streams of her subconscious mind. She saw herself walking alone within the misted fibers of her mind. She was a tall figure, clothed only in light and in her sacred collar as she moved slowly through wide, dark corridors of time beneath the huge, unblinking eye of the Watching Star.

Something wonderful loomed ahead in the darkness. She could not see or even begin to guess what it was, but she knew that she must possess it. As she drifted deeper into sleep, the eye of the Watching Star reddened then closed. The darkness thickened around her as she hurried on. Black, miasmic, it yielded no passage.

Suddenly she found herself sweeping through long strands of human finger bones, which clicked and sang like shards of volcanic glass in the wind. The sense of wonder was strong in her now as the curtains of bone fell away and dissolved into the night.

She came to pause before a gigantic juniper tree. Tall it was and as shaggy as a bison in winter. Its branches stretched wide and high, and its base was so massive, it would have taken ten men to encircle it with their arms. She stared at it, transfixed, then moved forward and, to her amazement, passed through it as though it were not there.

At last she stopped at the base of a great canyon. Even in the darkness she could see a waterfall plunging from one of many soaring cliffs that towered thousands of feet above the canyon floor. The air was sharp with the smell of roses and unfamiliar trees. Her nostrils expanded and drew in the scent of grazing animals—deer, pronghorn, horse, tapir, peccary. And mammoth! She caught her breath as a sense of wonder nearly overwhelmed her.

Then, suddenly, from directly behind her a lion roared. She whirled and stared. The sense of euphoria left her.

The taste of blood and salt filled her mouth. Sensing danger, she stepped back. A lion crouched above her in the branches. She knew this beast! He was a skeleton cat—old and headless and devoid of skin—and yet he spoke to her in the voice of a man:

"Do you imagine that Thunder in the Sky did not see who took the lead upon the last hunt? It was not you, Ysuna! And do you believe that the spirit of this lion—and of this wise man who died at Maliwal's hand by your command and was eaten by this lion—will allow you to forget us?"

Ysuna moaned against the dream. The headless lion prepared to leap. Within the capacious hollow of its skeletal chest cavity, the figure of an old man was curled like a fetus. Gut-wounded, bloodied, he stretched his corpse-pale, noncorporeal substance until he aligned his form to that of the lion. And now, as the great cat sprang out of the tree, it had the head of the old man. With fangs bared, Ish-iwi came for Ysuna and screamed for vengeance.

"I will have the sacred stone that you stole from me!"

"No!" she cried, and clutching her collar of sacred stones and human hair, she wheeled and fled deeper into the dream, racing headlong into the vastness of the canyon.

The lion did not follow, but the ghost of the old man called after her, "Run as you will, Ysuna. You have eaten of the heart and flesh of the meat eater that has eaten me. My spirit is within you now, and in the end I will have of you what I will."

Then the ghost of Ish-iwi laughed, a hollow cacophony that grew faint until it could be heard no more.

Ysuna trembled within the dream. She saw herself moving deeper and deeper into the canyon. Mammoth walked ahead of her, as many mammoth as there were stars in the sky. She salivated, tasting blood and salt again. She slowed her steps and followed the mammoth until he appeared—Great Ghost Spirit . . . Thunder in the Sky . . . a white mammoth, the source of all wonder. Her heart was pounding.

In her dream a man and woman rode astride the high, swaying shoulders of the mammoth. Their backs were to her, so she could not see their faces; but she could tell that they were young and strong, beautiful and without fear.

She was certain that the man was Masau. Who else but Mystic Warrior would be bold enough to ride upon the back of the god? And when the woman turned and looked back through the swirling, wind-combed black hair, she knew that she had to be looking at herself. The mammoth plodded on, leaving her behind as they followed Thunder in the Sky and the two who rode upon his back. She called out for the god to wait, but he did not. Behind him the ghosts of his many brides materialized to follow in a silent, diaphanous column until, once more, Ysuna was alone in the darkness of her dream.

Shivering, she knelt and looked down to see herself and the stars reflected in a pool of blood. Startled and appalled, she stared not at youth or at Daughter of the Sun. Her reflection showed the withered form of an ancient hag.

"No!" She screamed in horror and jumped to her feet.

Somewhere far away beyond the entrance of the canyon, a lion roared and an old man laughed.

Her hands flew to her collar of sacred stones. "No!" she cried again, and even as she spoke she felt the power growing in her.

The stars began to fall around her, and Thunder in the Sky appeared on the opposite side of the pool. He was alone now, a great white mammoth, massive and magnificent.

She stood motionless, then her head went high as she felt his power. She named him god and totem, and as she did he raised his massive head and pierced the night with his tusks.

The world shook. Falling stars turned red. Suddenly, as Ysuna screamed, the great mammoth collapsed and dissolved into the pool.

She stood alone in a rain of blood. She knelt again, made a cup of her hand, dipped it into the pool, then drank. The taste of blood was the taste of the white mammoth. She sluiced its hot saltiness through her teeth and savored the feel of its oozing down the back of her throat.

She looked into the pool, and instead of seeing the hag, Ysuna found a woman of eternal youth and beauty . . . an immortal clothed in the skin of a white mammoth. Masau, Mystic Warrior, stood at her side, and a golden grassland stretched out forever behind him, treed with the lodges of a people whose number exceeded that of the stars in the sky.

"Ysuna?"

Maliwal's voice drew her from the dream. She was shaken, not certain if she had heard it at all. She sat up in the darkness of her lodge. Her long, slim fingers worked the stones of her necklet. Beside her, lying on his side amid the jumbled bed furs, Mystic Warrior slept the deep, satisfied sleep of a man who has been mated well.

Masau had come into her twice this night. Both of them had burned and roared at the ecstasy of release. Nevertheless, she had been troubled by an uncharacteristic tenderness and solicitousness that had underlain his lovemaking. Her mouth turned down. Those emotions had always disgusted her; they were for the sick and the old. Is that how he thought of her? As the hag in the reflecting pool?

Revolted, she winced and then looked up.

Maliwal had drawn aside the hide weather flaps of her lodge and was looking in at her with lust and longing. "I have returned," he announced in a deferent and meaningful and hopeful whisper.

Disgust flared bright at his statement of the obvious. "Have you found the sign of mammoth to the south?"

"No. The smoke from your fire made me fear for the village and caused me to turn back."

She stiffened. "So you have failed me again. Can you do nothing correctly these days? The meat of the last mammoth kill is nearly gone from this village. Go! Do not return until you bring back word of that which I seek."

"But, Ysuna, I have only just returned. I have come far and driven my men and dogs without rest, and all in fear for you and—"

"Find me mammoth, Maliwal!" she hissed at him, and although Masau awakened and sat up with a questioning frown beside her, she chose to ignore him as she fixed her ire upon his older brother. "Go! Find me a new bride for Thunder in the Sky! One that does not scream! Find me another village that is made strong by the power of the sacred stone, and then bring that stone to me! And this time, Wolf, make certain that the village shaman does not see the treachery of your intent! Choose fresh men and dogs, and go now! Or perhaps you are no longer man enough for Ysuna, and it is time for me to send Masau in your place?"

"I . . ." Shattered, shamed before his brother, and completely taken aback, Maliwal failed to defend himself.

"My lodge is closed to a man who cannot work my will and blocked to a son who has drawn lions and ghosts to threaten my people and feed upon me within my dreams!" Ysuna shouted at him, then sneered with open contempt. "Prove your worth to me once more, Maliwal. Find me mammoth and sacred stones and a bride worthy of Thunder in the Sky—or do not come back at all!"

Dazed, Maliwal backed out of the lodge of Ysuna. For a long while he stood in stunned silence.

"I will find you mammoth," he grated. "I will find you a village that grows strong on the power of the sacred stone. I will find you new hunting grounds and a bride for Thunder in the Sky . . . a bride that does *not* scream. And when I have done this, I will come back. Your lodge will be open to me, and you will know which one of your sons is man enough for you—Masau the Mystic or Maliwal the Wolf!"

# PART III

# BLUE MESAS

# 1

In the late afternoon of the travelers' fourth day away from the Lake of Many Singing Birds, Cha-kwena paused at the edge of a vast, white, sweeping flatland to stare across miles of shimmering heat haze. The mesas appeared to float above the barrens a good day's walk ahead. Squinting against the glare, he was unable to make out the great rift that divided the ranges; they appeared to be a solid mass, miles long, cutting off all views of the north, and they no longer appeared blue at all. Disappointment became awe as Cha-kwena admired a range of dazzling colors: reds and oranges and yellows where the bare bones of the mountain walls lay exposed to the rays of the sun; purples in the shadowed canyons; greens on the high, forested foothills; and eye-burning white and uncountable variations of gray where gathering rain clouds had lowered to rest and growl upon the flat-topped summits.

"We may see rain before nightfall," Dakan-eh predicted as he came to stand beside Cha-kwena.

Hoyeh-tay paused between the hunter and the boy, drew in the scent and texture of the surrounding air, then shook his head slowly, lest he disturb Owl, perching on his left shoulder. "No, it is the rain spirits' way to gather on the heights of the Blue Mesas at the ending of many a summer day. They will pass the night there and be gone before morning."

Cha-kwena's face wrinkled with puzzlement. "Why do the mesas no longer appear blue, Grandfather?"

"A trick of the eyes and the miles," replied the old man. "Things always change as you come closer to them, Cha-kwena. Mountains . . . people—it is the same. If we were standing upon the mesa tops looking upon the land below, do you imagine that we would we see Owl and

81

three travelers from the Lake of Many Singing Birds? No. Through the haze of heat and the distortions of distance, we would see what appeared to be three ants and a mite standing on the white surface of a dead lake."

Dakan-eh frowned. "Was there not water in this lake the last time we trekked to the great pinyon gathering?"

"Yes, but not much," replied Cha-kwena, scanning the surroundings and surprised at how well he suddenly remembered the scenery. He had been only seven at the time of the band's last trip to the pinyon harvest. He smiled, envisioning himself as he was then: a small boy, as thin as a reed and as flexible. As on this day, he could feel the sun hot on his back while the boy in his memories waded knee-deep into the muck of the receding lakeshore with his childhood friends, joyfully instigating a mud fight that had driven their mothers to distraction and had inspired the men of the band to join them. In the end, the women and girls had joined them, too. He would never forget that day. It had been one of the best times of the entire journey—indeed, of his entire life.

Hoyeh-tay was staring straight ahead. He seemed disturbed and more than a little disoriented. "How many winters between now and then? Many. Three, I think."

"Six," corrected Dakan-eh, then reminded gently, "Usually the band makes the journey every third autumn; but in these past years of little rain the pinyon forests have produced a scant crop, one that could not justify relocating the entire band—"

"Six?" the old man interrupted with a shout of amazement. His mind had fastened upon Dakan-eh's first word; he had no interest in the rest. The number obviously had shocked him, but he covered his surprise quickly. "Yes, of course, six! That is what I meant to say. Does Bold Man think that I do not remember? Hmmph! I do not need you to remind me that pinyon trees tend to produce a bountiful yield every third autumn unless an early freeze takes the buds or there is too much rain or it does not rain at all! I know all! I see all! And I remember everything!"

Dakan-eh was astounded by the forceful reprimand, but that did not prevent him from sighing with strained tolerance and eyeing the shaman with pity. "Of course," he said with condescension.

Cha-kwena looked closely at Hoyeh-tay. The past days and nights upon the trail were telling upon the old man. He was slow of foot and increasingly slow of mind. Twice in one day he had stopped and hunkered on his heels, pretending to meditate, when it was clear to both Cha-kwena and Dakan-eh that he was exhausted and confused as to the way ahead. The boy was haunted by the memory of Tlana-quah's warning:

"Your grandfather is very old, and I fear that there may not be as much time as you think to learn from him all that will be necessary before you take his place in the band. Learn quickly and well from him, Cha-kwena. And be a gentle and understanding guide when his spirit wanders."

The words gripped Cha-kwena's gut like a spasm brought on by bad meat. *No!* his spirit cried in silent protest. *Hoyeh-tay is not so old! He will live long!* In defense of the old man, he blurted: "My grandfather speaks the truth. He has made the journey to the Land of the Blue Mesas every year, and it is his great wisdom that leads us now."

Hoyeh-tay, startled by the unexpected accolade, stood taller. His chin jabbed outward, and his mouth turned down into a scowl of pride. "Yes. It is so," he affirmed, less with arrogance than with relief. "And now we will go on."

In other days their route would have taken them along the south shore of Big Lake for many miles before allowing them to strike westward once again in a direct line toward their destination. Today, however, there was no lake to block their passage, and the way due west was open to them.

Nevertheless, Hoyeh-tay hesitated. His eyes narrowed to examine the distances of dry lake that stretched ahead. The region looked flat, white, shimmering in the heat of the afternoon, and hostile in the light of unfamiliarity.

"I do not know this land," the shaman confessed. "The old and proven paths of the ancestors are the ways we must follow to the Blue Mesas. Come, there is no use wasting time lingering here."

He would have led the others on along the old, circuitous route had Owl not risen from his shoulder and flown westward. It was an omen that took the old man's breath away.

Cha-kwena suddenly pointed off. "Look! Do you see? Out there on the dry lake bed in the shadow of Owl's wings? The tracks of Coyote and of Hare . . . no, more than one hare! And Coyote . . . he walks on three legs as he stalks his dinner to the west! There is enough meat for all. Come! Owl would have us follow to share Coyote's meat!"

Both Hoyeh-tay and Dakan-eh frowned, for they saw nothing in the shadow of the bird's wings.

Surprised by their reactions, Cha-kwena shook his head, walked a few more steps, and showed them what he thought was plain. "Look!" he said again, pointing to the footprints of a lone coyote in pursuit of at least two hare. "The tracks lead due west across the exposed lake bottom!"

His heart was leaping with excitement. What a tracker he had become, to have seen the tracks before Dakan-eh had noticed them! What an asset he would be to his band when he finally became a hunter! "You have taught me well!" he exclaimed to Dakan-eh, beaming, hoping that Bold Man would now say something to old Hoyeh-tay about his grandson's natural gifts as a hunter. When the man did not speak, Cha-kwena prodded eagerly: "Tell him what a good student I have been, Dakan-eh! Tell him that I was born to be a hunter, not a shaman!"

Dakan-eh eyed him briefly, coolly, then turned to Hoyeh-tay and said, "These tracks must be spirit tracks, or surely I would have seen them first. He must have magical powers."

Cha-kwena stared with disbelief at his ideal man. Betrayed and deeply hurt, he snapped, "Just because I saw them before you did doesn't make them magic! I am younger than you, Dakan-eh! My eyes are sharp, my senses quick!"

"Be silent, Cha-kwena!" Hoyeh-tay commanded. "Dakan-eh is right. There *are* omens to be read in the tracks of these spirits."

Cha-kwena gritted his teeth.

"A coyote who walks on three legs," injected Dakan-eh in the tone of an all-knowing seer, "and two—no, perhaps as many as four hare head west."

Cha-kwena was furious with him. "I already said that! But since you know so much, maybe *you* should be the next shaman!"

"Enough," Hoyeh-tay admonished quietly. He knelt and lay a questing palm over the tracks. Eyes closed, face set, he allowed the indentations in the surface of the lake bed to speak to him. "Coyote walks ahead of us on three legs. The spirits of pain may walk with him. But is not Coyote also trickster? Hare and his long-eared, grass-eating kind run before this lame Little Yellow Wolf Who Sings. Hare is in fear for his life, but he is quick and clever." He thought for a moment, then asked, "Does Little Yellow Wolf favor one hind paw because he walks with the spirits of pain? Or does he wish to fool Hare so that Hare will drop his guard and more easily become food for Coyote?"

Hoyeh-tay paused again. His eyelids quivered. "Perhaps Coyote is not pursuing Hare at all. It may be Coyote's purpose to lure us from the path of the ancestors with the promise of fresh meat."

"Every night since leaving our village my traps and spear have won fresh meat for us," reminded Dakan-eh.

Hoyeh-tay nodded. "Yes. This is so."

"*His* spear? *His* traps?" Cha-kwena was livid. "It is *my* spear that took last night's antelope!"

"A sickly doe," scoffed Dakan-eh. "Wasted meat. It was my kill that fed us."

"Armadillo, roasted in its skin! Yuk!" Cha-kwena felt a twinge of guilt. The armadillo had been as big as a goat and as tasty; they had stuffed themselves with it.

Hoyeh-tay was not listening. Visibly upset, he climbed to his feet and stood staring westward across the dry lake. "Omens . . . signs . . . would Coyote show us a new shorter route and be a helping spirit to us, or are there dangers to confound us on new paths, and does he make his song of laughter at our expense?"

Dakan-eh shrugged. "There are dangers to be found on all paths, Hoyeh-tay. But if you are still anxious about the well-being of your old friend Ish-iwi, consider that we will save much time by following Coyote."

The old man stiffened. His hand drifted to his throat, and his fingers curled around his medicine bag. "Ish-iwi. Yes. I *must* see Ish-iwi again. There is so much to talk about . . . so much that I . . . must know. . . ."

Cha-kwena saw that the old man's mind was drifting. The youth glared reproachfully at Dakan-eh and accused, "And you would choose the fastest way so that you can get back to Ta-maya before she changes her mind about you again."

"She will never do that!" declared Dakan-eh.

"Oh, yes, she will!" Cha-kwena shot back, and although the insult was based solely on his own momentary vindictiveness, he knew that somehow he had spoken the truth.

Ta-maya *would* refuse him. Bold Man would return to their village with gifts of gold and words that would make the daughter of Tlana-quah weep aloud with joy as she said yes to him. But then, before the day of their union came, as surely as sunrise followed moonset, she would turn her back upon him and accept another.

The vision, which must surely prove that old Hoyeh-tay was right about his calling to the shaman's road, left Cha-kwena dry mouthed and weak-kneed. He shook his head to clear it of unwelcome thoughts. *No!* he vowed. *I will* not *be shaman!*

The wind was rising. Owl had returned to perch upon Hoyeh-tay's head. The old man was lucid again, his eyes bright, his face relaxed, his mind made up. "If Owl, my helping animal spirit, has shown us the way, then we must follow. In the tracks of Hare and Coyote we will go; but while we walk let us sing songs of praise to our ancestors. We leave their way behind, and we would not wish to offend them or cause bad spirits to follow."

# 2

They followed the tracks of Coyote and Hare westward, mile after mile, across the enormous basin that once held the waters of Big Lake. Hours passed. They walked and rested, then walked again, but still the cloud-topped Blue Mesas loomed far ahead, floating on a haze raised by heat and distance.

Dry-mouthed and wishing that his fellow travelers and he had thought to bring water along, Cha-kwena began to wonder if they would ever reach the cool, spring-fed pools that lay in the pinyon-forested foothills of the distant mesas.

"Soon," assured Hoyeh-tay, either knowing his grandson's thoughts or anticipating them because of his own thirst. "Soon we will drink."

But despite the shaman's promise, the dry lake bed seemed to stretch on forever. Nothing grew on it except crystallized deposits of mineral salts. Cha-kwena had never seen anything quite like them. As white and delicate as solidified river foam, they twisted across the basin's surface like the raised cores of gopher tunnels left exposed after the melt of a winter snowpack. An inch to three inches in height, the labyrinthine encrustations appeared solid enough, but they crumbled beneath the weight of Cha-kwena's every step. And as his companions and he plodded on across the dry, hard-packed mud that lay beneath the salty rime, their footfalls roused a pale, powdery dust that stung their eyes, burned their skin, and caused them to taste a strange amalgam of sodiums whenever they licked their lips.

At last Dakan-eh shook his handsome head against weariness and thirst, paused, and, with an exhalation of acquiescence, drew three golden nuggets from the traveling pack that Ban-ya had given him. Ever since finding them, he had spent his evenings smoothing and polishing them until now they were round and shining nearly without flaw.

"Here," Bold Man offered, popping one into his mouth and handing a nugget each to Hoyeh-tay and Cha-kwena. "Suck on these, but carefully. Don't dent them. They will help you to work up enough spit to keep your mouth moist. And don't swallow them! I'll want them back when we find water."

Cha-kwena refused the offering. "I am not thirsty," he lied, and walked on without another word to one whom he no longer considered a friend.

At last the sun slipped behind the Blue Mesas. A soft wind whispered across the basin, raising dust devils on the dry lake bed. There was talk of resting for the night, but the prospect was not appealing. The temperature was still oppressively hot; there was no water or sign of game save the tracks of the hares that ran ahead of Coyote. Even though Hoyeh-tay was exhausted, the old shaman insisted that they go on.

"It is still light enough to travel." He pointed off. "Clouds continue to build over the Blue Mesas. The wind that will come down to us at nightfall will be sweet and moist with the scent of rain. In the cool of the night we will share our traveling rations, sleep, and dream away our thirst. Tomorrow we will put this dry country behind us. Tomorrow we will drink our fill at the springs of the People of the Blue Mesas."

They trudged on until dusk. For the first time since dawn, the mesas appeared blue again under their billowing cloud cover, and a cool wind that smelled of highland rain blew softly and tantalizingly across the surface of the dry lake.

Owl, perched on the shaman's head, stretched and yawned and picked his toes for a while before abandoning the callused bald spot that he had made upon the old man's cranium and flying off to the west.

The shaman sighed wistfully as he stared after his old friend. "Even as we watch, Owl reaches the mesas' cool springs. Ah, yes, he is there by now, winging high and selecting his perch. Owl will have wood rat for dinner. He will sate his thirst in blood and in the marrow of many little bones."

Dakan-eh eyed the old man drolly. Wiping sweat and dust and salts from his face, he hunkered on his heels, rested his spears across his thighs, and after taking the gold nugget from his mouth, said, "How fortunate you are to be a shaman, Hoyeh-tay. In the dark of this night you can fly away upon the wind to join Owl on his hunt. When you have had your fill of meat and blood, perhaps you will bring back a rat or two for us to 'drink.'"

Hoyeh-tay turned and eyed Bold Man. "Perhaps I will do just that," remarked the shaman in the same droll way. "But could you withstand the shock if I did?"

Dakan-eh smiled and was about to reply when suddenly four sharp-winged swallows appeared from the west and swooped low, heading directly for Cha-kwena. The boy ducked as the swallows banked and dove at him. In a flurry of wings and high, soft *chee*ing calls, they circled madly about his head until he whirled and slapped at them as though they were mosquitoes.

Despite fatigue, Hoyeh-tay guffawed merrily, then nearly choked on the golden pebble that Dakan-eh had given him to ease his thirst. Sputtering and gasping, he took the gold from his mouth and watched the swallows as they flew on, unharmed, toward the east. "Ah," he said, sighing as he fixed his grandson with watering, amused eyes. "You must thank your little friends, Cha-kwena, for bringing their message to you!"

"They are no friends of mine," protested the boy. "And they gave me no message. You are Shaman, Grandfather! If they had had something to say, it would have been to you, not to me!"

"Ah, Cha-kwena, Little Brother of Animals . . . " The old man clucked his tongue in loving admonition. "Why should the swallows not share their secrets with you? Has not Life Giver, the totem of our ancestors, allowed you to look upon his family and his little white son? Does not Owl share his thoughts with you and guide your eyes and tip his wings in your direction? Has not Hawk fallen from the sky so that you might heal him? Has not Deer entrusted her fawn to you? Have not Coyote and

Hare conspired to reveal their tracks to you before Bold Man and I could see them? The message of the swallows was clear enough, my boy. You did not even need to use your third eye to see that their beaks were glistening with wet, fresh mud."

"And where there is mud, there is water," put in Dakan-eh sagely as he got to his feet. "And if the mud looks wet, then water is very near."

Cha-kwena's face flamed defensively. "Everybody knows that! But how could I have looked for signs when the birds were swarming like biting flies all over me?"

"A hunter is always on the lookout for signs," replied Dakan-eh with cool dignity.

"But signs *come* to a shaman," added Hoyeh-tay with solemn emphasis, "as the swallows came to you, Cha-kwena."

"They came *at* me, not *to* me!" Cha-kwena was adamant. "Besides, it is too late in the summer for swallows to be gathering mud with which to build their lodges!"

"Yes, it is," affirmed Hoyeh-tay. "Nevertheless their beaks were thick and wet with mud—not for their lodges but as a sign for you. They have shown you the way to water, Cha-kwena. And I don't know about you, Grandson, but this old man is thirsty."

## 3

It was nearly dark when the coyote tracks led them to the place from which the swallows had flown. Frogs were croaking, and little brown bats were all around, diving and soaring as they feasted on insects.

Hoyeh-tay sighed and, smiling with relief, gestured wide. "The animal spirits that are brothers to my grandson have led us well!"

Cha-kwena was too parched and tired to disagree. Now that the heat was abating and the first stars were beginning to show, he walked eagerly with the others to the lowest portion of the great basin. Cha-kwena waved his way through airborne mists of biting flies and mosquitoes. What did a few bites and stings matter? The travelers had found water at last!

All that remained of Big Lake was a broad expanse of large, spring-fed brackish pools choked with sickly-looking water plants and stunted reeds and surrounded by broken, deeply eroded embankments softened by thick hummocks of long, weather-bleached grass.

The frogs stopped singing as the travelers approached, but the insects closed ranks and the bats continued to swoop and dive as Cha-kwena, Dakan-eh, and Hoyeh-tay ran joyously to the closest pond, threw down their spears, cast off their traveling packs, and prostrated themselves belly down upon the shore.

Cha-kwena had never been so thirsty. Eyes closed, he was just about to plunge his face rapturously into the water when an exclamation of disgust from Dakan-eh startled him. He opened his eyes and looked down. Revolted, he drew back. The pond was not water at all; it was a foul-looking pudding thick with yellowish-green algae over which flies and gnats were swarming while the bodies of countless of their drowned cousins floated in the muck. "We can't drink this!"

"If frogs live in it, we can drink it." Dakan-eh grimaced as he extended his right arm, put his hand into the pool, and with a slow, sideways motion swept aside algae and unidentifiable decaying organic matter. As a milky liquid bubbled to the surface Bold Man shook his head. "It isn't much," he conceded with disgust, "but I am thirsty enough to drink it—unless, of course, your old grandfather wants to fly off after Owl and bring us some *real* water from the springs at the base of the mesas."

"Hmmph!" the shaman snorted with annoyance. "A few hours ago you would have been satisfied to suck blood from a rat!" He knelt back and looked at the grass that grew all around. With deft fingers, he picked the greenest, softest stalks and wove them in the same way that women created mats for bedding and lodge covers.

"What are you doing, Grandfather?" Cha-kwena asked, wondering if Hoyeh-tay had lost his mind.

"Watch! Learn!" commanded the old man. "Here is a trick of the ancestors, one that Dakan-eh should have taught you and the other boys long ago. But I see from Bold Man's face that he has not learned this lesson. Or perhaps, like me, he has begun to grow old and has forgotten it!"

"Old?" Dakan-eh was openly irked. "Only eighteen winters have passed since I came into this world from between my mother's thighs! My thoughts, unlike yours, hold memories like a good, tight basket! I have forgotten *nothing*! Water is good, or water is bad. I know the ways to find it and to tell if it is safe. And I know how to drink it even when it is foul! Like this!" The declaration made, he scooped up a handful of muck and palmed it forcefully into his mouth.

Hoyeh-tay chuckled at Dakan-eh's expense as the young man did his best to keep from gagging against the rank taste. "That is one way, yes. I myself would not choose it, but . . ." He shrugged, and his mirthful expression vanished. "Long ago, my friend Ish-iwi taught me the way of those who dwell where there is much grass but little water. He showed me this way to drink clear water where there is none to be had."

The old man lay down again. Edging forward on his stomach until his head was well over the pond, he reached out with the gentlest of fingers, set the woven grasses flat upon the algae, then lowered his face to the little raft of grass. With his right hand maintaining his balance on the embankment and his left holding the matting steady on the surface of the pond, he pursed his lips and, while applying only the slightest downward pressure with his face on the little pad of grass, began to suck up clear water.

"Ah!" Cha-kwena cried, truly impressed. His grandfather had devised a crude but effective filter through which clean water could be sucked into the mouth while the thicker unwanted muck, algae, and insects were trapped below.

After rolling onto his side, the old man eyed Dakan-eh. "Come, Bold Man! Try this trick. I am too weary to fly off after Owl so that I might bring you rats to 'drink' or to fetch you better water than this to which Coyote, Hare, and the swallows have so generously led us."

Night came down slowly, setting itself silently upon the world. Frogs began to sing again. If Coyote was about, there was no sign of him. If Hare was near, he made no sound. Gnats whined, and mosquitoes droned. Flies sought rest under cover of the grass as bats continued their nocturnal dives. Something—a water snake, perhaps, or a large, sluggish freshwater fish—made a soft, slow, slurring sound as it cut a wake across the algae-thick surface of the pond. Stars gradually became brighter, except in the west, where they were eclipsed by the mountainous storm clouds. The boiling massifs and the distant flat-topped ranges that lay below were invisible until lightning flashed, illuminating them. Enthralled, Cha-kwena stared. Never in his life had he seen a display of lightning to equal this one, and now for the first time, in the livid, throbbing glare of the distant storm, he saw the rift that divided the Blue Mesas—a V-shaped notch a thousand feet deep and so narrow at the top that he wondered if a man might lean across it.

Hoyeh-tay, too exhausted to eat, now lay curled up and asleep under his cape of rabbit fur. Meanwhile Bold Man and Cha-kwena—with their own capes over their heads, and their faces and exposed skin slathered with mud to protect them against biting insects—consumed the last of their traveling rations in weary silence. Dakan-eh offered to share the remaining fillets of leftover armadillo that he had packed from last night's camp, but Cha-kwena, still nursing a grudge, refused it.

"As you wish," said Bold Man, consuming it all.

Cha-kwena swallowed the last of the delicacies that his mother had packed for him: seeds and berries and rancid antelope fat rolled into a ball. Days and nights on the trail had not improved the taste. The fat had gone soft and globular, and the berries were not fully ripe. The sourness made Cha-kwena's face pucker. In the darkness, however, Dakan-eh did not notice.

Licking his fingers clean of the last of the armadillo juices, Bold Man indicated the western horizon with a nod of his head. "As the old man promised, it is raining in the high country."

"The 'old man' is *Shaman* to you!" retorted Cha-kwena. He lay back and folded his hands beneath his head. "I wish it would rain here," he said, more to himself than to Dakan-eh.

"I doubt if it has done that for many a long moon," the hunter replied, having taken no offense. "Never have I seen a country so dry, so desolate. And this land was once rich with game and grass and welcoming with water. How strange it is to see it like this. The ancestors of First Man and First Woman came this way, following immense herds of mammoth, bison, horse, and three different kinds of pronghorn. The ancestors hunted an animal that I have never seen: a huge hairy pig with skin as scaled and tough as a lizard's and horns on its nose and a temper as vile as a fire ant's and—"

"Horn Nose." Cha-kwena spoke the name that his people gave to a creature that men of another age would call rhinoceros. "Old Owl told me that he saw one once, long ago, in his youth. He said that it was not as big as a mammoth or half so wise. His people drove it over a deadfall and killed it. They ate its flesh, but the meat was tough. From that day not a single other one of its kind has been seen in all the Red World."

"Yes." Dakan-eh's voice took on a dreamy quality. "The men hunted them with great, heavy spears and spear hurlers—much heavier and longer than the ones we use today. Oh, what I would not give to face down such a beast and kill it. I would bring the horn to Ta-maya. I would stand before Tlana-quah and demand to know who else could undertake such a challenge in order to bring honor to his daughter. Only Dakan-eh! Only Bold Man!"

Cha-kwena sighed at Dakan-eh's conceit. Through half-closed lids he watched the blue fire of lightning flare and subside within the distant thunderclouds. It was an awe-inspiring display. With each flash the clouds were illuminated in all their tumultuous glory while the flat-topped mountains seemed to pulse black and alive beneath them. The broad flatland that had once been a lake gleamed as white as the full face of Moon. How magnificent it was! He sat up, suddenly restless. "How far away do you think they are?"

"The clouds? A day's walk, no more. You and I could have been there by now. Your grandfather slows us."

"You are too hard on him, Dakan-eh."

"He is hard on himself—and upon the two of us—by pretending to be other than he is."

"And just what is that?"

"A man who is making his last trip to the Blue Mesas."

Cha-kwena was suddenly chilled to his heart. Dakan-eh had spoken the truth. He knew it as much as he hated it. "I wish he were young again! I wish that my father were here with Hoyeh-tay and me. And I wish that this stinking little pool before us were still a lake so that we could swim away across it all the way to the Blue Mesas. I wish—"

"Be careful, Cha-kwena. If the old man is right about you, who knows what kind of spirits may be listening?"

"I hope they *are* listening!" the boy snapped. "I long for rain! I long for sweet, cool water to drink. I *want* my grandfather to be young again! If he were young and strong, I would not have to be a shaman."

"If." Dakan-eh turned the word bitterly, then shrugged. "And if I, instead of you, had been chosen to be shaman, I would not have to worry over whether Ta-maya will change her mind again. If I were a shaman, not even the headman would dare to interfere, for I could turn the spirits against those who angered me. I would know the pathway to her heart as surely as you knew the way to water."

"But I didn't know the way!"

"Of course you did. You saw Coyote's tracks before I did."

"Only because you taught me how to look for sign!"

"No, only by a shaman's magic could a boy have bested me. The swallows proved that."

"Those stupid swallows prove nothing!" exclaimed Cha-kwena in frustration. "All of my life I have wanted to be a hunter like you, Dakan-eh. *No!* A *better* hunter, a *better* tracker. And most certainly a better friend to the boys who will look up to me and put their trust in me—as I have put my trust in you. You sided with Hoyeh-tay against me. Why, Dakan-eh? *Why?* I thought we were friends!"

Sobered by Cha-kwena's outburst, Dakan-eh looked steadily at the boy. "Learn one more lesson from me then, Cha-kwena. The blood of many generations of spirit masters flows in your veins. If Old Owl has said that you are to be

Shaman, then like it or not you *are* to be Shaman. Accept this. Take pride in it. And remember always that boy or man, hunter or shaman, you will never find a better friend than the one who tells you the truth . . . especially when you do not want to hear it."

# 4

Lightning continued to flash over the distant mesas. Thunder sounded across the miles. Cha-kwena observed the display and waited for old Hoyeh-tay to begin the story of the ever-battling twin war gods of the sky; full of conflict and thunder drums and flying spears made of lightning bolts, it was one of the few tales of the ancient ones that the boy actually liked. But beneath his cape of rabbit skins Hoyeh-tay snored on undisturbed while Dakan-eh stretched out beneath his own traveling cloak and, breathing deeply, twitched against his dreams.

Cha-kwena envied them. He was very tired, but try as he might, he could not sleep. Wide-awake and inexplicably restless, he sat cross-legged on the embankment above the pool. His cape was bundled around him like a little tent. Nearby, frogs croaked, while far away to the west, Coyote howled balefully and then began to bark.

Cha-kwena cocked his head. There was something imperative about the sound; he sensed a summons in it.

"Rise now, Cha-kwena!" implored Coyote. "Rise, Little Brother of Animals! Wake the others and hurry across the lowland and into the high hills!"

Cha-kwena slapped his hands over his ears, curled forward, and buried his head deep between his folded knees. "I am not your brother, Little Yellow Wolf! If you must howl in the night, howl to your own kind, not to me!"

But Coyote's barks became howls again, louder,

sharper, and even more imperative than before. "Come, Cha-kwena! Come to the foothills of the Blue Mesas. Come *now!*"

Cha-kwena cringed. "No!" he replied vehemently, whispering lest he wake the others. "You have led me far, Little Yellow Wolf, and I thank you if you have deliberately shown my companions and me the way to water. But I am tired. I must get some sleep."

His words settled in the darkness. Cha-kwena felt very foolish indeed, muttering in response to the imagined words of a coyote that was miles away. He sat up, pulled his knees to his chin, wrapped his arms around his folded limbs, and listened to the coyote's howls. He felt better. They were only howls now—no longer words. And yet only a few moments before he had been so certain that the animal had been addressing him that he had been foolish enough to answer back.

He sighed, disconcerted, as Coyote howled on and on. Soon, although Cha-kwena did not intend to do so, he found himself reasoning: *If you want to be my helping spirit, Little Yellow Wolf, then be quiet so I can sleep. Come to me in my dreams, in the vision that I have been seeking for so long! I do not want to hear you when I am awake!* He liked the sound of the words. Yellow Wolf would be a name worthy of a man of the People, a hunter's name that he would be proud to claim as his own.

"I will not be quiet! I cannot wait until you sleep before I may speak! You must hear me now!"

Cha-kwena was so startled by Coyote's reply that he jumped. He waited for more words, but only yappings and ululations came to him. He shook his head, again feeling the fool. Coyote's howling was so loud that the youth could not understand how Hoyeh-tay and Dakan-eh could sleep through it. And if Coyote had spoken with a human voice, how could a shaman of such power as Hoyeh-tay fail to have heard it?

*He is an old man,* the reply came from within his mind, an echo of Tlana-quah's last words to him, and of Dakan-eh's: *an old man who is making his last trip to the Blue Mesas.*

Cha-kwena felt sick with remorse. "I will not believe that. Because I am tired, my spirit is playing tricks on me!" He closed his eyes and yearned for sleep and for the visions that would prove that he was a hunter.

He sighed. The thought was pleasant. The voice of Coyote was fainter now. When the howls ceased, relief filled the boy. Sleep followed so abruptly that in seconds he was drifting in the complete darkness of a dream. . . .

Young Mah-ree was drifting with him, whispering, following close, trying to take hold of his hand. Many mammoth walked before them. Life Giver, with his little white son at his side, led them on. Somewhere up ahead torches flared bright and welcoming. Someone called. A man or a woman? He could not tell.

Suddenly it was dark again. Coyote was waiting for him in the darkness. Little Yellow Wolf was not alone. With him were Hawk and Fawn, Swallow and Hare, Bat and Horn Nose and a great assemblage of what seemed to be all the animals in the entire world.

"Brother." They spoke as one to name him that.

"No!" he cried aloud. This was not a dream he sought! This was a confirmation of the name he already possessed. Cha-kwena, Little Brother of Animals, a fitting name for a shaman—or so old Hoyeh-tay had said. "No! I will not have it!" he cried again in protest, and as he did, the dream collapsed around him, and although he slept, he knew no more dreams at all.

He was awakened by a sudden rush of air and a hard thump on the top of his head. Cha-kwena bolted upright just in time to see leathery wings brush past him as the dark form of a bat disappeared into the substance of the darker night. He tested his scalp with questing fingers. His skin was intact. The bat had done no harm, but why had it come so close? Strange, it was not like Leather Wings to misjudge his flight. Worse, he could have sworn that the bat had shouted at him as it flew by. Remembering his earlier confusion about the howling of Coyote, he would not give credence to such folly again. Cha-kwena yawned. How long had he been asleep? he wondered. He scanned the sky and noted that the stars had shifted considerably toward the west since he had last looked up at them.

Cha-kwena was suddenly uncomfortably aware of the

silence. There was no wind. The frogs had stopped croaking, and mosquitoes had ceased their buzzings. The last of the bats had disappeared. Quiet pressed against his skin and pushed against his inner ears . . . and yet from far away he perceived a low, completely unfamiliar *shh*ing sound.

Lightning flashed above the distant mesas. Thunder rolled. The storm over the flat-topped mountains was more intense than ever. Dakan-eh, on the verge of waking, made small sucking sounds with his lips.

Just then something ran across the back of Cha-kwena's hand, and in an instant, several more scooted across his legs. He jumped to his feet, slapping at another that ran across the nape of his neck and then squeaked as it plunged to the ground. Tiny, humpbacked forms of mice scurried out of the grasses and raced away in all directions across the basin.

"What frightens you, Little Long-tailed Ones?"

And then, suddenly, hackles rose along Cha-kwena's back as the answer became clear: Coyote, a solitary high-eared silhouette against the star-strewn sky, was standing across the pool from him. Its eyes were bright and steady. One hind paw was raised.

Cha-kwena stared. Coyote stared back. Seconds passed.

Far to the west, from the foothills of the mesas, someone shouted in dismay and warning. The cry was more imperative than Coyote's earlier howling. With a sudden snarl followed by a sharp bark, Coyote turned tail and was off at a three-legged run across the basin, his form illuminated by lightning flashes as he headed due east, away from the mesas.

Both Dakan-eh and Hoyeh-tay awoke, and Cha-kwena finally understood what Coyote had been trying to tell him. But he had heeded the warning too late. The flash flood was already upon them.

A terrible roaring filled the night. From north to south and all along the western horizon, the world went white as clouds of dust rose before the oncoming flood.

Dakan-eh and Hoyeh-tay were on their feet. Spear in hand, Bold Man reached for his traveling pack and began to sling it on, cursing loudly. Full and terrible understanding of what was about to befall them had dawned upon him.

"No time! No time! Run *now!*" old Hoyeh-tay commanded, taking off into the predawn darkness as fast as his scrawny limbs could carry him. "Follow me to the east, and whatever you do, do not look back! If the water takes you, go with it. Be a fish. Make fins of your arms and a tail of your feet and give yourself to the water. Be one with it, or it will drown you!"

"Come on, boy!" Dakan-eh shouted as he raced past Cha-kwena. "Run before it is too late! I warned you to watch your words! You wished for the lake to return, and here it comes!"

The roaring grew louder and louder, and the dust cloud grew higher and higher, but Cha-kwena could not run. He was transfixed by a numbing fascination. He remained as he was, staring toward the west, as though his limbs were rooted.

And then he could see it: Below the cloud of dust was a wave of water. It was no more than three feet high, but it stretched across the entire western horizon, and it was moving fast. His eyes went wide. The brown tide was coming for him. From horizon to horizon, its foaming lips were lifted back, preparing to swallow him.

"Stop!" he shouted at the oncoming flood, then waited for it to obey. When it did not, he turned on his heels and ran, wondering what had possessed him. Had he actually expected the flood to obey him?

Ahead, Dakan-eh had left Hoyeh-tay far behind. Bold Man was running so fast that Cha-kwena was certain that the hunter would outrun the flood. But he turned abruptly and raced back toward the shaman. With outstretched arms, Bold Man grabbed Hoyeh-tay just as the shaman stumbled.

Old Owl slumped in the embrace of the younger man and tried to remove the medicine bag from his neck. "The stone . . . you must save the sacred stone. . . ." implored the shaman, shouting to be heard above the roar of the approaching flood.

"And you with it!" cried Dakan-eh just as Cha-kwena caught up with them.

Breathless from his run and stunned by Dakan-eh's brave selflessness, Cha-kwena gasped, "I . . . I . . . will help."

"Go on! Run, boy! Save yourself!" Dakan-eh shrieked

in a fury as he slung the old man over his shoulders and raced on. "Run, Cha-kwena. If you have the power, use it now. Turn us three into birds so we may fly away above the water before it is too late!"

But it was already too late. One moment the boy was running on dry land, the next his legs went out from under him, and he was splayed flat on his belly, facedown, arms out, riding the onrushing surge of power that was the flash flood.

Desperately fighting to keep his head above water, he tried to become a bird, to transform his arms into wings that would lift him high above the waters. He tried and tried again but failed. He did not know the magic; the flood had him, turned him, twisted him. It scraped him along on his belly and back and side.

And all the while he fought for air, for life. It was no use. He went down again and again, and the last thing he saw was Dakan-eh and his grandfather being swept away by the churning waters.

*Be a fish. . . .* Hoyeh-tay's last warning filled Cha-kwena's mind as water filled his lungs. *Be one with the water or it will drown you!*

*But it is drowning me!* the boy thought. *I cannot be a fish. I have failed to be a bird. I am only a boy who will never be a man . . . or a shaman.*

# 5

Old men . . . grandfathers in paint and feathers and collars of silver sagebrush, adorned with beaks and berries and beads of stone and hard-shelled nuts . . . old men in towering headdresses of grass, festooned with multicolored plumage and the heads and feet of little birds and animals . . . tribal ancients who looked like strange half-human beasts and birds emerging from a tule marsh.

Old men . . . with blue faces, all of them scowling, all of them staring out of wet, rheumy eyes, all of them bending low over Cha-kwena. They circled him, chanting, blowing upon whistles of bone and reed, wafting the cool morning air across his face with long, sweeping fans made of the wings of golden eagles.

Lying flat on his back and shivering against an all-pervasive inner chill, Cha-kwena was already cold. Numb in body and mind, he stared up at the old men through a humming haze of semiconsciousness. They continued to circle slowly. They sighed and nodded as they moved, scuffing and sliding their sandaled feet, always to the left, in the opposite direction of the rising sun. *The left!* The realization was shattering. *The People circle to the left only when something unnatural and terrible has happened!* A bright white light blazed within his entire body. It burned him, hurt him, and he tensed against it even though he knew that his effort was in vain, for it was the light of truth. His panicky thoughts screamed at him: *The flood has drowned me! These old men are ghosts of the ancestors! They have come to greet you as you join them in the world beyond this world!*

"I am dead!" he shrieked, and sat bolt upright. A gut-twisting wave of nausea seemed to turn him inside out. He vomited up enough floodwater to create a minor deluge between his thighs.

The old men stopped circling and stared down at him. Then the tallest and most elaborately headdressed laughed aloud.

"He lives!" announced the tall grandfather, his blue face splitting from ear to ear with a broad, gap-toothed grin of triumph. "The ancestors have heard us! I, Shi-wana, shaman of the People of the Blue Mesas, say now that this boy has not gone to join the ancestors in the spirit world after all!"

"That's what you think!" wheezed Cha-kwena as, overcome by dizziness, his eyes rolled back in his head, and he collapsed backward into a dead faint.

He had no idea how long he slept. It could have been hours or days—it did not matter. He was alive! And he was awake . . . more or less. He sighed.

Naked and warm beneath a blanket of fur—rabbit, opossum, squirrel, and raccoon, from the smell of it—and comfortably stretched out upon a mattress of woven sweet grass, he stared up into the thick, interior darkness of a conical little lodge of bent branches, grass matting, and evergreen boughs.

He sniffed the air. *Pinyon boughs. Willow branches. Yes, definitely willow branches and freshly cut.*

The roof arched above his head in graceful curves, with slender branches interlacing like fingers. It was a well-made little lodge; he could see neither moon nor stars through the thick, rainproof overlayering of grass and branches that covered it.

He sighed again, closed his eyes, and drifted in sleep until the ache of an empty belly and the soft call of a woman roused him.

His lids fluttered open. He stared up blankly. Now, for the first time, it occurred to him that although the lodge was a familiar style, he did not know where he was.

*Home! Let me be home!*

"Cha-kwena . . ."

"Mother?" He propped himself up onto his elbows. Had U-wa just called to him?

"Cha-kwena, are you awake?"

He cocked his head. It was a girl's voice. "Mah-ree?" Disoriented, he frowned as he looked around. Then reality set in. He grimaced, realizing where he was. Beyond the walls of his little shelter the old men were singing. They were the medicine men with blue faces who had come from the far points of the Red World to meet with one another at the place where the two flat-topped mountains met.

"I am in their encampment. Now they will try to make me one of them. I have reached the Blue Mesas at last!"

Despite his best effort to remain irked, excitement touched him. Six years had passed since he had last visited the mesa country. He was nearly a man now. He would see everything with adult eyes. There would be things to discover and old places to reexplore.

His thoughts stopped. *Where is my grandfather? And where is Dakan-eh?* He realized that they might not have survived the flood. Shoving away his blankets, he started to rise and would have been out of the lodge in an instant had a hand not suddenly swept aside the entry curtain. A face peered in at him.

"Ah, you *are* awake!"

He blinked. Without waiting for an invitation, a young woman scooted on her knees into the lodge. She was naked save for an armload of translucent stone beads, and dimples shadowed full cheeks in a round face as she smiled.

"The Morning Star is going to its rest in the western sky. Soon it will be a new day," she informed him briskly, then swiveled around on her knees and leaned down as she reached outside, apparently to retrieve something.

His eyes widened at the sight of her bare buttocks. How round they were. And smooth. And . . .

"Here," she offered. "You are hungry?"

He gulped, tongue-tied as she turned around again, reached out with plump arms, and proffered a wide, flat basket laden with hot, steaming foods.

"You have slept long," she informed him. "Now you must eat. I have brought you cakes of black acorn meal and a roasted hare stuffed with pinyon nuts, onions, and purple sage. It is good. Eat all! I will tell the others that you have returned from the place of dreams. They—especially the old one who is grandfather to you, and the other who is guardian of you—both will be glad."

"They live!" Relief flared within him, but shame followed as he blurted, "What makes you think that I have need of a guardian? My grandfather is an old man who may have need of one, but I am young and strong. I am a man of the People. No one watches over me!" Somehow the words twisted around his tongue and came out as fast as the flight of hummingbirds and as hopelessly snarled as fishing line: "Wha-muk-a-thuk-ned-guard-I need? Old man grad-fudd ned-one-may, not care I a man of Pipple, otha-said not me strong!"

He blushed hotly. She was gone before he could speak another word, leaving the food and a giggle behind her.

Far away to the south, as a late-morning haze lingered over the waters of the Lake of Many Singing Birds, the women and girls of Tlana-quah's band gathered ricegrass and sweet tubers along the shore. A small group of bandsmen, meanwhile, kept watch for potential predators.

Knee-deep in cool water, Mah-ree stood beside her sister and stared toward the distant land of the Blue Mesas. The wide, flat gathering basket that she held braced against one hip was full of plump roots and long, heavy-headed stalks of grass. Like Ta-maya and the other women and girls, Mah-ree's face and body were coated with mud to keep away biting flies and mosquitoes. As she stared fixedly westward her short black hair was dusted with cattail pollen, which blew softly in the morning wind.

"What is it, Mah-ree?" asked Ta-maya, straightening beside her.

"I don't know. . . ." The girl sighed, for she did know. Clouds were rising within her mind, filling her with worry for those who were gone from the village. "There was a great storm over the far mountains last night."

"I, too, saw the distant lightning. Do you think that Dakan-eh is on his way home to us yet?"

Mah-ree frowned, suddenly irritable. Ta-maya had that sad, distracted look in her eyes again. The younger girl was grateful for the mud that hid her blush, for she knew that her own eyes must have held a similar look. "From the way you talk, one would think that Dakan-eh was the only one absent from our village! He is not alone, you know! Old Hoyeh-tay is with him, and so is . . . is Cha-kwena!"

Ta-maya smiled tenderly. "Yes, I *do* know, Sister. You miss our shaman's grandson as much as I miss my Dakan-eh."

"He is not your Dakan-eh yet!" snapped Ban-ya, standing close by. She glared at the sisters while remaining bent double, with her basket on her hip. With one hand submerged deep in the water and her bosoms hanging so low, she appeared to have three arms in the lake.

"Nor is he yours," answered Ta-maya sharply.

"No?" Ban-ya taunted. "You gave him no traveling gift, but he left this village with mine!"

"Only because I dropped my offering to him! Only because the shaman *made* him leave without it! Only because—"

"Girls! Stop bickering!" commanded Ha-xa. The headman's woman stood to the right of her daughters, close to the women of her own age. "The mammoth kind have eaten all the sweet grass and camas root that we have brought to the place where they are known to graze; but Great Ghost Spirit, Grandfather of All, has not come to feed upon our offerings. Our headman has said that we must bring the mammoth more and greener grass, and larger and sweeter camas root. Tlana-quah fears that the absence of our shaman has offended our totem. We dare not show further disrespect. This is no time to display rancor to one another. We must continue to bring gifts of food to the mammoth kind until Hoyeh-tay returns to make the proper songs and to dance the proper dances, and to bring other offerings—magic offerings—to the secret and most sacred spring, where Great Ghost Spirit may be moved to show himself to our holy man."

"We have sung the songs," interrupted Ban-ya, standing erect. "We have danced the dances."

"Yes, but *we* are not shaman," reminded Mah-ree sagely. "There is no magic in our dances or our songs. Only our shaman knows the whereabouts of the sacred spring and how to call Grandfather of All to the most secret place."

Ban-ya gestured to the other women. "Listen to Mah-ree, would you?" she said nastily. "One would think she was a shaman herself, the little stick!"

Mah-ree shrank at the insult.

Ta-maya hotly defended her younger sister. "The little stick will bud and bloom in time! But an overfilled bladder flask like you, Ban-ya, can only look forward to the day when your teats hang loose to your knees."

"Ta-maya!" Ha-xa silenced her elder daughter with a shout. "I will hear no more arguing from you—or from anyone else!"

The girl wilted, and Ban-ya glared at her with pleasure, as though imagining all the ways in which Ta-maya might possibly die.

Ta-maya stepped closer to Mah-ree. Her head was high again as she looked defiantly at Ban-ya; it was only out of deference to her mother's wishes that she remained silent.

"Back to work! Back to work!" commanded Ha-xa, assuming the authority of the headman's first woman.

The others obeyed—all except Mah-ree, who said worriedly: "Our father has us gathering more and more food for the mammoth, Mother, but no grass seeds will be left for us when winter comes if we do not set some aside now."

Before the girl could say another word, Ha-xa forcefully knocked her down. "You will not criticize your father! And you, Ta-maya, do not allow your father to see you slacking. He is watching us from the shore. He is not happy with you, you know. The continuing bad feelings between you and Ban-ya are not a good thing at all!"

"But, Mother, she has no right to turn her eyes to Dakan-eh or to bring him gifts or miss him when he is away."

"If Ban-ya yearns for Dakan-eh, it is your fault, Daughter, for having refused to accept him long before now. When he returns, Tlana-quah—not you or Ban-ya or even Dakan-eh—will decide which woman he will have. Is that understood?"

"Yes, Mother," Ta-maya whispered, heartsick.

Mah-ree looked up at her sister out of soft, consoling brown eyes, which gave her face the look of a little doe antelope. But Ta-maya had already turned obediently back to her work.

\* \* \*

On the lakeshore, perched upon a boulder apart from Tlana-quah and the other men, Kosar-eh the clown frowned as he saw Ta-maya's change of posture. He and the others were beyond range of the women's conversation, but it was apparent that an argument had just taken place and that Ta-maya had borne the brunt of it.

*Poor girl*, he thought, and looked at the headman's elder daughter with such wistful longing that, seeing his expression, the men around him laughed.

"Good old Kosar-eh! Always good for a chuckle!" chided Ela-nay, the man nearest to him.

"Better not let Siwi-ni see you eyeing Ta-maya!" warned another jokingly. "Your little woman's temper is well-known and much bigger than she is."

"Watch out for Dakan-eh, too," put in yet another.

"Dakan-eh is far away," replied the jester obliquely, and before he could weigh the judiciousness of his words, he added, "He does not care about her, not *really*."

"And you do, I suppose?" pressed Tlana-quah, obviously amused.

Behind his black and white face paint, the clown's scarred features remained set; only his eyes moved, narrowed, never leaving the slender form of Ta-maya as she bent like a supple reed to her work. "I am Kosar-eh, Funny Man. Of course I care. I care for all my people!"

"Have we found another would-be match for your elder daughter, Tlana-quah?" queried Ela-nay, gesturing toward the clown. "There is not a man here who would not gladly take such a fine girl to his lodge if she were willing. But our clown makes Bold Man seem a better bet, eh? I mean, just thinking of a beauty like Ta-maya with Kosar-eh, it's enough to make a man laugh—or squirm."

The clown did not move. His voice sounded oddly hollow as he affirmed Ela-nay's opinion. "Yes, looking at me is enough to make a man laugh. I am a clown, after all, and what would you all do for laughter were I not here to offer it up to you as one of the gifts of life?"

Tlana-quah scowled. He turned to take thoughtful measure of the painted man on the boulder before saying with an understanding that eluded the rest of the group, "Had there not been a Day of the Camel, our Funny Man might well have been the equal of our Bold Man. And yes,

I might well have smiled upon a match between my Ta-maya and him."

The clown's mouth worked, but into a smile or a frown, it was impossible to say. Suddenly he rose. "Ah, what *might* have been!" he shouted mockingly, shaking his limbs as he bent his good arm and twisted it into a grotesque imitation of the crippled one. Then, flapping both arms as though they were featherless wings straining for flight, he did a hop-legged dance, turning around and around atop the boulder. The others clapped and smiled and laughed at his antics. "I thank you!" he said, breathless, bowing to all, before seating himself once again and addressing the headman. "And I thank you, Tlana-quah, but I cannot accept your daughter. I have a woman! Siwi-ni is twice my age and half my size, and even when she is big with child, she is as wrinkled as I am scarred. People laugh when they see us together. A clown should have a woman who makes people laugh. What more could a funny man want?"

Tlana-quah's lids lowered. The others were laughing, but the headman shook his head sadly. "What might have been?"

Kosar-eh smiled wryly. He pointed at the headman and shook his own head. "It is I who am the clown, Tlana-quah. It is not your place to make me laugh!"

# 6

Dakan-eh was in a foul mood. He had lost his spears and spear hurler to the flood. Worse, the traveling pack that Ban-ya had made for him was gone, and with it the golden nuggets that were to have been a gift for Ta-maya.

Now, as he emerged from the communal lean-to under which he had passed the night with the other guardians of the Red World shamans, he was surprised when a man of his own age snapped to his feet and stood before him, flashing a congenial grin.

"I greet you, Bold Man! Have you slept well?"

"I have barely slept at all!" Dakan-eh replied sourly.

He scanned the encampment. It was a small assembly of neatly made conical huts of grass and twigs, set in a clearing amid a pinyon forest. High on the flank of the broad, flat-topped mountain that was the westernmost of the Blue Mesas, the settlement overlooked the country in all directions.

It was a good campsite. Water flowed nearby from a year-round spring, greening the rocky defile from which it sprang with moss, cress, a wild tangling of cucumber, and blistering oak vines. Depending upon the time of day, there were both ample sun and shade within the grove itself. From the look of the trees in the surrounding forest, however, old Hoyeh-tay's visions had been wrong once again: The stout, thickly branched pinyons with plump, resilient gray-green needles were nearly devoid of shapely little red-gold cones that yielded delectable nuts. There would be no Great Gathering this year.

"It has been my privilege to wait for you to come out at last to greet the day!" the young man rambled happily, eager to be friends with Dakan-eh. "The boy is awake and—praises be to the spirits of the ancestors—he is well! The one you call Old Owl has gone with the other wise men to the sacred grove upon the bluff. Their guardians are sharing our morning food. Come, you must be hungry, Bold Man. I will show you the way. My sister, Lah-ri, has prepared a special meal to honor your strength and valor. Usually she is not much of a cook, but she has outdone herself trying to please the many shamans and to prove herself worthy of being the wife of one of them. See for yourself. There are spitted lizards and rabbits and plenty of chia seeds and—"

"Wait." Dakan-eh signed the man to silence with an impatiently raised hand as he took measure of him. The hunter was big and solid and put together with all of the broad, hulking lines of a ground sloth. "Do I *know* you?"

"Yes, Bold Man, of course! Don't you remember? I brought you here on my back. I am Sunam-tu, hunter and protector of Naquah-neh, shaman of the People of the

White Hills. From the top of the mesa, in the bright flash of much lightning, we saw you and the others. We knew what must happen to those who—for reasons that remain a mystery to us—unwisely chose to pass the night in the middle of a dry lake during a mountain thunderstorm. We called and called, but only Coyote answered. Naquah-neh, Shi-wana, and the other shamans made spirit songs on your behalf. They asked the birds and beasts who were close enough to warn you. If they did, perhaps you did not understand. And so we—who are, like you, guardians of the shamans—came to help."

Dakan-eh heard the repudiation in Sunam-tu's statement. *Those who chose so unwisely to pass the night in the middle of a dry lake during a mountain thunderstorm.* Indeed! Cha-kwena and Hoyeh-tay and he had never seen a dry lake before. How could they have known that all the rainwater that fell upon the mesas would drain into it? A small, niggling voice prodded from within: *If Hoyeh-tay is still a shaman, he should have known. But the birds and bats went to the boy, not to the old man. And you, Dakan-eh, best and bravest hunter of your band, should have guessed after one look at the lay of the land its potential danger to you.*

"I have never seen anything quite so amazing," Sunam-tu was babbling on with barely a break for breath. "It was you who saved yourself and the others, Bold Man. Oh, yes, it was something to behold. At the height of the flood when a young, strong man might have outrun the deluge, you stayed with your shaman. You held on to him and kept his head above-water, even though you were hard-pressed to keep to the surface yourself. And when the boy was swept past you, you grabbed him by the hair and prevented him from being washed away. Truly, it was wonderful to behold. Had it not been for you, the others would have drowned long before we were able to come close enough to be of assistance."

Dakan-eh had never been one to resist flattery, especially when he knew the compliment to be the truth. His behavior during the flood had been more than exemplary; it had been extraordinary. He was delighted to hear that Sunam-tu realized it, too. He would be able to boast about his display of bravery for the rest of his life and never wear out the tale. But there was a deeper satisfaction in hearing others acknowledge it. Besides, he was paying for his selfless bravery. Not a muscle in his body did not ache, and his skin was marred by dozens of bruises, scratches, and abrasions. It would be weeks before he was fully healed. *Some sight you will be when you return at last to Ta-maya—black and blue and without a single gift to make her smile!*

"Perhaps tonight the sleep spirits will come to you, Bold Man, and then you will feel better. When the shamans meet in this place upon the Blue Mesas in years to come, forever shall they sing praise songs in honor of Bold Man, of Dakan-eh, who risked his life to save not only his shaman but also a boy of little worth."

Dakan-eh looked into the large, openly adoring brown eyes of Sunam-tu. It occurred to him that this was the proper time to inform him that the boy of little worth deserved some reconsideration. After all, the swallows and bats had flown to Cha-kwena. If the boy had failed to understand the magical form that the shamans' warning had taken, this was due to inexperience, not ineptitude. But to admit this now would overshadow Dakan-eh's own moment of accolade, and he was enjoying it far too much to risk bringing it to an early end.

And so Bold Man chose to keep silent on the subject of Cha-kwena. Dakan-eh stood a little taller. He threw back his shoulders and expanded his chest as he basked in the knowledge that Cha-kwena and Hoyeh-tay were alive only because he had risked his life to save them. He would be famous throughout the Red World. Men and boys would emulate his bravery. Mothers would look to their sons and tell them to eat well and obey their fathers in all things so that they might someday grow up to be as bold and powerful as Dakan-eh.

"Dakan-eh!" He spoke his own name aloud, proudly, arrogantly. Boastfully he spoke it, with his mouth down-turned and his chin jabbing defiantly upward toward the early-morning sky.

Sunam-tu cocked his head, perplexed by Dakan-eh's behavior. "You are all right, Bold Man?"

Dakan-eh laughed. Never had he felt more wide-awake or more rested. He slung a brotherly arm around

Sunam-tu's meaty shoulder. "Lead me to the food, Sunam-tu. We will eat together. I am starving!"

Sunam-tu beamed, eager to please. "I will be proud to eat with Dakan-eh. And my little sister, Lah-ri, will be honored to know that the food she has so carefully prepared will nourish such a man as you!"

Dakan-eh's smile was now so broad that it hurt; somehow the ache pleased him. The sun was warm upon his face and body. He had survived the flood! In this hunter from the White Hills he had found a new, adoring friend. As he strode toward the cooking fire where the guardians of the shamans of the Red World were assembled, his heart was singing. What more could he ask for? What greater gift could he possibly bring home to Ta-maya than the glory of his name?

He and Sunam-tu had reached the cooking fire.

"We may all eat now!" declared Sunam-tu. "Behold! I bring Bold Man to the feast that has been prepared for him."

"Welcome."

The word came not from the handful of men in their prime who rose as one to honor him; it came from the naked young girl who, on her knees before the fire, looked up at him and smiled. "Welcome to my fire," said Lah-ri.

For a long moment Dakan-eh stared down at her deferent and dimpled face and at her soft young body, which was as ripe with promise as the morning. And Ta-maya seemed very far away.

Something was wrong.

Hoyeh-tay sat alone and motionless in the wind on the outermost lip of the promontory on the sacred escarpment. He stared fixedly across the miles at that part of the horizon over which the morning star had disappeared. The star was long gone, and yet it lingered in the fabric of his thoughts, burning at the back of his eyes. Something was important about the star. Something *wrong* about it. But what?

"Hoyeh-tay, come join the circle. Bring the sacred stone of your people."

Who had called to him?

"Ish-iwi?" He turned to look at the gathering of

elaborately headdressed, blue-faced elders who sat a good distance behind him on a broad, flat, boulder-strewn area that was still on the promontory, but not so far out that it caught the full power of the wind. He could see the wizened old men well enough through the trees—they sat in a circle on folded limbs, their bodies as tough and lean as lizards', and skin as dry and loose. Did they imagine that their feathers and paint made them look younger, or only bigger and more impressive?

His hands drifted to explore his face and hair. He felt paint and feathers and great, upwardly blooming tufts of grass. He shook his head, took off the ceremonial bonnet, and stared at it. It was wonderful to behold, but he did not like the look of it. There were too many looped strings of dried berries, too many little fringes of white bones, too many beaks and beads and birds' feet. He put the bonnet down, knowing that one of the other wise men must have constructed it for him.

He sighed. *The spirits know us for what we are,* he thought. *How wise are we, eh? Down on the barrens, that which was dry beneath yesterday's sun is now a lake again. And although I am a shaman, I did not foresee the flood.*

Despondent, he slumped and mumbled to himself: "Ah, Ish-iwi, how sad it is that your old friend has been reduced to such a state!" He paused and looked for Ish-iwi among the gathering; but his old friend was nowhere to be seen. Disappointment touched him. The wise men of the Red World had gathered on the Blue Mesas, but his dearest friend was not with them. Perhaps he would come soon. Qu-on, shaman of the People of the Valley of Many Rabbits, had yet to arrive, as did Iman-atl, shaman of the People of the Place of Many Reeds. "Soon, soon they will come."

An empty feeling gnawed in his gut as he turned back toward the west, toward the horizon where the Morning Star had settled. He did not want to think more on the subject, and yet he could not help himself. Ish-iwi and Qu-on and Iman-atl were old. Had they died? Were they too frail to make the trip? Even so, if the spirits had summoned them as they had summoned Hoyeh-tay, the shamans would have sent a representative from their bands in their place.

He found himself thinking next of lions—big lions, as tawny as summer grass, rasping and working upon a kill—a human kill. Meanwhile, an old black-maned, stripe-bellied male stood apart, watching, waiting. For what?

"Hoyeh-tay, join the circle and bring your sacred stone."

"What?" Startled, he blinked. Who had spoken? "Nar-eh!" A father's longing for a lost son died as quickly as Nar-eh had died.

The other shamans were staring at him. He pretended not to notice as he fixed his eyes westward again, glad that he had not spoken too loudly lest the shamans think that he had lost his mind along with his powers. He wished that they would stop staring at him.

Then he forgot that they were there at all. Plucking at pebbles at his feet, he mused to one who was dead. "Ah, Nar-eh, my son, Mushroom Eater. You should see your father now! What a weary old fool I have become. But the boy, you would be proud of him! The spirits speak to Cha-kwena. He has looked upon Life Giver, and all on his own he has sought wisdom in the branches of the sacred tree. Perhaps the power has passed to him already. Perhaps I have come to the ending of my days. Perhaps you and I will soon meet again in the world of spirits beyond this world, my son . . . unless there are mushrooms there, and you have eaten the wrong kind again!"

He exhaled a short, bitter chuckle at this sad attempt at levity. He missed Nar-eh terribly. With the death of the son, a portion of the father's heart also died. It would never heal. In the cool morning air, his bones ached as deeply as his spirit. He felt old and tired as he watched his breath congeal into mist before his face, then vanish as it was consumed by the sunlight that warmed his back.

He turned yet again. Where was Owl? The bird usually returned from its nocturnal hunting before dawn; but dawn had come and gone, and soon it would be noon. Other birds were awake—day birds, seed and insect eaters. He listened bleakly to the familiar melodies of finches and chickadees, to the spiraling songs of warblers, to the flat, blatant calls of jays and woodpeckers, and to the throaty gawks of ravens.

"Hoyeh-tay?"

He looked up. Blue-faced and befeathered, Shi-wana, shaman of the People of the Blue Mesas, was standing over him.

"Come out of the wind, old friend. You do not look well. Perhaps you should have rested a day or two, slept more after your ordeal before accompanying us up onto the promontory."

"Yes. Perhaps I should have." He tried not to show that he was flustered. What ordeal was the man talking about? *Ah! Yes. The flood!* He remembered the flood, but he did not remember accompanying anyone to the bluff. Yet here he was. Distracted, he felt his thoughts drifting again and, almost in a panic, focused on the one that was clearest and most important to him: "Have you seen Owl?"

"There are many owls in the Land of the Blue Mesas."

"Not just *any* owl! *My* owl! My helping spirit! My friend and brother! The owl for whom I am named!"

"Was he with you before the flood?"

"Of course he was with me! Owl is always with me—by the light of day, that is. *Hmmm.* It is daylight now, isn't it? Yes, of course it is daylight. Owl should be here, perching on my head and picking his toes and—" His words stopped in midflow. A sudden pain exploded inside his head. He gasped. In less time than it took him to breathe out again, the pain was gone, but things seemed brighter, different from before. There was a faint buzzing in his ears. He shook his head, and the sound was gone, along with his memory. "Who are you, Blue Face? Where am I? What do you want? And what is that bird's nest doing on your head?"

"The 'bird's nest' is a ceremonial bonnet. You have reached the Land of the Blue Mesas, Hoyeh-tay. Surely you know me. I am Shi-wana, shaman of those who make their home in this country. You and I, we are on the great promontory where the spirits often speak to men of our kind. You are supreme wise man and elder of the People of the Red World. When I was only a child, you came to this place many times and called to the spirits, and they have answered you when they would speak to no other man. Look around you, old friend, and you will remember."

Hoyeh-tay looked. He saw. He remembered . . . and was ashamed. "Yes. *Yes!* I knew all that! I *did!*"

"No," corrected Shi-wana softly, caringly. "You did not remember, but now you do. Rest awhile more. Take hold of the sacred stone and ask its power to flow into you. Then, when you are yourself again, join the circle. There is much that must be spoken of, old friend. Many troubling things have happened in our world since last we met. Word has reached us that strangers have come from the far north into the land of the People. They have visited the most distant of our bands. Rumor is that some of our chiefs have allowed them take our daughters away with them. Since this has happened, the big lake has gone dry. The waterfowl and animals that were once food for us no longer winter in the shadow of the Blue Mesas. The trumpeting of Great Spirit has not been heard in this land for many moons. And only one small family of mammoth grazes in the dry scrub growth near the little highland lake to the north of my own village on the other side of the mountain. It is the same with all the other villages across the Red World. There used to be hundreds of mammoth in the land. Where have they all gone, and why? Have we offended them? We need the wisdom of Hoyeh-tay to help us understand the meaning of these things."

The old man's hands closed around his medicine bag. He trembled. The stone was still there; the flood had not stolen it. "The stone . . . the sacred stone . . . it will be for my grandson," he said.

"Yes," affirmed Shi-wana. "So you have said. But now the grandson is only a boy. It is Hoyeh-tay who is shaman. And with his coming to the Blue Mesas, the waters have returned to Big Lake. This is a wondrous omen, proof that Hoyeh-tay speaks well with the spirits, that his power is great and must be shared with the People."

Incredulous, the old man blinked. "Is it so?"

"It is so," affirmed Shi-wana.

Hoyeh-tay smiled. He felt better, younger, needed. With his right hand still curled around his medicine bag, he extended his left to Shi-wana and allowed the younger man to help him to his feet. "Come. I have rested enough. I will bring the sacred stone to the council of elders. If you have need of Hoyeh-tay, Hoyeh-tay is here. Calling the waters to return to Big Lake has tired me, but I am still Shaman!"

And in that moment, as though to prove the truth of his words, Owl flew out of nowhere to land upon his outstretched arm. Greatly pleased, the old man greeted the bird. "Where have you been? And what have you been hunting that has kept you so long from me?"

"A new shaman," replied Owl, chortling in that language that only he and a brother of his spirit could understand. "But I see that I have not lost the old one yet!"

"Grandfather?"

Hoyeh-tay was surprised to see Cha-kwena puffing his way out of the pinyon forest and up over the ridgetop that led down to the base of the promontory.

"Well, I see that Owl has decided to find a perch at last!" declared the boy, breathless and obviously annoyed. "Your spirit brother has been diving at me all morning. The moment I came out of the hut he was at me. People in camp were laughing, but it wasn't funny. His talons are sharp, and his beak drew blood! You can look at my scalp if you don't believe me! I tell you, Grandfather, it was either spear him or follow him. Odd, though, that Owl could not find his way to you without me."

# 7

They invited Cha-kwena to stay. It was a great honor and he knew it; but they were shamans, so he wanted no part of them.

"I will go back to camp," he said, sorry that he had come and sorrier still that he had advanced so close to the circle where Hoyeh-tay now sat among his peers.

He silently cursed the bird and eyed the holy men. He felt unbearably ill at ease in their company. Never before had he been in such close proximity to so many elderly men at one time. They sickened him; worse, they frightened him. Although they were cordial, with nods and smiles and gestures of continuing invitation, their appearance was, to his eyes, acutely threatening. He felt as if old age were a contagion, and he had to avoid contact with it.

"I . . . I . . . must go," he stammered. "I have no place here!" He began to walk hurriedly.

"Stop!" Shi-wana, shaman of the People of the Blue Mesas, was on his feet.

Startled, Cha-kwena obeyed. Suddenly his will to escape left him.

Even if Shi-wana had removed his elaborate headdress, he would have been extremely tall. He was also very thin. His ribs stood out like raised stripes on his narrow chest. Above the tightly drawn rabbit-skin belt of his loin cover, his concave belly looked thin-skinned and hollow. As he came toward Cha-kwena he resembled a great crested crane advancing through a marsh.

The man stopped and cupped two big, spiderlike hands about Cha-kwena's elbows. He did not look angry, only annoyed. There was command in his eyes, but no animosity.

"Your grandfather has said that you are to be one of us. We shall see. Come, Cha-kwena. You must join us in the sacred circle." Shi-wana lifted the youth straight off the ground, carried him to the circle, and set him firmly back onto his feet next to Hoyeh-tay. "Sit!" he ordered. With his palms now resting on the boy's shoulders, Shi-wana pressed him down hard.

Glumly, resentfully, Cha-kwena sat.

Next to him, on Hoyeh-tay's shoulder, Owl chortled, "Good boy. Be obedient for a change. Maybe you will learn something."

Before long, Cha-kwena was overcome by a strange mix of awe and puzzlement. He surveyed the blue faces of the old men and enjoyed the sensation of the morning sun striking hot upon his back. Sweat glistened on his skin while West Wind blew softly over him, cooling and caressing him, telling him that he had come home. But it bothered him that when Owl spoke, the magic men did not hear the bird's words.

The wise men were taking the sacred stones from the medicine bags that hung around their necks. Gnarled old hands fingered the infinitely older relics, then each man placed his stone within the circle.

Intrigued, Cha-kwena leaned forward and stared. These stones were not ordinary stones; these were spirit stones, the most sacred relics of the People. Some were round, others were oblong. Several were irregular lumps with no real shape at all. Some were no larger than a baby tooth. Others—like Hoyeh-tay's, which was the largest of the collection—were fanglike wedges about the size of a grown man's thumb.

Every man, woman, and child of the Red World knew that the color and texture of the stones was what set them apart and marked them as magic. They were not of flint or obsidian or white quartz or any other useful mineral for toolmaking. Indeed, when closely examined, the stones appeared to be not really rock at all, but bone—bone that had somehow been transformed.

"Behold the bones of First Man and First Woman!" exclaimed Shi-wana reverently.

And now, as Hoyeh-tay spoke, Cha-kwena could not help but recall the story:

"In the time beyond beginning, First Man and First Woman followed the great white spirit mammoth, Life Giver, across the world. From the far north they came. Across the Sea of Ice they came. Through the Corridor of Storms and into the Forbidden Land they came. Walking always into the face of the rising sun, they came.

"Spirits of Wind and Water and Ice and Fire did not like this. They did not know why Sun should call First Man and First Woman upon such a journey. They did not know why Life Giver should wish to protect them. The spirits asked to understand, but Sun and Life Giver would not answer. This made Wind and Water and Ice and Fire jealous. Many bad tricks did they play upon First Man and First Woman. But First Man and First Woman kept following the sun. Great White Spirit walked ahead of them to guard them from the tricks of the jealous spirits. Great White Spirit made them strong, and soon out of First Man and First Woman were the People born.

"First Man and First Woman were thankful for their many children. They sang praises to Life Giver and named the great spirit mammoth Totem. They promised never to eat the flesh of his kind. This was good in the eyes of Great White Spirit. This was good in the eyes of Sun, who offered them her blessing.

"The spirits of Wind and Water and Ice and Fire grew even more jealous. 'We will show Sun our power! We will thin the great herds of hooved animals upon which First Man and First Woman feed! We will make them hunger! We will send monsters to live among them!'

"And so, when Sun was sleeping on the far side of the world and the great white spirit mammoth was walking on his own for a while, monsters came to live upon the world. Soon, by trickery and deception, monster children were born to First Man and First Woman . . . twins . . . mammoth-eating brothers who fattened on the flesh of their totem's kind and grew strong upon the dissent of the band. Like spears of lightning were these twin brothers, piercing the hearts of First Man and First Woman. Fighting! Always fighting! Setting themselves against each other and the good of all until—*slash! clash!*—the world turned red with their blood. Their brothers and sisters scattered and fled from them, and the unity of the People was shattered."

When Hoyeh-tay paused, Cha-kwena looked up in a daze from the sacred stones. He had forgotten the spell that his grandfather could still weave when he told the ancient tales. Were the stones making the magic? he wondered. Were they granting the old man powers that he had lost long ago?

"Sun turned around and saw what these monster twins had done," the elderly shaman continued. " 'These cannot be the sons of First Man and First Woman to whom I have given all good things!' And now in anger Life Giver returned from his walk to find that many of his own mammoth kind had been slaughtered and eaten by the children of First Man and First Woman. And so it was that First Man and First Woman cried out to Sun and to Great White Spirit: 'Forgive our sons, for they have been made out of deceit and trickery by the spirits of this world. They do not act in our names or understand the bad things that they do!'

"But as all wise men know, some things cannot be forgiven. So it was that the power of Sun and the wrath of the Great White Spirit combined to hurl the twin sons of First Man and First Woman high and forever away across the sky.

"It was then that First Man and First Woman died. Together they died. In their sadness to see their sons cast away they died. In their grief at having borne children who had betrayed the trust of their totem and spurned the goodwill of Sun, they died. Great White Spirit carried them to a far place, which is known only to the mammoth kind. And there he mourned until Watching Star told him what he must do.

"And so it was that Great White Spirit took up the bones of First Man and First Woman, returned to the Red World, and divided the bones among their many children. From that day to this the People have been strong and unafraid and obedient to the sun, for the living spirits of First Man and First Woman are with us in their bones. The bones speak to us. The blood of First Man and First Woman is strong in us. Life Giver, the great white spirit mammoth, protects us still. As long as we remain grateful guardians of our totem, Sun will smile upon us and give to us all good things.

"But when the dark comes, we must look to the night and to the north. Watching Star is still there to remind us that we are her grandchildren. We must thank her for giving birth to First Man and First Woman, and we must remember that Brothers of the Sky are still above us in the night, still fighting, still clashing and slashing, still trying to kill each other with the terrible thunder drums and silver spears of lightning. If we do not honor the sacred bones of First Man and First Woman, if we forget our ancestors and fail to honor our totem, the brothers will fall from the sky and destroy us!"

On the far northern side of the sacred mountains, a golden eagle circled against the sun, and the cry of a man's name sliced through the midmorning heat haze.

"Maliwal!"

His aim ruined, Maliwal lowered the spear that he

was about to hurl at the eagle and snarled. Had Masau been following? For days Maliwal could have sworn that his brother was behind him, and truly he had *wanted* Masau at his back. Deep in his heart Maliwal nurtured the hope that Masau would care enough for the injured pride of a brother to leave Ysuna's side for his sake.

And yet, perversely, Maliwal had not slowed his pace. He had driven himself on, loping like the wolf he was, keeping his dogs and his scouting party close, covering mile after long mile, dozing only briefly and occasionally, and ignoring the complaints of his men.

It was Maliwal's intention to punish Masau, to run him to exhaustion, to shame him as he himself had been shamed, to force him to acknowledge who was the better man. But now, as Maliwal looked up and eyed the soaring eagle, he was certain that Masau had never been following him at all. His brother had attached himself to Daughter of the Sun like a lichen to a rock and was drawing all his strength and sustenance from the granite of her heart—as Maliwal had once done . . . and would gladly do again.

"Soon, Ysuna," he grated. "Soon you will see who is better."

As he watched the effortless upward spiraling of the bird, a hard, bitter lump burned hotly in his throat. He could neither speak nor swallow, his love for Ysuna was that intense.

"Maliwal!"

His fellow hunters were calling to him. Now, as they stopped at his side, they were panting and growling with resentment.

"By all the powers of this world and the next, Maliwal! What is this test?"

"No test. A game of will and strength. What's the matter, Tsana? And you, Ston and Chudeh and Rok? Aren't you men enough to play it?"

"You know we are!" Rok protested. "But look at your dogs, Maliwal! You'll run them to death if you keep up like this! And for what?"

Standing in the penetrating warmth of the morning sun, with the sweet smell of the grassland in his nostrils, Maliwal smiled. How many days had he been out from the village of his people? He had lost track and did not care.

He had been leading the others southward into unfamiliar country. The land ahead looked promising. The color of the foothills spoke of forest. There would be water in those mountains, and where there was water, there would also be game—and, from the smokes that he now saw rising from the scrub growth of the hills, people.

Maliwal looked down the mammoth tracks that had caused him to stop in the first place. His smile tightened with inestimable satisfaction as he pointed down with his spear and watched the expressions of his men.

"Mammoth tracks!" breathed Chudeh.

"Yes," Maliwal said, "and they lead toward the Blue Mesas. We will find what we seek there: mammoth, a new bride and sacrifice for Thunder in the Sky, and a sacred stone. All that will make Ysuna smile."

For a long while after the story of First Man and First Woman was told, old Hoyeh-tay continued to chant.

"Father Above . . . Mother Below . . . First Man, First Woman . . . we honor you. We await your sacred words."

"We wait. We wait," the other shamans sang.

Cha-kwena patiently waited with them. He watched as, from beyond the northern back of the mesas, a golden eagle soared upon the wind. Its wings were incredibly wide, and as this greatest of all raptors stroked across the face of the sun and then hung there, motionless, balancing upon the wind, its shadow swept across the earth below, causing daylight to tremble for a moment.

The shamans looked up. They stared in awe and introspective silence. They did not have to tell Cha-kwena that the eagle was sacred, solar, the symbol of light and power and life everlasting. To see it now, soaring into the sun like a black center in a golden eye in this holy place, was a special omen.

But what did it mean? Squinting, Cha-kwena followed the flight of the bird as the wind carried it high. It was banking to the north, now flying into the skies out of which it had come. It would be over Shi-wana's village on the far side of the mesas now. *Are Shi-wana's people looking up at it and pointing, wondering about its meaning*

*and asking one another what the shamans atop the Blue
Mesas will make of its flight?*

The eagle was banking again, dipping its wings, catching
a thermal updraft, rising with it . . . circling . . . touching
each of the sacred points of Creation that gave birth to the
four winds before veering away from the sun.

The shamans murmured softly in concern. "To move
against the sun, from west to east, from right to left, it is a
bad omen," they agreed.

Cha-kwena continued to stare upward at the eagle.
According to the stories of his grandfather, Life Giver had
led First Man and First Woman *into* the face of the rising
sun, toward that sacred place out of which Sun was born
and from which Sun began its holy ascent and descent into
the west every night. So, he mused, perhaps going to the
east was not always a bad thing. Perhaps . . . *What is the
matter with you?* Cha-kwena asked himself with a start.
*You are thinking like a shaman!*

He looked around. There was something special,
something magic, about this place. He wanted no part of
it.

"Can I go now?" he blurted, starting to rise.

"No!" the old men responded as one, and, without so
much as another breath, took up the cadence of their
chanting again.

Disappointed, Cha-kwena sat down. He was hungry.
He had not eaten since dawn. He thought about how good
it would be to eat again and to have the food served to him
by the smiling, dimpled young girl who had come to him
at sunrise.

A slow, pleasant warmth stirred unexpectedly in his
lower belly as his penis flexed and swelled. Startled, he
was grateful to be seated lest others see his condition.
What *was* the matter with him? He rarely thought about
girls in that way. In fact, U-wa openly worried about him.
In the village beside the Lake of Many Singing Birds,
when a boy's penis stood up and demanded attention, he
was sent by his mother to the widows for ease and
instruction.

Most boys went often for relief, but he had gone only
once—when he was nine, and U-wa, certain that his penis
would explode if he did not put it to use, had insisted.

Yet now, as Cha-kwena thought of the dimpled girl he had met that morning, his man bone was up and ready, as it often was when Ta-maya smiled at him. He swallowed. What would Dakan-eh think if he knew of Cha-kwena's feelings toward Ta-maya? The boy blushed. No wonder he disliked girls. They twisted his emotions until he could neither understand nor control them. He did not like the way any female made him feel!

He deliberately forced his thoughts back to the moment. The old men were still chanting, still holding their hands outward over the sacred stones. It was a pleasant sound, drifting languidly from the flow of words into a slow, constant, wordless rhythm. Cha-kwena did not know when he closed his eyes, or when he slept. . . .

He dreamed of the eagle circling high, flying over the Red World. He dreamed of a small family of mammoth. He dreamed of Life Giver plodding across the many miles that lay between the Land of the Blue Mesas and home. He dreamed that he was a small, brown, yellow-eyed bird, one of the kind that was always perched upon the head and shoulders of the great tuskers. He dreamed that he rode so high upon his totem's back that he was carried through the clouds.

He flew upward now, leaving behind the great white mammoth. He soared, he banked, then dove and soared again until he reached the upper limits of the eagle's flight. The eagle circled him. They were eye to eye, beak to beak, and the boy knew the raptor as the most transcendently beautiful creature he had ever seen.

"Are you not afraid, Cha-kwena, Little Brother of Animals?"

"I am not afraid," he replied, and to prove it he reached out and plucked the sun from the sky.

Suddenly, from somewhere far away at the edge of his dream, a wolf howled. Or was it a man? He could not be sure. A mammoth was trumpeting in pain, and a baby mammoth was bleating. A woman wept and children cried. There was the smell of smoke and fire and of burned meat . . . and the harsh cacophony of people screaming.

The expanding dream frightened him. He tried to

hold on to the sun, but it was too big! It was too hot! He flung his arms wide and released it. It fell and fell, and out of his dream he watched it plummet toward the world below. Then, with a gasp, he remembered that in this dream he was not a boy—he was a bird, a very little bird. And in that moment of revelation the eagle struck at him hard, gripped him with taloned feet, and pierced his flesh to the bone. Pain flared, and Cha-kwena cried out. The eagle was carrying him away, high and higher.

And then, suddenly, he was falling. He was following the sun as it plummeted to earth. He was crying out to his totem, but the great white mammoth was nowhere to be seen. He hurtled downward through space and fire until, with a shriek, the eagle dove at him again. He felt a rush of air and saw the shine of gold upon dark feathers as it swept past him and then turned. It flew toward him now with opened beak. Finally, with a woman's laugh, it swallowed him.

"Cha-kwena!"

He blinked. The dream dissolved. His vision swam. The grandfathers' blue faces were bending close around him. He laughed, a short, loud guffaw of relief. So much for boy-eating eagles!

"What vision have you seen, Cha-kwena?" his grandfather demanded.

"Vision?" Was it possible? Had the dream been a vision? Cha-kwena shook his head. No, it was a terrible dream. He refused to believe it. Besides, the hunters of the band had told him how it would be when he at last dreamed the special vision of a man. It would be fine and wonderful, of good things, a dream that would reveal his adult name and bring peace to his heart.

"No," he said, chafing against the truth, shaking his head, and rubbing his eyes with his fingertips. "I dozed off. It was only a dream."

"But you cried out!" said Hoyeh-tay.

"It was a *bad* dream," Cha-kwena added sharply.

"Perhaps you should let us decide if it was dream or vision," Shi-wana suggested.

The hair rose on the back of Cha-kwena's neck. He

did not like Shi-wana and did not find it difficult to lie to him. Now, as he looked up at the shaman of the People of the Blue Mesas, he spoke with an earnestness that seemed so genuine, he half believed it himself. "It was *not* a vision, Shi-wana, and it had nothing to do with you or with anything that should concern this gathering."

"Are you sure?" Shi-wana was not going to let the matter rest. "For many moons the omens have been confusing, both good and bad. I had hoped that all the shamans of the Red World would assemble here, but not a single shaman from the northernmost villages has come. So I ask myself, why have some of us been called to this place in their dreams, and others not? Never have we needed wisdom more than now, with the pinyons barren, mammoth disappearing, and lakes going dry. Perhaps if you repeated your dream, we could see things in it that you do not see."

"What good will it do?" snapped Cha-kwena, hating Shi-wana for maneuvering him into a corner. If he told them his dream, they were sure to find meaning in it—magic things of mystical portent. If they did not, they would not be shamans. But he was not one of them yet! If he kept the dream to himself, it would soon be forgotten.

"It may do more good than you know," said Shi-wana, giving the youth a third chance to relate the dream.

But Cha-kwena proclaimed more boldly and insistently than before, "You honor my grandfather's hopes for me by assuming that I might have a vision worthy of your concern! But you are wrong about me, Shi-wana. And Grandfather, you are wrong about me, too. Believe me, my dream was not important."

The sun was hot on the far northern side of the Blue Mesas. The hunters moved on their bellies through tall grass. They had tethered their dogs and left their traveling supplies in a thick grove of hardwoods at the head of a stream. Now, in silence, they approached a gaping ravine that cut across a benign stretch of hills. Although the fissure was a good half mile long and some twenty feet deep, it had been invisible to the hunters because grasses grew high all along its rim. The men discovered the rift when they paused at its brink. They stared, salivating, at the herd of mammoth that was grazing beyond the ravine, downwind amid a thick ground cover of scrub juniper.

"Tonight we hunt them," Maliwal whispered. "Tonight we feast on the meat of our totem."

His men looked at one another, and then at Maliwal as though he were mad.

"Maliwal . . ." Chudeh swallowed to clear his throat before repeating the name with tremulous emphasis. "Maliwal, in all respect, men cannot hunt mammoth in the dark."

"No?" Maliwal kept his eyes on the mammoth. The small herd, led by an emaciated, freckled old matriarch, had a few cows and adolescents, plus a young, enormously pregnant female that was even now huffing and circling restlessly, apparently about to give birth.

Maliwal's skin rippled with excitement. Such an animal was vulnerable. Whether she dropped her calf now or was still carrying it when the hunt began, she would possess no stamina for a long run. Experienced hunters could cut her from the herd and drive her straight toward the ravine. Once she went over the edge, the fall would either break or kill her. If she still carried her calf, its flesh would be a delicacy. His tongue traced the circumference of his broad mouth.

"That cow will be meat for us tonight," he told his men. "I am Maliwal. I am Wolf. I hunt when I will."

"We have come across the miles to find and hunt more than mammoth, Maliwal," reminded Rok evenly. He was a short, powerful man with muscular, slightly bowed arms and legs and a wide face that was oddly concave at the center. "We seek a village that possesses a sacred stone and a bride whom we may bring consenting to Thunder in the Sky. We must not place that mission in jeopardy. Now we have found that village, and tomorrow we shall go into the hills and meet with its people. The meat of mammoth is forbidden to all the bands of the Red World. If we hunt now and are seen by the villagers, they will drive us from their hunting grounds before we can seduce one of their daughters into coming north with us. We will have no chance of winning their shaman's confidence so that we may steal another sacred stone for Ysuna."

Resentment moved dangerously within Maliwal's eyes. "I do not need you to remind me of why we have come into this land, man of little vision. If we are to be strong of will and purpose in the days ahead, we must eat the flesh of the animal that is totem to us. Fresh meat is what we need. The village in the hills is yet far from us. We have moved wisely and with caution. Its people have not seen us, nor will they see us when we hunt under cover of darkness. The stars will allow us all the light we need. We have walked across this land by day and know its pitfalls."

Rok, ever sober, looked at him from beneath lowered brows. "We carry dried mammoth steaks in our traveling packs. Hunting at night is much too great a risk for fresh meat, Maliwal."

"My decision is made." He looked up, hoping to see the golden eagle again. It would be an omen to confirm his intent. But there was no sign of it. The soaring vastness of the flat-topped mountains drew his eyes higher until he saw an owl circling over the massifs. It was so far away that it was no longer than a stitch of sinew in the seam of his shirt. Nevertheless he knew it by the shape of its wings. His heart went cold. Among the People of the Watching Star, Owl was called Night Watcher, and Silent Enemy. What was the bird doing flying in broad daylight? Maliwal closed his eyes, then opened them again. The owl was gone. Relief shot through him. He had only imagined it.

"And if we *are* seen?" pressed Rok.

Maliwal glared at the man. He forgot about the owl and concentrated instead on the eagle, symbol of light and power and life everlasting. "We will *not* be seen," he said, staring off toward the mesas once again. The smokes of the hill village were rising from a cleft in the lower battlements, and from somewhere high above and far away there came the sound of singing.

# 8

The shamans, singing and chanting, kept Cha-kwena on the promontory for the rest of the day and into the beginning of the night. Owl circled restlessly, banking often to the north as though he wished to be followed. Hoyeh-tay took no note; he slept through most of the singing. At dusk Owl returned to perch upon the old man's head just as Dakan-eh escorted Sunam-tu and his dimpled sister up the trail to the ridgetop. The threesome paused a respectful distance from the circle; they did not set foot upon the promontory.

When Cha-kwena noticed the girl, he sat taller. The newcomers had baskets of food with them! Roasted seeds and meat—squirrel and rabbit and lizard, from the scent. He licked his lips, then blushed. The girl, licking her own lips, was looking at him. Slowly, very slowly, the tip of her tongue slipped along the wide, soft seams of her mouth. He found the movement fascinating. Somehow the motion of that little pink tongue warmed his belly, stirred his loins, and turned his penis hard and hot. Although he was not cold, he shivered.

She saw his reaction and offered a little smile of gratification. His heart leaped with delight. With a bold impetuosity that made him proud, he smiled back at the dimpled sister of Sunam-tu. Cha-kwena's right eyebrow arched upward, wrinkling his forehead with a speculation that astounded him. For the first time since Hoyeh-tay had dragged him by his hair from the boys' lodge, he found himself wondering if being a shaman might not have some advantages after all: Sunam-tu had been boasting all morning among the other guardians of the forest camp that he had brought his sister so that he could find her a shaman for a mate.

Standing close at her brother's side, young Lah-ri

held her head high and thrust out her small, firm bosom. Cha-kwena could not bring himself to look at anything else. Finally he noticed that Sunam-tu was beaming and urging her to turn around as he announced to all what a very fine cook and all-around woman his sister was.

The shamans frowned. So did Cha-kwena. He suddenly developed a profound dislike of Sunam-tu and definitely did not care for the way that Dakan-eh was eyeing the girl. Jealousy flared within him. How dare Dakan-eh look at her like that? Sunam-tu's sister was much too young for him! Besides, Dakan-eh already had Ta-maya, and Ban-ya, too, if he wanted her.

And why, he wondered, were the shamans measuring the girl with such open hostility? He felt fiercely protective of Lah-ri. It was a good feeling. It made him feel older, manly. He stiffened his posture and held his shoulders rigidly back. The girl seemed to notice the change in him, but he would never know for sure, for at that moment Shi-wana ordered the food bearers to take their burden and go away.

"This is a holy place, Sunam-tu!" rebuked the shaman of the People of the Blue Mesas. "You know better than to bring a female here. We call upon the spirits of the ancestors! This is no time for food."

The newcomers bowed, then obeyed, although Sunam-tu looked crestfallen. The girl's dimples were very noticeable as, pouting, she hung her head and walked away with Dakan-eh close at her side. His strong, sunbrowned arm was slung possessively around her shoulders.

Cha-kwena rose and started to follow.

"Where are you going?" Hoyeh-tay called.

"To . . . to get something to eat. I am hungry."

Shi-wana's eyes narrowed with speculation. "Yes. I imagine that you are. It has been many a year since I have known an appetite for that sort of food. It might be satisfying again with a girl like that."

Cha-kwena blushed bright red. He might well have flown at Shi-wana, but Hoyeh-tay, anticipating his next move, shouted imperatively: "Sit down, Grandson! Now! You may have an appetite, but the food that you require is not in the forest camp. It is here—spirit food—and equally nourishing for now."

Cha-kweña thought of rebelling but knew that there was no point; sooner or later he would be allowed to return to the forest camp, with or without the shamans. In the meantime, Sunam-tu's sister was not going anywhere. So, with a sigh of acquiescence, Cha-kwena re-joined the sacred circle.

Silent and obedient, he watched Night come down. The shamans spoke of many things, but mainly of the past and of how nothing was the same or as good as it had been when they had been youths of Cha-kwena's age. They urged him to learn from them, but he was tired and hungry and easily distracted.

They chanted until North Wind brought them the faint trumpeting of a mammoth. It came from somewhere very far, miles beyond the broad, soaring back of the Blue Mesas. Rapt, Cha-kwena listened; the shamans listened, too.

"Did you hear it? Pain was in the cry of our brother," said Naquah-neh, shaman of the People of the White Hills, frowning.

"Sister," corrected Shi-wana evenly. "A small herd of cows and little ones was grazing in the juniper scrubland several miles from my village before I left. A young female with them looked about ready to calve. Perhaps even now the cow gives birth. This would explain the sound of pain."

Hoyeh-tay nodded. "New life . . . always a good thing."

"Always the sound of mammoth is a good sound and a better omen," said Han-da, shaman of the village of the Blue Sky People. "There have been no mammoth seen in my part of the Red World for many moons. If your village were not so far to the north, Shi-wana, I would bring my people there, just to see them. I want them to know that our totem animals are still with us."

"Come south then, if you want good omens," invited Cha-kwena. Then he announced loftily: "Hoyeh-tay and I have seen Great White Spirit grazing at the mouth of the big canyon near the Village of the Lake of Many Singing Birds."

The information caused an instant and enormous stir among the shamans.

"What is this you say?" Shi-wana made no attempt to hide his incredulity or his anger.

"The great white mammoth walks once more in the Red World and Hoyeh-tay has not told us?"

Cha-kwena disliked the man more than ever. He had inadvertently put his grandfather at a disadvantage, and Hoyeh-tay suddenly looked lost, shrunken, very old. Shi-wana stared, pop-eyed, while the other shamans shouted, waved their fists, and demanded to know the reason for Hoyeh-tay's silence.

"I . . . I . . ." The old man's face went blank as, with Owl still perched upon his head, he sat hunched, desperately trying to gather his thoughts. "I . . . I . . ." Suddenly they came to him. He sat erect again, and his eyes went bright. "I am Hoyeh-tay!" he declared proudly, crossing his arms over his meager chest and sneering contemptuously into the wind. "I am Wise and Watchful Owl, but I am not so arrogant that I would flaunt my power. I was waiting for the right time to tell you about Life Giver. And now it seems that my grandson has found it for me."

Cha-kwena doubted if he had ever heard a more transparent excuse for forgetfulness. He frowned. The shamans were all looking steadily at his grandfather. He saw in their eyes that they had seen straight through the heart of the old man's lie. And then he understood that they cared enough for an old man's pride to accept his word without question or rebuke.

*Perhaps these shamans are not as bad as you think,* said Owl in that voice that only Cha-kwena could hear. *Your Dakan-eh would not be so kind. Come with me now. My old shaman is tired, and there is something that one of you must see.*

The youth chose to ignore the bird. It was easy enough to do, considering that he had no wish to hear Owl in the first place.

Hoyeh-tay was nodding, pleased with what he took to be the success of his deception. "Now," he said, "I will tell you of Life Giver and of how, on a night of spirit magic, our totem called my grandson through the darkness of our country to the sacred spring and . . . "

Cha-kwena rolled his eyes. The old man had not lost all his powers yet!

\* \* \*

On the north slope of the Blue Mesas, mammoth circled the young pregnant female among them as, with head hung low, she huffed and sighed against the pains of labor.

Staring through the darkness, Rok shook his head distastefully. "Maliwal, you cannot truly mean to do this."

"No?" Maliwal cast a withering look his way and snatched up his spears. With an exhalation of contempt, he trotted off to hunt under a star-filled sky. He carried a sack of extra spearheads at his side, and a spear hurler dangled from a thong at his wrist.

Maliwal could feel Rok glaring after him. He smiled, then counted his steps, certain that by the time he reached a number equal to that of his fingers, Rok and the others would follow. He was not mistaken; in a moment they were at his heels—like my dogs, he thought.

Grinning, he lengthened his stride. Man for man they matched it. His boldness inspired them almost as much as it shamed and worried them. They were right to be concerned, of course; what he was proposing was dangerous. But the barb of Ysuna's hurtful challenge had worked deeply beneath his skin and was like a burr in his spirit now. Mammoth were out there in the dark, more mammoth than he had seen in many a long moon. He would hunt them, and he would kill at least one of them—for *her*.

"Maliwal." Rok was at his side. "You cannot succeed at this alone."

"True," he conceded, and smiled his wolfish smile. "But I am not alone. You are with me, as well as Tsana and Ston and Chudeh. Here, run at my side. It is my plan to separate when we get a little closer, then to close in on this herd from three directions, leaving the fourth open so that the mammoth will run ahead of us, wherever we desire them to run. Do you see the young female? She still carries her calf! She will be easily driven toward the ravine."

They hesitated. Even the dogs seemed less than enthusiastic.

"Ysuna will know what weak-bellied men dare to call themselves hunters of the People of the Watching Star!"

Maliwal goaded. "Your women will weep in shame to hear how you have refused to stand with me this night!"

Against their better judgment but prodded by pride, they followed Maliwal across the land, separating and closing on the herd, charging in and feinting back only to charge in again, howling, yipping, and brandishing their spears.

As Maliwal had predicted, once taken by surprise, the old matriarch of the herd led her family off at a gallop. When the pregnant female veered away from the others, Maliwal laughed triumphantly, vindicated as the rest of the herd thundered on in blind panic, unaware that the young cow had fallen behind. Still in labor, exhausted from hours of pain, and confused in the darkness, she was easily driven toward the ravine. A spear hurled into her flank was enough to send her racing straight over the edge. She screamed like a woman as she fell, and Maliwal was not the only man to hear her spine snap and her legs break when she landed.

"Ho!" he roared. "Did I not promise that it would be exactly this way?"

Emboldened by their success, the other hunters cheered and praised their leader. Not one among them hesitated as Maliwal positioned them by the ravine so that they might hurl a few spears into the dying animal's vital organs.

"Now," he proclaimed, "all sit back and wait for the beast to grow so weak that she will be no threat to us as we butcher her where she lies and hack prime steaks from the unborn calf. Did I not tell you that it would be a good hunt?"

Not even Rok offered an argument. They placed their spears; but because of the way the cow had fallen, it was impossible to make a killing thrust. She raised her head weakly, waved her trunk, and bleated piteously, unsuccessfully trying to drive away her tormentors.

"She will be a while dying," Rok predicted, looking around nervously. "Perhaps we should go now, before the old matriarch of the herd returns."

"Go?" Maliwal was incredulous.

"It is the way of the mammoth to grieve for a lost member of the herd. They will linger nearby even after death has come," whispered Chudeh reverently. Fear lighted his eyes. "We have all seen it many times. Rok is right. We should go."

"We can return for the meat after the old cow at last goes her way and it is safe," added Rok.

Maliwal felt like spearing the man. "Nothing is safe in this life," he hissed. "The old cow will not return. She is miles away by now. There were calves in the herd. She will stay with the other mammoth to guard the little ones. That, too, is their way."

The words had barely left his lips when, with a gasp, Rok pointed off.

Maliwal turned to see the old matriarch of the herd was coming toward them. She paused—a mountainous mound of freckled, wrinkled skin swaying on stanchion limbs. Her head was out, her great ears were twitching, her trunk was uplifted, and her tusks were threatening. He could hear the other mammoth trumpeting from far away, in a place of safety to which the old matriarch had led them.

A growl rose at the back of Maliwal's throat. The matriarch's loyalty to a dying sister proved him wrong, and he did not like to be wrong. When Rok advised retreat once again, Maliwal told him to shut his mouth.

"Stay where you are!" he commanded. "Hold your ground. If she approaches, we will show her against whom she dares to come!"

"*If* she approaches!" Chudeh was incredulous.

"Maliwal, we cannot win at this," warned Rok, taking hold of the leader's arm and trying to pull him away. "If we move slowly and show no threat, we may be able to—"

"Get away from me! Go, run if you must!" Maliwal twisted free so violently of Rok's hold that the other man fell and landed hard on his back with a grunt. Maliwal did not care; he had had enough of Rok for one day. "No female—of *any* species—will send me slinking away like a frightened cur. I am Maliwal! I am Wolf!"

He faced the old mammoth, challenging her. "Come for me if you dare, old cow. The first man of Ysuna, Daughter of the Sun, does not fear you. He does not fear anything!"

What a lie that was. He was afraid; fear made the challenge irresistible. Rok led the others away in a prudent retreat. Maliwal stood tall as the old mammoth began to approach.

*The others will speak in reverent voices of the bravery of Maliwal,* he thought, readying himself for the attack. *How small and meek will my brother look in the eyes of Ysuna when she compares Mystic Warrior to the might of Wolf.*

"Come, old cow! Come for Maliwal if you dare!" he cried.

How slowly she moved. He looked disdainfully at her sagging skin and into her filmed, watery eyes and was so sure of himself that he decided to forgo the use of his spear hurler, which would have both lengthened and strengthened his throw. Instead he held two spears at ready in his left hand while he positioned the third across his right shoulder. Smiling, he had no doubt that he would have plenty of time to anticipate her charge and not only avoid it but make a killing thrust as she went by him.

It was his second and greater mistake of the night.

The hours passed slowly for Cha-kwena. For no reason that the boy could understand, Owl stayed upon Hoyeh-tay's shoulder, his feathered back turned to the gathering. It was as though he wanted no part of the assemblage. Now and then the old bird stretched a wing or extended a leg, but he did not fly off into the darkness to hunt among the stars.

Eventually the shamans dreamed the dreams of holy men. Cha-kwena rose and strode to the edge of the promontory as Owl came to light upon his shoulder. He waved the bird away, but Owl's strong talons gripped him and would not let go. Cha-kwena did not really mind; the claws neither bruised nor pierced his skin, and once it was evident that the bird was going to be allowed to stay, the grip relaxed. At his back, miles away across the northern edge of the Red World, the mammoth trumpeted again, and for a moment, he could have sworn that he heard the high wild shriek of a man.

"Listen!" cautioned Owl.

He stiffened. The mammoth trumpeted again; others of its kind answered from farther away. The man—if, indeed, it had been a man—did not cry out again, but the mammoth continued to call to one another. The sound was deeply disturbing; there was pain in it, and fear, and a heart-wrenching desolation that could only have been described as a lament. What was hunting them? Wolves? Lions?

"Men!" answered Owl.

"It cannot be. It is forbidden for men to hunt mammoth," he replied, not even aware that he had spoken aloud.

"Men of the Red World, yes," Owl agreed, "but there are others."

The premise was startling. Everyone knew that there were no other people in all the world except the People. Sons and daughters of First Man and First Woman, all bands were related. All shared the same blood and customs and traditions. The People did not hunt mammoth. It had been forbidden since time beyond beginning. And yet . . . had not one of the shamans said something about strangers from the north?

In the forest camp far below the promontory, a dimpled young girl was giggling. Would she smile at him again if he went to her now? There was only one way to find out. With a deep breath of resolve, Cha-kwena turned and strode out toward the forest trail as, *oo-ooh*ing in frustration and disgust, Owl left his shoulder and flew to land once more upon the nodding head of snoring, sleeping Hoyeh-tay.

"*Maliwal!*"

Well away from the ravine into which he and the others had just stampeded the pregnant mammoth, Maliwal heard his fellow hunters call his name. He could not answer, nor could he scream again. The old matriarch had him. He was clinging to the tip of one of her timeworn tusks, and she was lifting him, shaking him until his brains went to pudding inside his skull and his bones seemed to rip loose inside his skin.

Despite his best efforts, he could no longer hold on. Breathless, hurting, and more terrified than he had ever been in his entire life, Maliwal was hurled upward, sent tumbling into the star-filled night, and then falling through the darkness with blood in his eyes and the world coming up to meet him fast, much too fast.

He landed hard on his side. Stunned, he lost his grip not only on his spears but on reality. The old matriarch was pounding toward him. Without his spears, he had no defense. With a gasp of pain and terror, he rolled sideways, over and over until the earth dropped out from under him and he fell into the ravine and came to rest not far from the pregnant cow.

The stench was appalling. The young mammoth, broken and bleeding, had lost control of her bladder and bowel. She lay on a soggy mattress of her own urine and fecal matter. Breathing through his mouth, Maliwal wedged himself between her flank and the stony earth. If she tried to heave herself up by straining for leverage against the wall of the ravine, he would be crushed like a gnat. But what else could he do? The old mammoth was still coming for him. He could feel the reverberations of her footfall in the earth.

He wedged himself deeper and fought back the need to retch. The horror of his situation threatened to overwhelm him. He froze, his heart pounding in his ears, and tried to will himself into complete and absolute immobility and silence.

The old cow was at the edge of the ravine. She was not the largest mammoth he had ever seen, but she was large enough. He looked up. It was a mistake. The old cow's head came down, swinging from side to side. For an instant he saw himself reflected in elephantine eyes, and in that instant he knew that he had been seen.

The matriarch's head rose. She huffed once, and then, rearing back, she trumpeted, enraged.

Maliwal turned his head away. Perhaps, with eye contact broken, she would forget that he was there. But she did not forget. Her great forelimbs stomped and pounded at the edge of the ravine. Stones and earth cascaded over him. The world shook, and the air seemed to crack with the sound of her frenzied cries. And then, even in the darkness, through an avalanche of debris ripped from the earth, he saw her tusks thrusting downward, probing for him.

Too horrified to make a sound, he pressed himself still deeper between the dying mammoth's flank and the side of the ravine. With his back against the earth, he wriggled from side to side, desperately attempting to hollow out a space in which he could hide, driving himself straight back into the earth, away from the savage downthrust of the tusks. It was a futile effort, and he knew it.

He snarled as he remembered Rok's warning and kept jamming and twisting himself against the wall of the ravine until, with a gasp of surprise and relief, he slumped backward. The earth had yielded to the pressure and friction. It was just enough to grant him the space he needed.

He leaned back, breathless and for the first time aware of a deep, dull ache at the right side of his face. Again Maliwal willed himself to complete immobility.

He was not certain just when the matriarch's attempts to gouge him from the pit slackened. The sounds she made were low and labored. Somewhere above and beyond, men were shouting, and dogs were barking. They were very close—perhaps closer than they should be—but Maliwal knew no fear for them. His heart leaped with hope. *It is about time they found their courage and came to help me!*

They were harassing the old cow; in a moment they would drive her off, and he would be free of her threat, able to climb back into the starlit world and breathe untainted air again. But the mammoth, head down, tusks moving deep in the ravine, did not turn away.

Now and then the old matriarch exhaled a pained grunt or groan, and Maliwal, despite his situation, smiled as he envisioned spears striking her and dogs snapping at her side. But despite obvious weariness and discomfort, her tusks kept on probing. The hunter realized that she was not trying to impale him; she was attempting to lift her dying sister.

The wounded cow sighed in wan response. She was trying to rise. It was no good. She raised her trunk; it was all she could manage.

Maliwal squinted upward through darkness and saw that the trunks of the two mammoth were entwined above him. Silhouetted against the stars, they moved slowly as one, in an embrace or a last good-bye. Then, suddenly, the cow stiffened. She shivered and slobbered blood. She shifted her weight slightly to the left and sighed. All too close to her rib cage, Maliwal felt her die.

And now, for the first time since being hurled upward into the sky by the matriarch, he found his voice. He screamed and screamed again, for as the young mammoth exhaled her last breath, her body went completely limp and a portion of her flank sagged into the depression into which he had thrust himself. She would have crushed the life out of him had he not levered up in time, just enough to keep his head and torso free. Yet his limbs were held fast—burning, then going numb with so much weight against them.

His heart pounding, Maliwal saw the matriarch raise her head and turn away. She was leaving! The sound of men and dogs was all around now. It sounded as if half the hunters of the People of the Watching Star had materialized to assist the few who had accompanied him out of the village. Had Masau followed him after all? It did not matter, not now. The excruciating pain in his legs drove every thought from his head except the realization that when he had begun the mammoth hunt he had his skinning dagger at his side.

It was still there! Frantically, he loosed it from its sheath and began to slice and hack through the tough skin and flesh of the dead mammoth. At last his legs were free and, by the power of the Watching Star, whole and unbroken and ready to run once he rubbed the numbness from them.

This done, he started to pull himself onto the flank of the dead cow. Chudeh was already nearby, reaching down toward him. Shaking despite his best effort to appear unruffled by his close encounter with death, Maliwal took hold of Chudeh's strong hand and, with not so much as a grunt of gratitude, allowed the burly hunter to pull him up so that he might stand victorious upon their kill.

The sweetness of the untainted air was almost as staggering as the realization that he had come through the experience alive. He rocked on his feet for a moment before steadying himself.

A good distance ahead, the old matriarch was down. The dogs were at her flanks. She had so many spears in her sides that she looked like one of the large spiny mountain rats that his people valued for their quills. His men—and many others—were standing close to the dying mammoth. He frowned. His face was hurting badly now; he would have raised a hand to determine the pain's source, but he was too tired to lift his arms.

"So," he said, sighing, not looking at Chudeh or noting that he was the only man who had held back from the excitement of the final kill out of concern for his leader, "I see that Masau *has* followed, with many hunters."

"Masau is not here," informed Chudeh, his voice was low, worried. "The men you see are strangers. They are of the Red World, from a village in those hills ahead. These men were coming down from their own village to bring sweet grass to the mammoth when they saw us. They were hoping to stop us from hunting but joined us instead when they saw that we had a man in trouble. They are not at all happy about having to kill mammoth in order to save you, Maliwal. Two of their number are dead; another has been badly wounded. And Rok was crushed in the old cow's last foray. I slit his throat to end his misery before coming back to see if you were alive."

Maliwal was glad that Rok was dead. The man had challenged him and been proved right.

"Maliwal . . . are you listening to me, Maliwal?" Chudeh pressed earnestly. "What are we going to do now? These men know that we are mammoth eaters. We will not be welcome among them, and they will never give one of their daughters. It will be impossible to steal their sacred stone. Even now their shaman counsels with other holy men somewhere atop the twin mesas. According to the villagers, there is big medicine up there on the mountain—and bad medicine in our being here. I am afraid that once we leave this country, these men will warn every other village in the Red World about us. Ysuna is going to be very angry, Maliwal. Rok was right. We should have listened to him."

Maliwal stiffened as a rage of frustration built in him. "Rok is dead! If I hear another word from you about him, I will send you to join him in the world beyond this world!"

Chudeh gasped and took a backward step. His features expanded into a mask of horror. "Maliwal! Your face!"

Chudeh's expression alerted Maliwal to what he would

find before his hands rose to touch a truth that nearly dropped him where he stood. The right side of his face had been ripped from upper lip to ear by the tip of one of the matriarch's tusks. His ear, no longer attached to the side of his head, was dangling from a torn flap of scalp, tangled like a grotesque ornament in the blood-thickened strands of his hair.

"Ach!" He gasped, cupped the ear, and slapped it tightly back against the side of his face. He fought against shock but lost the battle as a wave of weakness brought him to his knees. "They . . . will pay for this. . . ."

"They? Who, Maliwal?"

He was cold. Shock numbed him. The ache in his torn mouth, cheek, and severed ear felt real enough but far away. A kernel of heat expanded within him, embedded deep, and burned hot within his spirit as he replied: "The herd whose matriarch has done this to me . . . and those who have nurtured that herd. They will pay."

"But the animal that wounded you has already paid with her life. And these men of the Red World have sacrificed their own brothers to save you."

"What matter? As you have said, these men will warn every other Red World village about us. They must die. But first we will take from them what we need—a bride for Thunder in the Sky and a sacred stone for Daughter of the Sun. After they are massacred to the last man, woman, and child, we will finish the herd that has done this to me. Ysuna will have the meat of these mammoth, and more. Yes, she will have much more." Suddenly dizzy, he leaned forward and braced himself upon his left hand.

Chudeh was kneeling beside him, gripping him, holding him up. "But ours is not a raiding party. We are few, while the men of this village are many. How can we hope to kill them all without risking ourselves?"

"We are warriors of the People of the Watching Star. The blood and flesh of our totem strengthen us! What threat can these lizard eaters be to us?"

Chudeh looked worried. "But they are not without weapons and resourcefulness. Always it has been our way to come into their village posing as brothers from a far land, to win their trust, and to leave in peace with one of their daughters. Only after she has been given as a consenting sacrifice have we returned with all the warriors of the Watching Star to claim the village as our own and to hunt the mammoth in the lizard eaters' hunting ground. Surely it is the only safe way to—"

"Ah, man of little vision . . ." The fingers of Maliwal's right hand were splayed across his ear and the ruined side of his face. His dizziness was passing. His face and ear ached cruelly now, but ideas were boiling in the storm clouds of his rage. He looked up past Chudeh to the towering flat-topped mesas and predicted darkly: "I have told you before, Chudeh, nothing is safe in this life. The spirits have led us well! We will return to Daughter of the Sun with all she has ever desired. Up there on that mountain, if what you have just said is true, the shamans of the Red World are gathered together with all the sacred stones of their people. Imagine it! *All* in one place, just waiting for us to take them, to claim their power as our own."

He paused, trembling—not against weakness and pain but against the overwhelming vision of what he now saw as possible for himself. Spurning assistance from Chudeh, he forced himself to rise. The effort cost him. His vision swam, and the earth seemed to drop beneath his feet. But his hand became a fist against the mutilated side of his face. "No man has ever brought a finer gift to Ysuna than the gift that I will bring to her now. This wounding will be nothing to her. You will see! She will not flinch from the sight of me. With the magic power that I will now bring to her, even such wounds as these will heal and leave no scars! Her lodge will be open to me, and never again will she have cause to doubt who is most worthy of her favor— Mystic Warrior or Wolf."

# 9

It was dark on the little wooded trail that led down from the promontory to the encampment in the pinyon grove. Cha-kwena walked cautiously. Something moved in the darkness up ahead. He stopped in midstep, and his heart quickened.

The forest was thick around him. Moon shone through breaks in the treetops and allowed him just enough light to see his way; nevertheless, he stood poised like a wild creature, holding his breath, listening to the rustle of branches and the soft sound of footsteps upon fallen pine needles. Something was treading lightly just off the trail directly ahead of him.

He had come a long way since leaving the old men to snore the night away on the heights of the mesa. He was not far from the encampment, yet he was not so close that he expected to hear a familiar voice, and that was what he heard now—the voice of Dakan-eh.

"I thought you might follow me," said Bold Man.

Cha-kwena allowed himself to breathe again. Greatly impressed that Bold Man had been able to recognize him, he was about to call out. But the giggle of a young girl stopped the words from leaving his mouth. Dakan-eh was not alone.

"My brother has sent me to follow you, Bold Man."

A strange and unwelcome coldness touched Cha-kwena when he recognized the voice of Sunam-tu's sister. Bold Man had not been addressing him at all.

"And why would he do that?" There was a flirtatious edge to Dakan-eh's question; he already knew her answer. "It could be dangerous for a young girl to follow a man into the forest at night."

"He knew that you would not go far. My dance by the campfire . . . you did not look away."

"From a young girl laughing and dancing naked in the firelight? The other guardians did not look away, either."

"But I danced for you, not for them."

"And why would you do that?"

"Because you are Bold Man. My brother says that since you have been in this camp, the sleep spirits have not come to you. My brother says that *I* should come to you instead. Because, he says, I am better than sleep."

"And are you?"

"Oh, yes! Much better."

Dakan-eh's voice was a low, husky invitation. "Show me."

Cha-kwena caught his breath. Neither Dakan-eh nor Lah-ri had seen him. He edged forward silently and peered through the small, leathery leaves of a smooth-barked manzanita bush. Dakan-eh and Lah-ri stood face-to-face in a small clearing beneath the stars.

Cha-kwena swallowed. How young she was, how small, like a child lost in the heavy folds of her ankle-length cloak of twisted rabbit fur. Shyly, she was holding it closed, the upper seam knotted in her little hands beneath her chin. Cha-kwena ground his teeth as loathing for Sunam-tu nearly overwhelmed him. It was obvious what was happening: The shamans had rejected Lah-ri, and now, in desperation to find her a man, her brother was forcing her to give herself to Dakan-eh.

Cha-kwena's heart swelled with pity as he waited for Dakan-eh to shame her with yet another rejection as he explained that he was already promised to another. But Dakan-eh did not reject her. Instead he reached down and stroked the robe . . . and the girl who hid so demurely within it.

"Show me," he commanded, his voice low. His eyes were intent upon her face as his hands curled over hers, opened the cloak, and drew it wide. He sucked air through his teeth, cast the skins aside, and demanded, "Dance for me, girl, now . . . here . . . alone. And then we will dance together."

Cha-kwena gasped raggedly as the girl turned and displayed herself. She cupped her hands under her little breasts and offered them up to Dakan-eh. "These were for shamans," she said, sighing. "But the shamans have sent them away. Will Bold Man also send them away if I dance for him?"

Dakan-eh's eyes were feeding on the body of the girl. Slowly, with his eyes still on Lah-ri, the warrior began to loosen the waist thong of his breechclout.

"No!" Cha-kwena cried, and hurtled through the manzanita bush. He stood breathless and fuming before Dakan-eh, feeling as bold as the man he now dared to confront. "She is not for you!"

Dakan-eh was taken aback. "I . . . What . . . How long have you been hiding in the dark?"

"What matter?" Cha-kwena shot back. "This girl is for a shaman, not for you. You already have a woman—*two* women, Ta-maya *and* Ban-ya!"

"I have not accepted Ban-ya, and Ta-maya has not accepted me."

"She will! You *know* she will."

Dakan-eh looked both irked and amused as he slung a proprietary arm about the naked Lah-ri and drew her close. "Go away, boy. Leave this man to his pleasures."

"She is for a shaman!"

"Ah, I see. And are you telling me that you are finally what your grandfather has wished you to be?"

"I . . . I, yes. I mean, no! I . . ."

Dakan-eh's laugh was particularly nasty, more of a snort. His hand caressed the girl's bare shoulder. "This boy would have you, Lah-ri. There are those who say that he will be a shaman someday. Of course, as you can see, he still has some growing to do. I, on the other hand, am a hunter no man can equal. I have saved this would-be shaman's life and that of his addlebrained grandfather. But if you prefer such a boy to me, how can I hope to stand against his powers?"

Cha-kwena was struck dumb by shame. Tears burned beneath his eyelids as something deep within his spirit ached and bled. He had once adored and trusted Bold Man. But now, for the first time, he understood that Dakan-eh had not risked himself out of compassion or concern for those who were dear to him. As in all things, he had been motivated solely by his amazing arrogance.

"What's the matter, Cha-kwena?" Dakan-eh goaded, openly enjoying the moment. "Speak up, boy! If you want something, you must let us know!"

Cha-kwena hated him. It was a new emotion to him, and it was so deep and dark and turbulent that he felt as though he were drowning in it. Looking away from the man he would never again think of as a friend, he stammered with defensive indignation to the girl, "You d-do not have to g-give yourself to him. He m-may be b-bold, but he is not worthy of you! If your b-brother must g-give you away, I would be p-proud to be your man. I would! W-with me you would b-be a shaman's woman. N-not right away, of course, but when my grandfather's spirit walks the w-wind. Maybe n-not for a long time, but f-for you, I *will* be shaman!"

Lah-ri dimpled and giggled. "Not for a very long time, I think." With her eyes on Cha-kwena's face, she snuggled against Dakan-eh's side and slipped her arms around his bare waist. One small hand opened and moved slowly downward across his belly until her fingers disappeared beneath the loosened loin cover.

Cha-kwena's eyes went wide. Dakan-eh's reaction told him where the girl's fingers had gone.

"Mmm . . ." She smiled dreamily as she sidled still closer to Dakan-eh. "He is hard and hot and moving in my palm. Let me see what *you* would offer me, Shaman Boy. You talk as fearlessly as Bold Man, but are you as big?"

Cha-kwena felt embarrassed, confused, ashamed.

Dakan-eh laughed again and in a single movement freed his loins, turned the girl inward, and lifted her high. "Go away, Cha-kwena. This little one and I will work our own kind of magic now, yes?"

"Yes!" she consented, and opened her legs wide and bent them around Dakan-eh's waist.

With his hips arched forward, Bold Man lowered her. Wriggling and giggling, Lah-ri accepted him as he thrust deep.

Cha-kwena caught his breath. His body was afire, but his mind was ice. How he wanted her! And how he hated her for shaming him and leading him to believe that she was in need of his protection.

She was looking at him now, laughing at him even as she "danced" upon Dakan-eh, her hands gripping the warrior's shoulders. Then Bold Man took her down, straddling her and mating her with a gasping, snarling, animal ferocity that sent the girl into paroxysms of gasps.

Stunned, Cha-kwena stepped back, stumbled halfway to his knees, and then, still stumbling, turned and ran.

"Stop! Where are you going? And who told you that you could leave the assembly of shamans?"

Breathless, his face streaked with tears, Cha-kwena stopped dead in his tracks. He glared up at Shi-wana and at the other shamans who blocked his way.

"You were all asleep," he defended. "What difference did my absence make? Here I am, on my way back to you!"

No one spoke. Why were they all looking at him so fixedly? A moment passed, and something cold flexed within his heart. Where was Hoyeh-tay? Something was wrong. Cha-kwena stiffened, then caught his breath as the shamans stepped aside. Hoyeh-tay was being carried by Naquah-neh, shaman of the People of the White Hills.

"Grandfather! Are you all right?"

Hoyeh-tay stared at him blank eyed.

It was Owl who replied. "Are you blind as well as stupid, Cha-kwena? Can you not see that my shaman is sick?"

"And where was the grandson when the grandfather called his name in need?" Naquah-neh spat the words with contempt as, with extended arms, he held the old man toward his grandson.

Cha-kwena's knees nearly buckled. The old man's expression was vacant eyed. He was drooling, and the left side of his face seemed oddly twisted. If Hoyeh-tay recognized his grandson, he gave no sign of it.

"A bad spirit has taken him," informed Shi-wana quietly. "A very bad spirit."

There was silence in the encampment. Wind moved softly through the pinyon groves, rousing no song from the sun-warmed pine needles. Cha-kwena sat alone on the bare ground in front of the little hut assigned to him. Dakan-eh and Lah-ri had not yet returned from the upland trail, and he did not care. He passed the time arranging and rearranging pebbles between his thighs.

When a shadow fell over the youth, Cha-kwena looked up. Shi-wana had emerged from the hut, where Hoyeh-tay lay under the care of the other shamans. "How is my grandfather?" he asked.

"The bad spirits are still with him," Shi-wana answered, "in his head and in one eye and the corner of his mouth. He talks of the past with a thick tongue. He speaks of old friends as though they were with him now. But he seems strong enough to travel. You and Bold Man can make a litter for him. Perhaps once Hoyeh-tay is home again, he will remember that it is today and not yesterday."

Cha-kwena cocked his head. Yesterday he had been in love. Yesterday he had thought of Dakan-eh as a friend. Yesterday old Hoyeh-tay had been well and strong. Today everything was different. A strange sadness overcame him. He felt empty inside, and home seemed far away.

"We must all leave this place and go back to our villages," said the shaman of the People of the Blue Mesas, staring with a furrowed brow across the encampment. "We must think about the omens and signs that have been a gift to us on this sacred mountain. I have thought only of my village, of my people, of the mammoth that were grazing in the scrubland before I left my lodge. Were my dreams the visions of a shaman, I wonder, or only an old man's restless longing to be home again?"

The silence that followed was heavy and troubling. Shi-wana had spoken to Cha-kwena as though to an equal. Somehow, the boy had felt more at ease when the shaman had behaved as an adversary.

Now, the tall, long-limbed man shook his head and said thoughtfully, "Of all the Red World shamans, Hoyeh-tay has always possessed the power of the ancestors most strongly. But now . . ."

Shi-wana paused, shook his head again, and directed his gaze downward to the boy. "Soon, much sooner than I would have wished, I will be supreme elder. And yet the sacred stones do not speak to me upon the sacred mountain. Perhaps there is a message in their silence?" He hesitated. "Could it be?" His features expanded into a smile of gap-toothed radiance. "Yes!" he cried, and continued in a rush of words, affirming his thoughts as he spoke them. "Through their very silence the stones speak!"

Cha-kwena did not share the man's enthusiasm, but the shaman did not give the boy a chance to voice his opinion.

"Since first the People came into the Red World," Shi-wana explained, "the many bands have assembled here every second, third, or fourth summer. Now six long years have passed since the last great harvest of pinyon nuts. In all this time, mothers have not seen daughters who have married into other bands, and the children born to these daughters are strangers to their grandparents. The People will soon begin to forget that once they were one band, all children of First Man and First Woman. This is the message of the sacred stones! Harvest or no harvest, next year there *will* be a Great Gathering. Ah, Cha-kwena, there will be dancing and singing and wedding feasts and baby namings! All the shamans of the Red World will make special magic for their people!"

"Hoyeh-tay is old and sick," Cha-kwena pointed out. "He may not be able to make the journey."

Shi-wana hesitated a moment before saying quietly, regretfully, "Hoyeh-tay has made his last journey to the sacred mountain, Cha-kwena. You will be bringing him home to die among his people. Learn from him what you can, and when his spirit leaves his body to walk the wind forever, seek wisdom and guidance in the counsel of Kosar-eh, the clown, for that good man might well have been a shaman had the forces of Creation not seen fit to maim him. Next year, when the Moon of Grass has risen and the Pinyon Moon is waiting to be born, take up the sacred stone of your ancestors and bring Tlana-quah and your band to the Blue Mesas. By then your people will have named you Shaman . . . although, in truth, my boy, you are Shaman now."

Cha-kwena would not believe it, nor would he allow Shi-wana to speak of it again. They made a litter for Hoyeh-tay, and rabbit skins were laid over its soft mattressing of fragrant, freshly picked pine needles. The old man acted like a happy child as he was settled upon it. He relived some ancient memory and talked to people who had been long dead.

"His spirit has gone to walk with the ancestors already," said Dakan-eh. "Perhaps it would be best to leave him in this sacred place so when the last of his life leaves his body, it will not become lost along the trail."

Cha-kwena glared at him. "He will not be lost as long as I am with him! I will drag his sledge until he is well again. And he *will* be well again. You will see!"

"As you wish," he said, shrugging off the boy's hostility.

After saying his good-byes to the shamans and other guardians, Dakan-eh would have walked off. But Sunam-tu called him back.

"Wait, Bold Man! My sister walks with you." There was a smile on Sunam-tu's face as he pushed the girl forward.

Lah-ri was bare breasted and wearing only a traveling backpack, sandals, and a short, see-through skirt of knotted cordage. "I come!" she declared proudly.

"I am honored, Sunam-tu, but I cannot take your sister," Dakan-eh said. "I have a woman—the headman's daughter—waiting for me in my village."

"You mate! You take!" demanded Sunam-tu, his smile gone. "Look! You wear my sister's armband around your wrist! You have accepted her!"

Dakan-eh's brows arched toward his hairline. "I took only what she gave willingly, what you offered—a token of appreciation from her, and from you, something to help me pass the night, not a wife!"

"It is the same!" insisted Sunam-tu.

"It is *not* the same," replied Dakan-eh coolly. "Bold Man does not accept as wife a woman who spreads herself as wide and easily as a well-worn sleeping skin!"

A snickering passed among the guardians. Their murmurs and exchange of glances shocked Cha-kwena as, with a start, he realized that Dakan-eh was not the only man to have passed a night with the little sister of Sunam-tu.

Lah-ri looked petulant. "Maybe you make a baby in me, Bold Man."

Dakan-eh shrugged. "Maybe."

One of the guardians snorted rudely. "It wouldn't be the first time."

Lah-ri's face tightened. "If Bold Man does not take me with him, I will kill his baby."

Again Dakan-eh shrugged. "If there is a baby, you may kill it or keep it. Either way it is the only gift that you will ever get from me."

"Then give me back my armband of white beads!" she demanded.

"No," he said coolly. "There is plenty of white chalcedony in the White Hills from which you come. Get some man to make more beads for you. I will keep these."

The guardians guffawed as Bold Man—head high and snorting in amusement—turned and stalked away.

Cha-kwena found himself gawking at her. Was this the same girl whom he had been willing to take as his woman only the night before? Pouting hatefully, Lah-ri looked as mean as a freshwater eel impaled on the end of a fishing trident.

Suddenly she turned, smiled, and ran to Cha-kwena. She threw her arms around him and rubbed her body against his. "You take me as your woman, Shaman Boy!"

"I . . . I . . ." He would have answered, but she was kissing him. It was a wide, openmouthed, all-too-experienced, tongue-probing kiss that made him flame with passion and confusion. But then the laughter and taunts of the guardians rose within his ears. He shoved her away. "No! Get away from me! You had your chance last night. What makes you think that I would want you now!"

A round of applause went up. The laughter that followed was at her expense, not at his. Cha-kwena stood tall. He had not been so pleased with himself for many a long moon.

"Good work, Cha-kwena!" called Dakan-eh, looking back over his shoulder and smiling with approval. "You learn quickly!"

"Yes, and that is a good thing," agreed Shi-wana, unaffected by all the laughter. He was staring down at old Hoyeh-tay. "You will have much to learn in the days and nights that lie ahead, Boy Shaman." He paused and drew in a deep breath. "Since no one else has spoken for the sister of Sunam-tu, I will take the girl back to my village to be my woman. Maybe, before I end my days, she will help me to remember what it was like to be young."

It was late in the afternoon when they put the Blue Mesas behind them and, in silence, headed eastward toward Big Lake. Han-da of the Blue Sky People, Qu-on of the People of the Valley of Many Rabbits, and Naquah-neh of the People of the White Hills walked with them for a while. Then the shamans and their guardians veered off toward their own villages after vowing to return again with the rising of next year's Pinyon Moon.

"May the harvest be great, may the omens for the People be good," Naquah-neh intoned before turning away. "And until we meet again on the sacred mountain, may the spirits of the ancestors deal kindly with my old friend Hoyeh-tay."

"May it be so," responded Dakan-eh formally.

"It *will* be so," emphasized Cha-kwena with an authority that he did not feel.

Naquah-neh grunted, then went his way. Sunam-tu followed for a few steps, then paused and turned back to glare with contempt at Dakan-eh. "When we meet again, you will treat my sister with respect," he growled. "She is now the woman of a great shaman—of a much better man than you could ever hope to be!"

Dakan-eh laughed in pure mockery. "And so much older, too! Certainly Lah-ri will be forever grateful to her brother. A man like Shi-wana must be every *young* girl's dream."

Sunam-tu's knuckles turned white around the shaft of his spear, and Cha-kwena felt certain that the man was going to attack Dakan-eh; but the moment passed, and Sunam-tu hurried off after Naquah-neh.

Amused and triumphant, Dakan-eh shook his head, guffawed as he admired his new wristband, and trotted on. "Come, Cha-kwena," he called back over his shoulder. "I want to put a few more miles under our feet before we rest for the night. If you want a hand with your grandfather's litter, speak up."

"I want nothing from you."

"So you say."

"And I mean every word!"

"So you say."

Cha-kwena ground his teeth and chewed on his anger as he dragged Hoyeh-tay's litter. Owl perched upon the old man's blanketed toes. Dakan-eh loped ahead and then burst into uproarious laughter.

"There is nothing to laugh about!" Cha-kwena shouted.

"Oh, yes, there is," countered Bold Man, turning,

walking backward, and smiling. "What a sweet time I had on that girl last night! And all the time she and her brother thought they had me trapped. Ha! I knew all along that Shi-wana had his eyes on her! Stupid old fool! She'll wear his man bone to the quick and then turn nasty on him when he objects to her opening herself to the young bucks of his band. Smile, boy! That troublesome schemer could have been yours!"

Cha-kwena was not amused. "I will never take a woman."

"No?"

"No!"

"You should thank me, Cha-kwena. You wanted her. You would have taken her. I have saved you a great deal of grief by sending you away instead of inviting you to share my pleasure on her."

Cha-kwena's face flamed because Dakan-eh had spoken the truth. He *had* wanted her. The thought of her as Shi-wana's woman made him sick with jealousy and . . . dread. The emotion jarred him. Suddenly the smells of smoke and fire and burned meat were at the back of his nostrils, and somewhere within his brain, he could hear people screaming as a golden eagle circled against the sun.

"Cha-kwena?"

Puzzled, he shook his head.

Dakan-eh was standing before him. "Are you all right?"

The sounds and scents and images disappeared. Cha-kwena's mind was suddenly very clear.

From his perch upon Hoyeh-tay's toes, Owl said, "Heed the vision that comes in the light of day, Shaman! Do not turn your back upon the girl! Danger walks beyond the Blue Mesas, boy!"

"I am *not* a boy! I am *not* a shaman! If Lah-ri were to die tomorrow, I would not care!"

Dakan-eh, unable to hear Owl's words, was taken aback by the outburst. He stared at the boy. "Let us be on our way, then," he said quietly.

Cha-kwena followed. When Bold Man began to chant the familiar, well-paced songs of the open trail, Cha-kwena sang with him, loudly, gladly, to shut off his thoughts and the continuing secret communications of Owl.

"I am Wise and Watchful Owl. I have taken Hoyeh-tay's spirit into myself. If I leave him, he will die . . . and then *you* will be Shaman."

"No!" A hot, thick lump swelled in his throat. The singing seemed to cool it.

"Shing . . . shing the shongs of the People!" commanded Hoyeh-tay from the litter.

As the miles slipped away Hoyeh-tay drifted in and out of dreams, alternately singing, talking to himself, and dozing so deeply that Cha-kwena paused more than once, fearing that his grandfather had died. At dusk, however, Hoyeh-tay was still alive and babbling.

"Rest, Grandfather. Sleep," Cha-kwena urged, setting the litter down by the Big Lake shoreline. "At dawn we will continue on toward home. By now U-wa will have stuffed your mattress with fresh sage and made your favorite cakes and broth and—"

"U-wa is a very pretty young woman, my son, but her cooking is not so good, eh? You are a good son, Nar-eh. You deserve the best. You should take another woman—a better cook. U-wa would understand."

"I am Cha-kwena, your grandson."

"Grandson? Ah, yes, I see you now, Ish-iwi! Always one for jokes. Grandson, indeed! Where have you been, Ish-iwi? At last we are together again, you and I! But do you hear? Many lions are hunting nearby."

"Grandfather, there are no lions. It is I, Cha-kwena!"

"Our mothers worry about us, Ish-iwi. They say that we are too young to swim unguarded in Big Lake. It is good to see you again, Ish-iwi. But so many lions! Why do they follow you? Uh oh, Nar-eh is eating mushrooms again. We must talk to him."

Tears stung Cha-kwena's eyes. "Grandfather! Ish-iwi is not here! And Nar-eh is dead!"

"Allow him his delusions, boy." Dakan-eh came close to place a consoling hand on Cha-kwena's shoulder. "I have seen this before. You can do nothing for him. He will die soon—perhaps even before we reach our village."

"No! I will take care of him! I will not let him die! Not ever."

Dakan-eh sighed and shook his head. "If you can accomplish that, then truly, Cha-kwena, you will be the greatest shaman of all."

\*      \*      \*

All night long Cha-kwena sat with the old man, listening to his nonsensical talk. Dakan-eh set a few light deadfall snares, and after finding a pair of suitable throwing sticks, Cha-kwena and he managed to brain a few rabbits. They skinned, roasted, and ate their kills, then tossed the snouts and feet to Owl.

After much coaxing, the old man downed a few mouthfuls. Toward dawn, he finally slept deeply, and a relieved Cha-kwena slept with him, but only briefly. He awoke to see Coyote standing at the edge of the little camp. The creature's head was down, and its eyes shimmered with starlight in the darkness as Owl circled high above. Cha-kwena, terrified, sat up.

"Grandfather!" he cried, certain that the old man was dead. "Come back!"

Hoyeh-tay did not respond until, on soundless wings, Owl banked sharply and returned to alight upon the old man's toes. As Coyote trotted away Hoyeh-tay stirred, yawned, and began to babble.

Cha-kwena sobbed with relief. "Thank you," he whispered to Owl.

"Strange . . ."

Dakan-eh had spoken.

Cha-kwena turned to see that Bold Man was standing and looking back across the way they had come. "Do you smell it?"

"Smell what?" asked Cha-kwena.

"The wind carries the scent of smoke to us from the sacred mountain."

"The guardians must have risen early to raise the cooking fires for their shamans."

"But the encampment was being dismantled even as we left it. By now the last of the holy men must be far away."

"Perhaps some of the shamans stayed behind."

Dakan-eh took a deep breath. "It does not smell like smoke from a cooking fire."

Cha-kwena inhaled. West Wind brought him the smell of smoke . . . of singed hide and hair, of burned grass and meat and oil. He tensed.

"I don't like the stink of it," said Dakan-eh. "Perhaps we should go back to see if everything is all right."

For an instant Cha-kwena was about to say yes, because he recalled his dream of a man-eating eagle. He thought of the dimpled young girl, giggling, dancing naked beneath the stars. But then he remembered the way that Lah-ri and Dakan-eh had mocked him.

"We must return to our people," he said hastily. "You are sworn to protect the shaman of our band. My grandfather must be brought home."

"Yes . . ." Dakan-eh conceded. "You are right. The shamans of the Red World walk under the protection of the sacred stones of the People. What could be wrong, eh? We will make an early start. If the spirits are smiling, I may be able to pick up a golden nugget or two in the same place where I found the last ones. Ta-maya will be pleased by such a gift."

Cha-kwena glared at him. "And what of Ban-ya?"

"She will be pleased, too, and not so angry when I choose the daughter of Tlana-quah over her."

"Will you tell the daughter of Tlana-quah about your new wristband and of Lah-ri and of the 'gift' you may have left with her in the grove upon the sacred mountain?"

Now it was Dakan-eh who glared. "That girl was nothing to me. *Nothing!* And if you want to live long enough to become Shaman, Cha-kwena, you will say nothing of Lah-ri to Ta-maya or to any other woman of our village! As for the wristband, it was a gift from a new friend in the White Hills. Who will say otherwise?"

Cha-kwena measured the threat and the man who made it. Neither was to be taken lightly. He turned his eyes toward his grandfather, who clutched his medicine bag in his right hand. If there was magic in the sacred stone within that leather pouch, why had it not protected Hoyeh-tay from the bad spirits that had rendered him blank eyed and drooling?

"Ish-iwi, beware of the lionsh, Ish-iwi!"

"Yes, I will beware," Cha-kwena answered with a broken voice.

He lifted the edge of the old man's sleeping robe and gently wiped his mouth. Smoke burned the youth's eyes, and his heart ached with pity and remorse. But the reply had soothed Hoyeh-tay. The old shaman sighed and relaxed. He smiled awkwardly, lopsidedly, and his grip around his medicine bag loosened. His clawlike hand drifted upward to touch the boy's face.

"Take me home, Cha-kwena. I would shee the shacred juniper and look onch more upon Life Giver before I die."

Joy filled Cha-kwena. Hoyeh-tay had called him by name! "You are *better*!" he cried, squeezing his grandfather's hand. "You are *not* going to die!"

Hoyeh-tay sighed again as Owl winged skyward. "Someday . . ."

"But not today!" the boy insisted, beaming. He rose and called triumphantly to Dakan-eh. "The spirits *are* smiling upon us, Bold Man! Hoyeh-tay's life spirit is fully back inside his body again!"

And so, with Owl flying ahead, they struck off to the east. This time Cha-kwena echoed Dakan-eh's songs with a light voice and carefree heart. Hoyeh-tay managed to join in, and the happy singing of the three travelers became so loud that only Cha-kwena heard the howling of an animal far away upon the Blue Mesas—the deep and hungry cry of a wolf howling in frustration over a kill that had eluded it. The boy paused to listen, but his ears were met with silence. After a few moments he was not certain if he had heard anything at all.

"What is it, my grandson?"

"Nothing," he said, fairly certain that he had spoken the truth.

"Too late! We are too late!" roared Maliwal. His ruined face was stitched and swathed in bandages of buckskin stolen from the village that he and the others had just raided. "They have gone from this camp and taken their sacred stones with them!" He stood seething upon the sacred mountain. The abandoned encampment of holy men seemed to mock him. "Burn the huts. Burn them all."

"But, Maliwal, we have already burned the village on the other side of the mountain." Chudeh looked distraught. His eyes still smarted and teared from the smoke of the decimated village left behind them.

It had all happened so quickly, without compromise: the slaying of the hunters who had come out to help them, the taking of the miserable little village, the killing of its inhabitants—except, of course, for a few choice female captives—and then the burning of the grass-covered huts. Chudeh still felt dazed by it.

Maliwal had been right—it had been an easy victory. The lizard eaters were a guileless, gentle folk. It was not the way of the lizard eaters to stand and fight; indeed, they seemed unable to understand that human beings were capable of killing their own kind. And so they had died gawking and disbelieving, picked off one by one at first, and then squealing like peccaries, scattering like rabbits, all to no avail. The spears of the hunters of the People of the Watching Star had found them easy targets.

Chudeh's brows furrowed. It was not his memories of the recent slaughter that disturbed him. He had killed lizard eaters before, and fired their villages, and sated himself on their stunned women and young girls before slitting their throats. But now, staring around at the neat assembly of small abandoned huts, he tried to put his thoughts into words. "The village was one thing, but this is a holy place, Maliwal. Let us return to the other side of the mountain. We have mammoth to butcher and captives to enjoy. Why should we burn these few little huts and risk offending the spirits of—"

"For my pleasure!" Maliwal interrupted hotly. "That is reason enough, Chudeh! If the spirits of this place had any power, they would have warned the lizard eaters of our intentions. They would have alerted the skinny old holy man to what he and his child bride would find when they blundered into their village. Isn't that true, Blue Face?"

"I am called Shi-wana." The shaman stood tall and proud, even though his long arms were bound tightly behind his back. His eyes took in the face of his captor from beneath battered lids. "The holy men of the Red World will not run before Brothers of the Sky."

Maliwal frowned at Shi-wana's dignity. "Brothers of the Sky?"

The old man's face was drained by sorrow and exhaustion, the blue ceremonial paint cracked and blotched. "Why have you come down from the sky?" he asked. "And how have we failed to honor the sacred bones of First Man and First Woman that have been entrusted to us?"

"What is he talking about?" asked Chudeh. He was being eyed by the dimpled young girl who cowered at the side of the holy man. Had the old shaman been lying when he swore that he had yet to couple with her? She was young and good to look upon, Chudeh knew, but something about her stance and expression told him she was no virgin. He would have had to have been a corpse to miss the invitation in her eyes.

He stood a little straighter and wished that she would look away. She made him hard with man need. Maliwal would be furious if he guessed as much, for he had forbidden any man to pierce her. She was for Ysuna—a new bride for Thunder in the Sky. Chudeh gritted his teeth as he appraised her. The god would be pleased by this one, but what a pity that he could not take his pleasure on her first.

"He talks too much," said Maliwal of the old shaman. "And he speaks of the wrong things." He extended his spear to press the tip of the lanceolate head against the shaman's belly. "I will ask you once more, Blue Face. Where have the others gone?"

Shi-wana's face tightened. He fixed his gaze upon the medicine bag that hung from a thong around Maliwal's neck. "Ask the sacred stone that you have stolen from me and from the People of the Blue Mesas."

Maliwal's eyes narrowed dangerously. "You will tell me what I want to know."

The old man's head went high. He did not flinch when the tip of the projectile point pierced his skin and burrowed deep into muscle. Blood welled and trickled down over his pale flesh.

The girl cried out, "The other wise men have gone away to their many villages across the Red World. They will return next year. There will be a Great Gathering of the People next year!"

"Well . . ." Maliwal smiled. "What a helpful little thing you are, and so caring of the life of your man."

She nearly swooned to see kindness in his eyes. "Do not kill me—er, us."

Chudeh nodded to himself. She was not helpful, nor concerned in the least for the old man. She was fighting for her own life.

Maliwal's left hand curled around the sacred stone

and other magic talismans that lay within the stolen medicine bag. "You say that the shamans will return here next year? *All* of them?"

"Say nothing, girl!" Shi-wana shouted. "You have already said too much! You will—"

His words were cut off as Maliwal pulled his spear from the old man's belly and used the weapon as a stave, clubbing Shi-wana hard across the side of the head. He fell, bleeding from ears and nose and mouth.

One might have expected the girl to drop to her knees to offer wifely commiserations to the shaman, but somehow Chudeh knew that she would not do this. He was not surprised when she frowned down at the shaman.

"He had no right to name me Wife." She pouted self-righteously. Then she looked at Maliwal and complained, "A wise man can do that, you know—just name a woman, any woman, and she must go to him. And so he took me away from my brother and my band. Even though he tried, he could not put his man bone in me. He was so old, you see, and I think that his man bone was even older."

Maliwal stared fixedly at the girl. "Has *any* man bone found its place within you, girl?"

Chudeh saw a muscle tighten at either side of her jawline. She was hesitating, deciding how best to answer the question. Any clearheaded man would have realized the truth at once. But, Chudeh knew, Maliwal was tired and in constant pain.

She said no and demurely looked up at Maliwal through the thick curtaining of her lashes. "Will you be the one to blood me? You are clearly the boldest of *all* men, and although I have no experience in these things, my mother has taught me the ways to please a man. I would never give you cause to regret that you have let me live to ease the needs of your man bone."

Chudeh clucked his tongue and could not help asking: "And what about your shaman? You speak of him as if he was already dead. He may be injured, but he is alive, and you are still his woman. Do you not wish to ease his wounds?"

She blinked, flustered, then sank to her knees and impatiently touched Shi-wana's face and belly. "He is dying!"

she cried in a high, frenzied tone that might have been caused by confusion . . . or relief. "Oh, poor old man. What shall I do for him?"

"Let him die," replied Maliwal, taking his hand from the medicine bag and extending it to the girl. "Come consenting to me and to my people."

This time the girl did not hesitate. She leaped to her feet and grasped at his hand as she might have clutched at a floating log had she been caught in a flood. "I do!" she said, and when he drew her close, she snuggled and giggled.

# PART IV

# YELLOW WOLF

# 1

Mah-ree dropped to her knees and then stretched out flat on her bare belly. She lay still, hidden among the meadow's grasses and horsetail ferns. As she peeked through reedy, summer-ripe stalks her heart was pounding, and she held her breath. There, straight ahead, moving through the sun-speckled shadows of the cedar grove, was a blur of white as tall as a mountain.

"Great Ghost Spirit . . ." she reverently whispered.

It was a rare occurrence when anyone other than Shaman saw Life Giver, so Mah-ree felt doubly awed. Her people's totem was huge, much larger than she had ever imagined! She fought the impulse to cry out in joy.

Her heartbeat quickened with sudden fear. He was so close. She was startled by how far she had walked in her game to catch a damselfly. A prickle of dread ran up her spine. She could not see the other women and girls. Had any of them noticed her absence? she wondered.

The girl shivered. What would happen if Great Ghost Spirit saw her? Would he be offended by the sight of such a puny girl? Surely she was unworthy of looking upon his greatness. Mah-ree visualized him charging out of the grove to crush her insignificant bones into the earth.

Mah-ree calmed herself with the realization that under any circumstances, a sighting of the great mammoth was considered to be the best of omens! Looking back over her shoulder, she longed to call to the others who had come out from the village with her to pick currants in the thickets at the base of the meadow. Great Ghost Spirit's presence would cause the entire band to rejoice. Ta-maya would cease brooding over Dakan-eh's absence; Tlana-quah would stop worrying over whatever it was that had been troubling him for the last few days and nights; and her own heart would sing, because surely the sighting of Life Giver was meant to assure her that Cha-kwena would soon return from the Land of the Blue Mesas! She trembled to think of it.

As Mah-ree lay motionless, watching Great Ghost Spirit, one of the blue damselflies whose flight had drawn her to this part of the meadow hovered before her face on netted, see-through wings. The girl blew outward, trying to send the insect away on the stream of her breath. It would not go; instead, it alighted on the tip of her nose. Mah-ree's eyes crossed as she puffed upward at it, but to no avail. It stayed a moment longer, then was gone at last on some whim of its own.

Mah-ree stared ahead through the horsetails and wetland grasses to the cedar grove that lay beyond. Life Giver, Grandfather of All, was still there, swaying, looking massive and magnificent. His huge teeth ground together like boulders as he fed amid the bracken fern beneath the sunstruck red pillars of the trees. He ate selectively, slowly, huffing low, swinging his head. Little yellow-beaked brown birds perched atop his head and along the pronounced ridge of his sloping back. Mah-ree laughed with pleasure.

Transfixed, Mah-ree smiled. How wonderful he was! She gasped in amazement when, with a single yank of his trunk, he uprooted a good-sized young cedar and began to suck upon it. Suddenly she felt afraid again, for she could feel his eyes upon her. Unable to look away, she met his gaze. What she saw in his eyes were wariness, wisdom, and something else—something that struck the girl to her core with deep, startling sadness. He was *old*!

Life Giver was as tall and broad as a mountain, but his wrinkled skin was scarred, grayed with age, and it sagged over his massive bones. Deep, lateral wound marks across his shoulders made her feel certain that he had been attacked years before by a great leaping cat, lion, jaguar, or bear. She frowned, observing concavities within his thighs and shoulders where once-powerful muscles had atrophied. His eyes were sunken and filmed, and the tips of his inwardly curling tusks were broken and discolored.

It saddened her when he huffed in pain, dropped the tree, and plodded away into the shadows of the grove, raising his pale trunk to disperse the birds and the cloud of blue damselflies that now hovered over him.

Mah-ree caught her breath. He was Totem to her people. He was Great Ghost Spirit. But in this moment she knew that he was no ghost. He was mortal and as old as the land. Someday, perhaps soon, he would die. Had not Shaman told the band that if their totem died, the People would die with him?

She rose, devastated and confused. What sort of an omen was this? Surely it was too much for one little girl. "Wait!" she called out to the great mammoth.

Inspired by her intensely nurturing nature and her dreams of being a shaman of the healing ways, the girl was unconcerned for her own safety. If Life Giver was in pain, she wanted to help him. "Do not go, Grandfather of All. Wait! I will gather willow leaves and shoots for you. They will ease the hurt of your teeth! You will be able to eat again, to grow strong and invincible again. Wait!"

But Grandfather of All plodded on, and the little brown birds winged after him.

"Mah-ree? Where are you, Mah-ree?"

Ha-xa's voice—imperative, radiant with joy and excitement—came from the lower reaches of the meadow.

Ta-maya's voice echoed their mother's. "Mah-ree, come, hurry! Dakan-eh and Cha-kwena have come home with our shaman at last!"

No one had time to listen to Mah-ree's excited babblings about having seen Great Ghost Spirit. Hurrying back to the village with the other women and girls, she was swept away by a tide of excitement.

"But he was in the upland grove. I saw him!"

"Later, girl. Tell us all about it later!" said Ha-xa. "Whatever you saw, we will take it as a good omen, a sure sign that the spirits of the ancestors are smiling upon the People."

"But Mother, he was so old, and it looked as though his teeth hurt him and—"

"Hush, child!" Ha-xa silenced her sternly as they reached their family's hut. "You are as bad as Cha-kwena, always imagining that some poor creature is in need of your ministrations! Of course Life Giver is old! He was born before First Man and First Woman. But his teeth cannot hurt him. He is immortal. When his last set of teeth has been cast off, he will grow new teeth . . . forever! So stop worrying about him. Comb your hair! Come. We must go out to greet those who return to us from the Blue Mesas!"

With a loud sigh of resignation, Mah-ree plopped herself down onto her bed furs. Ha-xa was right, of course. Soon Grandfather of All would be himself again. She smiled to think of it. Then, realizing that she would soon be welcoming Cha-kwena home from the far country, she picked up her comb of carved elk horn and was about to run it through the short strands when her sister came close, pulled her to her feet, and gave her a rapturous hug.

"They are back! Oh, Mah-ree, they are back, back, *back*!" Ta-maya planted a kiss on Mah-ree's cheek, then twirled her around in a dance of delight. She paused. "Oh, Mah-ree, do I look all right? Do you think he still wants me? Oh, Mah-ree, this time I will not say no when my Bold Man asks for me!"

The People went out in a joyous mood to greet the returning travelers. Kosar-eh, the clown, danced before them. His skin shone in starkly striped black and white body paint. Tlana-quah, tall and solemn and dignified in his feathered loin cover and jaguar-skin cloak, strode ahead of him. Directly behind the headman walked his family, and after them, at a respectful distance dictated by tribal decorum, followed the entire band. They shook rattles of bone and snake tails. Stepping high and clapping their hands, men, women, and children called out the names of those who had long been away, while U-wa, mother of Cha-kwena, snuffled in gratitude as she thanked the spirits of the ancestors for bringing her only child safely home to her at last.

Old Hoyeh-tay sat upright on his litter. He was not yet strong enough to walk, but he had recovered enough to raise one scrawny arm in greeting to his people. Owl sat perched upon his head. The old shaman declared that

Cha-kwena was returning to his People with newly discovered magic powers.

"Truly, thish shon of Nar-eh and grandshon of Hoyeh-tay will be Shaman!"

The youth cringed because his grandfather had yet to regain full use of his tongue. Beside him, Dakan-eh was strutting with his usual arrogance. As the crowd surged forward Dakan-eh seemed to grow taller and more confident until, at last, he stood before his intended bride and her family as though he, and not Tlana-quah, were headman.

Tlana-quah eyed him with characteristic stoicism, then looked away to nod graciously to Hoyeh-tay and the youth. "The People welcome those who return. Tlana-quah speaks words of greeting to Hoyeh-tay and to Cha-kwena and . . ." He paused. As though forced to deal with an unpleasant afterthought, he looked again at Bold Man. After a sigh that should have alerted Dakan-eh to the headman's feelings toward him, Tlana-quah included the warrior in the greeting.

Too taken with himself to notice the mood of the other man, Dakan-eh jabbed his chin toward the sky. After the most perfunctory of obligatory greetings, he looked brazenly down at Ta-maya and boasted about how he had risked his life and sacrificed gold nuggets, which were to have been gifts for his bride.

"Alone Bold Man stood against the raging waters! Alone Bold Man saved our shaman! Alone Bold Man kept Cha-kwena from being washed away! Mighty deeds has this man done! The shamans of the Red World were amazed by my bravery. In gratitude for my performance a gift was given . . . this fine wristband of chalcedony beads from the White Hills. Bold Man now offers it and the honor of his name and deeds to Ta-maya!"

A sigh went out of the crowd.

Cha-kwena looked up at Dakan-eh and decided that he was the most obnoxious human being he had ever known. Ta-maya obviously did not agree. The young woman allowed him to secure the adornment to her wrist, blushed, and lowered her eyes modestly. Standing just forward of the rest of the crowd, a sulking Ban-ya hung her head, certain that she had lost the man of her dreams to the headman's daughter.

But Tlana-quah raised his right hand, palm out, and said gruffly: "The People must hear the news of the far country and of the many bands of the Red World. The People must honor *all* those who return to us from the Blue Mesas. Now is not the time for you to talk of marriage to my daughter. Hold your words, Bold Man. I will not hear them now."

# 2

At the urging of the headman, Hoyeh-tay, Dakan-eh, and Cha-kwena shared in the recounting of the journey, each adding his own experiences to the delight of the villagers, who had gathered in a circle within the center of the village. As the sun grew hot the People donned conical hats and protective capes of woven grass and bark. U-wa brought hats and capes to shield Cha-kwena and Hoyeh-tay. Pah-la, mother of Dakan-eh, did the same for her son. The old widows, meanwhile, circulated among the gathering and offered hollow reeds filled with cool water, and wide, shallow baskets laden with hot roasted seeds and grubs.

Seated upon his extra-thick mat of plaited reeds, Tlana-quah was doing his best to ignore the moon-eyed way in which Ta-maya was staring at Dakan-eh from the women's side of the circle. The headman gritted his teeth because young Ban-ya was pouting prettily and trying to catch Bold Man's eye. Sooner or later, Tlana-quah knew, trouble was going to erupt over this.

*Trouble* . . . The word stuck at the back of his throat. *So the sacred groves will not yield a harvest again this year! The omens, then, are not right for marriage.*

At last the shaman announced that a great assembly of the tribe would take place in the sacred groves next year, regardless of the potential for a decent harvest. The People cheered this news, but Tlana-quah could not join in their declaration of joy.

Then, when a coyote yapped twice from east of the village, Tlana-quah believed that his troubled mood was affirmed.

"Dead lakes and floods and barren groves and a coyote calling in the light of day? . . . What kind of omens are these?" he asked Hoyeh-tay.

But the old man was exhausted. He thought and thought about the question, until it seemed that he had gone to sleep with his eyes open.

"Perhaps Coyote calls to Cha-kwena," suggested Dakan-eh. "It would not be the first time."

The headman turned his gaze to the youth and sensed in Cha-kwena's eyes animosity directed at Bold Man.

"Well?" prodded the headman. "Can you speak for your grandfather, Cha-kwena?"

"I can speak!" young Mah-ree answered. Rising to her feet beside her mother, she proclaimed, "They must be good omens, my father, for this day I have seen Great Ghost Spirit in the cedar grove! He was as tall as the sky and as old as the hills, and even though his teeth hurt him when he chewed, he—"

"Enough!" Tlana-quah raised his hands in a fury of sudden emotion. His expression sent his younger daughter shrinking back. "You have not seen our totem. Great Spirit cannot know pain."

Mah-ree's lower lip quivered, and she whispered: "I *did* see him. And he *was* in pain, my father. I could see it in his eyes. They were sad and tired and all misted over. I do not think that our totem can see very—"

"Do not say another word! Our totem does not appear to children! Great Ghost Spirit knows no pain. He cannot age or die. And if he does . . ." He paused, not daring to complete his thought: *If he does, the People will die with him.*

Mah-ree hung her head. But all other eyes went to the shaman. Hoyeh-tay's face had an oddly fixed look. A finger of spittle oozed from a corner of his mouth. Cha-kwena, seated beside him, hastily wiped the old man's chin.

"How many questions must an old man answer in one day?" the youth snapped defensively. "Can't you see that Shaman is tired?"

Tlana-quah nodded. "Cha-kwena is right. Escort your

grandfather to his cave and stay with him until he is rested. The day is still young. Now the People will hunt, and tonight we will celebrate the travelers' safe return. Go now, everyone. Leave me. I must think about what I have just heard."

Only Kosar-eh remained behind, hunkering on his heels, watching the headman from a respectful distance. The clown did not speak until Tlana-quah looked up at him out of troubled eyes.

"How may I cheer my headman?" the clown asked.

Tlana-quah repeated old Hoyeh-tay's words. " 'When we reached Big Lake, there was no lake, only a broad, flat plain of salt.' How can this be?"

Kosar-eh thought a moment, then shrugged. "The waters of our own lake have been shrinking. Perhaps, after the past six years of harsh summer sun and winters of little rain and less snow, Big Lake simply died of thirst?"

Tlana-quah sat unmoving, one hand idly stroking the worn pelage of his cape, his face set. "If our lake were to die, the birds and animals that are our food would cease to come to raise their young in the tule reeds along the shore. Since our ancestors first came into the Red World from the north, our lake has meant life to us."

The broad striping of Kosar-eh's face paint masked his reaction. "When I was with the People of the Blue Mesas, their shaman, Shi-wana, told of a time when there was only one lake—Big Lake. The Red World was entirely underwater except for the summits of the tallest buttes and mesas. Over many generations the waters gave themselves freely to the People who followed the sun. Then a day came when the one huge lake receded into many little lakes, and the first people divided into many little bands. Each lived by its own lake. No longer nomads, they were gatherers and foragers, eaters of rabbit and antelope, of lizard and fish and waterfowl." He paused, and his expression softened, the stripes sagging slightly. "It is a good life in a good world, Tlana-quah."

"Yes," the headman agreed, but his tone was bleak. "These past years, the world seems to be changing. We have never known a drought of such duration."

"Have the rains not always returned?" reminded the

clown. "As long as we respect the ancestors, guard our totem, and honor the sacred bones, why should the rains not return?"

"But how am I to be cheered by the omens that Hoyeh-tay has brought home?"

"The Great Gathering of the many bands next year will be a good thing for the People. And in a single night Hoyeh-tay's will and power have made the waters return to Big Lake. With such a shaman, need you fear for the future?"

Tlana-quah's mouth turned down. "You answer my questions with questions, Kosar-eh."

The clown hesitated. "It is my purpose in life to lighten the burdens of my headman, not to add to them. Should I not believe Hoyeh-tay's words?"

"He is weak, sick. His mind wanders, and he drools like an infant. Could such a man command the storm spirits to return the waters to Big Lake?"

"The boy will inherit the shaman's power."

"The boy is only a boy."

Kosar-eh's sad, gentle smile misaligned the black and white stripes so that his features seemed to move in two directions at once. "When the spirits of the ancestors call to Hoyeh-tay, Cha-kwena will become the man he was born to be."

Tlana-quah snapped to his feet, openly angry. "And in the meantime, what am I to make of the omens when I have no one to advise me except a drooling old man, an adolescent, and a cripple?"

Kosar-eh remained kneeling, but he stiffened. "You are a brave hunter, Man Who Kills Jaguar Alone. You are the leader of the people of this village, and many look to you for strength and courage. I am only a clown. I do not know the answers to your questions; I can hope only to amuse you and to make you smile."

Tlana-quah was not amused. He shook his head and lowered his voice. "Clown you may be *and* a cripple, but you are no fool. How can I smile when coyotes howl in broad daylight? How can I be amused by talk of floods and lightning storms, of sacred groves that remain barren, of shamans who fail to visit the holy mountain, and of strangers who have come from the north to marry into the most distant bands of the People. I ask you, Kosar-eh, how can this be? The People are *one*. They dwell in the Red World and only in the Red World. Beyond, there is nothing. Everyone knows that there are no people on the other side of the mountains."

Kosar-eh did not move. Dakan-eh and several other hunters had come into his line of sight and paused before a small group of women who were sorting out their hunting nets. Bold Man, grasping his rabbit-braining club, was ready for the hunt. With eyes afire, he looked down at Ta-maya, and she gazed up with open adoration at him. The clown could see that Dakan-eh was dedicating this day's efforts to her. Sick with envy, Kosar-eh looked back to the headman.

Tlana-quah had taken the posture of one who, having failed to make up his mind, had at least come to some sort of reckoning with his thoughts. "I will hunt now! Get up, Kosar-eh! Next year we will journey to the Blue Mesas for a Great Gathering of the tribe. That is something to look forward to and be thankful for. As headman, it *is* up to me to think about the omens, and so I have! I will concentrate upon the good ones and leave the bad to drift away upon the wind. Mammoth graze upon the offerings of the People, and our shaman has returned safely. True, his words confound me, but he *has* returned. This is a thing worth celebrating . . . isn't it?"

# 3

Old Hoyeh-tay's cave was a deep, south-facing hollow midway up the sandstone cliff that soared above a dry creek bed on the far side of the village. It had always been a magic place, from which a holy man might look across the village to the broad expanse of the surrounding Red World. A timeworn series of steps had been carved into the bluff, allowing access to the chamber.

Now, with old Hoyeh-tay snoring on his mattress at
the back of his refuge, Cha-kwena stood on the broad lip
of the cave and fairly itched with frustration as he saw his
people setting out for the rabbit hunt.

"You cannot join them. Your place is here," chortled
Owl, yawning on his perch, a horizontal pine root that
protruded from the stone wall just above the shaman's
bed.

Cha-kwena turned. "I do not need any comments
from you!"

U-wa, sitting nearby, looked up. Her summer-tanned
skin was smooth and red. Her square, handsome face
shone with sweat in the sunlight, for she had followed
Cha-kwena and Hoyeh-tay up the carved steps with her
back laden with bundles and baskets, her arms weighted
with sheaves of freshly picked sweet grass and sage. "I
have not said a word to you, Cha-kwena. And since when
do you take such a tone with your mother?"

"I was not talking to you."

"To whom, then?"

"To . . ." Cha-kwena frowned. "It doesn't matter,"
he said, not wishing to burden her with the revelation that
he had been talking to a bird.

U-wa indicated Hoyeh-tay's sleeping area with a
sideward nod. "How long has the old one been like that?"

"Since our last night upon the sacred mountain."

"You will be Shaman sooner than we thought."

"No. He grows stronger every day. He will not die."

"All men die, my son. Only our totem lives forever."
She rose to lay a hand gently upon his forearm. "Do not
leave him, Cha-kwena. He might walk off the lip of the
cave and never know that he has fallen until he hits the
ground."

"He is old and sick, but he would never do that!"

U-wa was a tall woman, and when she kissed her son's
brow, she had to lean down. "Not as long as you watch
him, Cha-kwena. He must die a good death so the omens
will be good for the one who walks the shaman's way after
him."

She made him feel young and inadequate, trapped by
responsibilities. Down in the sweet yellow heat of the
afternoon, the boys had taken up their clubs and killing

sticks and joined Dakan-eh, Tlana-quah, and the other men of the band. Cha-kwena could see them now, trotting toward the sage flats where the women and girls were busy setting up the snare nets. Soon the hunt would begin.

"Could you watch him for me?" he asked hopefully, yearning to take up his weapons.

"I could, but Tlana-quah has commanded you to stay with our shaman until he is rested. I would not encourage my son to disobey the headman, nor am I willing to offend Tlana-quah, who is close to my heart."

Her admission did not surprise him; he had suspected the truth all along. "Have you ceased to mourn for my father already?"

"It is lonely in the hut I once shared with him. I am too young to spend the remainder of my days in the widows' lodge. Why should I not turn my eyes to the headman? If he looks back, I will gladly go to his fire."

"But you would be second woman to Ha-xa!"

"Two women at a man's fire circle ease the work load for all."

"He already has Ha-xa and Mah-ree and Ta-maya. What good would you do him?"

"The daughters of Tlana-quah will soon choose men of their own, and Ha-xa will welcome me . . . as I have welcomed Tlana-quah when he has sought me in the loneliness of my hut. If the signs are right, I will be bringing a new child—perhaps a son!—as a gift to our headman." U-wa's smile softened. "You are inexperienced in the ways of a man. Soon may you know the joy of true affection for a woman—as lasting an affection as I now feel for Tlana-quah and as your friend Dakan-eh has for his beloved."

The words came before he could call them back. "Ha! Is that why he accepted Ban-ya's gift? Is that why he was after yet another girl in the sacred grove? I saw him take her down! With no thought of Ta-maya he took her down, and afterward he kept the wristband that she gave to him and shamed her before the entire assembly of the shamans. He shamed her and laughed at us both!"

"Both?" Her smile was gone, and her eyes took measure of him. After a moment she rested a loving hand upon his forearm. "I see," she said softly.

Cha-kwena blushed because he knew that somehow she did understand. He brushed her hand away and turned his back to her. From far away across the sage flats, he heard a series of high whistles—the women alerting their men that the nets were in place. The hunt would begin in earnest now. The men would surround their prey and drive frightened rabbits and hares toward the nets.

Cha-kwena sighed. If he could not hunt, at least he could observe. When he turned, he found that U-wa was gone. He was glad.

"I will *never* take a woman of my own," he vowed.

At the back of the cave, Owl chortled again. Hoyeh-tay moaned, then cried Ish-iwi's name.

Cha-kwena stared into shadows. "Ish-iwi is not here, Grandfather."

The old man propped himself onto an elbow. "We are in the village? We are home again?"

"Yes, Grandfather."

"Do you hear the lionsh, Cha-kwena? They are coming for ush."

The youth sighed. There would be no watching the hunt as long as the old man was awake. "Go back to sleep, Grandfather," he urged, then strode out of the sunlight to kneel beside Hoyeh-tay. "Truly there are no lions. You are safe. Rest now, for tonight there will be feasting and much good talk."

"Yesh, I will need my shtrength. There ish much that I musht teach you before the lionsh come."

Cha-kwena rolled his eyes. "I will protect you against the lions of your dreams, my grandfather."

The old man squinted up at the boy. "But who will protect you?"

"I am not afraid of dream lions."

"You should be," said Hoyeh-tay as, with a weary exhalation, he lay back, curled his good hand around his medicine bag, closed his eyes, and slept.

# 4

Ysuna was alone within the shadowed interior of her lodge, which was laced tight against intruders. After sending Nai, her attendant, away, she spread a striped, black-maned lion pelt on the floor and knelt and swayed on it. Save for a collar of bones and hair, she was naked.

She placed a broad, square swath of oiled leather in the center of the lion skin, and onto this she set a wide, flat stone. On this surface she raised a small fire of yellowed grass. Slowly, methodically, she fed leaves, seeds, tiny bones, and dried human fingers to the fire.

Finally Ysuna positioned herself, with her long, bare limbs spread wide above the smoke. It rose, caressing her inner thighs and genitals. It curled upward across her abdomen and rib cage and breasts. After spiraling along her upraised arms, it reached her face, and she breathed it in. "Smoke," she intoned, "heed the command of Ysuna. Enter me now as you return to the sky and to the sun. Fill me and bring back the blood of my youth!"

She sighed, hunched her shoulders, and bowed her head. A mass of black hair fell forward to surround her, barely escaping the flames. Ysuna moved within its shining dark caul and examined herself. "No blood," she murmured. "Again no blood. Never a baby in Ysuna's belly, and now, for how many a moon no blood?"

Daughter of the Sun straightened, parted her hair, and spread it back over her shoulders as she sat immobile, staring ahead, whispering ferociously to the smoke and the shadows. "There must be blood! Blood is life, blood is youth. Only the dead are bloodless, and only old, dry women do not bleed when the moon rises to mark their time of blood. It cannot be . . . it must not be. . . ."

She sat straighter. Her hands rose. One curled around

an acorn-sized white stone that was attached to her collar; the other pressed flat against her lower abdomen. "I will not *let* this be."

The priestess reached into her leather pouch and removed a lanceolate-shaped wedge of bone approximately the length of her palm.

"Yes . . ." the woman said, sighing. She stared at the blade, ran her thumb along its pale, sharp edges, and hissed in appreciation of its sharpness as she spoke to it. "No one may ever learn how you serve me now. I bring life to the People. I am not old. I am not dry. Once each moon, while Nai joins the other women in the lodge of blood, I have kept my own blood watch and put out the skins to be burned. The People consume the ashes and grow strong in the blood of my life! So shall it be forever!"

Ysuna rose and walked into the shadows at the far side of the lodge. When she returned to kneel upon the lion skin once again, she was binding the sides of the long, sharp dagger with thin, soft hide until only the dark tip of the blade protruded, beaklike, from the wrapping.

"Yes . . ." said the woman to the bloodstained sacrificial dagger of fossilized whalebone. "You will draw the blood I seek. Blood is sweet to you, as it is to me and to my people."

She positioned the dagger, pointed end up between her thighs, then lowered herself slowly, carefully, until, mated to the blade, she gasped once and stiffened against the pain. Finally Ysuna withdrew the dagger and, trembling, hunkered down on her heels. The weapon's hide wrapping was dark, soaked with blood. She set it on the stone in the center of the lion skin and, with the blade in her lap, smiled as the remnants of her carefully made fire hissed and went out, smothered by an ooze of blood.

"I *am* young, forever young, as long as I bring forth a woman's blood," whispered Ysuna, fingering her collar of sacred stones, bones, and tufts of human hair. The talismans soothed her.

Her smile deepened. Too long, she decided, had her people lingered in this encampment. It was time to break down the lodges, lay out the tent poles, spread the hides and expose them to the sun, beat them with pounders of bone, and scourge them with rubbings of hot ashes. Thus the People would kill whatever vermin were breeding within the crevices of the sheltering skins. Then it would be time to move on, deeper into the Red World, in search of a winter camp. They would find mammoth and brides for Thunder in the Sky and seek out the remaining bones of First Man and First Woman.

A cramp pulled at her lower belly. Blood and hot fluid gushed out of her and onto the leather square upon which she squatted. Something else followed—a warm, soft hemorrhagic mass. She felt it slide out of her and plop sloppily onto the hide. Curious, she leaned back and poked at it. Was it life at last? A child? Cast-off and ruined, but life?

She squinted down into the shadows between her thighs. There was no clot; there was no child. She had imagined them both. There was nothing on the leather but a dark stain, and the scent that rose from it was not the scent of womb blood; it was merely blood drawn by the questing dagger. She could just as easily have drawn it from her wrist. Her womb was barren, as always.

She closed her eyes. The cramp was passing. It was not a menstrual cramp—it was the reaction of her innards to the invasion of the knife. She clenched her teeth against disappointment and wanting. She no longer desired a child. She had her people. She had Maliwal and Masau. They had not gushed from her loins, but they were hers nonetheless. She had raised them to be the lions they were.

Ysuna raised her head high and tested the sharpness of the blade with her thumb. A thin, shallow line of blood and pain opened. She smiled, her thoughts clear, bright, and inspiring. The forces of Creation had not blighted her with sterility; they had *honored* her with it! She could not bear life because she *was* life!

The cramp returned. She curled forward against it as a nauseating wave of weakness swept through her, bringing a deep, enervating cold. She shuddered. Where was Maliwal? What kept him so long away from his people? Where were the sacrifice, the promised meat of mammoth, and another sacred stone to add to her collar? When she had these things, her strength would return and she would bleed again as a young woman bleeds, naturally and in rhythm with the moon. Then the sacred dagger would not be needed for any purpose other than that for which it was intended.

She moaned and gripped her belly. Startled by a sudden gust of air, she turned. Her eyes narrowed. She had laced the hide door flap with her own hands, but now the thongs were loose. The entry was open just enough to allow cooler air to enter.

The wind stirred the flap and folded it back to reveal a startled Nai. Knowing that she had been seen, the servant dropped instantly into a crouch, her chin touching knees, her forehead touching the ground.

Ysuna's suspicions were fully focused now. It was Nai's responsibility to remain close to the lodge of the high priestess at all times; but the girl's guilty furtiveness revealed that she had been doing more than staying close—she had been peering in.

"Assuming the position of a rove beetle will not make you invisible, Nai," Ysuna informed her coldly. "Get up. Come to me." Flustered, the young woman obeyed. She entered the lodge and paused, standing close to the door flap, ready to flee. She explained herself in an overly earnest rush of words. "I heard you moan. I thought that you had need of me, and so I came. A moment ago, only that, no more. Perhaps you would have me take the soiled strip of hide away for burning now?"

"But you have just come in. What makes you so eager to be away?"

"But I—I am not."

Ysuna glared at her. Nai was so young, so undeniably, unforgivably young. Envy squeezed the priestess's heart, then darkened, thickened, and congealed into loathing. "What have you seen, Nai, crouching beyond the shadows of my lodge? Why were you silent and secretive?"

"I have seen *nothing*, Ysuna!"

The young woman's words had been short little shrieks of ill-contained panic, which told Ysuna all she needed to know. The girl had seen *everything*. "Come closer, Nai. Secure the door flap behind you."

Nai, shaking, stood her ground. "Truly I have seen nothing, Ysuna!"

The priestess's face was impassive. "If it is your desire

to take away the strip of hide that has absorbed my moon blood, then come, I say. Do so now!"

Slowly, hesitantly, Nai tied the door skin's thongs, then moved forward and paused at the edge of the lion skin. The bloodied strip of hide lay in a bed of still-steaming ashes. It stank. Nai grimaced with revulsion.

"Well?" Ysuna demanded. "What are you waiting for?"

Nai looked up. The sacred dagger was still in the priestess's hand—a hand that was darkened with blood to the wrist, as though she wore a glove on it.

"The dagger interests you? Surely you have seen it before."

"Y-yes. At the sacrifices. Many times," she said faintly.

Ysuna smiled. She saw fear in the girl and reacted to it as she always did, with contempt and pleasure. "You have just seen me use it. On myself."

"No!" Again the girl's protest came out as a shriek.

Ysuna's smile broadened. "Will you keep my secret, Nai?"

Sensing entrapment, the young woman gestured outward pathetically. "I know of no secrets, Ysuna. I am only your slave."

Ysuna's smile disappeared. The girl's chest was heaving like a cornered animal's. Pleased, the priestess raised her head and appraised her servant thoughtfully. Although Nai had been loyal, Ysuna was aware of the girl's infatuation with Maliwal. He would be back soon, from the far country, with mammoth meat and sacrifices and an eye for youth.

A cramp stabbed through her belly. Weakness followed, then fear. Had she allowed the sacred dagger to seek too deeply within her loins?

"Ysuna! Are you all right? You look weak. Here, let me help you."

*Weak.* The word enraged her. Weakness came with age, and she would *always* be young! Had she not just bled as a young woman bleeds? As Nai bled? *Yes!*

While fighting against the agony of yet another cramp, she felt anger sear her spirit as the girl hurried to assist her. Ysuna's features twisted with rage as soft young arms went around her and sought to hold her up. Ysuna suddenly turned the girl, gripped Nai across the shoulders with her left arm, and pulled her close.

"I need no help from the dead," she grated, and, ignoring the frantic clutchings and thrashings of her captive, slashed the girl's throat from ear to ear.

The plains appeared red in the late-afternoon light. Masau, Mystic Warrior, stood motionless in tall grass. With Nai's body at his feet, he faced westward, into the wind, and wondered what the girl had done to offend the priestess. He was unmoved by her death. Taken captive as a child, Nai had not been the first young female honored to attend Ysuna; nor was she the first to die at her hand, nor likely to be the last. Her life was meaningless, her death less important than that.

At Ysuna's command, Masau had removed the girl's body from the sacred lodge of the high priestess. It was not an unfamiliar task to him; he had dragged her from the encampment and dumped her upon this open stretch of grassland, to be meat for whatever carrion eaters would come.

Mystic Warrior was not alone with the corpse. Families had followed him in solemn procession. Parents kept the children near as, in hushed voices, grandparents warned them always to show respect to Ysuna. Otherwise they would share Nai's fate.

A little girl began to cry. Her grandmother silenced her with yet another warning. "Yes! You should be afraid! For if you are not, you may forget your place and speak against the One Who Brings Life to the People! Ysuna is the strength of this tribe! Without her we are nothing. Without her we starve, as we starved long ago, before she was given to us as a gift from the sun."

Masau did not react to the words. Again and again Ysuna had spoken the warning; since the very first day she had taken Maliwal and him into her arms, she had told them that their lives would be forever strengthened and made meaningful by the esteem in which she was held.

His eyes, irritated by the continued intrusive glare of the sun, were smarting and tearing. Yet he could not look away. Maliwal was out there somewhere. Why had Ysuna forbidden him to go in search of his brother? Why was Maliwal so long in returning home? Masau was increasingly certain that something had gone wrong on his brother's trek to the south.

"She knows all."

"She is to be obeyed in all things."

"Or you will end up like Nai and Neewalatli and all the others who have dared to offend Daughter of the Sun."

The reverent litany droned on. Masau listened and, still staring at the sun, remembered the way that the young hunter Neewalatli had died with Ysuna's spear through his neck—a penalty for challenging her judgment, even though the boy's misgivings had been well justified.

Masau closed his eyes against the memory. Once again, as on the night after the lion hunt during which Neewalatli had died, dark spirits stirred in Masau's soul. He *did* have doubts about Ysuna. Today, when he had entered her lodge to remove Nai's body, he had been startled by the sight of the high priestess prowling naked in the shadows, pacing like a cornered animal, stressed and pale and *old*, although the lodge had stunk of the burned blood of a woman young enough to menstruate. Ysuna had looked so old that, struck to his heart with pity and remorse, he had turned his face away. She had sworn to him that she would live forever. Was it possible that she had lied? Could she be growing old before his eyes?

With a sharp shrug, he defiantly drove away the dark spirits of doubt. He had no right to doubt her. She had *not* lied. She had sworn that she would live forever . . . as long as she had the fresh meat and blood of the mammoth to sustain her. And this encampment was lacking in both necessities.

He drew in a deep, steadying breath and again stared toward the south. Where *was* Maliwal? And how strange it was, he thought, that so often these days he found himself suddenly transfixed, his attention called to the southern horizon by the stirring of grass, the rustling of leaves, or the bounding leaps of some animal.

Mystic Warrior scanned the southern skies. Thousands of migrating geese were flying in formation; he could not remember the last time that he had seen so many. Masau tried to calm his unease. The birds meant nothing. At this time of year, in what other direction would waterfowl be migrating? And with an older brother out from the village, it was not strange for Masau to turn in that direction, anticipating Maliwal's safe return.

Mystic Warrior nodded. His questions had easy answers, but he was not comforted. The birds' migration was premature; it warned of an early winter. And he knew all too well that something beyond concern for his brother drew his gaze to the south. But what? He had seen many visions lately—of an old owl, feathers falling out with age as it *oo-oo*ed solemnly from a perch in a cave above a snow-covered village . . . of a lone coyote answering the call with a high, threnodic song . . . of wind-driven storms, sacred stones, and carcasses in the snow . . . of Great White Spirit walking alone in the frozen whiteness while the People of the Watching Star, hungry and afraid, followed. And to the south they walked, always to the south, as though something important awaited them. It called across the miles to summon them and Mystic Warrior to some wondrous fate that would transform his people and him forever.

The sun was gone now, leaving a shimmering bloodred sky in its wake. The migrating birds were barely visible, but something else was clearly silhouetted against the curve of the horizon. Maliwal had returned at last!

With an arm raised skyward, he led a line of captives and his fellow hunters home. And even before Maliwal called out, triumphantly announcing his discoveries to the south, Masau knew what he would say and suddenly understood his visions' meaning. There were mammoth to the south. There were sacred stones and brides for Thunder in the Sky to the south. There was the blood of life to the south. Ysuna must go there, and soon, if she was to live and remain young forever.

# 5

"We musht leave this plash! The lionsh are coming!" cried Hoyeh-tay, sitting bolt upright on his mattress.

Cha-kwena was at his side in an instant. "You have been dreaming again, Grandfather."

Hoyeh-tay licked his lips. The dream was fading. He was glad; it had been a terrible dream. "Ish-iwi ish dead," he said quietly, his heart bleeding. "Shi-wana ish dead, too. Lionsh have eaten them both."

"You cannot know that."

"I am Shaman. I know." He looked up at the boy. "I have sheen much more than thish in my dreamsh, Nar-eh."

Cha-kwena exhaled audibly and rolled his eyes. It was difficult to remain patient when, from one moment to the next, Hoyeh-tay did not know to whom he was speaking. Far below the cave the village was ablaze with cooking fires. The hunt had been extremely successful; over three hundred fat rabbits and lean, long-legged hares had been snared in the nets and clubbed to death by the beaters. Tomorrow any meat that had not been consumed would be smoked and set to dry in the sun and then stored in grass-lined pits for future use. But now the feasting was almost ready to begin.

"Nar-eh? Are you lishtening to me?"

"Look at me, Grandfather. It is I, Cha-kwena! No one in this village has seen sign of lions. I do not know why your old friend Ish-iwi did not come to the sacred mountain, but I am sure that even the boldest lion would have a hard time sneaking up on Shi-wana, much less digesting him. He is far too resourceful and disagreeable."

"He ish dead."

Again the youth rolled his eyes. It was clear to Cha-kwena that Hoyeh-tay had lost his shaman's power. Now, in the meager firelight, he was merely an old man with a drooping face and a mind that kept turning back upon itself.

"Cha-kwena."

He turned, startled to see that Tlana-quah had come up the stone stairs.

"How is our shaman?" the headman asked.

"I am not deaf," replied Hoyeh-tay with a snap, "and I can still speak for myself! Hoyeh-tay does not need Cha-kwena to speak for him—at least not yet!"

Cha-kwena stared at his grandfather. The old man seemed to be his own irascible self again. Relief filled the youth. He looked up at Tlana-quah and smiled.

"I have come to invite and assist our shaman to the feast," Tlana-quah said. "In honor of those who have returned from the Land of the Blue Mesas."

"And what makes you think your shaman needs assistance?" Hoyeh-tay made to rise but discovered that only one leg would serve him. Tottering sideways, he would have fallen had Cha-kwena not come to his aid. "Hmm . . . leg's asleep . . ." he muttered. "And one arm, too."

Out of respect for the shaman's dignity, Tlana-quah averted his eyes. "Then I will leave you to make your own way with Cha-kwena. I will tell the women to prepare the place of honor for Hoyeh-tay."

On his feet now and clinging to Cha-kwena's arm, Hoyeh-tay scowled. "Who are these travelers who have returned from the Land of the Blue Mesas?"

"You and I and Dakan-eh," answered Cha-kwena patiently. The old man's mind was wandering again, but at least he was not rambling on about lions.

They feasted on the red flesh of hares and rabbits and on the pink flesh of flickers and quails and robins. Wide, flat woven trays heaped with hot roasted seeds, locusts, and crickets were passed, and similar but smaller trays went from hand to hand so that discriminating fingers might pluck up such delicacies as raw grubs and the eggs of spicy black wood ants and termites. Camas cakes pebbled with buckberries and currants were enjoyed by all, then washed down with a stone-boiled soup thickened with rabbit entrails, dried fish heads, and whole, gutted lizards made pungent with onions, sage, and the ripe fruit of roses.

Once again the people listened to the adventures of the three who had traveled to the Land of the Blue Mesas. As Tlana-quah listened he felt soothed by a new attitude. The omens still troubled him, but the spirits of the ancestors might still be smiling. After all, things were good for his people. Life Giver walked in the land, and as long as their totem was with them, the People would prosper.

Now, with their lips greased with fat from the feast, the People's faces shone in the firelight. Laughter came easily to them. Infants suckled happily at their mothers' breasts while some children sprawled asleep on the ground before the main fire. Others, older, giggled and wrestled with one another. The elderly watched them, ready to nudge them if their behavior became too rowdy, all the while nodding and smiling with memories of their own childhood. Young women circulated with food or sat with their mothers on the female side of the fire circle. They were dark eyed and lovely, especially his own two girls, the headman thought, feeling a father's pride. Even the old shaman seemed better.

Tlana-quah nodded, satisfied. Today's rabbit drive had been extraordinarily successful; there would be enough meat to last throughout the long, cold days and nights of winter and well beyond. Coots, ducks, and heavy-breasted geese were arriving in great numbers to winter at the western edge of the lake, where hot springs kept the water free of ice. They would be a ready source of fresh meat for the People, as there was every winter.

The rhythms of Kosar-eh's hand drum drew the headman's attention as the clown stepped forward to provide entertainment. In the firelight, in feathers and skins and body paint, Kosar-eh's scars and crippled arm were not apparent. His woman, Siwi-ni, sat straight and rigid with pride. Her fingers drummed the beat of his dance on her hugely pregnant belly.

Kosar-eh seemed both man and animal as he whirled and leaped—a powerful and potent rabbit, hare, and bird spirit, a force to honor the animals that the People had killed and eaten this day.

The People cheered him. The children awoke and sat upright. He danced the dance of Rabbit and Hare, of Flicker and Quail and Robin, and mimicked their ways. Then, from the darkness beyond the circle, he retrieved a net and a beater and symbolically reenacted the role of Man in the rabbit drive until he lay upon the ground, bound in the net, beating himself until the bone club fell to the earth and he lay still.

"Is he dead?" whispered a child.

"Watch," answered her grandmother.

Slowly the net unfolded, and Kosar-eh rose again. The children clapped their hands. The People cried out in delight as their clown took the skin of a rabbit from his head and presented it with a bow to his woman. "May you continue to birth our young with the same ease as does this rabbit," he said.

Siwi-ni blushed like a young girl, cuffed him playfully, and accepted his gift. She spread it wide upon her belly.

Next Kosar-eh slung off his cape of feathers, and he began handing them out one by one as gifts to the children.

"May the spirit of Red-Shafted Flicker live in you and make you strong and resourceful and caring of your future wives and little ones!" he said to the boys who received the red tail feathers of the woodpecker.

"And may the spirit of Quail live in you, so that you will always keep your future little ones following in the straight path to wisdom!" he advised the little girls to whom he handed the curling topknots of quails.

With giggles and grins the children accepted their presents. When all were gone save for a fan of magpie feathers, Kosar-eh danced to the women's side of the circle and paused before Ta-maya.

"And may one who already shines take the iridescence of Magpie to live within her. Let the feathers' iridescence be a bride gift from her to the one who will be her man and to his future children so that they, like their mother, will shine with the brightness of these feathers."

Ta-maya held up her hands and allowed the clown to place the gift upon her open palms. When she smiled at him, her face was transformed by gratitude and open affection. Then, with a deep intake of breath, the young woman was on her feet, standing next to the clown and extending her arms toward the men's side of the fire.

It was the moment that Tlana-quah had been dreading. It came and went before he could raise his hand or say a word to stop it.

"This woman offers this gift of feathers to Dakan-eh!" Ta-maya declared boldly.

On the opposite side of the fire, Dakan-eh rose, and without a moment's hesitation or so much as a sideways glance at Ban-ya he declared: "Dakan-eh accepts this gift. And he accepts this woman, Ta-maya, daughter of Tlana-quah and Ha-xa, to be his."

It was done. Tlana-quah felt sick with disappointment but could not say why. Ta-maya looked radiant, and Dakan-eh was the best man in the band. He knew it, Ta-maya knew it, everyone knew it—especially Dakan-eh himself.

Ha-xa had dropped her tray of grubs and ant eggs, then swept to her daughter's side to kiss and hug her in the way of mothers the Red World over when their firstborn daughter finally agreed to accept a man.

Tlana-quah frowned. He eyed Dakan-eh. Naked except for a short loin cover of antelope hide, the young man stood with head high and a confident leer on his handsome face. He had rubbed his skin with rabbit fat, and his skin glistened in the firelight. Every hard span and rounded curve of his musculature was defined. He was a man to envy, a man to make older men, fathers of young women, pull in their guts and expand their chests defensively. Tlana-quah's frown became a scowl. He disliked Dakan-eh. He disliked him intensely.

He took control of the situation and looked straight at Dakan-eh as he did so. "It is Ta-maya's right to name the man she will have. It is my right, as her father, to say when she will have him."

Except for the crackling of the fire, there was absolute silence.

The smile vanished from Dakan-eh's face, as it did from Ta-maya's and Ha-xa's. Tlana-quah felt the eyes of every member of his band upon him. Even Hoyeh-tay was watching him, although, from the blank look in the old man's eyes and the firelit tear of spittle on his chin, the headman knew that the shaman's mind had flown off among the stars. Tlana-quah nodded. The expression on the old man's face confirmed the rightness of the action he was about to take. The omens were not right for this marriage.

"Tonight would be a good night for a man and a woman to be together for the first time," said Ha-xa, her voice strained, her face tight.

"No," replied Tlana-quah, and knew that he would have to deal with his woman later. Resolute, he stood up. He had been dealing with Ha-xa for most of his life, and he would deal with her again, but not now. "This night, this feast, and this fire honor those who have returned to us from the far country. The giving of Ta-maya to her first man must have its own fire, its own feast."

"When?" demanded Dakan-eh.

"When the omens speak in favor of it."

"And when will that be?" Dakan-eh pressed hotly.

"Only our shaman can tell us that!"

Dakan-eh looked at Hoyeh-tay, then at Cha-kwena. Finally he shook his head. "What is this, Tlana-quah? I am Bold Man! Who is more deserving of Ta-maya than I?"

Tlana-quah controlled a desire to smile. Dakan-eh's arrogance was so ingenuous that he was amused rather than angered. "Who knows? Perhaps even now that man comes to us. From another band . . . or perhaps from out of that mysterious tribe of strangers that you have spoken of. Is it not possible that in all this world there might be a man whom I—or my daughter—might find more suitable than you?"

Dakan-eh stared, deep in thought. Then he said forthrightly, "No. I am the best man. Why would any woman want another when she could have me?"

Now it was Tlana-quah who stared. After a moment he did smile. "At the Great Gathering, if my daughter still wants you, let the joining of Dakan-eh and Ta-maya take place before the entire tribe."

Ta-maya's hands curled around the feathers that she had been about to give as a gift to her man-to-be. "Winter will have come and gone and many moons will have risen before then, my father."

"Many moons," Tlana-quah confirmed, still smiling. "Many, *many* moons."

"I will not wait!" proclaimed Dakan-eh, more hotly than before.

"Wait or choose another woman," Tlana-quah said sharply, no longer amused by the young man's arrogance.

Ban-ya, seated next to her mother and grandmother, stiffened and stared with sudden hope; but even as her eyes swept with longing over Dakan-eh her yearning was dashed by Ta-maya's response.

"With these feathers I have accepted him!" For the first time her soft voice held an edge of protest.

"No, Daughter," Tlana-quah disagreed. "The feathers are still in your hand. You have consented to accept him, and so you shall—at the Great Gathering." The headman looked his daughter up and down for signs of pregnancy. "You have never been in a hurry to say yes to him before. Is there a need to hurry now?"

Even in the firelight, her blush was evident. "No. No hurry."

"The lionsh . . . the lionsh are coming."

Distracted by the breathy croak of old Hoyeh-tay, Tlana-quah turned and looked down at the shaman. He was still blank eyed, and Cha-kwena was bending over him, wiping away the spittle with the back of his fingers.

"What did you say?" asked the headman.

Cha-kwena did not look up. His voice held worry and embarrassment as he answered, "Nothing. Pay no heed to him. His eyes are open, but he is still asleep. He dreams of lions and of old friends. What he says does not matter."

"You could have lied."

Ta-maya paused at the tone of Dakan-eh's words. Her right elbow was grasped in the cup of his hand, and he roughly swung her toward him. She looked up. He looked so stern, so angry, that she wished she had not lagged behind the other girls and women as they had left the feast fire.

The heated exchange of words between Dakan-eh and the headman had put an early end to the night's celebration. Kosar-eh had attempted to revive the festive mood, but the gathering had dispersed in hushed and troubled silence, and now the People were moving away to their family huts. With lowered heads and downturned eyes they passed Ta-maya and Dakan-eh in the darkness.

The young woman flushed, wondering what they were thinking. Then, suddenly frightened, she looked around for her father. He would be furious if he noticed that she was speaking with Dakan-eh when no woman from her family was present.

"Ta-maya . . ."

"I must go, Dakan-eh."

"All you had to do was tell him that I had put life in you, and this night you would be mine. Even now we would be alone together, lying together, and I would be deep inside you, moving on you, putting truth to the lie."

She gasped, and her face and body flamed at the images that he had so boldly put into her head. Yet when he tried to draw her closer, she pulled away. She did not understand him. To speak a falsehood was to offend the spirits of the ancestors. By even suggesting it Dakan-eh was dishonoring her and himself. She said as much.

He exhaled, impatient and annoyed. "What is the difference? Only you and I would have known of the deception!"

"The spirits of the ancestors would know. And I would not begin our lives together with a lie!"

His face twisted against anger. "Sometimes I wonder if you want to begin a life with me at all!"

Stunned, she watched him stalk off. He was so tall, so powerful, and so desirable that she ached for him and for herself.

"Once again I say that maybe he is not for you after all, eh?" The widow Kahm-ree paused beside her and smirked over her toothless gums.

Startled, Ta-maya stared as Ban-ya, linked arm in arm with old Kahm-ree, stared back.

"Maybe by the time of the Great Gathering he will not want you anymore," Ban-ya said with poisonous sweetness.

"He will always want me! Look! I wear his wristband! It is a sign of his love for me."

"We will see." With a toss of her head Ban-ya walked on with her grandmother, following quickly after Dakan-eh and leaving Ta-maya with tears in her eyes and the iridescent feathers of Kosar-eh's bridal gift in her hand.

Cha-kwena, hunkering on the lip of Hoyeh-tay's cave, listened to Coyote's familiar call from the far side of the lake and watched Tlana-quah and the elders bank the ceremonial fire. Lights were flickering within a few of the little thatch huts. He frowned. There would be low, troubled talk among the villagers tonight: talk of bold hunters who challenged their headman and of firstborn daughters who balked at obeying the will of their fathers.

"Little Yellow Wolf hash followed you acrossh the milesh," slurred Hoyeh-tay.

"There are many little yellow wolves in the Red World, Grandfather," Cha-kwena replied quietly.

His eyes cut back and forth across the near darkness below. Where was Dakan-eh? he wondered. He had seen him walking toward the longhouse of the unmarried hunters. Ban-ya and old Kahm-ree had followed close behind. But now there was no sign of him or the girl! The old woman was standing alone.

"Thish wolf knowsh you," said Hoyeh-tay.

Cha-kwena sighed, sorry that the old man had awakened. He himself was tired. Now he settled himself on his buttocks, pulled up his knees to his chin, wound his arms around his calves, and closed his eyes.

"Yellow Wolf hash followed you acrossh the milesh," said Hoyeh-tay.

"And why should he do that?"

"Becaush you are hish brother. Becaush he knowsh the lionsh are coming."

Cha-kwena sighed against sadness. He rested his right cheek against his knees. "It is late, Grandfather. Go back to sleep. I will guard the cave. And I have promised to keep you safe from lions."

"You cannot, Cha-kwena, not ash long ash you shtay in thish village. Not ash long ash you keep your inner eye closed."

"Whatever you say, Grandfather."

Cha-kwena was drifting off to sleep now and had not heard the old man's last words. He no longer heard the high, doleful cries of Coyote, nor did he see Owl sweep out of the night to alight on his perch at the back of the chamber. Darkness, deep and mellow, took him. He smiled in his sleep. Coyote did not come to him in his dreams, because he dreamed no dreams at all.

Hoyeh-tay sat up on his mattress, assumed the same position as the boy as he stared wearily at Owl. "The lionsh are coming," he said.

"I know," replied Owl. "It is too late to stop them."

"A white mammoth, you say?" In the center of the great meeting lodge of the People of the Watching Star, Ysuna stood rigidly.

"Yes," affirmed Lah-ri, the dimpled little sister of Sunam-tu. "The shaman boy told the others that Great Ghost Spirit grazed to the far south, by a village near a lake named for the singing birds."

Ysuna smiled with transcendent radiance. "You have done well, Maliwal!"

The man whom Lah-ri pretended to love stood taller. His face was still swollen with livid wounds that were hairy with sutures of blood-blackened sinew. "I have sought only to please Ysuna in all things."

"You have pleased me," she told him.

Masau looked at his brother. "It is good that Maliwal returns safely. As for Rok, we will make the songs to honor his life spirit. His woman will not mourn alone."

"He died bravely," said Chudeh, and began to recount the mammoth hunt.

But Maliwal cut him off. "What is the life of one man? Rok was nothing! *I* have found mammoth! I have *killed* mammoth! I have cached much mammoth meat to the south and have brought the prime portions, along with captives, to Daughter of the Sun. This Lah-ri of the Red World has come consenting to become one of us."

"Is that so, child?" Ysuna's smile eased into gentle affection. "Do you come consenting? After all that you have seen, do you not fear those who have taken you away from your own land?"

There was silence in the lodge. Lah-ri, seated on a soft pillow of rare, finely combed, long-haired mammoth hide, looked up at the tall, handsome forms and faces of the hunters who encircled her. "The men who have brought me north have treated me well, not as a captive but as an honored guest. The killing that was done in the Red World . . ." She shrugged. "I do not understand it, but since that day I have been given no cause to fear my captors."

"Nor shall you be given cause, Sister. You do not mind if I call you that?"

"I have never had a sister," said Lah-ri.

The circling faces expanded into smiles. For a moment the men looked like wolves leering over prey, and Lah-ri flinched.

"She will do," said Ysuna. "Yes, Maliwal, you *have* done well. She *will* do."

Lah-ri smiled. Since being taken captive, nothing had been denied her. When she was hungry, the man with the torn face and the patch where his ear should be had brought food to her. When she was thirsty, he had brought her drink. At night he had lain close beside her, forming a windbreak with his own body as he fondled her with his big, rough hands and smoothed her skin with mammoth oil.

His wounds stank and made his otherwise handsome face ugly, but he knew how to set fire to a woman's loins, and she would have opened herself to him had she not sensed that it was important to maintain the lie that she had never been penetrated by a man. So she had clenched her thighs and prettily begged him not to press her to completion. He had not forced her. He had played with her until the need for release was too much for him, then he turned away and drew one of the other captives close, leaving Lah-ri throbbing and envious.

She did not understand what made the men treat her with respect—even deference—while the other captives had been mocked and mauled and beaten until three of them were dead and several asked to be. From the first she had expected to be raped and killed, as the others had been raped and killed. Instead her captors called her Sister. And when at last they had entered the encampment of their people, Maliwal commanded women to bring forth the finest clothes and adornments so that his new woman-to-be might have her choice from among the best. She had chosen and chosen again. Never in her life had she possessed as many clothes, nose rings, ear pendants, wristlets, and anklets as she possessed now. Sunam-tu would never have given her so much.

It was enough to make her glad that she had been stolen away from her own people, from the handsome Bold Man who had humiliated her, from the young apprentice shaman who had spurned her, and from the skinny old blue-faced holy man who had barely had her out of the sacred groves before he was on her like a bear, in deep and thrusting hard from behind, spurting the juice of life into her. No youth had ever pumped so much hot, wet fire into her or taken as much pride in the accomplishment. She would miss the old man's enthusiasm for her favorite sport; but if his death could win her a beautiful necklace like Ysuna's, she would not think of him again.

Staring up at it now as it lay about the woman's shoulders, she smiled, recognizing the stones for what they were. "I know where you can get more white stones like those. If I tell you where, there would be enough so I could have my own necklace. Of course you would have to tell me what kind of bones those are, and from what animal you have taken the tufts of shiny black hair."

Silence settled like a dark, smothering, invisible cloak as the men exchanged glances with the priestess. No one spoke, yet somehow the girl felt that they were sharing a secret.

Suddenly on edge, Lah-ri frowned. "What is it? Have I said something wrong?"

A moment passed before Ysuna smiled. It was as full of secrets as the silence had been. She knelt, took one of Lah-ri's small hands, and gently stroked her fingers as, with her free hand, she reached out and toyed with a lock of the girl's hair. "What is this about stones, Sister?"

"I know where you can get more of them. All that you would ever want, all that there are."

It appeared as though an inner wind ran between the priestess's skull and the skin that covered it. Her face seemed to ripple over her bones as her eyes widened. She whispered flatly, hungrily: "Tell me."

But Maliwal spoke out before Lah-ri could answer. "I have waited until the last to be the one to tell you!" His voice was a lion's roar of pure pride. "The sacred stones,

the bones of First Man and First Woman—next year they
will all be in one place! The girl has told me that all the
tribes of the Red World will assemble on the flanks of
their holy mountain. All the shamans will be there, and
with the shamans, all the sacred stones."

Ysuna rose, slowly, as if in a dream.

Silence settled. All eyes were on her as she said
quietly, as though in prayer, "Then on that day we shall
be there, too."

# 6

The high priestess of the People of the Watching Star
emerged from her lodge to stand alone in the light of
dawn. Ysuna had not slept all night because a dull pain fed
upon the wound within her womb. She assured herself
that it was the mere pain of healing, even though her fever
warned her otherwise.

Restless, she moved soundlessly through the encampment of her sleeping people and toward the broad open
spaces beyond. She needed to think, to breathe, to stand
in open country. But there were so many lodges crowding
her! Their peaks pointed upward, and their support poles
jutted through closed smoke flaps like stiffly cross-laced
fingers.

To keep herself from feeling closed in, Ysuna counted
the lodges as she walked, but there were too many for
even Daughter of the Sun to sum in her head or on her
hands. She knew, however, from previous calculations
that there were three hundred of them in all.

On and on she walked. Movement eased her pain and
lightened her mood. She found herself taking pride in the
vast span of her village. Had her people raised so many
lodges when she had been a girl? No. Under her leadership
their number had burgeoned until sometimes the light

thrown from their many cooking fires obliterated the stars. Viewed by night by returning hunters from the surrounding hills, their encampment was a lake of light and warmth glowing in a hostile world that Ysuna had made their own. Her head went high with pride in her accomplishments.

The sound of her moccasins on the scattered stone nodules woke the dogs. They looked up and watched her as she passed. She sensed their wariness and felt strengthened by it. The dogs were big animals, wolflike, strong of back and fleet of foot. The pack had been bred for running down game and turning it toward the waiting spears of hunters and for trudging across the long miles that lay between each camp. The dogs were harnessed to sledges in the winter snows or carried side packs in summer when the terrain would not allow them to drag their loads.

Any one of them could have leaped upon her and torn her to pieces, but she had ordered her people to cull potentially troublesome pups from all litters. She herself had strangled more than a few and brained enough mature growlers and snarlers to have taught the survivors that they lived by her sufferance alone.

Of all the dogs, only Masau's shaggy, blue-eyed Blood rose when she came close to the lodge of the Mystic Warrior. Its flesh-colored nose worked from side to side, scenting her. A deep, warning vibrato sounded in the animal's chest, and the grizzled red hair along its spine rose. Head out, tail tucked, ears back, lips quivering and curled back, Blood showed the woman his teeth.

She paused, impressed.

Seeing her reaction, Blood took a step forward.

So did Ysuna.

The dog remained where he was, as did the woman. They eyed each other.

"You live only because you are *his*, Dog," Ysuna said, then walked on, widening the space between herself and the animal. By so doing, she canceled her threat to him . . . and his to her.

The morning star was still above the distant mountains when Ysuna finally put the last of the lodges behind her. She stared at it, waiting for omens. High, thin horizontal bands of cirrus clouds came instead, veiling the sky. Then they thickened, obliterating the star and assuming strange

shapes. The priestess blinked, stared again, and saw lions—
one of them headless—in the clouds. All of them followed
a herd of many mammoth across the sky. And then, as the
clouds moved and rolled and shifted, the many mammoth
became one mammoth—an enormous white storm cloud
of a mammoth.

She caught her breath, reached up to grasp at her
collar, at the sacred stones. "Thunder in the Sky . . .
Great Ghost Spirit . . ."

Even as she whispered the words the clouds rolled
and shifted again. The mammoth cloud collapsed and
dissolved. Then it was reborn, re-created as a tiny
mammoth, then as no mammoth at all but a huge owl
flying out of the mouth of a coyote. The owl flew high and
wide as it spread its cloud wings to engulf the Morning
Star.

Ysuna felt dizzy, feverish. There were too many visions
and too many omens in the clouds! And the pain in her
womb was back. She closed her eyes and forced herself to
breathe slowly and evenly.

"Ysuna."

She turned. Maliwal stood before her. He held out a
cup made from the hollowed tip of a polished mammoth
tusk. It held a steaming liquid.

"A morning gift from Maliwal to Daughter of the Sun.
Mammoth blood and marrow. I have heated it for you
myself. Drink."

Still clutching her collar, she shivered with revulsion
as she looked into his stitched and battered face. Needing
an excuse to look away, she took the cup and drank deeply.

"The blood is thick and the marrow is rich with the oil
of life. I have brought them far and obtained them at great
cost." He paused, then implored softly, tentatively, in the
way of a child standing before a parent whom he both
distrusts and adores: "Ysuna, heal me. Sutures of animal
sinew hold my cheek together and keep one corner of my
mouth from gaping wide. I carry my ear in a sack. Make
this torn flesh meld, Ysuna! Maliwal, slayer of mammoth,
would once again be pleasing to your eyes."

She was moved by his request and by his open and
unquestioning faith in her. Yet, suddenly, she felt sick.

The drink of blood and marrow had been too rich; it was all she could do not to vomit.

"Heal me, Ysuna," he beseeched. "I told the others that you would. I told them that this—" He paused, embarrassed, as he indicated his face with a stiff upward jab of his left hand. "I told them that this feat would be nothing to you. Heal me and show that you can do what I have sworn you could do."

She breathed shallowly. Nausea was passing, but the ache in her womb was deep and constant. Did he see her weakness? she wondered. She measured his ruined face, searching for guile and duplicity. Suspicion caused her to sense a trap, so she warned, "Do not dare to test me, Maliwal! I will not demonstrate my powers so that you may try to find fault in them and vindicate your lack of conviction in my abilities!"

"I—no, Ysuna! You misunderstand!"

She saw that he was both stunned and horrified by her accusation. Yet she pressed him. "Do I?"

She already knew the answer. She had sent him out to prove himself, to make up for past errors, to find and to kill mammoth, to discover a village in which there would be a sacred stone and a suitable sacrifice for Thunder in the Sky. He had done all this and more. And he had done it to please her as well as to satisfy his own combative nature. She knew this as surely as she believed that she could heal his wounds if she truly wished to do so. It should not be a thing of any great difficulty for her to heal a few wounds and take an ear from a sack and command it to adhere itself to the head of a man.

But experience had taught her that some challenges were best left scrupulously avoided. And so she asked, "What makes my son believe that he could ever be less than pleasing to my eyes? It is a good thing that you will be marked by scars. Everywhere you go, men, women, and children will stop and stare and know that you are Maliwal—Man Who Has Stood Alone Against a Great Mammoth . . . and lived to tell the tale."

He was not soothed. "Ysuna, *please* heal me."

She reached out and laid her hand lovingly upon his face. "This is a mark of your bravery and loyalty. It means everything to me, and I will not change it. Now go.

Awaken my people and bestir the captives and the girl whom you have brought to us as a sacrifice. The village must be broken down and made ready for transport into the south. There are mammoth and sacred stones in that land. You, my wolf, must show us where to hunt for them."

Maliwal watched her walk away from him—a tall figure in a flowing robe, with her hair cascading over her back to her heels and below. Her gait was smooth, determined, and yet he sensed a tightness in it, as though it hurt her to move as she strained to keep her back straight and her footfall long and even.

Masau, with Blood at his side, came from behind one of the lodges to stand beside his brother. "It is as I feared," he said.

Scowling, with a hand resting over the wounded side of his face, Maliwal eyed him darkly. "You heard?"

"And saw the weakness in her," Masau confirmed.

"Weakness?"

"It is growing in us all, Maliwal. We must find and kill the white mammoth for Ysuna. Our mother must drink its blood and eat its flesh before she grows old and the strength of the People of the Watching Star is no more."

Maliwal's scowl became a frown of perplexity. "Ysuna cannot grow old."

"She cannot heal your wounds. . . ."

"*Will* not!"

Masau shook his head. "So she would have you believe. I tell you, Maliwal, we must find and kill the white mammoth. And soon, Brother, before it is too late."

# 7

"Awake, Cha-kwena! Come! You must put your back to the North Star and follow me! You and your people must leave the Red World. Now!" The song of Coyote was a high, plaintive yowling.

In the darkness of a moonless midnight Cha-kwena awoke, startled and alert. He *had* only been dreaming again, and yet . . . was it not in dreams that a shaman heard the voice of vision?

After wrapping himself in his rabbit-skin blanket, the boy rose from his mattress of woven reeds and went to stand at the mouth of the cave. The night was clear and cool. Below the bluff, the villagers slept undisturbed. Cha-kwena drew in a deep breath and whispered: "Coyote, if you are my brother, if you are the helping animal spirit I have sought, and if—just *if*—I am to be a shaman someday, what kind of message have you sent me in my dreams? I would proudly call myself Little Yellow Wolf, name you as my spirit animal, and follow you into the worlds beyond the land of my ancestors. But my grandfather is sick, and I cannot leave him. The strength of my band lies in the Red World. Even now the People sleep in a camp full of meat. Life Giver has led us here. Since First Man and First Woman came walking across the mountaintops into this country, the spirits of the ancestors have lived with us and we have grown strong. We cannot leave the Red World."

He stared out across the little huts, over the lake and hills and great towering buttes and waited for Coyote to speak to him now as Little Yellow Wolf had spoken out of Cha-kwena's dreams. But instead, from somewhere far away across the lake, a mammoth trumpeted.

"Life Giver?"

Again the mammoth trumpeted. Cha-kwena felt certain

that it was Great Ghost Spirit. The totem of his ancestors had answered him! As long as Life Giver walked in the Red World, of what importance was the advice of an insignificant coyote?

Autumn lay gently upon the Red World. Blue jays scolded in the wide, flowering sage flats southwest of the Lake of Many Singing Birds. Red-capped woodpeckers screeched among the yellow pines above Hoyeh-tay's cave, rousing the shaman before dawn as they hammered out new holes and enlarged old ones, where they stashed their winter supply of acorns and assorted scraps stolen from the nearby village.

"Soon winter will be upon us. You have much to learn, Cha-kwena, before the first snow flies!"

Cha-kwena grumbled. The first autumn leaves had yet to fall, and already his grandfather was worrying about winter; nevertheless the youth did not complain. Hoyeh-tay was improving rapidly. His face still drooped, but he could speak fairly clearly again, and he no longer drooled. There were times when Cha-kwena felt almost sorry that the weakness was leaving the old man's bones, for now that Hoyeh-tay was feeling stronger, endless hours were spent in storytelling and instruction in the ways of the shaman's path.

Now Cha-kwena sat in the sun on the floor of the cave while Hoyeh-tay spoke on and on. The boy sighed, envying the villagers their work and freedom. Under the tutelage of the older men, his friends were now working stone into spearheads and carving bone fishhooks and fashioning spears and tridents and decoys, for now more than at any other time, the Lake of Many Singing Birds lived up to its name.

Great, honking rafts of waterfowl bobbed upon the blue deeps. Loons and bitterns called from within the tule brakes, and herons, storks, and assorted marsh birds fed along the shore. Horses and giant ground sloths came night after night to drink with camels and mammoth in the cool shallows.

"Cha-kwena!"

"Hmm . . . what?"

"You have not heard a word I have said!"

"I . . . I have heard every word!"

"Repeat them!"

"I . . . uh . . ."

Hoyeh-tay's expression informed him that there was no use trying to bluff it out. There was nothing to do now but pretend to be interested in whatever followed.

"We were talking about the coming winter, boy. Look to Spider for knowledge of changing weather. Until now she has spun her webs thin and high—summer webs. Now she spins them thick and low to the ground—winter webs. Yes, Cha-kwena, Spider tells this shaman that it will be winter very soon."

"High webs, low webs, what is the difference?"

The old man, vexed, rolled his eyes in the same way that the boy usually rolled his when irritated by what he took to be the thickheadedness of old age. "Think, Cha-kwena! When the weather turns cold, does a man stand upright and expose himself to the weather as he would to the warm rays of the sun? No. He turns his back to the wind. He wraps himself in thick garments. He hunkers close to the earth out of the cold and wet. Should Spider be less wise than man?"

The boy nodded thoughtfully. "How can you know if the winter will last for a long time? What signs tell you this?"

"White-haired Eagle has come a full moon early to gather with his family in perch trees in the old pine flats on the north shore of the lake. With his golden eye he can see far and deep into the water. There will be fish for him in the cold times, and the rich, red flesh of coots will make his heart glad. Blue Heron is here, feeding in the marsh above the hot springs. And mice are coming into the lodges now . . . fat little female mice looking for good, dry hidden places in which to store their seeds. But most of all, for those of us who are Shaman, the signs are here." He laid a fist against his heart, then raised his hand and let his fingers drift across his forehead. "The third eye, Cha-kwena. Remember the third eye! When it opens within a shaman, there is a sense of knowing, a perception of how things will or will not be. A shaman must give himself to this inner vision. He must ask for it to come to him, and he must be willing to accept its gift when that gift is a vision of something that he does not wish to see, or when the consequence of the vision is unknown to him."

The boy scowled. "You mean like following spirit voices that come in the night and tell you to run away from danger."

"Exactly! But as I have told you: It is too late to run away. Like the rain that will fall tomorrow, the lions will come."

Now it was the youth who rolled his eyes. "The lions always come to us at this time of year, Grandfather. They follow the browsing animals that winter with us in the Red World. The men of the band are alert to their presence. Besides, the omens are good for the coming winter. Everyone says so."

The old man's face was set, pinched. "Then why has our headman refused to allow his older daughter to be joined to Bold Man as his woman?"

Cha-kwena shrugged. "In truth, I do not think that our headman likes Dakan-eh very much."

Hoyeh-tay grunted. "He is too bold. Yet there is another who is bolder."

"Bolder than Dakan-eh? Impossible! No man could be more arrogant or—"

"No, the one I speak of does not wear the scar of arrogance. But he *is* bold. And he will have her."

"Who, Grandfather? No man in this band would challenge Dakan-eh for Ta-maya. And she wants no one except Bold Man."

"No, not a man . . ." Hoyeh-tay winced and sucked air through his teeth as his eyes went wide. He was suddenly shaking violently as he raised his hands as if to block the glare of a hurtful sun. "A lion . . . comes for her . . . for us all. Do you shee him, Ish-iwi? Do you shee him coming?"

Cha-kwena nearly cried. In one fleeting instant his hopes of reassuming a normal life were dashed as the old man began to drool and babble. "You are tired, Grandfather. You must rest. Here, let me help you to your mattress."

Hoyeh-tay did not resist. He clung to Cha-kwena's arm. "Ish-iwi, tell Tlana-quah! Let the union take plash now, before the lionsh come."

"Yes, Grandfather, I will tell him." There was no use

arguing. Cha-kwena led him back into the shadows and laid him down, covering him and soothing him.

Later, when the old man woke screaming in the night and the lights in the village flared, Tlana-quah came racing up the stone steps of the cave to find out what was wrong.

Cha-kwena did not know what to tell him. "The bad spirits have returned to our shaman," was all he could think to say. Cha-kwena hung his head, ashamed. The old man had lost control over his failing body. The hot, sweet stench of urine was overpowering.

Tlana-quah raised his head and said quietly, "After the others in the village have returned to sleep, I will bring clean blankets and matting. Set aside the soiled bedding for now. Ease him as best you can. In the morning your mother will bring fresh grass and sage cuttings to absorb the day's body leavings, as she always does, Cha-kwena. Burn this mess before your mother comes. Tell her it has been an offering of some sort. Then get some rest, young Shaman. No one need know of this."

Cha-kwena looked up at the headman's expression. Regret, sadness, infinite pity, and understanding all settled in the eyes of the headman. In that moment, Cha-kwena saw into the spirit of Tlana-quah and knew the innate goodness and kindness of the man. "My grandfather will be grateful."

The headman nodded. With bent head and stooped shoulders, he turned and began to descend the steps to the village.

Moments later Owl flew into the cave from out of the night and alighted on his perch. "I am still with you," said the bird to Cha-kwena.

Cha-kwena, cradling old Hoyeh-tay in his arms and rocking him, did not care about Owl. From out of the darkness of the star-strewn night, West Wind was carrying the scent of clouds and rain across the miles. A lone coyote howled in the hills to the south. Cha-kwena wept and did not hear him.

In the lodge of the bachelor hunters, Dakan-eh heard. Head high, eyes narrowed, he listened as the young men whispered of bad omens.

"Do you hear it, Bold Man?" asked a friend of Dakan-eh's.

"I hear," replied the hunter. "But in the Red World, it would be a bad omen if coyotes did not howl at night."

"But this coyote's call has an odd sound to it," said another youth.

In the deeper darkness at the far side of the lodge, another man of Dakan-eh's age stretched out on his reed mattress and, stifling a yawn, stared across the interior at Bold Man. "As long as Shaman remains sick and Coyote howls like that, Dakan-eh, Tlana-quah will never change his mind about you and his daughter."

Bold Man's jaw clenched. He knew the truth when he heard it. He also knew that although he could not make old Hoyeh-tay well, there were ways to silence coyotes who came too close to the village of the People.

# 8

A warm, soft rain fell before dawn. When it was over, a sweet, cool wind cleansed the earth and sky, and a towering band of many colors arched over the hills and buttes of the Red World and was reflected in the Lake of Many Singing Birds.

"Look!" said Ha-xa with delight. Pointing off, she came to stand close beside Tlana-quah just outside the headman's lodge. "Rainbow Woman walks the sky. It is the best of omens! Tlana-quah, let us talk once more of Dakan-eh and our daughter. When you are away from our lodge, Ta-maya weeps for want of Bold Man, and I often see him looking across the village at her—"

"No, Ha-xa. I have already spoken on this matter!" The headman glared from under lowered brows at the rainbow; he did not look at his woman as he added with great emphasis, "Until I see our totem walking again in the Red World, I can be sure of no omens."

Raindrops fell onto Ha-xa's head from the dripping roofline of the hut. Annoyed with them and with her man, she wiped her forehead. "But before the shaman left for the Land of the Blue Mesas, he and the boy saw Great Ghost Spirit!"

"Did they? Perhaps Shaman saw what an old man needed to see, and in the excitement of the moment, the boy imagined that he shared the vision."

"And I have seen Great Ghost Spirit," informed Mah-ree, peeking out from the entryway of the lodge and staring happily up between the two of them.

Tlana-quah scowled down at her. "No! I will not hear this again from you, Daughter. Our totem would not show himself to such as you when he has denied my eyes the sight of him!"

"But I have seen him!"

"Hush, Mah-ree!" commanded Ha-xa. "You know what I have told you about such talk!"

"But I know where he is. I can take you to him."

"Stop!" Tlana-quah was emphatic. "Our totem shows himself to holy men and headmen. Whatever you think you have seen, Mah-ree, I will hear no more of it! The omens are troubling enough to me in this village without your making them worse!"

Mah-ree shrank from the unexpected intensity of her father's anger.

Inside the lodge, she went to the bed of tule mats that she shared with her sister and sat down, pouting. "He doesn't believe me. No one believes me."

Ta-maya sat cross-legged and solemn in the middle of the mat. "Poor old Shaman cried out in his sleep last night. This has worried our father. You must be more understanding, Sister."

"You don't believe me, either." Mah-ree threw herself back on the mat. With a huff, she folded her slim arms across her flat little chest and closed her eyes. She envisioned him, the great white mammoth, Grandfather of All. "He is near," she said, and then, with an exhalation of pure determination, opened her eyes and sat up again. "If our father were to see him, too, he would believe me."

"See who?"

"Grandfather of All."

"Oh, Mah-ree, I am sure that you saw a mammoth in the cedar grove, but from the way you described him, you could not have seen our totem. Why would he appear to you and not to our father?"

"I don't know! But I did see him!" she insisted, then flinched and felt her face drain of all color.

Tlana-quah had entered the lodge. He had heard her every word! In his jaguar-skin cape, with his long face set and his eyes sharp with disapproval, he was a frightening figure. "I have heard enough. Come, show me! I will see with my own eyes, and you will see, too, that you have seen *nothing*!"


They walked out of the lodge together, hand in hand—the stern-faced headman and the frightened yet exhilarated little girl. Ta-maya followed.

"Where are you going?" Ha-xa asked.

"To see what walks in the cedar grove above the meadow where the roses bloom!" Tlana-quah replied angrily.

"To see the white mammoth!" Mah-ree declared.

Soon the entire band was following the headman as he strode purposefully toward the hills. Mah-ree stumbled after him, and Ha-xa and Ta-maya strained to keep up. Only Cha-kwena, standing on the edge of the shaman's cave, could not follow.

"Where is everyone going?" he called out.

No one answered.

With Mah-ree leading the way, the band ascended the rain-soaked meadow. The old people, wheezing and panting, fell behind as the girl ran straight toward the dark, west-facing, upland slope where the cedars grew thick and tall.

She stopped and stared. Tlana-quah was at her side. The sun was high above, bathing the meadow in its light. But the interior of the cedar grove ahead was gray and dripping and dank with mist.

Her heart was pounding. She squinted, straining to see a deeper, more solid bank of white moving within the gloom, but the grove was empty of all but mist. The white mammoth did not graze within it this day.

"Well?" Tlana-quah pressed.

Mah-ree hung her head, suddenly realizing the extent of her foolishness. "He is not here now. But he was here, within the trees. He . . ."

With an exhalation of disgust, Tlana-quah stomped forward into the grove. He crashed through undergrowth, waved saplings aside, looked for spoor, and, finding it, gestured everyone forward.

For a moment Mah-ree's heart leaped with joy.

Then Tlana-quah spoke. "Look at this: a torn tree, crushed bracken. But the undergrowth is too thick to hold a true track. And here, just as I thought—the stink of a sickly animal's urine. Is this what our totem leaves behind as sign for us? No! It is as I have said. My daughter may have seen a mammoth, but it was not Great Ghost Spirit. There is the smell of death in this one's passage. Our totem cannot die! If he does, the People will die with him! Let us return to the village. Let there be no more talk of this." He glared down at Mah-ree. "From *anyone!*"

Mah-ree stood solemn and contrite.

They were all returning to the village now, their backs to her, as though she had done some terrible thing. Grandfather of All may not have been in the grove today, but he was out there somewhere in the Red World, and she was certain that he was not sick or dying. He was simply looking for tender things to eat. If she knew where he was, she would bring him a mash of ground willow shoots to ease the ache in his great jaws; it would please her to do that. Perhaps if she were careful and placed her offerings in just the right places, he might come upon them. If his pain lessened, he might even come close to the village to see who had left all the fine healing foods for him. She would go out to him. She would stand respectfully before him—not too close, of course, but close enough to look into his eyes.

"It is I, Mah-ree, second daughter of Tlana-quah," she would say, "who has brought these good healing things to my totem."

Everyone would be amazed to see him standing before

her. Ha-xa would pale with motherly fear and call out a warning, but Mah-ree would not step back. As Cha-kwena and the hunters of the band gaped in awe of her bravery she would hold a basket of sweet cakes out to Grandfather of All, and he would eat from her hands. The children would *ooh* and *ahh*, and Ta-maya might even swoon.

Tlana-quah would set his eyes upon Life Giver and know that his totem was well and strong. He would look at his younger daughter and remember the day when he had refused to believe that she had seen Great Ghost Spirit in the cedar grove. He would proclaim to the band that he was sorry for ever having doubted her, and then he would call Ta-maya and Dakan-eh to him and tell them that now the omens boded well for their union. They would become man and woman together long before the Great Gathering convened in the distant pinyon groves of the sacred mountain. Shaman, restored to health by the renewed power of Great Ghost Spirit, would come down from his cave. Kosar-eh would dance and sing and make the People laugh. There would be feasting and many days and nights of celebration. Everything would be as it should be.

And everyone would know that all these wonderful things had happened because Mah-ree had brought Great Ghost Spirit to the village by the Lake of Many Singing Birds. No one would turn his back to her then.

Even Cha-kwena would look at her with admiration, and when she came close to him, he would not wave her away as though she were an annoying, flat-chested little mosquito. He would welcome her. He would walk gladly at her side. Perhaps he might even look at her as Bold Man looked at Ta-maya. Perhaps, someday, he would ask her to be his woman.

She sighed. Just thinking of it made her smile.

Day slipped into dusk, and dusk ebbed into evening, and soon it was dark again. Unable to sleep, Cha-kwena wrapped his blanket around his shoulders and went to sit glumly outside Hoyeh-tay's cave, as he had done every other night after the old man at last yielded to his dreams.

Moon was rising over the eastern sage flats. The village was hushed and sleeping. In the southern hills a coyote yelped sharply, as though surprised, and then was silent. Cha-kwena winced against the high, painful quality of the abrupt sound. He listened, waiting for Coyote to yelp again. Instead, a chorus of many little yellow wolves began to wail from the deep night shadows that filled the hollows of the boulder-strewn hills. The sound carried from the far buttes in a way that made Cha-kwena wonder if he had ever heard so mournful a sound in his entire life. The animals were crying across the miles, consoling one another.

Disconcerted, he shivered. *How can you know this?* he asked. He had decided that the little yellow wolf who had spoken to him in the past had really been old Hoyeh-tay, throwing his voice. And yet, as Cha-kwena listened to the wailing of the coyotes, a strange sadness swept through him.

He turned and stared into the cave. Owl was gone, and Hoyeh-tay was sleeping deeply, breathing loudly and rhythmically. Relief flooded through him; for a moment he had been afraid that his grandfather had just died. He shook his head. *It will happen someday, but not tonight. Not for many nights if I can stop it.*

He stared at the moon. As full and round as Siwi-ni's belly, Mother of the Stars rose slowly, spreading her light across the Red World.

The coyotes were silent now. A loon called on the lake; as always, it was an eerie sound. He listened, rapt, hearing the night sounds of coots and ducks conversing out upon the moonlit waters. At last the first risings of sleep touched and warmed him and made him yawn. He would have gone to his mattress then, but movement in the village caught his attention.

His eyes were drawn to where Bold Man had emerged from the lodge of the bachelors. He stood tall in the moonlight. Cha-kwena frowned. Something was unnaturally tense about the hunter's stance, something undeniably furtive about the way he looked around, then bent low and began to tread slowly across the village. He moved cautiously, silently. He had at least two spears with him, and what seemed to be a tool-carrying bag slung over his right shoulder. In a few moments he had disappeared into the darkness between the neatly arranged rows of huts.

Cha-kwena sat forward, waiting for Dakan-eh to

reappear. He did so much closer to the cave, out of the village and coming at a good pace toward the creek and the bluff. When he reached the creek bed, he paused and looked up toward the cave. Cha-kwena could not have explained why, but he scooted back, not wanting to be seen. He held his breath, wondering what Dakan-eh was up to.

He waited, but for what he could not say. He watched, half expecting Bold Man to come to the stone steps and ascend to the cave. The moment passed. *Probably because he does not see me and thinks he travels unobserved,* the youth thought ruefully as Bold Man kept walking. Puzzled, Cha-kwena moved forward again, watched him cross the creek and then head southward around the bluff for open country and the hills that lay beyond.

What was he doing alone in the dark? Cha-kwena wondered. Why was he moving with such stealth? Was he hunting? Was he seeking a surprise gift for Ta-maya, something that would please her and cause the headman to look upon him with favor?

Cha-kwena did not really care what Bold Man did. The boy was sleepy again, and too warm and comfortable to think of moving. He put his head down upon his folded knees and called for sleep. It came. . . .

And brought him dreams of Coyote, of Little Yellow Wolf, of Dakan-eh hunting his spirit brother in the moonlight, and of himself moving through a moonlit grove of cottonwoods. But he was not a boy in his dream; he did not walk upright. He moved through the woods on all fours, lithely, on clawed feet that were pawed and padded. He scented his surroundings through a long, slender snout while his furred, pointed ears pricked up at every sound that set the skin of the night vibrating and his own eardrums pounding. Onward he moved—slowly, not as a boy moves, not as Cha-kwena, Brother of Animals, would have moved, but as Coyote, Brother of Little Yellow Wolf—until at last he came to a place between the trees and saw what had drawn him there.

A lone coyote was hanging upside down, noosed by a hind limb, caught in a deadly tree snare that held him fast and high while Bold Man stood below. Ears back, Cha-kwena lowered his head and growled. He recognized his

spirit brother, but it was too late to save him. He felt the
pain of Dakan-eh's upward spear thrust as, without warning,
Bold Man drove his spearhead deep into the gut of the
snared coyote, twisted it, pulled back, and then drove it
deep to pierce the internal organs with a mortal wound
that would not damage the golden pelt. This he then set
himself to take for Ta-maya.

In the dream Cha-kwena howled. In the dream he
snarled and leaped at Dakan-eh. But somehow he was no
longer a coyote; he was transformed into a deer and a
hawk and every night animal that he had ever sought to
heal or comfort. In a confused flurry of wings and slashing
fangs and tearing beaks and striking hooves, he threw
himself at Dakan-eh with the intent to kill him . . . but
never reached him.

Cha-kwena awoke with a start. He was sweated and
dry mouthed, and his heart was pounding.

Loons were still calling on the lake. Moon was down.
The morning star was bright and steady above the western
buttes. He stared at it realizing that he must have been
asleep for hours.

Hoyeh-tay was beginning to stir on his mattress. The
faint glow of dawn illuminated the interior of the cave.
Cha-kwena saw that Owl had returned to his perch. One
tiny tail section of his midnight meal of mice protruded
from the side of his beak. Somewhere far beyond the cave
and the village, mammoth trumpeted to greet the onset of
morning. A lion roared.

Cha-kwena listened, breathless, waiting for the morning
barks and yaps of the little yellow wolves. But if coyotes
ran together in the predawn light of Morning Star, they
ran in silence . . . and somehow Cha-kwena knew that he
had run with them this night and that one of their number
would never run with them again.

# PART V

# LAND OF MANY MAMMOTH

# 1

"White Giant is walking somewhere out there to the south. I can *feel* it."

Standing next to Maliwal under the extended rain flap of her lodge, Ysuna showed no reaction to the man's words. "So you have assured me day after long day, night after long night. Yet there have been no sightings of mammoth as we have traveled to the south, and the sky continues to bleed rain, even though the one whom you have brought to me as a sacrifice to the god has yet to bleed at all. The moon has completed her passage from darkness into light and now begins to turn her face away from us again. When will this girl bleed so that she may be purified and offered to our totem?"

Maliwal looked worried. "Perhaps the shock of captivity has delayed her time of—"

"She vomits up her morning meals and swoons at the smell of the cooking fires!" Ysuna interrupted, her voice strained by impatience. "If she does not bleed by the time of the ebbing of the next full moon, I will know the truth—that you have brought me a pregnant liar, not a virgin fit to be a bride of Thunder in the Sky."

Lightning flared in the cloud cover to the west. It was a long, lateral veining of incandescence that stung the air and left the smell of ozone in its wake. Maliwal flinched, then squinted against the glare. Thunder followed almost instantaneously, causing the ground to shake. The track of the lightning bolt lingered in his eyes. Sleet and hail were thickening the rain now, pummeling the lodges of the People of the Watching Star, and pebbling the ground with a carpet of ice.

Maliwal barely noticed; his thoughts were in as much turmoil as the weather. Was it possible? he wondered.

Had the girl lied to him? If she had lied, he would make her regret the day that she had not been slain along with the blue-faced shaman and the rest of her people.

"As for the mammoth meat that you have stored in cache pits across the land—if the last batch is an example of the rest, it has begun to go bad. You were too quick in its preparation, Maliwal. This land of many mammoth of which you have spoken, just how far is it?" Ysuna stared off through the downpour.

Again Maliwal flinched, but this time it was against the question and the accusation that had come before it. Yes, in his haste to return to Ysuna, he had been in a hurry to prepare the meat for storage. And the band had been traveling for weeks now, moving from one cache pit and temporary hunting camp to another. But they never put enough miles between each encampment to satisfy him . . . or her.

Of course he could never tell Ysuna that she was the one who was slowing their journey to the south. She was not well; he could see fever in her eyes and worry in the drawn set of her features. And not once since his return from the far country had she called to him or Masau and commanded them to lie with her in the night. His eyes narrowed. Masau had been right: She was changing before their eyes—growing weak and old . . . and increasingly surly.

"How far?" she pressed again.

"Not far to men traveling lightly with their dogs, but very far to an entire village on the move with lodges and children and supplies to be dragged along."

The answer satisfied her. "Yes. We are many." Her eyes, scanning the encampment, narrowed thoughtfully. "It is good that you have found many mammoth in the land ahead. My people grow weary, Maliwal. The fresh meat will make them strong again."

He nodded, twitching against uneasiness. He wished that he had not exaggerated the number of mammoth that were to be found in the land that he and the others had reconnoitered. In his report to her he had put the number of animals within the herd at somewhere near ten times the number of fingers on both his hands. In truth, with the pregnant cow and the old matriarch dead, even if he counted the calves, the herd would total fewer than ten. Nevertheless, that number would make a great mound of meat—enough to last through the winter and beyond . . . or until they found the white mammoth.

"With your own eyes have you seen the great one, Maliwal?"

"No, Ysuna. I have not seen Thunder in the Sky, but the girl is sure that he is there."

She smiled. "He will live in all who eat his flesh—in me and in Masau. And in you."

"Yes, Ysuna," Maliwal agreed. Not once did he think to doubt her. When the white mammoth was slain, when all the sacred stones of the shamans of the Red World were in her hands, all that she swore would come to pass: She would regain her strength, look at him with clear eyes, and obliterate his scars to make his face whole again. Even Masau had vowed that this would be so. Mystic Warrior had seen the misery in his brother's eyes and, before setting out on a vision quest that had kept him away from his people for many days and nights, had vowed on his life that it would be so. Maliwal drew in a deep, steadying, reassuring breath of the wind and rain. Masau never lied. *Never.*

Snow fell in the high country to which Masau had traveled alone with his dog, Blood. It was said by the ancients that Thunder in the Sky and the spirits of the Four Winds drew the nourishment of life from the high places of the world, so men could commune best with them in the cold silence of the mountain snow, on the crags where eagles dwelled and could, if captured, become intermediaries between man, the sun, and the spirits.

For this reason Masau had sought the solitude of the heights. The wind and clouds and aches in an old hunting wound had warned him of the coming snow, so he was well prepared for bad weather when he left the encampment of his people. Now, as he stood on the mountainside with his dog at his feet, Masau appeared to be a creature of three species: man, animal, and bird. He was warm in a heavy traveling robe of bison hide; beneath this shaggy cloak, his body was wrapped in winter trousers and tunic of elk hide worn hair side in. His feet were encased in down-lined, trisoled moccasins. Across his upper back, the eviscerated body of a mature golden eagle lay belly down with its massive wings spread seven feet wide across his shoulders. Its clawed legs hung forward, and its head rested atop Masau's own, the beak extending over the hunter's brow. The effect was startling and magnificent.

Mystic Warrior had sought and killed the eagle during his second day upon the mountain; it had been a holy rite. Hot on the scent of badger, Blood had led him to a hollow beneath the roots of an ancient, lightning-blasted pine. Snow had not yet started to fall. Masau had eyed the tree and the surroundings and could tell that this was a place where eagles gathered. He had thanked the dog and the spirits that had led him to this spot and then, fasting, had settled in to pass the night in prayer.

The next morning he had smoked the badger from its den and speared it through the back as it had come snuffling and snarling into the cold light of dawn. This done, he had fed a small portion of the animal to Blood as reward for the dog's complicity. While the dog ate, Masau had worked to enlarge the hollow beneath the pine into a pit deep enough for a man to lie in. It was tedious labor. When he was finished, he removed all the stones, duff, and loose soil from the immediate area, hiding all beneath a nearby tangle of thornbush so no soaring eagle would notice his alterations of the landscape. Next he had felled a few saplings with his heavy stone fleshing knife, then placed them across the pit in such a way that birds in flight would see only leaves and branches. He had placed the dead badger securely atop the pile as bait and bound it fast with thongs.

Satisfied with the trap, he had raised another fire, then "bathed" himself and the dog in smoke so the scent of a predator would be taken from them. Then he had entered the pit, whistled to Blood, and after wrapping his palms with protective strips of leather, took his spear in hand. With the dog next to him within the hollow, he had lain down, adjusted the branches so that he could not be seen from above, and settled in for the wait.

Wolves had come—a mated pair. Masau, holding a snarling, slavering Blood under one strong arm lest the dog leap into a battle that it could not hope to win, had driven them off with his spear as he rose shrieking like a horror from another world.

"Find and kill your own meat!" he had called, laughing, as he watched their forms disappear across the stony slopes. "This badger's life was not taken as a lure to you."

It had taken him a while to calm the dog, but eventually Blood slept at his side. Masau lay motionless on his back, spear held upright, knees bent. He was not comfortable in the tight little hollow, but he was warm. When a light snow began to fall, only a few flakes penetrated the camouflage.

A raven was the next creature attracted to the bait. Masau had held his breath and then, soundlessly, reached up through the branches to grasp a dark stick of a leg. Taken by complete surprise, the bird cawed and shrieked and flapped its wings. Feathers flew as Masau yanked the raven into the pit. He snapped its neck and then rose to place it alongside the badger. When seen from above, the bird would appear to be feeding.

He settled back into the hollow once more. The dog relaxed again, and Masau thanked the spirits for the gift of the raven.

"Now our trap is twice baited. Our prey will see Raven enjoying a meal and come to steal it."

It had been exactly so.

The eagle had plunged with extended claws out of the clouds. It had alighted to one side of the raven, and Masau deftly snatched the eagle by both legs and pulled it down. He grasped its powerful body between his limbs and held it fast with the inward press of his thighs as his hands closed about its neck and crushed the life out of it.

Afterward, he placed the great bird upright on the ground and within a short time had put the heart of the badger and that of the raven within its golden beak. While Blood had watched, silent and perplexed, Masau had raised songs of thanksgiving to the spirit of the eagle. For hours he sang before he took the heart and eyes of the great bird and consumed them.

"May the heart of the man and the eagle be one. May they see with the same eyes across the land and sky, and may the spirit of the eagle bring down the spirits of the

Four Winds and of Thunder in the Sky . . . so they will hear and fulfill the invocations of this man."

He gutted the eagle, skinned it, and set the wondrous feathered pelt, legs and head attached, aside. He burned the flesh, releasing its power into the sky. Masau could not eat of it or feed it to the dog, for this would have been a dishonoring.

With the skin of the great bird attached to his robe and its hollow-eyed skull worn atop his head, Masau had raised a sacred fire and fasted and prayed . . . and prayed and fasted . . . through hours of daylight then darkness, through dawn and dusk, through noon and midnight—and yet he had seen no visions and had heard no spirit voices.

He scowled and squinted into the wind. More clouds were rising from the lowlands. Already it had been snowing for days. Winter had always been his enemy. If it came early this year, his people would be unable to continue their search into the Red World. If they could not find mammoth, Ysuna would die—he felt it in his bones and heart and spirit. For this reason he had come to the mountain to implore the spirits of the Four Winds to hold back the tide of winter for just a little longer, and to beseech Thunder in the Sky to manifest himself as the great white mammoth in order to be killed and to become the food of eternal life for Ysuna.

The latter premise was a new concept, and it unnerved him; but what Ysuna must have, she *would* have as long as it was within his power to secure it for her. But was it in his power? he wondered. There was a time when he would have said yes without hesitation; but now, exhausted as he was, he was no longer sure.

With a sigh that created a cloud before his face, he seated himself on a large protruding pine root just below the tree-clad summit and set himself to the task of vision seeking once more. He leaned back against a large boulder that would protect him from downdrafts from the mountaintop, then looked glumly through icicles that had formed on the beak of the eagle.

He had sworn to Maliwal that he would not return to the encampment until the weather cleared and he had experienced a vision. But the weather continued to grow worse, and the power of the eagle he had released into the wind had not convinced the spirits of Thunder in the Sky and the Four Winds to speak to him. How many invocations had he made over the past many days and nights? He had lost count. And still the weather worsened. The storm clouds were very low now and a dark, bilious yellow. *Why?* he asked himself. *Why!*

"Spirits of the Four Winds, Thunder in the Sky, my people have journeyed far across the land, but still there are no signs of mammoth or of the great white giant whose flesh must be meat for Daughter of the Sun. I, Mystic Warrior, ask you to send the meat of life to my people before it is too late for us, while there is still strength left in us!"

Suddenly his mind seemed to cut free of his body and drift away into the storm.

He gave himself freely to sensation, smiling a little, for he knew that at last it was the wind of vision that was taking him; he must yield to it or find himself back within the hollow shell of his body, earthbound and blind to the will of the spirits.

At his side, Blood looked up, whined, and rooted at his master's snowy, hide-covered thigh.

Distracted, Masau flinched, and suddenly the spirit of the Mystic Warrior plummeted through the clouds and snow to return to the body of Masau the man. He stared ahead, numb, exhausted, and unfulfilled. He was too tired to be angry with the dog for ruining that which he had been seeking for so long.

The air had turned so brutally cold that it hurt to breathe it in. The wind whistled around him and hurled hard white pebbles of snow against his robe. The past rose as a haunting within him.

*Father, please, it is cold. I did not mean to be afraid! Do not put me out of the band to die! Please!*

*You are not fit to live—you or the brother who has dared to defend you.*

*It's all right, Masau. Don't cry. Don't beg. I, Maliwal, will protect you against the storm. Let him go his way. We will survive. Someday we will find him. And when we do, he will be the one to cry and beg for mercy. But we shall give him none!*

He became aware of the distant rumbling of thunder—

but only that, no spirits, no answers, only memories that
were too bitter to hold.

The dog whined, scooted closer, and jammed its snout
up under the edge of the hunter's robe. Masau looked
down, pulled a portion of the robe over the dog, and
patted the sides of the animal. Loneliness overwhelmed
him. How long had he been out from the encampment?
How long since he had last eaten? The tight ache in the pit
of his gut and the lightness within his head told him the
answers: too many days, too many nights, and Blood had
been at his side for the duration.

"Yes, old friend," he apologized softly. "I know, it is
cold, and I am hungry, too . . . but for so much more than
meat!"

A flash of lightning illuminated the clouds directly
overhead. Thunder clashed simultaneously. Masau looked
up. The dog yelped, terrified. Another bolt followed. It
ripped through the falling snow to blast apart the tallest
pine on the summit. The hunter saw only a flash of white
incandescence as the world exploded around him, and the
impact of the lightning strike sent him sprawling into
unconsciousness. . . .

When he awoke, Blood was licking his face. His head
hurt, and his ears rang. He looked around. It was still
snowing, but the wind was down and the clouds seemed
less dense than before. He rose shakily and took up his
spear. The weapon seemed unnaturally top-heavy. Even
though gloved, his hand felt frozen within the stiff caul of
leather. Unable to close his fingers completely, he lost his
grip on the shaft. The spear fell to the snow.

He eyed it curiously. The upper half of the shaft and
the projectile point were encased in so much ice that the
spearhead was twice its normal size and length and as
translucent as pure white quartz. It was beautiful, but
Masau was not in a mood for beauty. He ached with cold.
Leaning forward, he shook himself to loosen the heavy
accumulation of snow that had fallen upon him while he
had been unconscious.

Snow sprayed from man and dog alike, but the heat of
the lightning strike had quickly melted the underlying
layer of flakes, which had frozen solid again almost
immediately. Thus, although Masau had shaken off a good

two inches of snow, the man's eagle skin and bison hide
remained stiffly rimed with ice, and Blood's fur showed
red beneath a layering of white.

Mystic Warrior's brow came down. *The colors white
on red, like the blood of a winter kill overlaid with snow.
Is there a vision in this? A vision of blood?*

He did not know the answer. Red was often the
underlying color of his visions and symbolized human
blood, the blood of the slain in the many villages that he,
Maliwal, and the men of his band had raided . . . the
blood of the many young girls who had come consenting to
their death by sacrifice.

The wind was shifting. Masau waited for the spirits to
speak and then wondered if they already had. The snowfall
was lessening, and the lightning bolt could well have been
Thunder in the Sky's tusk of fire ripping downward at the
world. But why? He was too tired to tell. Like Ysuna, he
was growing weak without the blood and flesh of a
mammoth.

In this moment bright beams of sunlight pierced the
clouds low to the west, and with their light a revelation
struck the Mystic Warrior. "Ah!" he gasped, startled. "The
colors! *They* are the vision! White on red—blood on snow!
The blood on the flesh of the great white mammoth!
Thunder in the Sky *has* spoken! The great white mammoth
*is* out there. It *will* die! For Ysuna, Thunder in the Sky
will come consenting. The god and Daughter of the Sun
*will* be one!"

He stood breathless, overcome. His enthusiasm soared,
then waned. "But how will this come to pass? Ysuna will
not be strong enough to continue traveling much longer.
She will die long before she heals my brother's scars or
finds the great white mammoth!"

The wind shifted again, gusted hard, and sent the
storm clouds streaming away to the south. *South!* With his
heart pounding, Masau knew that this, too, was a portion
of the vision. As on the day of Nai's death, as on the day of
Maliwal's return, when the spirits turned Masau's thoughts
into dreams, it was always to that portion of the world
where South Wind was born.

And now, as he stared down across the tumbled hills
to the snowy grasslands upon which his people had made

their encampment, he understood why and laughed with pure delight. He threw back his head, turned his tattooed face to the sky, and thanked the eagle and the spirits. He had not lost his powers after all! Winter may have come early to the land where Maliwal had led them, but at the base of the winter-whitened hills, a herd of mammoth was clustering around a broad, shallow lake within a grove of frost-denuded trees at the head of a dead-end canyon. Masau stared down at the gathering not two miles from the encampment. The place was a perfect killing site. The canyon was long and narrow, its neck like that of a hollow gourd; it could be easily blocked. The lake was thick with ice, its shoreline steep, the embankments treacherous with ice. He sighed in gratitude; had a mammoth hunter been allowed to choose a perfect place for a winter kill, this would be it. There was no white mammoth among the many gray cows and calves; but it was the largest herd he had seen in more moons than he would care to count— large enough to feed his people throughout the winter and for many moons to come.

"Come!" he said to the dog as he picked up his spear and jabbed the killing end of it into the snow to free it of ice. "We must tell our people what we have discovered! Tomorrow we will hunt! Tomorrow there will be the blood of mammoth in the snow! Tomorrow we will feast! Soon after we will raise a dais of their bones, and the blood of a new sacrifice will quench us all! Soon Ysuna will be well and strong, and Maliwal's face will be whole! And when the last of the winter snow has melted into the skin of the earth, we will strike out again, deeper into the Red World, to the sacred mountain where the shamans of the lizard eaters will be convening under the light of the Pinyon Moon. The great white mammoth will be there. And when we have taken the sacred stones of power, he will die and be reborn in Daughter of the Sun, as the eagle has died and been reborn in me!"

# 2

Winter came early to the Red World, but life was good in the village of Tlana-quah. The huts and storage pits were filled with meat and grains and berries. Old Hoyeh-tay was improving daily. While waterfowl rafted on islands of open water in the Lake of Many Singing Birds, animals grazed along its shore. Mammoth fed in the evergreens close to the hot spring, and now and again the tracks of a very large mammoth were seen and the people smiled with delight when they saw the little white calf grazing close to the flank of its mother. Although no one had yet sighted Life Giver, it was difficult for Tlana-quah to remain glum when both U-wa and Ha-xa informed him that they were with his child.

Now Tlana-quah shared his sleeping furs with two women, even though no official marriage ceremony had taken place; since U-wa was a widow, Ha-xa had simply extended a formal invitation to "the future mother of my husband's child," and the two had officially become "fire sisters." U-wa had packed her belongings, closed the entrance to the lodge in which she had dwelled with Nar-eh, and, after a solemn embrace from her son, said farewell to her old life.

"It is a good thing," said Ha-xa, looking at her man from beneath partially lowered eyelids. She put his right hand over her swelling belly and allowed him to feel their unborn child move as she teased him lovingly. "Two wives, both soon to be big with babies, a warm lodge full of many furs, a village full of meat . . . and a solemn headman who worries about the omens." She clucked her tongue and kissed his forehead. "Be content, man of my lodge. The spirits of the ancestors smile upon Tlana-quah, Brave

Hunter, Man Who Kills Jaguar Alone. Is it not time for you to smile back?"

"When I look upon the white mammoth, I will smile."

"Until then, I will smile for you. My life is too full of good things for me to doubt that our totem is not watching over us."

So it was that the long-unused cradleboard of choke-cherry twigs and painted antelope hide came to have a partner as it leaned upright against the headman's mattress and neatly rolled bed covers.

Tlana-quah's daughters giggled together in the night when soft, quick, breathless exhalations of amazed pleasure and long moans of ecstasy came from their father's side of the lodge.

"Maybe now that we have two mothers, one of them will give us a brother," whispered Mah-ree. She faced Ta-maya in the depth of a snowy night on their shared mattress beneath their thickly piled blankets of rabbit fur. "Ha-xa asks the spirits for a boy baby. I have heard her. And U-wa makes good sons!"

"She has but one," reminded Ta-maya softly.

"Yes. *Cha-kwena!*" Mah-ree sighed with open adoration. "He is the best of all sons!"

Ta-maya smiled at her little sister's infatuation. On their father's side of the lodge, the mounded bed furs were rising and falling to a noisy and familiar rhythm.

Mah-ree giggled again. "With or without bride gifts and wedding ceremony, I would go to Cha-kwena if he wanted me."

"I know, Mah-ree, and I will go to Dakan-eh when the time is right for us."

"Maybe our father will change his mind about you and Bold Man."

"Maybe . . ." Ta-maya yawned and nestled deeper into her bed furs. Sleepy now, she envisioned a wondrous wedding ceremony and fabulous gifts and magnificently attired guests, and an even more amazingly attired bride standing beside a befurred and befeathered Dakan-eh, who held his hands out to her and smiled as he had never smiled before. She saw herself take his hands. How warm they were! How steady, how welcoming. Imagining herself in Bold Man's arms, she sighed, and fondling the wristlet, which she had not removed since Dakan-eh had given it to her, she gave herself to her dreams. And yet, strangely, although she dreamed of a wedding, she did not dream of Dakan-eh at all.

Mah-ree lay awake beside her sleeping sister. It was quiet on her father's side of the lodge now. She listened, soothed by the sound of Tlana-quah's light snores.

A smile tugged at her mouth. This morning when she had crept from the village—as she did every morning to see if the great white mammoth had come to feed upon any of her secret offerings—the mash of ground camas and willow and the armful of sweet grass that she had stolen from Ha-xa's stores were gone. Armed against predators with a skinning knife and a fishing trident, she had knelt in the snow and laid her small hand within the enormous rounded hollow that was one of several mammoth tracks. Although her father would have said that the tracks might belong to any mammoth, her heart told her otherwise. With the exception of the two young bulls that were always seen feeding and traveling in each other's company, the mammoth herd grazed together; Grandfather of All was solitary.

Now, lying snug and warm beside her dreaming sister, Mah-ree sighed softly. *It was he. I know it!* she thought. *He is close to the village. He is grateful for the tender food offerings that I bring to him for his aching teeth. Tomorrow I will place my offerings even closer to the village. And the day after that, closer still. Soon the People will see him! Soon Tlana-quah will believe this daughter! It is because of Mah-ree that the great mammoth comes, and it is because of the great white mammoth that all is well with the people of this village! Maybe soon we will have our old shaman back, and then Cha-kwena will have time to walk and talk with me again!*

Mah-ree closed her eyes and gave herself to sleep. Unlike her sister, she dreamed of the one whom she longed to marry.

Old Hoyeh-tay was feeling so much stronger that he began a new ritual. It was simple enough: Every morning, with the aid of Cha-kwena and a stout stick of ironwood to steady his steps, the shaman came down from the cave to walk about the village. Owl perched upon his head, and Cha-kwena stayed by his side. When he grew tired, he would sit wherever he happened to be, and if the weather allowed, the old widows would raise a fire to warm his bones. The women would bring him good things to eat and drink, and mothers would tell their children to gather around him so that he could tell them the stories of the People and the ancestors.

"Hurry!"

"Go!"

"Sit with Shaman!"

"Why do you hang back?" Siwi-ni waved an admonishing finger at her four little sons as she watched the other women hurry their children off. She was so enormously pregnant that she could not raise herself from the pile of furs that Kosar-eh had arranged for her in the sunshine just outside their lodge. "Go, I say! Gah-ti, you are eldest. Take your brothers off and let your mother rest here while you listen to our shaman speak. There is much that you can learn from him."

Gah-ti pouted. "When Hoyeh-tay's spirit goes to walk the wind, Cha-kwena will tell the stories, and Cha-kwena will not forget when he is halfway through a tale and start all over again."

"I would rather listen to my father's stories. Kosar-eh makes us laugh!" Gah-ti's younger brother said.

"So does Hoyeh-tay when he starts talking to Owl and to people who aren't even here!" Gah-ti said with a sneer.

"Enough!" snapped Siwi-ni. "You must show respect for his age and sympathy for his illness. The son of U-wa is but a youth. His experiences and knowledge combine to make him like a tight springtime bud. He may be full of promise, but he's not a flower yet. Hoyeh-tay is like a winter flower—fully opened, every petal unfurled to the last warm rays of the sun and—"

"And beginning to turn brown and go to seed!" interrupted the boy. He followed the comment with high guffaws in appreciation of his own humor.

Siwi-ni was not impressed. "So you will be a clown like your father, eh? Time will tell. But now you will listen to Hoyeh-tay. He alone can tell you how things used to be when he was your age, and of how things have changed since the days of his grandfathers. Once, long ago, our shaman hunted the great horn-nosed pig and walked a world that was filled with lions and jaguars and giant armadillos and mastodons and beavers as big as men. There were three kinds of pronghorns and as many different kinds of camels and so many mammoth that they were as numerous as long-horned bison. But who sees many of them these days, eh?"

"Where did all these animals go, Mother? Why don't we see them anymore?"

"Ask Hoyeh-tay. Shaman can tell you of the great scoop-nosed bear that was bigger than a grizzly and could run down a horse. And of the giant teratorn, a bird bigger than a condor, and an eater of little boys who will not heed the advice of their mothers when they are told to listen to the stories of their elders!"

"Off! Obey your mother!" It was Kosar-eh.

She smiled up at him. "Help me to my feet so that I, too, may hear Shaman's stories."

Kosar-eh scooped her up in his one strong arm and, using the crippled one for balance, carried her to the circle of children where the old man was already engrossed in the story of how he had caused the water to return to Big Lake. They sat together, the little pregnant woman on the big clown's lap, engrossed in the story until other members of the band began to join in the circle. Then the clown's eyes moved to Ta-maya, and the expression on his scarred, unpainted face was one of such love and longing that Siwi-ni could not resist elbowing him in the gut.

"Ow!" exclaimed the clown, startled by the unexpected pain.

"Ow!" echoed Siwi-ni, but not in any mocking echo of her man. At last, suddenly and appallingly intense, her labor pains had begun. In pure reflex action, she found the strength and balance to leap to her feet and stand tottering, grasping her belly.

Everyone was staring wide-eyed with incredulity at her.

Siwi-ni stared back. Kosar-eh was on his feet, steadying her, but when she saw old Hoyeh-tay approaching her solemnly with Owl on his head, she nearly screamed. The

scrawny old man looked on the verge of death. She recoiled,
not wanting to be touched by him.

Nevertheless she was touched. The old man's right
hand shot forward. Palm down, fingers wide, it lay
questioningly upon her belly.

"No!" she cried. "Go away! You can do nothing for
me!"

His eyes narrowed. He stood taller, and his head
went high. "I am Shaman. You must not fear me, woman
of Kosar-eh. My spirit is back in my own skin now. I know
who I am and where I am, and I know what you need."

At Hoyeh-tay's command Kosar-eh stepped aside and
allowed the old widows to take Siwi-ni by the arms and
escort her into the birth hut that had been raised in
anticipation of Siwi-ni's delivery.

"Come, Cha-kwena!" Hoyeh-tay commanded, openly
annoyed and in absolute authority. "There are things that
we must do!"

As Cha-kwena followed in stunned amazement a new
Hoyeh-tay backhanded his way through the crowd and
stalked furiously across the village, leaving everyone gaping
after him as Owl fought and lost the battle to maintain
balance atop his head. With never a slip or a backward
glance, Hoyeh-tay pounded the snowy ground with his
ironwood staff and boldly stomped and sloshed across the
icy creek on the way to his cave.

"Grandfather! Wait! Let me help you! You will fall
and injure yourself."

"Bah! Can't wait! Won't fall!" Hoyeh-tay called back
without slowing his step or turning around. "There are
things to be done! New life is coming!"

Gasping for breath, Cha-kwena went up the stone
steps and caught up with his grandfather in the cave just
in time to see the old man grab his medicine bag and
snatch up a square of fur that he kept rolled up at the back
of the cave. Owl, clearly miffed, was on his perch with his
back turned to the both of them.

"Grandfather, wait!"

Hoyeh-tay was across the cave and heading for the
steps again. "Come, Cha-kwena! The baby will not wait."

Somehow they were across the creek and—with Cha-kwena soaked to the thighs and rubbing his right knee after a particularly nasty and embarrassing slip—they were back across the village and standing before the small hut into which the widows had brought Siwi-ni.

"Now behold, Cha-kwena. This is the role of Shaman when a woman of the People is called to bring forth new life!"

As all the members of the band—except Siwi-ni and the midwives—gathered to watch, Cha-kwena saw Hoyeh-tay unroll the fur that he had brought from the cave and lay it with great reverence upon the ground just outside the entrance to the birth hut.

"Cha-kwena, observe the alignment of the calling-upon-the-favor-of-the-spirits-for-the-good-of-the-mother blanket! It is made from strips of fur and hide taken from all the animals that are food for the People. Before a shaman seats himself upon it, he must thank the spirits of those creatures, and he must be certain that the corners of the blanket point to the north, south, east, and west."

These things done, Hoyeh-tay then sighed and settled himself, limbs crossed and hands resting upon his knees, to face the entrance to the birth hut. Exhalations of concern and wonderment went up from the people at Hoyeh-tay's back as he opened his medicine bag and withdrew many talismans of magic. One by one he laid them out: a rabbit's foot; an antelope's hoof; a dried, flattened frog; an equally desiccated toad and lizard; the claws and beaks of birds; a few oddly shaped pebbles; the feather of a hawk; a quill filled with pollen; and an eagle-bone whistle.

"Behold!" Hoyeh-tay took up the whistle and carefully emptied the contents of the quill into it. He held the whistle in both hands, moved it in the four directions from which the winds of life came to the People, and then blew through it strongly, releasing a spray of pollen that fell as a golden rain onto the closed entrance of the hut of birth.

"Let the pollen of life fly upon the Four Winds of the Red World and bring life to the child of Kosar-eh and Siwi-ni!"

Cha-kwena had never seen the old man in better form. The youth smiled; it was a warm, glowing, ear-to-ear smile generated by pride in his grandfather and by relief that the spirit of the shaman was back inside the old man's skin once more. Hoyeh-tay began to chant, and the People kept the rhythm. The youth stomped his feet and clapped his hands as loudly as any person in the band. He shouted the syllables of affirmation, not only of the old man's song but of what he knew must now be his own reprieve from the unwanted and long-lamented journey along the road of the shaman's way: "Hay yah hay!"

On and on went the song of the shaman, expanding, contracting, then swelling to pound the air with a sound that was that of a heart beating strong and sure. Then, suddenly, the old man's voice cracked, and with a gasp of despair, he reached out with a shaking hand for Cha-kwena.

"Come!" cried Hoyeh-tay. "My spirit weakens! Come, quickly! Join me upon the sacred blanket! Take up the rhythm of life that is the heartbeat of the world! Do not hesitate! The life of Siwi-ni and her baby depend upon our combined strength of will and power! You must become a shaman now!"

Cha-kwena's smile dissolved. He was horrified. To chant now would be an open consent to his role as shaman! Nothing would ever be the same for him. And yet, if the old man was right about the lives of Siwi-ni and her unborn baby depending upon him, how could he refuse?

"Cha-kwena! Chant!" implored Hoyeh-tay, still reaching shakily for his grandson's hand. "For the life of the child, chant! For the mother of the child, chant! For all that you will and must be, chant! I can no longer do this alone!"

A scream of agony from inside the birth hut jolted Cha-kwena into obedience.

He took his grandfather's hand. He went to his knees on the sacred blanket. He chanted. He raised his voice to the spirits of the night, and they came to him as a benediction. Calmness replaced turmoil in his soul. He sang, and his voice was the voice of a stranger . . . of a man who knew that nothing would ever be the same. He *was* a shaman now.

Within the hut of birth the woman of Kosar-eh gripped the birth pole. On her knees and strengthened by the chanting that was being raised to the spirits on her behalf, Siwi-ni gave a mighty push.

"It is good!" exclaimed Kahm-ree, bending forward as

she reached to cup the head of the infant so that she might guide its passage into the world. "Aieee, yes! It is very good!" she exclaimed again as the baby surged out of the mother on a hot tide of blood and fluid. "Another son for Kosar-eh!"

The midwives sighed and leaned close and nodded with approval.

"Look what a fine boy he is, Siwi-ni!" said Xi-ahtli.

Siwi-ni, sagging around the birth pole, held on tight and closed her eyes, listening to the old women as they praised her infant and exchanged stories about their own birthings. No one had suffered more than any of them. No one had endured longer labors. No one. Ever. In the history of the Red World since time beyond beginning.

With a grunt of annoyance, Siwi-ni looked up and asked to see her newest son—another fine, handsome, strong-lunged son for Kosar-eh. She smiled as he bawled and peed and clenched his tiny fists.

"Bring to me what I must have to cleanse him," she requested as, with gentle fingers, she checked his body for blemishes. Finding none, she rubbed him dry with her hair.

Siwi-ni cleansed her infant's navel with the powdery spores of a dried puffball, then put his umbilical cord into one of two identical little leather bags, each cut and fashioned to resemble a tortoise—one bag to hide his umbilicus from evil spirits, the other to draw the bad spirits to it, so that they might be trapped and burned and thus kept away from him forever.

"You must hide the good spirit bag and burn the other," Kham-ree reminded. "Then he will live as long as a tortoise and become as wise and inured to the hardships of life!"

"Look here. We have raised the little fire," added Xi-ahtli. "It is ready. Come. The empty bag must be burned before the evil spirits know of how we would trick them."

Siwi-ni nodded; they were right of course, but suddenly the sweet exhaustion that was the aftermath of a successful birth was upon her, and she set the bags aside. "Yes, in a moment." She would savor the pleasure of holding her little one for just a breath or two more of time. Life was good in the village by the Lake of Many Singing Birds. Whatever evil spirits might be looking for her son, surely they could not be near.

# 3

Smokes were raised in the sweat lodge of the encampment of the People of the Watching Star. The men came together to purify their bodies and their spirits. They fasted. They prayed. They invoked the blessings of Daughter of the Sun. Only then did they loose their dogs, take up their spears and hunting kits, and go forth to hunt the mammoth that Masau had seen from the mountain.

"Soon now you will become a bride," Ysuna said to Lah-ri, the little sister of Sunam-tu. The two females stood together at the edge of the encampment and watched the men and dogs disappear across the snow-covered hill. "When the mammoth have been slain, we will raise the ceremonial dais of their bones. But first you must be purified. First you must—"

"Why must you hunt them?" interrupted the girl.

"Their flesh is the blood of life to us, as it will be to you, also."

"The meat of mammoth is forbidden to the People of the Red World."

"So I have heard. But are you not *our* sister now, a sister of the People of the Watching Star? And would you not have this greatest of all gifts from us—the blood and flesh of our totem?"

"I . . . yes . . . if it would please you. But you have all been so kind to me and have given so many gifts to me already, I would go to Maliwal now and be his bride this very day. There is no need for him to risk himself hunting mammoth for me."

"He must. It is our way."

"But there is much other game available—small game, safe to hunt. I have seen much meat on the hoof and wing and paw as we have traveled southward."

"What meat would you prefer? Would you have the men of the People of the Watching Star hunt lizards and grubs for you, or weak-spirited antelope that often fall dead from the terror of the chase before a spear has even touched them? Or do you have a taste for brainless rabbits and muck-eating water birds? Word has come to me that before you at last entered the hut of blood, you set snares for ground squirrels and ate of that which is fit only for coyotes and badgers and foxes."

Taken aback by the unmistakable contempt that had flattened the usually mellifluous voice of the high priestess, Lah-ri gaped. "I— I—" she stammered, unable to form the words. She was stunned that someone had seen her at her squirrel traps and reported this to Ysuna. Had the high priestess also been informed of her recent act of deception within the hut of blood? No, it could not be! She had been so careful for the two moons she had not shed a woman's blood. No one could have seen her substitute the blood of a dead ground squirrel for her own nonexistent menstrual flow.

A muscle working high at Ysuna's jaw emphasized the increasing gauntness of the priestess's features. "Weakness, fearfulness, and unwillingness to risk pain or death for the sake of one's own are not qualities to admire in men or animals. That which we take into our bodies to nourish us is what we become. Men who eat lizards *are* lizards. Men who eat grubs *are* grubs. Men who eat antelope and rabbit are fearful creatures who flee from every shadow and from those more fit to survive than they. You have chosen wisely in Maliwal, Little Sister. He is fearless."

Lah-ri forced a smile. She could not tell Ysuna that she found Maliwal repugnant. The scars on his face were nothing when compared with the wound at the side of his head where his ear had once been; it still stank of flesh that would not fully heal. And yet she bore his presence bravely and even eagerly, for never in her life had Lah-ri been treated as well as in this encampment of strangers.

Yet how long could it last if she did not soon become a bride?

Now, standing in all of her new finery, the little sister of Sunam-tu lifted her chin and tried not to look worried. The other captive women were all dead now, save for one poor, mad-eyed girl. Now that the men of the tribe had tired of using her, she wandered the encampment scavenging for scraps of food. There was no lodge within which she was welcome. Ysuna had assured Lah-ri that the girl would die soon, that death was all she deserved since she had not been wise enough to ingratiate herself to even one among those who had been "caring" enough to bring her into their encampment and offer her a new life.

Lah-ri looked up at the priestess now. Ysuna did not look well, but she was still mesmerically beautiful in her long white robe of winter furs and feathers. Her skin was translucent in the cool light of morning, her eyes dark and steady, her mouth long and full and bent upward into a smile of loving radiance as she met Lah-ri's gaze. She enfolded her new little sister within the bend of one long, slender arm.

"Do I see worry in your eyes?" asked the priestess. "Ah, of course. You fear that Maliwal will come to harm during the mammoth hunt and leave this world without you—and you still a virgin who has had no knowledge of his body! You have not had knowledge of his body, have you?"

"No!" Lah-ri exclaimed. This was not the first time that Ysuna had pressed her on this point; why was it so important? She had not lain with Maliwal, but in a moment of supreme idiocy she *had* prayed to the spirits of the Four Winds that he would die on the hunt. Yet even as she had completed the prayer she had drawn it back, repentant and more than a little frightened as she begged the Four Winds to forget that they had ever heard her form such foolish words. She must marry him soon, she knew, before her pregnancy became obvious to all. These People of the Watching Star seemed unreasonably preoccupied with her virginity. Once it was apparent to them that she was carrying a child, they probably would no longer consider her a worthy bride. What would happen to her then, she wondered, after they realized that she had lied to them?

Would they send her away unprotected to walk the winter world alone? Or would they turn their backs upon her as they had the other captives, condemning her to death by starvation?

Lah-ri drew in a deep, steadying breath. As long as Maliwal returned safely from the mammoth hunt, everything would be all right. They would join together as man and woman, and he would never know that the child that she had been unable to expel from her womb with the usual herbal purgatives was not of his making.

She swallowed down her apprehension and looked up at Ysuna. "Maliwal has become so dear to me, I cannot wait until we become one. I so want to be a daughter of your people."

Ysuna's brows expanded outward across her forehead. "Do not worry, dear one. If the spirits do not choose to smile upon Maliwal and he fails to return, you will never want for anything as long as you live among my people. I have another son. Masau will take you as his bride."

Lah-ri's mouth dropped open. "Masau?" She was as terrified of him as she was fascinated by him; with his flowing hair and tattooed face and a body that moved like a cougar's, he was the most beautiful and physically exciting man she had ever seen. He had only to look her way, and her loins went hot and moist with longing. Again she secretly wished for Maliwal's death. "Oh, Ysuna, Masau would not want such a girl as I . . . would he?"

Ysuna laughed; it was a low, deep, throaty purr.

Lah-ri frowned, disconcerted. Lions purred like that, and lions were dangerous.

Ysuna saw the girl's reaction. "Have I upset you, dear? That is the last thing that I would wish!" She drew the girl closer, hugged her, and rubbed her shoulder in an open display of affection. "You are such a pretty little thing, so tender, so trusting. How glad I am that we are sisters now!"

The hug and compliment and warm reassurances relaxed Lah-ri; she sighed, content to be in Ysuna's embrace. "I am also glad!"

"Of course you are, and so you shall continue to be . . . as long as you live among the People of the Watching Star."

*     *     *

After reconnoitering the killing site and preparing it and themselves for the task ahead, the hunters divided into two main groups. Maliwal led one contingent, Masau the other. There were trees to cut and shrubbery to drag to the neck of the canyon, then kindling for fires to prepare. They worked in absolute silence, and when at last they were ready to begin the hunt in earnest, they moved in stealth, concealing themselves within a favoring wind, and kept muzzles on their dogs.

Snow was falling when Masau's group took its position upon the heights of the canyon walls and looked down to see the mammoth still grazing peacefully below the cliffs. The hunters removed the muzzles from the dogs, and as the animals caught the scent of mammoth, they barked and raced back and forth in a frenzy. The men hurled stones, spears, and flaming brands upon their startled prey.

Slipping and falling along the steep, snow-covered shoreline of the nearby lake, nearly half the herd fled in blind panic into the imagined safety of the lake and plunged into icy shallows or deep sink holes. The water was bitterly cold. Although strong swimmers by nature, the mammoth were quickly disoriented by the onset of hypothermia. Those animals that were not severely injured—or hopelessly mired in the ooze of a lake bottom thick with a sediment created by thousands of years of Ice Age erosion—tried to clamber back up the treacherous slopes. But their massive feet could find no purchase on the slick and icy surface of the shore. Even though they tried desperately to help one another, they slid, trunks entwined, calves bawling, cows trumpeting in confusion, back into the lake.

Trapped within the ice-thick water as a subfreezing wind blew hard out of the north, the mammoth circled for protection under a rain of spears. Old cows, outraged and in pain, flanked the calves. The injured beasts trumpeted and brayed in bewilderment as the hunters' dogs barked and snarled. The men called to the trapped and wounded animals from the cliffs, asking them to yield their spirits quickly to those who would honor their flesh by consuming it.

Meanwhile, the remainder of the herd had turned

and run for the neck of the canyon and thundered through to safety as Maliwal and his fellow hunters cheered and goaded them on from the heights.

"Go! Perhaps we will kill you another day!" cried Maliwal.

At the signal of his raised arm, those under his command hastily blocked the narrow entrance to the canyon with the young trees and thick piles of shrubbery that they had hacked down and dragged there for this purpose.

Maliwal nodded, satisfied. "When the mammoth turn back at the sound of their herd mates being slaughtered, this should keep them away. Make certain that the sharpened ends of the largest cottonwoods are facing outward and that the butt ends are well braced. If they still come, we will fire the scrub growth."

It would burn high despite the cold, he knew, for the hunters had underlaid it with kindling brought from the encampment and greased with oil and fat. If any mammoth dared to test the flames, they would meet the pointed ends of the braced trees and back off or be impaled through the chest and stomach, where their hide was thinnest. It was an old and well-tested hunting strategy.

"Keep to high ground," Maliwal ordered his men, "and when the mammoth come, be ready to place your spears well. Use your spear hurlers for added impact." His face contorted. "I want to see as many dead, maimed, and wounded mammoth as the spirits will allow!"

Maliwal was not disappointed. It had been years since the hunters of the People of the Watching Star had killed or wounded so many mammoth. Two mature cows, an adolescent bull, and three calves were slain at the neck of the canyon; ten more animals were killed in the lake. All but two could be butchered in the shallows, where their bodies were not entirely underwater.

A hugely pregnant cow with a broken hind limb had somehow managed to climb out of the water and stagger through the canyon in an attempt to follow those who had fled ahead of her. Hobbling now, her body riddled with spears, she finally sank to her knees to avoid further spear thrusts to the belly from the hunters who feinted in and out. Using their thrusting spears, the men tested their courage, timing their inward rushes in anticipation of the movement of her great head.

"Leave her!" commanded Maliwal.

His dogs and half a dozen others were on her back, savaging her. She was too weak to rise or to shake them off, and although she could lift her head, she did not possess enough strength to turn it far enough around to dislodge them with either her trunk or tusks.

Maliwal smiled. His hand strayed to touch his scars. He owed her kind a brutal killing that would satisfy his need for vengeance. The others stepped back as he advanced. The cow was weak and near to death, yet there was still enough life in her to present a threat to a man who faced her head-on. Maliwal was still smiling as he hefted a spear and, fitting it into his spear hurler, levered it upon his shoulder.

"Give me a thrusting spear," he demanded of Chudeh.

The man complied at once.

Now, as Maliwal saw Masau approaching the killing site from behind the downed mammoth, he held his stone-headed hurling spear in his right hand and raised his thrusting spear in his left as he shouted to his brother. "When I give the word, Masau, place a spear high at her back, behind the ear if you can. I will do the rest!"

Masau did not hesitate. They had challenged each other with this approach to a kill before—Ysuna had taught them the way of it.

"Now!" cried Maliwal.

Masau's spear flew. Impelled forward with the added strength of his spear hurler, the spear arced high and sang as it flew to its target. There was a *thunk* when it struck, and with a scream of pain and surprise, the mammoth threw her head back in agony.

In that moment Maliwal released his throwing spear, and even before the long, leaf-shaped projectile point of black obsidian pierced the mammoth's skin and carried the spear through hide and muscle and straight into the foot-long heart of the beast, the crazed hunter was howling, running to drive the second, shorter spear into the throat of the mammoth. He put all his weight against it, and then, in the second before she collapsed onto her side and died, he leaped away to stand triumphant before her.

*     *     *

An occasional rumbling of thunder was heard in the heavy snow clouds that had settled over the mountains as the men readied their butchering tools. Maliwal announced to all that since he had made the killing thrust, he claimed the honor of taking the heart and the fetus of the dead cow. With one of several palm-sized, bifaced butchering blades in hand, he set to work opening the belly, from the genitals to the rib cage. He changed stones whenever one became dull, and wiped the blades often to keep them from becoming bound up with excess tissue. Masau and Chudeh assisted by holding the incision open so that Maliwal could continue cutting back and forth. Six changes of stone blades were required before the thick, tough hide was laid wide.

Now, in a reverent conjoining, the hunters took turns dipping their hands into the wound and still-hot blood of the first kill that would be butchered this day.

"I told you that we would find many mammoth in the south!" proclaimed Maliwal with bold ferocity. "Many kills! Much meat and marrow and bone and blood for the People of the Watching Star!"

Masau looked closely at Maliwal; his brother's proclamation had been shouted in the way of one who has found need to cast aside earlier doubts.

"I will present the heart of the fetus to Ysuna!" Maliwal continued. "It is the promise of life coming forth from our totem and of life everlasting in our totem!"

"Two of the mammoth that lie dead in the lake were also pregnant!" announced Chudeh. "A good omen!"

"Yes," Maliwal agreed. "We will all eat of the meat of the unborn—of the future and all that is good. And Ysuna will eat and be strong! The bones of our many kills will be stripped and raised to form the dais. We will feast, and the sacrifice will be made, the bride given to Thunder in the Sky, who speaks in the mountains even now to affirm that what we have done this day is pleasing to him!"

And so Maliwal took the heart of the unborn mammoth and, with his dogs and several other hunters, jogged back to the encampment to announce the success of the hunt. He and the others sang as they went.

Soon he returned to the killing site with the women and children. His men carried Daughter of the Sun on a platform of mammoth bones and hide. Lah-ri, radiant in the knowledge that she was soon to become a bride, walked wide-eyed and jubilant beside Maliwal.

A butchering camp was set up in the snow, with lean-tos raised against the weather. Fires inside the shelters warmed the workers when they had need to come in out of the wind to rest.

The People did not roast the meat of the unborn mammoth. It was too choice, too pale and tender for that. They sliced pink steaks straight from the flanks and bellies of the fetuses pulled from the dead cows and gulped the warm, raw meat while it steamed in the cold air.

"Here, Bride. You must eat of the meat of your totem."

Lah-ri stared up at her man-to-be and tried not to vomit in his outstretched hands. She succeeded . . . barely. She accepted the meat he offered and ate a mouthful—no more than that. "It is unfamiliar to me, forbidden by my people. Please do not make me eat more of it."

He was grinning at her. His formerly wide, white smile was crooked now, distorted by the scars that maimed the corner of his mouth. "As long as you have eaten, it does not matter how much—it is enough," he said.

For days they feasted. And between the feasting they worked together, butchering, skinning, and extracting sinew from flesh and marrow from bones. The snow turned red with blood. They stuffed themselves with meat as they labored, and they thanked the wind spirits for bringing an early winter, for they could walk across the frozen lake and drag their precious bounty from the half-submerged carcasses upon sledges that made hauling easy. When dark came down, they feasted again and wagered among themselves who could eat the most meat. Maliwal held the record with ten pounds of raw steak and three more of liver and kidney consumed at one sitting until he lay back, groaning and belching with delight in his accomplishment. Children came forth to massage his belly, while the women sang songs of praise to his gluttony. Lah-ri stared, appalled, and tried—but failed—to take pride in one who would be her man.

Soon the usable portions of the slaughtered mammoth were dragged back to the main encampment. Meat, sinew, and fat were prepared for storage. The bones lay piled about the area in great tangled walls, and the skulls of the butchered animals were placed in a circle to touch tusks and stare at one another out of hollow eye sockets beneath the cold wedge of a winter moon.

Gradually the skies cleared. From the center of the circle of skulls, Ysuna stood in the path of shifting wind and observed the movement of the clouds, sun, moon, and stars. She remained distant and pale and silent despite the meat and blood of mammoth she had consumed. Not once did she call to her sons to come to her for pleasure in the night.

When three women separated themselves from the other members of the band and retired into the privacy of a small lean-to where they shed their moon blood, Ysuna commanded that a lodge be raised for her out of mammoth bones and hide. Into this she retreated for four days and nights of fasting. At dawn of the fifth day, when the morning star stood clear and bright above the western horizon, she emerged from the lodge and appeared even paler than before. Women hurried forth to attend her and to burn the skins onto which she had shed her cyclical blood; it was a small fire. She stood over it and grimly watched it burn.

After that, she called for meat and the heated blood of mammoth to nourish her. At last she walked through the butchering camp and entered the circle of skulls.

"Come!" she summoned her people. "Ysuna, Daughter of the Sun, has dreamed the dreams of vision! Thunder in the Sky, Grandfather of the People, White Giant, and totem of our ancestors has spoken to me! Thunder in the Sky smiles upon the flesh of the virgin who will be Maliwal's consenting bride."

All eyes went to the little sister of Sunam-tu.

"Thunder in the Sky looks with favor upon your presence among us and would have you consecrated to his name," Ysuna told her. "Will you come consenting?"

"I will," the girl responded, then smiled—less with gladness than with relief; under her smooth dress of fringed and beaded elkskin, a hard, elongated bulge had formed above her pubic bone, and her breasts were swelling as alarmingly fast as her waistline was expanding; it would be impossible to hide her pregnancy much longer. "Gladly will I come consenting to my wedding! And soon!" she added, and meant every word.

Ysuna's head went high. "Good," she said, and smiled for the first time in many days.

Now Lah-ri was drawn close into the inner circle of the women. They could not seem to have enough of her company. They touched her often, as though mere contact with her flesh would bring them favor from their totem. They put their babies into her arms and set their children on her lap. They shared their inner thoughts and most secret desires and told her that when the time came she must intercede on their behalf with the spirits of the ancestors because on the day that she became "the bride," she would have inordinate power.

"Truly?" she asked.

"Oh, yes," they assured, and mixed the blood of mammoth into her water flask, then urged her to drink deeply of it and often, for the potion would sweeten her flesh and make her pleasing to her new totem. She drank to make them happy. But when they brought her the meat of the mammoth, she remembered the way in which the fetuses had been pulled from their mothers and, secretly empathizing, could not eat. No one seemed to mind.

They were all so solicitous, so concerned for her well-being. Maliwal, slower of foot than he had been before his orgies of eating, nevertheless went out of the encampment and, to her amazement, ran down and killed with his bare hands a pair of small, dog-sized pronghorns and offered them to her.

"So the bride will not be weak with hunger when she enters upon her fast and days of purification . . . so the bride will be strong and steady of heart on the day of her wedding!"

The women would not allow her to prepare the meat. They took the little pronghorns from Maliwal and eagerly gutted and singed them. Then they stuffed the body cavities with sage and juniper berries before trussing and roasting them until their juices ran clear and the joint bones turned and came apart in the sockets.

"You are all so kind!" she declared as Maliwal brought her the meat on a platter of mammoth bone and watched her, smiling his ugly smile, as she consumed it.

"Yes, eat!" he urged. "Eat all that you can so that you will come well nourished and sleek of flesh and spirit to the hut of purification and the fast that you will endure within it. Eat! It will be your last meal . . . before you become a bride."

"Will the wedding be soon?"

"At dawn tomorrow you will begin your fast. After four days—one day to honor each of the Four Winds—you will become a bride."

Even as Maliwal spoke Ysuna stood alone within the circle of skulls and gestured to Masau to come to her.

"Sharpen your spear and prepare your ritual garments," she told him. "Tonight you will not eat or drink. Tonight you will stand with me beneath the light of the Watching Star. Tonight we will face to the north and give homage to the ancestors. At dawn we will turn to the Morning Star, the star of the future."

Masau nodded, well aware of the procedure.

"When the girl enters the lodge of purification tomorrow," Ysuna went on, "Maliwal will begin his fast, and you will guide the others in the raising of the dais and of the thunder drums. Now it is time for Daughter of the Sun to prepare herself. Soon I must ready the bride for sacrifice. Before we journey farther south, Thunder in the Sky must have the flesh of one of our own."

"Journey farther south? In the dead of winter? And leave a camp full of meat?"

"It is not the meat of the white mammoth."

"It is meat enough!"

"It is mammoth meat, but only that. It is no longer enough for me. It is not what I need." She looked deeply into his eyes. "Would you deny me what I need, Masau?"

He stared. In the cold light of the winter day, she was more beautiful than the light of the distant sun. And yet he saw the gauntness of her features and the fever in her eyes. "I would deny you nothing, Ysuna—nothing!"

"Then do as I say, Mystic Warrior. Do not challenge me again. When the sacrifice is made we will move south. The white mammoth, Thunder in the Sky, is waiting for us."

# 4

The meadow where summer's roses had grown was white and hushed now by early-winter stillness. A lone coyote hunted in the light of dawn, stalking nonhibernating ground squirrels, leaping onto the tops of their burrows, and dancing around them until the earth trembled and the rodents, curious, came up to investigate. That was a mistake—Coyote was waiting to pounce.

Unseen behind a snow-dusted thornbush, Cha-kwena leaned upon his spear and stood with his arm linked supportively through old Hoyeh-tay's. They silently watched the little yellow wolf devour its morning meal, and Cha-kwena wondered if this was the same animal that had once called to him and named him Brother. One step into the light of morning gave him his answer; the coyote stiffened, stared, then—with what was left of the ground squirrel still in its jaws—bolted across the meadow toward the cedar grove at the crest of the incline.

Cha-kwena felt a pang of disappointment and distress. Since the night that he had dreamed of himself as a coyote and had imagined one of his brothers slain and butchered by Dakan-eh, Coyote had not called to him or spoken his name.

"Cha-kwena, come. Let ush not linger here. I would resht and dream in the shadow of the shaycred juniper and walk one more time to the overlook above the shaycred shalt shpring before I die."

"You are not dying, Grandfather," replied Cha-kwena. He did not flinch against the lie; he spoke it too often these days, even though he and the old man knew it was wishful thinking.

"Shoon," said the old man with a sigh of resignation. "Shoon."

On Hoyeh-tay's fur-clad shoulder, Owl blinked and shivered. When he ruffled his feathers against the chill air of morning, several fluffs of down and a single flight feather wafted outward and then to the ground.

Cha-kwena stared down at the feathers in the snow and tensed against a coldness that had nothing to do with the early-winter morning—the bird was molting at the wrong time of year. There were bald patches on Owl's chest, and he looked nearly as scrawny as the old man these days. Since the birth of Siwi-ni's baby, Hoyeh-tay had been very ill, and Owl had not left the cave to hunt. He had perched upon the old man's blanketed toes or, when Hoyeh-tay lay upon his belly or side, on his head. Sometimes, as though the old man were a nestling to be kept warm and protected, Owl settled on his master's chest and spread his wings wide. Unaware of Owl's presence, Hoyeh-tay had slept and dreamed troubled dreams from which his grandson had been unable to rouse him, even though the youth had folded the old shaman's gnarled hands around the sacred stone and chanted every chant that Hoyeh-tay had ever taught him, and dozens of others that he made up as he went along.

Kosar-eh had come to him. "I can help you, Cha-kwena."

"Go away. You cannot cheer me now, Clown."

"No, but I can teach you how to cheer the People, how to give them heart in times like these. Have you forgotten that I, too, have been among the shamans of the Blue Mesas? I, too, have learned from them. Though your spirit bleeds with worry over your grandfather, now is not the time to brood and make chants of sadness. Now is the time to dance, paint your body, beat the drums, shake the rattles, and shout the songs. Now is the time to make smokes that will fill and rise beyond this cave into the winter sky so that when the People look to you, they will know that you are doing battle with the spirits for the life-force of your grandfather. Whether you win or lose is

not important. What matters is that the People know that
you are fighting, doing something—*anything*—in the face
of the inevitable death that must come to us all. The
functions of the clown and the shaman are much the same.
The clown's task in life is to distract his people with
laughter, while the magic man makes them feel less
vulnerable to forces they cannot change. If you can do
that, Cha-kwena, then truly will you be able to work the
most powerful and efficacious magic of all—you will give
to the People the gift of hope . . . as Hoyeh-tay has done,
and as countless generations of your ancestors have done
since time beyond beginning."

Now, standing with Hoyeh-tay in the dawn of this
cold winter day and staring at the feathers in the snow,
Cha-kwena was overcome by memories. One by one the
men of the band had visited the old shaman in his cave
and made what they had thought to be their final farewells.
They had observed the young shaman at his singing and
dancing and sacred-smoke making. If they found him
bumbling and inept, they were kind enough not to say so,
but he had seen the questions and worry in their eyes.

"Help me, Tlana-quah! I don't know what to do for
him!" Cha-kwena, desperate, had implored.

"Do as you are doing—as Old Owl and the shamans of
the Blue Mesas have taught you. No one can ask more of
you," the headman had replied somberly, then gone his
way, his shoulders hunched under the fall of his jaguar-
skin cape.

Afterward the women had come with food and broth,
and U-wa had brought the healing herbs for which Cha-
kwena had asked.

"Be strong, my son," she encouraged. "Whatever
happens, the spirits of the ancestors are smiling upon
you."

"Are they, Mother? I feel as though I have been
given a shirt that is too big for me."

"Cha-kwena, you are the son of Nar-eh, and the
grandson of generations of shamans before him. Listen to
your blood, Cha-kwena, and you will know what to do.
You will soon fill your grandfather's shirt. In time you will
even come to be comfortable in it."

"I will wear it only because I must. I will never be comfortable in it."

He shivered again and half closed his eyes, remembering now how the youths of the band had come in silence to offer their respects to the old shaman. He had turned his back upon his boyhood friends when he had seen awe and envy in their eyes. *Awe!* Of *him!* *Envy!* Of one who had been called to that which he abhorred. Gladly would he have changed places with them in that moment, for he had known then that the friendship they had once shared was ended forever. He was a shaman now! A man apart. A man alone. A man with the responsibilities of the ages upon his back.

Cha-kwena remained lost in thought as Hoyeh-tay sagged against his side and took hold of his arm. The youth barely felt the press of the old man's grip as he recalled how Kosar-eh had guided the children to perch like birds upon the upper steps to the shaman's cave. Wide-eyed and fearful, they had brought little gifts of their own making to the old man in the hope of cheering him. Then the clown had led the children in a sweetly deferent chorus of "Get Well Quick Please, Hoyeh-tay, Our Shaman."

When the song was over, Mah-ree, eldest among the youngsters, had shyly proffered a lidded basket filled with mice that she had helped the children capture just for Owl. It was no secret that the shaman's helping animal spirit had refused to leave Hoyeh-tay's side, even to hunt for food.

But even when tempted by live morsels of meat, Owl had refused to eat until, at last, Hoyeh-tay had suddenly awakened and looked around the cave. Whether he had been roused by Cha-kwena's chanting or simply by his own will to live, the boy could not know.

"What are you doing, Cha-kwena?" he had asked.

"Dancing! Raising smokes! And singing!"

"*Hmm*. Is that what it is? What are you burning? If you want me well again, get me shomthing to eat. But do not shing to me until you learn how."

And so it was that in a single moment the bad spirits of Hoyeh-tay's illness had once again flown from his body. Incredibly the old man spoke clearly and was strong enough to venture from the cave, walk about the village, and seek the sacred places that he had first visited when he had been Cha-kwena's age.

"You see, Cha-kwena," the old man said now as he drew in a deep and hungry breath of the morning. "I was right about you. The way of the shaman's path is your path. The power to heal and invoke the spirits of the ancestors is yours. I have not felt so well in many moons! This old man's spirit is back from the edge of the world beyond this world. If I could only look once more upon our totem, upon Great Ghost Spirit, perhaps I would be strong again." There was hope in the old man's voice. "Strong enough to live awhile longer and to teach you all that you still have to learn before the lions come."

The sacrifice went well. Lah-ri, the little sister of Sunam-tu and the bride of Thunder in the Sky, went consenting to her death. She smiled almost until the end. She felt smug and proud and self-satisfied until the sacred knife went deep. It found her heart before she could scream, and it was withdrawn so quickly that she had time for only a single gasp of surprise before her throat was cut and she was laid upon the dais.

Out of glazing eyes she saw Mystic Warrior as he stood above her and impaled her with his spear. If she felt pain, it was fleeting; if she thought of the many men she had known and the lies she had told in the shadow of the sacred mountains, her thoughts were as transient as her pain.

She was dead before the butchering began, before the high priestess of the People of the Watching Star removed her robe of feathers and donned another garment—a human pelt—and stood before Thunder in the Sky in the skin of the bride. Ysuna danced while the flesh of the sacrifice was portioned. Every man, woman, and child was given to eat a morsel of that which even now was nourishing the god.

And then, as the beat of thunder drums shook the world, Daughter of the Sun looked down at the remains of the sacrifice: bones, hands, feet, a scalped and faceless skull, a mess of innards to be tossed to the dogs so that they, too, would be made strong with the flesh and spirit of the bride. Ysuna peered through the bloody eye sockets of the mask of human flesh that she held before her own face. Then, her eyes narrowing, she bent lower and poked at the remnants of what had been a young woman.

She stiffened. She rose and cast off the skin of the sacrifice. She stared at Maliwal and pointed down. "This was no virgin. We have sent a tainted sacrifice to the god—a pregnant sacrifice!"

Everyone saw Maliwal blanch. "Impossible!"

Ysuna knelt again. She snatched up the proof and held it high. "A formed child . . . slain . . . as the mother was slain . . . by us, even though she was unfit for the slaying!"

Maliwal ducked the mass of blood and tissue that Ysuna hurled at him. "She swore that she had been with no man!" he protested in his own defense. "And *I* was never with her. She went to the hut of blood with the others. She could not have been—"

"Fool! All of us, fools! And I more than any of you. How could I not have seen what she was doing!" She paused but seemed to be railing in silence against her own thoughts for a moment before she shook her head and continued. "This sacrifice is an even greater offense than the last one to our totem! The totem of our ancestors has given us the flesh and blood of his children, and how do we repay him? With tainted meat! And all because of you, Maliwal! You are no Wolf! You are less cunning than the lizard eaters whom I have sent you to plunder! Look at you! Thunder in the Sky has marked you for what you are! I should have known when you returned with your face maimed and ugly and your ear in a sack that our totem had turned away from you!"

"Ysuna! How can you say this? I have won these scars while risking my life to kill mammoth for you! I have brought you yet another sacred stone! I have brought you word of where the White Giant walks, and I have led you into a land of many mammoth!"

"Your word of the White Giant, of our totem—how do you know that the sacrifice did not lie to you about that, too?"

He hesitated only for a second, but a second was too long. Ysuna was aware of its passage. Their eyes met. She saw uncertainty in him, and he was devastated by what came into her gaze; she had been angry with him before, but never like this. There was loathing in her eyes for him now, pure and undisguised loathing. "Ysuna . . ."

"No! I will hear no more from you. It was Masau, not you, Maliwal, who found the herd upon which our people have so recently feasted."

"But *I* told you that the herd would be here. I will find another sacrifice, Ysuna. I swear it on my life!"

"Yes." The expression on her face was purely carnivorous. "On your life," she said. "You may be certain of that."

Maliwal was shattered by the intensity of her ire. Everyone was staring at him, even the dogs. He hung his head, humiliated and confused. How could she have turned upon him like that? *How?* She and Masau were the ones who were supposed to see into the spirits of men and women, not he. If the sacrifice had duped Daughter of the Sun and Mystic Warrior, how could anyone expect the Wolf not to have been tricked?

His jaw clenched with righteous indignation; pain flared at the side of his head. Would the wounds never stop hurting! And how dare Ysuna call him ugly when, with only a word, she could have healed his face and made him whole again?

Maliwal looked up and found himself seeking Nai. She would not have found him ugly. She would have come to him and offered to ease the pain of his wounds and of his dishonoring. But Ysuna had killed her. At the time, he had been glad. Yet now he missed her, and worse than that, he recalled the expression of longing on her face when he had held her close on a firelit night. Although he had deliberately hurt her and smiled at her pain, she had looked at him with love and dared to speak to him against Ysuna.

"She does not want you anymore, Maliwal!" the woman had told him, "But *I* do! Behind your back she calls you stupid and arrogant and seeks her pleasure in the arms of Masau!"

He winced against the memory and looked to his brother. Mystic Warrior stood close at Ysuna's right. Masau was tall and unmoving, and his expressionless tattooed face was unscarred and handsome. Jealousy flamed within Maliwal. Once he, too, had been handsome. *Once.* But no more.

"We must burn the skin and remaining meat and bones of the sacrifice," Ysuna was saying now. "We must purge ourselves of all that we have eaten of it. We must fast. We must turn our backs upon this encampment and the meat of the mammoth children of our totem. We have shown ourselves unfit to eat it!"

A murmuring of surprise went up from the assembled people.

"It must be done," she said emphatically. "We will journey south toward the Blue Mesas that Maliwal has spoken of. If this is as mammoth rich a country as he has said, then we will hunt along the way and will know no hunger. If it is not as he has said, then we will all suffer the deprivation. Either way, when the lizard eaters from the far side of the world arrive at their holy mountain, we shall be waiting for them." She paused to fix Maliwal with eyes that speared him with contempt. "If there *is* a holy mountain!"

"Oh, there is, Daughter of the Sun!" Chudeh spoke up out of the crowd. "Tsana and Ston and I have walked with Maliwal upon its high summit and have seen the little huts of the holy men who convene there."

Maliwal was amazed by Chudeh's statement. The man had been annoying of late, but Maliwal could have kissed him now.

"It is exactly as Maliwal has said," Chudeh continued. "Before those men were slain in the village at the base of the mountain, they told us all that we needed to know. And the way that the old blue-faced shaman reacted to the girl's revelations affirmed the truth. There will be a gathering of the many bands of the Red World on the sacred mountain. It will take place at the rising of what the lizard eaters call the Pinyon Moon. All the shamans will be there with their sacred stones, Daughter of the Sun—except, of course, the old holy man with the blue face. Maliwal took the sacred stone from his neck and left him to die in the ruins of his burned village with a spear in his belly and a healthy terror of the People of the Watching Star in his heart."

"Left him . . . *alive*?" Her question was a slow hiss of incredulity.

Maliwal was suddenly overcome with anger. "Yes! Alive! Pinned to the earth with a spear through his gut. It pleasured me to kill him so, to know that he would die slowly, thinking of me and the power of my people as the life-force slowly bled out of him! He was a stubborn, uncooperative old fool."

She stared at him. Her eyes were fixed, her mouth set. Her pale flesh prickled with cold under the darkening, drying blood of the sacrifice, which had adhered to her skin when she had adorned herself in the girl's pelt. When she shivered against the cold of the winter day—or perhaps against the inner chill of premonition—Masau took up her cloak of feathers and placed it around her shoulders.

"It is all right, Ysuna," he assured her in a voice so low and tender with concern that only she could hear it. "What is the death of one old man to us? Was it not my brother's right to kill him as he saw fit? Maliwal may have chosen the last sacrifice unwisely, but there will be others, and he brought you the stone from around the shaman's neck. It is yours now, a great gift."

Her eyes were on Maliwal as her fingers sought the old blue-faced shaman's stone, her most recent acquisition. She nodded, almost satisfied. "Yes . . . perhaps. But many moons will pass between now and the rising of the Pinyon Moon."

The wind was blowing softly from the north. Ysuna turned into it, raised her face, closed her eyes, and drank it in. Her people watched her.

At length she turned to appraise them. She stood tall, with the wind in her hair and the soft brown feathers of her cloak ruffling as though being combed by invisible fingers. Her head was high, her shoulders back. When she spoke, it was with a strong, sure voice of supreme authority, and yet fatigue and illness—a gray wash beneath her feverish eyes and upon her long, dry lips—etched her still-exquisite face. "A storm is coming. We will move southward ahead of it and will hunt mammoth. As in the past, a small scouting party of men, disguised as traders, will travel ahead of us to find sacrifices among the daughters of the lizard eaters. *Perfect* sacrifices. *Unblemished* virgins. *Consenting* brides whose lives will atone for the travesty that has been done here this day."

Stung by yet another reminder of his past failures, Maliwal grimaced and felt bound to say, "Yes! And this time I will prove that the way of the Wolf is worthy of Ysuna! I will lead my men into the first unsuspecting village that I find, and I *will* bring back to Daughter of the Sun a worthy sacrifice!"

"No." Her voice was as cold as the north wind. "Twice now you have brought brides that have been unworthy of our totem. This time Masau will lead. Let Mystic Warrior be the eyes of the Wolf. Go, both of you. Bring me word of mammoth. Bring me sacrifices. And seek the white mammoth. I must know where he walks, and with my own hand I must kill him, for in his flesh lies the strength of the People of the Watching Star and eternal life and youth for Daughter of the Sun and for all who drink his blood!"

◆——————◆

# 5

◆——————◆

Hoyeh-tay walked so slowly that the sun was high in the sky by the time Cha-kwena, Owl, and he reached the ancient juniper. The bird flew ahead of them to a perch amid the vast canopy of evergreen branches. A few fluffs of downy breast feathers rained down upon the two human travelers as they paused below.

"Ah, at last," the shaman said, sighing with gladness, smiling, and nodding as he looked at the tree. It was as though he were looking at an old friend whom he had lost hope of ever seeing again. "It is good to see that some things in this world remain unchanged."

Cha-kwena slung off his back roll and laid it upon the snowy ground at the base of the great tree. He had brought food with him from the village: camas cakes spotted with chokecherries, and roasted lizard.

Hoyeh-tay and Cha-kwena ate in silence. They sat upon the raised, sprawling, sun-warmed roots of the ancient tree, their feet tucked under them. The old man's ironwood stave and Cha-kwena's spear leaned against the hairy trunk.

"You need not have brought your spear," the old man said. "I have told you before that the animals of the sacred wood will not harm their brother."

"You have yet to prove to me that I am their brother. And what happens when we are not in that portion of the woods that you consider sacred? Tlana-quah would skin me if I allowed harm to come to his shaman."

"Then he should have sent a man to guard us from what he imagines to be the dangers of the woods. But this journey you and I must make alone. We will come to no harm. We are both shamans now. Together our combined powers just about equal what mine were before I began to shrivel like a mushroom in the sun."

Cha-kwena opened his mouth to refute his grandfather's words, but old Hoyeh-tay, sitting there on the root of the tree, did resemble a withered mushroom. His leathery skin was pale to the point of resembling a fungus.

Owl spread his wings and floated down to land on the old man's head. Hoyeh-tay reached up and offered the bird a piece of U-wa's meat. Owl took it, blinked in surprise, then spat it out. Cha-kwena laughed heartily. His mother was not known for her cooking ability.

A pair of crested blue jays watched the threesome from the heights and hopped back and forth amid the branches, scolding as though they believed that the meal had been brought to this place just for them.

"Stupid birds," Cha-kwena chided. "When you get a beak full of my mother's cooking, you, too, will be sorry!"

"There are worse things," said Hoyeh-tay, and raised a frail hand skyward to offer a fragment of camas cake.

To Cha-kwena's amazement, the bolder jay swept down despite Owl's presence, snatched the gift from the shaman's hand, then disappeared into the canopy of the tree.

The youth frowned and his gut tightened, for the flight of the jay had drawn his eyes to another bird—black masked, hook beaked, gray and white bodied, dark winged, and sleek tailed. It watched from high in the branches. Its eyes stared straight down at Cha-kwena from either side of its curved beak.

A shrike. He had always hated shrikes. He knew that it was an irrational reaction. He did not loathe eagles or hawks or ravens or condors because they fed upon the flesh of other creatures; but Shrike looked like a songbird, so beautiful and benign and yet so insidious and unexpectedly deadly to the smaller, more vulnerable creatures of the world, and to his own kind.

Instinctively, the boy reached down, picked up a handful of snow, and hurled it, as forcefully as he could, upward at the bird. Inadvertently he had scooped up pebbles with the snow; he heard them *ping* against the bark. The bird, with a shriek of pain that made Cha-kwena exhale with gratification, took wing. But its flight was unsteady. The boy had injured it. Cha-kwena spotted what must have drawn it to the tree: Midway up the trunk, on a small spur of broken branch, a smaller bird—dead and impaled—was visible. Cha-kwena rose, then climbed the evergreen until at last he withdrew the tiny body of the chickadee from the snag.

"Shrike!" He spoke the name of the carnivore that had killed the chickadee and then impaled its body on the sacred tree so that it might return to feed upon it later. "Impaler! What makes a bird kill like this, Grandfather?" he asked after he had descended.

The old man shrugged. "Shrike is wise. You should not speak his name with such loathing, Cha-kwena. Like man, Shrike thinks ahead and kills for meat."

"I do not hunt and kill my own kind, and if I did, I would not hang my kill in a tree!" he exclaimed, seating himself and smoothing the soft feathers of the tiny chickadee as he held it in the hollow of his hand.

The old man smiled. "It is Cha-kwena, Little Brother of Animals, who speaks now. On long overland treks into country where there are many bears, have you not helped your people hang their meat in trees? And in our own village, have you not seen the skins and flesh of animals hanging on racks to dry in the wind?" He shrugged. "Of course you have. I imagine that if we could speak the language of those animals that we feed upon, we might hear the name of our kind uttered with revulsion and loathing. But in truth, the forces of Creation have made us all—seed eater and meat eater. There is a place for each in the world, including Shrike, who only does what he must to survive."

Cha-kwena dug a small hole in the snow, placed the body of the chickadee in it, and gently covered it.

"If the meat eaters of the wood do not find it, its life will have been taken for no purpose," Hoyeh-tay pointed out.

"Shrike will not have it."

"He will find other meat, Cha-kwena."

"Maybe I have killed him with my stones and snow."

"Maybe, but others of his kind will come. It is the way of life."

Cha-kwena was warmly clad in winter skins. Under his cape, the new vest that U-wa had made for him warmed his back and chest. Yet he felt suddenly cold. He looked up. High, thin clouds were drifting across the sun, making the disk glow pink within a vast, shimmering rainbow circle.

"It will snow again soon," Hoyeh-tay predicted.

"Yes. It is growing colder. We should return to the village."

"No, Cha-kwena. We will rest here, then go on to the sacred spring. I would see our totem."

"It is a long way to the salt spring, Grandfather."

"I know. But who can tell when I may pass this way again?"

The way to the sacred spring did not seem so long in the light of day as it had when Moon and Night Wind and Brother Bat had guided them. Now, moving slowly and carefully across the snow, Cha-kwena guided Hoyeh-tay, maintaining a strong grip on his elbow. And all the while Owl rode high upon the old man's head. Finally they ducked through a tangle of scrubwood, and the bird was dislodged with a squawk of protest.

Cha-kwena was enveloped by the good and heady scent of a wetland forest, of incense cedars and moist loam and fecal matter of grazing animals. He caught his breath as he came through the shrubs and trees to find himself suddenly on the brink of the vast chasm.

"Ah!" His response was the same as it had been before; an instinctive terror of plummeting into the abyss, as though some malevolent force swam unseen within the open space before him and might reach out to pull him down, down along the vertical white thread of the frozen waterfall, down along the black bones of the bare mountainside, down onto the stones at the base of the canyon. He took a step backward.

With a teasing twinkle in his eyes, Hoyeh-tay cupped the youth's elbow in his bony hand. "I will not let you fall, Cha-kwena."

The youth felt foolish. "Thank you, Grandfather." Lest he be shamed in his shaman's eyes, he stepped forward to stand side by side with Hoyeh-tay at the edge of the abyss. West Wind rose out of the depths to embrace him. "I am not afraid," he said, and was amazed to realize that he meant it. He could stand here forever; he could step out into space and spread his arms wide, and West Wind would bear him up, carry him high and away even as Owl was being carried now.

Overcome by the tumultuous majesty of the scene before him, Cha-kwena sank to one knee. Land . . . sky . . . he was a part of them both. There was no need for words. As on that moonlit night so long before, the presence of the old shaman filled the moment, although Hoyeh-tay was now silent. The truth revealed to Cha-kwena on that night was now like a song that beat within his mind: *There are places in the world that speak of magic, that touch and fill the heart until it aches with longing for all that is rare and wondrous and intangible to all but the spirit.*

This *was* such a place.

Far below, where the thickly forested floor of the canyon widened and the forest thinned, ice glinted on the pools. But if there were mammoth among the trees where the salt spring scabbed the walls of the canyon, they did not show themselves.

"We will wait," Hoyeh-tay declared, fingering the sacred stone that hung within its medicine bag by a thong around his neck. "We will wait until our totem comes."

"If we do not return to the village now, we will never be able to make it back before nightfall."

"I am not afraid of the dark. But I am tired. We will rest here awhile, until the white mammoth comes."

And so they stayed upon the overlook. Cha-kwena unrolled his traveling pack and made a lean-to of the skin.

All night long it snowed. They ate the remaining food that Cha-kwena had brought. They slept.

In the morning it was still snowing, and the canyon was more thickly filled with mist than before. Owl had returned and was sitting between them, shivering, trying to keep the bald places between his chest feathers warm.

"Take me back to the cave, Cha-kwena," said the bird. "I could find nothing to eat in this place. It is a sad situation when an owl lives to be so old that he grows bald and cannot hunt or keep himself warm! Take me back to the cave, Cha-kwena. Hoyeh-tay will not mind."

The bird had spoken the truth.

The old man awoke more tired than when he had succumbed to sleep. When he opened his eyes and looked around at the snow and clouds, he shook his head. "He is not here. I feel it in my bones."

"Our totem will be here another time, Grandfather. When the weather is better, we will come back."

Hoyeh-tay cocked his head. "Another time?" He rose so shakily that Cha-kwena had to reach out to prevent him from falling. "Without my totem to give strength to me, there will be no other time." He sighed. His hand was a fist around the sacred stone. "Soon this will be yours, Cha-kwena. Soon . . ."

"Enough of that sort of talk!" He lifted the old man into his arms. "Come on, Owl! We will go back to the cave now, while you still have some feathers left!"

They were more than halfway to the village when Hoyeh-tay began to speak of hearing lions again. This time Cha-kwena heard them, too. He set the old man down and gripped his spear. This time Hoyeh-tay's vision was real enough: An old lion stood in the snow at the base of the meadow where the women and girls gathered roses and currants each summer's end.

His mane was black and sparse and grizzled with age. His pelt carried many scars. The fur at the back of his legs was worn away, revealing dark calluses like those found at an old man's elbows. The loose skin of his belly hung almost to the ground, and when he roared, he showed a mouthful of stubs where fangs should have been.

And yet roar he did as he turned and began to bound

upward across the meadow, toward the solitary, fur-clad figure of a small girl who stood in the snow at the edge of the cedar grove. Cha-kwena recognized her by the cut and fit of her winter cloak. It was Mah-ree.

"Ish-iwi?" whispered Hoyeh-tay, staring after the lion. "Is that you, my old friend?"

At any other time Cha-kwena would have despaired of his grandfather's madness. Now there was no time. Mah-ree was facing away from the charging lion; she did not know that she was in danger.

"Mah-ree! Run! Lion!" Cha-kwena shrieked. Even as the warning left his lips he was running in pursuit of the beast. He brought his spear over his shoulder as he strained to close the distance so that he could hurl his weapon and cancel the threat to the girl.

Mah-ree turned and stared. "Cha-kwena?"

What was she waiting for? he wondered. Was she blind? "Run! Lion!" he screamed again.

This time she turned and fled into the trees, with the lion in pursuit.

Cha-kwena, heart pounding, adrenaline pumping in his veins, slipped in the snow. Somehow he rose, to run faster than he had thought himself capable. The lion was nearing the crest of the meadow, closing on the girl. He willed himself to run faster, and faster still!

*Spirits of my ancestors, you have chosen me to be a shaman, but make me a hunter now. For Mah-ree let me kill this lion, and I will never question your will for me again!*

He hurled his spear so hard that the action threw him off balance. From lying flat on his belly, he looked up and forced himself to rise as the weapon sped in a low, deadly arc. It sank through the lion's back. The angle and point of penetration caused the spearhead to emerge from the throat of the beast. The weapon must have coursed straight through the heart. The lion arched grotesquely upward from both ends, screamed, and twisted to be free of the spear.

Cha-kwena moaned with gratitude and disbelief. He had done it! He had just killed a lion! Or had he?

With a cry of sudden despair, he was running, for somehow the lion had not fallen dead. It was veering sharply to its left, and snow sprayed upward from beneath its racing paws. It disappeared into the trees on the downslope side of the crest of the hill.

"Climb, Mah-ree! Climb as high as you can as fast as you can!" he cried, loosing his dagger from the sheath at his side as he ran headlong between the trees.

After a moment he stopped and imagined death leaping out at him from every shadow. But wherever the lion had gone, he could find no sign of it—no tracks, no blood on the snow.

He looked up. Mah-ree was clinging to the top of a young fir tree, which was swaying dangerously against her weight. She looked like a frightened little gray squirrel. Suddenly the treetop snapped and deposited her in the snow.

He was at her side in an instant. "Mah-ree, are you all right?"

She sat up, shaking her head and spitting snow. "I . . . yes . . . " She stiffened, suddenly terrified. "Where is the lion, Cha-kwena?"

He took her arm and pulled her to her feet. "Didn't you see it after it entered the grove?"

"I did not see any lion at all."

"Of course you did. You ran away from it."

"I ran because you told me to run."

"But it was running right at you. It was hurt, speared right through its—" His words lodged in his throat. Just beyond where the girl had fallen, he saw his spear lying in a snowbank. He frowned. Still holding his dagger at the ready, he went to kneel beside his weapon. There were no lion tracks around it; there was no blood. The spear shaft and head were clean. "I don't understand. . . ."

In that moment Owl flew into the grove, and Hoyeh-tay came stumbling through the trees. He was wheezing, and his eyes bulged from the strain of an uphill run. But his ironwood staff was gripped like a stave in both hands. His ancient body was clearly ready to do whatever necessary to save his grandson and the daughter of the headman. When he saw that the girl was unhurt and that Cha-kwena, equally unharmed, was kneeling in the snow, he sighed with such relief that his entire body shook. "Ah, Cha-kwena . . ." He leaned on his staff. "I feared the worst."

"I don't understand. . . ." the boy said again. "I know I hit the lion. I saw my spear strike true. And I saw the lion carry it in its own body into the trees!" He turned, perplexed, and, hoping for an explanation, looked past Mah-ree to old Hoyeh-tay.

The shaman was standing erect, transfixed, with the most euphoric smile on his face that Cha-kwena had ever seen. "Look!" Hoyeh-tay exclaimed in wonderment as he pointed into the heart of the grove.

Cha-kwena turned and then stared with disbelief: The totem of his ancestors was staring back at him through the trees.

"That was no lion," Hoyeh-tay explained. "That was Ish-iwi's ghost, guiding us to our totem. A great magic have we witnessed this day. The great white mammoth comes to his people once more."

"He comes to *me*." Mah-ree corrected the shaman in a thoroughly respectful tone, which nonetheless held great pride. "He comes for the sweet and healing things that I have been leaving for him at the edge of the grove. Soon he will come to the village itself, and everyone will see him. Then Tlana-quah will know that Mah-ree has spoken the truth. By then Grandfather of All will be well and strong again, and all the omens will be good for our people once more!" Her enthusiasm was cut short by the sound of many voices calling from the lower flank of the meadow.

Cha-kwena recognized Tlana-quah's imperative shout, Ha-xa's resounding repetition of her daughter's name, and calling for him. And now and then the light, soft voice of Ta-maya could be heard.

The boy was still puzzled as, his spear in hand, he scanned the forest for signs of the lion. Could Hoyeh-tay have been correct? Could the animal have been the spirit of an old friend come to lead his boyhood companion to his totem?

Mah-ree turned and squinted off through the trees. When she turned back, hope blazed in her eyes. "I am glad that they have come! They will see now! Yes! Come, Hoyeh-tay! Come, Cha-kwena! Come, Owl! We will bring the headman into the grove and show him that our totem is here!" Then she was off, running like a deer through the trees, waving her arms, and summoning the others forward.

Cha-kwena was glad that Grandfather of All was grazing a good distance away. Even though he had seen this animal before, he had never been so close and had not realized that any creature could be so huge. The awe-inspiring height of the mammoth's great head and the impressive length of its tusks made the boy gulp, dry mouthed with apprehension.

And yet he knew that Mah-ree, as small and young as she was, had shown no fear of the mammoth. If she was to be taken at her word—and there was no reason to do otherwise—she must have been sneaking away from the village for some time now, carrying healing food for an ailing creature. It was not surprising; Mah-ree had always shown an interest in the ways of healing. Her behavior had required inordinate courage, for she had risked much. There was, he realized, more to her than met the eye. Not that *he* would not have done the same thing, of course; but he was skilled enough in the use of a spear to walk unafraid through the world and to slay invisible lions whenever he saw them.

He glowered at the idea. Mah-ree was out of the grove now. She had slipped off her winter cape and was waving it wildly. Her body was encased in a tubular dress of laterally joined strips of rabbit skin. Was it his imagination, or was he seeing the beginnings of decidedly feminine curves to her hips? No. She was still the same little stick. But how bold she was!

Cha-kwena's eyes went round, and a feeling of foreboding settled in his gut. Tlana-quah, wrapped in his jaguar-skin cloak, had brought half the band with him! One by one they joined Mah-ree at the topmost edge of the meadow.

The shaman, with one hand folded around the medicine bag at his throat, was staring into the grove at his totem. "He is so *old*," he said softly of the mammoth. His reverent tone was underlain by remorse and unwelcome surprise.

At that moment the great mammoth raised its head and, with a huff, turned away. Tlana-quah, guided by Mah-ree, was leading the others into the grove.

"Hurry, Father!" cried the girl. "Our totem is leaving!"

Cha-kwena watched as Tlana-quah followed her. His

women were at his side, and Dakan-eh led a sizable contingent of the band's hunters.

*Where is the lion now?* Cha-kwena wondered. *If only it were dead at my feet, my spear buried in its heart! How Dakan-eh and my friends would envy me such a kill! How proud U-wa would be!*

But the lion was not here, nor was there any proof that it had ever existed. Perhaps the bad spirits that walked in and out of old Hoyeh-tay's head were beginning to infect his grandson with their madness? Despite the chill of the winter day, Cha-kwena broke into a sweat just thinking about it.

He felt no better when Tlana-quah came to stand scowling before him . . . until the headman's gaze went straight over his shoulder and into the grove where the great white mammoth was still visible as it ambled downhill into the deep shadows of the trees. Tlana-quah gasped. Transfixed, he stared in open wonder.

"Come," Mah-ree urged, eagerly tugging at her father's wrist. "You will see that it really is Grandfather of All!"

Tlana-quah put a staying hand upon the child's head. "No, I see enough. If Grandfather of All prefers to be one with the shadows, let it be so. As Totem, it is his right to say by his actions when he will be seen and when he will remain unseen." And now, for the first time in all too many moons, the headman looked right at Ha-xa and grinned. "Did you see him, woman? Did you see how big he is? Like a mountain! No other mammoth could be so big!" He shook his head and laughed. "It is good to know that he is with the People. It is more good than you know!"

Mah-ree pointed. "He has been with us all along. I told you so, but you would not listen to me."

Cha-kwena could see that the headman was not listening to her. Tlana-quah had turned to extend his hand to Ta-maya. "Where is Dakan-eh?" he asked. "Ah, there you are, Bold Man. Come, stand beside my firstborn child. It seems that the omens do indeed smile upon this band. Perhaps it is time to assemble the wedding gifts and raise a new lodge for the two who would be one. It is time for the men to hunt and for the women to prepare a wedding feast. If Dakan-eh and Ta-maya would still be man and woman together, it will not be necessary to wait until the Great Gathering."

Ha-xa squealed with delight.

Ta-maya echoed her mother's cry of happiness and threw herself into her father's arms, hugging him hard. "Oh, my father, thank you! Thank you, thank you!"

Cha-kwena's heart made its usual *thunk* when he looked at her. How radiant she was! How perfectly beautiful. Was any female more deserving of happiness? But did she not deserve better than Dakan-eh, who found his own happiness in the arms of any woman who happened to be near enough to serve his needs at any given time? Who gave gifts to Ta-maya that had been given to him by another girl?

Envy and dislike of Bold Man caused Cha-kwena to turn his gaze from Ta-maya so that he might glare at Dakan-eh. Grinning from ear to ear, the hunter looked like a little boy who had unexpectedly been presented with a gift that he has lost all hope of winning. Then, suddenly, Bold Man remembered that he was Bold Man. He compressed his lips into a scowl of arrogance, threw out his chest, and replied coolly to Tlana-quah, "Yes. Perhaps it might now be a good thing."

"The best of things!" exclaimed Ta-maya, whirling away from her father to hug her man-to-be as though she would never let him go.

Cha-kwena was disgusted with her. What did she see in Dakan-eh? The headman, no longer smiling, was evidently thinking the same thing. He grunted the low, rumbling noise that a father makes when he knows that he has just acquiesced to his children in a matter that has made them deliriously happy even though it is not completely to his own liking. Tlana-quah's head swung back and forth, and he drew in a deep breath. When he exhaled, he also blew out all second thoughts about the union.

"Then let it be so!" the headman declared, raising his arms to the sky in a gesture of supreme beneficence. "In one moon's time, the wedding of Ta-maya and Dakan-eh will take place."

"One moon's time! An *entire* moon? Why so long?" Dakan-eh demanded sharply.

Cha-kwena was aware of the intake of many more breaths than his own.

The beneficence was instantly gone from Tlana-quah's mood. "One moon is better than the many that will rise and fall between now and the Great Gathering."

Ta-maya's eyes went wide with fright as she saw her marriage to the man of her dreams dissolving into ruins. "I would join with him now, Father! We need not wait! The omens are good, and we have all seen Great Ghost Spirit. Surely our totem would—"

"No!" Tlana-quah interrupted hotly. "Because the omens are good. Because we have all seen our totem, because you are my firstborn and my heart is soft in matters that concern you, I will allow you to join with this man who thinks too much of himself! But the traditions of the ancestors will be kept. Your mother has her heart set upon a wedding. In *two* moons time she will have her desire."

"*Two* moons!" blurted Dakan-eh, aghast.

"Yes, Bold Man. *Two* moons," reiterated Tlana-quah.

"But a moment ago you said one. Two are too many! It is—"

"*Three* moons then! And if you say one more word to me, as reward for your arrogance it will be four moons, and after that five."

Dakan-eh was livid.

Cha-kwena was delighted.

On Hoyeh-tay's head, Owl ruffled his feathers and shivered against the cold. "Take me back to the cave where it is warm," said Owl.

Cha-kwena ignored the bird. He had eyes and heart and ears only for Ta-maya as she laid her head upon Dakan-eh's chest and whispered soothingly, "Be at ease, Bold Man. Soon we will be one. What are three more moons to us now when we have already waited so long!"

# PART VI

# THE SHRIKE

# 1

The scouting party sent out by Ysuna came through the village of Shi-wana on a day of snow and wind, with the dogs dragging the bulk of their "trading" supplies and with ice riming the traces. The burned huts and long-dead corpses lay beneath a soft mantle of white. Only an occasional blackened ridgepole extended upward through the snow. It would take the hard rains of spring to melt the ground cover and expose the devastation that lay beneath. They paused and stared ahead to the wall of mountains that stood against the sky.

"There is the place where the holy men of the lizard eaters will gather at the rising of the Pinyon Moon," informed Maliwal.

Masau squinted through the wind and falling snow. "We will go on. I would look upon the land wherein the white mammoth is said to walk."

Maliwal shook his head. "We must wait out the storm, Brother. The way onto the mountain will be treacherous at this time of year. I doubt if I could find the way until the weather clears."

They set deadfall snares for whatever game might be about, then made a cold camp amid the ruins of the village, raising five two-man lean-tos against the wind and snow. The dogs drew close, and when darkness came down, the wind out of the north sounded like the ghosts of the slain villagers.

"How many died in this place?" Masau asked his brother as they lay in the darkness of their wind-whipped shelter.

"All except the captives we brought north with us."

"And you left the bodies where they fell?"

Maliwal nodded. "Most were burned in their huts.

What else should we have done with lizard eaters? They are barely human. Their corpses are fit for carrion, not for laying out with honor in the way of our ancestors."

"No, perhaps not."

"Perhaps? They *squealed* when they died, Masau. Not one man among them had the courage to rally the others against us. Creatures like that are not deserving of life."

"And yet does it not sometimes seem strange to you that the sacred stones of our ancestors are in their possession? And that the white mammoth walks among them? And that we offer their daughters instead of our own for sacrifice to Thunder in the Sky?"

"The ways of the forces of Creation are not for men—or wolves—like me to understand. It is enough for me to know that our mother sends us forth to do her bidding." He growled as he shifted his weight within his heavy winter traveling robe. "Soon my face will be made right. Ysuna has sworn it. She *has* sworn it, has she not, Masau?"

Masau did not respond. Ysuna had never sworn to accomplish that which his brother so desperately desired; Maliwal had merely assumed that she was capable of working such wondrous healing magic, and so, in a moment of compassion, Masau had assured him that it would occur. This was not the first time he regretted making that assurance. To avoid giving an answer, he feigned sleep.

The restlessness was on him again. They had come so far from the encampment of their people, and yet the weather had stood against them all the way. He closed his eyes. The majority of the sacred stones of power were still in the possession of lizard eaters, and the white mammoth walked in the land beyond the mountains. They must go there, and soon. Otherwise when they returned to Ysuna with all that she needed to remain young and alive, it would be too late.

"Three moons!" Ta-maya said the words and sighed again and again. "So long, so very long. How can Dakan-eh and I wait until our wedding day is here?"

And yet, even as she sighed, the intensity of her anticipation held such a heady sweetness that she found herself glad that the actual day had been postponed. Just thinking of it was somehow enough. There was so much to do!

Ta-maya busied herself at a hundred tasks. She assisted the women with the usual communal winter work and soon lost track of how many mounds of sagebrush and juniper bark she had shredded and turned into fiber for making sandals and cloth, or how many stalks of dogbane and milkweed she had cracked and peeled; or how many lengths of fine, tough thread she had spun against her palms from the filaments that she pulled from the stalks; or how many slender, braided ropes of cordage she had fashioned from the thread . . . because as she worked she daydreamed of all the wondrous things that she would make for Dakan-eh out of her allotted portion of the fiber and cord. At night, while her family slept, she sat in the light of her tallow lamp and sewed and wove and smiled to herself as her collection of presents for her man-to-be grew. She did not need sleep! There was too much to dream about when she was awake!

Sometimes she would tiptoe from the lodge and stand in the winter night. Twice she saw Dakan-eh walking past the widows' lodge on his way out of the village with his spear and knew that he could not sleep, either; he was hunting in the dark, checking his trap lines for the fine pelts that he would no doubt present to her on the day of their joining.

Although Ta-maya had come to see the wisdom of the waiting time that her father had prescribed, the third full moon was not soon enough for Dakan-eh.

"Ta-maya . . . " he whispered from behind a storage hut as she lagged daydreaming behind the other women when a heavy snowfall forced them to abandon their communal work circle. He caught her by the arm and drew her close. "Come . . . no one will see. Everyone has gone inside. Come away with me now, to the warm springs by the tule brake. I will spread my robe for us, and we will lie on it together. My need is great, Ta-maya."

"I will be missed, Dakan-eh."

"Yes, Ta-maya. We will both be missed. And as others call our names, I will put my life in you, and your father will know that we have been together. He will give you to me then. There is no need of ceremony. A man deep and hot in a willing woman—that is ceremony enough for me. I need no wedding, no gifts, no feasting. I need a *woman*, Ta-maya, a young, tight woman, not the old widows who beckon to me in the daytime and spread themselves at night so they can keep their eyes wide open when a man is on them and dream of their youth."

His words upset her, aroused and repulsed her. Had he been with the widows on the nights she had seen him passing their lodge? It was, she had to admit, his right. Her emotions flew within her like the stinging cold snowflakes against her face. "No, Dakan-eh. My father would be angry if I were to do as you say. My mother would be disappointed. And I am making many wonderful gifts for you and for our new life together."

"You are the gift. I need no more than this from you." His hands, palms up, lifted her breasts and worked them, and then, quickly, his arms moved down and back to cup her buttocks and pull her close against him. He arched his hips and moved so she could feel him, hard, high, and pulsing.

She caught her breath. Once again she was both aroused and repulsed. "Dakan-eh, I—"

He cut off her protest with a deep, hungry kiss of pure provocation. Despite her intentions to remain unmoved, when his tongue found hers, she yielded to the kiss until a chorus of giggles rose from the boys who had been playing some sort of game inside the storage hut. One of them, Kosar-eh's eldest son, threw a bone gaming piece at them; several more did likewise. And when Dakan-eh, cursing, turned on them, they all laughed and scampered off like rabbits.

Laughing and inexplicably glad to be free of Bold Man despite the passion that had almost overwhelmed her, Ta-maya turned and ran toward the lodge of her father. She called back over her shoulder, "Soon, my Bold Man, soon."

For days afterward she went about smiling, always thinking about him, but concentrating on the wedding itself. It was always in her mind, even when Mah-ree insisted that Ta-maya come along on her daily forays from the village. Tlana-quah routinely accompanied his younger daughter so that she might safely bring armfuls of sweet grass and a mash of pounded camas root, willow bark, and boiled yarrow juice to the places where Grandfather of All was known to roam. For such a young girl, Mah-ree had gained great status. The People called her Medicine Girl.

Dakan-eh usually found a way to be among the mammoth watchers on those days when the two sisters went from the village arm in arm. Ta-maya was easily distracted by his presence. This was the case that morning, when Mah-ree found the shrike with a broken wing. It was not unusual for the girl to nurture and heal any creature that she happened to find sick or wounded; she had always shared this interest with Cha-kwena. On this occasion Ta-maya had been too lost in Dakan-eh's yearning gazes to pay attention to her sister's unhappy discovery or to offer assistance. Mah-ree had been very upset with her.

And now, Ta-maya stood with her sister outside their family lodge and tried to make amends. Mah-ree, however, was not easily soothed; Cha-kwena also refused to have anything to do with the bird. As she held the shrike close in her winter cape she accused Ta-maya of caring for no one but herself.

"You could talk to Cha-kwena for me, Ta-maya. He likes you. He would take care of Shrike for *you*."

"It is just a bird, Mah-ree!" Since the fate of a shrike could neither add to nor detract from her wedding plans, it was unimportant to Ta-maya. "Cha-kwena has a great deal of responsibility these days. What can one bird matter to him?"

"I made a vest of rabbit skin for Owl so that his balding breast will stay warm this winter. Cha-kwena gladly accepted it, so a bird obviously can matter to him."

Ta-maya could not believe her ears. "You made a vest for a bird? Oh, Mah-ree, I wonder about you sometimes. If Cha-kwena is concerned for Owl, it is because Owl is his grandfather's helping animal spirit. The shrike is just another bird. You should not take it or yourself too seriously." Even as she spoke, the words seemed to be coming from the mouth of an unsympathetic stranger. "I'm sorry, Sister," she said, and was about to explain how she could think of little else except her upcoming marriage.

But Mah-ree was suddenly staring off, and her face was as red as a summer rose fruit. Ta-maya followed her sister's gaze. A sullen Cha-kwena was stomping toward them, and his face was also very red.

"My grandfather would see you," he said, stopping just out of arm's reach.

Mah-ree's face turned even redder than Cha-kwena's. "M-me? Shaman wants to see m-me?"

"My grandfather wants to see if Medicine Girl can learn how to set a broken bone. Although why he wants to help a bird like that . . ." He let the statement drift, then turned away and started back toward the cave.

Mah-ree reached for her sister's hand. "Please come with me, Ta-maya."

Feeling guilty about her earlier behavior, Ta-maya took Mah-ree's hand, and together they followed Cha-kwena through the village, across the creek, and up the steps to the cave.

Hoyeh-tay, bundled in his furs, was waiting for them. He shooed a fur-clad Owl from the top of his head. The bird flew to the back of the cave and landed upon a snarl of root that protruded from the rock wall. There, he began to peck at the rabbit fur that covered his chest. The old man bade Ta-maya seat herself on the topmost step while he gestured Mah-ree forward. "Come," he invited. "Come to me, child, and bring Shrike with you."

Mah-ree hesitated. "I . . . girls cannot come into the holy cave."

The old man sighed thoughtfully. "For a girl who makes vests for Owl and walks alone into the winter wood to bring healing foods to the totem of her people regardless of the risk to herself, Shaman can make an exception. Come, let me see Shrike. Cha-kwena, bring my medicine bag—the big one at the back of the cave."

Ta-maya sat motionless, proud of her sister. She watched Mah-ree sitting wide-eyed beside the shaman, taking in the old man's every word and action. This was an unprecedented occurrence.

"You must do now as I say, Medicine Girl," Hoyeh-tay instructed. "And you, Cha-kwena, hold Shrike as I tell you so that he may be healed. *Hmm* . . . how he has lasted so long in this cold weather with such a break, only the spirits may say."

Cha-kwena did as his grandfather asked.

"Now," Hoyeh-tay said to Mah-ree, "together we will straighten the broken bone . . . like this. Yes . . ."

Ta-maya held her breath. The scene transfixed her: the old man, the youth, the wounded bird—black masked, beautiful, and wild-eyed with pain and fright, its narrow hook-tipped beak agape—Mah-ree leaning close, her face pinched with concentration, her brow furrowed, the tip of her tongue protruding from between her set lips.

"Now, apply the splint as I show you. Now bind the thong. Lightly, lest the flow of blood be constricted and the green spirits come to feed upon the flesh of the bird. There. Good. Around the chest like that . . . ah, yes. Good girl!"

Then the shaman turned to look at Ta-maya. "You, pretty daughter of our Tlana-quah, you should marry soon with Bold Man."

Ta-maya was aware that Cha-kwena, who was reassembling the old man's medicine bag, had turned to gaze with interest at his grandfather. She replied, "In three moons, Shaman."

"Three?" Hoyeh-tay scowled. "Too long."

Ta-maya sighed wistfully. "I agree with you, Shaman, but my father has said three moons, and three it must be."

"No!" the old man shouted. He struggled to his feet and pointed a long, bony finger at Ta-maya. "You and Bold Man must marry now! Before the lions come!"

Frightened by the old man's ferocity, Ta-maya rose and backed down two steps as Mah-ree, staring in bewilderment, tried to help the shaman keep his footing.

Cha-kwena took over for her. "He'll be all right. You'd better take the bird and go," he said to the sisters. "When my grandfather starts talking about lions, it's best to put him to bed."

"You talked about lions in the grove, remember, Cha-kwena?" whispered Mah-ree as she looked up at him with unconcealed adoration.

He exhaled wearily. "Yes, I remember. Someone should have put me to bed, too. There were no lions."

"You were brave," said Mah-ree. "You risked your life to save me. I thought it was wonderful the way you ran and threw your spear and—"

Hoyeh-tay sagged against Cha-kwena and, gripping his arm, began to babble unintelligibly.

"You had better go," Cha-kwena repeated, and then, with a feeble attempt to inject humor into a humorless situation, he added, "Unless you want *me* to officiate at your wedding, Hoyeh-tay must have rest."

The storm clouds skeined southward over the crest of the Blue Mesas. Masau and Maliwal stood on the promontory and stared across the Red World.

"Which way now?" Maliwal asked, frowning. He had forgotten the enormity of the country to which he had led the others. The land seemed to spread out forever below the clouds.

Chudeh, Tsana, and Ston came up behind the brothers, with several of the dogs.

"The sledges are loaded and ready for travel," informed Chudeh.

Tsana laughed gruffly. "Laden with bright beads, quills, feathers, obsidian blanks, and all the pelts necessary to tempt the lizard eaters to trade with us. Let us praise the Four Winds for creating such gullible fools to serve the needs of the People of the Watching Star!"

The men laughed heartily. Only Masau was not amused. At his side, Blood looked up, sensing his tension.

Maliwal audibly caught his breath. "Look!" He pointed off to a low range of scrub-covered hills that flanked the great, mountainous sand dunes to the east. "A village! Do you see the smoke?"

"I see more than that," replied Chudeh.

"Mammoth!" exclaimed Ston. "Yes! I see them! A good-sized herd, too! Well, now we know the direction in which to go. You have led us well, Maliwal! Before the weather turns again, let us be off this mountain!"

"Wait." Masau's voice was as cold as the north wind. He pointed. "Ravens. Follow their flight. What do you see in the streams of sunlight that part the clouds to the south?"

"An eagle!" said Ston.

"A fishing eagle!" added Tsana. "Do you see the way the sun flashes on his white head and tail?"

"Yes, there is open water to the south," said Masau.

"There is a lake beyond the buttes and that canyon-cut range. A deep-water lake would welcome many an eagle to feed upon its fish, and many singing birds would find refuge upon its surface and along its shore in the dead of winter."

Maliwal gaped at his brother with open appreciation. "The lake that the captive girl spoke of? The Lake of Many Singing Birds that lies in the country where the white mammoth walks?"

"Could be," Masau replied obliquely. "It could be."

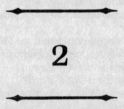

# 2

It was said by the ancients that time passes slowly for those who are eager for the coming of tomorrow, and so Ta-maya was puzzled that the days and nights seemed to fly by. Snow fell and fell again. Shrike was now strong enough to perch on Mah-ree's shoulder by day and to rest by night upon an alder twig within the cage that she had fashioned for him of woven willow branches. The lodge for the man and woman who would soon be one took shape and grew thick with thatching as the first moon went through its phases. Then the second moon rose new and unseen behind clouds and falling snow.

The men spent many hours in the sweat lodge now, and small, friendly groups of women came together in the various lodges to gossip and sew. A large gathering hut was assembled to break the monotony of the winter gloom, and within its warm interior the men and boys staged wrestling matches, and there were games of skill for all. Most popular were the guessing games and games of chance. Men and women wagered and argued hotly over the most boisterous game of all: Who Eats Who? It was a simple contest that involved the tossing and catching of dice made of beaver teeth. Each die was incised with the image of an animal, plant, bird, or insect, and each was worth a specific number of points, depending upon the place in the food chain of whatever was incised into it.

"Ha! My grub eats the bark of your mighty tree! I win the throw!"

"Oh, no, you don't! My bird eats your grub! I win!"

"No! My ant can eat your bird when the bird is dead and rotting in the ground!"

"Ha! And I say that my bird will eat your ant!"

"Only if he is alive!"

"And where does it say on this die that my bird is dead? He is standing on his two legs!"

"Turn the die around and he is on his back with his feet in the air!"

Because the arguments could go on for hours, Tlana-quah was often called upon to adjudicate.

"Ha! My lizard will eat your ant."

"My jaguar will eat your lizard!"

"No, he won't. When was the last time you saw a jaguar eat a lizard?"

"When was the last time anyone saw a jaguar at all? Since that day so long ago when Tlana-quah was forced to kill the beast whose skin now warms his back, there has been no sign of jaguars in the Red World. Maybe that die should be withdrawn from the game, along with the four-pronged antelope and three-humped camel? It has been a long time since anyone has seen any of these animals, either."

"Just because they have not been seen does not mean that they aren't still around! I saw a jaguar some moons ago!"

"Bah! How many moons ago was that? You are so old, Zar-ah, that you probably remember the days when mammoth wore hair!"

"With age comes wisdom! But I do not remember that far back, although my grandfather spoke of a hairy mammoth once. He said they had hair that was as long and shaggy and red as the bark of a juniper tree."

"I can't believe that!"

"Nor can I!"

And the arguments continued, except during those days or nights when Hoyeh-tay's spirit was not wandering.

Then he told wonderful stories. When he lost his way in them—as he always did—Cha-kwena took over. On such a night, with the people crowded around the fire, Ta-maya felt flushed by the onset of her time of blood and left the gathering hut to stand outside. Dakan-eh followed.

"Ta-maya, I have prepared fine sleeping skins as gifts for our new lodge. You may have them now. Just come with me. We will go into the night, and I will spread the sleeping skins so you may lie upon them and let me put my life in you. Now, Ta-maya. I cannot wait!" His hand was curled hard around her wrist, hurting her.

"Go away!" she told him. "I do not want you now! Not like this! In two moons' time, in our new lodge, then we will be man and woman together. Not before!"

His hand released her wrist as though her skin had burned him as hotly as had her words. With an exhalation of annoyance and disgust, he whirled around and was gone into the hut.

She stood still, feeling relieved and content to breathe in the cold air of night. Ban-ya suddenly appeared at her side.

"I would go to him if he asked me."

Startled and offended that Ban-ya had overheard her conversation with Dakan-eh, Ta-maya snapped, "Have you no suitors of your own? Must you always look hungry eyed after my man?"

"He is not your man yet."

"In two moons' time we will be one."

"So it seems. But tell me, Ta-maya, do you love Dakan-eh or merely admire him because he is bold and good to look upon? And is it a life with him forever that you really long for, or only the excitement of a wedding and a feast fire and the promise of many fine presents?" With this said, she turned up her nose and went back into the gathering hut.

For a long while Ta-maya stood alone in the darkness. Her heartbeat quickened with unexpected remorse. She frowned as she turned her face upward into the falling snow. Soon the second moon would turn its face away and go to sleep on the other side of the world. Then the third moon would rise. She was certain that she would feel better at that time, more sure of herself and her feelings toward Dakan-eh.

Lost in thought and fighting a headache, she returned to the lodge of her father and, bundling herself in her blankets, tried not to think of Dakan-eh's and Ban-ya's accusations as she drifted into sleep.

All night long snow fell, heavy and silent. Morning dawned clear and cold. Eagles swooped to feed upon even more hapless coots as Ta-maya rose early and went to spend her time of blood alone in the little hut that stood at the edge of the village. Ha-xa brought food, fresh swaths of skins to absorb her moon blood, and baskets of warm water so that she might keep herself clean. Three days later she emerged feeling much better, certain that her misgivings about Dakan-eh had been no more than the dark mood that often preceded her menses. When Ban-ya walked past her and entered the little hut, Ta-maya felt no resentment. How could she blame any woman for being envious of her coming wedding to the best and boldest man in all the Red World?

The morning was cold and beautiful. The morning star was still in the sky. Somewhere beyond the village, dogs were barking. Strange, she thought; one rarely heard or saw dogs in the Red World, and these sounded as though they were coming closer.

"Hurry, Ta-maya!" cried Mah-ree, running toward her. Shrike rode on her shoulder. "The most amazing thing is happening! Men with dogs are coming to the village from the north! Strangers! The most amazing-looking men you have ever seen!"

# 3

Cha-kwena emerged from the warm darkness of his dreams. He had been roused by happy, excited shouting and the sound of Mah-ree calling his name. Knuckling sleep from his eyes and pulling his blankets about his shoulders, he rose and went to stand outside the cave. When he saw Tlana-quah leading the strangers toward him, somehow he knew that nothing would ever be the same again.

"Lions?" Hoyeh-tay hobbled forward to stand beside him. Leaning unsteadily on his ironwood staff and holding his sacred stone, he asked, "Have the lions come at last, Cha-kwena?"

"No, Grandfather, not lions. Men," he answered.

And yet he knew that they were more than that. They were unlike any men he had ever seen: They were taller by a head than the tallest man of the People. They carried enormous back rolls attached to pack frames made of the multitined antlers of some sort of very large elk. Each pack appeared to weigh more than the man who carried it, but not one of the strangers slumped or appeared fatigued as he leaned forward against his load.

Nearly every inch of the men's clothing and hunting paraphernalia was beaded with bone or quills or freshwater shells or rare, wondrously colored stone. Even the side plaits of their hair, which looked as if it had never been cut—were festooned with beads, feathers, and quills.

Each man walked with a long, bold, earth-eating gait, and although the strangers were traveling across snow-covered ground, they seemed unconcerned about losing their footing. Cha-kwena marveled at the sight and stared unabashed as they came closer. Their boots extended to the knees and were cross laced with thong and fringed along the sides. The boots were apparently soled with

some sort of bone contrivances that cut into the icy surface
and gave them traction. Their tunics and trousers were of
fringed buckskin.

Their faces were painted with swirling patterns and
brilliant colors, their shoulders draped crosswise with the
skins of large predators. Each man affected his own style
and a different pelt. They carried the largest, longest,
heaviest-headed spears that he had ever seen. Each man's
spear shaft was painted or incised with a different pattern.
And even more amazing was the fact that they walked with
dogs—big, rangy dogs whose snouts were encased in
gloriously painted and beaded muzzles. The dogs were
strapped into trusses that bound them to long sleds that
were laden with great, fur-wrapped bundles.

Tlana-quah, in his jaguar-skin cloak, came slipping
across the creek. He was steadied by the tallest stranger, a
man with the skin of a golden eagle on his back. Its wings
were attached to his fringed sleeves, and its head was atop
his own. His extraordinarily handsome face was striped
bloodred beneath a black mask of tattooing that encircled
the upper portion of his face, in much the same way that a
shrike or a raccoon was masked. Cha-kwena caught his
breath. The effect was startling, frightening—until the
man smiled.

The tallest stranger now paused at the base of the cliff
and stood staring up with Tlana-quah and the others. His
smile was wide and positively luminous. He raised his
right arm, and his big, bone-shafted spear with its black
obsidian spearhead glinted in the morning sun.

"I, Masau of the People of the Watching Star, salute
the shaman of the people of this village."

His voice was deep, fluid, and soothing. Its melli-
fluousness made Cha-kwena think of a river running slow
and sure in the depth of a summer night. His words were
clearly spoken, and yet he turned each syllable with subtle
variances to his speech that might elude a man of the
People.

"This Masau is one of the strangers from the north
that you, Dakan-eh, and Cha-kwena were told of when
you last visited the Blue Mesas!" informed Tlana-quah in a
way that revealed that he was absolutely delighted. "You

were right, Shaman! There *are* other people in the world besides *the* People."

"It is so!" affirmed the black-masked leader of the strangers.

"The People are *one*," Hoyeh-tay said, solemn and angry. He pointed downward with a hostile jab of his staff. "You are *not* of the People! You are the Brothers of the Sky come down to destroy the sons and daughters of First Man and First Woman! You are lions! Go away!"

"You must excuse our shaman," said Tlana-quah sternly. "He has not been well." His eyes focused upward on the two who stood looking down at him from the mouth of the cave. "Masau is also a shaman, Hoyeh-tay. He has brought gifts to this people, and he has expressed a desire to speak with you."

The old man sneered, then mimicked Tlana-quah nastily: "When you have just told him that I am sick? Perhaps he would rather speak to the boy here?"

Cha-kwena's face flamed with embarrassment as, awestruck, he stared down at Masau. The man was so tall, so powerful and magnificent. Not even Dakan-eh could compare with him. Certainly no shaman of the Red World ever looked like this!

"I would counsel with Hoyeh-tay, elder shaman of the People of the Village of the Lake of Many Singing Birds," Masau said with infinite respect. "There is much that I would ask of such a venerable wise man."

"*Hmmm.* Venerable, is it?"

"Yes, Wise One, for I am young and surely inexperienced compared to such a holy man as you . . . and I have come far with these traders of my people to learn if what they have heard about the sacred stones of the Red World is true."

"Sacred stones? And what might they be, eh?"

Cha-kwena cast Hoyeh-tay a sideward glance. The old man was staring fixedly at Masau. Had he forgotten, or was he deliberately feigning ignorance?

Masau smiled; it was a knowing expression, as though he had seen into the heart of the old man and understood the cause of his defensiveness and unwillingness to speak. "I have heard it said that the sacred stones of the Red World are the bones of First Man and First Woman."

"Where have you heard this? And what are First Man and First Woman to you?" pressed the old man.

Masau gestured outward with his left hand. "My people call them Mother and Father, grandparents of all our generations since time beyond beginning. And my brother, Maliwal—"

At the mention of that name, a broad-backed man to Masau's right bowed his head. He wore a cape of wolfskin, with the head of the animal atop his own and the forelimbs dangling down over his ears to below his collarbone. He would have been handsome had it not been for the scarring of the lower half of his face. Cha-kwena tried not to show revulsion when he saw the extent of the recently healed wounds. From the spark of resentment that flashed in the man's eyes, however, the youth knew that he had failed.

Masau continued, "My brother, Maliwal, and I have led many a trading party into the far northern edge of your country. What a surprise it was for us when we learned that people were living beyond what we had always assumed to be the edge of the world! People who spoke our language! People whose tales of the past are much like our own! A bride was given to my brother from out of your land. And from her mouth we first heard of the sacred stones and knew that if the stories about them were true, then we must have brothers and sisters living to the south . . . for it is told to us by our ancients that once, in time beyond beginning, the bones of First Man and First Woman were given into our care. But over many generations, the bones were divided among the many bands of the People until they were lost to all but a few. If you possess these stones, then that would explain why you of the Red World are strong before the power of the Four Winds while, to the north, so many other peoples have been swept away into insignificance."

"Other peoples? Like yours? Hmmph! In your fringes and furs and feathers you do not look insignificant to me!"

Again Masau gestured outward with his left hand. "The power of the spirit is not to be found in fringes and feathers and furs, Hoyeh-tay, shaman of the Village of the Lake of Many Singing Birds. It is to be found in the flesh and blood and bone of the People. We should not be strangers to each other. We should eat of the same meat;

we should marry into each other's bands; we should gather to sing the songs of the ancients, to remember the way of the ancestors. And the power of the sacred stones should touch us all. It is said by the storytellers of my country that once, the People were one. It would be a good thing if it could be so again. First Man and First Woman will smile in the knowledge that their children are reunited."

Hoyeh-tay glared as he clutched the medicine bag within which the sacred stone lay secured against his throat. And then he shook his head with such vehemence that Owl did not even attempt to stay upon his perch. Raining feathers, the bird flew out of the cave and circled high. "You speak too many words, offer too many new thoughts, Masau, shaman of . . . ?"

"The People of the Watching Star."

"I have heard of that band."

"We are not a band; we are a tribe—a great tribe that dwells in a land of endless bison and horse and game beyond telling! We take our name from the star that stands constantly to the north as a reminder of the origins of the People. Is it not also said here in the Red World that your grandfathers came from the north, from out of the light of the Watching Star?"

"*Hmmm.*" The old man studied the strangers. One by one he fixed them with questing eyes. One by one he dismissed them with a snort and a toss of his head. But he made no attempt to answer Masau's question. "If there is so much game in your land of the North Star, why do you come here?"

"To be one with our brothers. To fulfill the desire of First Man and First Woman for their children. Too many generations have separated us. Too long have we walked in different ways. We have become strangers. This is not a good thing. It is time for the children of the ancestors to walk the same path. It is time for the People to be one."

Cha-kwena looked up as Owl came winging past the strangers to sweep into the cave and land on the old man's head. Before he did, more than feathers rained from the sky. Something white and of a substance that had no relation to snow landed with a splat on the wolf's head that adorned the man with the scarred face. He cursed, and when he looked at Owl, something in his expression set the finger of premonitory dread poking deep into Cha-kwena's gut.

"These men are not what they seem," Owl warned.

No one heard the bird except the youth and old Hoyeh-tay . . . and, it seemed to Cha-kwena, Masau. Startled, he saw the man react to the communication from Owl.

"You must trust me, Hoyeh-tay," Masau said in the smoothest, most ingratiating voice that Cha-kwena had ever heard. "I have come far to bring gifts of goodwill to your people, to trade many of the unusual things of the northern land for the things found in the south, and to proclaim a renewed and everlasting kinship between us."

The old man was upset and restless. When he spoke, it was to Tlana-quah. "This man greases his words in an attempt to oil this man's pride. Tell him to go away. He is not your brother. He is a lion hiding in the skin of an eagle."

Masau's eyes narrowed beneath the head of the raptor that shadowed his tattooed face. "Your old friend Ish-iwi would be sorry to hear your words."

"Ish-iwi!" Hoyeh-tay, already on his way back into the cave, turned so quickly that, had it not been for his staff and Cha-kwena's quick reflexes, he would have fallen.

"Yes," replied Masau. "My brother's bride was from his band. A good man was Ish-iwi, shaman of the People of the Red Hills. He came to the north to officiate at Ah-nee's wedding. It was his gift to her—a way to help her to feel at ease among strangers and a way of giving his complete approval of the joining of our two peoples into one."

"*Was?* You speak as though he was dead."

Cha-kwena saw his grandfather's face tighten with dread of that which he had so long feared and yet had somehow known.

"He was killed," Masau revealed with utmost sympathy. "My brother tried to save him and thereby won the scars that you see upon his face. But Ish-iwi died bravely. A shaman and a friend and brother of my people to the end, was he not, Maliwal?"

Maliwal stared at Masau as though he were having a difficult time understanding the question. The other men in the traveling party did the same thing. Then, suddenly, Maliwal smiled. "Yes. Absolutely! The old shaman *did* face death bravely!" His smile was gone as he turned his gaze to Hoyeh-tay and laid a broad hand over his heart to indicate complete sincerity as he added: "Believe me, I, of all men, can assure you of that!"

"How did he die?" Cha-kwena asked, and was immediately sorry, for when the answer came, old Hoyeh-tay moaned and staggered back.

"Lions killed him," Masau answered.

And a stunned Cha-kwena was there to catch his grandfather when he fainted.

"I am sorry about our shaman," Tlana-quah apologized. "Perhaps he will speak with you later. In the meantime, I invite you and your fellow travelers to accept the hospitality of my people."

They stayed, and despite Hoyeh-tay's rudeness, they were gracious and deferential in all ways. They admired Tlana-quah's cape, and he stood tall and proud as he boasted how he had slain the jaguar. Then he stood even taller when the newcomers told him that they had never seen so wondrous a creature as a spotted lion. They asked the headman's permission before spreading their trading goods upon fine, big pelts of bison and elk hides and gesturing the people forward. They had gifts for everyone: strings of tiny hematite beads for every child, earrings and nose rings of shells and feathers for every woman, and a chunk of black obsidian from which fine projectile points might later be cut and carved for each man.

By midafternoon they were gathered around a fire under clear skies, seated upon thick rabbit-fur blankets that had been spread over woven tule mats on the snow-covered ground. The girls circulated with woven trays piled high with rolled fried cakes, hot and fragile and taken straight from the stones upon which the batter had been poured, baked, then peeled away in thin layers. The women accompanied the girls with bowls of hot soup thickened with grain and marsh clay and strips of preserved meat. The last of summer's crisply roasted grubs, cicadas, lizard feet, and little brown rock spiders were added as a garnish. Although the strangers appreciatively slurped the soup, they ate sparingly and soon patted their bellies to indicate fullness. The people of Tlana-quah exchanged looks of approval of this great display of good manners and restraint. This was a winter meal, and it was apparent that the travelers sensed that to eat more than a little might be to cause hardship among their hosts.

"Truly we can eat no more," said Masau as Mah-ree paused before him with Shrike on her shoulder and a tray of fried cakes extended in her hands.

"There is plenty!" insisted Tlana-quah.

"Mah-ree, hand them out, hand them out!" Ha-xa insisted. "We would not have the cakes go to waste!"

The girl obeyed, and as she smiled at Masau, staring curiously at the tattooing around his eyes, he ate obligingly, observing the bird as curiously as the girl was observing him. When the shrike suddenly spread its now-healed wings and alighted on his shoulder, he stiffened and looked sideways at the creature.

"He likes you," said the girl. Then she added softly, "He even looks like you!"

Masau's brow arched toward his hairline. "Yes, perhaps he does."

"Shrike is beautiful. You are beautiful," Mah-ree whispered, and hung her head lest he see her blush.

"Mah-ree, just feed the man," scolded Ha-xa, then ordered the other girls to offer the rest of the travelers more cakes.

"You are too generous!" said Maliwal, raising a hand to ward off an offering.

"They are not to your liking?" asked Tlana-quah, concerned.

Masau took a cake from Mah-ree, tore off a piece with his front teeth, swallowed it without chewing, and then managed a polite, "The taste is unusual. Our women prepare nothing like this."

"No fried cakes?" asked Mah-ree.

"Not like these. The taste . . . it is . . . very different."

"It is my own special recipe!" informed Ha-xa. "You are fortunate, Man Who Wears Eagle. In dry years the fried cakes are always best. The locusts are so thick that we are able to flush them from the grass like quail."

"Locusts?" The word fell like a stone from Maliwal's mouth.

"Oh, yes!" Ha-xa went on in a burst of enthusiasm. "I have my girls scorch them separately for me in winnowing baskets."

"Separately? Separately from what?" asked Chudeh.

"From the seeds that make the bulk of the flour that forms the base of the batter."

"Ah, *seeds*." Maliwal sounded relieved.

"Oh, yes," continued Ha-xa. "Sweet seeds, bitter locusts, both ground together, mixed with heated water, and then—this is the real secret—before the batter is put to the stones, red-bellied ants are added. That is what gives the spice!"

"Indeed," said Masau.

"You must tell your own women of the fine cakes of the women of the Red World," Kahm-ree suggested, pausing in her soup serving to observe Masau thoughtfully. "A man like you . . . you must have many women, eh?"

Masau was staring at the fried cake that Mah-ree had just placed into his hand. "I . . . no . . . I have no women."

Kahm-ree froze. "None? Why? Is it forbidden for a shaman to have women where you come from?"

"Enough, Kahm-ree!" Tlana-quah scolded. "It is rude to pry. You have offended our guest."

"No," said Masau in a friendly way. "If we are to learn more of each other's ways, we must ask questions, and we must answer with an open heart. I am not offended. Among my people it is not forbidden for a shaman to have a woman. But I do not."

"Yet," said Maliwal, scanning the young unmarried women whom Tlana-quah had, for the sake of propriety, told to stand back from the others. When his eyes found Ta-maya, his expression changed. Beside her, Ban-ya stood taller and opened her cloak as though she was too warm in the chill air; but it was obvious to anyone who saw her that she was showing off the great, swelling mounds that strained the topmost reaches of her dress.

Masau was looking down at his portion of fried cakes again. "Yet," he echoed his brother, then folding the cake in half, put it into his mouth and ate it.

"Our mother looks after him," informed Maliwal.

Kahm-ree's fat face seemed to split in two with her grin. "Ah! It is good when a young man is close with his old mother."

"Yes," Ha-xa remarked. "I will be proud to share my recipe for fried cakes with the mother of Masau."

"Ysuna is not much of a cook," said Masau.

"All the more reason to share!" proclaimed Ha-xa.

"*Ysuna.* That is a pretty name," said Mah-ree. "What does it mean?"

"Daughter of the Sun. One Who Brings Life to the People. She is a shaman."

His statement caused an immediate response.

"Your mother is a *what?*" asked Ha-xa.

"A shaman," he replied evenly.

"In the Red World females cannot be shaman," informed Tlana-quah.

Mah-ree cocked her head. "I am Medicine Girl," she revealed. She put her basket down and scooped Shrike into her palms to hold him gently, even though he pecked at her with his hooked beak. "Like Cha-kwena, I, too, heal wounded things, like this bird. I am also Girl Who Calls Mammoth! They come to me, don't they, Father?"

Tlana-quah frowned, apologetic. "She is no shaman, but she does have the healing way, and our totem has come to her. That much is true."

"Your totem?" Masau asked ingenuously.

"The great white mammoth," Tlana-quah explained.

Masau and Maliwal exchanged quick looks. The other men in their party did the same.

"Well," said Masau with a sigh, "it seems we have not come all this long way in vain. We do share the same mother and father of the generations, as surely as we share the same totem."

"That is good!" exclaimed Mah-ree, as delighted with his news as she was obviously delighted with him.

"Yes, Little One," Masau replied. "That is very good!"

# 4

That night a high fire was raised by Tlana-quah and the men of the band in honor of the arrival of the travelers from the north. Kosar-eh, in full ceremonial paint and feathers, carefully ascended the icy stairs that led to Hoyeh-tay's cave and peered into the interior.

"Tlana-quah has invited Hoyeh-tay, the elder, and Cha-kwena, the novice, to join in the night's celebration," he said. "The strangers have hunted successfully with Tlana-quah, Dakan-eh, and the other men of the band. Tonight there will be great feasting, much dancing, and storytelling by the travelers. Tlana-quah would have our shaman join us to reveal the history of our people to those who claim to be our brothers from the north."

The old man was reclining against his backrest, with Owl perched upon his toes and his feet stretched close to the warmth of a small fire that burned blue as it fed upon old bones, pinecones, and deadwood. "Bah! Tell Tlana-quah there is nothing to celebrate. Go away, Kosar-eh. Ish-iwi is dead, and I must mourn."

"But *I* would go!" exclaimed Cha-kwena. "I would hear the stories of the men from the far country. Just getting out of this cave once in a while is celebration enough for me!"

Anger sparked hot within the sunken black hollows of the old man's eyes. "You will stay!" he commanded.

Cha-kwena looked crestfallen. "Please give Tlana-quah our shaman's apologies, Kosar-eh. Hoyeh-tay is too tired to leave his cave this night."

"No!" the old man shot back. "You will tell Tlana-quah exactly what I have said, Kosar-eh. We have no cause to celebrate—not over the coming of lions."

Kosar-eh stood a moment, then shrugged. "As you

say. Rest easily, old friend. I will miss your tales at the feast fire tonight."

"Then you will be the only one!" Hoyeh-tay retorted.

Kosar-eh was too honest a man to lie; instead of disputing the shaman's words, he said, "Listen to the singing, Hoyeh-tay. When you hear my voice and the beat of my drum, know that I am raising my song for you, to lessen the pain of your mourning for the loss of your old friend. Ish-iwi was a good man. To die as he died must be a bitter thing for a friend to hear."

"We were as brothers!" The old man began to weep like a child.

Kosar-eh nodded in sympathy. "Then my song will be for him, also—the happy song of a clown, made for an old friend and for all the good times that you once enjoyed together."

"You are a good man, Kosar-eh," said Hoyeh-tay.

With no further word except a brief admonition to Cha-kwena about the amount of ice that the youth was allowing to accumulate upon the stairs, the clown went his way.

Cha-kwena watched him go, and Hoyeh-tay, who could not help but sense the boy's longing, scowled with resentment. "Is it so difficult to stay here with me? I will not be in this world much longer. Soon enough you will be able to come and go as you will, for this cave shall be yours, and you shall be Shaman in my place!"

Cha-kwena whirled around. "You will never die, Grandfather. Your spirit may fly in and out of your head, but it always returns! I think that you will be Shaman forever. And I think that I will be here at your side, trapped within this cave, forever . . . doing your bidding forever . . . listening to your stories forever . . . taking care of you and cleaning up after you forever. And when I am old before I have had a chance to be young, you will be the one to take care of *me* forever! And then we will see how *you* like it! And then we will see how long it takes for you to wish *me* dead!"

The old man stared, appalled. Cha-kwena had never spoken to him as he had just spoken now. Hoyeh-tay's heart began to bleed, for he saw hatred and contempt in the youth's eyes.

"Forgive me, Old Owl. I did not know what I was saying."

"Yes, you did! You spoke from your heart," replied Hoyeh-tay.

The words did not come easily to the old man. He was deeply hurt, and only his affection for Cha-kwena and his understanding of the frustrations of youth allowed him to swallow his pain. Suddenly he was furious—not with Cha-kwena but with himself, with life, with the forces of Creation that had turned him into a sick old man whose needs and continuing illness had transformed a grandson's love and respect into loathing.

"You are right, Cha-kwena! It is not good to be old. The years sneak up on a man and turn him into what you see before you. Forgive me if I have made you feel trapped. It is not my intention. But, Cha-kwena, I *will* die, and when I do, you will be our people's only shaman."

Cha-kwena, kneeling beside him, took his bony hand and held it. "Yes, Grandfather, I know."

"I was right about Ish-iwi and the lions."

"Yes, Grandfather."

"And I am right about these strangers. They have bad eyes—wolf eyes, lion eyes, eagle eyes. Tlana-quah should have sought my advice before inviting them into our village. They may be the Brothers of the Sky."

"But how can we be sure unless we hear them out? Perhaps we should listen to their words and to their tales of their land?"

"The Brothers of the Sky are clever, treacherous, always watching for a chance to make trouble in the world. It was their eternal battling that brought disunity to the People and sent the many bands fleeing across the earth until the People were no longer one but many, strangers to one another. These travelers are perhaps enemies to us, as the lion and wolf are enemies of the antelope and hare!"

"The strangers are not animals, Grandfather."

"Do not condescend to me, Cha-kwena! You must remember the story of the Brothers of the Sky and—"

"I've heard the story so many times that I can tell it in my sleep, Grandfather." The boy stood and walked toward the entrance to the cave. "So many times that I—"

"Then you will hear it again! You will hear how the

People fled into the Red World! You will hear how the Brothers tried to follow! You will hear how Great Ghost Spirit grew so angry that he hurled the Brothers away into the night and—"

"And that is where they have been ever since—above us in the sky, always watching us, always fighting with each other. On nights of storm we can hear them battling with their terrible thunder drums and their spears of lightning. Is that not the way the story goes, Grandfather? Shall I repeat it to you from the beginning, or will that do?"

The old man, deeply hurt by his grandson's impatience, swung his head slowly. "It is the way the story goes," he allowed.

Hoyeh-tay was suddenly so tired that he could barely keep his eyes open. The fire that Cha-kwena had raised was burning high, sending long, languorous waves of heat through the bottoms of his feet and up through his legs and body. He yielded to the need for sleep until, from far away, mammoth trumpeted to one another in the darkness. Hoyeh-tay stiffened. He blinked, stared ahead, and curled both hands protectively around the sacred stone.

"Listen," urged Cha-kwena. "Our totem is out there. You have always told me that whenever Great Ghost Spirit walks, the signs will always be good for the People. So it is now, Grandfather. The visitors are only what they seem to be—traders from a far land and a distant people." Cha-kwena came to hunker down beside his father's father.

Hoyeh-tay grimaced against the pity that he saw on Cha-kwena's face . . . and against a deep pain in his chest. It passed, leaving his heart pounding and his breath coming so fast and shallow that he was frightened. He felt faint as he reached out and took hold of his grandson's hand. "You must remember all that I have taught you. Ah, Nar-eh, it is good when you come to visit with your father."

Cha-kwena smoothed and patted the gnarled hand that gripped his own so tightly. "You are tired, Grandfather. Lie back. Try to sleep."

"Sleep. Yes." Hoyeh-tay sighed and smiled with contentment. The fire was so warm, so soothing. . . . Then, as though stung by an insect, he winced and shook his head. Suddenly his eyes were focused and sharp. "No,

Cha-kwena! I cannot sleep! You must promise to remember all that I have taught you, for if you forget, the People will be lost and the Brothers of the Sky will send you wandering to the ends of the world."

"Our totem will protect us."

"No! You do not understand, Cha-kwena! We shamans are the guardians of our totem!" He snatched his hand free of Cha-kwena's soothing fingers and clutched the talisman tightly. "The great mammoth . . . his life is here. The last beat of his heart and the last breath of his spirit are in this stone in our care." He sighed again, so weak that he could barely keep his eyelids open. "As Grandfather of All watches over us, so must we guard and protect *him*." His eyes fluttered closed. His words followed his thoughts along a misted trail that led toward unconsciousness. It was so warm by the fire, so wondrously, relaxingly warm. "I will sleep now. You will keep me safe from lions and from the Brothers of the Sky?"

"Yes, Grandfather. I will keep you safe."

And so Cha-kwena sat by his grandfather's side, watching him sleep and tending the fire until the flames died. He banked the embers and then covered the elderly shaman with an extra blanket.

Far below the cave, Kosar-eh was singing loudly and beating upon his little drum. Laughter rose through the firelit darkness. Cha-kwena listened and yearned to join the celebration. Soon the women would serve the food, and then the storytelling would begin. What would the tales of such men as the traders be like? he wondered.

His belly gave an aching lurch, and he remembered that he had not eaten since morning. A slight wind gusted into the cave. It was a north wind, but instead of carrying the scent of snow, it brought the rich, heady scent of the meal that was about to be consumed. Overcome, he rose, snatched up his cloak, and slung it on.

"Watch him for me for a while, Owl. Just long enough for me to eat and hear a story or two."

"Do not be gone long," said Owl.

"No, just long enough," promised Cha-kwena, and, with that, was out of the cave and scrambling down the icy steps toward the creek and the village.

*    *    *

The villagers welcomed him. To the boy's amazement, when Tlana-quah saw him coming, he commanded that room be made for the boy in the shaman's traditional place of honor, at the headman's immediate right. Although Cha-kwena swore that he was not yet worthy of it, Tlana-quah insisted he stay.

"Hoyeh-tay is not feeling well. He is asleep," Cha-kwena explained. "I will stay just long enough to—"

"Long enough to eat!" The headman slung an avuncular arm around his shoulder. "Long enough to enjoy Kosar-eh's antics and the tales that our guests have volunteered to share!" He bent his head and confided, "I am glad that you have come, Cha-kwena. Let Hoyeh-tay sleep alone for a change. That old man has shamed me this day before my guests. If he were here to tell the tales of our ancestors, no doubt he would shame me again by forgetting the stories before he was even halfway done! You will be shaman for your people tonight, Cha-kwena. Sit tall and proud. If I ask you to speak, speak boldly, in the way that you have seen the shamans of the Blue Mesas speak. And watch the one who calls himself Masau. Ah, the magic that he works with his words and eyes and a turn of his hand! Pattern your style after his, and despite your youth there will not be a shaman in all the Red World who will not respect you."

Then Tlana-quah turned away to observe the antics of the clown. The fire was still high, and Kosar-eh was whirling and dancing around it as he blew madly upon a reed whistle and beat his drum with a hide-wrapped bone, all the while performing a series of clever mimes designed to prompt those who watched him into guessing the identities of the animals that he was impersonating.

"Lynx!"

"Sloth!"

"Antelope!"

"Bear!"

Whenever a correct answer was given, Kosar-eh would leap straight into the air, shake his feathered bottom, then pull on nearly invisible strings that caused a scattering of tiny presents—feathers and nuts and morsels of food and bits of colored bone and stones—for children and adults alike. The children squealed with delight, and the audience clapped their hands and laughed with pure pleasure at his skill.

In the merriment, Cha-kwena forgot all about old Hoyeh-tay. Kosar-eh was a sight to behold, despite his withered arm, strong and lithe and amazingly quick on his feet.

Cha-kwena found himself guffawing with pleasure. Tlana-quah sat tall with pride, his dark eyes shining, his shoulders thrown back beneath his spotted cape of timeworn jaguar skin. The strangers in their magnificent furs and paint were fully taken by the clown's performance. They laughed easily and applauded vigorously, urging Kosar-eh to continue the game until, at last, he feigned an enormous swoon and fell upon his back, legs up, squawking like a dying crow.

Children broke from the circle to swarm all over him, tickling him and grabbing the last of the gifts that were hidden within his feathers. When he was reasonably certain that every child had managed to grasp a bit of stolen "treasure," he scooped up an armload of giggling toddlers and rose, bowing mightily to his audience.

Now, as the clown took his place on the men's side of the fire, the women circulated with food. Cha-kwena ate greedily of his portion of roasted hare and peccary and slabs of sloth steaks. He listened wide-eyed as the men spoke of the day's hunt but soon noticed that Dakan-eh was unusually silent and morose. After a while, it became evident that Bold Man had nothing to brag about, for to hear it from Tlana-quah and the other men of the village, the strangers had outperformed him. The newcomers had set lighter-weight, more deadly snares and used their great spears in tandem with throwing sticks to take the huge sloth unaware. And then, advancing boldly on the peccaries, the northerners had provoked the boar to charge again and again as though its snorting, tusk-jabbing, potentially death-dealing feints were a mere amusement to them.

"How brave are the hunters of the north!" exclaimed Tlana-quah. "As for their leader, this shaman-hunter, Masau, never have I seen a man handle a spear with more accuracy . . . unless it is his brother. You must teach us the way of the spear whose head comes away from the shaft when a kill is made, so that the shaft may be withdrawn and refitted and reused on a new kill almost immediately after!"

The people murmured and nodded to show their desire to hear more about this innovation. Masau rose, took up his spear, and told them that the weapon's design was patterned after the spear of First Man.

"It is not for the killing of rabbits or antelope. It is for *big* game, for ma— er, mastodon! Yes! And for moose, horse, camel, bison, and elk! Do you see the head of the spear, how large it is and fluted along both sides to increase the flow of blood within a wound? And here, under the binding, the stone has been hollowed on both sides to allow for a tighter fit to the shaft and to eliminate any bulge in the wrapping that might prevent it from being driven deep enough into the body of its prey to strike a mortal wound. The shaft of the spear can be of wood or bone. This one is mastodon bone, which has been hardened and straightened in water and fire, obtained from life and reshaped to take life! And do you see the notch into which the foreshaft is fitted and bound to the throwing end? This, more than just its size and weight, makes the difference between this spear and yours—the foreshaft to which the hafted spearhead is joined."

The hunters of the band leaned forward so as not to miss a single word. As Masau spoke his fellow travelers passed around their long, heavy spears for the men of the Red World to examine closely.

"When properly mated to the foreshaft," Masau continued, "the main body of the spear can be quickly withdrawn, leaving the projectile point buried in a kill, while the shaft itself can be rearmed. This allows a man to carry fewer shafts but many spearheads. With such a spear as this, a single man can make many strikes with a single shaft and kill twice as many animals as could men hunting with spears such as yours. And for close-in work, when a big animal is down, and we wish to quicken its death without ruining good stone projectile points, we use the killing foreshaft. Show them, Maliwal."

The scarred man obliged by holding up a narrow, beautifully carved and painted length of deadly looking bone, approximately the length of his forearm.

Masau nodded, obviously pleased by the enthusiastic response of the men of the Red World.

Cha-kwena observed that the women of the village were also pleased by his presentation. Indeed, on the females' side of the fire, there was not a woman or girl who was not wide-eyed and fascinated by Masau's inordinate good looks and magnificent apparel. The old widows, bosoms rising and falling with quickened breaths, were gaping like virgins over his unmistakable virility. All mouths were smiling and all eyes were gazing at the glorious Masau.

Cha-kwena saw that Ban-ya was sitting with her little nose in the air and her great chest thrust forward, as brazen and pert as a jay in the way she held herself and stared provocatively across the flames. Beside her, Ta-maya was staring at Masau as if she had never seen a man before.

With a start, the youth realized that the man in the skin of the golden eagle was looking back at the older daughter of Tlana-quah. How could he not? In the light of the fire, her beauty was pure radiance. She might as well have been sitting there alone, for in the light of her perfection, no one else seemed to exist.

"That woman is mine! You will not look at her, Eagle Man!" Dakan-eh's declaration struck across the firelight like a well-hurled spear.

Ta-maya caught her breath and lowered her eyes.

Masau seemed to have a difficult time looking away from her and turning his gaze to Dakan-eh. "Then the forces of Creation have smiled upon you, Man of the Red World," he said graciously, inclining his head in deference. "My eyes have meant no offense to you or to your woman."

"My daughter is not your woman yet, Dakan-eh!" Tlana-quah declared hotly.

Bold Man reacted to the statement as though he had been slapped. He glowered and his jaw was set when Ha-xa came close to offer a conciliatory smile and another serving of boar meat. He waved her away angrily. "This meat is not to my taste! The flesh of the boar would be less tough and bitter had it been killed more quickly," he announced with a truculence that turned his mouth downward into a disdainful scowl.

Beside Cha-kwena, Tlana-quah stiffened. "I did not

see you rush into the scrub growth with the others to make the kill more quickly!"

Now it was Dakan-eh who stiffened. "These men of the north were having such a fine time antagonizing the boar, jabbing it, leaping over it like frogs hopping back and forth over a marsh lily, that I would not have presumed to end their pleasure in this strange sport . . . although what good it served, I cannot imagine—unless our northern 'brothers' prefer their meat tough and bitter from the terror that taints the flesh when a hunter fails to make a quick and clean kill."

Bold Man's criticism wrapped the gathering in a shocked silence.

Tlana-quah fixed him with a reproving glare. "You offend our guests, Bold Man. Take back your words."

"It is not necessary," assured Masau, raising his hands, palms out in a gesture of conciliation. "Among my people a man who speaks with a straight tongue is honored, even when his words may cause offense. That man is one whom others desire to have at their side on the hunt and in a council, for truly he is brave and bold and a seeker of truth, a man whom others may trust."

Cha-kwena saw Dakan-eh's face work against indecision as he tried to make up his mind whether to accept the compliment or challenge it. As always, his arrogance made the decision for him. "This is true. I am Bold Man. I am well named. It is my nature to be direct and unflinching and unafraid."

Cha-kwena rolled his eyes at Dakan-eh's never-failing conceit.

Beneath the head of the eagle and within the intricate black mask of tattooing that surrounded the upper portion of his face, Masau's eyes narrowed thoughtfully. When he spoke, his voice was soft and sure. "Among my people, Bold Man, it is indeed a sport to hunt boar as you have seen us hunt today. But it is not a game with us; it is a way in which we test and hone our courage as we leap before the threat of death. Unlike the lucky hunters of the Red World, we do not dwell in a gentle land where food for our women and children may be easily obtained within the hunting grounds of a single village, where the people have dwelled for generations. In the way of the ancestors since time beyond beginning, the harshness of our land has kept us a nomadic people. We follow the herds from one hunting camp to another, seeking big—often dangerous—game, to be food for our women and children."

He paused. Every eye was on him. Every breath was held, waiting for him to continue. At his side, his men exchanged glances, and his brother, Maliwal, seemed to be gloating with pride in him.

"Our ways are old ways, good ways," Masau told his listeners, and went on to speak of the north, of rich hunting grounds, of endless grasslands and snow-covered mountains, of bison and horse and mammoth, of lions and bear, and of the spirit of the golden eagle that was sacred to him and to his people. "Truly," he continued, "now that we have shared food and fire and long, good talk, I know that we are brothers and sisters beneath this sky. The People are one."

Now Masau was rising to his full height, and with his spear held horizontally between both hands, he lifted his arms and face to the sky and offered a song of thanksgiving to the forces of Creation, which had brought the children of First Man and First Woman together once again. The song, like the man, was overwhelming. Never—not even among the gathering of holy men on the heights of the Blue Mesas—had Cha-kwena ever heard a man speak with such commanding eloquence. The boy was transfixed. Masau's physical presence was so overpowering and compelling that the grandson of Hoyeh-tay stared at him in gape-mouthed awe.

*If this is what a shaman can be,* he thought, *then proudly will I walk in the shaman's way. The road that I walk need not be the road of the holy men of the Red World—it can be the way of Masau of the People of the Watching Star . . . hunter . . . traveler . . . trader . . . shaman. To be a man like him is to be the best of men— better than Tlana-quah or Dakan-eh or Hoyeh-tay have ever dared to dream of being!*

Cha-kwena was not the only one to follow the gaze of Masau, for the tall shaman was staring straight ahead, his face fixed, his body rigid. In the starlit darkness beyond the village and across the creek, old Hoyeh-tay was barely visible as he stood stiff bodied, leaning on his staff, at the lip of the cave.

A sinking feeling impelled Cha-kwena to his feet. "I had best get back! He should not be left alone. If he tries to come down the stairs without me . . ."

But in that very moment the old man turned and disappeared into the cave.

"Wait!" commanded Tlana-quah.

Cha-kwena obeyed.

"He will be all right," assured Tlana-quah. "He has lived most of his life without you, Cha-kwena, and you have spent the last many moons at his side. A few hours away from him and in the service of your people will cause him to take pride in you and in himself. It is time for you to show our guests what he has taught you and to share with them the stories of the People of the Red World."

Cha-kwena hesitated, but only for a moment. When he saw Owl follow the old man into the cave, he relaxed. Owl would watch over Hoyeh-tay. Owl had promised.

# 5

If Moon had risen, old Hoyeh-tay could not see her face. With Owl on his shoulder, he sat close to the embers of the fire. It occurred to him that he should build it up again; it was growing cold inside the cave, and Cha-kwena had arranged a sizable pile of well-dried bones and sticks and several small logs of ironwood beside the stone hearth—enough fuel to last the night.

Hoyeh-tay sighed. He was too tired to fuss with the fire, so instead he pulled his robe close and listened as Cha-kwena's voice came to him from across the creek. How much like a man his grandson sounded tonight—bold and almost sure of himself, his voice leading his listeners along the subtle pathways of the ancient tales.

Listeners? Why were his people listening to the boy while he was *here*, alone in the cave with Owl? Ah, he remembered now: He had been too weary to leave the cave. And strangers had come from the north.

Again the old man sighed, but this time he smiled a little. He had taught the boy well. Cha-kwena would make a good shaman and perhaps would be even better than that someday. Perhaps he would be a great shaman, as his grandfather had once been.

Hoyeh-tay's mouth pulled in against his teeth. Why had Cha-kwena left him alone for so long? Why did Tlana-quah not send the boy back to the cave?

"Hmmph! Tlana-quah!" He spoke the headman's name with a snort of annoyance, then looked sideways at Owl. "Did you hear the way he spoke to me in front of the strangers?"

"I did," replied Owl.

"Too often does Tlana-quah challenge me these days!"

"Too often," the bird affirmed.

"It is a shameful thing!"

"Shameful!" agreed Owl.

"That man was but an unborn spirit on the wind when I put my boyhood behind me."

"It was long ago, Hoyeh-tay. Tlana-quah is headman now. Tonight Cha-kwena is shaman. Tonight Wise and Watchful Owl sits alone in his cave with a balding old bird, and neither you nor I can make the People see that it is lions disguised as men who have come to them."

"Lions?" Memories flared and hurt so much that he refused to consider them. And yet a portion of them would not be ignored. Ish-iwi was dead, killed by lions! And those lions were in his village now! A moment ago he had risen, gone to the top of the stone steps, and watched the stranger in the skin of an eagle. He had known at that moment that he must go down into the village, stand against the man called Masau, and hurl every shaman's trick against him so that his people would see the intruder as an enemy, a destroyer! But in that very instant the man had turned and faced him in the dark. Their eyes had met, and a terrible feeling of weakness and impotence had overcome him. His mind had gone blank. Obediently, passively, he had retreated into the cave and had seated himself next to the fire. It felt as though the shaman of the People of the Watching Star had sucked the will right out of him.

Now the elderly man shook his head. The will of Masau was still working in him. His memory of the visitor blurred, then faded and vanished. His mind wandered back into time, into the careless days of childhood when life had seemed so easy. He smiled blissfully. He was a boy again, with Ish-iwi again, swimming in Big Lake.

And then, suddenly, even those memories blurred, and he was back in the cave. He knew that he thought too much of how it used to be, of then rather than now.

"Ish-iwi is dead," he said to Owl.

"Is Hoyeh-tay still alive?" asked the bird.

A sudden rush of apprehension made him shiver against the cold prickling of gooseflesh. "Yes. But for how long? And for what purpose when my headman calls a boy to be Shaman in my place?" He pulled his robe closer and stared glumly into the flickering flames. Abruptly, it seemed that tiny human forms took shape within the fire.

Hoyeh-tay's eyes went round with surprise. He had not called for a vision, but here it was—images of the village below the cave and of his people gathered around the feast fire. The young women of his band moved in the firelight while the strangers smiled wide, white smiles and watched them out of eyes as shining black as their spearheads.

The old man leaned closer to the fire. There was something both invasive and evasive about the eyes of the strangers. Although their lips were parted and their teeth were glinting bright, their smiles did not reach their eyes. And now within the vision Hoyeh-tay saw Ta-maya come forward to stand alone before the young women of the band. In the shadow of an eagle's wings she stood, with the skull of a mammoth at her feet. Strangers circled her . . . no longer men, but fanged and furred carnivores menacing potential prey. The stench of smoke, of scorching hide and fur, and of burning hair assailed his nostrils. He leaned even closer to the fire, trying to see better, to understand; but Owl's screeches and flurrying wings destroyed the vision.

Hoyeh-tay sat up, confused and perplexed as he warded

off the bird's frantic dives. "What . . . ?" He did not need to complete the question. Portions of his robe and the ends of his hair were smoldering. As quickly as his age would allow, he struggled to his feet and pinched and slapped out the potential blaze, then stood stunned, shaking, realizing that in his attempt to gain a closer insight into his vision, he had nearly set himself afire.

Owl, visibly upset and ruffling his feathers, was panting on the ground on the opposite side of the stones that formed the curbing of the fire pit. "Very impressive!" scolded the bird. "If you are hungry, there is plenty to eat in the baskets at the back of the cave! You do not have to roast yourself and me along with you!"

Hoyeh-tay was suddenly exhausted. He sat down, a good distance from the fire this time. He weakly held out his arm, and Owl flew to him. The bird was not as heavy as he had once been; nevertheless the old man had to bend his arm and rest it on his lap in order to support his old friend's weight. "I am tired," said Hoyeh-tay.

"I know, my shaman," said the bird. "We are both sacks of dried-up skin and brittle bones! But you cannot relax now. You must go to the People and tell them what you have seen in the flames."

"Go to the People for me. I must rest now. Warn them. Disturb the night for them. . . ."

"I have tried. They would not see or hear or heed me."

Hoyeh-tay hung his head and nodded, then lay down on his side. "So tired . . . " he whispered as Owl moved to sit upon his shoulder, spread his wings, and nestle close. The underside of the bird's beak rested upon the old man's cheek as Hoyeh-tay clutched the sacred stone, drew his knees up toward his chin, and exhaled a long, deep breath that seemed to be releasing most of his life-force along with it. "Must sleep just a little. I will ask the sacred stone for strength. Then I will go down from the cave. Then I will warn the People. But will they listen? And even if they listen, will they believe?"

For hours the feast fire burned. For hours the tale telling continued. Urged on by his listeners, Cha-kwena was soon so full of himself that when the last log had been burned and the fire was only a lake of sparkling light and heat in the darkness, he was the last one to fall asleep, warm in his cape, his belly full, and his head full of dreams.

Far to the southeast a mammoth trumpeted to the stars.

Masau sat up. He had not been sleeping; he had been waiting. Now, as silent as the night, he rose and moved around the sleeping revelers and through the village. When the mammoth trumpeted again, Masau stopped to listen. He stared fixedly past the creek and up at the cave of the shaman.

"It must be done."

He turned. Maliwal was beside him.

"Yes," Masau assented, his voice as low as his brother's. "It must be done."

"I could do it for you."

"You enjoy killing too much, Maliwal. I am the eyes of the Wolf on this journey, remember?"

"Yes, and what a clever wolf you are proving to be. The lies you spin, and the ease with which you spin them! Ysuna will be impressed."

Masau turned his gaze back toward the cave; he had no time for his brother's admiration or his envy. "There is power in that old man. He has seen straight through my words and has detected the scent of danger in us. Go back to the fire circle, Maliwal. What I will do now, I must do alone."

Hoyeh-tay slept deeply by the cold embers of his fire. Owl still nestled upon his shoulders. The shaman's gnarled fingers moved over the barely discernible indentations in the sacred stone.

Dreams came to him. He saw himself walking with the ancestors, with First Man and First Woman, across a white land and into the rising sun—an old man, an owl, a blue-eyed dog, a tall man in a lion's-skin garment with a wolf's-tail ruff, and an antelope-eyed woman with many children at her side, a necklace of shells at her throat, and a bola in her hand. The great white mammoth, Grandfather of All, plodded ahead of them, his massive tusks sweeping the pathway clean before the ancestors. Huge, magnificent, his body was swathed in long strands of mist—or was it hair? Hoyeh-tay could not be sure, but it did not matter. A little brown bird rode atop the mammoth's head. It was a sweet dream. First Man and First Woman seemed like old friends to him.

"The People are one," said First Man.

"Always and forever," added First Woman.

And the children smiled and ran on ahead until a pair of young boys, squabbling, shouting epithets at each other, broke away. Hoyeh-tay twitched against the dream. He knew these boys but did not want to know them—they were the Brothers of the Sky. They would grow to manhood and couple with monsters, and before they were hurled away across the heavens, they would destroy forever the unity of the family of First Man and First Woman.

Hoyeh-tay was suddenly cold and offended by the stench of burning feathers. He closed his nostrils against the unpleasant scents and reached to draw his robe and Owl closer. But the bird was gone.

The old shaman awoke with a start to find Masau kneeling across the fire pit from him. Owl was lying facedown with his wings spread wide over the coals.

"No!" the old man cried, and sat up, grabbing the bird from the firepit, but Owl was limp and lifeless in his hands.

"I could not let him speak to warn you of my coming," Masau said, and then, in the next instant, swooped across the small space between himself and the old man like a raptor hurling itself upon its prey. He had Hoyeh-tay by the throat before the old man knew what had happened. "Do not fight me, Shaman. I have always dealt quickly with those whose lives must end so that the goals of my own people may be served. There will be only a moment of pain as I crack your neck, and then it will be over. What fools your people are, to have had such wisdom as yours within their midst and to have failed to heed it. I must have their trust, but with you to speak against me, this could not be. And so, Old Owl, forgive me. I must see to it that you never speak again."

Cha-kwena was not sure what woke him. A sudden gust of wind? The cry of Owl in the cave? He sat up and looked around. Save for the occasional splash and low chortling of waterfowl on the lake, the night was unnaturally quiet. Masau was gone from the place that he had taken next to Cha-kwena at the height of the storytelling, but everyone else was still asleep.

Cha-kwena stared toward the bluff. For a moment, through a blur of sleep haze, he was certain that he saw Owl winging against the night, shadowing the village with wide, slurring wings, flying so low that he could feel the wake of the bird's passage. But when he looked again nothing was there—not even stars. Instinctively he knew that many hours had passed since he had left the cave. He knew that he should get back to Hoyeh-tay; he had been away too long. He was about to rise when Masau walked back to his place beside the fire circle.

"Where are you going, young teller of tales?" the shaman asked, settling himself close to Cha-kwena and explaining in a whisper that he was returning from relieving himself.

"I should get back to my grandfather. Just now I could have sworn that Owl flew over me, and it was as though he were telling me that Hoyeh-tay needed me and—"

Masau interrupted quietly but with great concern, "It is good the way you look after your grandfather. He is very old? Very frail?"

"Yes. Very old. Very frail."

"On my way back to the fire circle I saw an owl flying low. But do not all owls hunt by night and find their own meat?"

"Yes, but this owl is different. This owl . . . " He paused. Just thinking of the bird's special relationship with his grandfather troubled him. "I really should get back to the cave," he said again.

"It will be dawn soon. Will you not disturb your grandfather if you return now? Old men sleep lightly. Old men need their sleep . . . as do young shamans whose words have filled this night with magic!"

Had the compliment come from any other man, Cha-kwena might not have been taken in by it so easily. "Have I done that?"

"Ah, yes. Truly your people are doubly smiled upon by the spirits of your ancestors to have two such magic men as Hoyeh-tay and Cha-kwena. I was particularly taken by the tale of how your people came walking into the Red World over the mountaintops. It reminded me of a tale that my own people tell. Would you like to hear it?"

Dawn came up cold and cloudy. Cha-kwena awoke with a start. U-wa's piteous wails had awakened everyone.

"Aiyee-ay!" she sobbed. "Come! Come quickly! Hoyeh-tay has fallen from the bluff! He lies in the creek! His life spirit has left this world to join the spirits of the ancestors in the world beyond!"

# 6

The entire band and all the travelers from the north had gathered at the edge of the creek. Cha-kwena was in shock. Hoyeh-tay was dead. Owl was gone. And there was no sign of the sacred stone.

"It must have fallen from his neck into the creek when he fell," reasoned Tlana-quah.

"But the creek is frozen. The stone could not have washed away," said Cha-kwena.

Bereft and on his knees at the edge of the creek bed, holding the old man in his arms, the boy stared up at the headman and wanted to accuse: *You told me it would be all right to stay away! You told me that he would not need me! Now my grandfather is dead, and the sacred stone is missing! All because of you!* But he did not speak the words. How could he? He was the one who had chosen to stay away as long as he had. He had neglected to keep the stairs to the cave free of ice. And now Hoyeh-tay was dead, and it was his fault.

"You must not blame yourself," adjured Masau, lowering himself to one knee beside the youth.

Cha-kwena looked at the shaman from the north. The

man had understood his thoughts as surely as if he had spoken them aloud. "Who else is there to blame?" he asked Masau. "I left him. He asked me not to, but I left him. Now, because of me, our band is without a true shaman, and the most sacred talisman of my people is missing. You do not understand what this means to us, Masau. The very life and breath of our totem is in that stone. If it is lost, this band might be lost along with it!"

As Cha-kwena spoke, a murmuring of great worry and dread went through the crowd.

Tlana-quah made a face of profound irritation, gripped the edge of his spotted cape, and shook his head. "The omens have been good for this people! We will search the cave and the creek bed for the sacred stone. The old man was not himself these past many moons. For all we know he tossed it away as carelessly as he has thrown away his own life!"

"He would never have done that!" Cha-kwena said sharply. Even in death Hoyeh-tay's name was being blighted by the shame that his extreme age and infirmity had cursed him with during his last days; the youth could not—would not!—bear it. "I was the one who was careless, not Old Owl! He made me promise to protect him and to guard the stone. But I walked away. I left him to die—to die *alone*."

"It was his time to die, young teller of tales," said Masau with infinite kindness. "Nothing would have kept him safe. You must believe that. And he was not alone. His helping animal spirit was with him."

"Then where is Owl now?"

Masau's eyes narrowed speculatively. "That I cannot say."

Kosar-eh, standing beside Tlana-quah, replied softly, "Owl is where he was born to be: carrying the spirit of our shaman on his broad wings to the world beyond this world."

Masau glanced up at the clown. He carefully kept his tattooed face expressionless as he tensely measured Kosar-eh. Then he turned to look at the youth again. "Yes. Last night you said that you felt his wings stir the air above your face. Perhaps Hoyeh-tay was with him then, bidding you farewell as he and Owl took the sacred stone with them to the stars for safekeeping . . . until you, as the new shaman of your band, are ready to reach into the infinite and claim it as your own."

A sigh went up from the band. The words of Masau were magic. Yet, although Cha-kwena was soothed, he was also discomfited. The man's premise was as beautiful and comforting as his smiling face, but his reference to the stars called to mind Hoyeh-tay's warning about the Brothers of the Sky. Cha-kwena frowned and turned to see Masau's brother standing somberly among the other strangers from the north. The man's scarred face wore a most benign expression. He was big and powerful, but he seemed guileless enough now, with his hands folded before him and his eyes respectfully downturned lest they meet Cha-kwena's and intrude upon his grief. How could Hoyeh-tay have compared him and his brother with anything as disruptive and evil as the Brothers of the Sky?

Tlana-quah's next statement drove all further questions from Cha-kwena's mind. "You must go out from among us, Cha-kwena. You must seek our totem and the sacred place of dreams, which is now known only to you. Wear the robe and ceremonial bonnet of Hoyeh-tay. Take the medicine bag. These things are yours now. Go. Ask the spirits of the ancestors to show our new shaman where he may seek and find the sacred stone of our people."

Cha-kwena's arms tightened around Hoyeh-tay's shoulders. "I will not leave him." The old man must have landed on his back when he had fallen, for although the back of his skull was crushed and dark with blood as it lay against Cha-kwena's arm, his face was untouched by the fall. The timeworn features were relaxed, but his eyes were wide and staring, his mouth agape. It was a strange expression of surprise and disbelief, as though death had caught him unaware and he had done his best to fight it, but had lost the battle before it had even begun.

Cha-kwena gently closed the old man's eyes and mouth, then put his face against his grandfather's and whispered to the spirit of the dead man and to all who were close enough to hear: "I will be what Old Owl has wanted me to be. But if I were truly meant to be a shaman, I would not have to ask for the whereabouts of the stone. It would be here, around my grandfather's neck, waiting for me to claim it."

Tlana-quah hesitated, then knelt and laid a conciliatory hand upon the youth's head. "You will seek the holy place of dreams, Cha-kwena. You will fast, you will pray, and you will commune with the great white mammoth and the ghosts of Hoyeh-tay and Owl. In five days' time, the body of your grandfather will be set to flame so that all traces of his life-force may be free upon the Four Winds. On that day you *will* be Shaman, you *must* be Shaman—the only shaman your people will have to guide them in the days and nights ahead."

Cha-kwena felt as though a cold wind were stirring within his veins. Last night, when he had been called upon to tell the tales of his ancestors, he had felt bold and manly, full of himself and delighted by the adulation of his people and the strangers from the north. Now, with Hoyeh-tay dead in his arms, he felt lost and alone, as if a part of him had died with his grandfather. With that death he had become a little boy again, afraid of the completely unavoidable challenges and responsibilities that lay ahead.

"Without the sacred stone, how will I find the power to be what I will need to be?" he asked, and sighed, disconsolate.

"I could show you." It was Masau who replied, then turned to the headman. "Perhaps the spirits of our ancestors have sent me here to fulfill this purpose, to walk at the side of this youth as he journeys to the holy place of dreams and seeks the great white mammoth?"

"The place of dreams is only for shamans," said Cha-kwena dully.

"I *am* a shaman," reminded Masau, then added with a voice that flowed like sun-warmed oil. "Together the shamans of the People of the Red World and of the People of the Watching Star should commune with their ancestors. Together, if you lead me to the place where the great white mammoth walks, we will be strong in the power of our totem. Together we will find the sacred stone. Together the People *will* be one."

Cha-kwena looked up, startled. *The People are one.* It was as if old Hoyeh-tay had spoken to him through the mouth of the stranger. "Yes," he said, and felt much better. "Hoyeh-tay would like that."

Rain began to fall at that moment. Tlana-quah commanded Cha-kwena to carry Hoyeh-tay's body to the cave, then sent U-wa and the other women after him, to prepare the corpse for the mourning and funeral ceremonies. It was the only time that women were allowed within the shaman's cave. Once the old man's body was burned in it and his ashes scattered to the Four Winds, entrance to the cave would be forbidden to them once again. It would be the domain of the new shaman, Cha-kwena.

"You have made your mother proud, Shaman-to-be," said U-wa as Cha-kwena laid the old man gently upon his mattress. "In five days' time, return to us. Be strong and resolved in your calling. And find the sacred stone, or omens will be very bad for your people!"

The man and the youth walked in a driving rain into the hills. Cha-kwena wore the cloak and feathered bonnet of old Hoyeh-tay. After a while, even though the cape was soon waterlogged and the bonnet was sodden and heavy upon his brow, he barely felt their weight . . . or the weight of his grief over the death of his grandfather. Masau distracted him with endless questions about the customs of his people, and when he had exhausted this topic, he wanted to know who was the best hunter in the band, how far he could hurl his spear, and if he had skill with a dagger in a close-in fight with another man.

"Why would he want to fight with another man?"

"To . . . to test himself against the potential charge of a large predator."

"Dakan-eh is good with any weapon—unless it is a big spear like the one you and your fellow travelers have brought from the north."

"*Hmm.* And the other men of your band? Who among them challenges Dakan-eh?"

"They hunt together most of the time. All do their best."

"I see." The answer seemed to satisfy him, but his questions did not abate. Did the People always build their lodges with the entrance facing due south, he wanted to know, and how many hunters went out from the village at any given time? How had Kosar-eh become a cripple, and

what was his function in the band aside from making a fool
of himself? What were the circumstances surrounding the
new lodge that was being assembled in the village, and
what was the meaning of the name of the exceptionally
pretty girl who stood with the unmarried women apart
from the other females of the band at last night's festivities?
Was she—or were any of them—still virgin?

"Her name is Ta-maya." Cha-kwena stopped to stare
worriedly at Masau. "The name means Most Favored Child.
She is Tlana-quah and Ha-xa's elder daughter. She will
soon become the woman of Dakan-eh. The lodge that is
under construction will become Ta-maya and Bold Man's
shelter after their wedding. In winter it will open to the
south, like all the other lodges, to catch the sun. In
summer it will open to the north, to drink in the shade.
The fact that there will be a wedding speaks for the
virginity of the bride; but if we do not find the sacred
stone, there might not be a wedding, for the omens will
be dark and the very life of our totem will be threatened.
Why do you ask so many questions, Masau?"

"Because I would learn about my new brothers and
sisters and because as you answer my questions your words
draw you from your troubled thoughts and become a balm
to your spirit. Talk is good medicine, Cha-kwena. This
would be the first lesson that I would teach you. Did you
say that if you do not find the sacred stone, the wedding of
Ta-maya and Dakan-eh will not be allowed?"

"Yes. The stone is the heart of this band. There can
be no wedding—or celebration of any kind—if the people
have lost their heart."

"I see. . . ."

Cha-kwena shook his head. "No, I doubt if you could."

And so he explained it all to him. As they walked on
in the rain, Cha-kwena told Masau of the stone's significance,
its power, and all that it had ever meant to the People of
the Red World since time beyond beginning. He told him
about his journey to the Blue Mesas, the meeting of the
shamans, and how they would meet there again in a great
assembly that would unite all the bands and bring together
all the holy men and their sacred stones. He told Masau
about Grandfather of All and how Hoyeh-tay had told him
that as long as a single stone remained entrusted to a

single shaman of the Red World, their totem would live—
but if the stones were lost, the great white mammoth
would die. "And then the People of the Red World will
die."

"Yes," said Masau. "It will be so."

Cha-kwena stopped dead. "It *will*?"

Masau paused beside him. His eagle-skin cape and
hood formed an effective raincoat. His face was dry and his
features set, infinitely caring. "If all the stones are lost." A
strong hand found the youth's shoulder. "You are Shaman.
I am Shaman. Too often it is a lonely life. I promise I will
not leave you until the sacred stone has been found and all
due respects have been paid to your grandfather's spirit. I
will remain at your side until you are at ease in this
shaman's skin that you must now wear."

"I do not think I will ever be at ease in it," Cha-
kwena confided.

Masau nodded. "In time you will. But come. I have
promised Tlana-quah that I would accompany you to the
sacred place of dreams and to that place where the great
white mammoth walks."

The wind was down and the rain had stopped by the
time they reached the ancient juniper and paused beneath
its sheltering crown.

Masau stood with his neck craned back. "I have never
seen so large a tree!"

Cha-kwena levered himself up through the lowest
branches. "Spirits live in it—tree spirits, forest spirits.
They speak in this place, but I have never heard them.
Perhaps that is because I have never really listened." He
was climbing easily and gracefully until he found a familiar
limb and sprawled belly down. He nearly sobbed as he
closed his eyes and remembered his grandfather standing
far below with Owl perched upon his shoulder.

*Cha-kwena! Cha-kwena! Where are you?*

*I am here. You are Shaman, my grandfather. Find me
if you can!*

He opened his eyes. Hoyeh-tay was not there, nor
was Owl. Masau was looking up at him, and Mah-ree was
with him; the shrike was on her shoulder. Cha-kwena sat
up abruptly and glared down at the girl.

"What are you doing here . . . and with that bird?" he demanded angrily.

She pouted. "I am Medicine Girl. I am a shaman, too. I want to help. And Shrike goes where I go."

"You are a girl, Mah-ree. You cannot be a shaman, and you cannot come with us to the sacred place of dreams. Does Tlana-quah know that you have followed us?"

"He is too busy making ready for all the sad songs and dances that must be made for Old Owl. I was careful to leave many tracks. By the time my mother misses me, everyone will realize that I have gone off with the two shamans."

"Go away, Mah-ree," Cha-kwena insisted. "You have no cause to be with us."

"But I do! For many days, there has been no sign of our totem near the lake or in any of the usual places where I leave my offerings. I think that he is with the other mammoth at the sacred salt spring. Only you know where it is, Cha-kwena. But Grandfather of All comes to me, not to you. If I am with you, maybe he will tell you where the sacred stone is."

Masau went to one knee beside the girl.

"Is this true, little daughter of Tlana-quah?" he asked.

"Oh, yes!" She looked at him with open adoration. "Is your mother truly a shaman, Man Who Wears Eagle?"

"A great and powerful shaman."

"Then tell the boy up in the tree that although I am a girl, I can be a shaman, too! Our totem eats of the food that I bring to him! Old Hoyeh-tay welcomed me into his sacred cave! If he were here now, I know he would let me come with you!"

Masau looked up at Cha-kwena. "If we send her back, one of us will have to go with her."

"Why? She came this far alone!"

"She is a child, Cha-kwena."

She frowned. "I am almost *not* a child."

"Yes," said Masau, and as he spoke his voice had an odd, pinched tightness to it. "I can see that. Perhaps someday you will grow up and live to be just as beautiful as your sister."

Cha-kwena found the statement disquieting. *Perhaps you will grow up? Live to be as beautiful as your sister?*

What a strange way to order the words. Unless he was implying . . . He left the thought unfinished. Because the sacred stone was lost, was the future of his people lost along with it?

Mah-ree's head went high. "I will be different from Ta-maya. I will be Medicine Girl! And I will know how to make up my mind about things."

One of Masau's eyebrows arched toward his hairline. "And what is it that Ta-maya cannot make up her mind about?"

Mah-ree, enraptured by her audience, betrayed a confidence. "Dakan-eh."

Cha-kwena was not sure what bothered him more: the forwardness of the child or the fact that she seemed to have switched her affection so easily from him to another. He knew only that Masau was shaking his head and smiling with a bemused sort of downward twist to his mouth as he rose and extended his hand. "Come, Girl Who Walks with Shrike. You have come too far to return alone. It is time for us to go on to the place of dreams. If the shaman of your people welcomed you to his cave and if your totem has truly come to you upon command, I do not think that Cha-kwena will mind if you come along."

Cha-kwena did mind, but it did not matter. Masau had consented to Mah-ree's company, and so she was with them every step of the way, wide-eyed, eager to please, and obedient.

It was a time of fasting, but Mah-ree made no complaint. She set herself to do without food as resolutely as she had followed the two shamans into the hills. Now was a time for silence, for communion with the spirits of the dead and of the upland forest.

Cha-kwena guided Masau and Mah-ree on and on, through the scrub growth, up and over the hills toward the overlook. The girl was scrupulous in maintaining a suitable distance between herself and the two shamans. She watched them from afar, never allowing them out of her sight. Cha-kwena could feel her behind him, moving as silently and consistently as his shadow, keeping up, falling back, stopping when he stopped, moving on when he moved. He smiled. He had to admire her; there was

more to Mah-ree than met the eye. It pleased him also to
know that he was ordering her for a change, even if it was
as subtly as setting their pace.

After a while he forgot that she was there at all. And
then, at last, they reached the overlook, and as Masau and
Mah-ree came through the thornbush behind him, he
spread out his arms to keep them from advancing over the
edge of the abyss.

Each of them gasped when confronted by the vast
maw of the canyon and the astounding view that lay below.
Now, as before, Cha-kwena felt the magic of the place.
Ghosts were at his side—Hoyeh-tay's and Owl's, and the
ghost of the youth whom he had been when he had last
stood here. Now, as he stared across the chasm, he knew
that he was here to accomplish more than mourning and
invoking the spirits of the ancestors so that they might
lead him to discover the whereabouts of the sacred stone.
He was here to say good-bye to his youth and to all the
boyhood dreams that had led him to imagine that he might
ever be anything other than Shaman.

He knelt. The sun was setting beyond the western
walls of the canyon. It would be dark soon. And there,
moving below the soaring crowns of the ancient cedars,
firs, and pines that grew at the base of the canyon, was
what he had come to see.

"Great Ghost Spirit . . . " he whispered in absolute
reverence, and pointed downward so the eyes of Masau
and the girl would be drawn to the mammoth's pale,
towering back.

"Grandfather of All." Mah-ree intoned the name as if
it was that of a beloved friend. "I knew he would be here.
And look—he is not alone. His 'women' and 'children,'
and his little white 'son' are with him in this sacred place.
It is a good sign, don't you think, Cha-kwena?"

Cha-kwena found himself comforted by the sight of
the herd clustered, protected by the soaring walls of their
secret refuge within the canyon and the towering pillars of
the trees. Hoyeh-tay was dead and the sacred stone missing,
but Grandfather of All still grazed in the Red World with
his family and his little white son. All was not lost. Was
this the sign he sought?

Beside him, Masau went to one knee and leaned

forward to gain a better view. "The great white mammoth! And a calf—a *white* calf, offspring of the totem!" Masau exhaled the words in such a low, deep tone that they set up reverberations in his throat and chest; he sounded like a lion purring . . . or growling in contented anticipation of a meal.

Cha-kwena, suddenly troubled, appraised Masau as he stared fixedly downward, his eyes narrowed, his mouth drawn back from his teeth. In profile, with the head of the eagle extending over his own, Masau looked like some sort of magnificent carnivore—half-man and half-bird, or half-animal and—What had Hoyeh-tay called him? *A lion hiding in the skin of an eagle.* Now, as Cha-kwena stared at Masau, he seemed to be everything that his grandfather had feared.

Blood welled behind his eyes in a sudden red flare of a vision. Red on white. Blood on the hide of the white mammoth. He caught his breath so sharply that both Mah-ree and Masau turned to look at him.

"What is it, my young brother shaman?" queried Masau.

"I have no brother!"

Masau's face seemed to expand upon his skull as though the youth had both surprised him and hurt him to the quick. "Are the People not one? Are those who are called to the shaman's way not united in spirit as well as in blood? What should I call you then, Cha-kwena?"

*Enemy. Destroyer. Lion!* whispered West Wind as it swept into the canyon.

But Cha-kwena was looking into Masau's eyes. How dark they were, how filled with infinite kindness, affection, and genuine concern. The vision of blood faded as did his feelings of trepidation concerning the man. With Masau looking into his eyes, Cha-kwena could not bring himself to look away.

"I . . . I don't know," the boy said. "Maybe I should not have brought you here. It is a sacred place to the holy men of the Red World, not to the People of the Watching Star."

Masau held his gaze. "Does the Watching Star not rise over the Red World? Does the great white mammoth not walk within its light?"

Cha-kwena, his eyes still locked to Masau's gaze, felt suddenly sleepy, beyond argument. "Yes, it is so."

On Mah-ree's shoulder, Shrike had managed to tear through the sinew that held him captive. With his one good wing spread wide, he risked the flight to Masau's knee and managed a landing.

"Shrike names you Brother," said Mah-ree.

Had Cha-kwena not been so groggy, he would surely have found significance in the moment; but Masau's eyes had somehow lulled him into a mood of such heavy-bodied tranquillity that, with a sigh, he lay down onto his side and excused himself. "I must rest. The need for sleep has overcome me."

# 7

For four days and four nights the shaman Masau supervised the fasting and praying of Cha-kwena and Mah-ree. For four days and four nights, they were led in awe along the paths of the shaman's way as the man of the People of the Watching Star guided them into mystic worlds on the wings of his words. He took them into the clouds and through the very heart of the sun . . . across the Red World and over the moon and the great open grasslands of the north . . . above tumbled, timber-clad hills and soaring mountain peaks heavily laden with the remnant massifs of glistening ice fields . . . and through broad, cold lakes that were all that was left of a dying age, an age of ice.

And then he left them in solitude to their dreams as he stood alone at the very edge of the overlook. With the sacred stone of Hoyeh-tay curled within his hand, Masau watched the great white mammoth grazing with his herd in the depths of the canyon far below. The man missed nothing—not the number of animals or the way they positioned themselves around the pools and within the

trees . . . not the way that the great white mammoth
tended to stand alone or the way two cows—one young,
one very old—always set themselves to watch and nurture
the little white calf. And certainly not the steep battlements
of the dead-end cirque in which the mammoth gathered
and from which there would be no escape from the hunters
whom he would bring to this age-old sacred refuge. It
would, in the end, prove no refuge at all, but a death trap.

In the predawn darkness of the fifth day, Cha-kwena
awoke from dreams of coyotes and swallows, of bats and
leaping hares, and of Owl swooping at him from the stars.
He sat shivering in old Hoyeh-tay's damp robe. All attempts
to dry it had failed; the robe had absorbed too much
water. It would take many days in good, strong sunlight to
restore it—if, in fact, it could ever be returned to its
former condition. But because it was Hoyeh-tay's robe,
rain damaged or not, he would wear it as long as a single
stitch held together.

Now, with Mah-ree sound asleep in a little nest of pine
boughs that she had made for herself, and Masau off dream-
seeking in the woods, Cha-kwena rose and walked to the
overlook. Standing alone in the dark, he was dry mouthed
and thirsty but somehow beyond hunger despite his days
and nights of fasting. He doubted if he had ever felt more
lonely. He closed his eyes. A terrible sadness was his as,
once again, he awaited the vision that he had yearned for
all his life—the vision in which his helping animal spirit
would come to him and give him his adult name and totem.

The waters of his mind rippled, and with a start, he
saw Coyote standing at the edge of the lake, just as he had
stood on the far side of the pool so long before, staring,
golden eyed, at him from out of the night . . . watching
but silent. Then, with a little yip, Coyote turned and
disappeared into the vision, only to be followed by the
usual assortment of creatures that all too often came to
Cha-kwena in his dreams. First Deer, as tawny as summer
grass, came wading into the lake of his phantasm. Her
great liquid eyes were full of starlight, her ears turning as
she asked, *Why do you turn away from me, Cha-kwena? I
and my kind will always remember Little Brother of
Animals, who healed the fetlock of an injured fawn when*

*others of your kind would have put an end to me and added my flesh to the drying frames within their village.*

Next Hawk came to land upon the hindquarters of Deer. Broad of wing, red of tail, his one good eye as gold and bright as sunlight in contrast to the darkness of the dream, he said, *And surely you must remember me, Cha-kwena. As I and my kind will always remember Little Brother of Animals. You picked the fly larvae from the ruined eye of this injured hawk and kept me warm and safe from your mother's stewing bag until the fever was gone from my flesh and I could fly away . . . one-eyed but well and strong again, able to hunt with my own kind once more.*

Bat swooped low, leaving a long, lean tracing of his path upon the surface of the lake, and said, *Do not forget me, Cha-kwena. I and my kind are forever watching the ways of Little Brother of Animals. You once took it upon yourself to say nothing of this stunned bat when you saw me lying at the base of a great pine while other boys of your kind passed me by. They would have killed me, for it is the way of boys to harry and kill wounded creatures, which they then may bring back to their mothers' boiling bags. But this has never been the way of Cha-kwena, and so Bat will always be here in the night for you, to put himself between danger and his human brother.*

Swallow followed the wake of Bat. Pale of breast, pointed of wing, she twittered as she alighted on the head of Deer. *Remember me, Cha-kwena, as I remember Little Brother of Animals. When you and Dakan-eh and Hoyeh-tay were encamped in the middle of the great dry lake, how could I not have warned you of danger? I have seen you lead others of your own kind away from the nests in which my children were being nurtured.*

Hare came bounding to the edge of the lake of vision and sat with Mouse and Rabbit and Lizard. *Remember us all, Cha-kwena, as we will always remember Little Brother of Animals. Although you have killed our kind and eaten of our flesh, you have never carelessly set a snare lest you cause us to suffer. And you have never killed us only for the sake of your own pride. In times of abundant meat, you have let us go our way. You have healed our brothers and sisters when you have found them wounded, and for our sake you have endured the laughter of others of your own kind.*

And now Cha-kwena saw a gray blur in the darkness. The perpetually molting, balding, irascible Old Owl winged over the lake in his vest of rabbit fur.

*I am still with you, Cha-kwena. We are all with you. . . .*

The air before Cha-kwena's face was stirred by a sudden gust of wind, as though a winged creature had passed close by and then suddenly banked and flown away.

Cha-kwena opened his eyes. The vision was gone. The strong stink of burned fur and feathers hung in the air. The youth looked to the fire pit. It was cold; no scent rose from it but the acrid smell of ashes. He stared straight ahead, then looked all around, disturbed by the lingering, unexplainable stench of charring and half expecting to see Owl flying toward him or perching in the trees or scrubwood. If the bird was near, there was no sign of him.

"What is it, Cha-kwena? Does the dream that you seek still elude you?" Masau was coming toward him. The Morning Star glinted in the sky over his head, and Shrike was sitting on his shoulder in the same way that Owl used to perch on the shoulder of Hoyeh-tay.

The comparison depressed Cha-kwena. Disconsolate, he shook his head. "I dream the same old dreams, Masau. I think my grandfather was right about me. I think I will be Cha-kwena, Little Brother of Animals, forever."

"It is not a bad name for a shaman."

"So my grandfather said, although I am not so 'little' anymore."

"No. You are young, but I can see that you are a man. Your grandfather saw this, too. He had great powers of discernment."

Cha-kwena looked up bleakly. "Do you think so, Masau?"

"Oh, yes! I was sure of it the moment our eyes met. But Hoyeh-tay had lived out his time—and then some. The power that was his must come to you now, Cha-kwena. Now let us wake the girl. You must come with me. I have just returned from the sacred juniper, and there is something there that you must see."

\* \* \*

Wan and silent and reflecting upon his dreams, Cha-kwena followed Masau away from the overlook and back across the hills toward the sacred tree. It was Mah-ree who first noticed the object to which Masau had led them. She would have run forward, but Masau held her back.

"This is not for you, Medicine Girl. This is for Cha-kwena. This is a gift for him from the spirits of the ancestors and from old Hoyeh-tay."

Cha-kwena's heart was pounding. He moved forward slowly, hesitantly, until at last he paused at the base of the great tree and stared down. Nested in a fluff of owl feathers on the wide, curving musculature of the massive root was the sacred stone of his ancestors.

Masau, at his side, placed his hand on Cha-kwena's shoulder. "Today is the fifth day. Today your grandfather's body will be given to Fire. In the meantime his spirit has looked upon you and has seen into your dreams. He has found them worthy of a shaman. And so it is that Hoyeh-tay and Owl, his helping animal spirit, have returned to your people that which they must have to make them strong. The sacred stone is yours. Take it. For now, truly, you *are* Shaman."

Their gaze met and held. Masau was smiling. It was reassuringly radiant, but somehow his eyes remained dark, wary, watchful—a predator's eyes . . . a lion's eyes staring out from beneath the raptorial head of a golden eagle. Cha-kwena could not look away.

For a moment suspicion ran wild within him. Had Masau stolen the sacred relic and, for reasons of his own, placed it at the base of the juniper, and then led him to it? But why would he have done that? And if he had, would he not be implicating himself and perhaps his fellow travelers in darker, more insidious deeds—such as the death of Hoyeh-tay and the disappearance of Owl?

The questions were too appalling. He would not give them credence. In these last four days and nights Masau had been as a brother to him, offering comfort and advice and a depth of friendship that Cha-kwena had never known—not even from his own father or Hoyeh-tay himself. He would think no ill of Masau; it was not in his heart to do so.

For a long time Cha-kwena stood before the great tree and gazed at the sacred stone. The thong that had held it safely around Hoyeh-tay's scrawny neck was gone. How small the talisman looked! A lump the size of the stone suddenly formed at the back of Cha-kwena's throat, and hot tears stung beneath his eyelids. Trembling, he reached down. Cha-kwena let the tips of his fingers touch the stone and lay lightly upon it. He was ready to pull back, but nothing unnatural happened. He swallowed and advanced his fingers forward until his palm lay over the stone. And then, still waiting for extraordinary things to happen, he dared to curl his fingers and ease them under the stone, slowly . . . so slowly . . . and then he picked it up.

He gasped, not at the shock of any monumental sensations but at the lack of them. Nonetheless, a sense of awe and wonder filled him. This sacred stone was a part of First Man and First Woman, an undeniable link with his past, a talisman within which lay the determining life-force of his people and of their totem. It—and they—were in his safekeeping now.

"Am I worthy?" he whispered as he turned his hand, opened his fingers, and stared at the sacred stone as it lay in the hollow of his palm.

"Oh, yes, Cha-kwena . . ." whispered Mah-ree adoringly as she stood at his side.

"A shaman *makes* himself worthy," said Masau.

Calm and assurance flooded through the youth. Then he was shaken by a strange chill. It was the breath of new life rising in him, an acceptance of everything that he had fought against for so long but now consented to with all his heart.

"For Hoyeh-tay," he proclaimed. "For Owl, for First Man and First Woman, for all the ancestors and the spirit animals who speak to me in my dreams, and for Great Ghost Spirit who is Grandfather of All, I *will* be worthy! I am Cha-kwena! I *am* Shaman!"

# 8

Hoyeh-tay's funeral pyre lit the night. The People gathered below the cave to watch it burn.

The women had cleansed the old man and laid him on a bier of split logs and abundant kindling mattressed thickly with fragrant sagebrush. They had oiled his body, festooned his hair with feathers, and painted him with precious ocher so that the blood of the earth would be his in the world beyond this world. They had wrapped him in a shroud of dry reeds and placed a feather-filled bag as a pillow beneath his head. Presents were brought by every man, woman, and child, in little funerary baskets, so that his spirit could take all good things to share with the ancestors in the spirit world. They had placed the laden baskets all around and over him.

When everything was in readiness, Cha-kwena ascended the stairs to the cave and, before kneeling, stood for a long while over the body of his grandfather. At last he knelt, and with Hoyeh-tay's bow drill, he set fire to the kindling that would ignite the larger logs and send the beloved old man's spirit to the world beyond this world. When the flames were so high and their heat so intense that he could no longer bear to stand close, he left the cave and joined his people.

Now he stood before them, arms held high to the infinite, his voice raised in the songs that old Hoyeh-tay had taught him. Every member of the band listening to him knew that a part of the old man had been reborn in his grandson. None had cause to doubt for so much as a moment that Cha-kwena was truly Shaman at last.

Standing apart from the members of the band, the traders kept a respectful vigil.

A scowling Maliwal confronted Masau. "The new sha-man wears the sacred stone." In a lowered voice he de-manded, "How has it gone from your keeping to a place of honor around his neck?"

"I left it in a place where he could find it."

Maliwal was confused. "You killed the old man; you took the stone. Why give it back? Ysuna will want it. If we don't have it when we return to her, she will want to know why."

"It grows increasingly clear to me why I was the brother chosen by Ysuna to be Shaman. You are named for the wolf, Maliwal. Can you not think like one? Ysuna *will* have her sacred stone. In time it will come to her of its own accord. The boy will bring it to the gathering place where the people of the Red World harvest pine nuts under the light of the Pinyon Moon. In the meantime he will wear it with honor. If we are to maintain the trust of the lizard eaters and assure the complete success of our journey in this land of fools, the stone serves us best around his neck."

The other men in the party, having overheard, ex-changed looks of amusement and approval.

"Have you chosen the one we will take back to be a bride for Thunder in the Sky?" asked Chudeh.

"I have," replied Masau.

Maliwal was staring off toward the assemblage. The women stood apart from the men, and Ban-ya was looking over her shoulder in his direction. Although her posture seemed properly demure and downcast for a funeral, her brazen eyes were searching and provocative.

"Look at her. . . ." Maliwal sighed and ran his tongue over his lips as though he were appraising a future meal. "Now there's a girl who would come consenting with just a little effort on our part."

"Perhaps," Masau allowed. "But this sacrifice must be perfect, the best of their women." His eyes fixed on Ta-maya. "For Ysuna's sake—and for ours—the next sacrifice must be perfect."

"That one is promised to the bigmouth," reminded Maliwal.

"Yes," assented Masau. "But the little girl has said that her sister is not completely certain of her commitment to the one who is so full of himself. Ta-maya is the one whom I have chosen, and she will come to me. As sure as sunrise, she will come."

In that moment, aware of eyes upon her, Ta-maya turned to see who was staring. When he smiled, she lowered her head and looked away. But then she turned back and returned his smile for a moment before looking away again.

"She will be the one," vowed Masau. "She will be the one."

The weather was fitful in the days that followed. On snowy days, when the headman went to sit in the sweat lodge with the strangers from the north and the other men of the band, Ta-maya was content in the lodge of her parents. Now it was always a happy lodge, with her mother and U-wa and Mah-ree busy at their sewing and weaving and easy talk.

"It is a good thing that Dakan-eh and you have not rushed into the wedding," Ha-xa said. "Now that these traders from the north have come to us, look at the many wondrous gifts that your man will be able to bring to his bride—such fine furs and beads for the daughter of the headman!" The woman went on to speak endlessly of her own wedding and of the many gifts that she had received and of her first night with Tlana-quah, who had been her first man. "Your father will talk to Dakan-eh about this. He will tell Bold Man to pierce you slowly, so there will be as much pleasure for you as for him. Young men must be instructed by their elders in such things; they have little experience with women their own age."

"Dakan-eh needs no advice on the ways with women," U-wa said with a little snort of mixed disapproval and admiration.

Ta-maya looked up from her own sewing, so disconcerted, she pricked her thumb. "Oh!" she exclaimed, sucking on the wound and letting her work—a beautifully pieced tunic of egret skins for Dakan-eh—fall into her lap. U-wa, Ta-maya realized, had been a widow for many months! Had Dakan-eh come to her to find a man's pleasure? She could not bring herself to ask.

U-wa saw it in her face, however, and clucked her

tongue. "No, dear. He never came to me. I was not widowed long enough, nor was I old enough to be sent to live with the widow women. Besides, Tlana-quah's eyes made it clear to all the younger men that I would not live alone for long after my man's death." She paused, obviously proud of this fact but not insensitive to Ha-xa's reaction to it. She looked at Tlana-quah's first woman with a fond smile and reached to squeeze her hand. "You and I were best friends as girls, Ha-xa. I think that the spirits of the ancestors always wanted us to live as sisters!"

Ha-xa nodded in affirmation. "True enough. And a good thing it has turned out to be for us!" There was a merry twinkle in her eyes as she patted her belly and chuckled. "So many years have I desired to have another child. Now that my man has two women, he performs even better than before! Look at us! What life makers we have proved to be for our man, eh?"

Ta-maya took her thumb from her mouth but did not pick up her sewing, for now U-wa reached across the little family circle to pat the girl's knee and remark with a knowing wink, "If the talk of the widows is to be believed, you will not long enjoy a flat belly once you share the bed furs with Bold Man. His needs are strong. He will put many babies inside you! Many sons!"

Ta-maya blushed deeply and lowered her eyes.

Both older women chuckled lasciviously. "What should we expect from such a hot-blooded young man when all he has ever had to ease his man bone are well-used flabby old widows!" exclaimed Ha-xa. "I must admire him for waiting for my Ta-maya for so long, especially when that brazen Ban-ya has been ready to spread herself for him like a fox in heat! How he must long to lie on a tight young woman, and how his blood must heat at the thought of being with a first-time girl like my Ta-maya! Ah, Daughter, you will have to forgive him if he cannot hold back his passion when he first pierces you."

U-wa said soothingly, "I do not think that Ta-maya will have to worry about that. Bold Man had a young girl when he was with the old shaman on the sacred mountain— and had her quite thoroughly, if you know what I mean. Cha-kwena told me. Hmmph! I think my boy had an eye for the girl himself. He was not too happy with Bold Man because of it. But young men away from home . . . you know what is said about that! More babies are born after a Great Gathering than at any other time, and none resemble their father! Do not look so glum, Ta-maya. If your Bold Man has a healthy appetite, you are fortunate! Your mother and I will teach you all the little tricks that a woman needs to know about how to keep a man hungry—and herself well fed! Now my own first man . . ." She stopped. Obviously not wishing to speak ill of the dead, she at last added circumspectly, "Let me just say that he was a good hunter who might have made a better shaman. But he was no magic maker when he lay upon the tule mattress he shared with me. I often am amazed that I was able to give him a son at all!"

"Cha-kwena!" Mah-ree sighed happily as she spoke his name. "The best son in all the world—next to Masau, of course. Masau is the most beautiful man I have ever seen! His mother must be very proud!"

Ha-xa frowned. "Masau was too lenient with you! He should have brought you home where you belonged rather than take you along on a shaman's journey!"

"He was wonderful!" Mah-ree swooned back onto her sleeping furs. "I told him about the mammoth and Grandfather of All and—"

Ta-maya felt an unfamiliar rush of heat to her loins at the mention of Masau's name; nevertheless, as her little sister babbled on in a state of bliss, her face paled as she pressed U-wa, "You say that Dakan-eh had a girl at the Blue Mesas? Actually *had* her?"

"He is a man, my dear, and you have long denied him." Ha-xa wagged an accusing finger.

Mah-ree sat up. "I told her not to, Mother, but she never listens to me!"

"But before Dakan-eh left, he swore that he wanted no one but me."

Ha-xa shook her head. "Wanting is one thing, Ta-maya, and waiting is another. If this girl at the Blue Mesas was willing to open herself to Dakan-eh, why should he have denied himself pleasure? A man must have his release."

U-wa nodded sagely. "It has nothing to do with affection."

Ha-xa laughed. "If it did, then I would seriously

worry about his going to the widows nearly every night! But, truly, Ta-maya, they are no competition."

Suddenly flushed, Ta-maya jumped to her feet. "He doesn't! Not every night! He couldn't be! He is out hunting! He is—"

"But he *is*, dear. What matter?" asked Ha-xa. "Three lonely, barren old women are pleased to hold youth in their arms once more, and a young buck in rut does not go about the village behaving like an elk in velvet, ready for a fight all the time! It is a good thing, a wise custom."

U-wa saw the anguish and confusion in Ta-maya's eyes. "No doubt he imagines that he is with you when he is with them, darling. Soon it will be so, and he will lie with them no more."

Ta-maya felt angry and upset—not with them, not with Dakan-eh, but with herself. They were right, of course: She had made him wait. Because he was much older than she, he had declared his desire for her before she had even come to her time of blood. She had wanted him from the first, but she had wanted a wedding more, and so she had made him wait. And wait. And wait. She had wanted the wedding more than she wanted the man.

"Oh!" Ta-maya's eyes scanned the hut, the two women, her little sister, the bed furs, and the assembled wedding gifts. "Oh!" she exclaimed again, an exhalation of pure self-deprecation because she realized her mind had not changed.

Loons were calling on the lake. She went to the entryway of the lodge, brushed aside the door skin, and stood looking out. The glow of interior fires illuminated both the sweat lodge and the widows' hut. Across the creek and on the bluff, a fire burned in the cave of Cha-kwena. Just thinking of the cave as belonging to him made her feel disoriented. During these past moons, the order of her world seemed completely undone. Since she had come to her first time of blood, everything had changed. *Everything!*

She drew in a deep, steadying breath of the night air. Snow had turned to rain. It was almost warm outside. The Lake of Many Singing Birds was nearly free of ice. Soon it would be spring, and the cattail shoots within the marsh would be ready for picking. Soon the third moon would rise, and soon after that, she would be Dakan-eh's bride! Would the widows be glad for her or sad for themselves? She did not care. At this moment she hated the widows, and if the truth were told, she hated Dakan-eh for going to them. She sighed resentfully and watched her breath form a diaphanous little cloud before her face as she listened to the loons.

"*Haoo-oo-oo*," they called to one another. "*Haoo-oo-oo*." They wailed almost in the way of the women of the band when someone died.

Sadness touched her. Within a short time she had witnessed the burnings of three people: her dear, sick grandmother Neechee-la; proud, careless Nar-eh; and now Hoyeh-tay. Somehow she had imagined that he would live forever. The old man had been like the main ridgepole of every lodge; if the pole cracked, it was caulked and bound with strong girdings of sinew and thong, which made it stronger. It was impossible to think of a lodge with a new mainstay ridgepole, and it was equally impossible to think of her band without Hoyeh-tay. Now that he was gone, Ta-maya thought, a portion of all that linked her people to past generations had been cut away forever.

Behind her, within the lodge, Ha-xa and U-wa were singing a careless round. Mah-ree must have fallen asleep, or she would have joined in. Ta-maya's frown deepened. Mah-ree was growing up fast. In just the past few moons the changes in her were evident. She was developing hips; soon her breasts would follow. Soon she would be a woman, and then, like Ta-maya, she would become a bride. A bride became a mother in nine moons and sometimes a widow in as many years. Perhaps the older people were right when they claimed that life was short—short and wonderful and as full of color as the Red World itself; until this moment, however, she had not believed it. Yet now, standing in the lodge entryway, she knew that it was true and—even more sobering—for the first time she realized that she was not exempt from the finality of it. She was fifteen, a woman. She would not live forever. When the third moon rose and completed its phases, she would go to Dakan-eh rejoicing, and she would tell him that she was sorry for having made him wait so long to begin his life with her.

She bit her lip. She was *not* sorry.

*Why?* she wondered. *What is* wrong *with me?*

The loons called again in the darkness, this time in high, maniacal cackles that sounded too much like laughter. And in that moment Ta-maya knew the answer to her question.

The figure of a naked man emerged from the sweat lodge. She recognized him by his height, the breadth of his shoulders, the leanness of his hips, and the length of his hair. It was Masau.

Her heart was pounding.

The loons were laughing on the lake.

*This* was the man she wanted. This was the man she had been waiting for, without ever even knowing that he was coming into her life.

She frowned again. But how could this be? He was not of her band, nor even of the People of the Red World. But what did it matter? She was promised to Dakan-eh. He would claim his bride—and how could she refuse him now, after she had made him wait so long?

# 9

Soon the third moon would rise. Cattail shoots were greening in the marsh. The new lodge was finished. All was in readiness for the wedding.

And in the deep dark of a warm and windless night, Dakan-eh awoke, restless with yearning for Ta-maya. Finding no cause to deny himself, he rose and went once more to the hut of the widows to ease his man need amid grasping arms and wide-spread limbs. Quickly sated on such as they, he knelt back and accepted the basket of hearth-warmed water and proceeded to clean himself with soft buckskin cloths. He was aware of the old women moving in the darkness, murmuring, then giggling as they stroked his back and took the cloths from him.

"No need for you to soil your hands with this," whispered Xi-ahtli. "Here, let me help you."

"We will miss you after the wedding when you come to us no more," said Zar-ah.

"Others will come," he told them.

"They will not be Bold Man," said Kahm-ree.

The words pleased him, as did the strokings of their wise, well-oiled hands. He closed his eyes and imagined that it was Ta-maya touching him, massaging him with moist warm cloths—his back, belly, inner thighs, and man bone, working it, making it hard again, ready again. "No wonder you have outlived your men," he said.

"They went to the world beyond this world with no complaints—that is true," boasted Kahm-ree, leaning close, allowing her great breasts to sag upon his folded limbs. "My Ban-ya . . . I have trained her how to please the man she will have. She would be a better girl for you than the other. All the men, even the traders, look at my Ban-ya. Maybe she will go away with them, eh? Would you miss her as much as I?"

"Ban-ya is free to do as she chooses. Whatever her decision, it will have nothing to do with me."

"But it will."

The voice had not been that of an old woman. A draft of cool air from behind chilled Dakan-eh. Shivering, he turned to see that someone had opened the door skin. The old women ceased their ministrations quickly, as though on some unspoken command, chuckled, and scurried out into the night. And as another figure entered, Dakan-eh clearly heard Kahm-ree say, "He is ready for you. Remember all that I have taught you. You will not have a second chance."

The door skin closed.

Ban-ya stood before him. "No man has yet had me, Dakan-eh," she informed him, and allowed her robe to fall away.

He stared. Somewhere over the edge of the world the sun was rising, so the darkness beyond the hill was taking on the milky look of dawn. Enough light penetrated the hut's thatching for him to make out the contours of her tight-skinned, meaty little hips, her thick, wild hair, her taut belly, her breasts . . . ah, her breasts. The sight of them weakened him.

"Go away, Ban-ya. I do not want you," he said, and quickly folded his hands across his lap lest she see the truth jabbing up at her.

It was too late; she had seen. She did not move. "Ma-nuk has asked for me. So has Omar-eh."

"Both are good men and excellent hunters. Not as good as I, of course, but either one will make you happy."

"The hunters from the north have also looked at me. I may be tempted to go away with them."

"Would you not miss your people?"

"Perhaps, but traders have many fine gifts to give a woman and a good life to offer in a land of endless game. The one with the scarred face looks hungry eyed at me all the time. And the beautiful one has said that he has no woman. I have thought that if I cannot be your woman, maybe I will be his. In his world he is the best of men, and I would have only the best. Would that make you angry, Dakan-eh? It would make Kahm-ree angry. She does not want me to go from the village. She has said that it is not yet done between Ta-maya and you until you lie down together or enter the new lodge together. I would lie down with you now, Dakan-eh. I would let you be my first man."

"Tlana-quah would skin me if I were to choose you over Ta-maya. And he would skin you, too."

"Maybe he would. Maybe he would not. You are the best and boldest hunter in the Red World. Why should you fear Tlana-quah?"

The question irritated him. "A hunter must show respect to his headman."

"*Hmm* . . . and what kind of daughter does he have? A girl who makes Bold Man consort with old widows rather than open herself to him. I will open myself to you, Dakan-eh. I will open myself now. And after you have been with me, maybe you will not want the headman's daughter anymore."

His mouth had gone suddenly dry. If only she would put her robe back on! "I will have Ta-maya, Ban-ya. When the moon stands full in the sky, on that night it will be done between us."

Her face twisted into petulance, but only for an instant. She arched her back sensuously and shook back her long, untamed hair. She sighed and began to circle him. As she walked, she ran her small, pudgy hands from her armpits to the high points of her hips. Her palms smoothed her breasts, then lifted them, held them high, and pointed the nipples right at him. "Can she offer such as these to you?" she asked, pausing directly before him.

"No woman in all the Red World and beyond can offer such as those, Ban-ya."

She smiled tightly as she knelt. "And does she come to you as eagerly as I come to you now? And how does she thank you for going off hunting, finding bride gifts for her? Does she long to open herself to you, as I do, or does she long only for the gifts that you will give to her?"

"She wants a wedding. She is virgin. It is her right."

"Yes, but she looks at *him*, the beautiful one with the face of a shrike. Everyone has seen her . . . haven't you? Don't you mind?"

Anger pricked him. She was taunting him, and he knew it. But yes, he *had* seen it. And yes, he did mind. He was Bold Man! How could any woman refuse him? How could any woman look at anyone else? There was no man to equal him in the Red World. But the strangers from the north had made him seem small in her eyes. He would show her, he vowed, and them.

"Masau has looked at her," Ban-ya continued. "And she has looked back."

He was livid with frustration and anger. "When she sees my gifts, when I take her into the new lodge and put life into her, she will have no cause to look at any other man ever again! I will be enough for her. I am enough for any woman."

"You are enough for me, Dakan-eh." Ban-ya was looking straight at him. Her face was set, expectant, full of open adoration. "Maybe I am enough for you, too? How would you know unless you try me? There is much more woman here for you than you will ever have with Ta-maya. If you still want her afterward, I will not complain . . . for I will have had you first."

"Go away, Ban-ya." His command was a croak.

"Later," she said, and did not go away.

So it was that neither Dakan-eh nor Ban-ya was with the happy assembly of people who walked out of the village in the first sweet hours of sunlight. The villagers had their spears and gathering baskets, and the dogs walked leashed at the sides of the men from the north as Tlana-quah led them toward the marshes to gather some of the new greenery of the season. Cattail shoots, crisp and sweet, were highly prized once the outer leaves were stripped away.

"It is good that you have decided to wait until warmer days before beginning your return journey to the country of the People of the Watching Star," said Tlana-quah with a smile of assurance, even though he could not keep himself from casting a worried eye at the dogs. He strode out with Masau and Cha-kwena on his right, and Maliwal, Chudeh, and the other traders to his left. "You will enjoy this morning, Brothers from the North. Never to have eaten of the first cattails of the season . . . that is something that no man should have to say! But—" He cast a quick look over his shoulder to where Kosar-eh the clown was walking with the women and children, then directed his gaze back to Masau. "Perhaps it would have been better to leave your animals tethered in the village. I . . . the women worry about their being so close to the children."

"These dogs are not animals," corrected Masau politely. "Just as the sacred stones have been with the People of the Red World since time beyond beginning, so dogs have walked as brothers of the People of the Watching Star ever since First Man and First Woman named them so."

Maliwal was shaking his head at what he obviously took to be Tlana-quah's ignorance. "How do you travel without dogs to carry your loads? And how do you hunt without dogs running ahead? What man among you is as swift a sprinter, or has ears as sharp, or a nose as keen as a good dog's?"

Cha-kwena shrugged. "Dakan-eh can outrun an antelope and bring it down bare-handed."

"And speaking of Bold Man, where is he this morning?" asked Tlana-quah.

"Probably still out hunting," said Cha-kwena. "Or working on his bride gifts for Ta-maya."

"*Hmmph!* More likely with the old widows," snapped the headman with obvious disapproval.

"No," said Cha-kwena, "they are behind us with the other women."

"She is a rare beauty, your elder daughter," said Masau to the headman. "If I had hope of winning so fine a woman to my side, I would have no stomach to take my ease on old women while a virgin waits and keeps herself for me. No, I would keep myself apart from all. I would go to the sweat lodge alone. I would fast, and purify my body and my spirit; for as the bride does this for the husband, should not the husband do as much for the bride? I would bring many gifts to Ta-maya and honor her family. I would lay fine pelts and much meal before their lodge. And I would do more than run down an antelope to impress her."

Tlana-quah looked at Masau with open interest. "Would you?"

"Any man would do as much for Ta-maya," said Cha-kwena, and then quickly stared down at his feet, openly embarrassed for having spoken at all.

Tlana-quah chuckled at his expense. "You are Shaman now, Cha-kwena. Behave with authority. Do not stare at your feet like a blushing boy. Why have you not spoken if you wanted her? A little competition might have done our Bold Man some good."

The youth's head came up so fast that for a moment it looked as though it would fly off his neck. "She is for Dakan-eh. She has always wanted him. He spoke for her many winters ago, even before she became a woman. How could I compete with him? He is the best and boldest hunter in all the Red World."

Tlana-quah raised a telling brow as he looked first at Masau, then at the other men from the north. "Not anymore," he said, and when Maliwal snickered and the other traders walked a little taller, he imitated them, well satisfied for having won approval in their eyes.

By midmorning the baskets and the bellies of the gatherers were full. They sat along the shore while relaxing, picking shreds of succulent cattail stems from their teeth, and talking easily to one another. The children stared at the dogs, and the dogs stared at the children. Masau watched them until, at last, he shook his head and went to where Blood was tethered with the other dogs. Patting a noticeably pregnant female, he knelt. The bitch happily thumped her tail. Blood looked at Masau expectantly.

Fondling the head and ears of both dogs, he said: "Each day I see the children of the Red World looking at these dogs, and I see their mothers watching with worried eyes and keeping the little ones close. I hear the mothers whisper: 'Stay away from the dogs! They are like wolves! They will eat you!' Now I must ask, do you believe that your brothers from the north would bring wolves or *wild* dogs among you?"

Maliwal and the other traders exchanged questioning looks. The women looked embarrassed and the children curious.

As Blood sagged blissfully against Masau and raised his head so that his chin might better be stroked, Masau said, "Do you all see how much of a brother he is to me? In the villages of the People of the Watching Star, dogs guard our children. Come closer, children and mothers, but not too close. He is no wild dog, but he has much dignity and, just like you, is wary of strangers. If I were to extend my fingers too close to your face, would you not snap at me and turn away frightened and confused by my intent?"

Ta-maya, seated next to Kosar-eh, Siwi-ni, and their new baby, watched the children and their mothers timidly come a little closer to Masau. How wonderful he was with them, she thought. How patient and caring, and how modest when he went on to say, "I admire the bravery of your hunters, who have the courage to hunt without dogs. Who runs ahead of you, across unknown ground, to scent out your prey? Who warns you of vipers in tall grass, or of lions or leaping cats hiding in the scrub growth? If you happen upon a great bear, who brazens forward to confuse its charge? Who runs into a herd of antelope and turns it toward your waiting spears? All this do you do by yourselves, without dogs."

Ta-maya found herself breathless with awe of him.

Without a single boast, he had just painted a wondrous picture of the way in which he and his people lived and hunted, as though man and beast were of one family. She was reminded of Hoyeh-tay and Owl, of Cha-kwena and his special relationship with animals, and of Mah-ree, who even now sat with Shrike tethered to her shoulder. Truly, there *was* a bond between her people and the people of the north. She sighed, enraptured by the grace, eloquence, and humility of the shaman of the People of the Watching Star, who had made her understand this. What an extraordinary man he was.

Ha-xa, sitting with Mah-ree, U-wa, and the widows, directly across from her elder daughter, clucked her tongue. "You already have the best man in the Red World, girl. Do not look at another man like that! Dakan-eh would not like it."

Ta-maya was deaf to her words. Dakan-eh was not here, and she was glad.

"He is so beautiful, Mother," Mah-ree said of Masau.

Ha-xa looked to Kahm-ree and suggested, "Now there's a man for your Ban-ya! Where is she, anyway?"

"My Ban-ya? Ah, poor child, she was not feeling well this morning." Kahm-ree lied for her granddaughter as easily as she drew breath. "Perhaps she will join us later."

Zar-ah and Xi-ahtli tittered at some amusement that they did not choose to share.

Kahm-ree gave them a venomous hiss. "You two! What are you laughing at? And you, Ha-xa, how can you say that a trader from the north should be for my Ban-ya? How would you like it if Ta-maya or Mah-ree were to go off from the village forever with some stranger to a land about which you knew nothing, and to a people whom you have never heard of before they came here!"

"The People are one," said Mah-ree. "That's what old Hoyeh-tay taught us. And it is what Masau says, too. The strangers are our brothers, aren't they, Kosar-eh?"

The clown seemed surprised to have been drawn into the conversation. "Who else could they be?" he asked, and yet he was not looking at Mah-ree or the other women. When he spoke, he was looking at Ta-maya, who was still staring adoringly at Masau . . . who was looking back at her as though no one else in the world existed.

*    *    *

They headed back to the village toward midday. Peace had been made with the dogs, who were unleashed and running ahead of the children. The woman chatted and carried their wide, circular baskets high on their heads. The men positioned themselves protectively around the little group, and the entire time Tlana-quah talked of his world, his people, their ways, and the good life that had always been theirs. He spoke of how much richer things would be now that they could enjoy a beneficial commerce with their newfound brothers from the far north.

When mammoth were heard trumpeting ahead, the traders called the dogs and leashed them. The People paused and waited, breathless. Soon the entire herd of mammoth crossed before them, the great, lumbering bodies parting the winter-pale tule brakes. All but the calves and the little white "son" made the earth tremble as they passed.

No one spoke when the great white mammoth paused close before them. His height and girth and the length of his tusks caused even Maliwal to take an inadvertent step back. Masau's eyes rounded with incredulity, and every man in his party stiffened and sucked in a little breath of terror at standing so near to an animal of such inordinate size and obvious power. The dogs growled and strained against their leads. Their ears were back and their tails were tucked.

Only Mah-ree did not drop to her knees in abject awe when the mammoth huffed and lifted his head and looked in their direction. She set down her basket and, smiling, raised one arm in greeting as she tried to calm the terrified shrike with her other hand. "I greet you, Grandfather of All! How good it is to see you feeling well enough to move once more among your women and children!"

Ha-xa reached out and took hold of the bottom edge of the girl's tunic lest she move forward into danger.

Mah-ree turned and frowned at her mother. "He would not hurt me. He would not hurt any of us!" With an impatient tug she freed her garment, and with her left hand gently pressing Shrike into submission, she quickly bent to snatch up a handful of cattail shoots from her basket with her right hand and was off before Ha-xa could stop her. A few strides brought her within reach of the mammoth.

His head went high. He swayed and huffed and stared straight down the length of his trunk and tusks at her.

Behind Mah-ree, Tlana-quah snapped to his feet. The other men followed his example. Even Kosar-eh was up and ready to defend the girl, although he had no weapon. All the villagers had followed Mah-ree to the various places where she left food for the mammoth, and this was not the first time that any of them had been close to their totem. But never before—at least when they had been watching— had the girl ventured within the fall of his shadow.

The traders had their spears positioned. Masau had leaped to put himself between Ta-maya and danger, and Cha-kwena frantically wondered what Hoyeh-tay would have done to keep his totem in a mild mood. He stood tall, raised his arms, threw out his chest, and let loose a great booming, "Hay-yah-yah yah-hay."

Startled, the mammoth blinked. It raised its twin-domed skull higher. Its ears twitched.

Mah-ree glared over her shoulder. "Oh, Cha-kwena, stop that noise! And you, brave men of my band and of the north, put down your spears! How can you threaten that which is Totem to you!" The admonition given, she turned and held up her palm to the mammoth. "Here, Grandfather. Do not be offended by the shouting of our shaman or by the raised spears of the hunters. They are all very brave, but you are so very *big*, you must not blame them for being frightened into disrespectful behavior. And our shaman is new. Although he means well, he does not know what he is doing. Forgive him for making so much noise. Here, I bring you good things to eat!"

Cha-kwena stifled his chanting. Everyone was holding his or her breath, gaping in disbelief as the mammoth lowered its head and reached out with its trunk to test the contents of Mah-ree's upheld palm. As she yielded her offering to her totem, her arm and hand curved to embrace its trunk. The mammoth lowered its head and came forward slightly. The creature enfolded the girl within its trunk, drawing her close and allowing her to guide the cattail shoots directly into its mouth.

"Good!" She exhaled with delight at the display of

affection, rubbed the mammoth's cheek, and leaned close. "Ah, your breath is sweet! I see that your new teeth have grown in at last, and your old gums are no longer sore!"

The mammoth shook its head and, with the little girl standing on the curve of its trunk, rocked her gently, as a parent might cradle a favored child in the curve of an arm.

"Ah, she *is* Shaman!" breathed Maliwal, his eyes bulging. "If Ysuna could only see this!"

At that moment one of the mammoth cows trumpeted, and the little white calf bleated. As though responding to a summons, the old white bull set Mah-ree down. It stood erect again and gazed at those who stared up at him.

Only the hunters from the north still held their spears. Sunlight shone red on the dark obsidian projectile points, making them appear wet and glossy, as if they had been carved out of liver or clotted blood.

The mammoth's eyes seemed to refract the color through the mists of its ancient corneas. Sensing danger, it suddenly swung its great head, loosed a high, nasal shriek, then threatened with a brief feint forward that had Mahree on the ground and all the people screaming and running away. Finally, with a huff of defiance, the great mammoth flicked its tail and turned away in the very moment that Masau was about to launch his spear.

Ta-maya's hand stayed his. "Wait!" she implored. "He is Totem! He goes his way. No one has been hurt. Look, Mah-ree is all right."

He did not look. He did not even care. He was lost in her eyes. He was made breathless by her touch. Her hand had closed about his wrist; how cool her fingers felt, and yet his flesh burned against hers. His mouth was suddenly dry, and his heartbeat quickened alarmingly. And although he wished to speak, he could not form a single cogent word or thought. Never had a woman elicited such a reaction from him. *Never.*

"You placed yourself between me and what you thought would be a danger to me. I thank you," she said.

Her voice was so soft. He could not look away from her face, her exquisite and caring face. As he lowered his spear arm her hand remained about his wrist. He could feel his pulse pounding against her palm, and yet, although she stirred the man need in him, his reaction was wholly unfamiliar and disturbing. There was more to his wanting than the simple need to take her down and invade her body with his own; but he did not know what it was. All he understood was that he wanted to share more with her than that which he had shared with Ysuna since he had been little more than a boy and Daughter of the Sun had eagerly led him with mouth and tongue, with seeking hands and welcoming arms and open thighs to discover the pure joy of sexual explorations that ended in explosive, howling fires of exhaustion and release.

His reaction startled him. How could he feel this way? True, Ta-maya was the most perfectly beautiful and wholly lovely young woman he had ever seen, but it was for those very reasons that she *must* be the next sacrifice. Without her blood and the blood of the white mammoth, Ysuna would wither and die, and all that he had ever known and loved would die with her. Ysuna was the living heart of the People of the Watching Star, and he, as their shaman and Mystic Warrior, lived only to protect them and make them strong.

It was the shrike that shattered his thoughts and caused him to step away from the girl. The bird had freed itself from Mah-ree and flew to Masau's shoulder.

Mah-ree came quickly after it. She scolded it gently for flying away from her.

"If you would make the right knot on his leg noose, he would not fly away all the time," said Cha-kwena.

Mah-ree defended herself. "He keeps pecking at the knot until it comes undone. I think he wants to be yours, Masau. You both wear masks. Maybe Shrike thinks you are his brother?"

"Hardly a compliment," Cha-kwena remarked.

Masau and Ta-maya were gazing at each other again. When Tlana-quah chewed his lower lip with pleased speculation, Ha-xa came sweeping forward and firmly took her daughter by the arm.

"Come away now, Ta-maya! The third moon will soon be full, and there is still some last-minute sewing to do on the gifts that you will give to Dakan-eh."

\* \* \*

It was Blood who first caught scent of the lion. Masau leaped ahead of Tlana-quah to place the first spear as the lion charged out of the scrub growth not far from the edge of the village. With this strike he inflicted a mortal wound that brought the animal down. When the beast lay on its side, limp and gape jawed and bleeding, the headman swore that Masau had saved his life.

"That lion would have had me had it not been for you and your dogs!"

But Cha-kwena was not so sure. From where he had been walking with Kosar-eh, it appeared that the lion had no intention of leaping at Tlana-quah. It had been headed straight for Maliwal and Masau. It was an old lion, black maned, scarred, sag bellied, with a mouth of stubs where fangs should have been. Two suppurating, half-healed wounds—one high at his back and the other at his throat—marked the entry and exit points of a spear that should have killed this animal long ago. As the barking, slavering dogs were waved away from the beast and the people came close to observe the kill, Cha-kwena frowned deeply. He knew this lion! The scabbing, necrotic wounds on its back and throat had been made by his own spear! This was the same animal that had led him uphill and across the meadow toward Mah-ree, then had led him into the grove where the white mammoth grazed. He *had* wounded it, after all.

"This animal has been dying for a long time," said Masau, kneeling beside the lion, touching the throat and back wounds. "A spear did this. A spear of the type made in the Red World. Whose?"

"Bold Man's no doubt," answered Ha-xa before Cha-kwena could reply. "Dakan-eh has been hunting for pelts that will be bride gifts for my Ta-maya!"

Masau nodded; nevertheless, his face was set and stern as he looked at Tlana-quah. "Your Bold Man should have pursued this animal to the end. To leave a big carnivore wounded like this is to invite it to come close to the dwelling place of men. It was only a matter of time before any one of you could have been attacked—especially your children."

It was Mah-ree who spoke, not in Dakan-eh's defense but in Cha-kwena's. "It was our shaman who threw the spear that injured the lion. He saw it coming after me and warned me to run. I never saw the lion with my own eyes, but after Cha-kwena's spear was cast, he did go after it, into the cedar grove, alone and armed only with a dagger. He would have made the final kill at the risk of his own life, but it was such a cold day and the snow on the ground within the grove was as hard as stone; the lion left no tracks or even a trail of blood by which he could follow it. You should have seen Cha-kwena! How bold he was! How wonderful!"

Cha-kwena felt himself flush with both pride and embarrassment as all eyes turned to him.

"My son," U-wa said haughtily, "has always said that although he has been chosen to walk the shaman's path, he would prefer to be a skilled hunter. And so he is. I, for one, am not surprised in the least!"

Tlana-quah eyed Cha-kwena with new respect. "Well done, Cha-kwena. But why did you say nothing of this to me or to anyone else?"

"Because I found no blood and no tracks, I was not certain if I had actually struck at anything more substantial than my own imagination. Besides, there was no sign of the animal later on, no sound to make me think that it might be lurking anywhere about."

Maliwal bent closer to inspect the wounds. "A clean piercing—so clean that at first there was probably no hemorrhage. That is why you found no blood, Cha-kwena. And in a grove where the snow has lain long upon the ground after many days and nights of extreme cold, even a big cat like this might leave no tracks."

Cha-kwena stood a little taller. The expressions of open adulation upon the faces of his people were so wonderful to him that he chose not to mention the fact that when he had found his spear lying in the snow, it had been clean, devoid of blood or tissue. He was Cha-kwena, Brother of Animals, Shaman, and now . . . *Hunter of Lions*! He wanted nothing else in the world except to have the moment last.

Tlana-quah slung an arm about the youth's shoulder and drew him close in a congratulatory hug that affirmed not so much one man's affection for another but kinship and profound respect. "You *are* Shaman! And as good a man with a spear as Dakan-eh!"

Cha-kwena's spirit soared with delight. *As good a man with a spear as Dakan-eh!* His lifetime dream was realized. He knew that he was beaming like a boy who had just won his first race or wrestling match; he did not care. "Like my headman, Tlana-quah, Brave Hunter, Man Who Alone Kills Jaguar, I, too, faced a lion and was unafraid."

"Yes," affirmed Tlana-quah, his tone suddenly tight and oblique. He turned his attention to Masau.

"You stepped into the path of the lion and risked yourself in order to place the spear that saved my life. What would you have as a show of thanks from me? Some gift . . . *any* gift."

"You need feel no obligation to me, Tlana-quah," replied Masau evenly, a muscle working high at the line of his jaw as he looked down at the lion. "You would have done the same for me had you, and not I, held the heavier spear and been in a position to do so."

Across the carcass from him, Maliwal eyed his brother watchfully. "Tlana-quah has offered you a gift—*any* gift, Brother! Do not insult the man by refusing his generosity."

Masau drew in a deep breath. He held it for a long time before exhaling. Then, still staring down at the lion, he said, "I want no gift save friendship from you, Tlana-quah . . . for aside from that, the one thing I desire from you with all my spirit is something for which I cannot ask."

Tlana-quah frowned and thought very hard. His face was set, his eyes somehow focused inward. Then, with a sigh of affirmation, he slapped his jaguar-skin cape. "The cape of the spotted cat? It is yours! From this day forth you will wear it as a sign of everlasting brotherhood with Tlana-quah . . . as Tlana-quah will wear the skin of the lion that Masau has killed for me."

Masau rose quickly and stayed the headman's hand as Tlana-quah reached to undo the bone fastener that held his cape secure upon his shoulders. "No, Tlana-quah. Proudly would I wear the spotted-lion cape of the headman of the Red World, but I would not ask so much of a brother!"

Tlana-quah was incredulous. His fingers remained poised above the bone clasp. "You do not want my cape? Every man in the Red World envies me my cape!"

"It is not the gift that I would ask for . . . if I dared to ask at all."

"Dare!" insisted Tlana-quah. "Name it, and it will be yours!"

Masau looked at Maliwal.

"Name it, Brother!" insisted Maliwal. "Do you imagine that the most honorable Tlana-quah would deny you that for which you have secretly longed since we first came to be his guests?" He looked at Tlana-quah and shook his head. "My brother hesitates to offend by asking too much of his host."

"Your brother has saved my life! He offends me by his reticence. There must be something in this village that he would have as a reward for his bravery! Pelts! Food! Adornment!"

"It is a gift that must come consenting, or it would be no gift at all," said Masau.

"I do not understand," replied Tlana-quah. "How can a gift consent to be given?"

Masau exchanged looks with Maliwal again.

"Go ahead!" prodded the older brother. "Ask him!"

Masau hesitated, then shook his head. "I cannot ask for what cannot possibly be mine. I cannot ask for one who is promised to another. I cannot ask for Ta-maya . . . although if she were to consent to come with me, she would be cherished and honored above all brides. She would enjoy a good life among my people. Together we would assure that the People would be one forever, and . . . and I would bring her to be with her family at the Great Gathering of the tribes in the shadow of your sacred mountain under the light of the Pinyon Moon. *This* is the gift that I would ask of you, Tlana-quah. The *only* gift. But although my heart urges me to ask this of you, she is promised to another, so I cannot."

Stunned, Cha-kwena caught his breath, as did everyone else.

"No! You cannot! She is *mine!*" declared Dakan-eh angrily, elbowing his way forward through the people who clustered around the dead lion.

Ban-ya followed close at his heels, and as she met Ta-maya's wide-eyed stare her chin was in the air and a smug grin of satisfaction dimpled her love-reddened cheeks. The look on her face revealed everything that had happened between Bold Man and her even before she declared, "As am I!"

Dakan-eh whirled around and ordered her to shut her mouth. "You are nothing to me! Ta-maya is my woman!"

Ta-maya paled, stiffened, and then trembled. "You and Ban-ya have been together?"

"It was nothing!" he shouted.

"Nothing?" Kahm-ree was openly furious. "How dare you insult my granddaughter like that!"

"Nothing?" Standing with the other women, Xhet-li spoke out in a rare display of concern for her daughter. "*My* Ban-ya is the best of all women! Ban-ya is—"

"*His.*" Ta-maya's voice was unnaturally low and flat. "This day he has chosen her over me."

Dakan-eh was livid. "I have lain with her, but I have chosen you!"

"Yes. You have." She spoke quietly, with sadness and regret. "But I have not chosen you. I see that now. I have said yes to you, and then soon to you, but I have made you wait and wait because, perhaps, all along I have known that you were not the man whom I have wanted at all. It has been wrong of me, and I beg your forgiveness. Here is the man I will have: Masau, Shaman of the People of the Watching Star. He has saved my father's life this day, and if I am the gift that he desires from Tlana-quah, I will go consenting to be his woman and his reward."

# 10

And so it was that when the third moon rose full above the village by the Lake of Many Singing Birds, Ta-maya prepared to make good on her word to accept a man, but the man would not be Dakan-eh. She sat naked on folded limbs within her parents' lodge, allowing Ha-xa, U-wa, and Mah-ree to fuss about her hair and rub oil into her just-bathed skin. It seemed as if everything that was happening was unfolding within a dream.

Ha-xa was beside herself. "I don't like it!" she said. "I know it's too late to turn back now—your man-to-be is fasting in the solitude of the mountains. The men of the north are out with their dogs hunting in preparation for the feast. Baskets bulge with food to be cooked and served at tonight's celebration—but after your first night with Masau, you will go away, and I will not see you again until the Great Gathering. I cannot bear to think of it!"

"Many girls marry out of their band and do not visit with their loved ones until the Great Gathering," Ta-maya pointed out. "But Masau is a trader; he travels all the time. We will come often to see you. I will make sure of that!"

"Are you not afraid to go so far away from home, Ta-maya, and with strangers?" U-wa asked.

"*I* would not be afraid," assured Mah-ree. "As long as Masau was with me, I would not be afraid of anything!"

"You don't know your own heart anymore, girl," teased Ha-xa. "One day moon-eyed over Cha-kwena, the next day sighing over any stranger who happens to come along!"

"Masau is not just any stranger, Mother!" reminded Ta-maya. "He is Shaman. Father names him Brother. Cha-kwena likes him. And I am glad that my sister approves of our union."

"Hoyeh-tay did not trust him! Kosar-eh does not like him!" said Ha-xa.

U-wa clucked her tongue admonishingly. "That is not fair, Ha-xa. Old Hoyeh-tay did not know whether it was day or night or whether it was yesterday or tomorrow. And poor, dear Kosar-eh . . . his heart is full of Ta-maya."

"I know," she said with a sigh. "And my heart is full of Masau. The children adore him. He will be my man— not because my father wants it, but because I want it. You must accept this, Mother."

She was surprised by the cool authority of her own voice; deep down there *was* fear. Whatever happened from this day forth would happen in another life, far from home and from all whom she knew and loved. But somehow that fear was unimportant. Just thinking of Masau eased her doubts. She had not seen him since he had taken his dog and sought the solitude of the mountains. Maliwal had followed soon after, in the company of the other men of the north. They had been gone from the village for several days now, hunting with their dogs for meat that would be their contribution to the marriage feast. Tonight they would all return.

Her heart leaped in joyous anticipation. How she longed to see Masau again, to be joined to him as his woman! With Dakan-eh, there had always been uncertainty; with Masau there was only eagerness. Had he asked her to go away with him without a wedding at all, she would have said yes, and now. It was all so strange, so unlike her usually hesitant and indecisive nature; but when she looked into his eyes, nothing else but love mattered. She knew that she must go to him and be his, whatever the terms, whatever the cost.

After days and nights of brooding, Dakan-eh was enraged, ashamed, and disconsolate. When he heard from the boys posted as lookouts that the men of the north were on their way back to the village, their dogs dragging crossed poles laden with meat, he cursed them all. In a frenzy of temper, he gathered up the bride gifts that were to have been for Ta-maya and, staggering under the weight of the many rolls of fur in which they were wrapped, stalked to the headman's lodge and, with every step he

took, roared out the name of Tlana-quah's elder daughter.
Alerted by his shouts, people dropped whatever they were
doing and followed to see what he was about.

"Ta-maya! Firstborn daughter of Tlana-quah! Come
out!" he bellowed.

"What is this, Bold Man?" Tlana-quah, annoyed, came
hurrying from where he and some of the other men had
been preparing the feast fire.

"I would talk with your elder daughter!"

"It is not fitting!" said the headman.

"Nothing is fitting for me these days!" Dakan-eh said
with a sneer. "You have given away my woman!"

"She was not your woman."

"She would have been!"

"Perhaps." Tlana-quah measured the younger man.
"And what is all this that you bring?"

"Gifts for the bride! In hope that I may have one
more chance to make her change her mind and come to
me instead of to *him*."

Tlana-quah raised his eyebrows at the contemptuous
way in which Dakan-eh had formed his reference to Masau.
The man's audacity and arrogance were unaltered by Ta-
maya's rejection. Although Tlana-quah disliked the young
man, he knew that he himself would have felt equally
hostile in a predicament similar to Bold Man's. He decided to take pity on him. "A few words. No more," he
said, and called to Ta-maya.

She appeared, wrapped in her bed furs, with Ha-xa
and U-wa and Mah-ree standing behind her. Her lovely
face softened when she saw the misery and wanting on
Dakan-eh's face. Then she flinched, for without warning,
he hurled his gifts at her feet.

"What can he give you to compare to these!" he
demanded, and without so much as a single word of love
or tenderness, knelt to unroll a length of pieced rabbit fur
that was filled with earrings and necklets, with wristbands
and belts and feathered hair adornments that he had made
for her. "Who could make better than these? No one!"

He moved to a second roll of fur, unwound it furiously, and smirked with pride over the beautifully displayed needles of bone and thorn, at awls of exquisitely
worked stone, at thimbles and palm pads and all the

necessary paraphernalia that would ease the labor of a woman as she sewed. With this spread out before her, he opened the largest of the furs and raised yards and yards of intricately woven cording.

"Can *he* weave for his bride as fine a net for the catching of rabbits and hares? No! Only Bold Man can weave like this! And this! Can he match this?"

Now he took up yet another large roll of pieced rabbit skins and unfurled it before her. Laid out upon it were the pelts of rabbit and raccoon, of skunk and fox, of lynx and badger, of opossum and coyote, and the skins of birds and fish, all stretched and fleshed and cured to the softest perfection, ready for a skilled woman to fashion into clothes and adornments and whatever else might suit her fancy.

"All this I have made for my bride!" he declared, standing now, throwing out his chest, jabbing his chin at her in defiance of her rejection. "All this I have hunted at night for you and worked secretly for you. And for your parents I have brought together other things—so much meat and so many pelts that I could not carry them all—all to make you smile with pride in me on this day that should be mine!"

Her eyes went round. "Yours?"

"Yes! Mine! I am Bold Man! You are Best Woman! Who else is fit to share a lodge with me?"

Her brow furrowed slightly; she looked at him as though she had never seen him before and, in the seeing, understood him for the first time. "Perhaps you should marry yourself, Bold Man. Then all your efforts in assembling these many fine gifts will not be wasted upon someone less capable of appreciating them than you yourself."

Mah-ree stifled a giggle. U-wa did the same. And at Dakan-eh's back, most of the villagers tittered openly.

Furious, Bold Man turned. Cha-kwena was standing close by. Dakan-eh pointed a rage-stiffened finger at him. "Tell them! Tell *her*! Tell them all what you have seen me do. I have saved your life, and that of the addlebrained old fool who was Shaman before you! Tell them that I am the best and the boldest man in the Red World and beyond! Tell them! Go ahead! What are you staring at? Tell them!"

Cha-kwena did not speak. He was staring past Dakan-eh to where the fur of a coyote lay tumbled loosely over the other gifts. It was a golden fur, with head, tail, and paws still attached. One paw was slightly crooked and smaller than its mate. He stared at the pelt, and then he stared at Dakan-eh. "My dream was no dream. You have killed my spirit brother. You gutted Little Yellow Wolf and left him to hang, and smiled as you did it."

Bold Man cocked his head. "What are you talking about? It was just another coyote. Of course I smiled as I skinned him. His is a prime pelt! What's the matter with you, Cha-kwena?"

The young shaman shook his head as though to free it of an unpleasant memory. "I will not speak for you," he said. "Any more than you spoke for me upon the sacred mountain."

Dakan-eh looked wary. "What is this, Cha-kwena?"

"I am now Shaman of this band, Dakan-eh, as you assured me that I must be someday. You found pleasure in shaming me—and Ta-maya—with the sister of Sunam-tu. Look—even now Ta-maya wears a wristband that was given to you by another woman. And even now you continue to degrade the good name of my grandfather with insults. So now do I take pleasure in shaming you. I have not forgotten that humiliation on the sacred mountain; I have learned from it. Maybe now you also will learn from humiliation. A man cannot always have what he desires. And although you believe yourself to be the best and the boldest man in the Red World and beyond, the truth is that there are others who are bolder and better. Ta-maya has found such a man in Masau. He has been as a brother to me. He has killed a lion and saved the life of our headman. I will not speak against his union with Ta-maya."

Dakan-eh's face went purple with rage. "Why you little—" He cut off the epithet before it was formed and glared at Tlana-quah. "When the traders return to the north, who will kill lions for you then, Headman, if Bold Man is not here to do it for you?"

"I am here," responded Cha-kwena coolly. "And you are not the only hunter of worth within this band."

The other men of the village murmured responsively to the compliment, and the women sighed as Ta-maya removed her wristband and handed it to her mother, who returned it to Dakan-eh. Bold Man threw it to the ground.

Tlana-quah's eyes narrowed with dislike as he fixed his gaze on Dakan-eh. "What is this talk of not being here? Are you planning to leave us?"

"There are other villages in the Red World! Other bands!"

"Go, then. Join one! Do what you must do, Bold Man! I have had enough of your mouth for one day. A wedding will take place in this village at the rising of the moon. We must make ready! We must prepare!"

"Do it without me!" Dakan-eh ground the wristband into the earth with his heel, then kicked out savagely at the furs, sending the gifts flying in all directions. Leaving them where they lay, he stalked out of the village without another word to anyone.

The wedding of Masau and Ta-maya took place under the full face of a silver moon. Dakan-eh was not there to see it, nor was Ban-ya; but before she surreptitiously dared to follow Bold Man into the night, she waited until all the celebrants were gathered and the new shaman was in his best and loudest form.

West Wind whispered all around the village. Ha-xa wept in the way of all mothers at the wedding of their firstborn, and Kosar-eh performed clever and lascivious dances to inspire the bride and her new man. If loons called on the lake, no one heard them, for the sound of drums and whistles and rattles filled the night. There were too many songs to be sung, and too many dances to be danced.

The People of the Red World and the traders from the People of the Watching Star ate and drank together. When the bride and her new man were escorted to their lodge, Tlana-quah folded his arms across his chest and watched them enter.

"Now," he said with great satisfaction, "the People of our two worlds will be one."

At last Ta-maya, trembling with eagerness and apprehension, lay in the arms of Masau within the new lodge.

"Be at ease, Ta-maya. That which has been celebrated tonight cannot be consummated until we return to my people and receive the blessings of the high priestess of my own land. I will live with a virgin bride just a while longer."

On the newly woven mattress of reeds and sagebrush, warm beneath the finest blankets of rabbit fur, her hand strayed to his bare chest. "Must it be so?"

"Are you not afraid of your first piercing, Ta-maya?"

"I have not wanted it . . . until now . . . with you."

He looked at her in the firelight, then touched her face, kissed her brow, and moved to seek her mouth. Lightly. So lightly. He sighed, trembled, and with a long, low exhalation he turned his back to her. "Sleep now, my bride, if you can."

She swallowed down her disappointment. Understanding, she stroked the curve of his back and felt his skin ripple beneath her touch. "I will dream of you, Masau, and of how it will soon be with us when we reach the land of your people. Will they like me?"

"They will find you as I find you—a perfect bride."

"And your mother, the great lady shaman, she will not be angry that you have brought to her a woman of another people? And what of your father? Is he a shaman, too?"

"I have only Ysuna."

"Daughter of the Sun . . . One Who Brings Life to the People . . . is she as beautiful as her name?"

"Ysuna is beautiful."

"She must be very wise."

"It is so. She is wise. She is beautiful. And soon she will be as powerful as the white mammoth."

"What if she doesn't like me?"

"She will love you, Ta-maya. Believe me when I say that you are all that she has ever wanted for me."

The next day the People of the Red World assembled to bid good-bye to Ta-maya and the traders. Maliwal told his man Tsana to stay by the fifth sledge, which was carefully covered with hide to protect its cargo.

"Must you leave so soon after the wedding?" Ha-xa's eyes were red rimmed from a night of weeping.

"We have been too long from our own country," explained Masau. "Now that the weather is improving, we must journey north. It is our hope to stop in as many of the villages of the Red World as we can. I would like to trade some of our black obsidian for a good supply of that rare, translucent stone that your people have told me is common in the White Hills to the west. But we will meet again at the Great Gathering under the light of the Pinyon Moon. In the meantime, I, too, have a mother, Ha-xa! How she will rejoice in this bride and in the rare gifts I bring to her from the Red World! Until then, I have a gift for your people. Maliwal, bring forth that which was delivered into our care during the light of last night's moon."

Maliwal complied. Chudeh and Tsana assisted, each man clutching a corner of a large stretch of hide, upon which lay the pregnant female dog that usually kept close company with Blood. The bitch was no longer pregnant. The result of her whelping lay at her belly, milk new and sucking, as blind as newborn mice—thirteen pups.

"This dog is too weak to carry her own weight on the journey to the north. Her name is Watching Star. She will stay with you until we meet again at the Great Gathering. The pups are yours, our gift to you. Their mother will show them how to hunt. Care for her as though she were the daughter who now walks to the north with us. If lions come close—even if Dakan-eh does not return—she will know what to do to warn and protect your villagers. And any pups of Blood's and hers will have the heart in them to do it."

Kahm-ree's eyes were as red as Ha-xa's from crying. "You will look for my Ban-ya along the way?"

"She is with Bold Man, old woman," Tlana-quah said impatiently. "In time he will bring her home again. She is his woman now. Is this not what you have wanted all along?"

Kahm-ree snuffled. "Only with the two of them living close, making a new family for me."

"We will look for Ban-ya and Bold Man in every village," assured Maliwal.

"And when you see them, tell them that all is forgiven," the headman said, shaking his head as though he could not believe his own generosity. "It has been a good year, all in all—good omens, our totem close by, my firstborn daughter married at last. Dakan-eh has a big mouth and enough love for himself to make himself pregnant with it; but he has lost a good woman in my Ta-maya, and I cannot blame him for reacting badly to his loss."

Ta-maya shook her head. "I am the one who has treated him badly, to have made him wait so long and then to have accepted another instead."

"He did not exactly wait for you, Ta-maya," reminded Cha-kwena, darkly eyeing Kahm-ree and the other widows. "Did he, old women?"

Kahm-ree hung her head but did not speak.

Kosar-eh, still in body paint from the previous night's festivities, held his new baby in the fold of his one good arm as he and Siwi-ni came close to say their good-byes. "Take care," he said to Ta-maya. "And may the spirits of the ancestors walk with you."

"And you, old friend," she said, and stood upon her tiptoes to place a kiss upon his cheek. "Until we meet again under the light of the Pinyon Moon."

With a heavy heart, Cha-kwena watched them go. Mah-ree came to stand beside him. Shrike, untethered, was perched upon her shoulder. "Ta-maya has married the best man in all the world!" she declared.

"I thought *I* was the best man in all the world as far as you were concerned, Mosquito."

"Masau would never call me that," she said with one of her pouts. "He calls me Medicine Girl and his new little sister. And his brother has told me that if I am not careful, next year he will come back and take me away with him to be his bride!" She wrinkled her nose. "I would not go, of course—not with him. I don't like him. But his brother . . ." She sighed. "The spirits of the ancestors are smiling upon Ta-maya!"

Cha-kwena shivered but could not say why. He felt as if a cold wind had suddenly risen to chill him. He looked around. There was no wind to speak of. The day was clear and warm, ripe with the promise of spring. Shrike flew off after the travelers. With a sigh, Mah-ree watched the bird until it alighted on Masau's shoulder. Mystic Warrior turned to look back at her.

"He is your brother, not mine!" cried the girl. "He has chosen the way he will follow!"

Again the cold wind stirred within Cha-kwena. His hands rose to press the sacred stone closer to his breast.

As he did, mammoth trumpeted somewhere in the hills off to the northwest. A good omen! He willed himself to take heart. The Great Gathering of the tribe would take place in autumn. He would see Masau and Ta-maya again before next winter. It was not such a long time.

Soon wintering birds would leave the lake, and summer migrants would arrive by the tens of thousands. There would be eggs to gather and decoys to set, and then, before he knew it, the Cattail and Duck moons would shine only in his memories, while the Fish Moon would show its face. It would be time to leave the village and travel to the river where huge schools of trout were spawning. Then, in warming days, the People would return to their lodges under the light of the Grass Moon, and it would be time once more for gathering and threshing and winnowing. And finally, at long last, the Pinyon Moon would rise, and it would be time to begin the long overland trek to the sacred mountain.

Cha-kwena drew in a deep breath. He suddenly felt wonderful. All seemed right with the world at last. The white mammoth grazed in the far hills, and the sacred stone was safe about his neck. If only old Hoyeh-tay and Owl were here to share it with him!

# PART VII

# BROTHERS OF THE SKY

# 1

They traveled west toward the White Hills, with Shrike perched upon Masau's shoulder. There was no sign that Dakan-eh and Banya had passed this way. The sun rose high, and Ta-maya was happy and excited.

"Ha-xa has an aunt in the White Hills," she told her new man, looking forward to showing him off to her relatives there. "And my father has several cousins. Tlanaquah has sent gifts along for them. It will be a good time for us. It is a small band, but we will be welcomed with gladness."

The sun slipped toward dusk. They made camp to the lee of a towering red butte, and Ta-maya smiled at the beauty of the land of her people: the red earth, the great soaring mesas, the sage flats and forested foothills, and a small shallow lake reflecting the colors of the approaching sunset in its calm waters.

Masau scanned the landscape from under furrowed brows. "It is good country with plenty of water," he said. "Lakes everywhere. Good potential deadfalls in the stream channels. But there is not much grass for big game."

"There is plenty to browse for antelope and deer," Ta-maya told him, smiling enthusiastically. "Mammoth sometimes pass this way. Bison, too, and horses and camels. Look to the summits of the tallest buttes. There, where thunderclouds often gather to make rain on the summits, you can see the marks of the ancient waterline of Big Lake. I always imagine the children of First Man and First Woman coming over the tops of the mountains, as though they were stepping-stones across which the ancestors could follow the great white mammoth into this new land. There was only one lake back then, but with so many fish waiting to be caught that although the People were hunters of big game, they stopped their wandering and settled in to eat fish instead. Many generations later, when the waters of Big Lake went up to the sun, the children of First Man and First Woman had forgotten the big-game-hunting ways of their ancestors. Antelopes and rabbits came down to the Red World to feed the People. Hares came, too, and lizards and toads, frogs and—"

Maliwal grunted rudely, shivering with revulsion as he spoke. "That is not meat, girl! Now that you are in the company of men of the Watching Star, you will learn soon enough what real food is."

Masau raised a warning brow. "Be at ease with your words, Brother. We would not want our Ta-maya to regret her decision to come north with us. Besides, it will be some time before any of us eat any meat at all. You, Chudeh, unpack the fourth sledge. The hides for our shelters are there, and the thongs and support poles."

Ta-maya scanned the darkening sky. "It will be a clear, warm night. We could sleep under the stars and save your men the trouble of putting up shelters for my sake."

"We will be here awhile, Ta-maya," Masau told her. "When the sun rises tomorrow, you will need shade. Chudeh will raise a shelter for you before he joins me and the others. Rest now. Be comfortable. Enjoy the sunset, then try to get some sleep. Whatever you see, do not concern yourself with it. Tomorrow will be a long day."

"And you?" she queried, openly puzzled.

"Before we go on, my men and I must tend to certain duties. I will explain later, but we have been long in the country of your people, and we must pause to cleanse ourselves."

"Of what? Only yesterday you all enjoyed our sweat lodges and—"

"Please, Ta-maya, I will explain later. For now, stay here. The dogs will keep you safe."

She obeyed, watching as Masau trotted off toward the lake. Shrike flew away as the man began to peel off his garments. Masau discarded them in a pile along with the clothes of all the other men.

Ta-maya stared, curious and amazed. With the exception of Chudeh, who was raising the lean-to, every man in the trading party was stark naked and gathered into a circle. From the way they stood, she could see between them. Their discarded clothing was in the center. Maliwal hunkered down and worked a bow drill until a spark flashed within a nest of kindling that he had taken from one of the sledges. The man named Ston was now splashing oil onto the clothing from a bladder flask that had appeared out of nowhere.

"What is he doing, Chudeh?" she asked, frowning. "Why are they burning their garments?"

"Take no offense, Bride, but before coming into your village we paused here and between those boulders over there stashed fresh clothes and supplies, purgatives, and the makings for fire."

"Why? My people would gladly have provided you with all that you might possibly need. And what need have you of purgatives?" Worry leaped within her. "Are you sick?"

"Not exactly. In a way you might say that we are . . . not so much sick as sickened. Your people were generous, Bride. Many are the fine gifts they have given us. But our ways are very different ways, and so is it that these things and all that we wore while in contact with your people must be burned, and all that we have eaten must be purged."

Before she could ask why, the pile of clothes was a smoking pyre. As she watched in growing perplexity, Masau, with noticeable reverence and hesitancy, placed his eagle skin atop the pyre. Then the men ran to the lake and plunged headlong into the water, diving and splashing and scrubbing themselves with a vengeance.

After the lean-to was hastily assembled, Chudeh left her to add his garments to the pyre and join the others in the lake. They shouted and shrieked with relief, then emerged from the water. Masau loped from the shore to the boulders, where he retrieved several rolls of darkly furred hide. One he unwrapped as he returned to the others, then handed out some dried leaves. All accepted an equal portion and drew in a steadying breath of resolve before eating. Soon every man was violently sick.

Frightened and confused, Ta-maya fought against her desire to go to them and offer help. But Chudeh had said that they must be purged, and Masau had told her to stay where she was while they cleansed themselves. Masau was Shaman. Whatever he had given them might make them suffer, but they would not die of it.

The sun was down now. The world was turning gray as the traders of the Watching Star moaned and vomited in abject misery. Ta-maya felt a twinge of resentment. Those were Ha-xa's camas cakes they were deliberately regurgitating, not to mention the bowls of good lizard soup with brown-spider garnish, and roasted ground squirrels and rabbits and cattail shoots plus grubs hard won from the stumps of rotting pine logs!

"Purged indeed! Cleansed indeed!" she exclaimed, insulted and angry to see such a wanton waste of excellent food. Her twinge of resentment solidified. Angrily she clenched her teeth, turned away from the sight of so many retching men, and stalked through the watching dogs to seat herself within the lean-to.

"What kind of ungrateful men are these into whose band I have married?" she wondered aloud in the thickening darkness.

Blood came to sit before her, his head cocked, ears up, eyes looking at Shrike as the bird perched on one of the support posts. The sight of the little masked creature made her think of home and of Mah-ree.

*You have married the best man in all the world!* her sister had assured her.

"Oh, Little One . . ." Ta-maya sighed and tried not to think of Dakan-eh. "I hope you were right!"


"Why did you follow me?" Dakan-eh's question was a shriek of rage in the darkness of the woods.

"It seemed the best thing to do at the time," replied Ban-ya bitterly.

"I will not take you back to the village."

Ban-ya wore only sagebrush sandals and a short skirt of blue-jay feathers. Around her shoulders was a single pelt—the yellow skin of a coyote. She shivered so violently that her teeth clicked in her head. She sat on the ground, her arms wrapped around her lower legs, her knees drawn up to her chest, and her back pressed to an ironwood tree. "I should have brought more of the gifts that you threw away—the blankets, anyway. We would be warm, at least."

"They were not for you. They were for *her*. It is not cold, so stop complaining! And take off that coyote hide. I never want to see it again."

She shook her head and exhaled in misery. "You are never cold, Dakan-eh. The pelt is warm. I will keep it. If you don't want to see it, then don't look at me."

"That will be a pleasure. If I never set eyes on you again, it will be too soon! I should leave you sitting right where you are, to be meat for whatever is hunting in the forest this night. It is all you deserve after what you have done to me! How could you come into the widows' hut and force me to take you when it was *her* I wanted, only her—*never* you!"

Ban-ya glowered in the moon-shadowed light of the forest. "You wanted me as much as I wanted you. We took each other. Until now I have not been sorry."

"You should be, because you can sit there and whine all you like, but I am not going back to the village ever again. The next time I see Tlana-quah, I will be at the Great Gathering. I will have found another band to call my own. What headman would not want such a bold hunter as Dakan-eh to live among his people? What shaman of any worth would look at Bold Man and dishonor him by denying him that which was his by right?" He was completely taken by his rhetoric. His nostrils were flaring; his lips curled back to show his fine white teeth. "I will go to the far side of the sacred mountain, to the village of Shi-wana, shaman of the People of the Blue Mesas. It is the farthest of all the villages, but now that Hoyeh-tay is dead, Shi-wana has become supreme elder of all the holy men in the Red World. He will appreciate the news. He will make me welcome. He was such an old man. Perhaps he will be tired of his young woman by now."

Ban-ya, hurt and resentful, stared up at him. He looked like a healthy young animal standing there, snorting his defiance into the night. "I will go with you, Dakan-eh, back to the village or anywhere else you decide to go. Just don't leave me behind. I am afraid of the dark."

\* \* \*

Ta-maya awoke in the thin light of dawn, after a miserable night spent listening to the traders of the People of the Watching Star being sick. After the men were internally cleansed, they were ready for another bath. Their splashing and low, deep masculine talk roused her from troubled dreams.

Now, in the light of the rising sun, they were coming from the lake, shivering and *brr*ing and shaking themselves dry. From where she lay within the lean-to—on her side with her head propped onto a folded elbow—she could see down across the long slope that led to the lake. She watched them take up fresh clothes from their cache and put them on, then kneel to eat of the dried provisions left here for this purpose.

"Eat lightly. Our bellies are tender now," she heard Masau advise.

"And there will be no more of this kind of meat until we can hunt again," added Maliwal. "That which we carry on the fifth sledge is for Ysuna."

"There was sign beyond the boulders—fresh, too," Chudeh said.

"With so many ravines in this land, with any luck by nightfall we will be well fed and well rationed for the long trek ahead," added Tsana.

"I say we go back now and finish what we started and take all of what we have come for! That will be the best meat, eh?"

Ta-maya flinched at the rough intensity of Maliwal's voice. *Take what we have come for.* What did he mean by that? she wondered.

"Lower your voice, Maliwal. Would you wake my bride?"

Maliwal said something about thunder and Ysuna and omens being right again, but Ta-maya could not make sense of it.

"I have never seen a more perfect girl." It was Chudeh.

"Nor have I," replied Masau.

Ta-maya smiled. *Nor have I ever seen a more perfect man*, she thought, content, as she wondered what kind of meat they were eating. Whatever it was, she was going to have to learn how to prepare it in ways that would make Masau smile, for if she was to judge from his behavior of the last few hours, he was not going to be easy to please when it came to cooking for him.

"When we have finished here, Maliwal," Masau was saying, "you and the others take up your spears. See what you can find while I attend to things here."

Ta-maya's heartbeat quickened. He was sending the others away with the dogs! He would come to her now. He would bring her food and drink, and they would be alone together. Perhaps he had changed his mind about waiting to join with her until they reached his village in the distant northland.

She sat up and smoothed back her hair. Her stomach gave a loud lurch of hunger, and to her surprise, Blood awoke with a start and growled back at it. She stared, frightened at first, because she had not been aware of the big dog lying close at her side. Now, after sniffing her covers and finding nothing worth attacking beneath them, Blood yawned and stretched out again, thumping his tail and rooting under her hand for a pat.

"Well, well, have I found a friend in you?" she asked happily. She reached carefully to touch the massive head and scratch through the red fur.

Cha-kwena awoke with a start. Terror ran down his throat like a mouse down a tunnel when a hawk is after it. He stared straight out of the cave and into the light of the rising sun. It burned his eyes, but still he stared straight at it. A dark form was winging northward. An eagle or an owl . . . or only a figment of his dreams?

Troubled by dreams and as inexplicably restless as he had been for days, he rose and turned to stare into soothing shadows within the depths of the cave. He drew in a deep breath. It still made him uneasy to think of the cave as his, and yet he knew without a doubt that it was, for the fire that had consumed Hoyeh-tay had blackened the interior and seared all traces of Owl's perch.

After the burning, Cha-kwena had remained in the cave as tradition mandated, maintaining a small, constant fire, laying sagebrush over the coals so that the fragrant smoke would take away the rank, lingering smell of the funeral pyre. While the little fire had smoked and sparked, he had used the sharpened scapula of an antelope to scrape away most of the oily sediment that had remained upon the walls and ceiling. Although the chore was tedious, there had been a soothing rhythm in the work. After a while, despairing of removing all the greasy residue of death, he had left narrow tracings of it upon the rock. They followed the irregularities in the stone, to assume shapes in the firelight or when sunlight blessed the interior.

Later he took a sagebrush branch, burned one end until the carbon on it was thick, and, with this, embellished the tracings with bolder lines of black. The curvilinear patterns and forms were inspired by whims that he did not even try to understand. Coyote was there, watching. Owl was there also, in his vest of fur. Bat flew with Swallow across the ceiling. Mouse sat with Hare under a natural bulge in the rock wall so that Hawk could not see them. Deer leaped high, extending her slender limbs and stretching her long, lean belly over the round face of Moon. West Wind was represented by long, whirling lines, and mammoth plodded around the interior's entire circumference, led by Grandfather of All, whose body Cha-kwena had filled in with a colorant of white clay. With the exception of a single drawing of a shaman in ceremonial raiment, his hair streaked with gray, nothing of Hoyeh-tay was left within the cave except his ruined robe and bonnet and the sacred stone.

Cha-kwena's hand went to his throat and closed around the talisman. Something was wrong. But what? The sun was rising. The women were up, and the aromas of cooking fires and breakfast were rising in the morning smokes. Within the lodge of Tlana-quah a woman laughed, and in front of the lodge of Kosar-eh, children were already at play. In the tule brake at the far side of the lake, a mammoth trumpeted.

"Life Giver . . . Grandfather of All . . ." Cha-kwena exhaled forcefully. What could be wrong on a morning such as this? Dakan-eh had not yet returned, nor had Ban-ya; but they were no doubt together, and Bold Man would look after the girl almost as well as he looked after himself.

The mammoth trumpeted again. The great one had not been close to the village for several days. Others of his kind answered his call from somewhere far away; distance warped their voices into a doleful threnody.

Cha-kwena listened, touched by a terrible and unexplainable sadness and sense of loss, until he saw Mah-ree, with an armful of pups and a concerned mother dog panting nervously at her side, emerge from the headman's longhouse. The girl sat down; the dog lay beside her. In a moment the animal was nursing, and Mah-ree was stroking her, assisting the pups to find their way to the nipples. She showed no interest in the lowing of the mammoth; she was far too happy and preoccupied with her new little family.

Cha-kwena smiled. What could be wrong on a day such as this? *Ta-maya no longer lives in this village.*

He had not realized until this moment just how deeply he felt about her. But she was on her way to a new life with the man she loved, and they would all meet again in the rising of only a few moons. There was nothing wrong with that, nothing at all.

Yet when Cha-kwena turned and looked back into the cave, he could have sworn that he saw the image of Shrike upon the wall, a black-masked bird flying in pursuit of the leaping Deer. He blinked and looked again. The image was gone. It had been only a trick of the rising sun.

"I wish I had killed that bird," he muttered, then turned.

U-wa was coming up the stairs with his breakfast.

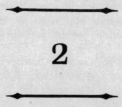

# 2

Masau was standing between Ta-maya and the sun. The girl raised her right hand to block the light. How tall he was, how magnificent in a simple tunic of buckskin. His limbs and feet were bare, his ankle-length hair loose. Shrike flew close and tried to land upon his shoulder, but he impatiently backhanded the bird away. Drowsy, Ta-maya stretched, smiled sleepily, and told him that she had never seen a man with hair as long as his.

"How long has it been since you last trimmed it?"

"The People of the Watching Star do not cut their hair, Ta-maya. This is one of the things that gives us strength. My hair is an extension of my living spirit, that part of my life-force that will stay longest with my body. After I am dead, it will grow even as my flesh withers and begins to dry in preparation for blowing away upon the wind."

She sat up, wide-awake and horrified. She touched the ends of her own hair. "Do you believe that, Masau?"

"It is a true thing. From this day until your last day among the People of the Watching Star, your hair shall remain unshorn—a visible, outward manifestation of the health and vitality of your spirit." He glanced around. "Come. The others are gone. They hunt. They will not be back until the sun stands high. Greet the day with me and be purified in the way of my people."

She was horrified again. "I do not want to eat things that will make me sick, Masau."

"I'll be with you."

She was not happy about his request, but as her eyes met his she yielded to his desire. She reached for his hand. When he moved his arm suddenly away, she realized that he would not touch her until she was purified. She rose on her own, not liking the turn of events. Blood was at Masau's side, watching her, tongue lolling in a way that made the animal appear to be smiling. She smiled back wanly and then, feeling foolish, wondered why she had done that.

"Because he is now your brother," Masau answered as though she had spoken aloud. "Blood is one with the People, a member of your new tribe. It is all right to smile at a relative, Ta-maya."

She was so taken aback by the realization that he had read her thoughts that she was only vaguely heartened by his rare attempt at humor.

"Come. We will go to the water," he urged gently. "Now that you are a woman of the People of the Watching

Star, you must be cleansed of your old life before I can take your hand and touch your lips with mine again."

The words set fire to her loins. She blushed, embarrassed by her flaming cheeks and by her desire. "I . . ."

"Come. Take off your garments. Let me look at you as you bathe, Ta-maya."

She hesitated, but only for a moment. With her head down, she stared at her feet as she undid the ties of her dress and allowed it to fall to the ground. Her face was burning. Nudity was commonplace among her people in the late summer months; every man in her band had seen her body. But the man before her was not every man. She looked up at him.

His face was rapt, transfixed, and his breath came shallowly, almost as though it hurt him to breathe at all. "*Ah . . .*" The exhalation was almost a sound of pain as he turned away and gestured for her to proceed to the lake.

"Masau? Am I less than you imagined I would be?"

"No. You are more. You *are* perfect. Go, you burn my eyes and heart and spirit. I cannot bear to look at you! Go!"

Tears stung her eyes as, uncomprehending, she ran to the lake's edge and waded out. She dipped beneath the surface and gasped against the cold. All the while she bathed, she kept her back to him, just as he kept his to her. The smell of smoke intensified her hunger, and she assumed that he had begun to prepare a hot meal for her. She called out to him, asking him to bring her a rabbit skin with which to dry herself, and some of her new clothes so that she might dress.

"They are in the second travois, there—"

But the words stuck in her throat, and her heart sank. When they had left her father's village by the Lake of Many Singing Birds, two travois were needed to carry her bridal gifts, and another was required for her clothes and personal belongings. Now she realized that Masau had not been preparing a meal for her; he had dragged "her" travois away from the others and had set all three ablaze.

"Oh, no!" she cried, sloshing toward shore as fast as the water would allow her to move through it. "My bride gifts! Stop! Masau! What are you doing?"

He had her by the wrist before she was even aware of

trying to run past him. "You have left your old life behind. You can no longer wear the skins of birds and fish and animals unworthy of your tribe. You are beginning a new and better life, one worthy of a bride of Thunder in the Sky."

"Of *what*?" The name struck terror to her heart.

"When you accepted my people and me, you also accepted the great spirit of the People of the Watching Star—Thunder in the Sky."

"Our totem is the same!"

"But venerated in different ways."

Weeping, she strained to move past him. "Oh, Masau, my beautiful things . . . my mother's handwork, and U-wa's and Mah-ree's. Put out the fire! Please! I want my gifts. Do not let them burn!"

Without a word, he turned her toward him, lifted her slowly, and moved her body upward against his until, bending his head, his mouth found hers, and his arms folded across the small of her back.

It was a kiss that shattered her senses, dissolved her will to resist, and obliterated all concern for everything except the moment, the joining of their lips and hearts and spirits. Thrilled, she flung her arms around his neck, and when at last the kiss was done, she sobbed with joy and buried her face in the hollow of his neck.

He carried her to a blanket of unfurred hide and laid her down upon it. "I will stay with you throughout the purging. It must be so, Ta-maya, if we are to be one."

He gave her the purgative herbs. She ate them. Afterward, throughout the long ordeal, he stayed beside her and stroked and soothed her. He offered encouraging words that were so solicitous of her discomfort that when at last she lay spent and exhausted, she fell asleep on the clean blanket of finely combed bison hide that he brought to her.

By late afternoon she was awake and feeling better. Masau carried her to the lean-to. "Now, for the new woman, *I* have a gift that will make even this bride smile!"

She sat up, feeling almost well again. She watched eagerly as he brought a large pack and set it down before her. With deft fingers he unlooped the ties. To her amazement and delight, it contained clothes for her: a wonderful

dress made of fawn skins, beautiful moccasins, shell brace-
lets, a quillwork browband and matching necklet, and
pretty little thong ribbons onto which small brown feathers had been stitched. Suddenly suspicious, she frowned.
"Where did this come from?"

"From the cache that we left here when we were en
route to your village."

"I don't understand. Were you *planning* to find a
bride on your journey to the south?"

"Not planning—hoping. For in truth, Ta-maya, a wondrous dream led me away from the country of my people.
In this dream I found a bride—a perfect bride, you, who
are truly worthy of Thunder in the Sky."

She could not help but be flattered, but she was
discomfited by his strange name for their totem. "You
make Life Giver, Grandfather of All, sound angry. I like
our names for him better. And really, Masau, I do not
understand how a girl can marry a totem. I am for you."

"In the end it will be the same."

She smiled. "I am glad that I am to be your woman,
Masau."

"What a waste!" exclaimed Maliwal, brought short by
the sight of Ta-maya sitting naked in her lean-to as he and
the others came near.

Ta-maya grabbed the dress that she had just been
given and held it up. "Go away! I am not for your eyes!"

Masau turned and eyed the others curiously. There
was blood on their clothes, and their spears were stained
halfway up the hafts; even the dogs were bloody. "Well! I
see we will have the meat we have sought on the spits at
tonight's fire?"

Maliwal nodded, obviously pleased. "More than we
could ever hope to eat. There were three of them. We
followed them up a ravine and drove them straight over
the edge of a natural deadfall at the end of it. There wasn't
one that didn't break bones in the fall. Two were still alive
but weak enough to butcher safely. It looks as though this
site has been used before, and for the same prey."

Ta-maya's empty stomach gave another lurch and growl.
"What have you been hunting, Maliwal?"

Maliwal looked at Masau, and then all the hunters
exchanged meaningful looks.

"Mammoth," Masau answered bluntly. "The men and dogs of the People of the Watching Star have been hunting mammoth."

She would not join them in their feast. She sat in her lean-to and watched them haul great, bleeding slabs of meat to the fire, which they raised much too close for her comfort. When Masau came to her, she shrank back in horror.

"Go away! What you are . . . what you eat . . . is forbidden! How can you eat the flesh of our totem?"

He thought a moment. "As you worship our totem from afar and in spirit, Ta-maya, we worship it in communion with its living blood and flesh. In this way do we partake of its wisdom, strength, and power. When we came into the land of the lizard eaters, we knew that we could not speak this truth to your people. Those who feed their spirits with the blood and flesh of squirrels and grubs and chuckwallas have become passive and weak, while we—still on the move, still hunting our totem—are men of power! Because I am a mammoth eater, you have been drawn to me—to my strength, my wisdom, and to a power that is not mine at all but that of our totem—mine *and* yours!"

Tears filled her eyes. For a moment she thought of asking him to take her home. They were only a day's journey from the village. They had not yet joined together as man and woman. She could still go as a virgin to Dakan-eh. But Dakan-eh had run off with Ban-ya. And after having lain close to Masau in the night, after having been kissed by him and held by him, she desired Dakan-eh even less than before. Besides, even if Bold Man had returned to the village with Ban-ya, he would never forgive her for the way she had behaved toward him. She had shamed him. And she would shame herself and her entire band if she returned home to inform her father that her new man was a mammoth eater who spoke contemptuously of her people and who found the ways of the Red World revolting. She hung her head and quivered with misery.

He reached out and raised her chin. "Had I told you

that I was a mammoth eater, would you have come away with me?"

"Never."

His expression was one of infinite compassion. "Have I lied to you, Ta-maya?"

She thought, then shook her head. "No. You have not lied. But you have not gone out of your way to tell the truth."

"But I have! I could have told you that my men were eating camel or horse or elk. I could have called you forth to the fire and asked you to eat of your totem. You would never have known the difference. I could have contrived a way to destroy your belongings that would have led you to believe that the loss was accidental. But you are my bride. I have shown you what I am and explained to you why I feel as I do. My revulsion toward your people's ways has not caused me to turn away from you. But if you find me so contemptible that you cannot overlook our differences, I will return you to your village, Ta-maya. Perhaps this will be best, for you obviously do not desire our union as much as I."

For a moment, images of home and smiling faces and familiar scenes flared bright within her memories. She almost said yes; but his hand caressed her face, and suddenly she was in his arms. He was holding her, and the homesickness was gone. "I want you, Masau! You! Nothing else matters!" she cried.

He was stroking her back. "Of course it does. I will not bring an unhappy bride to my people. What would Ysuna think of me? Here, dress now. I will catch you a fish and roast it for you, and you will regain your strength for the long journey ahead."

That night the stars shone, and the traders rested around a warm fire. Shrike perched amid a tangle of nearby thornbush, and as the moon rose a high-flying bird passed before it and cast a shadow upon the earth below.

Ta-maya looked up. "An owl . . ." She sighed wistfully and smiled somewhat wanly at Masau. "Do you think that the spirit of Hoyeh-tay is accompanying me to my new life?"

Startled, the traders looked from one to another.

A frowning Masau shook his head. "It was only an owl, Ta-maya. Hoyeh-tay's companion was not the only such bird in all the world."

Again she sighed. "I know, but it eases me to think of him in the sky, watching out for me—an old friend who understands my spirit in a world that will be new and frightening."

Maliwal was chewing on a well-gnawed bone. He looked straight at his brother. "You must see to it that the bride is not frightened, Masau."

Masau moved closer to Ta-maya, put an arm around her, and held her close. "I will protect you. Until our last moment together in this life, you need have no fear."

She snuggled close. The effects of her purging had wearied her. She looked tired, and her muscles ached. "Do not speak of endings, Masau," she requested, and raised a small hand to cover a yawn. Heavy-lidded, sleepy, she stared into the fire. "Our life is just beginning."

He carried Ta-maya to the lean-to and gently put her down upon the bison hide. For a long while he stood staring down at her as she slept, and then he grimly walked back to the others.

"You risk too much with her," said Maliwal.

Masau shook his head. "No, the more she knows now, the less she will have to be suspicious of later."

"She *is* a rare beauty," Chudeh remarked.

Maliwal threw the bone across the fire at him and laughed. "So you keep saying! She is for the god, Chudeh! Not for any of us. But looking on her body today . . . By the wrath of Thunder in the Sky, were you all as hard and ready for a woman as I?"

Tsana feigned shock. "What? You weren't tempted to ease yourself on the old hags in the village of the lizard eaters? Tlana-quah offered them; isn't there one among us who took up his offer?"

"I would rather have rammed one of those dying mammoth back in the ravine!" replied Maliwal.

They were all laughing low, shaking their heads—except Masau. He was staring fixedly into the fire. "There are women in the White Hills."

Their laughter ceased. They looked at him with interest.

"According to Tlana-quah, it is a small village," the shaman said, still staring, unblinking, into the flames. "But there is a sacred stone in the keeping of its holy man. And enough opaque chalcedony in the hills to meet my needs."

"Which are . . . ?" pressed Maliwal, curious.

Masau snapped to his feet, paced, then paused. "The white mammoth—you all saw its size, its girth, the thickness of its skin . . . and its majesty."

Now the hunters were sobered.

"It will not be easy to kill," said Ston.

Maliwal growled in open disagreement. "I still don't know why my brother refuses to let us make a move against it. The girl need never know! We could go back and kill it right now and take its hide and heart to Ysuna, along with the sacrifice! If the lizard eaters stand in our way, what matter? We can kill them and take back the sacred stone that Masau returned to the boy."

Masau shook his head. "No. The boy will bring the stone to the sacred mountain. All Ysuna wants from us is word of the white mammoth's whereabouts. She plans to make the kill herself."

He paused and stared down into the fire again. They had cleared the small area for the fire circle and rimmed it with rock, most of it veined with rich intrusions of white quartz. He stared at the rocks and the flames and the shimmering glow of firelight dancing on pale crystal. There was a vision in the flames. Masau opened his mind to it, and it flowed through him . . . the culmination of many moons of phantasm building upon phantasm since he had gone onto the mountain in a snowstorm to ask the spirits for direction. They had answered him on the wings of a raven and an eagle and in a lightning bolt that had nearly killed him—and left his spearhead encased in so much ice that the projectile point had been twice its normal size and as translucent as the finest chalcedony.

He caught his breath. *That* had been the vision! He had not realized it then, but he knew it now with a clarity that stunned him. "That which brings down the white mammoth must be sacred, worthy of the kill. It must be a spearhead unlike any that has ever been made before—as huge and perfect and white as the animal whose life-force it will seek out."

He drew his eyes from the fire. He looked at the assembled men, then allowed his gaze to settle on his brother. "Go to the village of the People of the White Hills. Steal the sacred stone from their shaman. Take the women whose bodies please you. When you have finished, leave no one alive. Return to me then, and I will go alone into the White Hills above the village. The spirits of our ancestors will guide me to what I need."

# 3

Ta-maya slept well that night. When she awoke, the sun was well up, and ravens and red-tailed hawks were circling the kill site. She sat up, peered across the little camp, and was surprised to see that save for Masau and Blood, there was no sign of any of the hunters or dogs. While she had been asleep, drying frames identical to the ones her own people made had been raised. They were simple four-sided structures, vertical posts of saplings cross braced with lighter-weight laterals to which meat was skewered and hung.

She frowned, knowing that she must have been exhausted to have slept through the noise that always accompanied the placement of the frames. The big red dog was lounging next to the nearest. Its front paws were folded protectively over a partially denuded bone, which was bigger than the dog. Masau was standing nearby, busy skewering long, thin strips of meat and setting them to dry in the wind. From the amount of meat on the frames, he had been at his work for some time. She watched him and wondered if he would ask her for assistance. She shivered with revulsion; even the thought of touching the flesh of her totem was repugnant.

Aware of being observed, Masau looked up from his work and turned toward her. Her heartbeat quickened. She would never have enough of looking at him.

He neither spoke nor smiled to acknowledge the meeting of their eyes. Expressionless, he held her gaze and then, gesturing her forward, walked to the place where he and the others had made their fire circle. The flames were banked, but a roasted fish had been left for her on one of the curbstones. Now he bent, picked up the long stick upon which the fish was impaled, and held it out to her.

She went to him but scrupulously avoided the drying frames and the large, boneless sections of mammoth meat that lay piled on the ground, waiting to be cut into smaller portions for drying. As she sidestepped the great mounds of air-darkened flesh she tried not to think of its source but failed.

"Oh, Masau . . ." she said, "it is not going to be easy for me to live with mammoth hunters."

He raised the skewered fish. "No one will ask you to eat the meat of your totem, to touch the flesh or bones or hides, or to do anything that displeases or offends you."

She was grateful; nevertheless she wanted to say: *Everything about the killing of mammoth displeases and offends me.* The words begged for release as she looked at him. The blood of her totem was on his hands. And yet he had brought gifts to her people and been tender with their children. He had fasted and sought visions with Chakwena and consoled the youth during his greatest mourning. He had led the young shaman to the sacred stone after it had been lost and guided him in his first, most difficult steps along the shaman's path. And Masau had risked his own life to save her father from a charging lion. Mammoth hunter though he was, as she continued to look into his eyes, nothing about him displeased or offended her; she accepted the fish with thanks and, kneeling beside him, ate gratefully before asking him where the others had gone.

"They are hunting," he replied.

"For Dakan-eh and Ban-ya?"

"No. There has been no sign of them. Wherever those two have gone, it was not in this direction. Is the fish to your liking?"

She nodded. It would have been impolite to tell him that it was overdone and that when he had gutted it and cast off the intestines, he had discarded the best part. "I don't understand," she said. "They have killed three mammoth. Why do they need to hunt for more?"

"I have sent them to seek a different type of meat."

His reply sent relief surging through her; for an instant, a terrible suspicion flared within her mind: They were only a day's journey from her village; the hunters could easily have doubled back to seek the mammoth that grazed within the hunting grounds of her people. The thought was chilling. She remembered how Masau had been ready to hurl his spear at Grandfather of All. She had not understood then how he had been able to take such an aggressive stance against their totem; but now she knew that the killing of mammoth was second nature to him, as it was to his fellow hunters, who had driven three hapless mammoth into a ravine so that they might enjoy a few steaks and a fresh supply of their favorite meat to carry along on their trek north.

*So much waste!* she thought, heartsick. *They could never hope to carry it all away with them.* But at least they had not gone after more. That made her feel better.

"I do not eat much, Masau. I am happy with this fish. And I am happy to be with you."

"Good." He got to his feet and walked back to the drying frames.

Puzzled and disappointed, she tried not to be hurt by his curtness as she followed. Ta-maya paused as close to him as her abhorrence of the piles of meat would allow. "I would help you with your work if that which you touch were not forbidden to me."

"I know that, Ta-maya."

"What will you do with the meat when we come to the Village of the White Hills? The People will not welcome us if we come carrying the meat of their totem."

"I would not bring it anywhere near them, Ta-maya. We will pack some of it along with us and cache some of it here. But most will have to be for carrion."

She was shocked. *"Most?"*

Her reaction surprised him. "Of course. Since we cannot carry it all or take the time to cache it all, what else can be done? Many a creature with beak and fang and claw will thank us when we leave this place."

She was not happy about this. She wanted to say, *Creatures with beak and fang and claw can find their own meat. They do not need men to provide it for them.* But to express her opinion would have been presumptuous.

He saw the worry in her eyes and raised a telling brow. "Unlike your people, hunters of big game cannot always determine the number of animals that will fall prey to their spears. When a man pursues mammoth or any other big herd animals, he cannot trap them with simple snares of sticks and cording, nor can he drive them into nets as though they were rabbits! But drive them he must—into boggy lakeshores, in which they become mired, and over deadfalls, in which they break their bones or simply cannot heft their own weight. There they soon die, asphyxiated by the pressure of their own tonnage. Sometimes a weak bison or elk or horse can be cut from its herd, and then it is with us as it is with wolves—a pack hunt, running the animal to exhaustion.

"With mammoth, though, it is different. Mammoth are wise and wary, and they will work together to protect their own. I have seen them run down many a dog and all too many a good man. And so we hunt them as we do. Often, as with the animals in the ravine back there, many more are killed than can be eaten.

"But do not look so distressed, Little One. When I was a boy living with the Bison People, hundreds of animals would die on a single drive—so many that we never saw half of those killed because we could slaughter only those that fell on top. When the deadfall was big enough and long enough—the best were chasms up to a quarter mile long and a good twenty to thirty feet deep—the bison would pile up. Sometimes five animals were layered one on top of another. It was something to see . . . to take pride in."

"Your people . . . there must be as many mouths to feed as there are seeds of grass upon the wind in autumn!"

"Yes, we are many. But not all the bands of your world and mine put together could ever put an end to the amount of meat that walks on the hoof in the great grassland to the north. In recent years most of the mammoth, horses, and camels seem to have come south. But the number of bison remains endless—long horned, short horned, high humped, whatever kind you prefer. There was so much meat that we took only the most desirable—hump meat, haunches, tongues, livers, eyes, and intestines! The rest was left for carrion. Sometimes the plains stank for months after our kills.

"But the bison is a stupid animal. It is better to take mammoth. There is power in the flesh of our totem and satisfaction in killing an animal that challenges a hunter to be daring and clever. Since time beyond beginning it has been the way of the hunt. You will get used to it. And in the land that lies under the Watching Star, Ta-maya, you will never be hungry enough to look at another grub or spider or lizard and think of it as food. In time, even fish such as that which I have caught and roasted for you will seem undesirable. You will eat as we eat, Ta-maya. You will be one of us."

His words left her breathless. She tried to visualize hundreds of big animals being killed at one time, and then she tried to understand why the hunters would take pride in leaving the bulk of the meat for vultures and hawks and lions. But she could not understand. Life was good in her Red World; nothing was wasted there. She shook her head. "I will try to be all that you wish me to be, Masau. But I will never eat of the flesh of my totem or understand why men who are as daring and clever as their prey cannot find ways to hunt only those animals whose lives are necessary to give nourishment."

His brow came down, and he looked at her speculatively. "Those who are not wise enough to recognize danger when it threatens do not deserve to live," he said. "That is the way of life both among animals and among men."

The day passed slowly for Ta-maya. Masau worked the meat. Blood gnawed on the great bone, occasionally growing angry with it and dragging it around by one of several grotesquely dangling tendons, shaking it and growling, and now and then backing off and barking at it, as though he wished it would come to life and do battle with him.

It was a warm day. The first insects of spring were

buzzing over the lakeshore. Ta-maya walked back and forth, tossing pebbles in the age-old game of stone skipping, flinging them sidearm, and finding pleasure when she succeeded in making them bounce across the surface of the water several times before they at last settled to the bottom with a *plunk*. Intrigued, Masau joined her at the water's edge.

"I know this game!" he told her.

They competed against each other five times in a row, and each time the match was a draw. Excited, they continued the game, goading each other until he was flushed and laughing along with her. At last his stone skipped across the entire surface and ended on the far shore.

"Oh!" she cried, impressed and delighted and determined to try to best him at least once. Choosing another pebble, she tried a running throw but lost her balance and fell in a tumble, laughing as the stone sang across the water.

He was at her side in an instant, his features stressed with worry. "Are you injured?"

"No." She laughed at herself. "Just clumsy."

They were very close. For a moment she was certain that he was going to sweep her into his arms and kiss her. Overcome by her love for him, she kissed him instead. Had she thrown water into his face, his mood could not have changed faster. His mouth tightened. The laughter was gone from his eyes. He helped her to her feet, bent to check her ankles and smooth her calves, and then straightened to feel her wrists in the way of one who checks for breaks. "You must not be so careless, Ta-maya. I would not bring you to Ysuna with broken bones."

His concern touched her deeply. "You are too good to me, Masau."

"It will always be so, Ta-maya, until the end of our days together." The statement caused a sudden tension in him. "Rest in the shade of your lean-to for a while," he commanded and, without another word, went back to his work at the drying frames.

She rested. She told herself that she would soon become used to his ever-changing moods. She dozed, then woke to pick at the remains of the fish that she had been unable to finish in the morning. As she ate she saw Shrike fly to Masau's shoulder, only to be backhanded away. She frowned. Mah-ree would not have been happy to see her feathered friend being harshly rejected. But since the bird could fly, perhaps Masau was right to drive it away. It should be seeking its own kind, not lingering in a camp of people with whom it should have no affinity. She watched the bird make several unsuccessful attempts to find a perch on the man. Only when Blood took notice and began to jump at it did Masau allow the shrike to alight on his head.

She laughed. "You look like old Hoyeh-tay. Is this a new type of ceremonial bonnet that every shaman must wear? A living bird on his head?"

He did not seem amused. "If Blood catches him, he won't be a bird much longer." He commanded the dog to retreat.

Blood obeyed instantly, but not without visible reluctance. Annoyed at having been denied a new diversion, he returned to harass his bone, but only halfheartedly.

Ta-maya smiled. "Your brother dog *is* like a man in many ways—or perhaps more like a sulky boy who has been turned away from a game."

"On the hunt Blood has the heart of two men. If it were not for your sister's affection for this sack of feathers and scrawny feet that has taken a liking to me, I would gladly allow the dog to have it."

"Mah-ree would smile to hear that you care enough to remember her concern for Shrike."

His expression changed. He reached up, took hold of the bird, and lowered it to its long-fought-for perch upon his shoulder. "Mah-ree . . . can she always call the great one as she did that day?"

"She has an extraordinary way with all living things. It is something that she has always shared with Chakwena. I think they will be man and woman together someday. It would be a good thing, don't you think?"

He seemed mesmerized by the idea. His eyes narrowed within their mask of tattooing. "Together they might someday have much power—enough to stand effectively against any enemy."

"*Enemy?*" The word was unknown to her. "What is that?"

"Another band that might come to the village to do them harm."

The idea was so preposterous that she laughed again. "Why would anyone want to do that?"

Her question seemed to unsettle him. "Do none of the bands of the Red World ever make war upon one another?"

"*War?* I do not know that word. Do you mean 'battling,' as Brothers of the Sky are eternally battling with each other in the stars above?"

"Brothers of the Sky? That's what Hoyeh-tay called my brother and me. What did he mean?"

She was amazed when he informed her that he did not know that story. She told him the legend and then, with a lowered and earnestly apologetic voice, confided, "I am afraid that Hoyeh-tay believed that you and Maliwal were the Brothers of the Sky come down to earth to destroy the People. That was why he was rude to you. He was seeing things in his last days, if you know what I mean. It was very sad."

"Yes, very sad."

"Masau?" She was worried now. "In the land beneath the North Star, are there bands who would make war on the People of the Watching Star?"

He looked straight at her and replied forcefully, "No, Ta-maya. No one makes war on the People of the Watching Star."

Three days later Maliwal led the dogs and other men back to camp. They brought several small, gutted pronghorns with them. The hunters looked tired, and there was blood on their clothing; but satisfaction lighted their faces. Ta-maya thanked them for going out of their way to bring meat for her.

"It was no trouble," said Maliwal, smirking. "It was a pleasure for us all. More pleasure than you will ever know!"

The others seemed amused by his remark. She waited for them to share the source of their merriment, but when they did not, she did not press them. Men had a right to their secrets, just as women had.

So it was that she did not question Masau when he

drew his men aside, and after a brief conference during which Maliwal made a show of placing some sort of necklace over Masau's head, he hefted his spears, slung a traveling pack over his shoulder, and left her alone in the care of his fellow hunters.

"Take this time to skin the antelopes and prepare the meat for the journey ahead," he told her. "I will be gone for two days. Be ready to leave this camp when I return. For now I must seek solitude in the hills."

She watched him walk away, with Blood trotting at his side. The adornment that Maliwal had given him was hidden beneath his fringed, hip-length shirt. Immediately she felt lonely without him and uneasy in the company of his scar-faced brother and the other hunters. She envied the dog its closeness with Masau and wished desperately that he had asked her to accompany him. If he had need of time and space within which to call upon the spirits of his ancestors, she would not be a distraction to him. He was her man. Her desire was to please him. So she kept silent and willed herself to be content.

For a lone man and a dog it was only slightly more than a half day's travel to the Village of the People of the White Hills. He did not bother to go all the way.

"Veer to the east before you reach the village," Maliwal had instructed him. "You will know the place because the earth becomes very red, and strange gray plants grow flat to the earth. You will pass through many wide stretches of land that is yellow with leafless blossoms no bigger than the end of your thumb. The hills beyond are the ones you seek. Follow the ridge where the juniper trees stand like men keeping watch. Then look due north, for as though it were a signpost to our people, you will find the white rock that you seek. It is in great exposed blocks as big as the village of lizard eaters who once cut it from the earth and traded it with those to the south. At the base of these broken white cliffs is much scree—loose stones, perfect nodules for flaking. Take what you will. We have left no one alive to stand against you."

He found what he was looking for at a quarry that must have been in use for millennia. When sunlight struck the bare rock, it blazed white and hot on cliffs of opaque quartz twenty to fifty feet high. Beautiful veins of color, pale pink and muted green, ran through the rocks; but it was the pure, milk-white crystal that he sought. He found it while scrambling upward across a broad scree slope.

Masau's footfall crushed low-growing gray sage that would blossom purple in late summer; the air grew heady with the scent of bruised leaves, which were releasing intensely fragrant oils. He breathed in the scent and then stopped abruptly, brought up short by a viper as thick as his forearm.

As he held Blood tightly by the scruff of the neck he hunkered down and watched the snake. It was curled on a heart-shaped nodule of pure, translucent chalcedony, approximately the size of the shaman's head. The nodule had perfect dimensions from which to cut blades of the proportions that Masau had in mind.

This early in the season, with frigid nights and mornings, the snake was sluggish. It had, Masau supposed, only recently emerged from hibernation. The man and the dog were close enough for the viper to have sensed their body heat, even if it had not felt them clambering up the hillside toward it. Yet, with its head up and the tip of its multibeaded tail relaxed, it swayed dreamily, seemingly mesmerized by the revitalizing warmth of the sun . . . until the dog barked.

Suddenly alert to danger, the snake's tail shot up and began to buzz madly; the sound sent vibrations of warning through Masau's skin. He counted the beads on its tail—as many as he had fingers on both hands. There would be much venom in a snake that had managed to live so long. And from the advantage of its coiled position, it could strike outward with exquisite accuracy to a third of its body length. Masau's eyes narrowed as he tried to calculate its maximum range. His gut tightened. He was too close, much too close.

Masau held the dog in the bend of his left arm and managed to get a good grip on Blood's snout. He pressed it down and shut. The excited animal struggled against the restraint, but within seconds the dog recognized Masau's actions as a command for obedience. Blood relaxed, but only a little; the deep vibrato of a growl was a constant resonance against Masau's palm as he held his breath and stared straight into the snake's eyes.

At last he felt the spirit of the animal. Then, just as he held the dog with the power of his body, so, too, did he hold the snake, but pinioned with his mind. Finally, weakened by the superior force of will, the rattler lowered its head and began a slow, undulating retreat.

Masau put down his spear, picked up a fist-sized rock, and got to his feet. Still holding the dog, he hurled the rock with all his strength. It flew straight to its target, smashed the fragile skull of the viper, and killed it almost instantly.

"Those who are not wise enough to recognize danger when it threatens do not deserve to live," he said quietly, recalling the words that he had told Ta-maya.

Only after he had cut off the snake's head and hurled it away did he release the dog. The body of the viper was still flexing. Blood went after it with a vengeance, as if to prove that although the man had killed it once, he was capable of killing it a second and final time.

Masau left the dog to pull the rattler to pieces. He did not take the tail as a trophy. An animal that was stupid enough to bask in the sun while predators approached— and then was so passive as to allow itself to be stared into retreat when it had been in a position to strike and kill— was not an animal whose death he wished to commemorate. He turned and went to retrieve the stone upon which the viper had been lying.

Again he knelt. He hefted the stone in both hands, turned it, and examined it for cracks. Then he tapped all around with a smaller stone while listening for the sharp clarity of sound that could only come from an unflawed nodule. He felt satisfied; the piece was true to its core and would yield many fine, long blades. He held it up to the sun. It resembled a chunk of ice—glistening, translucent, almost clear in places. It reminded him strongly of his night on the mountain, when all had been encrusted with a thick layer of ice.

Chalcedony was more difficult to work than most stone, he knew, and certainly trickier to flake than fine-grained obsidian or flint; but once heated over a meticulously banked fire and allowed to cool, its crystalline form would harden and become more malleable. With care he could end up with spearheads that were nearly as long as his forearm and as wide as his palm at their apex. He nodded, remembering the way his ice-encased spearhead had looked after the lightning bolt had struck the mountain. Out of this stone he could fashion spearheads as awesome looking as that—they would be long enough and heavy enough to slice deep through the toughest skin and muscle and, with enough force behind the shaft, to sever tendons and break bone. Not even the great white mammoth could stand against such devastating weapons. The chalcedony spearheads, he realized, would require special shafts—thicker, longer, than the conventional ones the hunters used now. And once hafted, the spears would be too heavy to use with a spear hurler. The kill that would be made with them would require close-in work.

He drew in a ragged breath, then exhaled, troubled, as he set the nodule of white crystal down between his feet. He stared at it. The spearheads that he would fashion of this translucent white stone would be the spears of his thunderstruck vision upon the mountain. If the great white mammoth totem could in fact die, these spears would be the ones to kill it. But Ysuna had demanded that she be the one to deal the death blow to the great white mammoth. When the time came, would she be strong enough?

He picked up the stone, got to his feet, and called to the dog. "Come, old friend. There is no time to waste. We must return home."

# 4

"But I don't understand," Ta-maya said. She tried hard to swallow disappointment but failed. "Why must we head north so soon? I thought you intended to stop in as many villages of the Red World as you could. And the Village of the People of the White Hills is so close! The rare white chalcedony that you seek is there. They would be happy to trade for it, and I have so looked forward to a visit with—"

"The many bands of the Red World will assemble at the Great Gathering," Masau reminded her. "Look forward to that instead, Ta-maya. Now we must go on."

They set their backs to the White Hills and, heading due north, passed the ravine into which the hunters of the People of the Watching Star had driven the mammoth. Ta-maya was stunned by the amount of meat left on the carcasses. As the group traveled on she was further upset to see Maliwal's earlier statement about the location confirmed: The site had been used before, and for the same prey. As they advanced along the back of the ravine she could see into the depths of the mile-long defile. Sickened, she turned away from the sight of enormous tanglings of huge bones and tusks protruding from the scrub growth at the bottom.

She nearly wept; it would not have been an exaggeration to estimate that hundreds of mammoth had died in this place. "Oh! How can there be so many? Until you came, no one hunted mammoth in this country! No one!" She was so distraught that she could not keep herself from speaking out. "And now your spears pierce the flesh of more of my people's totem. What must Grandfather of All think of this?"

"Even Great White Giant must walk in fear of the People of the Watching Star!" Maliwal proclaimed proudly.

She was appalled, then angry. "No, I saw *you* step back in fear of our totem when you saw him face-to-face for the first time! He was not afraid of you!"

Maliwal's face tightened with resentment. "He should have been."

Masau glared at his brother. "What would you have my bride think of us, Maliwal?" To Ta-maya he said, "Pay no heed to my brother, Little One. But know that this second kill site has nothing to do with us." He was looking down, apparently intrigued by the bones within the ravine. A moment later he climbed down to take a closer look. "See this? Old shrubs grow out of the bones, and in some places the bones are buried deep in the runoff of uncountable seasons of rain and snow." He knelt and sifted the earth through his fingers. "I cannot be sure, but it seems that many of them lie beneath the ground. And the texture of the bones is like nothing that I have seen before . . . except—" He paused. His hand drifted upward, to the throat of his tunic. Then, lost in thought, he lifted a fist-sized rock, which he brought down with a sharp *whack* against a section of weather-brittled bone. The bone broke—not with the dull crack of fracturing calcified tissue but with the hard, clear sound of fracturing stone. As Masau continued to pound it, it disintegrated into a pebbly rubble from which he withdrew a complete spearhead.

Clambering up out of the ravine, he paused before Ta-maya and held out his palm. "Tell me what you see," he requested.

"A spearhead such as your people make."

"Yes." He nodded. "But my people and I have never been in this land. And I took this point out of a kill that was made so long ago that a forest of artemesia and manzanita has grown to maturity on top of it. Look closer: Had this kill been made recently, the sinew that once secured the spearhead to the foreshaft would still be bound tightly in place. But there are no traces of sinew or of the foreshaft. And the bones of the slain mammoth are so old that they have become one with the earth within which they lie partially buried—no longer bone at all . . . but stone. And examine the color of the spearhead. What color do you see?"

"Dark green with flecks of deep red," she replied.

"Yes, green! But the projectile points of the People of the Watching Star are black obsidian, made of cores taken in a place far from here. This spear is made of flint, as are most of the spearheads that I have seen here in the Red World. Here"—he pointed—"at the base of the head, the stone has not been blunted to lessen chafing against the binding sinew. That is the way of the projectile points of the Red World."

Ta-maya frowned. "What are you saying, Masau?"

"I am saying that my fellow hunters and I are not responsible for the bones that lie below. We killed three mammoth at the head of the ravine. Three. No more, no less. These animals died very long ago, killed by spears that did not belong to the People of the Watching Star. These mammoth may well have been killed in the days when the children of First Man and First Woman came walking across the mountaintops into the Red World . . . before the children lost their nerve to hunt mammoth and settled down instead to become lizard eaters."

Ta-maya caught her breath. "No!"

"Yes," said Masau, taking her hands and gently pressing the spearhead into her palms. "Feel the edges. They speak in as sharp a tongue as they did on the day the spearhead was first made. The stories that your old shaman told were true, Ta-maya. In time beyond beginning the People *were* one. Now, at last, it shall be so again. You must know no fear of your new tribe. You are not journeying into a land of strangers; you are coming home."

A murmuring went up from the others.

Ta-maya blushed. "If I were not eager to be joined to you and to your people, I would not have come north with you at all." She added softly as she handed the spearhead to him, "I will walk with you, I will live with you, and if the forces of Creation smile upon us, I will give you many children. And someday, if the forces of Creation are still smiling, I will die at your side, and our grandchildren will sing the song of our life and take pride in us. But because this is now, not the time beyond beginning, I will not eat of the flesh of my totem, Masau, nor will I ever pass the bones of any of the mammoth kind and not feel sad."

\*     \*     \*

They struck out toward the great dune fields that Ta-maya's people called the Mountains of Sand, then continued northward through the broad, open country that lay beyond. Days and nights passed in rhythm with the rising and falling of the sun and stars. The Hills of Many Rabbits lay to the west, their rounded slopes thick with low-growing oak woodlands and occasional groves of scrub pines. When darkness came and the wind was from the west, the travelers could smell the cooking fires of a distant village.

Masau sat apart from the others, working on his spearheads, and Ta-maya stood alone, drawing in the familiar scent of her kinsmen's fires and thinking wistfully of home. Already she longed for the day when her family would be reunited.

Soon the Hills of Many Rabbits lay far behind. Ahead lay the Red Hills—big, bare, stony intrusions of ancient lava flows and cinder cones, surrounded by the softer lines of older hills furred with thick woodlands. It was country rich with game, but the traders preferred their traveling rations of dried mammoth flesh, even when they set the dogs to flush fresh meat for Ta-maya. She did not rebuke them for their preference, but she turned her back to them when they ate.

On and on they walked. The traders went out of their way to make the long trek pleasant for Ta-maya. They rested often, and at every fire there was a fresh hare or rabbit or squirrel on the spit for her. They told stories and sang songs as they walked, and soon she learned the words and could join in.

Soon the Red Hills were behind them, and Maliwal spoke of the need for a council. While Ta-maya roasted her evening meal the men gathered into a circle. They kept their talk low, but from the tone of their voices and from their gestures, it soon became clear to Ta-maya that there was disagreement over which direction they would take from this point. It became apparent that Maliwal wanted to cut due west toward the Blue Mesas, while Masau was adamant in his desire to continue north.

"I thought that you were in a hurry to get back to Ysuna, Brother."

"And so I am, Maliwal. But to go through the sacred

mesas, other things will be seen . . . would not risk . . . she must have no cause to fear . . . dangerous . . ."

"But how do you know that we can get through the mountains that lie ahead?"

"We will find out."

From the surly look on Maliwal's face, it was obvious that Masau's route would be the one they would follow. Ta-maya was content, certain that her man had chosen a way north that would offer a minimum amount of stress to his bride.

The next day, however, her contentment began to wane. As they headed north the land rose with every step. At last they crested a wide range of hills, and Ta-maya paused, terrified by the scene that lay ahead. To the east and ranging along the entire horizon from north to south, towering, heavily glaciated peaks formed a snaggletoothed wall.

"What is it, Bride?" asked Masau.

"Those mountains," she whispered in awe. "It is said that the world ends where they begin. Surely we cannot go on!"

"I would not let you fall off the edge of the world, Ta-maya."

She was not heartened. "But, Masau, the mountains blocking our way to the north are so high. How can we walk over them?"

"We will walk *through* them." He pointed. "Look ahead. You can see the pass through which we will travel."

"I am afraid," she told him.

"Why? I promise that no harm will come to you in the shadow of these peaks. Come," he urged. With Blood at his side and Shrike trying unsuccessfully for a landing on his shoulder, Masau took her hand and led her on.

Now the travelers quickened their steps. The dogs seemed to take on renewed energy. Every step was uphill, across long sweeps of open alluvial plain cut through by a misty river along which hardwoods were now in full leaf. It was a high, cool, glorious land of sweeping vistas, soaring heights, and tumultuous watercourses. At length, after entering a massive canyon and following the curving banks of the river for many miles, they crested a broad pass, and Ta-maya gazed back with longing.

"Look there." She pointed off when Masau came to stand by her side. "You can see the entire Red World from here. The Red Hills, Big Lake, the Blue Mesas, the Mountains of Sand, the buttes that stand between us and the village of my father. Oh, Masau, it is so beautiful . . . and so far away. Will I ever see it again?"

"You must learn to live for the moment, Ta-maya. You must learn to enjoy what you have now, rather than long for what the future will or will not bring."

She was disturbed by the bleakness of his tone. He was in one of his somber, contemplative moods, but he put his arm around her waist. They were so very close that when she turned, she could see herself in his eyes and feel the warmth of his breath upon her face.

"I long for you, Man of My Choosing," she revealed shyly, then added with all her heart, "I long to take the sadness from you . . . to make you smile and laugh in the life that we will share."

Scowling, he reached to brush a windblown strand of hair from her cheek, and suddenly his expression changed. His hand lingered and tenderly caressed her face.

"You are so young, so trusting, so beautiful in all ways," he said softly, huskily, almost as though it hurt him to speak. The tips of his fingers strayed across her features and moved lightly upon her mouth.

She gasped as his touch set fire to her. How she loved him! How she wanted him! Her hand rose and pressed his fingertips to her lips; she kissed them. Again and again she kissed them.

He caught his breath and pulled his hand away. "Enough! You would drive Ysuna from my mind and cause me to forget that I must bring you virgin to my people or be dishonored before Daughter of the Sun."

She was stunned by his sudden anger. "I—I wish only to please you, Masau."

"Then do not thrust yourself upon me!"

Tears stung her eyes.

The sight of them roused even greater anger in him. "Do not look at me like that, Ta-maya. Do not look at me at all! Set your eyes to the north. The land of the People of the Watching Star lies ahead!"

\*     \*     \*

"Be still," Dakan-eh commanded.

Ban-ya's mouth pursed resentfully. "But my feet hurt."

"You will have more than that to complain about if you do not shut your mouth!"

Since consenting to her company, Dakan-eh had joined with Ban-ya every night—and several times each day— taking her down and handling her great breasts and thrusting his organ deep, reminding her over and over that it was Ta-maya who should be writhing beneath him, wrapping her limbs about the small of his back, and whooping with delight when he came into her again and again. After a while her whoops had become moans of discontent, and she had bruised his back and arms with hard pummelings of her fists as she had tried unsuccessfully to keep him off her.

Now, with the girl standing beside him, he felt troubled as he stared ahead through the soft, fragrant shade of the pinyon grove. Dusk's lingering light allowed him to see that the little village of holy men was just as he remembered it: The temporary shelters had been broken down; all that was left of them were neat circles on the ground, which marked where the postholes had been set. The larger, permanent huts were closed and the exterior fire circles banked, waiting to be brought back to life when the shamans of the Red World returned in the autumn with their bands. Dakan-eh relaxed, realizing that it was only natural for a deserted village to be silent.

"I'm hungry," Ban-ya moaned.

He ignored her. Crested jays were hopping about in the trees, cawing to one another and at the trail-weary couple that had just intruded into their midst. Irritated, Dakan-eh shouted at them. The birds flew off.

"You make more noise than I do," said Ban-ya petulantly.

Again he ignored her. The wind was strong from the northwest. He cocked his head, realizing that this was what had been worrying him: The northwest wind should be carrying the sounds and scents of the village that lay on the far side of the mesas. True, it was miles away, but it was a big village. The cooking fires would be high by now, and the wind should be ripe with the smell of smoke and cooking meat and steaming boiling bags. Children would be laughing and shouting. He strained to hear them. There was nothing but the wind.

"Where is everyone?" asked Ban-ya.

"I already told you. The village we seek is on the north slope of the mesas. This place is where the shamans come. It is not for us. The trail to the village of Shi-wana begins over there."

She sighed in abject misery. "I am not going another step today, Dakan-eh!"

He ignored her. He struck out along the trail that led from the heights of the sacred mountain to the Village of the People of the Blue Mesas. It was a long, downhill hike in the growing darkness, but for once Ban-ya did not complain. She clutched the coyote-skin robe around her shoulders and kept up with Bold Man every step of the way. He gave her no time to rest, but she stuck to his side like a shadow.

Several times they lost the trail and had to backtrack and search for it in the darkness. By the time they reached their destination, they were exhausted. The first light of false dawn was showing above the mountainous horizon to the west. Suddenly Bold Man's eyes went round. At the edge of the village, where the largest of the permanent huts formed an effective windbreak, was something that took his breath away.

"What are you staring at?" she demanded. Her pretty face twisted into a scowl of absolute annoyance until, following his gaze, her own eyes bulged and she screamed.

The body of a dead man sat upright on the ground. His back leaned against the hut, one long leg was extended, his arms lay lax at his sides, with a long spear shaft protruding from just below his ribs.

With Ban-ya clinging to his side, Dakan-eh moved slowly toward the corpse, then paused before it. Wind and weather and the gnawings of animals had stripped most of the flesh from the bones. Although there was enough tendon and tissue left to hold the skeleton together, the feet and most of the right leg were missing. Both hands were gone. There would have been no way to identify the body had it not been for the ruins of an enormous ceremonial bonnet of grass, feathers, and woven reeds, which had somehow remained firmly fastened about the head, and for a few patches of blue skin that still clung to the uniquely gap-toothed skull.

"Shi-wana . . ." Dakan-eh whispered the old shaman's name.

Ban-ya buried her face in his arm. "Oh, Dakan-eh! The poor man! He must have fallen on his own spear! How could his people have left him like this?"

A wave of cold like an ice storm went through Dakan-eh and chilled him to his heart. Scowling, he freed himself of the clinging young woman and knelt to examine the body. The spear had been thrust through the man's now-vanished gut, entering the abdominal cavity with such force that the projectile point had sliced clean through it, cleft the man's pelvis, and pinned him to the earth.

"This was no accident," he said grimly as he took hold of the spear shaft and pulled back sharply. His effort jerked the spearhead free of the earth but not of a portion of the bone into which it remained embedded. He held it up and darkly eyed both shaft and spearhead. "The People of the Red World do not make spears like this. Look at the length and girth of the shaft and at the size and shape of the head."

Ban-ya stared, disbelieving. "The shaft is made of bone, and the spearhead is cut from black obsidian!"

"Yes," said Dakan-eh hefting the weapon. "It belongs to the People of the Watching Star. But what is it doing here, in the belly of a shaman of the Red World?"

They stood in horrified silence, then continued on, into the heart of the village. There they stared at burned and ravaged huts, at all that was left of weathered bodies upon which birds and small animals had been feeding, at scattered bones and skulls, and at the occasional telltale spear shaft that remained buried within the sad remnants of what had once been human life.

When Ban-ya began to cry, Dakan-eh did not silence her, nor did he speak a single word of repudiation. He threw down the spear that he had taken from Shi-wana's body. There were tears in his own eyes as he drew Ban-ya close and held her. He did not feel bold. He did not feel brave. And perhaps for the first time in his life he did not feel arrogant. He felt confused, numb. He held on to

Ban-ya as though she were the only thing in all of this scene of devastation that could keep him rooted to sanity.

"Men have done this killing," she whispered, incredulous.

"Men of the Watching Star," he affirmed.

"But how can men raise their spears against other men? *Why?*"

His arms tightened around her. The ice storm was loose within him again. He was shivering as he said, "Because Hoyeh-tay was right about them. They have come to destroy the People."

"But *why*, Dakan-eh?"

"That I cannot say. But they have killed Shi-wana, and because of me, the little sister of Sunam-tu was with him. Her bones are probably spread out before us now—such willing, pretty little bones. And . . ." His voice caught then broke in his throat as he gasped: "Ta-maya has joined with their shaman!"

Within his embrace, Ban-ya stiffened. "We must find her, Dakan-eh! We must bring her back to our people before they hurt her—if they have not done so already!"

"Find her? Bring her back? Why should I do that?" The words sounded as cold as the ice storm of emotion that had spawned them. "Of her own will Ta-maya turned her back upon me. If she has chosen to go off with Brothers of the Sky, why should I care what happens to her? They are ten men with many dogs, and I am one man. Even if I knew where they have gone, why should I risk myself for the sake of one who has shamed me?"

"Because you are Bold Man."

"Bold, yes. But not bold enough for her, eh?"

Ban-ya looked up at him as though fearing that a stranger had taken his place. "They will have taken her to the north, Dakan-eh, beyond the Blue Mesas. They called themselves the People of the Watching Star. We can seek them there, under the light of the one star that is always constant in the sky."

He was suddenly deeply angry with her—or with himself; he could not tell. Although her words made sense, he did not want to hear them. He put her away from him. "*We?* Since when are you so brave? And since when do you care about Ta-maya? You have wanted nothing so much in this world as to hurt her by seducing me away from her."

The flush that reddened her cheeks and the tip of her nose was so intense that it was visible even in the false dawn. "Seduce *you*? That has been no trick! Anything female—young or old—can wave a breast or open a leg to you, and despite all your words of love for Ta-maya, you are ready to come into her, like this!" She snapped her fingers and sneered up at him contemptuously. "And I have always been brave, Dakan-eh! Brave enough to try to take the man of my choosing from the headman's daughter because I imagined that he would make a better mate for me than for Ta-maya! But it seems that she was right to hesitate before giving herself to such a man as you, who loves her so much that he is willing to abandon her to a life among men who can do this to their brothers!" She gestured outward and shivered violently. "Oh, Dakan-eh, do you think she still lives?"

"Why should you care?"

Her face went blank with disbelief. "Ta-maya and I have worked and played in the same village since we were born. I only wanted her man—not her life!"

"And now you have her man. Now she has chosen her life. I can do nothing for her."

"But—"

"Be quiet, Ban-ya. Let me think." He looked around. The devastation was almost too much to stomach. His mind was racing. "We must go back to our village. We must warn our people. The Brothers of the Sky have come down from the stars and may return to the Lake of Many Singing Birds. If they do, we will know them for what they are."

"And then?"

"Tlana-quah is headman. He will know what to do."

"But in the meantime, what of Ta-maya?"

"If Tlana-quah wants to go after his daughter, the decision will be his. She has chosen the man with whom she will walk and with whom she will lie down. She has not chosen wisely. She has not chosen me."

# 5

The travelers paused on the heights of a tall hill and gazed down. The world below was a vast, round-shouldered, high-breasted land of green grass surrounded by the distant blues, purples, and soft grays of faraway mountain ranges.

Ta-maya caught her breath and exclaimed with delight and wonder. "It is like a great blanket of green fur!"

"In summer it will be the color of the sun," said Masau, scanning ahead. "In winter it is as white as the face of the moon—and as beautiful."

She looked up at him, pleased by his unexpected expression of tenderness and affection for the land of his ancestors. She felt overwhelmed by happiness because he was at her side and talking to her once again.

"Look to the west." Maliwal's voice was tight with excitement.

Ta-maya squinted into the setting sun. A long dusky cloud was visible along the curving line of the horizon.

"Bison!" said Maliwal. "A huge herd!"

Chudeh was not the only man to lick his lips in hungry speculation. "At this time of year there will be many calves."

"Surely you do not hunt the little ones?" asked Ta-maya.

"The meat of the young is the best meat!" replied Maliwal with undisguised enthusiasm.

Something about the way he looked at Ta-maya made her cringe.

"If the spirits of the hunt are with us, we will roast you a calf tomorrow," Chudeh promised. "Then you will see that what Maliwal says is true."

"In the Red World, when the men pursue antelope and deer, Tlana-quah forbids the taking of does and little ones, to assure the replenishment of the herd," she told him.

They all laughed.

Even Masau was openly amused as he gestured to the broad horizon. "The bison are as many as the stalks of grass that green the plains, Ta-maya. They will last forever! Maliwal, we must return to our people. We will not go out of our way to hunt them."

They spent the night on the hill overlooking the rolling landscape. A cold wind blew from the north, carrying the scent of new grass, of watercourses running fast and clear within the clefts of green hills, of dust, of grazing animals on the move, and of smoke from the cooking fires of men.

"Are we nearing the village of your people?" asked Ta-maya, excited but suddenly filled with nervous apprehension.

Masau saw the worry in her eyes. "No, not near yet. The smoke that you smell comes from a hunting camp of the Bison People. They follow herds in the spring. Sleep now. My village lies a few days to the north. I would not have my bride looking weary when at last she comes to her new people."

She smiled. "I am glad that you are no longer angry with me, Masau."

"I have never been angry with you, Little One. I have been angry with myself."

She did not understand. She tried to rest, but she could not sleep except fitfully. She dreamed of home, Ha-xa and U-wa at their sewing, Cha-kwena sitting outside his cave and looking pathetic in his new role as shaman. She dreamed of Mah-ree being held in the curl of Grandfather of All's trunk. She dreamed of the little white mammoth standing close to the two great cows who mothered him. And she dreamed of Kosar-eh, whirling and dancing in his black and white body paint, with sprigs of sage and rabbit brush protruding from his waistband as he paused before her to offer a gift of precious magpie feathers. He had told her to give the feathers to the one who would be her man.

She sighed. What a good and caring man was Kosar-eh! What would he say if he knew of the fate of his gift? She had packed the feathers along with the rest of her belongings from home, with the intention of offering them proudly to Masau. Now the feathers were burned. Again she sighed, then moved restlessly in her sleep. The rumbling and lowing of the distant herd of bison filled her dreams. She awoke trembling but did not know why.

It was nearly dawn. Masau was awake, sitting apart from the others as he often did when he chose to occupy his time in camp by stone working. She listened for the sound of his hammerstone but could hear only the occasional slip and glide of his antler-bone awl. She knew that he was fluting the edges of one of the projectile points he was making. Although he was secretive about the work, she sat up and looked his way. His back was to her. For a moment she considered going to sit beside him, but then thought better of it. As long as he was working stone, he would send her away.

Ta-maya drew in a breath of the rising wind and, shivering against the cold, bundled herself in a warm sleeping robe of elkskin, which Masau had given to her. It was a beautiful garment, but she missed the light, airy, familiar comfort of her own cloak of twisted rabbit skins. Ha-xa had worked so hard to make it for her. What would she have said had she known that it had ended up in flames?

Ta-maya resolved not to think of home as she watched the cool, blue light of dawn pour over the eastern rim of the world and bathe the rolling terrain in light. How wondrously vast was this land! It was as big and as handsome as the men of the People of the Watching Star. As the sound of the bison herd drew her eyes northward, for first time she could clearly see its enormity. It was a brown river of life, miles wide, miles long, pouring over the undulating landscape. Masau had been right—the bison *were* as many as the blades of grass that greened the plains. No one could ever hunt them all.

They broke their fast with a light meal of dried meat— mammoth for the men and dogs, rabbit for Ta-maya. By the time the sun was standing on the edge of the eastern ranges, the group was on its way north.

Ta-maya found it strange going, like walking over the waters of a wind-riled lake—up over the waves and then down into the troughs. She had no idea how far they had gone before the first of the Bison People appeared ahead of them on the crest of a particularly high sweep of hill.

The hunters stopped dead to stare up at the strangers who stood silhouetted against the sky. There were ten of them, all broad-chested, wide-faced men with black eyes slitted watchfully against the rising sun. One was noticeably older and taller than the rest and was as lean as the land and as handsome, despite the weathering of his face. His right arm was raised to hold his spear laterally in his closed fist. It was a weapon almost identical to those carried by the men with whom Ta-maya traveled. Each stranger carried several such weapons. Each man wore a leather loincloth and a robe of bison hide.

Not one of them looked friendly, and Ta-maya was afraid. She stepped closer to Masau. When she looked up at him, she saw that his face had gone as tight as the skin of a drum. With his eyes fixed on the strangers, he put her behind him and, shifting two of his spears into his left hand, impatiently backhanded Shrike from his shoulder as he hefted the third spear and aimed it at the men on the hilltop.

Blood growled. Masau silenced him with a single word. At Masau's right, Maliwal hissed an unspoken epithet through his torn mouth; his spear was also leveled, as were the spears of every man in the traveling party.

"Who dares to cross the land of the Bison People without consent of Shateh?" the older man shouted in a loud, flat, contemptuous voice.

"Masau! Mystic Warrior! Shaman of the People of the Watching Star!" Masau shouted his reply in an equally contemptuous tone. "Would Shateh stand against me?"

"I am ten men strong!" boasted the older man.

"As am I. But do not imagine yourselves our equal!"

"Ha! Why has no man killed you yet, Masau?"

"You have tried once and failed, Shateh! Come! Try again, if this is how you would end your days!"

Maliwal's scowl seemed to cut his face in two. "You have lived long enough from the looks of you, old man!"

"Ah, Maliwal is with you. You would both be dead by now if I wanted your lives! And from where I stand here above you, I hold the advantage. I could have come upon you from behind and had my spear in both your backs before there was a need for words between us. But I have chosen to come to you with the sun in my eyes. It is a sign of peace. Shateh has grievance with few tribes, and he seeks no trouble from yours." He lowered his spear arm. "Come! Join us! My people prepare for a hunt."

"We journey north to join Ysuna," said Masau, lowering his own weapon. "We have no time to hunt with you."

"No time or no inclination? Do those who walk with Daughter of the Sun still find our ways beneath contempt?"

"We do!" Maliwal could not have been more emphatic, yet he spat on the ground to add emphasis. "Only old women and cowards follow the bison when there are mammoth to be had!"

Peering out from behind Masau's back, Ta-maya went cold with fear as the men on the crest of the hill closed ranks. Their spears were up again.

The older man took a decisive step forward and rammed the butt end of his spear into the grass. It was a moment before he spoke. "The medicine pole is raised in the place of death. Do you still fear it, Masau?"

Ta-maya's left arm was around Masau's waist; she felt him stiffen against a tremor that shook him. And yet, when he spoke, his voice was calm and even and as resolute as before.

"I fear nothing that you ever put before me, Shateh. Not even death."

"Prove it!"

The old man's challenge struck Masau with the full force of a gale; he stood against it.

Maliwal shook his head and cautioned, "Do not risk it, Brother. We must get back to Ysuna."

"Yes! Get back to Ysuna!" mocked Shateh. "Tell her that her shaman has no more courage now than he had as a boy! Tell her that the headman of the Bison People has humiliated you, that you quaked in fear of the challenge of the medicine pole. I accept it boldly and without fear, as I have always done!"

Masau's mouth was white as his lips compressed over his teeth. "One day here," he told Maliwal. "That is all it will take. Then we will go on."

"Accept his challenge and you may not be here to-morrow!" warned Maliwal under his breath.

"I cannot refuse."

"Masau?" Sensing imminent disaster, Ta-maya stepped out from behind him and looked up at him imploringly. "I do not understand. What is happening?"

He turned toward her. With his spears resting against his chest, he put both hands upon her shoulders as his eyes held her face. Then he bent and kissed her gently, upon the brow and then upon the mouth. That last was a long, deep, hungry kiss—the kiss of one who is saying good-bye.

Terrified, she reached up and flung her arms around his neck, held the kiss, and returned it in a way she had not known herself capable of; she felt his response and then gasped as he broke the kiss and shook his head.

"Be brave, Little One," he said. "Maliwal will watch over you until I return to your side. And if I die, do all things he says. He will take you to Ysuna. Do not be afraid. She will be as a sister to you until the ending of your days."

Masau spoke briefly with Maliwal before leashing Blood, handing the lead to his brother, and then joining Shateh, who sent several of his warriors ahead to his village to announce the coming of strangers.

"When we get there, say nothing, eat nothing, touch nothing," Maliwal warned Ta-maya. "And no matter what you may hear, pay no heed."

Blinking and dazed, she walked close beside him as she followed Masau and Shateh toward the great, dusty, tumultuous hunting camp of the Bison People. Her eyes widened at the scene before her. It was not difficult to obey Maliwal's instructions. The camp was a huge, squalid settlement of bison-hide lean-tos set amid the smoke of many carelessly made cooking fires. Dogs and children were everywhere.

The villagers fell to silence when their headman approached. They stared at the strangers who were led not through but around the peripheries of the village. Their hostile expressions became strangely curious and almost pitying when their eyes fell upon Ta-maya. A ragged-haired young girl came close to gawk, then shrieked in terror when she inadvertently placed herself within the fall of Ta-maya's shadow. An old woman screamed and chased the child as she ran away, squealing. When Ta-maya slowed her step and looked after them in perplexity, a scrawny old man came forward to shake a scrotum rattle aggressively in her face.

"Away, Bride! Away!" he commanded.

Maliwal snarled at the man, then hurried her on. Feeling very upset, she was only too glad to oblige. How had the old man known to call her that? she wondered as she walked on, clinging to Maliwal's strong arm.

The women of the band whisked their children out of her way and quickly averted their gaze when her eyes strayed toward them.

"These people hate us," she whispered in a quavering voice to Maliwal.

"They *fear* us," he corrected.

"*Why?*"

"Because they are weak. Because they know that they live only because we have allowed it."

She could not grasp such talk. The members of the Bison Band were certainly dirty but did not appear weak. They were a large, robust people, and despite the chill of the morning, they all went virtually naked. They made her feel small and vulnerable, and anxious to be away from them.

"Where is Masau going? What is the challenge that he has accepted from the old one who calls himself Shateh?" she asked Maliwal.

"You will see. Come along. But do not speak."

With the women, children, and old people of the Bison Band at their heels, they walked for perhaps half a mile, then stopped on high ground at the edge of a tall bluff. It overlooked a wide area of broken country and a long, ugly, precipitous ravine. Masau, Shateh, and the men and dogs of the Bison Band had gathered within the draw. The herd of bison was approaching the ravine from the west.

"Now . . ." The voice of the old man who had shaken the scrotum rattle at Ta-maya rasped over his timeworn larynx. "We will see what the shaman of the People of the Watching Star is made of."

The medicine pole had been placed at the very center

of the ravine. It was a cottonwood tree, which had been stripped clean of all but the topmost branches. Four feet of its lower trunk had been buried deep in the earth, but still it towered twenty feet aboveground. Surrounded by Bison Men and their dogs, Masau ascended easily. Shateh watched him climb.

"Just as it once was long ago," recalled the older man with visible satisfaction and more than a little bitterness. "The eagle-bone whistle awaits you. There it is, hanging from the branch to your right."

Masau did not reply. He grasped the whistle and tested it; its song was a high, thin pipe. Shrike winged to settle on the highest branch.

At the base of the tree, one of the men of the Bison Band lifted the end of his spear and brained the nearest dog. The grizzled old animal fell over dead before even having a chance to yelp. As Masau watched from the top of the tree, Shateh knelt, and using a well-honed palm dagger, he carved the dog into sections and set them around the bottom of the pole.

"Many a hunt did this courageous dog participate in," said Shateh. "Never once did he swerve from the path of the brave heart. Let his spirit strengthen your own on the hunt, Mystic Warrior . . . if indeed that is what you are. Or do you and your brother hunt only unsuspecting, unarmed men and lure their guileless young women to their deaths with your mysterious ways, as we have heard from those fortunate enough to have survived the raids of your people?"

Masau's mouth turned downward at the deliberate insults. Yet he did not speak. He had not seen the older man in more years than he cared to remember, but despite the gray strands in Shateh's hair and the deep gougings that time and weather had worked into his once-flawless face, he was the same. And now, as Masau looked down from the top of the pole at him, he hated the man even more than when he had last seen him.

"Call the bison if you dare!" commanded Shateh, and with a broad gesturing of his arms, he sent his many men and dogs out of the ravine and off across the land.

Some circled downwind of the distant bison herd; others placed themselves within full view of the approaching animals. Once seen, the warriors shrieked and waved their arms and cloaks of bison skins until the herd panicked and stampeded, fanning out in several directions. A good portion of them headed straight for the ravine, with the screaming men and barking dogs racing at their heels.

From the top of the medicine pole Masau could see it all—exactly as he had seen it once before, on a bleak and freezing winter day, with Maliwal and Shateh clinging to the branches beside him. His gut tightened at the memory. His mouth went dry, his heart hammered. The palms of his hands were wet.

In a few moments the stampeding bison would be pounding straight at him, running in blind terror ahead of the men and dogs, thundering toward the ravine, seeing it only when it was too late to stop. Unable to turn away in time, they would fall into it, collapsing one on top of the other—two deep, then three, then four, then five, until their combined weight stressed the pole and shook it to its foundations. If it did not hold, Masau would topple into the ravine. It had not held once before, for another of the shaman's line, for Masau and Maliwal's older brother. And when the bellowing of the dying animals fell quiet at last, when the hunters pulled him from the pit, he would be lucky if anyone would be able to tell his mangled body from those of the beasts.

"Go ahead!" Shateh taunted. "Blow the whistle! Call forth the bison to die for the People! Tell them that you are not afraid!" The man was shinnying up the pole, climbing with the strength and ease of one half his years. At last, with one foot braced on a substantial stub of branch, he faced Masau and goaded nastily, "Or would you rather run? Climb down quickly, Mystic Warrior, and knock me to the bottom of the ravine, as you did once before. Maliwal did not panic until you screamed and scrambled for your life. You nearly killed all three of us that day, Masau, as the bison turned and ran. Not one animal fell into the trap. The People went hungry because you were afraid."

"You should have thought twice before sending little boys to do a shaman's work, Shateh."

"Our shaman was dead! You saw your older brother die. You and Maliwal were next in line to be Shaman. I had no choice; we were starving." He laughed harshly. " thought my three sons would make me strong. But they were weak. They sapped me of whatever power I might have had that day."

"And so, as punishment, you put your surviving son: out of the band and abandoned them to certain death. And thus drew into yourself the power of headman and shaman."

"You do not look dead to me. But yes. And I was right to do so. You were trouble from the first—a left handed boy. Soon after you were abandoned, the bison came."

"And there was food enough for all," Masau said bitterly, "but you kept the band moving and never looked back, *Father*. To think that I once called you that, and trusted you . . . as you should not have trusted me this day."

Shateh's face collapsed into a frown that held wariness, surprise, and terror. It was in this moment that the surging tide of bison reached them. For the last few seconds the men had been shouting to be heard above the thundering roar of the beasts' pounding hooves. Now the ground shook. Savaged earth and grass exploded upward to form a cloud of debris as the stampeding animals saw the ravine and tried to jump, but too late. The bison—all high humps and horns wider than most men were tall, eyes rolled back, tongues flapping, saliva spraying like spume on a flood-maddened river—screamed and bellowed piteously and fell headlong into the ravine.

The medicine pole swayed against the storm of flesh and bone, of hide, hoof, and horn. Shrike flew for safety and never looked back. Safe on the bluff, Ta-maya screamed and Maliwal cursed and called out his brother's name they could not be heard above the earsplitting din.

The pole shook violently. Masau gripped it hard; he was beyond fear now. Shateh's expression was as gratifying as sexual release, for there had been a time when he had lusted to seek out his father and kill him; but Ysuna would not have it.

"I always wondered what I would do if we ever met again," Masau bellowed. But the noise of the dying bison was so profound that he could not hear his own words, and the pole was shaking so ferociously that he could not form any more of them.

Ysuna had said that she would not raid the camp of the father of her "sons." She had chosen to allow Shateh life, for it had given her pleasure to know that somewhere across the plains, a man trembled every time he heard of the deeds of those whose lives he had so callously cast away. But now that they were face-to-face at last, Masau had no intention of allowing Shateh's life to continue. He reached out and struck the man with a sideward blow across the neck that sent him reeling just as the pole went over backward.

Too stunned to scream, Masau fell. For a reason he would never understand, he curled his fingers into Shateh's hair and kept the man from dropping straight down into the ravine and certain death. The forces of Creation intervened, angling the pole not into the draw but onto the plain. The tree was so tall that when it struck, its topmost branches landed well free of the chasm, which was now filled with a hideous living stew of broken bones and churning horns and bleeding hide.

Masau landed hard on solid ground, but the medicine pole was beneath him and took the brunt of the impact. He lay spread-eagled over the man he had just attempted to kill.

Shateh grunted and turned his face sideways. There was blood coming from his nose and ears as he stared up at his son out of disbelieving eyes. "You . . . have . . . saved my life. Why?"

Masau closed his eyes. His father's question had been a good one; even if he had not been on the edge of unconsciousness, he would not have been able to answer it. As he drifted in and out of blackness all he could think of was that a madness had come over him when he had found himself confronting his father—and in this state of delirium, he had put Shateh's life and Ysuna's wishes that the man live above his own lifelong desire for vengeance. He would never forgive himself.

Ysuna was Daughter of the Sun. She was growing old and ill for want of the flesh and blood of the white mammoth. It was in his power to give her both. And give them to her he would.

As soon as he was able to will his body to rise he would turn his eyes toward the village of the People of the

Watching Star. Ysuna was waiting for him. Ysuna *needed* him! And if she was going to live long enough to see another winter, Thunder in the Sky, the god of their ancestors, must have his bride.

Later that day, Shateh came to Masau as the brothers prepared to resume their travel north. Ta-maya stood apart, still upset by the wasteful hunting methods of the people of the north. Close to fifty animals had gone into the ravine—cows, bulls, and calves. But as she observed, the men, women, and children of the Bison Band set themselves to butcher only the top layer of bison. And it was obvious that they were taking only the choicest cuts of meat.

"You have not killed me this day," Shateh said.

Masau eyed him coldly. "Apparently not."

Maliwal measured his father with the same amount of affection that he might have shown a foul-smelling rack of meat. "Go away, Shateh. Go far and fast. We are no longer your sons. We are Ysuna's! And someday, when my brother's will does not bind me, I will see you dead!"

The man's eyes narrowed at the threat, then he turned and looked to where Ta-maya stood alone with Blood at her side. "Is she to be the new bride for the totem who speaks with the voice of thunder and assures the meat of endless mammoth to your people?"

Masau leveled a scrutinous gaze at him but said nothing.

"The wind speaks of many things to men in this land of grass and mountains," Shateh continued. "It speaks of troubling things, which bring pain to a man's spirit in the night—of vanished daughters, of blood and death. It speaks with the voices of those few who have escaped the wrath of Thunder in the Sky." His head swung slowly back and forth. "Is this what your totem spirit truly wants of his people? How many brides will Ysuna cause to be brought from the south before the bloodletting ends?"

Masau's face darkened. "Be grateful that Ysuna has seen fit to exclude your daughters from among the chosen these past many years. With each new bride, Thunder in the Sky speaks from the mountains and smiles upon his people. With each new bride a new herd of mammoth is always found. With each new bride Ysuna grows strong, and her people grow strong along with her."

Shateh gestured to his own people and to the butchering site. "Once we, too, hunted mammoth. But mammoth are few in the land these days. So now we hunt the long-horned bison. We follow the herds, and on this meat have my people grown numerous and strong. Perhaps it is time for Ysuna and her people to seek a new kind of meat. This day, Masau, you have saved my life. Stay with this band. Hunt with us. Let your lovely bride *be* a bride, and let the blood that she sheds for your people be the blood of childbirth—that is pain and sacrifice enough for any woman. Let her live, Masau. Bring your people here and be a tribe with us. Tell Ysuna that our ways are good ways, that our meat is good meat, and that we do not need to marry our daughters to Thunder in the Sky in order to win his favor or the favor of any other totem."

"Nor do we," protested Maliwal.

"No." Shateh shook his head with droll admonition. "You marry the innocent daughters of other tribes, of bands that know nothing of your ways. It is their flesh that feeds Thunder in the Sky, not yours. You may owe your lives to Ysuna, but do you believe that Thunder in the Sky does not know what you do in her name? Do you think that even Daughter of the Sun can deceive the great spirits of the mountains, the wind, and great Father Above, who has made us all? And do you not imagine that the spirits of the ancestors of those brides you bring north may be watching you? Be careful, my sons. Someday they may follow and prove to be greater than you think."

Maliwal's face contorted with anger. "Are you threatening me, Bison Eater?"

"No," said Shateh sadly, "I am warning you. This day one who was once a son to me has given me a gift of my life. Perhaps my words may save his someday."

Masau was not moved. He scanned the encampment. There were days of work ahead for the people of the Bison Band. This had been a good kill. Already fires had been raised and bones cracked so that marrow could be melted from them in great bison-paunch boiling bags. Hunters—three or four men to an animal—were crawling over the bloody carcasses, hacking out hump steaks, pulling out intestines, and opening throats so that the tongues, which were a special delicacy in any band, could be easily removed and consumed raw upon the spot. Young boys had been set loose to crack open skulls with stone pounders so that their mothers could get at the brains inside and set them aside to be used later, after the hides were stretched and ready for tanning.

No doubt the meat was, as Shateh claimed, "good meat." But it was not mammoth meat. Masau said as much, then frowned as he appraised the slovenly appearance of the people and the lack of ritual that was accompanying their work.

"You have abandoned the ways of our ancestors, Shateh. I will not hunt with you. I will not stay so much as a single night in this camp, nor will I or any of those who walk with me eat of this meat. The great white mammoth—the source of my people's strength—walks to the south with its herd. It must be hunted. It must be killed by Ysuna herself. Then it *will* be eaten so the mammoth herds will return to the land of the People of the Watching Star. In great numbers will they come. Ysuna, Daughter of the Sun, has sworn it."

Shateh shook his head again. "Has she? It is a strange logic. I do not understand how killing and eating your totem and all of its kind will bring the mammoth back into the land of grass between the mountains. And we have not abandoned the ways of our ancestors—we have found *new* ways. Once the mammoth were many. Now they are few. I do not understand why this has come to pass. I know only that once my people were few, and now they are many. This is a good thing! It has been said since time beyond beginning that the tree that bends before a storm is the one that will not break before it."

Maliwal eyed the sky. Incapable of subtlety, he snorted in derision. "There is no sign of storm!"

Masau ignored his brother. Grasping the headman's double meaning, he eyed Shateh keenly. "There will be no storm," he replied, then added dangerously, "unless I bring it. Beware, Shateh. The next time I set eyes upon you or this band, you will die—all of you."

# PART VIII

# THUNDER IN THE SKY

# 1

"It cannot be true!" The words ripped from Cha-kwena's throat. Within the curl of his right hand, the sacred stone seemed to be burning straight through his palm.

"It *is* true!" Dakan-eh insisted. "Do you think that I would have returned to this village if it were not? I tell you they were dead! Every lodge had been burned, sometime before last winter's snow from the look of it. All that was left were charred postholes, human bones, several broken spear foreshafts, and one spear—and that was protruding from the midsection of a dead man!"

Beside him a dull-eyed, haggard-looking Ban-ya shook her head to clear it of bad memories as she echoed, "Bones . . . everywhere. Only bones . . ."

Tlana-quah's face had gone tight with apprehension and disbelief. "And the headman of the village, what had he to say to this?"

Dakan-eh exhaled through his teeth. "You are not hearing me, Tlana-quah. They were dead—*all* dead beyond recognition, their bones scattered and picked clean by meat eaters. But there was no mistaking old Shi-wana. His body was apart from the others. I would have recognized his bonnet anywhere, even though it was broken and half-eaten by rodents. And despite the fact that his skull was stripped of nearly all skin, what was left of it was still painted blue, and the spaces between his teeth spoke his name to me. The spear we found had been thrust through his gut, and it was fitted with a killing foreshaft such as the traders carried. It was made of carved and painted mammoth bone, with the colors of the scar-mouthed man, Maliwal."

The people stared, gaped, and tried to grasp the implications of the news that Dakan-eh and Ban-ya had brought to them. They stood together in the gathering hut. Its winter covering of antelope skins had been removed from the conical thatched walls, and the birds' singing and the lake waters' gentle lapping at the reed-bound shore could be heard clearly in the sudden silence. Beyond, a mammoth trumpeted.

Cha-kwena winced. His head was spinning, and he felt sick, disoriented. Although he was Shaman, he was as much at a loss as anyone else to comprehend the horrific images that Dakan-eh's words had evoked. He kept staring at Ban-ya's coyote-skin cloak. The soft fur was the color of summer grass; the limp, slender front limbs looped over her shoulders; the delicate forepaws crossed and dangled over her enormous chest—the cloak was all that was left of Little Yellow Wolf, of Brother Coyote, who had come to him in his dreams and in the waking hours of long-gone nights to warn him of danger . . . and who, even in death, somehow had found a way to warn him still.

"Men do not hunt other men!" Tlana-quah was adamant. "The traders from the north brought gifts to us. They called us brothers and sisters. They ate our food, they hunted at our side, and they contributed meat to our feasts. It was Masau who found the sacred stone when Cha-kwena had given it up as lost. And it was Masau who put himself between me and a charging lion. I owe that man my life. I think that you have not understood what you have seen, Bold Man. Perhaps there was a fire in the village. Perhaps lions came, or a great bear. Perhaps the men of the north tried to drive the meat eaters away, and Shi-wana put himself in the way of a spear. Perhaps—"

"Then why did they not speak of this to us?" Dakan-eh challenged. "They made no secret of the fact that they were trading among the various bands in the northern half of the Red World before they reached us. Yet they made no mention of the fate of the People of the Blue Mesas, even though we found plenty of sign of the northerners amid the burned rubble of the lodges and among the bones and skulls of dead men and women and children."

Tlana-quah raised his hands to silence Bold Man as he fixed him with troubled eyes. "Dakan-eh . . . are you saying that the men of the north did this—this *death* to the shaman of the People of the Blue Mesas?"

The silence was palpable.

"Old Hoyeh-tay did not trust them," reminded Dakan-eh. "He warned us about them. He thought they were Brothers of the Sky."

"Do you think this?" pressed the headman.

"I do!" answered Dakan-eh hotly.

"Then why are you here? Why have you not gone after my Ta-maya? Why have you come here to speak to me when she is far away and in danger?"

"Because she *is* far away. It was my first thought to pursue her, but I had no idea where to look for her. And I feared that you, that the entire village, might be in danger!"

Ban-ya looked up at him with a frown.

Clearly flustered, Bold Man ignored her glance as he snapped churlishly to Tlana-quah, "I can tell you only of what I have seen." His mouth was a narrow white line of frustration and resentment as he compressed his lips and turned his gaze to Cha-kwena. The venom of hatred twisted his mouth downward when he said, "It seems that my word is worth nothing in this band! Ask Cha-kwena if you want answers. He is Shaman. He knows everything—or so he says. But if my eyes have spoken the truth to my spirit, then you may blame him for approving the marriage of your daughter—and the woman of my choice—into a band of strangers who have slain our brothers and sisters and burned their village to the ground."

Ban-ya hung her head.

Ha-xa moaned and swayed and whispered Ta-maya's name with longing.

Seated between her mother and U-wa, a distraught Mah-ree cuddled her favorite of the pups that Masau had left in the care of the band. "It could not be!" she exclaimed. "Dakan-eh, you must be wrong! Masau is good! His men are good! We will meet with them and Ta-maya at the Great Gathering, and you will see that this is so!"

"Perhaps we had better see before then," Kosar-eh suggested grimly. "When the men from the north left this village, they were headed for the White Hills. Let us send men there. Let us counsel with Hia-shi, headman of that village, and with Naquah-neh, shaman of that band. Let us see what they have to say about the People of the Watching Star. And let us at least know in our hearts that Ta-maya was safe and well when she reached that place."

Unimpeded by heavy loads, they went from the village in somber moods—Tlana-quah, Dakan-eh, Cha-kwena, and a small, select group of the best hunters of the band. They carried their spears as though they expected to be attacked by bears or lions, and with every step they made toward the White Hills, Cha-kwena kept hearing old Hoyeh-tay's voice:

*Beware, Cha-kwena! You must warn the People before it is too late. The lions are coming. These strangers have bad eyes—wolf eyes, lion eyes, eagle eyes. They are the Brothers of the Sky come down out of the stars to destroy the People.*

He was not sure just when Kosar-eh, without his clownish body paint and feathers, came to join the sullen, introspective little group. He had a traveling pack slung over his shoulder, a sheathed dagger looped to his waist thong, and three spears grasped in his good hand.

"Go back," Tlana-quah told the man quietly. "You have not been a hunter for many years, Kosar-eh. The women and children need their Funny Man to cheer them."

"I will have no heart to cheer anyone until I know that Ta-maya is safe," he replied.

Dakan-eh eyed Kosar-eh's scars and crippled arm with open revulsion. "We will bring news from the White Hills soon enough. Go back to the village where you belong, Funny Man. We have no need of a clown to slow us upon this journey."

Kosar-eh was used to Dakan-eh's hurtful tongue; nevertheless he appraised the man with more than an equal measure of the distaste that Bold Man had just shown toward him. "I will not slow you. I have lost most of the use of one arm, but I have another. I was once as bold a man as you, Dakan-eh. I am a clown only because I was not as lucky. I am still bold when there is need. And I have never stopped being a man. If Ta-maya is in danger, I must know. Unlike you, had she been promised to me, I never would have allowed her to leave the village with strangers."

"You could not have stopped her," Tlana-quah said ruefully.

Kosar-eh ignored the headman as he continued to look with cold disapproval at Dakan-eh. "Had she been promised to me, she would never have wanted to leave."

Dakan-eh snorted with pure mockery. "Ha! I have told you, we have no need of clowns upon this journey!"

"It is you who are the clown, Dakan-eh," replied Kosar-eh. "Can you not see yourself for what you are? You may blame Cha-kwena for failing to see through to the heart of the strangers, but not once have you seen into the heart of Ta-maya. Everyone in this band knows that it is your arrogance, your selfishness, and your overbearing ways that drove her into the arms of another."

Bold Man stopped dead in his tracks. "She had the best man in the Red World or in any other world when she chose me!"

Now Tlana-quah paused and glared furiously at Dakan-eh. "Man in Love with Himself . . . *that* should have been your name, for by the spirits of the ancestors, I understand now that my disgust for you allowed me to see my girl married to a stranger! Better had she gone to any hunter in this band—even to Kosar-eh—than to such an insufferable man as you!"

Dakan-eh stiffened. "I have not come back across the long miles to listen to this!"

"Then leave us! Go away and take with you the bad words that you have brought to shadow the lives of your people!"

Dakan-eh was incredulous. "You still don't believe me?"

"My eyes will tell me what to believe. The words of Naquah-neh, of Hia-shi, the shaman and headman of the People of the White Hills, will speak a truth that I will trust."

Dakan-eh's eyes were bulging with fury. "Then go to the White Hills without me! Seek word of Ta-maya and the strangers, but hear it without me. And if by some chance the men of the north are still there and in a mood to do to you what they did to the men of the Blue Mesas, I will thank the spirits of the ancestors that I will not be at your side to put my life at risk for you!" He turned and stalked off toward the village, with his head high and his chin jabbing the air.

The men looked at one another and shifted their weight restlessly from foot to foot.

"We may need him," said Ma-nuk.

The others murmured in agreement—all except Chakwena, who stood looking after Dakan-eh. The young shaman was still dazed by the events of the past hours, still hearing old Hoyeh-tay's ghostly voice of warning, still not wanting to believe it.

Tlana-quah was livid. He stood tall, threw back his shoulders, and slapped his left hand hard across the jaguar-skin covering of his right shoulder. "Why would the men of this band need Dakan-eh when they walk with me? I am Tlana-quah! I am headman! I have stood alone against a great spotted cat! With my own hand and skill I have killed the beast whose skin I wear! Have you no confidence in your headman . . . or in yourselves?"

A muscle was throbbing high at the line of Kosar-eh's jaw. "I will not go back to the village, Tlana-quah. Before the Day of the Camel turned me into a clown and a cripple, I was the 'bold man' of this band. I will go with you to the White Hills. If I find that Dakan-eh has spoken the truth, if Ta-maya has been harmed or placed into danger by these men of the north, he will not be the only one in this band to answer to the name of Bold Man for her sake!"

It was not difficult to pick up the way that the traders of the People of the Watching Star had taken toward the White Hills; their sledges had left deep gouges in the earth.

"They do not walk in stealth," observed Tlana-quah, taking this as a good sign. "And look, Ta-maya walks with her new man. Here are her footprints. She wears new sandals! They were part of Ha-xa's great mound of bridal gifts! No woman makes sandals as well as my Ha-xa."

Heartened, he set the pace that allowed them to proceed with little need for rest. Before dusk they found the abandoned first encampment of the traders and stood in shock.

"Mammoth bones? Are these *mammoth* bones amid the bones of fish and pronghorn?"

Cha-kwena went cold at Tlana-quah's unnecessary question. The awful truth was there for all to see: piles of mammoth bones. No other animal had bones of such size. Gnawed on by dogs, cracked and fleshed by men, the bones were unmistakable even before the men found the ravine.

"They have killed and eaten of our totem animals!" cried Tlana-quah in despair.

"They are mammoth hunters!" Kosar-eh shook his head and sighed as though he could not believe his own words.

Cha-kwena was so staggered that he was sure he was going to be sick. "It cannot be," he said.

But it was, and he knew it.

They did not stay at the camp, because it was a foul place to them. Traveling by night as well as by day, they hurried on, worried by the fact that now the footprints of Ta-maya were recognizable only by their small size, for when she had left the place of the mammoth slaughter, she was no longer wearing Ha-xa's sandals; her feet were clad in leather as were those of the men in the company of whom she traveled.

## 2

They approached the White Hills on a fair, clear, sun-struck day. A man was waiting for them; they felt his watching eyes for a long time before he showed himself above them on a boulder-strewn hill. Tlana-quah raised his arms in greeting. The man stood motionless, his broad, burly form leaning forward in the way of one who is poised and prepared to flee from danger.

At length Tlana-quah called out to him. "Ayee-aye! You, on the hill! Tlana-quah, headman of the People of the

Lake of Many Singing Birds, comes to counsel with Hia-
shi, headman of the People of the White Hills!"

The man remained where he was, swaying and making odd, grunting noises. At last he ambled down from the
hills and yelled, "Come! Come!" again and again and bade
them welcome with outstretched arms. He moved quickly,
with the odd, awkward, heavy-footed gait of a ground
sloth.

Cha-kwena recognized him. It was Sunam-tu. He appeared to be in good health, but his smile was fixed and
his eyes were big and bright—too bright. It was not until
he paused directly in front of them and leaned close—
staring and sniffing like a wolf or a dog after the identity of
a questionable pack member—that they saw the madness
in him.

"Have you seen my sister?" he asked, then lowered
his head and stared at them from beneath partially closed
lids. "We will go to the Great Gathering now," he confided in the way of a conspirator. "Yes, I have been
waiting. All the bands will go. They will be there, too. Oh,
yes, they will be there."

"They? The traders of the People of the Watching
Star?" pressed Tlana-quah. "They were here, then?"

"Oh, yes. They were here." Sunam-tu's eyes were
enormous.

"And my daughter Ta-maya was well?"

Sunam-tu's face went blank. "Daughter?"

Tlana-quah's brows came together at the bridge of his
nose. "The bride of the man with the tattooing around his
eyes. A small girl, very pretty."

"A small girl? Very pretty? You *have* seen my sister!"
Sunam-tu declared, much relieved.

Tlana-quah shook his head. "No, my daughter. Her
name is Ta-maya. She was the only woman traveling in the
company of the men of the north."

Sunam-tu sighed. It was a sound of infinite disappointment. And then, suddenly, a laugh burst out of him.
It was a high, loonlike, maniacal laugh. He gave it no
chance to subside before he stifled it and informed in a
low, triumphant whisper: "They went away. They did not
see me! But it is all right now. I am still here, and they are
gone. Come. Let us go to my village. I will make you

welcome. Hia-shi will be glad to counsel with another headman of the Red World." He squinted at Cha-kwena, then nodded in excited recognition as though remembering him was a great accomplishment. He pointed at the youth. "Shaman Boy! Have you seen my sister?"

"Not since the Blue Mesas," said Cha-kwena with a scowl.

Sunam-tu wailed, then pressed his hands over his face as he shook his head violently. "She is with *them* now. Yes, she is with them, with their shaman forever. I heard them say so. But is this not what I always wanted for her? When a man has no mother or father to care for his sister, he must be a good brother and see to it that she finds the right man to care for her." He peeked at the others through the slits of his fingers. "Is this not so?" Giving them no chance to reply, he flung his arms wide. "But you have not come here to talk of Lah-ri! Come! You must come to the village!" He turned, ran off a few steps, then turned again and gestured them forward. "Why do you not follow?"

As the once-proud hunter and guardian of his people's shaman led them to the village, he talked constantly in the way that old Hoyeh-tay had done at the ending of his days—addressing people who were not present, laughing out loud when no one had made a joke, or simply rambling along courses of conversation that involved subjects that eluded his listeners.

Soon enough they understood why. They smelled the village before they saw it. The stench of putrefying flesh was so strong that they held their hands cupped over their noses and mouths as Sunam-tu hurried them on past the first of the small, neatly made lodges and then into the central compound of a village that was almost exactly like their own, save for the silence and the absence of all signs of life.

The sense of foreboding was almost as overpowering as the stench. Tlana-quah and the others paused.

"Come, come!" urged Sunam-tu. "Hia-shi awaits you within the gathering lodge. Naquah-neh is with him. They are all with him, except the women and children. They are asleep in their own family lodges. All sleep since the strangers went away. Maybe they will come out later. But do not worry. I know that you have come far to speak with my headman. I will see to it that you are fed. I have been feeding everyone since the women went to sleep. I do not mind. After all, I was Naquah-neh's guardian when he journeyed to the Blue Mesas, and now I guard him here. Now I guard them all!" He smiled broadly, displaying his teeth. They clicked as they came together, and he tittered at the sound. "Come!" he beckoned, still giggling as he proceeded to the main lodge, where he held the woven entry cover back for them. "Come! Come and see how well I have cared for my people!"

They entered the lodge together.

They stopped dead in their tracks together.

Small, dark, long-tailed rodents ran across their feet and scurried for the safety of the shadowy interior of the lodge as Cha-kwena took an involuntary step back. His companions did the same.

"Rats!" he exclaimed, then sucked in his breath with horror—not at the rodents but at what lay before him. The air that he had drawn into his lungs weakened him. He staggered, feeling faint.

Sunam-tu pulled the entry cover even wider. Light streamed into the lodge.

Cha-kwena stared ahead. All the men of the village were there. They stared back at him out of sightless eyes. They were dead, propped up in a circle, leaning against woven backrests as though in the midst of a council. Incredulous, he saw that there were baskets of food before them and haunches of freshly roasted hare in each man's hands, although it was obvious that they had been dead for days. Dried blood was everywhere. Most of the corpses had smashed skulls. Their necks and chests were dark with blood that had gushed from slit throats, and there were gaping wounds in their arms and chests and bellies.

"You see?" said Sunam-tu, still standing at the entry. "They are all here. I brought them inside after the strangers left. I thought they would have need of a council."

Cha-kwena was shaking uncontrollably.

Tlana-quah's voice came in short gasps. "How . . . did . . . this . . . happen?"

Sunam-tu's smile never left his face. "Nothing has happened. The strangers came, then they went away.

Now the men in my band sit at council, and the women and children sleep."

A terrible wave of nausea rose in Cha-kwena. He recognized Naquah-neh—the shaman's wide, perpetually scowling features, his broad nose, and wide and fleshy mouth—only now the once-sleek, shiny, well-fed skin had lost its gloss and was sunken over the bones of his skull. The fleshy lips were gone, as were the eyes. A rat peered at Cha-kwena from one of the empty eye sockets. Shocked and sickened, he cried out and turned and, backhanding Sunam-tu out of the way, fled from the lodge. He gave up the contents of his stomach and then, shaking, sank to his knees.

The others were beside him.

Sunam-tu had followed. "Go back inside," he urged. "It is cool inside. You cannot hold a council with the men of my band if you're out here in the sun."

"I cannot hold a council with the dead!" snapped Tlana-quah. "Yet in truth they have told me most of what I need to know. Ma-nuk, go and check the lodges. See if there is sign of Ta-maya."

Kosar-eh reached out and snatched Sunam-tu by the hair, pulling him close with his one good arm. "What happened here? Where are the women and children? Tell me," he threatened, "or you will join the others inside the gathering lodge, and when we leave this village, the rats will be feeding off you as they are feeding off your bandsmen!"

Sunam-tu seemed puzzled. "The women were tired when the strangers left. They and the little ones just lay upon the ground, so I carried them all in their lodges and put them to sleep. Go, see for yourself!"

Ma-nuk emerged tight-lipped from one of the lodges. "They are not sleeping," he said, his face working against revulsion. "They have been dead a long time."

In a frenzy, Tlana-quah ran from lodge to lodge in search of Ta-maya. When he returned to stand with the others, he was breathless with what seemed to be both worry and relief. "She is not here. But the others are all slain, even the babies."

"Dead?" Sunam-tu mewed the question. "No one is dead here. The women and children sleep. The men keep

council. And the strangers are gone. They have taken their
long, bright spears and gone away. But they will be at the
Great Gathering. I heard them say so. They will be there.
Waiting."

Kosar-eh's face twisted with fury as he hurled Sunam-tu
to the ground. "For what will they wait?"

The man landed hard beside Cha-kwena. Stunned,
Sunam-tu lay on his back in a pool of vomit but did not
even seem to realize it as he stared up at Kosar-eh. For a
moment the madman's eyes cleared, and his face twisted
in an agony of remembrance. "They wait for the shamans
of the Red World to come together upon the holy mountain. They wait to claim the sacred stones as their own.
When they have all the stones, they will go south. They
will seek the white mammoth and kill it. Then they will
eat of its flesh and drink of its blood so the strength of the
totem will become their strength. The People of the Watching Star will be many, and no one will be able to stand
against them as they move out across the world in search
of endless brides for Thunder in the Sky."

"No . . ." The word sighed out of Cha-kwena. Somewhere deep within his heart and spirit something had
begun to bleed; it was the last of his youth, the last of his
innocence, the last tender portion of his willingness and
ability to put his trust in any man—especially in himself.
As it seeped out he clung to it desperately. "No. It cannot
be. You are mistaken! Look. Do you see this? Around my
neck I wear the sacred stone of my band. The men of the
north made no attempt to take it from me."

Sunam-tu cocked his head. "You say that they had
one of the daughters of your village with them?"

"Yes." Tlana-quah's voice seemed to come from a
bottomless abyss of dread. "My daughter . . . my Ta-maya."

"A young girl? Pretty? A virgin?" Sunam-tu saw the
answer to his questions in Tlana-quah's eyes. "They eat
them, you know. The men from the north seduce the
young virgins away from their families and then, when
they come consenting to their wedding day in the Land of
the Watching Star, they kill them and divide their flesh,
and the woman who is Shaman dances in their skin."

The sound that escaped from Kosar-eh was not human. Then he screamed, "No!" and with the side of his good hand, he struck Sunam-tu across the face.

The man fell sideways, then propped himself onto his elbows and, looking both hurt and perplexed, rubbed his jaw. "Hitting me will not change the truth of what I say. From the scarred mouth of the one who led the others into the village, I heard the words. The strangers came so quickly. They killed everyone before we could understand and react to what they had in mind for us. I do not know how I escaped unseen, but somehow I managed to hide myself in the hills until the screaming stopped.

"When it was over I returned, thinking that they were gone. But they were not gone. They were still sating themselves on the young girls of my band. I watched, afraid to come forward, for I had run off without so much as a fleshing dagger with me. When they had had enough of the girls, the men cut their throats and all but one went away. The scar-faced man lingered, standing over Naquah-neh. The shaman had a spear straight through his belly—so deep that he was pinned to the ground but was not quite dead.

"The northerner mocked him, told him all that I have just repeated to you. He said that he and his men were no longer strangers to the Red World, that they had been to the Red Hills and the Blue Mesas and to the Lake of Many Singing Birds and had taken brides from each of those villages and had made a sacrifice of all but the last. Before he went his way, he took the sacred stone from Naquah-neh's neck and drove his spear deep again—once, twice, and then a third time before he left Naquah-neh to die. That's when I came out of hiding. It took four days for my shaman's spirit to leave his body. He told me to go, to warn the People of the Red World; but I am the guardian of my holy man and could not leave him or my people. They . . . they were tired. They needed to be put to rest. Now I must guard him and them until they wake up again. They will wake up again." A spasm of grief and guilt shook him. "I was trained to protect my shaman from bears and lions, not from men! I cannot be blamed for what happened! I am Sunam-tu! My sister was given to the shaman of the Blue Mesas. Have you seen my sister? I am tired now. I would like to sleep now. I do not want to talk to you anymore. Go away." With a moan of abject misery, he lay down on his side and, tucking his head to his folded knees, wrapped his arms about his lower limbs.

Cha-kwena got to his feet.

"What will happen if they come south again?" Ma-nuk asked Tlana-quah.

"They will seek the white mammoth," replied the headman. "They will know just where to look for it. They will come to the village beside the Lake of Many Singing Birds, and after they have killed my people, they will kill our totem."

Cha-kwena was trembling. A cold wind rose within him. It seemed to carry him away from the others and set him apart from them and from himself. Old Hoyeh-tay seemed to be speaking out of his mouth as he said: "And if they succeed, not just our band but all the People of the Red World will die."

"Ta-maya is with them now. We must go after her and bring her home." Kosar-eh was emphatic. Mammoth— totem or otherwise—were the last things on his mind.

"And if we are killed in the attempt," asked Tlana-quah, "who will warn the People of the danger that will soon come to them from the north?"

No one spoke.

Tlana-quah stared to the south, toward home and family and people and totem. He quivered in frustration under the weight of his responsibilities as headman and father. "The People must be warned," he decided. Then he turned to the north and looked achingly across the miles over which his beloved child had gone her way with the murderous strangers, having the full consent of her father and blessing of the shaman of her band. When he closed his eyes, he exhaled a long, bitter sigh of acquiescence to her fate. "Those who have gone ahead have put many days and many nights between us and them."

Kosar-eh's face worked against incredulity. "You are not going to abandon her to man-slaying mammoth hunters! Not you! Not Brave Hunter! Not Man Who Alone Kills Jaguar!"

Tlana-quah winced. His eyes opened. "I . . . I . . ." He seemed about to speak, then changed his mind. His eyes settled on Cha-kwena. There was no anger in his gaze—only sadness and infinite regret. "You told us that you were not born to be a shaman, and you were right. A man born to walk in the way of the wisdom of the ancients would have foreseen this tragedy. He would have known—as old Hoyeh-tay knew—what these men of the north were. He *was* Shaman to the end, but we would not listen to his warnings."

The wind that had risen within Cha-kwena was a gale now, a storm of flying hooves, furred backs, and flurrying wings as the voices of Deer and Bat, Hawk and Swallow, Mouse and Hare and Owl shrieked within his head. They rode the tumultuous back of West Wind, and a lone coyote howled at him, *You* knew! *All along you* knew! *But though we led you to the truth again and again, you turned away and would not see!*

"No!" he cried, and now both of his hands were curled around the sacred stone. He held on to the talisman as though it alone in all the world could keep him safe from the devastating storms of revelation sweeping through him. *It cannot be true! Whatever happened here, Masau could not have been a part of it. I trusted him! I trust still. He would not bring harm to Ta-maya or to any of the People of the Red World.*

And yet, as he pressed his palms against the amulet, the stone burned him with recollections of Lah-ri and Shi-wana, of Naquah-neh and all the men and women and children who now lay dead because the men of the north had come to the Red World. He thought of Hoyeh-tay lying broken and bloodied in the creek bed below the cave. He saw the old man's timeworn features contorted by a strange look of surprise and disbelief, as though death had caught him unaware and he had done his best to fight it to the end.

Cha-kwena caught his breath. He saw the face of Death. It wore a mask of black tattooing. It was the face of Shrike, it was the face of a carnivore smiling at him from within the skin of an eagle.

"Masau?" He spoke the name of the man whom he had trusted and come to love as a brother. He spoke the name of Death. And still he would not believe it.

Suddenly there was the strong scent of charred feathers within his nostrils. He gasped, for now he saw the scene that must have transpired within the cave while he had been asleep at the feast fire: He saw Masau moving like a lion in the darkness, stalking Hoyeh-tay, grasping Owl as the bird had flown at him, pushing the bird into the fire pit, pressing down, burning it, hurting it even as he broke its back and its neck, and then turned in murderous intent to the old man.

"No!" he moaned.

*You could have stopped it,* said the voices of all the animals that had ever named him Brother. *Had you listened to us and chosen to believe, you could have stopped it!*

The accusation was more than he could bear; he refused to hear it.

Hoyeh-tay's warning filled his consciousness and cut straight to his heart. His grandfather had urged him to remember all he had been taught about the shaman's path, or the People would be lost. The old shaman had cautioned that as long as the great white mammoth lived among the People, the People would be strong; but when he died, the People would die with him. And as long as a single stone remained within the keeping of the shamans of the Red World, the totem would live forever.

"Cha-kwena?"

He blinked and emerged from the trance. He stood stunned by it. It was a few moments before he was aware of being surrounded by his fellow travelers. Kosar-eh's strong good hand was pressing his forearm imperatively.

"Are you all right, Cha-kwena?" asked the clown, his face grim with strain and worry.

Cha-kwena looked at him and then at the others. They seemed like strangers to him until he realized that he himself was the stranger—lost, bewildered . . . no longer a boy but not quite a man . . . a shaman whose visions continued to lead him along a path that he could not bring himself to follow. "You must go after Ta-maya," he said dully. "If all this is true, you must bring her back to her people."

"*If* it is true?" Kosar-eh could not believe his ears. "Surely you do not doubt it? Look around you, Cha-kwena! Breathe in the stench of death! Dakan-eh spoke the truth, as did your grandfather! These strangers from the north are not men; they are lions, feeding on our people at will, killing our shamans, stealing the sacred stones of our ancestors, and robbing our totem of strength even as they seek him out with the intent of killing him!"

The words struck Cha-kwena with the force of a spear thrust. The pain was blinding. Breathless, still gripping the sacred stone, he whispered, "No, I will not believe it. Go, follow Ta-maya if you must. When you find her, you will see that she is safe. In the meantime, I will go back to our village. I will tell the People of what we have seen here and of what Sunam-tu has said to us. But as long as a single sacred stone remains in the hands of a shaman of the Red World, our totem is safe! Whatever has happened here and in the Village of the People of the Blue Mesas, it was not of Masau's doing—it could not have been."

Tlana-quah eyed the youth soberly. "Of all the words of wisdom that old Hoyeh-tay spoke to me in my lifetime, I should have heeded all except the ones that named you Shaman. You are no man of vision, Cha-kwena. You are a blind fool."

# 3

Cha-kwena did not walk back to the village by the Lake of Many Singing Birds. He ran. He loped like a wild thing, and all the while the spirits of Deer and Coyote and Hare and Rabbit ran behind him. Mouse scurried along at his heels, and Hawk and Sparrow and Owl and Brother Bat flew overhead, repeating the words of his headman: *You are no man of vision, Cha-kwena. You are a blind fool!*

He went on, lengthening his stride, telling himself again and again that Tlana-quah was wrong, that when the others overtook Ta-maya and the traders, they would see that he had been right. Whatever had happened in the White Hills and in the shadow of the Blue Mesas had nothing to do with the men of the People of the Watching Star. Others had done the killing.

As to the mammoth that they had found butchered in the ravine and the encampment of the northerners, perhaps the men had come unexpectedly upon the mammoth, and the animals, startled, had charged, forcing the men to spear them. Perhaps they had some covenant with the spirits of their own ancestors that in such a situation, the meat of the slain mammoth might be eaten. It was the only explanation that Cha-kwena could find acceptable. In any event, he did not want to think about it. The truth would be made known soon enough, and he was confident that his faith in Masau and the men of the north would be justified.

He ran faster, pausing only to drink and to gnaw on an occasional strip of dried meat. Day wore toward dusk. Darkness brought him to a stop. He hunkered on his sandaled feet and dozed just long enough to ease the fatigue that might have slowed his steps.

He started again under the light of the star children of the moon. He moved more slowly now. Night Wind rose to blow softly at his back, as though hurrying him on his way.

"It is dark," he said to the wind. "I cannot see well enough to move more quickly."

"Use your third eye to find your way, Cha-kwena! Do not lag behind, boy, or Great Ghost Spirit may not be at the salt spring when we arrive!"

He stopped and turned to squint into the night. Who had spoken? He suddenly went cold. The ghosts of the past were all around him. Hoyeh-tay was beside him. Owl perched upon the old man's head. Cha-kwena closed his eyes so tightly that his lids ached. When he opened them again, the ghosts were gone. He went on and was not sure just when his steps had taken him wide of the well-worn trail to the village of his people. Without meaning to, he was headed for the salt spring.

He stopped again to look around. He frowned. It would take him an hour or more to backtrack and pick up the trail to the village. He sighed. It was very late, and he was tired and thirsty. He decided to drink and sleep for a while by the pools below the salt spring. He doubted if there were more than a few hours until dawn. In the light of the morning, he could proceed up the canyon and on to the village by way of the overlook.

He continued forward, uphill now across a broad, stony stretch of plain that shone blue beneath the stars. The multiveined arm of the river was to his left, approximately a quarter of a mile away. It was full now with spring runoff, and he loved the cool, clear *ssh*ing sound that it made. Had it been closer, he would have cut due east and sought to refresh himself in its shallows, then slept along the shore. But the canyon lay ahead, black against the shimmering campfires of the many children of the moon. Night Wind was soughing in the tall pines and cedars and hardwoods, and he could hear the waterfall and smell the good, heady scent of forest.

He hurried his steps and smiled with the tug of affectionate memories of Hoyeh-tay. He had found his night eyes, perhaps even the inner third eye that his grandfather had told him of, for although he was moving through woodland, his step was long and sure and without error. Hoyeh-tay would have been proud of him.

He was deep into the canyon now. Night Wind rushed on ahead, then turned back to bring him the scent of the pools, of the ferns and duff, of the first tender green uncurlings of mountain columbines . . . and of something else, something dead.

Cha-kwena stopped. Somewhere in the darkness ahead, a mammoth huffed, then moved off. The boy listened and waited. He heard the footfall of massive feet on heavy undergrowth and the sound of branches parting. He squinted into the night and saw a dark mounded form swaying off into deeper darkness. Then he caught a glimpse of three smaller mounds moving on either side of the larger one.

"The herd . . ." Cha-kwena sighed the words as though he were intoning a prayer. The women and children of Great Grandfather of All walked ahead of him. He followed unafraid, although he frowned now against the unmistakable stench of rotting flesh.

He did not cry out when he saw it.

He was too appalled even to breathe.

The partially skinned butchered body of the precious

little white mammoth lay half-immersed in the shallow waters of the lower pool, along with that of the great gray cow that had been its mother.

"What gifts do you bring to Ysuna from the land of the People of the Red World?" asked Ta-maya as she stood in the light of the rising sun and watched Masau and the others begin to unpack one of the sledges.

"Rare things," he replied. "Maliwal and I will bring them to her for all our people to see. But why do you stand there watching? You must prepare yourself to meet Daughter of the Sun. Comb your hair. Plait feathers and beads into it. And put on the dress with the many fringes. I would not have Ysuna think that I have chosen an unworthy bride. I'll send for you soon."

After Ta-maya went to obey, Masau, his brother, and the other hunters traveled the short distance into the encampment of the People of the Watching Star.

Ysuna came toward the brothers out of the sun in all of her ceremonial attire to greet them. Her people stepped aside to part the way for her. Never in all of Masau's dreams of her had she looked more beautiful.

"My sons return to me at last. What do you bring Ysuna, Daughter of the Sun?"

"A bride for Thunder in the Sky!" replied Maliwal with boundless enthusiasm. "A sacred stone for the One Who Brings Life to the People! News of the whereabouts of the white mammoth! And this: Behold the hide and heart of its son!"

Her head went high. Backlighted by the morning sun, she stood outlined by a shimmering aura of red and gold. She watched expressionlessly as they unrolled the hide and laid the heart upon it.

"I have killed this little mammoth while the villagers thought I was hunting for food for a wedding feast!" Maliwal said, gesturing proudly to his treasure. "I have smoked its heart in the heat of fires fed with sacred sage. Eat and grow strong, Ysuna!" His hand rose to the side of his face. His features were engorged with hope. "And then you will show everyone that you have the power to make my face whole again!"

She appraised the pale hide and the organ that lay

upon it, then eyed him darkly. "That was a very small mammoth, Maliwal."

"It is the little white son of Great Ghost Spirit."

"It is not the one I seek."

"It is the offspring of the great one!" he protested, hurt and passionate in his desire to be believed and appreciated.

Masau was measuring Ysuna thoughtfully. Her face was set. With the sun shimmering at her back, her unlighted features were uniformly gray. His brow came down. His heart made a leap of terror in his chest. Never had she looked more beautiful—or more haggard. There were dark hollows beneath her eyes and vertical shadows at the sides of her mouth. He knew illness when he saw it. It was severe illness, approaching death.

His mouth tightened with revulsion and horror. He could smell the sickness on her. Now his heart was pounding, deep and steady with ever-intensifying resolve. "We have seen our totem, Ysuna. We have been so close to him that we could feel the heat of his breath and could have touched him had we wished to do so. He is great and powerful and is the one you seek. We could have killed him for you. But the blood and heart of the great white mammoth must be for Ysuna's hand to take. I know where you may hunt him, and I have fashioned the spearheads with which to kill him."

He knelt. Slowly, reverently he removed the projectile points of white chalcedony from their carrying case of lion skin. There were four spearheads in all, one to honor each of the Four Winds. Each spearhead, as long as his forearm, was wrapped within a protective folding of buckskin. In a moment all four lay exposed and gleaming in the morning light. Ysuna gasped in amazement as he held up the palest and allowed the sun to stream through the milky substance of the stone.

"When I have hafted these for you, that which you seek will be defenseless against Daughter of the Sun."

Her eyes widened. She paled. When he rose and placed the spearhead in her hands, she held it balanced across both palms, then tested its weight.

"I will need all my strength if I am to honor this gift," she said, shivering. Her breathing quickened as she handed the projectile point back to him. "Where is the sacred stone that you have brought to me?"

Frowning, Masau took it from his neck and placed it around hers.

She trembled, touched the talisman with eager fingers, then crossed her hands over it and pressed it against the woven collar that lay over her shoulder blades. She closed her eyes and breathed hard, like a sexually excited mare after a long, uphill chase by a stallion—lower lip down, nostrils wide, drawing in great drafts of air and shivering with every revitalizing pull. "Yes! I feel its strength! It pours into me like blood sucked hot from a still-living kill!"

She opened her eyes to stare straight at Masau. "Where is the bride? If I am to hunt the great white mammoth and be reborn through his death, there must be a sacrifice."

Something ugly turned within Masau's gut. It shadowed the morning sun, and it stung his belly like the well-placed fangs of a viper, injecting venom deep into the moment, poisoning it. The sacrifice . . . in his joy at being reunited with Ysuna, he had momentarily forgotten about Ta-maya.

Maliwal grasped the opportunity to respond for his brother. "She is behind us, on the hill beyond the encampment. She awaits your summons!"

"She is perfect?" Ysuna's eyes fixed upon Masau's.

"She is," he replied quietly. "Perfect."

"Then bring her to me," Ysuna commanded. "Thunder in the Sky has been waiting too long for his bride."


As she walked toward the encampment of the People of the Watching Star with Chudeh to her left and Tsana to her right, Ta-maya knew that never had she seen such a great village, smelled the smoke of so many cooking fires, or imagined that so many lodges could be assembled in one place. Not even at the Great Gathering had all the people come together into one huge camp. The bands would assemble, each occupying its own section of woodland or open space, until all across the base of the Blue Mesas there were many small villages. The air would be resinous with the scent of burning pinyon wood, and at night individual little cooking fires would cause the hills to glow as though festooned with stars. But here the lodges were like strange, tall trees growing one next to the other for as far as the eye could see. There were hundreds of them! And they were not at all like the neat, small round-topped huts of her people. They were upside-down cones of various sizes—all very large—with support posts protruding from the pointed tops. There was not a bit of thatching to be seen on any of them. Instead they were covered with large, well-fleshed hides, skin side out, and each was painted in wondrously bold designs of black and white and many bright colors. She thought of Kosar-eh and smiled. How the clown would delight in the sight of these lodges! She was sorry that he could not be here to share the spectacle with her.

Homesickness dulled the happy edge of her excitement and anticipation of her wedding. *If only my mother were here!* she thought. What was Ha-xa doing now? And U-wa? Was Mah-ree with them, or was she off on some errand of mercy to the animals of the Red World, walking with Cha-kwena and the pups, bringing good things to eat to the great white mammoth, and peering through the tule reeds at the herd and at the little white son of their totem? The thoughts filled her with longing for home and family, for the familiar surroundings of her village, and for the teasing banter of the old widows, and even for Dakan-eh. She wondered if he had made peace at last with her memory. She hoped so. When she met with him again at the Great Gathering, she would try to make amends, to bring some special gift for him and for his new woman, Ban-ya. She owed them both an apology, something that would show them that she was truly sorry for having been so selfish and callous about their feelings.

"Come, girl. Ysuna waits!"

Chudeh's sharp voice jerked her from her reverie. They were close to the village now. A teeming throng of people and dogs had assembled on either side of the tusked skulls and piled bones of mammoth, which lined the pathway into the heart of the complex. As she walked on she tried not to look at the bones or to remember that she was marrying into a tribe of mammoth hunters. She gritted her teeth and resolved to be strong.

These were a handsome people, tall and strong. Even

the dogs seemed overjoyed to see her. She smiled as the villagers called out to her.

"Welcome, Bride!"

"Welcome!"

"Come gladly to the People of the Watching Star!"

"We greet you with happy hearts!"

"Behold! The sun shines on the new bride!"

"Welcome to the new daughter of the People of the Watching Star!"

It was impossible not to be thrilled and grateful for the tumultuous reception.

*May the totem of my ancestors be glad for me! May Great Ghost Spirit understand and forgive me! What has been done cannot be undone! I did not know that the one to whom I would give my heart would be a mammoth eater. I have consented to become his woman. I will live at his side. I will bear his children. I will be a good woman to his people. But I will not eat of the flesh of my totem, nor will I touch its hides or meat or drink its blood. This I swear on the sacred bones of First Man and First Woman! This I vow to Grandfather of All, who is Life Giver to my people!*

She walked in silence between her two escorts. The children of her new tribe were throwing sage leaves and small, fluffy, brilliantly colored feathers before her, strewing her pathway with fragrance and downy plumage that had been tinted red, blue, green, and yellow. She walked through a rain of perfumed color and upon a carpet that made her think of the petals of springtime blossoms. She smiled more sincerely as the rising wind of morning blew some of the fluffy feathers against her. They clung to the fringes of her fine new dress, tickled her face, lodged in her hair, and brought to her nostrils the sweet, heady scent of the purple sage leaves with which they had been mixed.

Ahead, the bone-lined pathway ended before a great lodge. Masau, with Blood at his side, stood with Maliwal before its closed entryway. A tall post was directly behind them. Feathered and bone-beaded strips of thong streamed from the top of it in the breeze. A woman stood between the brothers. She was the tallest, most astoundingly clad, and amazingly beautiful woman Ta-maya had ever seen.

Overwhelmed by the woman's magnificence, the girl caught her breath. The priestess raised her arms, palms up, and smiled radiantly as she gestured Ta-maya forward.

"Come to me, Bride. Come to Ysuna. Come to Daughter of the Sun. Come and be one with your new sister and the People of the Watching Star."

# 4

Cha-kwena did not know how long he had stayed beside the pool. In a daze he looked around. It was midmorning. What he had not believed by night and had questioned during the dawn still lay before him.

Now, in the full light of the well-risen sun, he could no longer deny the truth: The little white mammoth was dead. The men of the People of the Watching Star had killed it and its mother. By the look of its decomposing body, he guessed the men had killed it when they had gone hunting before the wedding feast. Two broken spear shafts remained within the unbutchered carcass of the cow. A cracked foreshaft protruded from the skinned rib cage of the calf. He recognized their colors and carvings: One spear was Tsana's; the other spear and the foreshaft were Maliwal's.

The boy stared straight ahead, taking it all in, believing it at last. Hoyeh-tay's worst fears had come to pass. Lions in the skins of men were loose within the Red World, hunting and feeding upon the People and upon their totem animals. They had come to kill the little white mammoth in this sacred place, of which they would never have known had a blind fool not ignored Hoyeh-tay's warnings and shown their leader where it and its sire might be most easily hunted. How clear the lies and the deceptions were to him now.

*Maybe I should not have brought you here.* He heard his own voice echoing to him from out of the past.

Cha-kwena looked straight up the canyon walls and through the trees, to the place where Mah-ree, Masau, and he had knelt together upon the overlook. He saw Masau as he had seen the man that night—a lion in the skin of an eagle, with the face of a predator.

*What is it, my young brother shaman?* Cha-kwena remembered Masau's query as clearly as he recalled his own defensive reply.

*I have no brother,* he had responded.

And now he remembered the mesmerizing black eyes watching him from within the even blacker mask of Masau's tattooing and recalled the wide, white perfection of the man's compelling smile. *Does the Watching Star not rise over the Red World? Does the great white mammoth not walk within its light? Are the People not one? Are those who are called to the shaman's way not united in spirit as well as blood? What should I call you then, Cha-kwena?*

Now, as on that night, West Wind was sweeping into the canyon. It was warm and promised a golden day. Nevertheless, Cha-kwena shivered as he got to his feet. Tears were spilling from his eyes, but he did not feel them fall. He was numb, emptied of all emotion, as, staring at the slain mammoth within the pool, he spoke aloud to the shrike-faced specter of the past. "You have done this, Masau. You have betrayed me. You have murdered my grandfather. You have killed Owl. You have butchered the little white mammoth and its mother, as you have butchered my people in the White Hills and on the far side of the Blue Mesas. You have seduced Ta-maya away from all those who love her, not to be your woman but to be meat for the perversions of those who call themselves the People of the Watching Star. And when you have finished with her, you will bring your people from the north to hunt and kill the greatest mammoth of them all."

He curled his right hand around the sacred stone and turned his eyes once more to the overlook. Now, not for the first time, but for the first *acknowledged* time, a vision came to him. It was similar to the vision he had experienced long before, when he had been seated with the other shamans on the holy mountain.

He saw an eagle circling high, flying over all the Red World. He saw Life Giver and his little family plodding across the land of his ancestors. The little white son was not with them. He saw himself as a small, brown, yellow-eyed bird, riding high upon his totem's back.

He saw himself take wing and fly so high that he could look down upon all the Red World and beyond. He could see the women and girls of his village gathering ricegrass and tubers as they waded knee-deep in the waters of the Lake of Many Singing Birds. Ta-maya was not with them. Mah-ree, shadowed by the wings of the soaring eagle, looked up and waved. But in his vision Cha-kwena, still a bird, turned away. He soared. He banked. He dove. He flew high again, pursuing the eagle to the upper limits of its flight until the eagle circled him, eye to eye and beak to beak, the most transcendently beautiful and dangerous-looking creature he had ever seen.

"Are you not afraid, Cha-kwena?" the eagle challenged.

"I am not afraid," he replied.

The eagle mocked him with the laughter of a woman, and then, as can only happen in a vision, the eagle became a shrike, masked and taloned. It impaled him through the heart upon a thorn that was a spear—a spear of bone, with a head of black obsidian.

And now, within the vision, he heard a mammoth trumpeting in agony as a baby mammoth, lost and dying, bleated and cried for a mother who could not rescue it from its pain.

Somewhere beyond the caul of blue mist a woman wept. He knew that it was Lah-ri and that he could not help her; she was beyond help. She had chosen the way in which she would walk, and now, like Hoyeh-tay and Owl, like Shi-wana and Naquah-neh, she had blundered into the path of lions and and had died.

The vision was expanding. The wind held the smell of smoke and fire and burned meat . . . the stench of death and destruction—the decimation of the People of the White Hills and of the People of the village that lay beyond the Blue Mesas.

He gasped because the People of the Village of the Lake of Many Singing Birds would be the next to suffer. He saw his people dead, their lodges burned. He saw their totem slaughtered and reduced to a pile of bloodied bones upon which ravens fed.

The vision swept him away, then transformed him. He was no longer a bird; he was Coyote, Little Yellow Wolf. He was wise and wary and fleet of foot as he led his pack across the Red World, not away from danger but into it . . . above it.

Deer and Hare and Rabbit and Mouse ran at his heels. They were all somehow a part of him. Hawk and Swallow and Brother Bat and Owl flew above him, and yet he saw the world through their eyes. At last he saw himself upon the promontory. Lions circled below, howling in defiance, roaring in frustration, because, try as they might, they could not ascend the heights. The People, alive again, were with him on the promontory. They hurled spears and rocks and bladders filled with hot oil.

As suddenly as it had come, the vision vanished. Cha-kwena stood in silence. He was shattered but strengthened and reborn.

"I am not your brother, Masau," he declared aloud. "I am Cha-kwena. I am Hawk. I am Owl. I am Deer. I am Hare. I am Mouse. I am Rabbit. I am Swallow and Bat, and, yes, I am Eagle. I am Mammoth! I am Coyote! I am Brother of All Animals, and Guardian of both the sacred stone and the totem of the People of the Red World. I am your enemy, Masau. And when you come south, I shall find you and shall drive you from this land. And if Ta-maya has come to harm because of your betrayal of my trust, I will see you dead for what you and yours have dared to imagine as your destiny. I am Cha-kwena! I am *Shaman*! And I am your enemy!"

Thunder growled over the distant mesas, but Masau did not hear it. In the company of Blood, he had been walking since noon outside the village of his people and trying to shake off the deep discontent that had come upon him when Ysuna had embraced Ta-maya. By now the daughter of Tlana-quah would be in the priestess's lodge and under her spell. Having been introduced to an eager and influential friend and supposedly guileless confidante, Ta-maya would forget her fears of his people. By now all would be in readiness for her to be prepared for the day of her wedding . . . and of her death.

The shaman of the People of the Watching Star walked with a long, tendon-straining, earth-pounding ferocity that sent the blood surging in his veins and caused his breath to snag in his throat as he exhaled angrily through his teeth. Puzzled, the dog looked up at him. Masau paid no attention to the animal; he was unaware of all but his own tormented thoughts.

The hut of purification had already been raised. Tomorrow the construction of the great dais would begin. After the rituals were observed, the girl would go to her fate.

This time he, not Maliwal, would paint his body gray, don the skin of his totem, and dance before his bride. This time Mystic Warrior, not the Wolf, would lure the girl onto the dais and accept the sacred dagger from the hands of a willing sacrifice.

His jaw tightened. He thought of the way in which he would kill her—quickly, so quickly that she would suffer neither pain nor terror before she died. There would be no hesitation on his part. This time the bride would go cleanly to the god. This time the offering would be perfect. This time, when Ysuna ate of the heart and drank of the blood of the sacrifice, the youth of the girl would pour into the veins of Daughter of the Sun. This time when the One Who Brings Life to the People danced in the skin of the sacrifice, she would be transformed, strengthened, made young again.

He longed for Ysuna's restoration to youth and health and beauty. And he trembled against the astounding pain that the price of it was costing him.

"Ta-maya." As he spoke her name a rush of bitterness soured his mouth. His lips turned down. How beautiful she was! How kind and caring and infinitely trusting. He despised her for the very attributes that made her the perfect sacrifice. Like her sister, Mah-ree, and the youth Cha-kwena, Ta-maya created a softheartedness in him that shamed and demoralized him.

He could not rationalize his feelings toward her. He knew only that when in her company he felt disoriented, and his eyes went blind to all that mattered in this life. No doubt it was because of her nearness that instead of killing Shateh, he had saved the man's life. It still enraged him to think of it. It would be good when she was dead. It would be good when they were all dead—all the guileless, passive lizard eaters of the south, and all the compromising, ancestor-defiling bison eaters of the plains . . . especially his own father. Only then would he find relief and be a man again.

Again thunder rumbled in the mountains. This time Masau stared in the direction from which the sound had come. He frowned. When he had left the village, the sky was clear. Now, however, clouds were building over the southern ranges—dark clouds, full of the fury of a rising storm. He scowled, recalling Shateh's last words to him:

*It has been said since time beyond beginning that the tree that bends before a storm is the one that will not break before it.*

His reply came back to him as he repeated, "There will be no storm—unless I bring it."

Yet now he heard the snarling roar of distant thunder and saw storm clouds rising against the sky. Windblown, they assumed strange shapes, the forms of animals and birds . . . and of a young man leaping toward him with winged arms stretched wide, his face transformed into that of a coyote. The voice of Cha-kwena came to him across the miles:

*I will see you dead for what you and yours have dared to imagine as your destiny!*

At the shaman's side, Blood looked up, startled, because Shrike—unseen for days—suddenly flew close and attempted a landing on the shaman's shoulder.

Masau's face contorted into a mask of pure malevolence as he snatched the bird and, with one twist of his hands, broke its back. With an exhalation of contempt he hurled the bird to the ground and stomped it into the earth with his heels.

Unnerved, Blood took a backward step and lowered his head.

Annoyed by the dog's reaction, Masau shouted, "The bird was of the Red World. Like the girl, its life means nothing to me. Nothing! When the daughter of Tlana-quah is dead, you and I will lead Daughter of the Sun to the white mammoth. On that day the lizard eaters will die, the People of the Watching Star will be reborn, and Ysuna will be assured life everlasting."

Once again the sound of thunder echoed across the land. Then, with a start, the shaman realized that it was not thunder at all. Within the village, men setting up the ceremonial drums and beaters were testing the sounding quality of the skins. As Masau listened a terrible darkness settled upon his mood. It was as black and full of unwelcome shapes of portent as the clouds above the mesas.

"Come," he said impatiently to the dog. "This night Ysuna will wish to counsel with Maliwal and me. Before then I would seek a true vision within the hills."

He walked on. It was a few moments before Masau realized that the dog was not at his side. He looked over his shoulder to see Blood loping toward the village. It did not take a shaman's insight for him to know that the dog would be heading straight to the lodge of Ysuna, where he would enter if he could, or find a place outside, where he could be close to Ta-maya. In the long days and nights of traveling out of the Red World, Masau had noticed Blood developing some sort of affection for the girl, often choosing to walk at her side and to curl up against her back when he sought sleep.

His brows came together into a frown of annoyance. "Soon the sacrifice will be offered," he said to himself, eyeing the clouds and then shaking his head as he walked on. "Soon the girl will die. But it will not be soon enough for me."

# 5

It was nearly dusk when Cha-kwena reached the outskirts of the village. Mah-ree, perched on one of the big, lichen-covered boulders that stood along the well-used trail into the hills, was waiting for him. A pair of pups slept on her lap.

Her smile of welcome vanished when she saw that he was alone. "Where are the others?" she asked.

"They have gone in pursuit of the men of the north. They will try to bring Ta-maya home."

Her eyes were enormous. "But *why*?"

He did not slow his step as he walked past her. "It is as Dakan-eh has told us it would be, Mosquito—only worse, much worse."

She slid from the boulder and, cuddling the pups, fell into step beside him, too shaken to protest the hated nickname. "I do not understand," she said.

"You will," he told her.

Suddenly, as they rounded a bend in the trail and entered the village, people were all around them. Someone was calling for Dakan-eh.

In a moment Bold Man, tall, impudent, majestically scornful, appeared and strode to face the young shaman. "Well?" pressed Dakan-eh. "Where are the others? Did Naquah-neh and Hia-shi of the White Hills have good words to say about our 'brothers' from the Land of the Watching Star . . . or were they still there, so Tlana-quah decided to stay for a pleasant visit with our 'old and trusted friends'?"

Cha-kwena did not flinch. For a moment it occurred to him that he should ask Dakan-eh what he was doing here, but he already knew the answer: Before committing himself to another trek across the land—when only the spirits of the ancestors knew what he would find waiting for him in any of the other villages—Bold Man was skulking around, no doubt waiting to see if the headman would return. So Cha-kwena replied evenly, "Tlana-quah has led the others to the north. He found no friends in the White Hills. The men of the north had been there and gone, leaving Naquah-neh, Hia-shi, and every man, woman, and child of that village dead—save one. Sunam-tu, guardian of the shaman of the White Hills, told us what happened. You spoke the truth to us, Dakan-eh, when you informed us of what you found in the village on the far side of the Blue Mesas. It was the same in the White Hills."

Vindicated, Dakan-eh snorted nastily.

The People were too stunned to speak as Cha-kwena told them what they must know. He spoke quietly, forthrightly, leaving out only those details that would surely terrify the children and set panic loose within the hearts of the women. He informed them that Tlana-quah and the others had gone ahead to steal Ta-maya away from mammoth-eating liars and murderers with whom no daughter of the Red World could ever hope to make a life lest she defile the traditions of her ancestors. Cha-kwena chose to make no mention of the fate that lay in store for her if the men of his band failed in their intent. He said coolly, "It is the plan of the northerners to be waiting for us on the promontory when the bands of the Red World gather there under the light of the Pinyon Moon. They hope to steal the sacred stones from our shamans. If we stand against them, they will kill us. Perhaps they will kill us anyway, before they journey farther south in search of the white mammoth. When they find our totem, they will slay him and eat him and claim the Red World as their own."

Dakan-eh's head went high. In Tlana-quah's absence, his arrogance allowed him to assume authority as though he were born to it. He spoke as though he were headman, and indeed, in this moment, with no man bold enough to challenge him, he was. "Then we will abandon this village," he declared. "We will go into the hills. Cha-kwena will lead us to the secret place where the mammoth go, to the place that only shamans and our totem know of. The men of the north will not find us or the great white mammoth."

Standing close to Cha-kwena, Mah-ree bit her lower lip. "Oh . . ." she moaned, distraught as she looked up at Cha-kwena. "But they will. We took him there. He knows. . . ."

"He?" pressed Dakan-eh.

"Masau," Cha-kwena responded. "He is Shaman. I trusted him. I led him to the heart of the Red World, to the secret place where our totem and his kind shelter against storms and drink from sacred pools that are sacred no longer. He has betrayed me and all who have named him Brother. He and those who walk at his side have slain mammoth in that place. The pools are red with the blood of the little white son of our totem. Masau has proved my grandfather right—he and his men are the Brothers of the Sky. They have come from out of the Watching Star to destroy the People of the Red World."

The awful words hung heavily in the air. The People were breathless, staggered by the revelations that had suddenly come to them.

"Then we will go south," Dakan-eh said. "You, Mah-ree, have brought Grandfather of All close to this village so that he might eat of your medicine food. Now you will make him follow us as we leave this place."

Mah-ree's eyes were enormous again. "I have sought to heal him, Dakan-eh, but I can *make* him do nothing. He is Totem."

Dakan-eh was not pleased with her. "You will try!" he commanded.

Then Ha-xa spoke as one who is coming out of a bad dream. "Since time beyond beginning our people have dwelled in this village. We cannot leave it. Tlana-quah would never consider such a move!"

"Tlana-quah is not here," Dakan-eh retorted. "He is off chasing Ta-maya when he should be with his people."

Ha-xa blinked. Righteous indignation sparked hot within her eyes. "And what father would not do the same!"

Dakan-eh thought a moment, then shrugged. "If there is a man here who would speak in Tlana-quah's place, then let him come forward. If not, I am Bold Man, and I will tell you all that Ha-xa is right: In the time beyond beginning the ancestors came to this place to escape the Brothers in the Sky. We all know the story. Old Hoyeh-tay told it often enough!" He seemed to be growing taller with every word he spoke. His chest expanded, and his chin poked higher and higher until his head was tilted so far back that he had to look down his nose to see those who were staring at him. "Now the Brothers of the Sky have discovered the children of First Man and First Woman. How can we stand against them? You all have seen their spears. I, for one, have no wish to die. We will abandon this village. The time has come for this people to walk in the way of First Man and First Woman. We will leave the Red World. We will escape the Brothers of the Sky."

"No," dissented Cha-kwena. There was no hostility in his voice—only weariness and sadness. "You are not Shaman, Dakan-eh. By what right do you recount the genesis of the People? I, Cha-kwena, grandson of Hoyeh-tay, am the shaman of this band. The blood of all the generations of the magic men of the People flows in my veins. I will tell you that although First Man and First Woman came into the Red World to escape the Brothers of the Sky, they came following their totem. I ask you: Where walks the great white mammoth now?"

Dakan-eh scowled, resenting Cha-kwena's intrusion into his mastery of the moment. "How should I know? He is around someplace. He is always around someplace!"

"Does he walk into the sun?" Cha-kwena asked.

"He walks the lakeshore and the hills," answered Mah-ree, "and he circles back toward the sacred place. He's always circling these days." Then she added guiltily, "He has trumpeted in the night and called to me in my dreams, but I have been too busy with the pups and Mother Dog to heed him."

"He has not needed you, dear," soothed U-wa, consoling the girl as though she and not Ha-xa were Mah-ree's mother.

"But you have needed *him*," said Cha-kwena, not only to Mah-ree but to all who had gathered around him. "I, too, heard his trumpeting in the night but paid no attention. Now I know that he was mourning his lost son and its mother. He was calling me to the sacred place so that I might see with my own eyes the treachery of the men of the north. Had I listened and heeded, I would have followed him . . . I would have seen . . . and we could have gone after Ta-maya and stopped the Brothers

of the Sky from taking her away from the Red World.
Perhaps we might even have found a way to save the lives
of the People of the White Hills."

Ha-xa moaned and swayed, unsteady on her feet.

U-wa embraced her. "Our man will bring Ta-maya
home. Won't he, Cha-kwena?"

Dakan-eh's head came down. "Your man is headman,
U-wa, but he cannot see where his responsibilities lie. I
say that we follow the sun or risk ending up dead, like the
People of the White Hills and those on the far end of the
Blue Mesas!"

Ban-ya, standing with her mother and grandmother,
glowered at him with disgust. "It is always so easy for Bold
Man to run away," she accused venomously.

He stiffened and stared at her with an equal measure
of poison. "What else is there to do? We are few; they are
many. Their weapons are magic. Ours are—"

"As long as a single sacred stone remains in the possession of the bands of the Red World, the power of our
totem will be with us," Cha-kwena interrupted. "If we
flee, who will warn the other bands? If we run away, will
we not hear the death lamentations of our brothers and
sisters and be haunted by their ghosts in whatever land we
may find and claim as our own? And will Dakan-eh assure
us that our enemy will not pursue us as surely as the lions
pursue the antelope when it takes flight?"

"Why would they follow us?" Dakan-eh asked, sneering. "We are but one small band! They will choose instead
to seek the sacred stones of all the others upon the sacred
mountain."

Cha-kwena caught his breath, taken aback by the ease
with which Dakan-eh dismissed the lives of the other
people of the Red World. "The People of the Watching
Star hunt the power of the sacred stones, but they also
hunt the meat of our totem," he stated grimly. "They will
find him and kill him. And on that day all the People of
the Red World will die. And so I say that we send runners
to the other bands. I say that we alert the headman of the
Blue Sky People, the People of the Place of Many Reeds,
the People of the Valley of Many Rabbits, the People of
the Red Hills, and the People of the Mountains of Sand. I
say that we call together all the hunters of the Red World

and unite upon the sacred mountain to await the coming of the People of the Watching Star. No one can come against us there without our first seeing their approach. If the bands of the Red World stand together upon the sacred mountain, the Brothers of the Sky cannot prevail. And stand against them we must, for I tell you now that from what I and Dakan-eh and those in Tlana-quah's party have seen of the People of the White Hills and the village beyond the Blue Mesas, we must stand against them or die."

"What of Ta-maya and the others? We cannot just turn our backs upon them and walk away." The question had come from Ban-ya.

Cha-kwena looked at her with surprise. The effects of her long overland trek with Dakan-eh still showed on her face. She looked tired, thin, almost frail. And yet her expression was one of such earnest concern for her friend and the missing members of her band that he could not help but take pride in knowing that such a woman was of the blood of his people. "If there is a way to bring Ta-maya back to the band, Tlana-quah will find it," he said, and wished that he felt as certain as he sounded.

"Of course he will!" seconded Siwi-ni with absolute certainty. She held her baby to her breast as her other sons stood around her like a bastioned wall of tender saplings. "My Kosar-eh is with him! Our clown may have lost the use of one arm, but no man is braver or more resourceful."

Annoyed, Dakan-eh eyed the aging little woman. "He should be here with you and his sons to cheer his people in their hour of need, not off chasing another man's woman!"

Siwi-ni's eyes went small and sharp with anger as she chirped out as pugnaciously as the little bird for which she was named, "In this hour, which brings us word of death and danger, not even Kosar-eh could cheer his people! And what would his sons have to say of their father if he turned tail like a frightened rabbit and ran away to safety while others stood bravely beside their headman and risked their lives for Ta-maya's sake? She is more than a child of our headman. She is a daughter of this band! Her flesh and blood belong to all of us! But you would not understand this, Dakan-eh. You are no longer Bold Man. You are Rabbit Who Runs Away! You cannot think beyond your own damaged pride."

Dakan-eh's face congested with fury at the unexpected insult. "They will never bring her back! They will all die, just as the people died in the village beyond the Blue Mesas! All of them!"

The little woman's features puckered into a knot of defiance and pride. "Then we will honor their brave spirits as they walk the world beyond this world. And in the meantime, I say that we heed the advice of our shaman rather than that of one who would turn his back upon the other bands of the Red World and upon a woman whom he once claimed to love." She turned her back to Dakan-eh. "Cha-kwena, would you have us wait for Tlana-quah to return before we leave for the holy mountain?"

The question was as pointed as it was unexpected. It struck the young man hard. His right hand rose and curled around the sacred stone. He closed his eyes. He called for a vision, and it came. The corners of his mouth turned upward into a smile, for he was not alone. Hoyeh-tay was with him, and Owl sat upon the old man's head. They were in the cave. Clearly he heard himself say, *But how do you know how to understand the signs, my grandfather?*

*Because he is Shaman, stupid boy!* retorted Owl.

Hoyeh-tay, ignoring the bird, had advised Cha-kwena to trust the third eye, which would lend a sense of knowing, a sense of how things will or will not be. He had urged his grandson to accept the gift of inner vision, even when it showed something he did not wish to see or when the consequences were unknown. The old man had paused, looked straight at Cha-kwena, and said, *You are Shaman now.*

The images of the cave, the owl, and the beloved old man dissolved. The inner eye opened wide within him to recall the vision that he had experienced by the pool. He saw himself upon the promontory. The eagle was flying above him. The bands of the Red World were assembled all around him. Far below, hundreds of lions were gathering, all coming from the north . . . coming now.

He opened his eyes and stared straight ahead. When he spoke, it was with a calm authority that overrode Dakan-eh's earlier blustering. "The men of the north will not wait for the rising of the Pinyon Moon. We cannot wait for Tlana-quah's return. We must leave for the Blue Mesas now."

"But what have you seen for my Ta-maya, grandson of Hoyeh-tay?" Ha-xa was near to tears with worry.

Cha-kwena shook his head. When he spoke, it was with a solemnity that caused his heart to ache. "I have seen nothing, Woman of Tlana-quah," he replied, averting his eyes from hers, for the absence of a vision concerning Ta-maya seemed a vision in and of itself; the implication was more than he could bear.

It was warm within the lodge of the high priestess. A small fire glowed within the hollow of a large stone lamp. Ta-maya sat near it, next to the priestess, with the newly arrived dog Blood lounging close to her bare, folded limbs. The lamp fascinated her. She had never seen anything quite like it. The hollow was filled with melted tallow, and the scent of the burning wick of twisted forest lichen was strange but pleasant.

Thunder growled in the distant mountains. A mouse scurried along the heights of the ridgepole. Ysuna, the dog, and the girl all looked up. The mouse vanished.

Ta-maya smiled wistfully. "It will rain soon. My mother always said that mice move about in daylight before a storm if they are unsure of the safety of their nest. And my little sister said that—"

"You must think of me as your sister in the days to come, dear one."

Ta-maya sighed gratefully. The mother of Masau was so kind! So solicitous! It was difficult to imagine ever having feared meeting her. She had been within the lodge of the high priestess for hours, and even though nearly everything within it was composed of mammoth hide or bone, her initial revulsion had been soothed by the caring woman's deferential manner. Other women had followed them inside, carrying food and paunches of warmed water. After Ysuna had sent them away, she had eaten of what seemed to be some sort of blood meat. She had offered it to Ta-maya but had not pressed the girl when, instinctively knowing that it was mammoth meat, she had refused it. After consuming her portion, the priestess had seen to it that Ta-maya strip naked and wash her body and hair.

"If you will not eat, then you must bathe. The warm water will relax you after your long journey. How fair you are, and without blemish. Masau has chosen well," the priestess said now, and Ta-maya blushed with pleasure at the compliment and felt overwhelmed by the woman's concern. Ysuna took it upon herself to assist Ta-maya with her bath, moistening soft buckskin cloths and dipping them in a fragrant paste made of some sort of root that turned white and frothy, like bubbles in a fast-flowing stream, when mixed with warm water.

"Here, let it be as though you were the daughter of my own body," Ysuna had urged, and Ta-maya yielded gratefully to the priestess's overtures of friendship.

Ysuna's long fingers had worked the fragrant paste into a lather upon Ta-maya's head and had massaged her skin with such skill that the girl had found herself giggling and protesting that she would surely dissolve away into nothing if Ysuna did not stop.

The priestess smiled patiently. "Like Masau, I am Shaman. You must yield to my magic," she said softly. Her ministrations continued until Ta-maya closed her eyes and drifted in a blissful limbo of complete relaxation. The long fingers of Daughter of the Sun moved over every inch of her skin, soothing her slender arms and soft breasts and massaging her back and limbs until Ta-maya found herself sighing with delight.

Then, scrubbed and clean, with the dog at her side, she knelt naked before the priestess while the woman combed her hair with the many-tined, intricately carved comb of antler. Ysuna was beautiful despite the wear of age. Ta-maya felt saddened, for Ysuna's body gave off an unpleasant necrotic scent, which no amount of fragrant oils had been able to mask. Probably the effect of some sort of lingering illness, Ta-maya thought. The girl's heart went out to her. She could not keep herself from confiding, "Oh, Mother of Masau, I will try to please you in all ways. You are so good to me! You make me think of home. I miss my family so much."

"Of course you do, dear one, but you must know that you have a new family in my people, in my sons and in me."

"I am very grateful."

"We do not wish you to be grateful. We long only for you to come to us with a happy and consenting heart, to be filled with gladness and eagerness on your wedding day."

Ta-maya looked down into her lap and blushed. "I am eager to become the woman of Masau," she admitted.

"He is the most perfect of all men. And you it seems are indeed the most perfect of young women."

"No, surely not. But I will try to be perfect for him."

A female voice spoke the priestess's name from beyond the shelter's closed door skin.

"Enter," Ysuna called.

A young girl complied. She came on her knees into the lodge. Not once did she look at Ta-maya or the priestess as she placed a neatly folded leather parcel onto the hide-covered floor. Then she scooted out as fast as she could, still on her knees, with her head bent so low that her nose touched the floor.

Ta-maya had never witnessed such subservience. It puzzled her. "Can she not walk?" she asked.

"Yes, dear one, she can walk. In my presence, deference is required of many. My powers are great."

Ta-maya tilted her head. "Is she afraid of you?"

"She does not know me as you do. But here, let us unwrap her offering. She had brought food and drink to us."

"I . . . I mean no offense, but as I told you, I cannot eat of the meat of mammoth."

"Nor would I ask you to, dear one. Here, look: A fat rabbit has been caught and cooked for you. And here is a flask full of a drink that is traditional among my people— the fermented juice of chokecherries, bison berries, currants, rare roots, and fungi, spiced with the sap of pinewood. Drink deeply. You will find it soothing to the mouth and blood."

Ta-maya drank deeply. She found the liquid soothing to the mouth and blood . . . and to the brain. "Oh!" she exclaimed, suddenly light-headed and flushed and thick tongued. Her vision swam. She blinked. Ysuna seemed to be rippling before her. The most extraordinary warmth was filling her body, numbing her mouth. She licked her lips and was not certain if they were still in front of her teeth. "I . . . feel . . . so strange."

Ysuna smiled. "Yes, I know. You are sleepy now, in need of rest."

"I . . . yes . . ." With a sigh, she lay down onto her side, wrapped an arm around Blood's shoulders, and succumbed to a deep, drugged sleep.

Ta-maya did not hear the low, warning growls of the dog or feel the touch of the priestess's hands or the questing invasion of her body, affirming her virginity.

"Do not growl at me, Dog, or Masau will need all his powers of inner vision to know what has happened to you after I have smashed your skull, dismembered you, and fed you to your brothers!" The words hissed from Ysuna's mouth.

Blood lowered his head. His muzzle quivered as he showed his teeth.

But Ysuna was not intimidated. Her face was transformed as she lowered her own head, displayed her teeth in warning to the animal, and growling, sent the dog moving back on his haunches . . . but only a little. He was still close enough to Ta-maya to spring to her defense. Ysuna's brows went wide. "You are loyal to the sacrifice, I see. Or has Masau sent you here to watch over her? There is no need. She is safe. For now."

The dog laid his head upon his forepaws and stared at her. There was no trust in his eyes.

Ysuna gazed down at Ta-maya. "So young . . ." Again she hissed her words, and again her face was transformed, but this time into an expression of jealous loathing as she withdrew her noticeably aging, high-veined hand from between the smooth flawlessness of Ta-maya's inner thighs.

Her own flesh had once been as smooth, as flawless, as sweet . . . her own body as incomparably, heartstoppingly young and perfect in all ways.

"No more . . ." She trembled against the truth.

Kneeling back, she could feel the ache of sickness in her loins, the low heat of fever that burned constantly beneath her skin and eyelids. When she drew in a breath to steady herself from the dread of ever-increasing illness, she caught the foul stench of the warm purulence. It had been oozing from her womb since she had last sought to draw moon blood from it with the questing tip of the sacred dagger.

A spasm of revulsion shook her. "I *will* be young again!" The words were a declaration of pure frustration.

Blood's head went up. His ears went back, his snout shot up, and his teeth were showing.

Ysuna paid no heed to the animal. She moved angrily to roll the girl onto her back. When the dog rose and growled again, Ysuna, with an upraised palm and a tone of indisputable and fearless authority, commanded him to stay. He obeyed, but every hair was standing upright along the line of his spine.

"No harm will come to her. She was born for this," the priestess assured quietly, gently, soothingly as she leaned forward to caress the girl, to run her hands covetously over her face and throat, along the curve of her shoulders and sides, over her belly and limbs and breasts. "So fine . . . so young . . . so beautiful . . ."

Suddenly her face worked with hatred and envy. Her hands closed into hurtful knots over Ta-maya's breasts. The girl moaned from the pain. Ysuna's fingers flexed, then twisted cruelly. She smiled when the girl sighed and tossed in her sleep and tried to rouse herself, to move away from the pain.

The dog barked sharply once and lunged to position himself between the girl and the priestess.

Ysuna, startled and off balance, knelt back. She eyed the dog dangerously. "Move against me, and it will be the last move you ever make. Masau may name you Friend, but I do not. With my bare hands I will tear out your throat."

Blood growled. He lay down where he was and stared at the woman as though challenging: *Try me. I am not afraid.*

Ysuna rose. She stood above the dog and girl and looked down at the daughter of Tlana-quah. Never had she seen a more perfect young woman. *Never.* Masau *had* chosen well. Her mouth pressed inward against her teeth. Would he hesitate to place the dagger when the time came? Had his spirit, like that of the dog, been touched and turned by this exquisite offering of flesh and bone and blood, which he had brought to her across the long miles? Her lips tightened into a scowl. He had turned away when she had embraced the girl. He had strode out of the village as though impelled to do so.

Her eyes narrowed. Soon he would be back. Soon she would summon her attendants, and they would carry the unconscious girl to the hut of purification. Ta-maya would pass the night there alone, drugged and dreaming the mindless, meaningless dreams that mindless, meaningless girls had been dreaming since time beyond beginning. And while the girl slept Ysuna would counsel with her sons, and together they would formulate the future of the People of the Watching Star. She exhaled deeply and ran the sound back and forth through her larynx until it became a purr, like that of a lioness.

Blood's ears went back.

Ysuna ignored the animal as she spoke softly to the sleeping Ta-maya. "You have drunk of more than the blood of berries and pinesap this day, dear one. The blood of mammoth was also in that flask. Now it is in you. In the eyes of the god it makes you one of us."

Beyond the lodge, beyond the village, beyond the broad plain of grass, thunder rumbled over distant mountains.

Ysuna tensed, listening. The sound was an affirmation of her intent. Thunder in the Sky, the great spirit mammoth that walked hidden within storm clouds in the world beyond this world, was waiting for his bride.

The priestess, quivering, raised her head, closed her eyes, and whispered to the totem of her ancestors, "Yes, she is for you. Soon she will come. You will be pleased by this sacrifice. She is the best and most perfect of all!"

The dog watched, unblinking, alert, scenting danger and death within the woman.

Ysuna opened her eyes and fixed her gaze past the dog and upon the girl. "Soon I will drink your blood. Soon I will consume your flesh. Soon I will dance in your skin. And then I will bleed again, as you and all the young women bleed, in rhythm with the rising of the moon and without the aid of the sacred dagger. Soon I will be well and strong. Masau will look at me as I have seen him look at you, for your strength and youth and beauty will be mine. Soon you will be dead, and I will be reborn. Then my people will leave this camp and journey into the land of the great white mammoth. When I find him, I will kill him. His power will become my power. And then, unlike you, I will live forever!"

Blood was growling again, snarling, showing his teeth again.

She looked at him and snarled back. "And on that day you will die, too, Dog . . . if you live that long!"

# 6

The people of Tlana-quah immediately sent runners to the various villages of the Red World. Two days later, laden under heavy packs and dragging their belongings on thong-lashed frames made of hardwood poles, the villagers turned their backs upon the Lake of Many Singing Birds and upon the settlement that had been their home for generations. It was an appropriately lugubrious day—gray, humid, and overcast. Thunder was booming on the far side of the mountains.

"It will be raining on the Blue Mesas," said Dakan-eh with a scowl.

"It will be raining everywhere until we drive Brothers of the Sky from the Red World," replied Cha-kwena glumly.

"And until Tlana-quah returns with Ta-maya and the others," added Ha-xa hopefully.

Cha-kwena nodded bleakly.

"How will he know where to look for us when he returns?" U-wa asked.

"Our trail will be easy enough to follow," he replied, grateful for the woman's optimism. Neither had the slightest doubt that the headman would return from the north. He wished that he shared their confidence. "Come," he said. "It is a long way to the holy mountain."

Wearing Hoyeh-tay's robe and bonnet, Cha-kwena led his people on.

"There are too many of them."

Tlana-quah lay belly down upon the crest of the hill. Kosar-eh lay to his right, and the other four men in his traveling party were spread out in a single line to his left. The encampment of the People of the Watching Star was below them. The headman knew that he was not the only one to feel sick with fear at the sight of it.

"Their numbers are like blackflies hovering over a marsh—too many to count, too many even to imagine," said Ma-nuk, gape jawed with awe.

Tlana-quah knew the truth when he heard it. His mouth was dry, his belly was queasy, and the palms of his hands felt like the skins of dead fish.

"Ta-maya is there somewhere," Kosar-eh said through gritted teeth.

Tlana-quah swallowed; his spit went down hard. He had hoped that they would catch up with the travelers before they reached their destination. At the back of his mind he had envisioned himself slipping into the encampment in the deep darkness before dawn, slapping a hand over Ta-maya's mouth as she slept alone beneath the stars, and then hefting her over his shoulder and carrying her away before anyone noticed his presence. It was an ill-conceived vision, but he had known that all along. It was unlikely that his daughter would be sleeping anywhere except at the side of the shaman; with Masau beside her, Tlana-quah's chances of abducting his daughter were minimal . . . even if she wanted to come with him. Besides, the men of the north had dogs with them. The dogs would bark and growl if a stranger came uninvited and unannounced into their midst.

Ma-nuk was shaking his head. "If Sunam-tu spoke the truth, Ta-maya could be dead already."

"We do not know that!" Kosar-eh was emphatic.

Ma-nuk kept shaking his head. "We can't just walk into that camp and ask for her."

"Why not?" Kosar-eh asked.

Tlana-quah darkly eyed the clown. "Because they will want to know why we have followed them. What will we tell them? That we want my daughter back for no reason other than reconsidered affection for her? They would never believe us. And if she has somehow come this far with them in ignorance of what they are, she will not want to leave her new man."

Kosar-eh's brow was down, and his lids were slitted as he stared ahead unblinking. "We could tell them that her mother is ill, having her baby too early. Or we could say that Mah-ree has been injured by the great mammoth. If Ta-maya is still alive, she would return with us without hesitation."

"And if she is dead?" asked one of the other hunters. "We will have risked our lives for nothing. They will kill us as they have killed the men of the White Hills."

"For her sake it would be worth the risk," replied Kosar-eh.

"If you are attempting to play the clown in order to cheer us, you are failing," said Tlana-quah coldly. "Is your life of no meaning to you? Have you forgotten that you have a woman and children waiting for you back in the village? Have you forgotten that these men of the north have left a trail of dead mammoth and dead people behind them? By whatever ruse we enter their encampment, they will know that we have followed them. They will know that we have seen the slaughtered mammoth and the slain men and women of the White Hills. They would never allow us to leave their encampment alive."

Kosar-eh's head turned. He leveled a steady gaze at Tlana-quah. "I have not forgotten these things, Tlana-quah. Have you forgotten that Ta-maya is your firstborn daughter, that you are Brave Hunter, Man Who Alone Kills Jaguar, headman of your band . . . and that these men of the north have dishonored you?"

"Better dishonored than dead," Ma-nuk muttered.

"I say we go back," said the man next to him. "We can do nothing for Ta-maya here. Come, Tlana-quah, you have done all you can. You have another daughter, and two women big with babies await your return to the village."

"Go, then," goaded Kosar-eh. "I will stay. I will discover what has become of her. I will bring her out from among them if I can."

"You will die," warned Ma-nuk.

"Then I will die," Kosar-eh snapped contemptuously.

With the bright light of the sun beating down on his jaguar-skin cape, Tlana-quah stared at the crippled clown and went cold with shame. The cape—not the man—was shaming him. It was reminding him of a lifetime of lies: of a dying old jaguar, of a solitary, terrified young hunter approaching the animal and then hooting with joy at finding that the great spotted cat posed no threat. Only then did he hurl his spear, then hunker down at a safe distance to wait for the animal to die.

*Brave hunter!* he thought in disgust as he recalled it all—the long hours of waiting, the impatience that had prompted him to cast another spear, then throw stones at the head of the incapacitated cat until its skull was a bloody mash of ruined skin and fractured bone.

*Man Who Alone Kills Jaguar!* he thought, repulsed. He had been alone that night, but that's all that was true in the tale. He envisioned himself tiptoeing close—but only after the jaguar had breathed its last. He had withdrawn his spears and then placed them again and again. With what care he had placed those spears so that any experienced hunter would be able to study the resultant wounds and name them fatal.

He shuddered. His shame was terrible, heavy, as crushing as the weight of the carcass of the jaguar as it had lain warm and limp and painfully heavy across his shoulders as he carried it back to the village, proclaiming for all to hear, "Behold! I am Tlana-quah! I have killed the great spotted cat! No more shall it be a threat to the women and children of this band!"

Three moons later, when the old headman had died, Tlana-quah had been named headman in his place. No one had spoken against him. No man was more fit to lead the people than Tlana-quah, Brave Hunter, Man Who Alone Kills Jaguar!

Ma-nuk and the others were slithering down the side of the hill, moving away from the encampment of the People of the Watching Star and back along the route they had taken out of the Red World. Only Kosar-eh remained at Tlana-quah's side. The headman unflinchingly met the eyes of the clown, then scanned the hillside and the camp below.

"We will wait until night," he decided. "Perhaps we will see her by then. If not, we will go among the people in the dark before dawn and look for her."

"It will be dangerous," warned the clown.

"Is Kosar-eh afraid?"

"Yes."

Tlana-quah appreciated the man's honesty. He was aware of the jaguar skin lying warm against his own. It lay lightly upon him now, no longer oppressive with the weight of shame. "It is said that fear makes men wise. It is said that fear makes men move with caution."

"Are you suggesting that we go back with the others?"

"No. Not until I can do so with Ta-maya at my side . . . or the blood of her killers on my spears and the satisfaction of their death on my spirit. I must not dishonor the skin of the beast I wear."

Kosar-eh nodded. "You have not done so to this day," he said.

Tlana-quah did not reply; some truths were better left unspoken. He was headman. He was Man Who Alone Kills Jaguar. Now, for Ta-maya's sake, it was time to be what he had claimed to be all along: a brave hunter, a great hunter, a hunter bold enough to risk his life for the sake of the band.

The skin of the little white mammoth was spread across the floor of the lodge of the high priestess. The spearheads lay upon it, each projectile point facing in the direction of one of the Four Winds. Ysuna, Maliwal, and Masau knelt beside the skin of the calf.

Ysuna was pleased. It lighted her face. "You have done well," she said softly. "Both of you."

Maliwal's head went high with pride. He looked straight into her eyes; the pupils were enormous. He knew that she had been drinking deeply of the ceremonial liquid, which had earlier sent Ta-maya into unconsciousness. The girl was so small that her body had no defense against even a meager portion of the drink; it was always so with the brides. Ysuna had summoned two young women to carry the girl from the lodge, and Ta-maya had been as limp as a new corpse in their arms . . . and so lovely to look upon that every man in the band had come close to feast his eyes upon what would soon be meat for the god.

Maliwal's loins warmed at the memory. At Ysuna's invitation, both Masau and he had then taken the girl's place within Ysuna's lodge. His brother had just returned to the village. He had been in a surly mood, so surly that when his dog had trotted toward him from the hut of purification into which Ta-maya had been carried, he had commanded Blood to stay away from him. Ysuna, however, had seemed extremely pleased. She had offered the flask to them. Each had sucked off a deep draft. They were big men, so the brew did little more than heat their blood, pleasantly warm their genitals, and loosen their tongues.

The need to speak was strong in him now. And so Maliwal urged boldly, "Heal me, Ysuna. Heal me now! Before the bride is given to Thunder in the Sky, take the scars from my face. Let me officiate as a whole man at the sacrifice, and as unblemished as the bride."

Her mouth tightened. Her eyes narrowed. Wariness and resentment swam in the pupils. "Do you still test my power, Maliwal?"

"No, Ysuna! It is my very faith in your power that prods me to speak! And my need to be whole again—a man from whom others will not turn away in disgust when I take my wolf's cloak off and bare the place where my ear once was!"

The priestess's eyes settled on Maliwal's face. She smiled at him. There was neither warmth, affection, nor compassion in her expression. Ysuna's smile was the smile of a drowsy viper coiled on a rock, the long mouth closed and stretched wide, the eyes unblinking, fixed, staring. "Why do you care so much about the thoughts of others, Maliwal? I look at you and do not turn away. What more do you need to satisfy you in this life?"

His breath was a ragged exhalation of disappointment. "I have killed mammoth for you, Ysuna. I have brought you sacred stones and slain men and women and children in your name. I have killed this calf so that you might eat of its heart and look upon its hide and know in your spirit that its sire lives and will soon be yours for the taking. I have done all this. All I ask in return is a little magic from you, so that my man's pride will be restored and—"

"But I have already given you my magic, Maliwal. It is because of my magic that you are alive. Without me you would never have grown to manhood, let alone have experienced a man's pride! You need not ask for what you already possess, Maliwal. Are you not the Wolf of Ysuna? On this last venture to the south you have proved your worth to me once again. You are no longer in my disfavor. Your scars are as beautiful to my eyes as is the perfection of your brother's face and body."

The comparison wounded him.

Embarrassed by it, Masau lowered his eyes and avoided looking at his brother.

Ysuna measured them both. The bladder-skin flask of ceremonial drink was in her hands. She drank, then replaced the bone stopper and tossed the now-flaccid vessel onto the mammoth hide before them. "Drink, both of you."

They obeyed. Then, slowly, she rose, and as she did so her hands untied the claw-tipped thongs that held her cloak. The feathered garment fell to the floor. Tall, proud, she stood naked before them. In the warm, dusky shadows of the closed interior, she appeared to be as she had always been—young and strong and beautiful beyond measure or comparison.

"As the bride awaits her wedding day in the confines of the lodge of purification, so, too, must Daughter of the Sun be made ready for the ritual," she said huskily. She cupped her breasts and raised them. Then she turned and moved slowly to the wide, soft mattress of piled furs and hides that was her bed. She turned again to face the brothers. She knelt on the mattress with her limbs spread wide, her hips moving, and her hands smoothing her breasts. "Come to Ysuna, both of you. Come, fill me with your youth and power. Fill me now. Put life into me, as I have given life to you."

# 7

Darkness was falling upon the land of grass.

Ta-maya awoke to the sounds of drums and to a woman's screaming. The girl propped herself on an elbow, looked around the firelit little lodge, and wondered where she was. She rose, drew a soft bed fur around her nakedness, then moved across the lodge and paused at its entrance. She swept aside the weather baffle and looked outside.

She caught her breath. Fires blazed throughout the village. The drumbeat had stopped. People were busy at what seemed to be a thousand unfamiliar tasks as they worked together to assemble an enormous structure of bones. *Mammoth bones!* She recognized ribs and leg bones and saw that the two halves of a huge tusked skull that had somehow been cleft was being raised by ropes and pulleys to a platform made of gleaming white femurs and polished pelvic bones.

"Go back into the hut, Bride. This is not yet for your eyes."

Ta-maya blinked. A girl of her own age had spoken to her. She deliberately blocked Ta-maya's view across the village.

"Please," the girl implored. She was pretty but pinch faced with fear as Blood, growling, looked up from where he lay across the entryway. Not daring to take another step lest the dog attack her, she said, "You must go back inside, Bride. Ysuna will cut my throat if she knows that you have looked upon the dais."

"Ysuna would never do such a thing!"

"Please, Bride, call back the dog and return to the hut. You must drink more of the juice of dreams that the

priestess has left for you. And later, if she asks, pretend
for my sake that you have seen nothing!"

A woman screamed again, and hackles rose at the
back of Ta-maya's neck. The cry had come from the lodge
of Ysuna. She recognized the voice as the priestess's. It
was a high-pitched shriek of agony, and yet, somehow,
intermittent laughter rose through it, along with moans
and the frenzied, savage howls of pure orgasmic release.
These fell away into long, wailing ululations. Never in
Ta-maya's life had she heard a human being make such
sounds. All across the village, people had paused in their
work to listen and to mutter to one another as the screams
went on and on.

"Please . . ." whispered the girl. "Please go back into
the hut."

But Ta-maya could not move. The shrieks continued—
now cries of pain, now cackles of laughter, now mad,
incendiary roarings. Appalled, she would have gone to
Ysuna, but the girl risked the ire of the dog to take hold of
her arm and stop her.

"Stupid girl, stop! She is not alone! Don't you know
the cries of a mating when you hear them?"

"Mating? She screams with pain, not pleasure!"

"Pain and pleasure are one and the same to Daughter
of the Sun!" declared the girl vehemently, attempting to
turn Ta-maya around and force her to reenter the hut.

Blood got to his feet. The fires of the village reflected
in his eyes. The girl wisely released Ta-maya's arm and
took a step back; Blood kept on growling, head down, tail
tucked, the hairs on his back standing straight up.

Ta-maya laid a soothing hand upon the animal's head.
Her touch gentled him instantly. She was relieved. He
had frightened her as much as he had frightened the girl.

"Please, Bride, before someone sees you, you must
go back into the lodge."

Ta-maya, staring ahead, suddenly felt cold. From where
she stood, she could see the lodge of the high priestess . . .
and the naked man who emerged from it wore his long,
black hair like a cloak streaming down his back.

"Masau?" She was shaking as she spoke his name.
"Has he joined with his own mother?"

Beside her the girl trembled. "Yes, and Maliwal is

still with her. Masau and his brother are more than sons to
her; they are life itself."

He had seen her and was striding toward them. Within
moments he was standing before the girls, his body rigid,
his face livid.

"What has she seen?" he demanded of the girl of his
band.

She could barely speak. "I . . . I . . . it is not my
fault. The screaming of Daughter of the Sun woke her and
I . . . I—"

"Get out of my sight." His words held both warning
and command.

The girl ran off.

Stunned and quivering, Ta-maya looked up at him.

His face was set, his eyes were dark with anger as he
placed a hand upon her shoulder and, without another
word, escorted her into the lodge. He led her to her bed
of furs. She knelt with her back to him and stared into
shadow. Tears were running down her cheeks.

"I do not understand," she quavered. "Among my
people, it is forbidden—*unthinkable*—for . . ."

"The People of the Watching Star are your people
now, Ta-maya." He had knelt behind her. Now he reached
to turn her toward him, then raised her face to his with a
gentle hand. "Look at me, Bride. What do you see?"

She swallowed. In the darkened interior of the lodge,
she saw a shadowed face . . . masked perfection . . . the
man she loved, and yet a stranger, someone from another
world. "I see a man whom I do not know very well."

His hand moved to stroke her face. "I name Ysuna
Mother," he told her quietly. "She has given life to me
and to Maliwal. But, in truth, my flesh is not her flesh.
The woman who gave birth to my brother and to me died
many moons before either of us was old enough to speak
her name. Ysuna took us when we had been abandoned by
our own tribe and by Shateh, the father whose life I hold
in contempt and yet chose to save when we were among
the Bison People."

She stared at him. She felt amazed, relieved, yet
confused and hurt. "Am I to be second woman to Ysuna
then?" she asked in a small voice.

"You will be second woman to no one, Ta-maya."

There was a hardness to his tone that put her on edge
as he said quietly but fiercely, "She was once as young as
you, and as beautiful and without blemish. Now she grows
old and sick before my eyes, and I feel that her heart
bleeds with fear of death as much as mine bleeds as I
yearn to restore her to youth and life. There is nothing
that I would not do for her. Can you understand this,
Ta-maya?"

She nodded. She could understand. She did understand. Her eyes sought his. "I am very young. You have
seen many more moons than I. Someday, when you become old, my heart will bleed in fear of your death, and
there will be nothing that I will not do for you . . . as
there is nothing that I would not do for you now."

He tensed, sucked in a quick, jagged breath, and
stared down at her.

Now, for the first time, she realized that she was as
naked as he. Her face flamed; she was grateful for the
shadows as his hands reached out to her . . . touched her . . .
traced the contours of her body . . . and then laid her
back. Her heart was pounding as he looked down at her.
She could see that the anger had gone out of his face.
Sadness had replaced it. Her hands took his, raised the
fingers to her lips, and kissed them, tasting the saltiness of
them with her tongue.

The change in him was instantaneous. "Ta-maya, you
do not make this easy for a man."

She smiled. Now he would take her. Now he would
join with her. She wanted him. She was ready for him. Yet
he did not move to join with her. He drew his hand from
hers and slowly traced his fingertips over her body.

Her skin rippled beneath his touch. No man had
ever caressed her as Masau was now with his gentle
movements. His tracings became long, sure, tender
strokings. She trembled. Her body throbbed, moving to
inner rhythms that she did not understand. When at last
he bent to kiss her, it was not upon the lips, but upon the
brow and cheeks and the lobes of her ears, and then her
throat and breasts and belly. She gasped as he opened her
thighs and moved to enter her gently with his tongue,
savoring the sweet warmth of her virginity, setting fire to

her senses so that with a cry of bewilderment she arched to him, opened to him even as he moved away.

He assumed a seated posture and gazed down at her as his hand resumed its slow, wondrous trespass. The tips of his fingers entered her, then moved, and probed, leading her in a tumultuous, solitary dance of passion until she fell back, sweated and trembling, awash in sensations that she had never experienced or even imagined before now.

He continued to look down at her. "At least you have had this much of a woman's joy before you become a bride, Little One," he said huskily, then turned away to reach for the flask that had been left by the side of her sleeping furs. "Here, drink deeply, then sleep. Dream of all that will gladden your heart and make you smile."

"I will dream of you," she told him, sitting up and drinking deeply as she held the flask to her lips.

"When Ysuna comes to you tomorrow to begin the ritual of purification, make no mention of what has passed between us—or of what you heard . . . before," he said, easing her back and gently placing the soft sleeping furs over her. "You are still virgin. Thunder in the Sky will not be denied his pleasure, as I now leave you and turn away from mine."

For a long time after he left her, Masau stood outside the lodge of purification. Blood watched him from the defensive position that the dog had taken beside the door. Masau was aware of the animal's eyes upon him; the man gave no sign of recognition, nor did he make an overture of friendship. Blood had chosen to place his loyalty with Ta-maya. Masau's mouth turned down. Soon the animal would have no cause to concern himself with her.

The encampment was alive with firelight and life. The dais construction would be complete by the time it was needed. Men were busying themselves with it while women were dragging bones and wood across the village to assemble two great pyres, which would burn high on either side of the dais when the time came for them to be ignited. The keepers of the thunder drums had raised the huge hide-covered disks of bent willow wood and hung them from posts of mammoth bone over meticulously banked fires; the heat of the smoking coals was slowly drawing the moisture from the hides. Now and then a man struck a drum with a padded beater to test the resonance. The sound was deep, invasive.

Masau flinched against it and the loud growls of a man coming to sexual release within the lodge of Daughter of the Sun. So Maliwal, the shaman thought, was still with Ysuna.

Masau frowned and shook his head. How could his brother bear to be in close company with her for so long? Perhaps Maliwal hoped that if he came into her enough times, she would be so gratified by his performance that he would heal his face. Masau's lips pressed against his teeth. A terrible bitterness filled him. Ysuna would not heal his brother. How could she? She no longer possessed enough power to heal herself!

Although she would not speak of it, although she would surely deny it, although she raged because of it as she opened herself to her sons and commanded them to fill her with life and youth even though their penetration of her body caused her to scream in pain, the stench of truth pervaded her lodge and had driven him from it. Darkness and scented smoke and oil had not been able to hide it. That which had once been beautiful, that which once had been beyond the corruption of age and illness, now reeked of both. The stench of Ysuna's body had sent him recoiling in revulsion. Withering, his organ had been unable to come to completion, and he had been incapable of doing anything but feign illness of his own. Ysuna was dying, and he knew for a certainty that he was dying with her.

And so now he stood motionless in the dark, grieving for her and for himself, and for the guileless, trusting little creature in the lodge behind him. Touching her young, healthy body had soothed his spirit and cleansed him somehow. Being with Ta-maya reminded him that he, too, was young and strong, virile and years away from the corruption of the flesh that was destroying the one who had given him life.

His jaw tightened. When all the sacred stones were gathered upon the holy mountain, when the white mammoth was slain and its flesh and blood were consumed by Daughter of Sun and the People of the Watching Star,

only then would Ysuna be healed . . . transformed . .
made young and strong again—a woman who would hun'
lions at his side again . . . and lie beneath him as swee'
fleshed and fragrant as a summer's dawn.

He closed his eyes and conjured memories of hi
past—of the woman who had battled the will of her tribe
to save the lives of two small boys . . . who had loved
them and cherished them when their own people had
abandoned them to be meat for the starving carnivores o
an endless winter. He owed Ysuna his life.

He opened his eyes. Although he stood as a grown
man in the encampment, the bitter winds of that long
gone winter of his youth chilled his soul.

Chudeh was coming toward him. He gave the traditional greeting and said, "The work on the dais goes well
At dawn tomorrow, when the morning star stands on the
horizon, all will be in readiness."

"Good," replied Masau, and tried not to think of the
tender, trusting heart and yielding body of Ta-maya when
he added, "The sacrifice cannot be made soon enough."


"Cha-kwena!"

He stopped dead in his tracks. Who had called? He
turned and scanned along the way that he and the others
had traveled. The night had not yet reached the peak o
darkness, and the stars were very bright. The milky path
by which the spirits of the ancestors made their way across
the heavens from one ghostly, starlit camp to another was
a river of light beneath which his people were plodding
behind him. They walked silently, staring disconsolately
at their feet, in the way of weary trekkers who knew that
they have no recourse but to continue and have resolved
to make no complaint.

They had walked far since leaving the village. Although they had rested often, in their need to reach the
Blue Mesas as quickly as possible, they had agreed to
make no traveling camps and to walk by dark—when
moonlight and the lay of the land allowed—as well as by
day, and to carry their little ones and drag their elders
upon their travois when exhaustion claimed them.

The soft, familiar hills of home were far behind them
now: the boulder-strewn ridges where lizards warmed them-

selves in the summer; the fragrant sage flats and wind-combed tule marshes; the deep blue waters of the Lake of Many Singing Birds; the meadow where the roses grew; the cave of Hoyeh-tay; the darkly forested mountains that concealed the secret canyon of the shamans and the ancient juniper and the sacred spring . . . all were part of a world that they carried with them in their hearts and minds. With every step they took away from it, every man, woman, and child thought of home and longed for the day when they might return.

But first the Brothers of the Sky must be driven back into the stars from which they had somehow plummeted to earth. Otherwise none of them would ever see home again.

Cha-kwena frowned. Who had called his name? His people had fallen well behind. They were trudging on, slump shouldered, their feet shuffling beneath the weight of heavy loads. If any of them had beckoned him, no one raised a hand in acknowledgment.

"Cha-kwena! Brother of Animals! Guardian of the sacred stone and of the breath and heartbeat of your totem! The sun rises out of the east and warms its house in the fire of the south wind!"

The voice stunned him. It had come from beside him—a deep, masculine whispering of power and warning. But no one was standing beside him.

"Heed us, Cha-kwena!"

He winced. A second voice, a female's, was speaking now, from somewhere very close. He caught his breath. His right hand shot up and pressed the sacred stone that lay against his throat. The voice was coming from the talisman!

"As the ancestors came walking into the rising sun, so must it now be for the People and for their totem. Heed us, Cha-kwena! Walk into the sun with First Man and First Woman! You cannot stand against the north wind, and the west wind speaks only of endings."

His heart was racing. Within his palm, the contours of the sacred stone seemed to meld with his flesh to cast images into his mind of a man and a woman. Clad in unfamiliar furs, they moved toward the rising sun through icy mists and a haze of distance that his mind could not grasp. The North Star stood above and behind them. Owl flew before them. Hoyeh-tay walked at their side.

"Come, Cha-kwena, come walking with us into the sun!" called the old man, while strange and familiar animals ambled and leaped and ran before him and First Man and First Woman. There were odd, hook-nosed little antelope; strange deer with antlers as huge and complex as the branches of wind-torn trees; grazing sloths, prong-horns, and camels; horses, short-legged wolves with massive jaws, and long-horned bison; and slope-headed mastodons, lions, and leaping cats with fangs like crescent moons. He recognized the lumbering girth and dancing gait of the leather-skinned creature that his people called Horn Nose.

Then he caught his breath as, from out of the clouds of his vision, he saw a blue-eyed, wolflike dog walking beside a mammoth unlike any he had ever seen. It was immense. Its tusks cleft the mists, and its body was furred in long shards of ice. When it trumpeted, the sound of its voice shattered his vision.

Cha-kwena's heart went cold. He did not understand. Had First Man and First Woman and Hoyeh-tay asked him to turn back from the purpose to which his earlier vision had called him? He had already committed himself and his band to the northward trek. If they turned now and ran before the Brothers of the Sky, they would be pursued—hunted and slaughtered as the People of the White Hills had been slaughtered.

Confusion swarmed in his head like winged insects hatching on a summer pond. It could not be! Surely fear of the unknown had caused his thoughts to turn toward home. But even as he looked in the direction to which First Man, First Woman, and Hoyeh-tay had called him, the mountains that now stood between his people and their beloved village by the Lake of Many Singing Birds were like a great black, featureless wall rising against the stars. Deep within the soaring darkness of that range were the canyon, the overlook, the waterfall, the pools, the sacred spring, the bones of the little white mammoth and its mother, and the great white giant himself. If the People of the Watching Star came through the mountains into the Red World, they would find him there. They would kill him.

"Did you hear him, Cha-kwena?" asked Mah-ree. The weary girl had come to stand before him.

"I heard . . . something. . . ."

"Grandfather of All awaits our return from the north."

His head went high; there seemed to be a message in her statement. "Yes . . ." he agreed, realizing that perhaps the vision made sense, after all. "Mah-ree, we must return to him."

He felt a little better as he looked down at her. Even in the darkness he could see the fatigue on her face. The big female dog, Watching Star, was heavily laden with side packs and stood at Mah-ree's side; nevertheless, the girl was bent nearly double under the weight of the backpack that was almost as large as she was. Many small baskets filled with personal belongings dangled from thongs, which had been attached to the willow-wood frame. Lashed to that were several tightly rolled tule mats and antelope hides; one large, lidded basket was conspicuous among all the others, and a puppy managed to poke its head through one of the small holes in the ventilated lid. The bright, curious eyes of the little animal were full of starlight as it looked at Cha-kwena from over the top of Mah-ree's shoulder.

"Are you carrying all *thirteen* of the puppies?" he asked, incredulous.

"Of course. No one else wanted to help me with them. Dakan-eh said that they are of the Land of the Watching Star and should be left behind. But I would not abandon them. Look at their mother! See how strong she is? See how proudly she carries my burdens? When the pups are grown, they will carry the burdens of the band, and when we journey to the Blue Mesas for the autumn gathering, we will be the envy of the tribe!"

Her enthusiasm annoyed him. She had spoken as though nothing had changed, as though they were not fleeing for their lives. He glared down at the dog and remembered that on the same day that Masau had given it and its pups as a gift to the band, the strangers had taken Ta-maya away to become meat for their totem. There was no cause to doubt him. But Cha-kwena could not bring himself to tell Mah-ree this or to scold her for bringing the pups. Instead he said tersely: "You carry too much as it is."

The girl's face puckered with righteous indignation. "Ha-xa and U-wa are both big with babies. I carry things for Ta-maya as well as myself. My sister will need them when we find her."

The words struck him to his heart. *If* we find her, he thought, turning away and staring ahead again. Big Lake was up there somewhere; he could smell it. If only it had disappeared as it had once before, leaving the way to the sacred mountain open before them.

"Do you smell water?" Dakan-eh had caught up with them. He seemed unaffected by the long walk. "Yes." He answered his own question. "I smell a thick dampness in the air. By the ancestors, that is a big lake! It will take a long time for the entire band to get around it." He eyed Cha-kwena nastily. "Make a wish, Shaman! You made the waters return to Big Lake once. If you are what you claim to be, now is the time to make them go away!" This said, Dakan-eh readjusted the weight of the single traveling roll that he carried slung over his shoulder and continued on.

Disgusted, Cha-kwena watched him walk away. Lightning pulsing above the Blue Mesas caught his eyes, and thunder rolled far away, miles away.

Where was Ta-maya now? he wondered, and felt sick with misery. Where were Tlana-quah and Kosar-eh and the others? *On the other side of the sacred mountain, too far away for me to help them even if I could!* He trembled with hatred and frustration.

"You shiver, Cha-kwena. Are you cold?"

"Yes, Mosquito," he said, and loosened the basket of pups from her back and slung it over his forearm. Then he put his arm around her shoulders as he began to walk again. "I *am* cold. Let us go on. We have a long way to travel and much to do before we can follow the sun back to our totem."

"Do you think that my father and Kosar-eh have led the others to Ta-maya by now, Cha-kwena?" she asked softly.

"That is the dearest hope in my heart, Mosquito," he replied. And yet, even as he spoke, he winced against premonitory dread and somehow knew that this would never be.

Maliwal's spear flew like a silent, deadly hawk in the darkness. Tlana-quah cried out, struck through the upper back before he even realized that he was being stalked.

Kosar-eh heard the high, thin song of the weapon as it passed overhead and well to his left. He could not identify the sound until it ended in a dull, meaty *thwack* and Tlana-quah's explosive exhalation of pain and shock rent the night as surely as the spearhead had rent the jaguar-skin cloak and the flesh and muscle and bone of the man within it.

The clown lay still, holding his breath, pressing himself to the earth, and hiding within the tall grass and darkness. Tlana-quah's deep, garbling chokings were those of a man drowning in his own blood. Another spear sang in the air close by. This time when Kosar-eh heard it strike, the exhalation that came from the headman was not followed by an intake of air. Kosar-eh waited. Although he knew that Tlana-quah was dead, he ached with the need to find a way to force the headman to breathe. But Kosar-eh dared not move, dared not breathe.

Moments passed. Soundlessly he exhaled and then drew air back into his lungs. His heart was pounding. He wondered if the predators could hear it. They were coming closer. He could hear them clearly: *Three men, perhaps four. And dogs!*

He cursed himself for not having picked up the sound of their approach before the attack on the headman. Tlana-quah and he had been so careful as they had at last begun their own slow, meticulous advance toward the sleeping village at the base of the hill. When the men had inadvertently flushed a ground-dwelling bird from her nest of grass and twigs, dogs had begun to bark in the village below, prompting Tlana-quah and Kosar-eh to remain motionless, as silent and patient as the night itself. They had waited, watching, until the dogs had become quiet again. At last the men had moved forward, inching their way on their bellies down from the hill.

So intent had they been in their purpose to rescue Ta-maya that they remained ignorant of the men who, with dogs evidently muzzled beside them, had circled to come upon them from behind. Their scent and the sound of their footfall were blown back and away by the night wind.

Kosar-eh did not hear the flight song of the third spear, but he felt its impact as the projectile point sliced through the skin of his upper arm and straight into the ground beside him. He felt no pain, yet his senses were screaming in a silent confusion of amazement, terror, and relief. Had the aim of the spear thrower been only slightly to the right, the weapon would have broken his arm and pinned him to the ground. As it was, the strike had done no more than damage the skin and topmost layer of muscle of an already unserviceable arm. He was hurt, but not badly; he could still evade the fate of Tlana-quah!

The realization made him sneer with the pleasure of defiance as, with a hard twist to the right, he propelled himself downhill, rolling faster and faster until—with an agility that could only have been achieved by exposure to extreme danger—at exactly the right moment, he dropped the spears that he had managed to grip tightly to his body with his left hand, leaped to his feet, and broke into a mad run.

Someone angrily commanded him to halt. Then a spear hissed over his left shoulder. Kosar-eh dodged right, raced forward a few paces, and then dodged left, bending so low that his knees banged his chin as he ran on, hoping to lose himself in the rolling contours and high grasses of the hills.

He might have won the race had they not turned the dogs loose. The animals were on him in moments. Raging in a fury of frustration, Kosar-eh curled himself into a tight, protective ball as they savaged his back and shoulders until his pursuers pulled the beasts back.

"What have we here?"

Kosar-eh recognized the voice of Maliwal before the man pulled him by his hair and then kicked him so hard in the side that he momentarily lost consciousness.

Seconds later he was looking up at the scar-faced brother of Masau and three of the men who had been with him in the Red World. They smiled viciously when they saw that he recognized them.

"I thought I smelled the stink of lizard eaters when the dogs started barking," said the man named Tsana.

Maliwal growled in amused speculation. "Who would have thought that the cripple would be man enough to follow us, eh? But then, we all saw the way he looked at her. He wanted her, as though a girl like the headman's firstborn would ever have looked back at such a freak. Why ever did they let you live, Clown?"

"So that someday I could face you down and kill you if you have harmed her!" He knew that the threat was useless, but he did not care. He tried to rise. They let him get to his knees, then tripped him and sent him sprawling.

"He *is* amusing!" exclaimed Tsana vindictively.

"The other one's dead," Chudeh retorted.

"And his cloak?" asked Maliwal.

"Here. It's torn, but it can be mended if you still want it," replied Ston.

Maliwal snatched the jaguar skin and held it up to Kosar-eh. "Recognize this? It's mine now. What do you think of that, eh?"

Kosar-eh told him without words. He stood and spat in Maliwal's face.

Maliwal threw him to the ground and kicked him in the gut so hard that, once again, the clown lost consciousness.

When he awoke, he saw that Maliwal was wearing Tlana-quah's cloak and standing over him, watching with satisfaction as he rolled onto his side and was violently sick.

"It will be dawn soon," Chudeh remarked. "This will be our last chance to rest before the ceremony begins."

Maliwal growled again. "After these past hours with Ysuna I have need for rest—and a sweat bath. But first we must deal with this clown."

Kosar-eh was too weak to move, and yet he tried to rise, to get away. When Maliwal kicked him again, he lay still, and waited to die. He willed himself to do so like a man, not like a clown, without giving these killers any cause to laugh.

*Once I was a hunter, as bold as Dakan-eh and as strong.* He thought of his woman, Siwi-ni, and their baby and of Gah-ti and the other boys. He said a silent good-bye to them. *Tonight your father will die, but I will die bravely. And not before I try one last time to warn Ta-maya—if she is still alive. For if I can buy her life with my death, then I will die laughing.*

And so, twisting inward, he bellowed her name quickly, before anyone could stop him, "Ta-maya! Beware! They have betrayed you! They have killed Tlana-quah! They will kill you! Run while you—"

Once more Maliwal kicked him, then again and again, until Koser-eh relaxed and lay prone. And then he was kicked again, in the face.

He remembered no more until he awoke on the hill-top. He was seated on the ground with his hands bound behind his back to, he guessed, some sort of stake. His mouth was gagged and, from the feel of it, stuffed with the leaves of stinging nettle; the pain was excruciating, but not nearly so deep as the pain that emanated upward from his side and belly. He looked down . . . at the spear that pinned him to the ground.

"This will keep you in one place until you die," said Maliwal, taking hold of the shaft and wiggling it until Kosar-eh lurched and cried out in agony behind his gag. "What's wrong? Can you find nothing amusing in your situation, Clown?"

"Maliwal," urged Chudeh, "kill him and have done with it."

Kosar-eh tried to focus on the man through a blur of pain; he did not know whether to curse him or be thankful to him.

"Why?" asked the brother of Masau. "He will die soon enough. But not too soon. Do you see where I placed my spear? It's low, between belly and groin and away from the big vein. By tomorrow he will want to die, and if he has not done so, I will kill him. But not before he has seen the 'entertainment.' "

# 8

The sound of thunder drums shook the earth. All day long the world was filled with their resonance; but in the lodge of purification, a drugged Ta-maya slept soundly, and hearing nothing, she dreamed of home and the white mammoth and smiled.

In the sweat lodge of the men of the Watching Star, Masau and Maliwal sat alone.

Masau looked at his brother across the large steaming fire pit, in which heated stones glowed pink in the gloom of the closed lodge.

"Ysuna will not be pleased to know that you have taken the spotted cape of the lizard eater."

"She need not know from where it comes."

"Ysuna knows all things."

"Then why will she not give me back my face? Or cause my ear to grow upon the side of my head? Nothing in this world do I want more than these things. Why will she not give them to me?"

"When the sacred stones of the Red World are hers and the great white mammoth is dead, she will accommodate you. The power will be hers."

Maliwal's eyes narrowed. "Then when the sacrifice ascends the dais, do not hesitate to do what must be done, Brother . . . for Ysuna's sake and mine."

"I will not hesitate."

"She is rare, this bride. You want her for yourself. I can see that in you."

Masau made no comment. He reached out, lifted the water scoop that was fashioned from the cranium of the last sacrifice, dipped it into the large mammoth-hide water container, and then tossed the liquid onto the stones. They hissed and steamed as though in anger. He stared

493

expressionlessly into the mists, weighing the halved skull, his eyes half-closed and unreadable. "When next we sit together in this lodge, the skull of the new bride will be in my hands, and it will mean no more to me than this." He hurled it so hard into the fire pit that it cracked as it landed on the stones. "The girl is nothing to me. Daughter of the Sun must have the blood and flesh of this sacrifice. With my own hands will I offer this new bride to Thunder in the Sky and be glad in my heart when the one who has given life to me dances in her skin!"

All day Shateh of the Bison People sat alone, listening to the sound of the drums, which rode the dry, cool, rising wind from the north.

The previous night, after he had seen fires burning on a distant mountain, his women brought meat to him; but he would not eat. His children brought water to him; but he would not drink. His people and the elders of the tribe watched him in troubled silence. They said nothing. Their worried sighs whispered like the rising wind.

When the youngest of his wives came close and knelt to put his robe around his shoulders, he shivered, put his face in his hands, and would not look up, for his wife reminded him of the bride who had been taken north and of all the young girls who had gone before her to Thunder in the Sky.

At length the father of his second woman came with the other men of his band and stood around him.

"Soon another captive will die," said Father of Second Woman.

The eldest hunter of the tribe spoke. "One day the drums will sound, but we will not hear them, for the People of the Watching Star will have come against us, and it will be one of our own daughters who is fed to Thunder in the Sky."

"The younger two sons who were born to your long-dead first woman eat of the flesh of their own kind, Shateh," said the firstborn son of his second woman. "How many bands have they raided in their endless search for sacrifice? How many villages have we seen destroyed? How soon will it be before they must seek a new source of meat

and come for us and for our daughters? We all heard
Masau's last words to you. His threat was clear enough."

"We are many," added Eldest Hunter. "Perhaps not
as many as the People of the Watching Star, but we are
strong and unafraid. Those who were once put out of this
band should not be allowed to live as lions while we stand
back and allow them to offend the very forces of Creation."

Shateh looked up. "What are you saying?"

"You asked Masau and Maliwal to join with us. Instead they spurned you and our ways. They are no longer
your sons, Shateh. They are Ysuna's and warriors of the
Watching Star. Masau has vowed to kill us all. It is time
for Maliwal and him to die the death that should have
been theirs long ago."

"To the east and west, along faraway river crossings
and over distant hills, bands of this tribe have spoken
many times with you and the men of the Land of Grass
about them," said yet another of Shateh's sons. "They
have said that when the People of the Watching Star have
burned the last village in the country of the lizard eaters,
when they have eaten of the last mammoth, then they will
come to hunt the Bison People until we and the animals
upon which we feed are no more."

Shateh's face was tight and hard as he stared off
through slitted lids. "Masau had my life in his hands when
we clung together to the medicine pole. He gave me back
my life."

"And in return will you give him our lives when next
you see him?" asked Eldest Hunter. "The day will come
when you must ask yourself this question, Shateh."

Shateh scowled and shook his head. He rose to his
feet and exhaled decisively. "I have warned them. I have
urged them to bend against the coming storm, to turn
their backs upon Ysuna and the ways of the People of the
Watching Star. Now thunder drums are heard once more
upon the land. Tomorrow another captive will die. The
day that you speak of is here." Folding his arms across his
chest, he looked at the men who stood around him. "You
and you, go to the bands of the west. Tell them what I say
now. We must all take up our spears. We will make of
ourselves the storm that must come against those who will
not bend before the wind."

Eldest Hunter faced to the north, listened to the drumbeat, and shook his head with grim regret. "Their camp is far. Will the captive die before the storm sweeps the land?"

Cha-kwena felt relieved when Big Lake lay behind them at last; the People had rounded its easternmost shore and turned west toward the Blue Mesas. The choppy waters glistened gold in the light of the setting sun. A strong wind was sweeping down upon them from out of the northern ranges, riling the surface of the lake, driving sizable waves onto the shore. Cha-kwena listened to the unfamiliar sound of the surf and, when the wind was right, to the occasional sound of distant drumbeat.

"It must be coming from the mesas," Mah-ree said, looking wearily ahead. "There were fires on the sacred mountain last night. Our runners must have brought some of the other bands there ahead of us."

"No, the sound of drums comes from much farther away, from beyond the mesas," disagreed Dakan-eh.

"I have never heard drums like that," said Ban-ya, in her coyote-skin cape. "They sound like thunder rolling in the sky, yet there are no clouds." She was wan and wide-eyed with fatigue. The long trek was costing her. Ever since they had left the village, the girl had been unable to sleep well when the band stopped for brief rests, and she could not hold down much more than water.

Old Kahm-ree looked at her, then eyed Bold Man with a suspicious scowl. "We should rest again. My Ban-ya is tired."

"She is not the only one." U-wa sighed.

"Yes, Bold Man!" snapped Kahm-ree. "You should carry some of my Ban-ya's load."

"She is not my woman!" he snapped back, and stalked on.

Cha-kwena shook his head at the man's nastiness, then readjusted the weight of his own load. The Blue Mesas lay directly ahead, but the way would be uphill from now on, and it would soon be dark. "Let us go a little farther. The land rises ahead. We will stop at nightfall, get a good night's sleep, and then go on at dawn."

Ban-ya sighed a weary assent.

Cha-kwena tried to smile in encouragement in her direction; Ban-ya had made no complaint about the way she was feeling. Cha-kwena did not need to be a shaman to suspect what old Kahm-ree and the other women were already fairly certain of: that Dakan-eh had put life into her while the two of them had been alone and away from the village. If this was the case, she would be miserable whether they went on or rested; either way he would see to it that she try to make more of an effort to eat.

"Here," he said, and went to her. "Let me lighten your pack for a while."

Although Mah-ree frowned and jealously shadowed him, he took no notice.

Ban-ya turned so that he could remove a pack roll or two from her pack. She had adjusted her cape so that the attached head of the coyote folded back over the top roll of matting. The wind twisted it around, so Cha-kwena found himself staring at the upside-down face of Little Yellow Wolf.

*Come walking into the rising sun, Cha-kwena. You cannot stand against the north wind. Grandfather of All waits for you, and the west wind speaks only of endings.*

Startled, he stepped back. Little Yellow Wolf was dead; Dakan-eh had killed him. Coyote could not have spoken! But Cha-kwena was shaman now, and he knew that Coyote indeed had.

"We must go on," he replied, unlashing the top. "The People of the many villages of the Red World await us on the Blue Mesas. We will be safe there. From the heights we can combine the strength of the many bands to prevent the People of the Watching Star from coming through the sacred mountains into the Red World!"

*There is another way into the Red World from the north,* said Coyote, but even as his spirit spoke Ban-ya turned her head and looked at Cha-kwena so sadly that he heard nothing but her question:

"Do you think that we will ever see Ta-maya again, Cha-kwena?"

"Of course we will!" put in Mah-ree a little too aggressively. "Tlana-quah and Kosar-eh will bring her back to us! She may be waiting for us on the sacred mountain even now!"

\* \* \*

Ta-maya awoke to the sound of drums and to the low, dulcet sound of a woman singing. She sat up with a start, looked around at her surroundings, and, recognizing them, breathed out with disappointment.

"What is it, dear one?" asked Ysuna from where she knelt beside the small fire pit. She was arranging heated stones upon a bed of well-laid embers, using tongs of green willow wood.

"I was dreaming of home. I thought I heard Kosar-eh, our village clown, calling out to me."

"It is only natural for you to long for home at such a time as this, dear one. Here now, smile for me. I have brought a special gift for you." Ysuna held out a timeworn dagger of bone.

Ta-maya looked at it as it lay across the woman's palms. It was long, gracefully carved of bone, and yet, like the sacred stone that she had sometimes seen around Hoyeh-tay's neck, it possessed the texture of polished stone. It appeared to be very old, very valuable.

"Take it," urged Ysuna.

Ta-maya obeyed. It was heavy.

"It is for the bride," Ysuna explained. "Do you see the incised places on the blade? Yes? It is difficult to make them out. They are worn by time, dear one, carved by magic in days when the mountains walked and all the People of this world were one. Touch the carvings. Feel the power of the stone. As I make the sacred smokes of the bridal sweat bath for you, you must bathe the blade in the sweat of your body and polish it with your hair. Keep it close to your flesh during the coming hours of purification. Let it feel you and know you as its own. Then, when the wedding takes place, bring it forth to Masau, as a gift for the one to whom you will give yourself."

Ta-maya thought that she understood the significance of such a gift. "As a sign that I consent to be blooded by him?"

Ysuna smiled. "Exactly," she said, and the tip of her tongue emerged to moisten the circumference of her long mouth. "As a sign of your consent to be blooded."

# 9

"Great Spirit . . . Grandfather of the People . . . White Giant of many names, hear and behold me. I call to you in the name of the daybreak star. I raise my arms. I turn. I set my face toward the four corners of the world, where the spirits of the wind are born and where you, Thunder in the Sky, walk in the flesh of clouds and in the shadowing power of eagles. Behold me. I am Ysuna, Daughter of the Sun, wisewoman of the People of the Watching Star. On this dawn I bring to you a gift of life. On this dawn I bring to you a bride. May the blood of this people and of Thunder in the Sky be one."

At the sound of Ysuna's last words, a shiver of delight and expectation ran beneath Ta-maya's skin. The girl stood just outside the hut of purification. The night had passed so quickly! Ysuna had left her in the care of a new and silent attendant. In preparation for the ceremony, Ta-maya had been sweated and rubbed clean, and then, instead of being given a new dress to wear, she had been ceremonially painted from head to toe with a fragrant oil that had been colored red with powdered hematite and ground willow buds. Her hair had been combed, and a fragrant crown of silver-leafed purple sage had been placed upon her brow. Save for this one adornment and the glorious swirling patterns of the colored oil, she would go naked to her wedding.

Her heartbeat quickened. At last it was dawn. Soon the sun would rise above the curve of the hills. Soon the daybreak star would fade from the sky. And now, in this moment, she was about to become a bride.

The drums were sounding so loudly that they shook the world. Ahead of her, the entire band had assembled on either side of a long carpet of shaggy hide. At the end, Ysuna stood before the dais with her back to the crowd.

The platform was of overwhelming magnitude. Huge bonefires were burning on both sides of it. An amazing replication of a living mammoth, elaborately adorned with long strands of eagle feathers, multicolored tubular beads, and disks of bone, towered above the ground. Masau, his body painted gray, was ascending the broad stone steps that led to a raftlike platform, which was positioned between two halves of a severed mammoth skull. On either side of him, the hollow eyes of the skull stared sightlessly, and its massive tusks extended forward like two polished white tree trunks.

Fear fluttered like a caged bird within Ta-maya; she told herself that she had no cause to allow it freedom. She knew what these people were. Their ways, their customs, their beliefs . . . they were all entirely different from those of her own band. But she would become used to them in time.

"Ta-maya! Ta-maya!" The People of the Watching Star had begun to chant.

Every man, woman, and child had put on ceremonial paint and feathers and garments of pigmented skins in honor of the occasion. Even the dogs had been adorned. She smiled when Blood, a collar of eagle feathers around his neck, came trotting up to her.

"Will you walk with me to my new man on my wedding day, Friend Dog?" she asked him.

He nuzzled her hand.

Now Ysuna turned. She was in full ceremonial regalia, with her hair shining like the wings of a raven and her astounding cloak of feathers sweeping the ground at her feet. Nevertheless Daughter of the Sun looked old and ill, gaunt and as pale and hollow eyed as the skull of the mammoth beneath which she stood.

Ta-maya's heart went out to her. When Ysuna extended her hands and spoke her name, it was all the girl could do to keep from running to her side. But Ysuna had instructed her in the way in which she must behave as she approached the dais. With her gift for Masau in one hand and a sprig of juniper in the other—she had learned that juniper was sacred to the People of the Watching Star because mammoth favored it as food—she stood her ground and waited for the ritual to begin in earnest.

"Come to us, Ta-maya!" Ysuna summoned. "Come consenting to become the bride!"

"I come," answered Ta-maya in the way and with the words that Ysuna had taught her. "I come consenting to become the bride!"

As she began to move forward the change in the atmosphere of the assembly was instantaneous. The beat of the drums grew more intense; it seemed to permeate her skin, pound within her veins, and quicken her senses. On either side of her the faces of the People of the Watching Star seemed to float by. Such serious faces! she thought, their mouths set, their eyes full of secrets and anticipation, their pupils black and dilated, and their eyelids virtually unblinking. She noticed for the first time that there were no elderly or infirm among them.

"Behold!" they cried as one.

The beat of the drums quickened.

"Behold the bride!" the men shouted in unison, extending their hands and shaking scrotum rattles close to her face. The men reached to touch her as she passed.

She saw Maliwal standing back amid the throng. He stared hungry eyed, wolf eyed. She blushed and looked away. But then she looked back, startled. A spotted hide lay over one of his broad shoulders. A jaguar skin! The sight of it instantly recalled home and father.

*Oh, Tlana-quah, if only you and Ha-xa and Mah-ree could be with me now, to know that your daughter has chosen well in her new man and in her new people!*

Maliwal stepped back into the crowd. Now she recognized Chudeh and the other men who had accompanied her from the Red World. They all looked proud and openly approving. She was glad. From this day on they would be her brothers in this band, and each would hold a special place in her heart because he had been a part of bringing her to a new life among the People of the Watching Star with the man she loved. She smiled at them. When they averted their eyes, she was perplexed but not offended. Everything was so wondrous!

Ysuna had spent hours explaining the ceremony, but nothing had prepared Ta-maya for the spectacle before her. She realized that she could not possibly hope to remember every nuance of these people's complex traditions. She walked on, hoping that she had not unwittingly violated a taboo. Later she would ask Masau. Later. Now they must be joined as man and woman. Now she must become a bride.

The beat of the drums grew louder.

"She is beautiful! She is perfect! Behold a worthy bride!" proclaimed the women, trilling their tongues with an unnerving ferocity. They, too, reached to touch her as she walked by. She looked for Wehatla, the tremulous, talkative girl who had been her attendant when she had first awakened within the hut of purification; she had not seen her since the night when Masau had sent her running off in tears into the darkness. If Wehatla was among the throng of female faces, Ta-maya could not find her.

Still the beat of drums grew faster, louder.

"She comes!" the youngest children piped. Like their mothers and sisters, they reached out to touch her until it seemed as though every inch of her skin had been host to questing fingertips.

The drums stopped abruptly. The sudden lack of sound rocked her as she paused. She had reached the base of the dais. Ysuna stood directly before her. For a moment Ta-maya could not take her eyes from the collar around the wisewoman's neck and shoulders. It was the first time she had looked closely at it: the many stones, each so much like Hoyeh-tay's sacred talisman . . . the long, plaited strands of human hair . . . the many jointed bone beads, so much like human fingers that she frowned and strained to look closer. But then, from high above her on the platform, Masau called her name.

She looked up at him. Dawn was growing gold and soft pink behind his back. He was standing dead still, arms out, long hair blowing in the wind, his naked body glistening gray with oil, his arms and limbs resplendent with the colors and patterns that symbolized life to his people, and a pale cape of mammoth hide upon his back.

"Dear one, at last the moment comes!" Ysuna was radiant as she spoke.

Ta-maya sighed with pleasure as the wisewoman swept her into a brief but loving embrace. She could hold no rancor toward Ysuna for what had transpired between her and Masau and Maliwal. Masau had explained how it had been between them, so the incident was all but forgotten. She stepped back from Ysuna and stared up at Masau. How magnificent he was! No one in all of this world or the world beyond could equal him. And he had chosen *her* above all others to be his woman. Her heart filled with pride and love and desire.

Ysuna reacted visibly to the expression on Ta-maya's face. Her head went high. Her nostrils expanded. Her long eyes narrowed. A pale blue vein pulsed in the exposed length of her throat above the magnificent sprawl of her sacred collar. "Let it be done!" she called out. "The moment has come. Are you now my sister, Ta-maya? Are you now a daughter of the People of the Watching Star? Does the bride come consenting to her moment of union with us and with our totem, Thunder in the Sky?"

Ta-maya smiled. They had asked her that question repeatedly, and now the answer came as easily as the exhalation of her breath. "Yes. I come consenting to be the sister of Ysuna, to be the daughter of the People of the Watching Star, to be the bride of—"

"So be it!" Ysuna interrupted. Her features expanded into a mask of triumph as she flung her arms high and cried to the Four Winds, "Ta-maya, daughter of the People of the Watching Star, comes consenting to Thunder in the Sky! Let no man or woman or child ever say that it was otherwise!"

The drums began to beat again, very loudly, very fast, then even faster. They kept rhythm with the pounding of Ta-maya's heart. Elated, she almost laughed with pleasure as Ysuna stepped aside and urged sweetly, "Go to him, dear one. Go of your own will! Go to that which awaits you in the arms of Masau, Mystic Warrior and shaman of the People of the Watching Star!"

As Ysuna took hold of Blood's collar to prevent the dog from ascending the dais, Ta-maya went eagerly up the bone stairs. She did not notice the many ceremonially painted and feather-adorned spears that had been placed on either side of the bone stairway. With the juniper bough in one hand and the dagger in the other, her small, bare feet fairly flew as they carried her to her waiting man-to-be.

At last she stood before him. The daybreak star was fading in the west, and the rising sun was at Masau's back. She looked up into his face and, as Ysuna had instructed, held out her hands to him, to offer the juniper bough and the dagger.

He stared down at her. His mouth was set. His expressionless eyes looked through her, focusing on Ysuna. He did not move. He did not extend his hands to accept her gifts.

Her smile faded. Was he going to refuse her? She was aware of a stirring, a murmuring, a sudden restlessness among the assembled crowd behind her.

But then, with a ragged exhalation, he took her offerings. He closed his eyes and drew her close. The dagger was in his left hand. She could feel the coolness of the blade pressed flat beneath her breasts. She knew no fear of the blade. She was relaxed and yielding in his arms, until, at the base of the dais, Blood went wild.

Ta-maya turned her head and looked straight down the bone stairway to see the dog snarling and slathering, twisting violently against Ysuna's hold on his collar. When the collar suddenly snapped, Blood snapped with it. He was a wolf now, turning to savage Ysuna's hand and in the next instant pounding up the bone steps, his front paws slipping on the narrow stairs, his hind limbs pushing him forward. He was barking in a frenzy of intent that Ta-maya could not understand.

But she could understand the look of hatred and fury that transformed Ysuna's beautiful face into a twisted mass of ugliness as she snatched up not one spear, but two. And although her right hand was bleeding badly, she ignored Masau's command to hold and hurled the weapons with her left. In an instant, one after the other, the spears struck the dog through the spine midway up his back, passed partially through him, and lodged beneath the stairs, effectively holding him in place.

With a high, squealing yip of pain, he went limp, then whined piteously as he hung suspended, dying. And yet, even though his hindquarters were paralyzed, he still tried to move, to pull himself up to the platform to protect and defend his Ta-maya.

Masau had gone rigid. He dropped the juniper bough. Ta-maya felt a tremor shake him. He stepped back from her, moved her gently aside, and, with the dagger in his hand, descended halfway down the stairs and knelt above the dog. He laid his free hand upon Blood's head. The dog whined piteously and licked his hand. A sigh of remorse went out of Masau as the dog continued to reach with its front paws for purchase on the stairs.

"Enough, old friend. Be at ease now. You can do no more for her . . . or for me."

Ta-maya's eyes widened. She could not comprehend the meaning of Masau's words. His back was to her, but the set of his shoulders told her that he was struggling to contain his grief. She had not thought him capable of tears, but somehow she knew that his eyes were burning with them as he used the dagger to end the dog's agony. Blood's whines ceased, but Masau remained as he was, stroking the now-lifeless body of the dog whom she had more than once heard him call Brother.

Sobbing, she quickly descended the steps to bring her to his side. She knelt to lay a gentle hand upon his shoulder and upon the dog's.

At the base of the dais, Ysuna looked up and hissed malevolently, "That dog has needed to die for a long time now. It pleased me to kill it. But that which has begun this dawn has not yet been finished, Masau. Finish it. Finish it *now*, before the Morning Star fades from the western sky, before the god turns away in anger from his people once more."

For the first time, the bird of fear spread its wings and flew wildly within Ta-maya. The woman who stared up at her now was a stranger—an evil hag with death in her eyes.

Masau ignored Ysuna's command. Working in silence, with deliberate slowness, he drew the spears from the dog, desecrating the body of the animal no more than was necessary.

The drums were silent. Every member of the tribe was watching him. No one spoke. No one seemed to be breathing. The only things that moved in the entire village were the wind . . . and Ysuna's eyes as they narrowed and held upon him, skewering him with unspeakable rage.

Hefting the spears in his left hand and the bloodied dagger in his right, he rose and stared down at her. The light of the rising sun was in her eyes; but not even those soft, benign colors could dispel the blackness and cruelty burning from between her half-lowered lids. Her mouth was a downturned scar that seemed to cleft her face in two.

His brow came down. Did he know this woman? Was it possible that he loved her? A terrible weariness swept through him. He gazed down at the dog. Blood had known full well what he had intended for Ta-maya; the dog had witnessed many a sacrifice.

"Masau, the Watching Star is setting. The sun is standing on the horizon at your back. Ascend the dais. Thunder in the Sky is waiting for his bride." Ysuna's words were a warning as dangerous as the look in her eyes.

He stood motionless and remembered the viper on the rock. He took Ta-maya by the wrist and led her back up to the platform.

"Masau?" She spoke his name tremulously as she followed.

The drumbeat began again. Someone threw bundles of dried sage onto the bonefires to rekindle their blaze.

"Masau, I am afraid," whispered Ta-maya.

He did not answer. They were on the platform now. He released her wrist, shifted his spears and the dagger, positioning the sacred blade for use in such a way that the girl could not see what he was doing. "What do you fear, darling one?" he asked at last.

"Ysuna. The people. The way they look at me."

"Do you not fear me, Ta-maya?"

"I love you," she said simply and without hesitation, and then looked down and around, her face tightening with worry. "Are we not yet man and woman in the eyes of your people? What must happen between us on this dais before I become a bride?"

"Only this," he said, and drew her close. She came against him easily, eagerly. She put her arms around his waist and held him, pressed her face against his chest and kissed him. Even when she felt the dagger resting upward against her flesh, she did not draw away.

"Now!" Ysuna roared like a riled and impatient lioness. "Now, Masau! Quickly!"

He closed his eyes. His arm tensed. His hand tightened on the stone haft of the blade.

"Now!" he said, and suddenly, with a roar that put that of the woman to shame, he pushed Ta-maya away and behind him, dropped the dagger, and took a spear into his left hand. "Yes! Now Thunder in the Sky shall have the supreme sacrifice, the perfect bride, the only woman in this world who is truly worthy of such a bloodthirsty god as he!"

Ysuna's face went blank.

Maliwal was racing through the throng.

And Masau's spear was flying straight at its target.

# 10

He fled with Ta-maya into the dawn, carrying her in his arms as he ran. He cut sharply southward toward the broad, rolling hills across which he had led her out of the Red World.

"I will take you back to your people," he said as he paused for a moment, setting her onto her feet so that he could catch his breath and scan the way they had escaped. A good-sized group of men was in pursuit.

Masau cursed as hope and dread stirred simultaneously within him. He had one spear with him; it would have to be enough. He had managed to put a considerable distance between himself and the men who were following. As drugged as they all were from partaking of the ceremonial brew, they must have hesitated before coming after him. Maliwal's blood would be thick with it. Masau's head was as clear as the wind that blew out of the north.

From what he could see, his brother was not with them, nor were the dogs—a sure sign that the pursuers wanted to capture the girl unharmed, that it was still their intent to sacrifice her.

Masau's mouth tightened. His brother would be with *her* now, with Ysuna. She would never heal the face of the Wolf, even though she would live to be as old and powerful as the great white mammoth. Even as Masau had leaped from the dais he had known that his spear had gone wide and failed to strike her through the heart. But had he struck a mortal wounding? He might never know. With a stab of pain, he realized that he was glad. He wanted her dead and yet . . .

"Come," he said to Ta-maya. "We must go on."

He took her hand and looked down into her face. His actions since the rising of the sun had cost him everything he had ever lived for. But as his eyes met Ta-maya's he had no regrets. He loved this girl more than he loved his own life. *Love*. He did not understand the emotion. It was a gentle thing and very unlike anything he had ever felt for Ysuna. His love for Ta-maya soothed him, comforted him. He had saved the girl's life, and yet, deep within his spirit, he knew that it was he who should be grateful to her, for when he had stood for her against Ysuna, he had also saved himself. If only he could find a way to elude their pursuers . . . He hefted her into his arms and began to jog again upward across the long slope of the hill.

"You cannot carry me all the way to the Red World! Put me down, Masau! I am your woman, not a child! I will run at your side!" she proclaimed with a fervor that amazed and delighted him.

"Naked and barefoot you cannot go far, Little One. We have many miles to cover before you are once again safe among your own people!"

"The People of the Watching Star will follow us. We will never be safe."

"Have hope! I will teach your people how to be lions instead of rabbits! I will teach them to stand and fight against the predators of the world! Besides, if Ysuna dies and can no longer control Maliwal's actions, my brother will not have the heart to lead the others against me!"

Just saying the words heartened him. Once Ta-maya

and he crested this rise, the downhill lay of the land would ease their escape. To the east lay a wide, broken stretch of rain-eroded arroyos, beyond which ran a good-sized river. Beside that was the cover of thick, sheltering woodland. He planned to conceal their tracks along the stony shallows of the riverbed and confound those who followed. Within the cover of the trees, Ta-maya could rest while he hunted for food and the makings of some sort of foot covering for her. By then, with Ysuna wounded and perhaps unable to lead her people, Maliwal would probably call off the search, and then, Masau hoped, he and Ta-maya could continue on in safety. The thought was invigorating. He lengthened his stride.

The north wind was strong at his back, urging him forward. Beyond the crest of the hill, ravens were circling and diving ahead of him. He could hear their cawing. He frowned, for the birds reminded him of Wehatla, the young attendant, Yatli's only daughter, whom he had been forced to strangle the other night. Otherwise she might inadvertently have revealed to Ysuna that Ta-maya had seen the dais before the dawn of her sacrifice—and that he had gone into the lodge of purification to spend forbidden time with her after leaving Ysuna's bed. *Ravens*, he thought, cringing. *Omens of death.* He should have named them Totem! But no, no more: The birds would be feasting on the corpses of Tlana-quah and Kosar-eh; he had nothing to do with those deaths. He could not lead Ta-maya near the bodies. He need not burden her with news of her father's and friend's death just yet.

He changed direction to cut sideways across the slope. He would carry Ta-maya out of harm's way, no matter what the forces of Creation might put in his path. In days to come he would consider himself favored by the ghosts of his ancestors if the lizard eaters of the Red World would forgive him for all that he and his people had done against them. He would humble himself before them and beg them to allow him a new life as one of them, far to the south, in the sunstruck land of dreams.

"He must die. The girl must die with him!" Ysuna lay upon her piled sleeping furs. Her eyes were fixed and glaring, her jaw was clenched.

Maliwal knelt beside her, packing a salve of spider-webs and willow oil into the severe gash that Masau's spear had made in her upper right arm.

"The girl is the one to blame, Ysuna," he said gruffly, completing the packing and setting himself to suturing the wound with a bone needle and sinew thread, talking all the while to distract her. "She and her lizard-eating people and that boy shaman of theirs worked some kind of magic on him."

"A boy shaman?"

"Yes. And a girl, too. A pretty little thing. She could call the great white mammoth, and he would come to eat out of her hand."

Ysuna sat up as though the words had stabbed her. "You saw this?"

"I did! It was magic. She and the boy must have used it on Masau. Had he truly wanted to kill you, Ysuna, his spear would not have gone wide. It would have found its mark."

"And had you not cried my name in warning, I would not have turned away in time. I would have taken the full impact of the thrust. It was you, Maliwal, who kept his spear from striking me. Masau would have had my life in exchange for hers, despite all that I have been to him and done for him."

She paused and watched his ministrations dispassionately, without visible reaction to pain; it was as though he were suturing someone else's arm. "Now I will have them both. Yes, with my own hand I will offer them to the god, and you will stand beside me and be the first to taste their blood as I gut them. Thunder in the Sky will see how severely the People of the Watching Star deal with those who dare to offend him and his supplicant, Daughter of the Sun!"

The stitching complete, Masau laid fresh willow leaves over the wound, wrapped it in wide strips of buckskin, then folded her hand upward and secured it in a sling of the same clean, soft elk hide. "Now let me see to your hand. Ah . . . it will also need suturing."

She watched him thoughtfully as he tenderly salved the puncture wounds and slashes that Blood's teeth had made in her flesh. "It is Masau who should be tending my wounds, Wolf."

He looked up at her with a start and frowned. "It was Masau and his cursed dog who inflicted them! I may answer to the name of Wolf, Ysuna, but I would never turn on the one who has given life to me!"

"You are a loyal son, Maliwal."

"Yes!" he agreed, growling a little with hurt pride. "I am."

One of her brows arched speculatively as her free hand reached out to stroke the cape that he had neglected to remove from his shoulders. "A spotted pelt . . . I have never seen the like. Where did you get it? It has the look of extreme age."

His face tightened defensively. "It is the last of its kind. I took it off the corpse of the headman of the band from which we took the last sacrifice. He boasted of it when he was alive. He said that he had killed it when he was a youth and that it was the last of the great spotted lions that his people called Jaguar. I wanted it. I took it. It did not belong on the back of the lizard eater!"

Ysuna's hand strayed back and forth over the time-worn pelt. "The great cat that walked in this skin must have been beautiful."

Maliwal knelt back to sit stiffly on his heels. "As you are beautiful, Ysuna." Without hesitation, he took the cape off and wrapped it gently around her shoulders. "I should have given it to you before," he said, then lied as easily as he drew breath, "but I did not think that Daughter of the Sun would want something that had once belonged to a man of the Red World."

She smiled benignly. "The men of the Red World will soon kneel at my feet as you are kneeling, Maliwal. But they will not be my sons; they will be my slaves. Their women will be for the pleasure of the men of the Watching Star. Their daughters will be meat for Thunder in the Sky." The words excited her. Her face was pale from her ordeal, and the whites of her eyes were filmed with fever; but there was a deeper heat of ambition and resolve in them. Her hands drifted to her collar. "When I have the sacred stones of the Red World and the flesh and blood of the white mammoth, I will not forget this son—this Maliwal, this Wolf. You shall live forever at my side. No longer will you carry your ear in a sack. On the day that I am reborn into youth and immortality, your face will be restored and will rival the splendor of Daughter of the Sun's."

He trembled.

She saw his reaction. She nodded, affirming the vow. "It will be so, Maliwal. *Soon.* Leave me now. Bring Masau and Ta-maya to me. After I have killed them, we shall go forth to the sacred mountain. When all the holy men of the Red World are dead, you will lead me to this girl shaman who can call the great white mammoth. She will call him for me. After I take his life, she will die, for from that day there will be only *one* shaman, Ysuna, Daughter of the Sun!"

The drums had been silent in the village for some time, but Kosar-eh's heart was pounding. Maliwal's so-called entertainment had gone wrong. Had the clown's circumstances been different, he would have been rejoicing now.

Strange men were all around him, but they had not come from the encampment at the base of the hill; they had come in stealth and silence upon the People of the Watching Star, as he and Tlana-quah had come, and from the south. They carried many spears. They had spear hurlers with them, and larger versions of the braining clubs that the People of the Red World used on rabbit and hare drives. Their faces were painted in bold streaks of color. From the look of them they had come far and in haste. Hidden in the tall grass, they went unnoticed by anyone in the chaotic village below. In a daze Kosar-eh tried to count them. There were far too many.

"The hunt begins. . . ." whispered their leader, a man in a distinctively painted robe of bison hide. He tested the weight of the spear that was in his right hand and stared ominously toward the village.

"Good," said a much younger man who resembled the one who had just spoken. "May the spirits of the ancestors be with us, lest we all end like this poor man."

Several tall, big-boned men circled Kosar-eh, knelt around him, and shook their heads in sympathy and muted anger that was obviously directed against those who had done this to him. One of them began to loosen the thongs that held his wrists. Another untied his gag. He would have spit the nettles out, but his mouth and tongue were so swollen and enflamed that he could not. A second later it did not matter. One of the men pulled the spear from his body. The pain was so intense that Kosar-eh screamed. The nettles went flying from his mouth as he swooned forward into the arms of a stranger who clasped a wide, callused hand across his face.

"No use!" exclaimed Eldest Hunter. "They heard his cry!" He exhaled a wordless epithet. "And look! The men who are out of the village and moving toward the southern hills have seen us!"

The knuckles of the leader's hand whitened as he gripped the haft of his spear. "Then they have seen their death!"

Kosar-eh looked up through a haze of pain and queasiness and confusion. What was happening? Who were these men? It did not matter. All that mattered was that they were obviously enemies of the People of the Watching Star. Perhaps there were benevolent spirits in the world beyond this world, after all! Perhaps they actually did look down upon the world of men and hear the invocations of their priests and clowns. How many times since Maliwal had impaled him and left him to die had he implored the forces of Creation to take that man's life and save Ta-maya? And now it seemed that both would happen! If only he could shout the words that were swelling in his heart: *May I live to thank Masau for what he has done this day! And may I live to see Maliwal, that wolf-faced slaughterer of men, women, and children, die slowly!*

Someone was examining his wound, saying something about the spear having missed the vein and penetrated straight through to the ground without striking bone. "The totem spirits of your ancestors have been with you this day," said the man, offering a waterskin.

Kosar-eh tried to drink. The nettles had done their work, however; it would be hours before he could swallow without severe pain. He tilted his head back and tried to relax enough to allow the liquid to pour straight down his throat. And then he choked.

"Masau!" The name exploded from the leader's mouth.

"I gave him warning. Too many young women have gone at his hand to Thunder in the Sky! I, Shateh, will not allow him to shed the blood of another. He should have died long ago!"

The men around Kosar-eh broke ranks and hurried to stand beside their leader. From the way they positioned themselves, the clown could see past them to the next hill. Masau, with Ta-maya in his arms, had just crested it. When Masau saw the group, he put the girl down and stood tall. His spear was in his left hand. He appeared to say something to Ta-maya. Distance made it impossible for Kosar-eh and the others to hear the words, but his left arm moved.

In that instant Shateh released the spear with which he had already armed his spear hurler. The strength of the man was as amazing as were the extra speed, power, and distance that his spear thrower gave to his weapon. Not even in the most fanciful tales that Kosar-eh had invented for the children of the band had he ever conjured a spear that could fly so far—or with such deadly accuracy.

On the next hill, Ta-maya screamed. It was too late. Spun around and knocked back by the impact, Masau went down with Shateh's spear through his chest. Ta-maya cried his name and threw herself across his body as though her own flesh and bones would be enough to ward off the seeking head of another spear.

Stunned and half-disbelieving, Kosar-eh watched Shateh nock the butt end of another spear to his spear thrower, level it over his shoulder, and prepare for another assault.

"No!" The word ripped out of Kosar-eh as he managed to rise, stagger forward, and hurl himself against the back of Shateh's knees, knocking the man forward and to the ground before he could loose another spear. The weapon scudded forward. Kosar-eh lurched after it, grabbed it with his one good hand, and, sobbing against excruciating pain, managed a complete about-face. Crouching, the clown pointed the end of the spear straight between Shateh's eyes.

The man stared and gasped. His men closed around him.

With swollen tongue, Kosar-eh managed the threat; it was garbled but audible: "Raise a spear against her, any of you, and your leader will die before you can put an end to me."

Shateh's eyes fixed him unflinchingly, then stared straight down the length of the spearhead and shaft. "It was not my intent to harm the girl. We came to end Masau's life before he took hers. Even now many more hunters of the Bison People will be coming to this place from the west and north to stand with me against the People of the Watching Star. We will kill the madwoman Ysuna. We will send Maliwal and Masau back to the spirit world, to which I sent them many a long winter ago. We will put an end to their depredations and see to it that they will never again attack our people and steal our daughters to become meat for their totem!"

"Masau risked his life to save Ta-maya." Weakness and pain were threatening to overwhelm Kosar-eh, but he was aware of the stunned murmuring at his back.

"What does it matter now?" demanded one of the other men of the Bison Band with nervous irritability. "Look: The men of the Watching Star have turned back to their village. They will warn their many brothers that we have come. All hope of taking them by surprise is lost. Let us turn back and take cover in the woodlands along the river until the others of our tribe come to strengthen our numbers. We must act now, before it is too late."

Still staring unblinkingly at Kosar-eh, Shateh saw the weakness in the clown. He reached out and reclaimed his spear with a forceful jerk. As he got to his feet he said to the others, "Yes, because we have been seen, we must act now. We must attack now because we will be expected to run away! Too many times have I turned my eyes away from these People of the Watching Star. You, Firstborn Son of Fourth Woman, you and the other young men have been lusting for a fight! Go! Your spears are as sharp as your readiness! Lead the others. Eldest Hunter and I will see if my son Masau is dead. If he is not, this time I will finish him. Then I will join you."

"Stay away!" Ta-maya's voice was steady, her face set, and her dark eyes were wild. She awkwardly held Masau's heavy spear in both hands. She marveled at the ease and accuracy with which the hunting men of the northern grasslands hefted and hurled these weapons. She doubted she would be capable of putting enough force behind this one to prove much of a threat with it. Nevertheless she stood her ground before Masau's curled-up body, jabbed forward at the Bison Men who were coming toward her, and warned them back again.

The incredulous men stopped and stared past her. Masau groaned, fought to rise, and managed to sit up. He gripped the spearhead, which protruded from his upper chest just to the right of his armpit.

"This son of mine is not easy to kill," grumbled Shateh, his mouth tight across his teeth.

Beside him Eldest Hunter's face expanded in the way of a man who has just been given a vision by the spirits. "Perhaps he is what they say he is: Mystic Warrior, invincible like Ysuna. Perhaps he cannot die."

Shateh squinted with disbelief as he appraised Masau's wound. "He bleeds." Something changed in his face as he appraised his son. There was a softening about the mouth, a sudden sadness in the eyes. "That which bleeds can and will die."

When he began to advance, Ta-maya feinted forward with the spear. "Come no closer!" she warned, but Shateh ignored her. He approached so quickly that before she knew what had happened, he had ducked the jab with which she had intended to pierce him and deflected her spear with a hard sideways swipe of his forearm. She cried out as the weapon flew from her hands.

"Stand back, girl!" Eldest Hunter reached out and pulled her against him into the bend of one strong arm.

"No!" she cried, fighting to be free as Shateh came to pause above Masau. The head of Shateh's spear pointed straight at the wounded warrior's heart.

"As you would have pierced my breast, Masau, with your spear as you stood upon this hill and looked across to me, now I shall at last put an end to you with my mine. Then I will join my men and bring the gift of death to Ysuna and the People of the Watching Star!"

"No!" screamed Ta-maya. "He was raising his arm to you in greeting, not in threat! He said to me that he would never raise his spear against you! He said that it was time to heal old wounds between you!"

Shateh's spear arm remained poised and ready to strike; but he flinched at her words. There was unmistakable hesitancy in his stance as his eyes met his son's. "Is this the truth she speaks?"

"I gave you your life on the medicine pole, Shateh." Masau was fighting for the words. They emerged as pained suckings. "Take the girl to a place of safety. If you and the Bison People fail, the People of the Watching Star will come for her. They will kill her."

"We will not fail!" Shateh vowed.

Masau, wheezing, his face gray and with blood bubbling at the corners of his mouth, strained to move into a position from which he might look toward the village. The Bison People had attacked. Drumbeats were sounding below. War whoops and shouts and the screams of frightened women could be heard in the encampment. But even from this distance it was clear that someone had rallied the forces of the People of the Watching Star. They outnumbered the invaders three to one. And on the platform of the dais stood Ysuna, one arm bound, a spear in the hand of her other arm, her hair and feather cloak streaming behind her, and Tlana-quah's spotted cape upon her shoulders.

"You cannot be victorious as long as she lives." Masau's statement hung in the air.

Shateh's face twisted. "We will win!"

Eldest Hunter held Ta-maya so tightly that she could barely breathe, yet still she strained against his hold and wept—with both joy and sorrow—when Kosar-eh, leaning heavily on a hunter's arm, came hobbling into view.

"You *must* win," the clown managed to say. "If you do not, they will move to the south. They will slaughter the great white mammoth, and then every man, woman, and child left alive in the land of the People of the Red World will know the same fear that has driven the Bison People with their war clubs to this place."

Ta-maya could barely breathe. "No! It cannot be!"

"It is," replied the clown grimly. "Your father is dead, Ta-maya, slain by Maliwal before my eyes. Look: In the village the priestess wears his cloak, and here at your feet Masau wears a cape made of the hide of the little white son."

She went limp in Elder Hunter's arm. "Masau," she sobbed, "tell me that this is not true."

He looked at her for a long time before he pulled in a series of broken, shallow breaths and then exhaled with the wheezing rasp. "Shateh, this time you *have* killed me, but I am not yet dead. Pull this spear from me. I will take it to the village. This time my spear will not miss its mark."

## 11

They took the spear from him, but they did not send him back to the village with it. He collapsed in Shateh's arms, and the chief of the Bison People declared that this was a good thing; Masau could not feel the searing agony of the cauterization of his wound. He was also spared the pain that would otherwise have been his as, at Shateh's command, instead of being "finished," he was carried on the back of Eldest Hunter into the sheltering woods along the river. Ta-maya followed, helping the wounded Kosar-eh along. For hours they were too stunned by the events that had preceded their escape to speak.

And for hours the battle raged in the village, a series of bold skirmishes and well-timed feints back into the hills, with men on both sides dying until the Land of Grass was red with blood. The smoke of burning lodges rose into the air, and the ravens that had been feeding upon the bodies of Tlana-quah and Wehatla, the daughter of Yatli, wheeled over the encampment of the People of the Watching Star in numbers so great that their wings shadowed the world.

Far away upon the Blue Mesas, the people of Tlana-quah's band set up a small, disconsolate camp amid the sacred pinyon groves. Other bands were already encamped, but their greetings were circumspect in light of the situation. Soon the shamans were gathered in council on the promontory, and Dakan-eh and the other hunters were busy fortifying the various approaches onto the mountain with snares and pit traps designed not for animals but for men.

The wind was strong from the north, and the sun was angling toward the west. Cha-kwena, in his grandfather's robe and bonnet, sat with the other holy men and placed his sacred stone in a circle with theirs. He tried hard not to remember the last time that he had been here—a callow boy in the company of a beloved old man and an owl, both of whom had been making their last pilgrimage to the Blue Mesas.

The shamans were talking in low, purposeful tones. Their talk was of death and dreams . . . of Shi-wana and Ish-iwi and of Hoyeh-tay . . . of old friends who would never sit in council with them again in this world.

The wind held the scent of smoke. Cha-kwena shivered as he recalled what he had seen in the White Hills. He wondered what Sunam-tu was doing now. The deranged man had refused to leave his village. Was he still hunting and feeding the dead, guarding Naquah-neh and the rats that feasted off the corpses in that place? Cha-kwena shuddered.

The old men were chanting, calling upon the sacred stones to give them answers to a thousand questions. He listened, then chanted with them, even though he knew that they already had the answers that they sought.

Hoyeh-tay had warned them: Brothers of the Sky had come down to walk upon the skin of the earth. Soon they would come to the holy mountain. The people of the Red World would stand against them—or die.

In the red light of the setting sun, Ysuna saw it all from her place upon the dais: blood, fire, and black, stinking smoke rising from dozens of burned lodges. Dogs skulked around what was left of the village, making quick meals of the dead before the living cursed and kicked them away.

Leaning on the single spear that she held upright in her unbandaged hand, the priestess rocked on her heels

with the weakness that had been threatening for hours to
overwhelm her. Through pure, rock-hard will she managed to maintain her balance as Maliwal slowly climbed
the bone stairs and came toward her.

"How many dead?" she asked.

Sweated, covered in spattered blood and gore, and
carrying a war club that she did not recognize, he spoke
the numbers and names.

She recoiled, staggered, then caught herself before
falling off the platform and remained on her feet only by
the grace of the spear. "So *many*! And among the enemy?"

"More! Many more! I myself took this braining club
from the hand of one of them. Twelve men went down
after that." He was beaming. "They have followed the
shadows into the hills. We have driven them off for this
day and will be ready for them if they dare to come back
tomorrow! Now, like dogs, they hide and lick their wounds.
I could take men and go after them if it would please you,
but in the dark they will have the advantage of cover. I am
your Wolf, Ysuna, but I prefer to see my prey's face in full
light when I kill him!"

"Yes. I have taught you well, Maliwal."

He stared at her. She looked like one of the corpses. Her
face was ashen; her eyes were glazed and staring. When the
wind gusted at her back, not only her hair and robe and
jaguar-skin cape swayed. He quickly closed the distance
between them and reached out to steady her. The wind
brought her scent to him. He was appalled by the sweet
heaviness of advanced necrosis.

"You must rest now, Daughter of the Sun! Your wounds
have weakened you. You *must* rest." *Or how will you live
long enough to heal my face?*

He helped her to her lodge. The Bison Eaters had not
come close to it; nevertheless it stank of smoke and the
death that had been brought into her encampment this
day.

Soon she slept. The hated and beloved dream came to
her again, of the past, of youth and deprivation, of
cold and hunger, and of a longing for life and sunlight
and the meat of mammoth . . . of a young girl shivering
in the white darkness of an endless winter while visions of

the white mammoth led her on through storms of swirling snow to discover food and salvation for her people. . . .

Her eyes opened. Night had fallen, and it was dark within her lodge. Beyond the hide walls women were keening their dead. Men were offering death songs for fallen sons and brothers and comrades. One of the drummers had taken up his beater and was sounding a slow, steady rhythm of mourning.

She closed her eyes again. She remembered Maliwal's words about a girl shaman who could summon the white mammoth.

"It is I," she murmured. "No, it is another, an enemy. She saps me of my strength and turns the Great White Giant from my people."

She sighed and drifted into another sleep and along a familiar course that took her through the misted fibers of her mind. A tall figure was clothed in light, in her sacred collar, and in a cape of a spotted lion that lived in the land of her ancestors no more. It was she.

On and on she walked, through wide, dark corridors of time beneath the huge, unblinking eye of the Watching Star. Red and bleeding, it stared down at her, and then it closed.

She walked on through darkness. Long, spidery arms reached to enclose her. Ensnared, she cried out. The darkness thinned. She passed through it with ease now, through a curtained wall of long strands of human finger bones, which clicked and sang in a rising wind like shards of volcanic glass.

It was all familiar, this dream trail that she had walked before, past a great juniper tree, toward a deep ravine, and into a wondrous canyon where the white mammoth awaited her at the far side of a reflecting pool. But as before, she sensed danger. There was a lion on this trail, and then another and another. They lay above her, sprawled in the branches of the great juniper.

They spoke their names to her: *Ish-iwi. Shi-wana. Hoyeh-tay. Naquah-neh.*

She did not recognize the names. She clutched her sacred collar and tried to shift the dream; it would not be shifted.

"Beware, Ysuna, Daughter of the Sun. The sacred

stones you wear belong to us. We will have them from you in the end!"

"Never!" She stood alone and breathless within the canyon of her dream. The Watching Star was opening again. Red, so red! She looked up, distracted by the shadow of an owl. Its great round eyes stared down at her. Its broad, silent wings oared the darkness as it opened its beak, swallowed the Watching Star, and—with a shriek— regurgitated a river of lesser stars before banking upward and leaving her to stand alone in a cool, glittering rain of incandescent light.

She basked in the glow. She opened her mouth and drank it in. She became the light—a star more brilliant than the sun, and ageless, immortal, progenitor of all life. Ysuna, mother of lightning, Daughter of the Sun . . . and now the Sun herself!

She moved deeper into the canyon. Mammoth walked ahead of her—as many mammoth as there were stars in the sky. She salivated, tasting blood and salt in her mouth.

Lightning flashed, and thunder rolled. The great mammoth trumpeted as though in reply.

She spoke his name. "Thunder in the Sky."

He stood before her across a lake of blood. She looked down. Her image shimmered up at her, but it was not the image of youth and beauty. It was a withered, sickly hag.

"No!"

Lions roared, and old men laughed. Her hands flew to her collar, but even as she clutched the sacred stones a shaft of lightning rent the pool. The world shook, the skin of the night gushed blood, and the great white mammoth dissolved into the pool.

She stood alone in a rain of blood. She knelt, made a cup of her hand, dipped it into the pool, then drank. But this time no rejuvenated young woman appeared to look back at her from the pool. Though she drained her palm a thousand times, the hag in the pool was still there, as hollow eyed and skeletal and devoid of life as the mammoth skull that stood upon the dais.

Across the pool a young girl watched and smiled.

"Grandfather of All is not for you. I will protect him!"

"You will die!" screamed Ysuna, and tore herself from her dream.

*    *    *

"Ysuna?" Maliwal knelt by her side. He had never seen her like this. She was sweating, drooling, shaking like a terrified child. The darkness of the lodge could not hide what she had become. She was old. She was ill. She was repulsive. "What is it, Daughter of the Sun? What troubles you?"

"The girl . . . the girl who walks with mammoth . . . she is stealing my life from me."

"She is far away. She is a child."

"I was a child once. I was wise even then, Maliwal. Oh, yes. But no one knew how wise I was. Although they tried to kill me, I would not die. The spirits of the ancestors were with me. Thunder in the Sky was with me. I knew that I must live. I knew what I must become for my people. I had to survive for them. It has all been for them. You know that, don't you, Maliwal?"

He frowned. Her good hand was gripping his forearm. He could feel how thin and sharp her bones were. The fingernails curled into the heel of his palm. Like the talons of an eagle, they pierced his flesh; he did not have to look to know that they had drawn blood.

"I can feel her, Maliwal. She is shrewd, this girl who walks with our totem. She thinks that she will suck my spirit out of my head when I dream. But I know what she is, and I know what she wants. She longs for my power. From this moment I will not sleep. I will not let her have it."

It occurred to him that she was mad; but madness was a thing of the spirits, and Maliwal believed in spirits. The way Ysuna looked, the way she smelled, told him that something malevolent was eating at her. Besides, her words confirmed what he had suspected all along: The headstrong younger daughter of Tlana-quah was no simple-minded little creature. She had to be a shaman; why else would the great white mammoth have come to her? And how else could a mere girl have possessed enough courage to walk in the shadow of the great white mammoth, to yield eagerly, without fear, to the embrace of its trunk, while he and the boldest of his hunters had stepped back in terror of the potentially deadly power of the totem.

"I must have the sacred stones soon, Maliwal. Especially the one that belongs to her band. She draws her power from it. I can feel it. This one stone is greater than all the others."

His eyes widened at the words. "Masau had it in his possession, but he returned it. I did not understand then why, but I do now. It was the stone itself working on him through the girl."

Her clawlike fingers tightened on his wrist. "I must have it, Maliwal! Otherwise, there will not be enough strength left in me to pursue the great white mammoth . . . or to heal you, my son."

"Soon his strength will be your strength, Ysuna!" he assured her. "After we have routed these Bison Eaters we will go south and take the sacred stones from the shamans on the Blue Mesas. The one you seek will be with the boy Cha-kwena."

"The girl does not wear the stone?"

"No. It is Cha-kwena's now. But he is nothing! He has no power that I could see. The power is with the girl, and she will be with her people by the Lake of Many Singing Birds. Where you find her, you will also find the white mammoth."

A spasm shook her, but of pain or happiness, it was impossible for Maliwal to tell. "Then we must go to her, you and I. We cannot wait. This village is finished. Call together the People of the Watching Star. Tell them that we will abandon this place tonight. We will leave the Bison Eaters to lick their wounds and plan tomorrow's attack. By the time they come against us, we will be gone. I doubt if they will follow us. Why should they? They will think that they have driven us away in fear of them!"

Disappointment shot through him. Leave the Bison Eaters when the killing had only just begun? He said as much, then added, "What about Masau and Ta-maya? Even now they may be in the camp of the Bison Eaters. Are their deaths no longer important to you?"

"If they follow us, they will die." Her eyes narrowed. Her hand withdrew from his wrist. "And if they do not follow us, there will be no place in the Red World or the world beyond in which they will be safe from me." She reached to the side of her sleeping mattress, fumbled in the leather parfleche that lay there, and withdrew one of

Masau's nine-inch-long chalcedony spearheads. "Here. Haft them for me. There are four of these. Magic blades, your brother said, for a magic woman, so that I would not fail to kill a magic mammoth. This I will do. You will stand with me, Maliwal, and together we will eat the flesh and drink the blood of our totem. Then we will put these spearheads to another purpose. They will seek the lives of those who have betrayed us—the spearhead that killed the mammoth totem will also be for the bride. The second will be for the girl who would dare to be shaman in my place, the third for Masau. He has chosen the way he will walk and the way he will die! With his own hands, he has fashioned the spearhead that will kill him."

"And the fourth spearhead?"

As she looked right at him, her smile broadened. "A purpose will be found. In the meantime, tell my people to break camp in absolute silence. It is time to journey to the sacred mountain."

He obeyed without hesitation, glad to be away from her odor.

She watched him as he left her, her viperish smile settling into a vindictive expression. "Stupid man, the fourth spearhead is for you. After I kill the white mammoth I will have no need of you. You are not Masau. You are not Mystic Warrior. He is the only man who was ever fit to rule at my side over the People of the Watching Star."

# 12

It was nearly dawn. At the base of the promontory on the holy mountain, the wind continued strong from the north, and the shamans of the Red World were still talking.

Cha-kwena listened. He watched the old men in their paint and feathers and collars of silver sagebrush, adorned with the beaks and heads and feet of little animals, and with berries and beads of stone and hard-shelled nuts. The grandfathers had painted their faces blue in honor of this sacred place. The color basket had gone around when they had first arrived. Cha-kwena, one of them now, had dipped his fingertips into the greasy paste of antelope fat, water, and ground duck manure. The last ingredient had lent the substance its fine, rich color. He had smeared it onto his face without restraint as he thought of Hoyeh-tay. The old man would be proud if he could see his grandson as a shaman at last.

Now, sitting cross-legged and back-weary before the little fire and the circle of sacred stones that had been laid reverently around it, he stared into the flames. The talk went on and on, circling around the stones.

"I do not like this talk of men hunting men," said the shaman from Red Butte Lake. "The People are one. Perhaps if we sought council with these northerners, they would agree to change their ways."

"Brothers do not do to one another what the men of the north did to the People of the White Hills," said Cha-kwena.

Iman-atl of the Place of Many Reeds nodded emphatically in agreement. "I say that it is a good thing that we make a stand here against the Brothers of the Sky. They deserve to die slow and painful deaths. The hearts of the young men of my band sing with anger. They work happily with Dakan-eh. Bold Man is not afraid; anger makes him strong. Although I am old, I become strong and courageous while watching Bold Man. I will stand with the young men against the northerners, and I will urge the women and children of my band to rain hot stones upon them and pour boiling oil from the paunch bags onto their heads!"

Han-da, shaman of the Blue Sky People, shook his head. "If these men are the Brothers of the Sky, we cannot fight them! Better to run away!"

Cha-kwena closed his eyes. The argument went on and on. The old men seemed incapable of understanding. He spoke with elaborate patience. "If we run, the men of the north will follow. If we do not stop them here, they will destroy our way of life forever." How many times must he repeat the warning before they believed it?

"If we fight them and lose, will we not die forever?" pressed Han-da.

"As long as a single sacred stone remains in our possession, the People cannot die. You know this."

"Hmmph!" Han-da was not happy. "Ish-iwi is dead. Shi-wana and Naquah-neh and Hoyeh-tay are dead. I will take my stone and go from this place. I will lead my people to a new village away from all this trouble, to the hills above the western edge of the lake that fronts our ancestral home. If Brothers of the Sky come our way, we will see them in plenty of time to run away. Besides, the lake is nearly dry now. Perhaps the spirits of First Man and First Woman are telling us that it is time to move on. It is a different world. Once, this was a land of much water and many trees and of grass and big game; now it is dry, and the People who once hunted horse and camel and elk now eat rabbits and grubs and ask themselves where all the animals have gone."

Cha-kwena was troubled. "If the People of the Red World scatter in panic . . . if the bands move off—one to the west, another to the east, others to the north and south—how long can the People hope to remain one? And who will protect our totem against the Brothers of the Sky?"

Han-da thought for a moment, then shrugged. "There is an old saying among the People, Cha-kwena. 'In changing times, men must learn new ways.'" He let the words settle, then nodded, affirming them to himself. "There are few mammoth left in the world. It is time for our totem to protect us against the Brothers of the Sky. If he cannot do this, then perhaps he is Totem no more."

Appalled, Cha-kwena stared at the man.

He was not alone in his amazement. Han-da was resoundingly rebuked by nearly all. Then the shouting died down, and the shaman from the Red Buttes spoke in Han-da's defense.

"I, too, will take my people from this place. We will move our village farther into the hills. For many summers now our lake has been dry, and too often have we gone thirsty. If Brothers of the Sky are coming to the Red World, the People of the Red Buttes will move out of their way."

"And abandon the rest of us to defend the villages and traditions and totem of our ancestors!" Cha-kwena leaped to his feet. "What animal will you name totem in your new world? *Rabbit?*"

Han-da replied evenly, "Rabbit is wise and wary. Rabbit knows when to stay and when to run away. There are many rabbits in the world. But where have all the mammoth gone, Cha-kwena?"

"The People of the Watching Star have killed them!" he shot back. "As they will kill you and your band if they catch you."

Han-da shook his head. "They hunt mammoth and the sacred stones, Grandson of Hoyeh-tay. They do not look for rabbits." His brow came down. He was thinking very hard. Then, he bent forward decisively, lifted his sacred stone from the circle, and, after a moment of solemn contemplation—reverently placed it into the fire.

Cha-kwena made a dive for it as the other shamans wailed in protest at Han-da's sacrilege. The heat of the little fire was intense, and Han-da's sacred stone was very small. Cha-kwena's fingers plucked at it, but it evaded his grasp. The youth flicked at the flames and poked at the coals, but it was no use. Han-da's sacred stone had vanished.

"It is done," said Han-da. "It is you they will kill, Cha-kwena, and all others who stand in their way."

Incredulous, Cha-kwena stared at the man. "You have destroyed a part of First Man and First Woman, of all that we are, of all that we have ever been! You have weakened us and our totem before our enemies. Since time beyond beginning the People have been one, Han-da; but you have put yourself outside the sacred circle. Go! You are no longer our brother."

There was tense silence on the mountain. For a moment even the wind ceased its dry, hard breathing, and in that moment there was not a man at the fire circle who did not know that the youngest and least tested among them had somehow become spokesman for them all.

Han-da was on his feet, glaring at the others as the wind rose again. "Does this inexperienced boy speak wisdom for his elders?"

Iman-atl sneered at the man. "This boy is the grandson of Hoyeh-tay. This boy names the mammoth Totem. This boy stands into the north wind and is unafraid. This boy is Shaman, guardian of the sacred stone and of our totem, Life Giver! This boy is no boy."

They were wrong—Cha-kwena *was* afraid. Han-da's band was of considerable size, as was the band of the shaman of the Red Buttes. When they left in the morning, many a strong hunter and valuable spear would go with them. Cha-kwena was concerned that others, seeing this, would lose heart and follow.

Later, alone and restless, he left the little grove where the holy men were resting and walked back through the woods and onto the heights of the north face of the mountain. He suddenly became aware that Mah-ree was following him. He turned.

"Cha-kwena, I have to talk to you."

"You should not be here."

"I had to come."

He did not slow his pace.

"Cha-kwena, Grandfather of All has followed us! He grazes at the base of the holy mountain. Cha-kwena, did

you hear me? He is here! If we fail to stop the People of
the Watching Star, they will see him and kill him!"

He paused. He had reached the highest point of the
broad, flat top of the mesa. The Land of Grass lay far
beyond. Instinctively his belly tightened. They were out
there somewhere. Soon they would come. He half closed
his eyes. The wind of warning was sweeping through his
spirit, and North Wind was whispering all around: *They
are already on their way, in great numbers. Will you ever
be able to stop them all?*

"They are not there," Shateh said with disgust. "They
have left their dead and wounded, abandoned the village,
and gone south."

"We must follow," said Kosar-eh, on his feet in an
instant despite his heavily bandaged side.

"They are many miles ahead of us. Besides, you are
not fit to travel," Shateh told him. "Perhaps it is for the
best. There are many dead and injured in this camp. It is a
time to mourn, not to fight. The girl is exhausted from
tending my wounded warriors. Look how she sleeps! As
for Masau, let my son's troubled spirit leave his body in
peace. If we have driven the People of the Watching Star
from their village and made them know that they will have
to pay for what they do, all has not been in vain."

Propped upright against a tree, Masau opened his
eyes. "I am not dead yet," he said. "And they have not
fled in fear; they have gone to avoid a further confronta-
tion that would keep them from their goal. You cannot let
them reach the sacred mountain of the Red World."

Kosar-eh nodded vigorously. "He is right, Shateh. If
they reach the sacred mountain, many holy men will die.
If we reach it first, we can send runners into the Red
World to warn—"

The leader of the Bison Band made a face. "They are
your holy men, not mine!"

"The People are one," Masau said hoarsely.

Ta-maya, wrapped in Shateh's robe, stirred on a mattress of leaves, which the headman had gathered for her in
gratitude for her concern for his men. Since Kosar-eh's
revelations, she had been in shock. She had not spoken a
single word to Masau, even though she knew that he lay

near death. She stared at him now, her eyes haunted by fatigue and grief. "Your people are *not* one with mine! They have killed my father, and you . . . are . . . are—" Her voice broke, and she hung her head.

Shateh frowned, for he had developed a deep liking for the girl. "They are your holy men, too?"

She nodded.

He eyed Masau. "For her I will go."

"I will go, too," said Eldest Hunter, and was echoed by every man present, except those too weakened by injuries to speak.

Shateh was impressed. "The wounded will stay behind. Eldest Hunter, you and this girl will care for them, and ten men will guard you until the other bands of the Land of Grass arrive. Their hatred for the People of the Watching Star is no less than mine. They will follow us. They will want to kill Ysuna as much as I do."

"No . . ." said Masau.

The headman growled. "You cannot save her."

"I do not want to save her. It is by my hand that she must die."

"You will be dead before you get there!" warned Shateh.

"I am Shaman, Shateh. I may surprise you."

"You always have." The headman went to Masau, knelt, and checked the shaman's wound and his brow for fever. "You may yet do so again, but only if you stay here. The bleeding has stopped. I can feel only a little fever. But you have two broken ribs, and this lung . . . Well, perhaps it is not punctured. I cannot tell. *Hmm*. If you have rest and proper care, Masau, maybe I will have failed again to kill you. In the meantime, Kosar-eh, the spirits of the ancestors have saved your life for good purpose. You must come with us. Prepare to travel. We will make a litter for you. We will be strangers to the People of the Red World, and we will need you to speak for us, to tell them all that you have seen. If it comes to fighting, I will try to protect you."

Kosar-eh raised a brow with bitter resolve. "I may have lost the use of one arm, and now I have a wounded leg that will barely support me. But I have learned that I am still the man I was. I can face my enemies as bravely as any of you. If it comes to fighting, give me a spear. I will protect myself."

They left Masau in the cover of the trees, with Eldest Hunter standing close and Ta-maya watching them walk away.

"They are brave men. The spirits of the ancestors will walk with them," said Masau.

She eyed him darkly. "Whose ancestors? Yours or mine? Do not speak to me again, Masau. You are the cause of this. It pleases my heart to know that you are in pain. If you die of your wounds, my spirit will sing with joy to know that you are dead."

From that moment on she turned her back to him and worked with Eldest Hunter to ease the pain of the others who had been left behind. The guards sat sullenly around, making no secret of the fact that they would be best pleased if Masau died. By midmorning he was not only still alive but noticeably improved. By midafternoon, when a disappointingly small party of six armed men approached from the west, led by a pair of hunters from Shateh's band, Masau was on his feet, leaning on his spear and staring to the south.

"Where are the others, the many men of the bison country to the west and north?" Eldest Hunter asked the newcomers.

"They would not come. They smile upon Shateh's venture and say it is a good thing. But they told us to tell Shateh that they have moved their villages into high country now in order to avoid Ysuna and her people. They have all lost daughters and suffered because of her treachery and will not risk their sons in a battle against her."

"Then Shateh and those who follow him go alone against Daughter of the Sun." Eldest Hunter swung his head and indicated Ta-maya. "A man—a cripple—was bold enough to accompany his headman in defense of that girl. Because of the bravery of two men, she is alive. And because of the bravery of Shateh and his hunters, soon the People of the Watching Star will be no more. But know that when this comes to pass, those who failed to stand with him will not be welcome in his lodge."

"We came to bring news, old man, not to trade insults."

"Then consider your mission fulfilled. Go. We have no need of cowards in this camp."

They left without another word.

Masau watched them go, then again turned his eyes southward.

By nightfall he was gone.

# 13

It has been said that madness makes one strong. This was so of Ysuna. They made a four-poled, fur-mattressed litter of mammoth bones for her, upon which she rode, seated upright, carried by four strong bearers whom she goaded on and on until sweat ran down their backs and they began to wheeze and stumble. She mocked them then and climbed down to walk, wild-eyed, her skin dry with fever, endlessly whispering to herself. She had the strength to stride ahead of her people, to urge them on until even the young and strong among them strained to keep up with her. She insulted them and, head high, lengthened her stride.

Ysuna wore her sacred collar, her feather robe, and the jaguar-skin cape, draping the spotted pelt so that it covered the sling for her wounded arm and hand. She carried the sacred dagger sheathed at her side, slung from a thong loop sewn into the girdle of shaggy black lion skin that encircled her hips. She used her spear as a staff, driving the butt end hard into the earth with each step. It was a newly hafted spear with a massive shaft that was nearly as tall as she was. The head of translucent chalcedony was as long as her forearm and as pale as the skin of the white mammoth.

Women, some with little girls riding on their backs, walked behind her, supervising other little girls who had been chosen to hold up the feather-festooned ends of the high priestess's hair lest they drag over the ground and snag in some obstacle. When one child became tired, another was lowered to take up these duties. Not once did the priestess look back at them—until a child tripped and fell forward upon Ysuna's hair, jerking her head back and causing her to turn in a fury.

"Please, take pity," stammered the woman who was closest to the child. "The pace is too hard on the little ones, Daughter of the Sun."

Ysuna kicked the prone child off her hair and ignored the little girl's frightened cries. Then she struck the woman across the face with the side of her spear. So hard was the blow that the woman, her cheekbone and jaw shattered, collapsed in a heap.

"We go south!" Ysuna raged at her.

As another woman quickly bent to scoop up the stunned child and warn her to silence, a man raced forward to kneel by the woman who was on the ground. The man was Yatli. His sons were at his back as he tried to help his woman to her feet; but she would not or could not rise. Her nose, one ear, and the corner of one eye were oozing blood. He tried to sop it up with his fingers; it was a pathetic attempt as he apologized to Ysuna.

"This woman of mine is not as young as she once was. She is made weak by the child that grows in her belly."

Ysuna eyed him without pity and the woman with contempt. "Six sons and two daughters have not been enough for you? This is no time to be weakened and puking with pregnancy! If she cannot keep up, leave her. Take another woman, a younger one! One who is worthy of the People of the Watching Star." This said, she looked away from them and squinted into the glare of the southern ranges. "Last night I heard a mammoth trumpeting to the south. The great white mammoth awaits Daughter of the Sun on the far side of the mesas. Last night there were many fires on the holy mountain. The shamans of the Red World are gathering. Tonight, we shall reach our destination. Come, the sacred stones will soon be mine!"

A low whistle of amazement escaped from Dakan-eh as he scanned the darkness and the grassland that lay far below. The enemy had arrived under the cover of night.

Beside Bold Man, Cha-kwena shook his head. "So many campfires. So many enemies. And since Han-da left, all but two bands have followed the rabbit off the mountain. Their shamans have fed their sacred stones to the fire and gone with them. Perhaps I was wrong. Perhaps we should not have brought our people here. Perhaps Han-da is right. The world is changing. There is still no sign of Tlana-quah, Kosar-eh, or Ta-maya. Perhaps it is time for us to become rabbits and run away from danger."

Dakan-eh raised a disapproving brow. "If you say the word *perhaps* once more, I will kick you off this ledge. No one ever told you that being shaman would be easy, Cha-kwena. You have had a vision; now follow it. I am not the only one who has faith in your power. I saw your magic the night that you and I and Hoyeh-tay and Owl camped in the middle of Big Lake. I have not forgotten how the animals and birds were with you, leading you to water, warning you of danger. Because I envied you, I was not a friend to you or to the old man. I may die soon, so I want you to know that I regret my actions."

Cha-kwena was taken aback. "You saved my grandfather's life and mine that night, Dakan-eh!"

He shrugged, and his chuckle, at his own expense, was barely audible. "What else could I have done? How would it have looked to the spirits of the ancestors and those watching from the sacred mountain if Bold Man had turned into a coward? What I did I did for myself and for my pride. And what I do now I also do for myself. I have done much thinking over the past many risings and settings of the sun. I think that I have been bold, but I have not been much of a man. But it pleases me to be here, to be strong for my people, to hunt and be ready to kill whatever—or whoever—comes against them. Han-da has done a shameful thing by breaking the circle of the sacred stones. He has weakened our totem and the tribe. Never again will the People of the Red World be as they were. But he was right the other night when he announced to all that it was time to look forward, not back."

On the far side of the mountain, a mammoth trumpeted, and several answered. A terrible bleakness swept through Cha-kwena. "Forward to what?"

Bold Man's eyes narrowed with stern contemplation.

"You have brought me here to see the many fires of our enemies. All right, I see. But I stand above them in a place of strength. I wonder if the People of the Watching Star have raised those fires to warm themselves or to turn us cold with dread." He paused and smiled. "Maybe there are not so many of them as they want us to believe. Possibly they have raised those many fires to rouse the rabbit in us all, to send us scampering off the mountain so that they can cross it at will into the Red World, follow us, and pick us off one by one with little threat to themselves. But if we stand against them here, on high ground, many of them will die if they try to ascend this mountain. If they knew that we were armed and unafraid and waiting for them, we might give them second thoughts."

The idea caught fire within Cha-kwena. "We will bring wood and kindling to this place. We will set so many fires that the sight of them will fill our enemies with the same dread that they have heaped upon us. For all that they have done, it will please me to know that they look to this mountain and know that men, not rabbits, stand against them. Lom-da and Iman-atl are still with us. Their headmen and the men of their bands are brave hunters."

Dakan-eh slung a brotherly arm around Cha-kwena's shoulder. "Yes! And even their women are ready for a fight! Now that my Ban-ya is feeling better, she works with the other women to gather great heaps of rocks, which they plan to hurl upon any man foolish enough to come against us from below. Have you seen them at it? They are looking forward to smashing a few heads! As am I!"

"*Your* Ban-ya?"

Dakan-eh looked embarrassed. "I *have* put life into her, you know." A droll smile tugged at the corners of his mouth. "I *like* to put life in her."

"Is there a woman alive you don't want to put life into, Dakan-eh?"

"No, it is true, I like to lie on women—young, old, fat, thin—it is a weakness in me. But I like Ban-ya best of all. I like the feel of her big breasts. I like the way she fights me. I like the way she is willing to fight life itself for what she wants and for those she loves! She will make bold sons for me. I am proud to know that she is my woman now—but do not tell her that I have said so. I would not have her think less of me."

Across the long miles, Masau moved like a wounded lion—long strides when he could bear it, brief rests prone in the grass. He sucked in shallow breaths, gasping with pain, and dozed only lightly until he had summoned the strength and the will to stumble on.

By day and by night he moved, following the People of the Watching Star. Even with Ysuna driving them, they rested at night, raised fires, hunted small game, cooked the meat, and sang the songs of death and conquest. They slept, and then rose with the dawn to move on again.

At last he was within sight of their encampment near the base of the sacred mountain of the Red World. On this night Masau lay in the grass beneath a clouded sky and listened to the beat of drums and the high, piercing shrieks of whistles. To the south, high upon the mountain wall, fires were also burning. Were the shamans gathered there, he wondered, was Cha-kwena, as guileless as ever, or had he at last dealt with and accepted his true nature? Did he look down into the Land of Grass, observing death as it came to them? His eyes narrowed. The girl, the little one who walked with mammoth, would she be there, too? She would be a shaman someday, a wisewoman of the healing ways—if she lived long enough.

The moon, a curving band of silver revealed now and then by the scudding clouds, was rising over his shoulder. He lay still and felt the light moving over him . . . gray . . . soft . . . soothing until it was eclipsed by cloud shadow. He looked up into the darkness.

Was the god watching him? Would Thunder in the Sky be loyal to Ysuna this night?

His eyes closed, and he recalled the body of the broken-faced woman that he had come across earlier in the day. He had recognized her as Yatli's wife. Abandoned by the People of the Watching Star, her eyes had been open, her mouth agape. Ants streamed in and out through her nose and ears. She had not been dead long. Yatli had already lost a son, Neewalatli, to Ysuna after the boy had challenged her judgment on the long-ago lion hunt, and Masau had strangled the man's older daughter, Wehatla. Who had killed Yatli's woman, Masau wondered, and why?

He drew in a breath and stiffened. He knew the answer to his question. Why had any of them died—the young girls . . . the children who accidentally strayed into Ysuna's shadow . . . the men and women in all the villages that had been raided for captives . . . the old people whose appearance offended Daughter of the Sun and were put out of the band to die—it was always at Ysuna's whim and for Ysuna's pleasure.

"No more," he vowed, and, thinking of Blood, sighed with grave intent. Yet another memory rose in him: *Am I worthy?* It was Cha-kwena speaking to him across time, staring at the sacred stone as it lay in the hollow of his hand. And yet it was not Cha-kwena; it was another young boy, unsure and untested.

*Am I worthy to be shaman, Ysuna?*

*A man makes himself worthy to be Shaman, Masau.*

His jaw tightened. Thunder rolled in the storm clouds that had gathered above the mountains. Somewhere far away, a mammoth trumpeted. Raindrops began to fall. They pounded Masau's cloak—all that was left of the little white son. The raindrops were cold where they struck the bare skin of his arms and legs. He tensed. Memories filled him, of the village by the Lake of Many Singing Birds, of the gentle, caring People of the Red World, of Tlanaquah, of Cha-kwena, of Mah-ree, and of his beloved Ta-maya.

"Ta-maya, may you remember me for what I do now and for all that I might have been had Daughter of the Sun not put her mark upon my life. This night Ysuna will die. And by this one act will this shaman at last be worthy to call himself a man."


Ta-maya awoke with a start. "I cannot stay here."

Eldest Hunter opened one eye and looked at her sleepily. "The men of Shateh go to fight. You cannot follow."

"But I let Masau go without a word to him. I let him walk away."

"You could not have known that he would go."

"I should have known." She sat up and pulled Shateh's coat more tightly around her shoulders. "Do you think he will be all right out there alone in the dark, Eldest Hunter?"

"Masau *is* the dark. He brings it to all he touches."
The man shook his head. "But this time, girl, I think he
will die in it. I *hope* he will die in it. Do you no longer
want this for the man who killed your father and betrayed
you and your people to Ysuna?"

A terrible emptiness opened within her. It was black,
cold. She thought she would drown in it, and then was
sorry she did not. "I have never been very good at knowing what I want, Eldest Hunter. But, no—no matter what
he has done, I do not want him to die."

It was raining harder now. The People of the Watching Star erected hasty shelters for themselves and a secure
lodge for their priestess. Maliwal brought food and drink
to her. He was grateful when she said that she would be
alone on this last night before their attack on the mountain.

"Soon all will be as I have promised."

"Yes, Ysuna, soon." He left her with his hand braced
against his ravaged face and missing ear. "We will both be
healed through the blood of the mammoth, the possession
of the sacred stones, and the death of the lizard eaters.
Soon!"

Alone at last within the lodge, Ysuna removed her
feathered cloak and her jaguar-pelt cape. She drew the
sacred dagger from its sheath, tucked it into the fold of her
sling, then removed the square of lion skin from her hips
and placed it on the hide-covered floor. After retrieving
the little stone lamp from her belongings, she knelt. With
one arm still in a sling, she could not make the necessary
ceremonial fire, but she could sit motionlessly, staring at
her lamp, holding the dagger across her thighs, watching
imaginary flames, smelling imaginary smokes, and listening to the rain as she thought about how things would soon
change for her.

"I will be young again. I will bleed again. When the
next full moon rises, I shall walk forth reborn and eternal
among my people."

Thunder growled on the mesas. Ysuna felt the power
of the sound and trembled. She looked across the lodge to
where her new spear lay braced upright next to the closed
cold flap. She smiled. How beautiful a weapon it was.

Even now Maliwal would be hafting the others, working the mammoth long bones that he had chosen and brought from the last encampment, straightening them, smoothing them, hardening them in fire.

A bolt of lightning illuminated the night. The flash was so intense that it penetrated the hide covering and filled the lodge with momentary brightness. Thunder followed. It was so loud, so earthshaking, that she cried out, then laughed at her foolishness.

"Yes, Thunder in the Sky, I hear your voice! You are near! You are life! You are death! You are Totem! And I am Ysuna. Fire eats at my command. Grass burns, the wind blows, and men and women live and die, all at my will. Soon I will walk at your side, and your lightning will live in my spears as I slay lions and men and cause all living things to quake in fear of my name!"

"In your dreams, Ysuna. Only in your dreams."

Masau's voice followed so close on the sound of the thunder that she could not tell which had come first. She looked up at him with a start.

"Masau!" She spoke his name in surprise and dread. One look at his face had her instinctively positioning the dagger for use as she rose to her feet. Her eyes narrowed. This was not the son she had raised and nurtured and manipulated to work her will and serve her pleasure. This was the lion whom she had seen growing in the skin of the man. This was Mystic Warrior. He had become Death. And he was coming for her now.

"I have told you before, you cannot follow." Eldest Hunter was adamant. "Besides, it is dark, and from the look of the far horizon, it is raining on the mesas."

"I am not afraid of the dark, and I've walked through rain before!" Ta-maya controlled her temper. The man could not keep her here against her will. Nor could any of the Bison Men left behind as guards detain her . . . or the sixty armed and painted warriors who had just arrived from various bands across the Land of Grass. Shamed by Shateh's message, they had reconsidered their earlier decision not to make war on the People of the Watching Star. Now they would follow; now they would fight; now they were ready to die.

"I will go with you!" she declared. "I *must* go with you!"

"This is a war party. There is no room for women in it," said their leader.

"I am young and strong. I will not slow you."

"They walk into danger," warned Eldest Hunter. "If you try to leave this camp, I will tether you as though you were a dog that does not know its place!"

She matched his threat with a stare of unshakable determination. "I have tended your wounded, Eldest Hunter. I have snared meat for them and cooked for them, and I changed the dressings of their wounds. In this I have repaid Shateh for his kindness to Kosar-eh and me. But I have done enough! The shamans of my people are under attack, and if Shateh does not reach them in time, they will die and my village will be overwhelmed by enemies!"

The elder hunter gestured outward with telling hands. "Yes! Exactly! And so it is that Shateh has commanded you to stay here with us, in a safe camp!"

Her head went high. There was no indecision in her voice or in her heart. "I am a woman of the Red World, not the Bison Band. I do not wish to be safe among strangers. There is no honor for me here. Every hand may be needed to save the village of my people."

Eldest Hunter looked at the leader of the newcomers. "She was to have been the latest sacrifice. It is said that Masau turned on Ysuna in order to save her life. It is easy to understand why."

"And where is Mystic Warrior now?"

"He has gone to kill Ysuna," informed Ta-maya.

The dark eyes of the newcomers narrowed with disbelief, and the leader snorted nastily. "More likely he has gone to join her."

"No! He would not!" she shouted.

"What difference?" asked the leader of the war party. "When we find him, we will kill him." He looked at Ta-maya with a odd, twisted expression of pity and admiration. "After what he and his people have done to my people and yours, your heart should be hard toward him. Yes, I say that you *should* come along, to see what we will now do to those who have given us cause to avenge our dead."

Masau had his spear at ready and could have impaled Ysuna where she stood. But as he stood looking at her nakedness, a bright, bruising flash of lightning enabled him to see her as she was—old, sick, dying, and afraid. Despite himself, his heart lurched with a son's love and pity. And in that moment, the weakness in him was in his eyes and softened his expression.

Ysuna began to approach him slowly, moving as a lioness, one cautious, measured step at a time, staring, locking her eyes to his, drawing his spirit into her soul where she held it captive.

Safely past his extended spear, she stood face-to-face with him. Her long mouth pulled wide. Her lips parted. She was smiling at him, showing her teeth. Suddenly, without word or warning, her good arm pulled back and then snapped forward, driving the point of the sacred dagger toward his heart.

But he lurched back, grabbed her wrist, pulled sharply back on it, withdrew the dagger, and prevented it from penetrating more than skin and surface muscle. She had broken her own spell. Her actions had named him prey. Although he, too, was weakened by wounds and fever, he was in his prime. His natural, superior strength gave him the advantage.

She fought him, seeking desperately to place the blade again, then screamed in rage when, still twisting against his hold, her wrist was crushed and her hand went limp.

He had the dagger now. It took only a single second to turn it, to place the point below and between her breasts, to drive it upward, hard, with a ferocity that stunned them both.

Her knees buckled, and she sagged in his embrace. In the instant before her head went back, her eyes bulged and fixed on him; then the pupils contracted and suddenly went wide. They did not move again, and a sound of disbelief went out of her. The stench of her dying breath was that of someone who had already been long dead inside.

He held her. He felt numb, beyond emotion. Lightning flashed, and thunder rolled. Rain pounded on the hide covering of the lodge. He picked her up and carried her to the lion skin, kicked aside the unlighted lamp, and put her down upon the pelt. He remembered the day that she had taken it. It could have been his—*should* have been his, but he did not want it now.

In the sporadic, livid glow of lightning, he stared down at her. She was ugly in death. Had she ever been beautiful? Yes, once, like the viper on the rock or the lioness on the plain—beautiful, but deadly . . . and never his mother, always his enemy.

He closed his eyes. She was dead, and he was glad. He had killed her, but he felt no guilt. Now, at last, he was free of her. He could walk as a man. He could be a shaman who would lead his people in the way of life, not of death.

He opened his eyes and spoke softly to the dead woman at his feet. "At last I have made myself worthy of the life you had returned to me. You did it not out of concern for an abandoned child but in perverted fulfillment of your own dark needs. It could have been different, Ysuna, for both of us. And now it *will* be different, for me."

With a deep, steadying breath, he turned away from Daughter of the Sun and thought of Ta-maya and of the life he would try to lead with her . . . if she could forgive him, accept him, and understand why he had been what he had been and done all that he had done.

He became aware of the sound of hard, driving rain. It was a good sound, like a spring rain falling on the mountain heights. Lightning flashed. How beautiful was the light! Then he noticed Yatli standing just inside the entrance of the lodge. How appallingly ugly was the expression of hatred that transformed Yatli's face as he hurled the spear that he had snatched up from where Ysuna had left it standing upright beside the cold flap.

Masau felt no pain, only wonderment and disappointment as the great white spearhead of chalcedony penetrated his heart. Death came in a bright, explosive shattering of hope as the spear drove straight through him and took him down. He fell beside Ysuna, but he had Ta-maya's name on his lips. The last thing he saw as his spirit collapsed and fell away into inner darkness was Yatli standing above him in triumph, shouting the names of his dead wife and of his son Neewalatli and of his daughter Wehatla, the frightened young attendant whom Masau had left to be food for carrion at the edge of the encampment not so many nights before.

"No!" Maliwal stood in shock.

Yatli's shouts had brought Maliwal to the lodge of Daughter of the Sun. Now Yatli lay dead at his feet, strangled. But Maliwal's quick retaliation could not restore the lives that Yatli had so unexpectedly taken.

"Ysuna!" Maliwal wailed, and struck to the heart by unbearable grief, he turned and ran into the driving rain, calling to Chudeh and to any other man who could hear. "The sons! Where are Yatli's sons?"

Unaware of what had just transpired, one of the young men stepped forward. In an instant Maliwal's hands had crushed his throat and sent him to join his father in the world beyond this world.

"Bring the rest of them to me," commanded Maliwal. "They must die, all of them, including the young daughter. And their dogs. Kill their dogs."

Mad with grief, he stopped. The rain was pounding the earth all around him. He could feel it running down his hair and face and soaking his body. The people were all out of their shelters now. Circling him in shocked silence, all of them stared wide-eyed at Maliwal as his hand flew to the side of his head, to touch the ugly, scar-rimmed little hole where his ear had been. "My face! Now she will never heal my face!"

He sank to his knees in the rain and sobbed like a baby. Suddenly the idea came to him. It was an epiphany that had him on his feet again. He ran back inside the lodge of Daughter of the Sun. He ripped the sacred collar from her neck, put it around his own, then—wearing her feathered cloak and the jaguar-skin cape—went out into the rain again.

"It can still be!" he cried to his assembled people. "I, Maliwal, will lead you now!"

# 14

The rain had stopped. The sun was shining through broken clouds, and yet the storm had only now struck full force against the mountain. Last night strangers had circled around the encampment of the People of the Watching Star and come toward the mesas. Cha-kwena had sensed their presence before their signal fires were seen. Dakan-eh had armed himself and gone down in stealth with several other hunters. He returned grim faced, with the strangers following and carrying Kosar-eh on a litter. The clown's woman and children had run to embrace him, fussing over his injuries, until he told them all that he had endured, and what he had seen, and how Tlana-quah had died. And then they wept, and all the People of the Red World had wept with them.

But now the time for grief was over. The strangers—men from the Bison Band,—had offered to join ranks with the two remaining bands of the Red World and had promised that more men, from the Land of Grass, would be arriving soon to come to their aid.

Mah-ree, holding a basket of rocks, stood in shock upon the north wall and looked straight down from the heights. Her heart was pounding so hard, it felt as though it must knock her down. Never in her life had she seen so many people . . . on the mountain or off! The men of the Watching Star were climbing the flank of the mesa while their women and children stood in a great rank behind them and pounded on drums, blew on whistles, screamed, shouted, and howled like wolves. "Throw your rocks or get out of the way, girl!" demanded Ha-xa, hefting her own basket on her hip. Off balance because of the great mound of her pregnancy, she half stumbled to the edge of the wall, then pitched the load with all of her might.

Far below, a man screamed in pain.

"Ha! Take that in the name of Tlana-quah," bellowed Ha-xa, and turned on her heels. Wearing a look of pure, mad delight and satisfaction, she headed back for the rock pile and a new supply of armaments.

Mah-ree could not move. Her mother looked like a stranger to her; all her people looked like strangers. Inspired to the heights of battle frenzy by Kosar-eh's revelations, their eyes and faces aglow with the hatred of vengeful purpose, the women pitched basket load after basket load of rocks and fecal matter down at those who dared to come against them. They sloshed paunch after paunch of boiled oil and urine onto their attackers.

All the men and boys were following Dakan-eh. In Tlana-quah's absence he had become headman. Even Shateh and his men and chiefs of Lom-da's and Iman-atl's bands were obeying him, drawing inspiration from him, leaping upon the heights, contemptuously displaying themselves, shouting insults, whirling stone-laden bolas, and throwing the many spears that they had made for this occasion.

"Look at my Bold Man!" Ban-ya was actually weeping with pride as she ran past Mah-ree. "He is all and more than he ever claimed to be!"

Suddenly, from far below, a spear came arcing upward and landed with a *thunk* at Mah-ree's feet; it might have struck her had Cha-kwena not seen it coming and yanked her away.

"What is wrong, Mosquito? You stand like a stone! If you are too frightened to help us, place yourself out of danger. Here, give me your basket."

He pitched its contents over the edge of the wall. More than one man cried out from below. Cha-kwena laughed at their expense, then turned, picked up the spear that had nearly struck Mah-ree, and went forward again, took aim, and threw.

The garbled cry of a mortally wounded man caused him to raise his arms in joy.

"That is one more lion who will not hurl a spear against the People of the Red World!" he declared.

She stared at him. "I do not know you anymore, Cha-kwena."

"I am the same, Little One."

"No, you are not acting like a shaman."

"I am Shaman, Mah-ree. And now I am also the hunter that I always knew I must be."

"You are hunting *people*!"

"Yes, Little One, because they have hunted and killed too many of my people and because now they are hunting me!"

"But look at yourself, Cha-kwena! By the look on your face, it is obvious that you *like* what you are doing! All of you, you *like* it! Look: Over there, Kosar-eh has propped himself against a rock. The children are handing him spears and—"

He was annoyed. "We have no time for this. We must turn back the Brothers of the Sky! Now help us, or get out of the way."

Her lower lip was trembling. She knew that she was about to cry. She stomped her foot in frustration. "You were wrong that night upon the mountain long ago when you told Masau that you were not his brother. You *are* his brother, Cha-kwena! All of you, all the men and women of this band. You are no different from the People of the Watching Star! You are all Brothers of the Sky!"

At the base of the mountain, Maliwal took a break from the battle and saw the familiar figure of a little girl turn and run away, leaving her people swarming on the heights. He could not believe what was happening: The lizard eaters were driving back the men of the Watching Star! They were winning the day. The numbers of his dead and wounded were staggering.

Chudeh, stinking of the urine and excrement that had been rained upon his head, came close. "Maliwal, our men are breaking ranks. They have had enough. They are tired from the battle with the Bison Band, then the trek to get here. Not all the sacred stones in the Red World are worth this!"

"There is power in the stones," he growled.

"Yes, and aside from the stones that you wear around your neck, the majority of that power seems to be with *them*!" He jabbed a thumb upward as Tsana came to stand beside him.

"Well?" drawled Maliwal. "What 'good' news do you bring to me?"

Tsana's face puckered with fury and revulsion as flicking the remnants of a shattered turd from his shoulder, he stared up with hatred at the mesa. "There is not man, woman, or child up there whom I would not see dead for this shame that they hurl upon us. But it was Ysuna who had need of the sacred stones. What are they to us that we should risk our lives and our pride at the hands of lizard eaters? We are mammoth hunters, no shamans."

The words pricked Maliwal. The pain was sweet to him, as sweet as the sudden insight that caused him to tremble with near-orgasmic pleasure. "You are right! I will remember you well for your words this day, Tsana. We *are* mammoth hunters! Why do we waste our strength here, when the greatest mammoth of all walks the Red World beyond the Blue Mesas? There is another way through the mountains to him. The pass, the pass through which Masau led us!" He laughed. His eyes were alight. He was nodding, thinking out loud. "I will leave the majority of our hunters here, under your command, to harry the lizard eaters and to keep them occupied while we tend to more important work!"

Disappointment took the smile that had just come to Tsana's face. "The men will not stay. . . ."

"They and you will do as I say!" Maliwal roared in sudden anger. He shoved Tsana so hard against the shoulder with the heel of his left hand that the man staggered.

"You are not Ysuna!" Tsana retorted, his eyes flashing.

Maliwal measured the look in the man's eyes. He was on the point of rebellion. Maliwal realized that if he were to exact what he wanted from the man, he would have to deal with Tsana differently. He smiled and gave a brotherly pat to that portion of Tsana's anatomy that he had just bruised. "I am now the leader of the People of the Watching Star," he reminded affably. "With Ysuna and Masau both dead, who else will guide the People, eh? And who else would I leave in command of my forces when I am away but one of my most experienced men?"

Tsana was soothed but not happy.

"What are you saying, Maliwal?" asked Chudeh. "What is this 'more important work'?"

Maliwal smiled; he was in control now. "Ysuna's spirit speaks from within me. We will hunt and kill the great white mammoth. As she had need of its flesh and blood, so, too, do we. When the strength of our totem flows in me, I shall return with its heart to you. We shall feed on it together, then ascend with ease to the heights of the Blue Mesas. We'll laugh in the faces of the shamans and the lizard eaters of the Red World, for I will have stolen the source of their power. The great white mammoth will live in me. I will be totem! And the sacred stones will leap into my hands of their own will!"

The north wind had dropped noticeably by the time Ta-maya and her fellow travelers reached the encampment where Ysuna had died. They had passed the corpse of a woman on the trail, and circling ravens and a pair of red-tailed hawks told them that death had walked yet again in the land ahead. The bodies of several men and a girl and a few dogs lay in the open. Ta-maya was told to stay where she was while the warriors went to make certain that they were not being led into a grotesquely baited trap.

Tired and afraid of what they would find, she obeyed. They had come far since she had begged to be allowed to join them. The leader of the group had commanded one of the smaller men in the party to give her his extra pair of moccasins. Even when stuffed with grass, the shoes were still too large; nevertheless she had not complained.

Now, with the wind gusting restlessly around her, she turned her face to the sky rather than look at the corpses. How blue it was! How clear after last night's rain. It was impossible to tell that there had ever been a storm.

The leader of the traveling party called to her from the entrance to the only lodge in the campsite. "Young woman, there is something inside here that you should see."

"Mah-ree!"

The girl looked up. Cha-kwena was summoning her to the top of the mesa and a day-end meal of thanksgiving.

Mah-ree frowned. Armed men of the Watching Star were still camped on the northern flank of the mountain. Many had broken ranks and been driven away, but as long as any remained, she could not feel thankful. Everyone else was so sure that the People of the Red World had won the day, that tomorrow their attackers would lose heart and run north, where they belonged. She hoped the predictions were correct, but hoping was not enough. She could not eat; she did not want the company of others—not even Cha-kwena's. In the last few hours he had become a stranger. As a result, she did not answer him.

She sat in the fading light of day, with the basket of pups and Mother Dog, just outside the little cluster of hastily thatched huts that her people had erected in their traditional camping spot high on the south-facing flank of the sacred mountain.

Mah-ree sat on a big, lichen-clad boulder. It was as large as three or four lodges put together, oddly shaped, and set amid a jumble of other similar boulders. For generations the women of the Red World had cracked pine nuts and ground mountain acorns on these rocks; but she was certain that never in all of those generations had they sat upon these boulders after a day like this one.

With her knees pulled to her chin, Mah-ree wrapped her arms around her calves. She could hear singing from the top of the mesa. *Singing!* Her father was dead, Kosar-eh badly injured, and Ta-maya was still not reunited with the band. Only the forces of Creation knew how many men were dead on the north slopes of the mountain. True, they were not men of her tribe; but they were men just the same, and the People of the Red World had killed them!

Appalled, she listened as they sang of the treacherous strangers from the north, of their own bravery and cleverness, and of their newfound friendship with the men of the Bison Band who tomorrow would help them drive their enemies from the land of the ancestors.

But what if they failed? What if the Bison Band turned on them as the men of the Watching Star had done? What songs would they sing then?

She shivered. "Listen to them, Mother Dog," she said, unable to bring herself to use the animal's given name, Watching Star, lest by doing so she speak the name of the people who had betrayed her band. "We called those who gave you to us our friends, but look what they turned out to be. You are an exception, of course." She reached out and fondled the dog's shaggy ears. The animal whined appreciatively, then suddenly went rigid and began to growl.

Trudging to a halt in the pinyon grove below was the great white mammoth.

Mah-ree hushed the dog. "I greet you, Grandfather of All," she said to her totem. "I am sorry that I have not brought you good things to eat. Life has been bad on this mountain. You should not be so near. If things do not go well for us tomorrow . . ."

"Things *will* go well!" Cha-kwena had discovered her whereabouts and was standing atop the next boulder. "Today my vision has been fulfilled. Tomorrow we will drive off the men of the Watching Star."

Mah-ree did not like the ease with which he gave his assurance. "How can you be so certain?"

"I am Shaman!"

The mammoth huffed and circled restlessly.

Mah-ree watched him, troubled. "I am afraid for him, Cha-kwena. He should not be here."

He eyed the mammoth thoughtfully. "He is here to prove the rightness of my vision. I saw it all: the spears, the heated oil, the people rallying together, and the coming of the bison hunters. I saw them as lions, and lions they proved themselves to be!"

"Hoyeh-tay warned us to beware of lions."

Mah-ree's statement took him off guard, then irritated him. "I have finally accepted my calling to the shaman's path. I do not need a mosquito to sting me with doubt now." He shook his head. "And Ha-xa is worried about you. She sent me to find you. Are you coming?"

"No."

"Then stay here and go hungry. You are an annoying little nit, Mah-ree, and I do not care what you do!"

For a long time she sat on the rock, nursing her nicked pride, idly running her fingers through the fur of Mother Dog's neck. She noticed after a few minutes that the mammoth was gone. One moment he had been facing her; the next he turned away. She rose. She could see him

moving off through the trees, heading downhill to the
south. Somehow she knew that he would keep going until
he reached the high forested hills above the meadow near
the abandoned village by the Lake of Many Singing Birds.

"Wait," she called after him, hefting the basket of
pups. "I am coming with you! Let us go home together.
We will wait there for our people to return. Maybe they
will be themselves again, and we will know them again
when they get there. In the meantime, you will be safer
away from this place."

Mah-ree clambered off the boulder, then turned back
and waved Mother Dog forward. "Come! You and I and
the pups will walk with Grandfather of All as he journeys
home to his family! No one will miss us!"

# 15

In the thin gray light of false dawn the first group of
runners from the combined forces of the Bison Bands
attacked the men of the Watching Star who were still
encamped at the base of the mountain. They came in
stealth. They came with spears and war clubs and flaming
brands.

Before the sun was up, the fighting spirit of the men
of the Watching Star had faded even though the star itself
was bright in the sky. Disheartened, without Ysuna,
Maliwal, or Masau to lead them, they broke ranks, abandoned their dead and wounded, and fled with their women
and children.

Hours later Chudeh brought some of the men together into a dispirited cold camp, where they salved and
stitched one another's wounds.

"They think they have beaten us, but they have not,"
said Chudeh. "They have shamed us with the power of
their totem. I, for one, cannot retreat into the land of our

ancestors with this stain on my spirit. I say that we gather those of us who are willing to fight on. I say that we follow Maliwal. He is strong. He is *Wolf*. We will run with him in a pack and hunt the great white mammoth. Then, after we have killed and eaten it, we will return to this place and make the lizard eaters and bison eaters regret the day."

Silent, pale, and brokenhearted, Ta-maya was escorted back to her people by several of the men of the Bison tribe. She stood with them in the camp within the sacred grove. So grateful was she to be alive and among her own once more, she could barely speak. She made no mention of Masau's name or his death. She knew that there would be no mourning, except in her own heart, in this camp for Mystic Warrior.

Ha-xa wept with joy to see her. Ta-maya looked for Mah-ree, but U-wa's embrace distracted her, as did all the hugs of the women and girls and the three old widows.

She saw immediately what had blossomed between Dakan-eh and Ban-ya, for although he came to place two strong hands upon her shoulders and told her that his heart smiled at her return, Ban-ya held back until he called her forward, proudly informing Ta-maya, loudly enough for all to hear: "Ban-ya is my woman now! I have put life into her. I have decided this a good thing!"

Ban-ya looked Ta-maya straight in the eyes and said with an open and unbegrudging heart, "He is my man now. But if he still wants you, and you still want him, you will always be welcome at our fire and in the bed furs of our lodge as second woman."

Ta-maya was taken aback. She had heard no smugness, no gloating in Ban-ya's voice—only a flat but genuine offer of friendship . . . on her own terms.

When Dakan-eh flushed with sudden temper and sternly castigated his new woman for a loose tongue and angrily warned her to allow her man to speak first in the future, Ta-maya at last understood him well enough to realize that he had intended no shame to her or Ban-ya. He was simply a boastful man who was insensitive to the pride of others while being painfully in need of constant bolstering of it in himself. She had taken his pride away from him once; she gave it back to him now, without reservation. "Ta-maya's heart smiles to see that Bold Man has forgiven her for what once came between them. But now events that have nothing to do with Dakan-eh take the gladness from my heart. Ta-maya will sleep under the bed furs of no man."

Hearing this, Siwi-ni, woman of Kosar-eh, came fluttering forward to kiss her cheeks and bring her little ones close so that they might hug the returning daughter of Tlana-quah. "Be brave, elder daughter of our headman. Be proud. On this day your father's life spirit smiles once more. Although he has died in a far land, his actions against the enemies have brought you safely home to us!"

Ta-maya returned Siwi-ni's kiss; the little woman's cheek was dry, as furrowed by weathering as an eroded creek bed. Ta-maya embraced all the children except Gah-ti, who blushed in her presence and, by his posture and haughty expression, made it clear to her that he was too old to show affection to a female. She grinned at the youth. He had changed since she had been away; he had grown up. Sadness touched her. They had all changed, all grown up, all come to see the world with different, older eyes.

"Everyone must take pride in the memory of my father," she said to the eldest son of the clown. Then, feeling the eyes of Kosar-eh upon her, she turned and looked toward him. He leaned on a crudely made crutch of pinyon wood, with rabbit fur softening the arm brace. "We must also know that had it not been for the bravery of Kosar-eh, the Bison Men would not have known of our plight and the men of the People of the Watching Star might now be sitting in this camp among our dead, drawing power from the sacred bones of First Man and First Woman, and readying themselves to hunt Grandfather of All."

Absolute silence prevailed among the assemblage.

"I did only what any man would have done," Kosar-eh said modestly.

She would not allow it. "You twice risked your life so that mine might be saved: once when you chose to stay at Tlana-quah's side, and again when you put yourself between me and the spear of Shateh when you feared that he might impale me with it."

"It is true!" affirmed the leader of the Bison Band. "He is a brave one, this Kosar-eh."

The people murmured. All looked at their clown with astonishment and wonder. Siwi-ni stood as tall as her birdlike form would allow and harrumphed as though to say that she could not understand why anyone had ever supposed that her man had been less than a hero. The eyes of Kosar-eh's sons went round with newfound pride and respect.

Kosar-eh was openly embarrassed. He made a face and an undirected gesture. "What is all this? I am a clown! I am Kosar-eh, Funny Man, a teller of tales, and, when this wound of mine is healed, a dancer who will lighten the hearts of this People and make them smile in times of need. Every band of the Red World must have its clown! I had to come back. Who else would make you laugh?"

Ta-maya shook her head. "You are more than a clown, Kosar-eh. You are a *warrior.*"

He was openly flustered, as red-faced and blushing as a boy as his people cheered him. To everyone's amazement, Dakan-eh came forward and laid a hand upon his shoulder.

"In times when Brothers of the Sky have come to walk in the world, I am proud to know that in this band there are many brave men and two hunters, Dakan-eh and Kosar-eh, who can answer to the name of Bold Man!"

After a brief and solemn council, it was decided that the dead enemies would be left on the other side of the mountain where they had fallen. As for the wounded men of the north, some among the People of the Red World spoke in favor of bringing them into the sacred groves and tending them as best they could.

"They have shown no mercy to our people," reminded Dakan-eh.

"Nor to Tlana-quah," added Kosar-eh grimly. "Or to me."

Shateh nodded. "When they have come against encampments in the Land of Grass, they have killed all they could, allowing life only to those whom they took as slaves.

Because children and women are present, I will not describe these deaths or the fate of these slaves. Instead I will say that these warriors of the Watching Star have chosen their own fate. Let them die as they have lived. Let the wounded lie unattended with their dead brothers. If you bring them here to be healed, how will you deal with them when you have made them well and strong again? They will be predators loose among you. No woman or child in this camp will be safe, and no man or boy will ever again be able to sleep without his spear at his side. They must be left to die."

Ha-xa was extremely disturbed. "We cannot leave injured men to be fed upon by beasts."

"Why not? That was what they had in store for me." Kosar-eh's voice was more harsh than any of his people had ever heard it.

Cha-kwena said gently, "Had you walked among the dead of the White Hills, Ha-xa, you would feel no pity for those who have reveled in death as though it were meat and drink to them."

Her face was pinched with grief, but not with indecision. "They have killed many of my people. They have taken the life of Tlana-quah. But somewhere out there to the north, their women and children await their return. Soon they will mourn, as I mourn now." She drew in a deep, steadying breath as she looked straight at Shateh. "Your words are wise, Headman of the Bison People, but you have never borne the life of another in your belly. As a mother who even now carries life within me, I ask this of you and the men of my band: Do not let it be said of my people that in this moment of decision over life and death, we were as cruel to our enemies as Brothers of the Sky have been to us."

Shateh's brows came together. "What do you ask of me, Ha-xa? These men have killed your man! These men have killed my *son*!"

She hesitated, but only for a moment. "I ask only this: If these sons of the women of the People of the Watching Star must be meat for the animals of the earth and the birds of the sky, then kill them first."

Shateh and the men of the various bison-eating bands were awed by the strength of will that had been displayed by the widow of Tlana-quah. Equally impressed were they by the resolve of the men of the Red World, who took up their spears and war clubs, which, in the main, were only rabbit-braining sticks. Together they went down from the top of this flat-topped mountain, walked among the wounded and dead of their enemies, and killed without mercy.

When at last the moon rose full out of the western sky and the night wind whispered softly across the northern flanks of the holy mountain, there was not a Brother of the Sky left alive in that place to enjoy the clean, cool breath of the wind or to look up and appreciate the moon's beauty.

Together the men of the Red World and the men of the Bison Bands ascended the north trail. There was low, tired talk of "work" well done, of enemies who had died well or badly, and of those men of the Watching Star who had shown the good sense to turn and flee the day before.

Cha-kwena stood alone in the darkness, his bone braining stick in his left hand and the sacred stone at his neck within the curl of his right hand. He doubted if he had ever been so tired. His bones felt heavy and his spirit seemed numb as he looked down along the mountain wall.

How many men had he slain tonight? Only two. Dakan-eh and the bison eaters had done the bulk of the killing. Nevertheless, now that he thought of it, two dead men seemed an infinite number when he added it to the others whose lives his spears and stones had ended since the assault on the mountain had begun.

But the two men he had killed tonight had been mortally wounded and posed no threat to him—at least not at the moment of their death. Each had looked right at him, guessing his intent. One, in fact, had sneered at him in open contempt; the other had merely closed his eyes and looked away. Cha-kwena had smashed their skulls without hesitation, as though they meant no more to him than a pair of hares or rabbits trapped in a snare net. No, he realized. That was not true. He had never enjoyed killing an animal; but he had found pleasure in the deaths that he had dealt this night. He had enjoyed killing these two men.

Somewhere far away, a mammoth trumpeted and a coyote howled, and a young man asked out of the depths of Cha-kwena's spirit: *Am I worthy?*

And the ghost of one whom he had once named Brother whispered on the wind: *A shaman makes himself worthy, Cha-kwena.*

"But worthy of *what*, you stupid boy?"

The question stung him as the silhouette of an owl flew across the face of the moon.

He gasped. The bird was flying toward him. Somehow the moon and stars shone right through it. In a moment it would fly straight into him. He moved to the side. The bird altered its course and kept coming. Cha-kwena threw himself to the ground, tossed away his braining stick, and then put up his hands to deflect the certain collision. But the bird passed through his flesh and bone to disappear into thin air, as though it had no more substance than the wind. And yet Cha-kwena felt the rush of wings and the warm exhalation of mocking, raptorial chuckles as the spirit of Owl vanished into the eastern sky, leaving a rain of feathers and a warning in his wake.

"Stupid boy! You are Shaman at last! But you still do not understand the path to which you have been called!"

Once more he heard the trumpeting of the mammoth and the call of a coyote. He sat up. When a bat dipped low out of the dark and grazed his head, he barely felt it. In the darkness in front of him were Deer and Hawk, Swallow and Hare, Rabbit and Mouse.

"Is this Cha-kwena, Brother of Animals, whom we see sitting on the ground?" asked Deer.

"It is Shaman, Slayer of Men," responded Hare, shaking his head sadly.

"I do not know him," said Rabbit.

"Is he dangerous?" asked Mouse.

"Only to his own kind and to himself," answered Hawk.

"By my actions I have saved my people!" Cha-kwena angrily told the animals. Then he blinked, frowning, as another bird joined the others. It flew gracefully out of the night to alight on the head of Deer.

"You have not saved them all," accused Shrike, cocking his black-masked head and looking at Cha-kwena out of shining black eyes as bright as polished obsidian. "A shaman makes himself worthy, Cha-kwena. Where is Mosquito tonight? Where is the great white mammoth? And where walks the Wolf named Maliwal?"

The youth's heart went cold. He knew his path now, the path to which he had been called. It took him to Dakan-eh and Shateh and the gathering of hunters. He was not alone when he faced them. Owl and Bat, Deer and Hawk, Swallow and Hare, Rabbit and Mouse, Coyote and even Shrike were gathered around him.

"My spirit brothers have spoken," Cha-kwena told the men. "We must leave this mountain and go to Tlanaquah's village. We must protect the great white mammoth and Mah-ree from the Wolf. And we must go *now*!"

# 16

The way to Tlana-quah's village seemed longer than Maliwal remembered, the land steeper, the mountains colder, the river wider. He paused only long enough to draw in a deep breath of resolve before stalking on, paying no heed to the complaints of the dwindling number of his followers.

"If we stop to rest and eat, it would go easier with us all," said Ston.

"We will rest after we have killed the shaman girl and the great white mammoth. We will eat when we feast upon his flesh and scrape the marrow from his bones."

"But, Maliwal . . ." It was Chudeh now, wheezing with exhaustion. "Maliwal, slow down! I have brought these men far in order to walk with you. We have come miles without a rest. We must—"

"Keep up or fall behind!"

Suddenly furious, Chudeh stopped and shouted, "Half the men you started with have already done just that! Or haven't you noticed?"

Maliwal whirled around. He carried three enormous spears of mammoth bone and white chalcedony. His eyes were red and wild in a face strained with fatigue. In his feathered cloak and jaguar-skin cape, and with Ysuna's collar embracing his neck and shoulders, he had a deranged look about him.

Chudeh took an involuntary step backward. "Maliwal, old friend, we have walked many a long mile together and hunted many a beast and made many a kill together. But I cannot keep up with you if you continue at this pace."

"The stones of Ysuna give me power."

"Perhaps, but they do nothing for me or for the others. We must rest, eat, and offer up songs of mourning to honor our many dead so their spirits will be with us as we continue."

Maliwal's face twisted. "Now that the sacred stones of Ysuna are mine, what are the spirits of the dead to me? When the great white mammoth is dead, all will be as it once was: my face, my ear, and the dead—maybe they will rise again, I do not know. But you must have faith in me, Chudeh." He paused, measured the hunter with suspicion and then with compassion. "You have always been too cautious, Chudeh. Do you remember how it was on that night many moons ago when you said that I could not hunt mammoth in the dark? But I did, and later we burned a village of lizard eaters and took their women and—"

"The night that Rok died? The night that the old cow mammoth took your ear and ripped half your face away?"

Maliwal's compassion was replaced by hostility. "The mammoth kind still have a debt to pay to me for that night. They will pay, and so will you with your life if you slow my pace or try to turn me from my purpose again!"

With Life Giver walking ahead of her and Mother Dog and the pups gamboling alongside, Mah-ree jogged steadily toward home. At first she had hoped that Chakwena would follow in an attempt to bring her back to join the others . . . not that she would go. She never wanted to set eyes upon the sacred mountain again, nor did she wish to think of what might be happening now upon its heights. Besides, as long as there was the slightest chance that

Grandfather of All might be at risk, he must be kept moving away from his enemies.

A day passed and a night. The great mammoth trudged on as though he had no need of rest. Puzzled by his behavior, she kept up with him and ate lightly off the land as they traveled. She carried the pups in their basket when they grew tired. Mother Dog never fell behind; her impetus was the fact that Mah-ree had control of her offspring.

At last the girl had put Big Lake behind and was moving across familiar country on the last stretch of her journey. The forested mountains ahead were those of home; beyond lay the village and the Lake of Many Singing Birds. The mammoth seemed to sense this. As day ebbed into dusk Grandfather of All settled into an evening of grazing that allowed Mah-ree much needed sleep. She awoke hours later, thinking that someone had called her name.

She sat up, listening, looking around in the impenetrable dark, thinking of Cha-kwena, missing him, hoping that he would come to her with good news. The wind was out of the south, so if anyone were coming from the mesas, it would be difficult to hear them unless they were very close. But they could hear her, so she called out once, twice, and then again. No one answered.

Grandfather of All was circling restlessly. Mother Dog was sitting up, ears pricked, staring to the northeast.

Mah-ree shivered, suddenly afraid. *Do not be foolish,* she upbraided herself. *You walk in the presence of your totem. Nothing can harm you as long as you are with him!*

If Chudeh and the others had been allowed a little rest and a bit of food, they might well have followed Maliwal until the end. Nor did he provide them with a little of that which any wise leader grants to those who willingly walk with them into danger: a pretense, at least, of respect, loyalty, and consideration. But Maliwal had never been wise, and his respect and loyalty and consideration for anyone other than himself had extended only to Ysuna.

Now, his men looked back to see the combined forces

of Shateh and the murdered Tlana-quah advancing toward them.

"They do not give up, these lizard eaters," observed Chudeh with visible apprehension. "Now they are many, and we are few. Maliwal, what is the plan of attack?"

He stood like a riled, gut-wounded bull bison—head out, nostrils flaring. He was breathing hard and deep and shaking his head in a fury of frustration. "Hold them off. I will go on alone ahead of you and do as I have vowed."

His men exchanged dubious glances.

"How do we accomplish this?" asked Chudeh.

"When the mammoth is dead, no one will be able to stand against you!"

"And in the meantime?"

"Just do your best! And I will do mine!"

"But you will be out of the range of their spears."

"I will be hunting the greatest mammoth of them all!"

"You cannot kill him alone."

"I am *not* alone! I wear Ysuna's sacred collar. I carry the spears of Mystic Warrior."

"And what do we have to protect us?" pressed Chudeh.

"Someone other than you to lead this force while I am on the hunt!" replied Maliwal, and before Chudeh could react, he had a spearhead of white chalcedony buried in his gut. "I warned you that you would pay with your life if you chose to stand in my way again." Maliwal jerked the projectile point free of Chudeh's belly; the man stood, stunned, staring with disbelief as he dropped his own spears and grasped at his wound to keep his innards from burbling out of it.

"Now," Maliwal said, "I will hunt the great white mammoth!" He went on without a word.

His men stared after him, then looked to the advancing force of Shateh and the lizard eaters. They, at least, knew where their loyalty lay. They left Chudeh where he stood and ran for their lives.

# 17

A storm was building over the buttes and mountains of the Red World. The Lake of Many Singing Birds spoke to the gathering night in a constant, wind-whipped imperative of slurrings and slappings along the shore. A fish jumped. Ducks scattered and flew off to land again farther out.

Exhausted from her long walk, Mah-ree lit a small fire, then slept deeply in the lodge of Tlana-quah. She did not hear the distant voices of men raised in warning; she did not hear the barking of Mother Dog or the animal's yelp of pain as the butt end of a spear shaft made of mammoth bone crushed her skull; she did not hear the yip of the puppy that Maliwal took from her basket before stooping to enter the lodge and stare in at her.

"You! Shaman Girl! Wake up!"

She stirred groggily at his sharply spoken command, then sat upright with a cry of alarm and dismay when a pup with a broken neck was thrown onto her bed furs.

"They will all end like that if you do not show me where he is."

She picked up the limp little form and held it close, as though cuddling might revive it. "He? Who? I am the only one here! What do you want, Maliwal?"

"Do not pretend innocence with me, Shaman Girl. You will tell me where he is—your totem, Life Giver, Great Ghost Spirit, Thunder in the Sky."

She saw that he had her puppy basket slung over one shoulder by its carrying thong. And then, with a start, she saw that he was wearing Tlana-quah's cape. Her eyes widened. "My father is dead. How did you come by that?" she demanded, pointing.

He smiled. "I took it from him. He did not need it anymore, and he was not fit to wear it in the first place."

As he spoke he opened up the wide lid of the basket, groped into the interior for another pup, and pulled one out. With a flick of his thumb, he snapped its neck and with a laugh tossed it at Mah-ree.

"How many more of these do you want to see dead? Believe me, Shaman Girl, I will kill them all as easily as I killed your father unless you tell me now where to find the great white mammoth."

She felt light-headed, nearly overcome by despair and anger and fear. "You will kill Grandfather of All."

His eyes narrowed. "Yes, I will. He is old. It is time that he shared his power."

"He is Life Giver. He already shares his power with all the people who name him Totem."

"Too many people name him Totem. That is why he grows old and weak. That is why he must die. Ysuna knew what must be done, and somehow you realized her intent. That is why you set yourself to destroy her—to protect him and yourself. But all that is over now. I have come to take his life and his power into me. And then *I* will be Life Giver. My ear will grow back. My scars will disappear. Ysuna swore that it would be so."

Mah-ree blinked and tried hard not to show emotion. He had changed drastically since she had last seen him. She had disliked him before; she hated him now. His words confused her. His expression terrified her. She knew that if she said the wrong thing or looked at him in a way that offended him, he would kill another pup. And he would kill her, too; she could see it in his eyes.

"Where is he, Mah-ree Who Walks with Mammoth? Tell me. I will find him with or without you. He is too big to hide."

Had he made an attempt at humor? Yes. She saw his mouth twitch into a smile. He had smiled when he had spoken of her father's death. He had smiled when he had killed the last pup. And now he was smiling as he reached into the basket for another.

"Wait! I know where he is. But you will never find him—unless I show you the way. And if you hurt another of my puppies, I will not show you at all!"

He laughed at her. "Ah, of course! He is at the secret spring! I should have guessed!"

"No, he is *not* there."

"You lie. I can see that by the way you look at me with such earnestness. How obvious! Ha! He *is* at the salt spring. And I *do* know how to get there: up the canyon to the pools where I slaughtered the little white calf and the cow. But there is a shorter, secret way. Masau told me of it. He also told me that you knew the path. You will show me now, before your people and Shateh's men arrive. Do not stall, Shaman Girl. Remember, I am Maliwal. I am Wolf! I was suckled at the breasts of Ysuna, and her magic was not wasted on me!"

And so, fearing for her life and for the lives of the pups, Mah-ree was obedient. Disconsolate, she led him through the village and into the benighted hills, walking heavily, sobbing openly, occasionally stumbling in the dark. Her tears and obvious misery pleased him. In his eagerness to keep her moving toward his goal, he clouted her when she tripped and cursed her for her clumsiness and never once noticed that she was leaving a trail clear enough for other men to follow in the dark.

They walked in grim silence through the night. Cha-kwena led the men on. Dakan-eh was with him, and Lom-da and Iman-atl and Shateh and many of the bison eaters and men of Tlana-quah's band. All those creatures that roamed the woods by night were at Cha-kwena's side, urging him on, guiding his steps, and seeing to it that he did not falter. He dared not take a wrong turn or a hesitant step, for once Dakan-eh picked up Mah-ree's footprints and they followed them a few paces beyond the village, Cha-kwena knew where she was going. His heart turned to ice as he gripped the sacred stone in his hand and implored all the powers of Creation for their aid. *First Man and First Woman, be with me! Grandfather! Walk at my side! Old Owl, do not let me be a stupid boy! Mah-ree is taking Maliwal to the sacred spring. Mosquito is leading the Wolf to our totem. If I do not reach her in time, both she and the great white mammoth will die.*

Mah-ree lost her way several times. He struck her. Her nose was bleeding, perhaps broken; she could not tell and was beyond caring.

"I have only been this way once. Please, be patient with me!"

"Patient?" he growled. "So that we may be overtaken?"

Something—a night hawk, perhaps, or a bat or flying squirrel—passed low over his head. He swatted at it in the darkness, looked nervously up and around and back over his shoulder. He was by nature a man of the open country; confined spaces unnerved him. He growled again, then shoved Mah-ree forward so hard that she went sprawling. "Get up! Get moving! Or shall I kill another pup?"

She struggled to her feet and, with the heels of her hands bleeding and raw, went on without complaint. It seemed hours before her nostrils picked up a subtle change in the scent and texture of the air. She heard the waterfalls and smelled the scent of cedars. A moment later they heard the low huffing of large animals.

Maliwal stopped dead. "Mammoth?"

"At the pools," she told him miserably. "They are just ahead, beyond those shrubs."

With a sound of barely contained ecstasy and anticipation, he cast off the basket of pups and threw it down. She heard the surviving little dogs yip in surprise as the basket fell to the ground. Then he backhanded her aside with such strength that she was lifted from where she stood and landed hard a few feet away.

Maliwal, holding two spears in his left hand and hefting one into throwing position over his right shoulder, hurried forward. She could actually smell his excitement as his sweat took on the stink of it. He was running now, parting the scrub growth with his left hand. A branch snagged Tlana-quah's jaguar-skin cloak and snatched it from his shoulder; he did not notice. He was breathing hard, so eager to see his prey that he never noticed the chasm before he plunged into it.

Mah-ree watched him disappear, then she closed her eyes. She did not have to see him fall; she heard his bellowing scream of shock and disbelief as he plummeted into the abyss, down, down along the vertical black walls of the mountainside . . . down through the crowns of the towering cedars and firs and onto the rocks that rimmed the pools below, where mammoth that were still mourning the dead cow and the little white son raised their tusks in savage and uncompromising greeting.

"Mosquito?"

Startled by the sound of Cha-kwena's voice, she opened her eyes and turned. He was standing in the clearing behind her. Even in the dark she could see the worry on his face.

Shakily, she stood and faced the men.

"What has happened here?" asked Dakan-eh.

She thought a moment, then replied matter-of-factly, wondering why she trembled so, "This mosquito has stung a wolf and led him over a deadfall. I told Maliwal that the prey he sought was not here, but he would not believe me. So I brought him where he would go. Now the wolf is dead, and Tlana-quah's jaguar-skin cape has been returned to the People!"

"And the white mammoth?" asked Cha-kwena.

"Grandfather of All grazes in the meadow where the roses bloom. You are Shaman now, Cha-kwena, you should not have to ask this mosquito that!"

# 18

For four days and nights the storm lay upon the world. When at last the rain stopped, lakes that had been dry were full again. Rivers ran high, and the sacred pools within the great canyon overflowed their embankments. All that had lain within was washed away. Of the sacred collar there was no trace. The land was cleansed of death, and Brothers of the Sky were seen no more.

In the days that followed, the People who gathered by the Lake of Many Singing Birds were of many bands, and only three of them were from the Red World.

"Come, Cha-kwena! Come, Shaman!" invited Dakan-eh. "Tell us of the People! And tell us how the lizard eaters of the Red World and the bison eaters of the Land of Grass came together to drive Brothers of the Sky back into the stars!"

And Cha-kwena came forth to recount a bitter tale that would long be remembered. It began as Hoyeh-tay had taught him:

"In time beyond beginning, the People were one. Then First Man and First Woman followed the great white spirit mammoth, Life Giver, across the world. From out of the Watching Star they came. Across a Sea of Ice they came. Through a Corridor of Storms and into a Forbidden Land they came, walking always into the face of the rising sun . . . until the Brothers of the Sky were born and the unity of the People was shattered. But now it is so no more. The People have come together to face a common enemy, to drive them from this land, to fight together against them, even if it may take forever. . . ."

Ta-maya could not bear to hear it. She stood and walked from the circle. A golden eagle flew above, and she could not help but think of Masau and weep for her loss of him. She wondered what he might have been like had he been born into the Red World instead of into the savage land of golden grass to the north.

"He will live in your spirit, Favored Child," soothed Ha-xa, knowing her daughter's thoughts as, wearing Tlana-quah's cape, she came to stand beside her and watch the eagle. "Remember your Mystic Warrior, as I remember your father. Remember your love, and as long as you live, it will never die."

# EPILOGUE

The Pinyon Moon rose and fell over the Red World. No one had the heart to journey to the Blue Mesas again. They were a place of death now. A new source of pine nuts was sought in other ranges to the west.

Kosar-eh's wound healed slowly. He took advantage of the time to listen to the many colorful and intricate tales of the men of the various bison bands who chose to linger in the Red World when they heard talk of mild winters.

"Maybe I will bring my women and children and winter with you," said Shateh. "I am not so young as I once was. In the Land of Grass, the Snow Moon is bitter. We would not hunt the mammoth in this country unless we fell upon starving times. In summer, when the Red World burns, you would be welcome to bring your people north to be brothers and sisters with us, to trade, to hunt the bison, or to hunt those people of the Watching Star who have escaped us. They should not be allowed to go unpunished, or they might raise up a new generation and attack us again."

Dakan-eh was supportive of the idea. When he spoke, his words were met with great enthusiasm. "We should hunt them as they once hunted us," he urged. "We could take many women as slaves. Slaves would not talk back to us or to our wives. It would be a good thing! Our women would not have to work so hard."

Cha-kwena listened and grew restless. He sought the cave. He painted new images on the walls—strange images . . . disturbing images. At night he could not sleep, and by day, when he dozed, he dreamed terrible dreams, of lions and rats peering at him from the eyes of the dead.

\* \* \*

The Rabbit Moon rose and set. The yearly rabbit drive yielded few rabbits. There was talk that Thunder in the Sky had drowned them all. Shateh's men, not impressed with rabbit meat, left for the north. Dakan-eh and many of the hunters of the Red World went with him. They returned with slaves and bison steaks but told of how the herds were not coming as far south as they once had. The grassland seemed to be shrinking, and even in a wet year, the bison were staying far to the north.

"Our old headman, Tlana-quah, feared that the land was changing," revealed Dakan-eh. "As new headman, I do not fear this."

He allowed the statement to settle, waiting to see if someone would challenge it. No one did. Tlana-quah was dead, and Dakan-eh was a bold man in changing times that demanded bold men.

"The People must change with the land," he added in the tone of a sage. "It is a good thing."

This said, he gestured across the compound to his lodge, where two naked young women sat awaiting his command. They were survivors of the decimated People of the Watching Star. He had taken them captive on his journey north; there had been three of them initially, but one of them had been damaged during the raid and had taken ill on the trip home. Since she was useless to him, he abandoned her at the suggestion of the bison eaters. It had proven to be an excellent tactic; the other two girls had been quick to obey him after that. Now they scurried inside to await his pleasure.

Ban-ya had no objection. She was growing big with child now, and when the slaves were not spreading themselves for Dakan-eh, they were doing all the work for her. She found this such an amazing boon to her daily life that she wondered why her people had never thought before of raiding other bands for slaves.

"Because we cannot make slaves of the People," Kahmree told her. "It would not be right. But these sons and daughters of the Watching Star are not really people. They fell from out of the stars with the evil Brothers of the Sky. They are lucky that we allow them to live at all. We can do with them as we like—hunt them, train them to be beasts of burden like the dogs they brought to us, or even kill them if they are disobedient. We can always have our hunters go north to bring back more of them for us."

Winter came early that year and stayed long. The bison eaters watched the herd of mammoth grazing in the sage flats and were overheard speaking of how they had been mammoth eaters once.

"To have so much meat available and to eat dried grubs and seeds instead, surely this is an affront to the forces of Creation and an insult to the mammoth themselves! I can understand why you do not hunt and kill the old white one that is Totem; but there is an entire herd out there. True, it isn't a big herd—I doubt if there is such a thing anymore—but you could take that young pregnant cow and feast on her for the entire winter and savor the delicacy of the unborn calf as well."

Dakan-eh and the hunters agreed with their brothers the bison eaters.

On the day the cow was to be hunted, the sun shone on new snow. The wind was mild, and all the omens were favorable, despite the warning of the shaman.

"You are young, Cha-kwena!" insisted Dakan-eh. "Too young to make such decisions for the People. Shateh and his hunters have shown us new ways to hunt, to make a winter kill with ease, and to assure our people a new source of meat."

"It is forbidden!" cried Mah-ree.

"You will hold your tongue. Your father is no longer headman, Mah-ree. I am. The People have spoken in council. Just as Han-da said on the sacred mountain: In changing times, men must learn new ways."

"Yes," agreed Cha-kwena. "But you are turning your back upon all the traditions of the ancestors and on First Man and First Woman. Han-da destroyed the sacred stone of the People! And in council you ignored the advice of Kosar-eh and of your own shaman by planning to hunt pregnant cows. Tlana-quah never would have allowed it!"

"As I have said, Cha-kwena, Tlana-quah is no longer headman. Kosar-eh may be a bold man, but he is still a cripple. His word in council is invalid, and as far as I am concerned, yours is worth little more. It has been decided: It is no longer a good thing for us to be content to feed upon lizards and rodents. Mammoth graze in our hunting grounds, and we will hunt them and eat them. We are not going after Grandfather of All. He will always be Totem."

"And when you have killed the last mammoth in this herd—or perhaps in all the herds—what then? Will you seek out the lost spearheads of Masau and hunt our totem, too?"

It was Shateh who answered with an air of amused tolerance. Whatever he had felt for Masau and Maliwal, he had made no mention of either of his sons since their deaths and showed no reaction to Masau's name now. "Cha-kwena," he said, "things are changing all around us. Animals die. Men die. But one thing I know—there may be wet years in which rivers flood and dry years in which lakes vanish; there may be winters of plenty and winters in which the People ache with hunger; but there will always be mammoth and bison for men to hunt."

Cha-kwena's eyes shot to where Ha-xa, wearing Tlana-quah's cape, stood with the women. "And Jaguar, the great spotted lion, will always walk in the Red World!" he said sarcastically.

There was nothing more to say. He watched the hunters leave, then he went to his cave. He could not sleep. He could not eat or drink. He raised a fire, and with the carbon-blackened end of a willow stick, he made more images on the wall—stick figures of angry men hunting other men and of men hunting mammoth. The hunters leaped and danced and exulted in their kills as their victims moved before them, speared, wounded, dying. . . .

He turned away in anguish. "Hoyeh-tay, Grandfather, Old Owl! Help me! Please! I am a man of the People of the Red World! But how can I be Shaman? Mah-ree was right upon the sacred mountain! My people are strangers to me. I do not know them anymore. They *have* become Brothers of the Sky!"

They hunted on a day when the old white mammoth was grazing, as alone as he often was when he sought the meadow beyond the village and where even in the depth of winter a mammoth's tusks could root up tender sleeping shoots and saplings.

The men surprised the little herd. They rejoiced in

the thrill of the chase. Not one cow but two were panicked by the cleverly designed ice-slick sides of a long, V-shaped embankment of snow that the hunters had labored many days to raise on the lee side of a run of hills that the mammoth were known to use as shelter against strong winds.

It was a winter trap often used in bison country, and it proved equally effective for mammoth. Slipping on a surface that had been meticulously wetted down under subfreezing temperatures, one cow fell atop the one that was pregnant. The impact fractured the pregnant cow's hip and rendered her immobile. Off balance, the topmost animal took the brunt of the hunters' spears. She hobbled off, trailed by a pack of men who harried her every step and followed her for hours until, at last, she dropped.

Stopping now and then to rest and eat of traveling provisions, they rose to the game of the kill when the mood moved them, driving the long, bayonetlike lance tips of their spears deep into whatever vital organ they could reach.

Back at the snowslide, the rest of the hunters went to work on the pregnant cow. The band had joined them and made a camp. The butchering would begin the next day, whether or not the mammoth was dead.

Cha-kwena went out into the hills alone and did not look back. He walked the familiar trails in silence, as though in a dream of old friends who were now enemies, and of enemies who might, under different circumstances, have proved to be friends.

It was snowing hard when he reached the shaggy-barked old juniper and climbed back within the branches, then stretched out like a young lynx and called back through time, "You are Shaman, Hoyeh-tay. Hear me! Find me if you can."

Snow fell silently within the wondrous webbing of the branches; but if the spirit of Hoyeh-tay was there, he did not come to Cha-kwena within the arms of the ancient tree.

Cha-kwena climbed down and trekked on. He reached the overlook and carefully made his way down to the pools; it was a treacherous descent. By the time he reached his destination sunlight was breaking through the snow clouds. He allowed the living heart of the sacred stone that he wore about his neck to lead him, and there, amid deep drifts of snow, he searched for what reason told him he should not find and yet somehow knew that he must find. The great rainstorm had washed away the bones of mammoth and of Maliwal. But there, wedged high on the embankment of one of the pools, out of the weather and beneath a granite cornice, the spearheads of the Mystic Warrior lay gleaming, encased in ice. The hafts and sinew joinings had been cracked and torn away, but the projectile points were intact.

*Take them,* a voice said. *They are as I first saw them in my vision.*

*Masau?* Cha-kwena wondered as he reached for them. Then hesitating, he drew back.

A voice spoke softly. "You *are* worthy, Cha-kwena."

He looked up.

Mah-ree was smiling at him from the opposite side of the pool. "He would want you to have them, to take them where no one will ever find them and be able to use them against our totem."

"How is it that you are always able to follow me without my knowing it? And why do you so often understand my thoughts better than I know them myself, Mosquito?"

"Because I am Shaman. And I am a part of you, as you are a part of me. You don't have to like me, but it is true."

"I do not dislike you, Mosquito."

"Then call me by name. I am not a mosquito! I am Mah-ree, Girl Who Walks with Mammoth. Grandfather of All awaits us in the meadow where the summer's roses will grow. He will walk in the Red World no more. Ha-xa, U-wa, Kosar-eh, Ta-maya, Siwi-ni, and the babies and children and pups are with him, waiting for us. We have sledges piled high with food and all the other things we will need to make a new life and a new People. We will walk in the manner of First Man and First Woman, into the face of the rising sun, to the east beyond the Mountains of Sand and over the edge of the world where Brothers of the Sky will never think to follow."

He rose. Clouds had obscured the sun again. It was

snowing harder now. "You cannot leave all that you have ever known and loved, Mah-ree."

"But do it of my own accord. My mother and sister come. And I will walk with Cha-kwena and with Life Giver. That is all I have ever wanted."

He did not know what to say, and so he said nothing.

She stood patiently as he bound each spearhead carefully in the lengths of thong that he had brought for this purpose, and then placed all three into the special parfleche that he had fashioned.

They went on together in silence. Somewhere along the way, she took his hand, and he did not pull his away.

It was cold and silent within the canyon. There are places in the world that speak of magic, and this was one of them. A young man and a girl walked toward a new life in a new world, and somehow an old man walked beside them and a balding owl in a rabbit-fur vest sat upon his head.

*Ah, there you are, Cha-kwena. I have found you again at last!* said the old man.

*Stupid boy! It took you long enough to find the path of the shaman's way!* mocked the Owl as Deer and Mouse, Hare and Rabbit, Sparrow and Hawk, Brother Bat and Little White Son, and Coyote and a redheaded dog named Blood all walked or flew or hopped along behind. Somewhere far ahead, Life Giver trumpeted in the meadow where, in summer, the roses grew, and Shrike, resplendent in his black mask, flew overhead.

*Come walking into the rising sun, Cha-kwena,* said Shrike in the voice of Mystic Warrior. *You cannot stand against the north wind. Grandfather of All waits for you, and the west wind speaks only of endings. You are worthy at last, Cha-kwena, Brother of Animals, Grandson of Hoyeh-tay, Little Yellow Wolf . . . Guardian of the last mammoth . . . Shaman. . . .*

# AUTHOR'S NOTES

*The Sacred Stones*, like the four previous novels in THE FIRST AMERICANS Series, has attempted to reconstruct the migration of man into the Americas. The plot and lifeways of the characters within this book have been drawn from the archaeological record and from the mythology of those Native Americans whose languages and cultures link them most closely with the pre-Athabaskan-speaking people who were the first Americans.

The People in this story are the direct descendants of the first bands of Paleo-Siberian big-game hunters who walked out of Asia some forty thousand years ago. Among the diverse cultures of the Americas, all who refer to themselves as "the People" share a common linguistic and racial stock. All speak of "coming from the north," of "First Man and First Woman," and of twin war gods who are often called "Thunder Beings" or "Brothers of the Sky."

The Morning Star ceremony is not my invention. It appears to have ancient roots, and one variant of it was practiced (using arrows instead of spears) by the Pawnee until the nineteenth century. Various forms of the ceremony survived in Mexico, Meso, and South America until well after the European conquest.

Ritual eagle killing occurred exactly as recounted in this novel, but not always for purely spiritual purposes. Golden eagles were valuable trading items. It has been said that among the northern Blackfoot tribes, sometimes as many as forty birds were taken in a single day. Four golden eagles were the standard trading value for one horse.

The "magic" spearheads of Masau have been patterned after real projectile points that were carved of pale chalcedony by a left-handed master stone knapper some 11,200 years ago, then abandoned along with other Clovis tools at a site in what is now East Wenatchee, Washington. Their enormous size mystifies scientists, but S'uski, the little Zuni coyote fetish who stands guard atop my old Mac 512K and summons the spark of creativity from my word processor, assures me in the resounding spirit voice of Song Dog that they can have been made for only one purpose: "magic" spearheads to slay a "magic" mammoth. And so, with Coyote guiding me as he has guided Chakwena in this novel, I have tried to tell a story of what might have been.

In waves of migration that coincided with the ebb and flow of glacial epochs, generation after generation of Paleo-Indian big-game hunters followed mammoth and the great herds of the Pleistocene "Beyond the Sea of Ice" and across the exposed seabed of the Bering Strait. These bands traveled ever eastward through Alaska and Canada until they were eventually forced southward through open grassland and along a vast "Corridor of Storms," which lay between the Cordilleran and Laurentide ice sheets that buried most of North America. The hunters trekked southward through an unknown and "Forbidden Land," which lay along the exposed eastern spine of the Rocky Mountains, and by the time they became "Walkers of the Wind" and eventually emerged onto the northernmost edge of the Great Plains, many millennia had passed. They were a new people entirely, with a new and redefined gene pool and with a way of life as perfectly honed to their surroundings as their uniquely tooled weapons of stone.

Within less than a millennium, the descendants of these first Americans had penetrated both continents. Their fluted spearheads and dart points are evidence of a single unifying pattern of culture that extended across the breadth of North America and well into both Central and South America. But the projectile points of this ancient people are also indicative of something equally as amazing as their trek from the north, as shattering as the best of their hammerstones, and as ominous as the smoke of the grass fires before which they drove their prey into extinction.

Clovis Man (named after a town in New Mexico where his unique projectile points were discovered in an ancient kill site amid the bones of his favorite meat: mammoth, horse, and bison) was not merely a predator; he may well have been (Allosaurus and Tyrannosaurus Rex not withstanding) the most *destructive* predator that has ever lived.

In the approximately one thousand years that it took for Clovis Man to hunt his way southward from the Great Plains to the southernmost tip of Tierra del Fuego, his burgeoning numbers, profligate hunting methods, and apparent preference for the meat of young animals, combined with changes in the world's climate, accomplished a mass extinction of not one species of herbivore, but of entire genera of large North American mammals—mammoth, horse, camel, and giant sloth all fell to the predations of Clovis Man. It was inevitable that the large carnivores that had come to depend upon these animals as a ready source of meat—great American lion, the North American short-faced bear, and the saber-toothed cat—would soon vanish with them.

On the southeastern edge of the Rocky Mountains where forests and grasslands were becoming deserts, the disappearance of the great ice sheets and inland seas of the Pleistocene forced all living things to adapt to radically altered and increasingly arid environs. Clovis Man was a slow learner. It is now generally agreed that his hunting techniques may have been the critical factor that resulted not only in bringing about the extinction of the megafauna of the Pleistocene but in dooming his own way of life to extinction as well.

In this last decade of the twentieth century, when man stands on the brink of a new millennium, the lifeways of Clovis Man and his negative impact on his environment should give us all food for thought. Once the last mammoth was gone, the culture that depended upon its existence had no way to survive. On the surface this may seem a moot point, for Western civilization is currently expanding into a world culture increasingly bound to technologies that set us apart from the natural world. Yet few would deny that despite all the wonders that this civilization has wrought, our behavior is systematically polluting our planet and dehumanizing our lives even as it prolongs them. Perhaps it is time to remember what Clovis Man forgot—that we can survive only as long as does our "meat."

Like the first Native Americans who were forced to abandon the exclusivity of big-game hunting and evolve into multivarious hunter-gatherer and, eventually, farming and husbanding traditions, we must see that it is time to look for new paths . . . or perhaps to rediscover some of the old ones.

The cultures of Native Americans are as varied as the land that has shaped them. Yet they share an innate spirituality born of their belief that this planet is Mother to us all, that man is not master of his world but only one of its many children, and that he is as much a creature of spirit as of flesh—the two are one, inseparable; and without a strong sense of spiritual kinship with the natural world, something essential to the human life process begins to die.

The spirit of Chief Seattle of the Suquamish still speaks: ". . . all things share the same breath, the beast, the tree, the man . . . the wind that gave our grandfather his first breath also receives his last sigh. All things are connected."

While the wind still sings to our children of open places where the forests grow tall and the wild grass grows sweet, while the living creatures of this earth still bear young in hope of tomorrow, let ours be the generation that is wise enough to learn from the past. Let us remember that in "time beyond beginning" the ancestors of *all* mankind were tribal peoples who praised the forces of Creation under an open sky and upon an earth that was sacred to them. Let there be no last mammoth for us. Let the sun be shadowed by the wings of eagles, and may the sky tremble at the trumpeting of wild elephants . . . forever.

The author wishes to thank Dr. Michael Gramly, Curator of Anthropology at New York's Buffalo Museum of Science and Clovis Project Director at Richey Clovis Cache, in Wenatchee, Washington, for his gracious sharing of precious newfound data that has greatly enriched the story line of *The Sacred Stones* and confirmed—as well as challenged—many of this writer's hypotheses. Thanks must also go to the research and editorial staff of Book Creations, Inc., especially to Laurie Rosin, Senior Project Editor; Betty Szeberenyi, Librarian; Judy Stockmayer, Associate Editor and liaison; and Marjie Weber, Copy Editor.

More thanks are due to Donald B. Fisher and Cathy Anne Burton of Nearly Native for all the information gleaned on Paleo/Archaic Indian lifeways during a weekend of Ice Age sleuthing, atlatl hurling, cordage making, and trap setting at the Soda Springs Desert Research Station of the University of San Bernardino at Zzyzx, California. Thanks also to Jacques Devaud, president of the Friends of the Big Bear Valley Preserves, for sharing his enthusiasm and knowledge of the wintering bald eagles of Big Bear Valley, and to the Natural Science Council of the Palm Springs Desert Museum for the inspiration given by speakers at their seventh annual science symposia, especially to Drs. Ruth DeEtte Simpson, San Bernardino County Museum; R. Scott Anderson, Northern Arizona University; Thomas R. Van Devender, Arizona-Sonora Desert Museum; and George T. Jefferson of the George C. Page Museum.

William Sarabande
Fawnskin, California

January 1991

# THE WORLD OF
# THE FIRST AMERICANS

A monumental epic, **The First Americans** chronicles all the passion, danger, and adventure from the dawn of the Ice Age. It was a time when humans walked the world and when nature ruled the earth and sky. For the people who lived then, it was a time of mystery but also of wonderment and discovery. In this stunningly visual and powerfully dramatic series, the bold young hunter Torka his incredible journey into the vast unknown.

## BEYOND THE SEA OF ICE

*In Book One of this breathtaking series, a crazed mammoth rampages through Torka's village and kills all but three people. Torka and two fellow hunters, unaware of the band's decimation, are stalking game far from the encampment and battling their own superstitions.*

The brothers nodded, one to the other, acknowledging their unspoken thoughts. An Arctic hunter's ability to communicate without sound was a sixth sense, as it was with all predators whose survival depended upon their ability to hunt in packs. To speak was to alert prey to their presence, and to break the concentration of others when game was being stalked was unthinkable.

It was hunger, coupled with exhaustion, that put the word on Nap's tongue. He did not know that he spoke until the wind blew his voice back into his face and slapped him with it.

"Caribou . . ."

The enormity of his transgression hit him at once. He sucked in a half-strangled gasp of alarm, as though he might draw back his utterance, but it was too late. The word was out, running free upon the wind.

Torka and Alinak stook stunned to silence. Nap had just broken one of the most ancient taboos of the Arctic. They all knew that to name a thing was to give it the spirit of life. And life spirits had wills of their own. If called forth without the proper ceremony or chants of respect, they were dishonored and would seek to punish those who had shamed them. In the case of game, they might not come forth at all, thus punishing the transgressors through starvation. Or they might transform themselves into crooked spirits, half-flesh, half-phantom . . . clawed, fanged, invisible, and malevolent . . . big enough to make prey of men and eat them . . . slowly.

Nap felt sick. He could see Alinak's wide face scowling at him out of the shadowed recesses of his antlered headdress. Torka's hood was fashioned from the pelt of a dire wolf, with the tail of the beast stitched end to end to form an encircling ruff, within which his face was but a pool of darkness in the meager light of the morning; but Nap did not have to see the strong, even features to know that Torka's dark brows had merged into one black sprawl above his all too expressive eyes. He could visualize the well-formed mouth snarling back from the white teeth as Torka hissed an exhalation that was more damning than any rebuke.

Torka did not have to tell Nap that what he had done was unforgivable. His lapse might well cost all three of them their lives. And if, by some chance, they *did* manage to get safely back to the winter encampment of their band, Nap's reputation as a hunter would be sullied forever. Yet, as the initial flaring of his anger cooled, Torka could not condemn Nap for his blunder. They were *all* exhausted, *all* hungry and dangerously near starvation. It was said that starvation fed the light of vision. It was also said that hunger made men careless. Any one of them might have blurted the word of longing and thus, inadvertently, broken the ancient taboo. But if Nap *had* loosed a crooked spirit, it would be a separate entity from the one that Torka sensed stalking them. *That* phantom had been following them for hours. And whatever it was, Torka was now more certain than ever that it was no herd of caribou.

The three hunters stood immobile. They all saw specters, listened for the voice of danger, and imagined that they saw death stalking them in the wind-driven mists.

Torka stood with his fleshing dagger in one hand and his stabbing spear balanced and at the ready in the other. He could taste bile at the back of his throat as he recalled the words of old Umak, the grandfather who had raised him and taught him to hunt after his parents had been killed: *There is a light that burns at the back of a man's eyes when death is near, stalking, waiting for the hunter to make the final error. The hunter must face into this light. Only by facing death may his spirit overcome it.*

The light that burns. Torka could feel it now. It seared the back of his eyes and transformed his vision. The world was ignited by it, bright, as white and bold as the great white bear of the north, and he thought: *Whatever is out there, the wind is in its favor now. It will have our scent. And if it is a bear, it will be mad with hunger after months of living off its own fat. It will come for us, even here upon high ground. It will come.*

Restlessness ran in his blood, heating it. Despite the cold, he could smell the acrid scent brought on by his tension. He wished that his grandfather were with him now. Alinak and Nap were both in their prime and experienced hunters, but when old Umak was at his side, Torka always felt that he had the courage and the wisdom of two men. But Umak had injured his leg while chasing down a steppe antelope earlier in the season. Now he sheltered within Torka's pit hut back at the winter camp with Egatsop, who was Torka's woman, their newborn infant, and Kipu, their little son.

Kipu! The boy grew paler and weaker every day. And here was Torka, the brave hunter, dry-mouthed and in fear of an unseen prey whose flesh would feed his son and save his people from starvation. Self-revulsion caused him to scowl. What sort of a man was he? Why was he standing here in silence when he should be making the chants that would summon the unknown prey to him?

But what if the prey was a crooked spirit? Or worse, what if it was a bear? He had seen what the great white bear could do. When Torka was a child he had seen his father slashed and torn by those great paws. He had seen his father die as many others were mauled, until at last the huge, short-faced, lumbering marauder had been driven off. Later it had been found dead from wounds it had suffered in the encampment. The surviving members of the band had eaten it, but the bear had ruined ten spears and taken the lives of three hunters and one woman, Torka's mother, to the spirit world with it.

The memory roused anger and a fully formed resolve that drove away his fear. Umak had stood against that bear. Umak's courage had enabled him to place the killing spear. Not even the great white bear had been bolder than Umak. *And I am Torka. I am the son of Umak's son. I can be bold. I, too, am mad with hunger after months of living off my own fat.*

The wind was gusting now, its power ebbing as morning claimed the tundra and banished the terrors of the dark. Torka's black eyes stared into the settling ground snow, searching for a bear that was not there. Nap and Alinak frowned into the distance, expecting crooked spirits to take shape and come at them to take their lives. But to their infinite relief, there was only the familiar, empty tundra spreading out before them, with the mountains circling the far horizon and, on that horizon, the frozen jewel of a shallow little lake glinting in the cold colors of the morning. The lake was at the base of the shouldering rise of a terminal moraine, no doubt the result of the recent thaw and ensuing freeze. A huge embankment of loose stones and rocky debris rose at the foot of a glacier. And mired at the edge of the lake, its shape a dark scab upon the ice, was a corpse whose color was unmistakable. Red. Deep red, the color of blood rising from a wound.

The hunters exhaled in disbelieving unison. The terrors of the night and caution were forgotten. Hunger took complete control of their senses as they realized that at last they had food enough to gorge upon until they were sated and still have more than enough to bring back to their starving people.

Torka laughed with relief. So his instincts had failed him at last! What a fool he had been! The only thing that had stalked him in the night had been the beast of his own fear! The light that had burned behind his eyes had only been the color of that fear!

"Do you see it?" questioned Alinak softly, as though he dared not trust his own eyes and feared a negative answer.

"I see it!" Torka affirmed, and put a name to that which lay before them, obviously dead, fresh-frozen in the ice, waiting to be taken. "Mammoth!"

Nap winced, but Torka reached out and gave him a friendly shoulder jab that told the other man that everything was going to be all right. Nap *had* broken a taboo, but it seemed as though the spirits were going to overlook it.

*Nap and Alinak are also savaged by the killer mammoth. Torka returns to the village to find that only his grandfather Umak and a young girl, Lonit, have survived. The threesome travel into a realm of mystery and danger, where they come upon the boy Karana, abandoned by his father, the headman Supnah, to die. Karana joins Torka's tiny group.*

# CORRIDOR OF STORMS

*The adventure continues in Book Two as the four travelers arrive at a winter camp where many bands gather to hunt the great mammoth. Here Torka and his followers meet the evil magic man called Navahk, who maintains his power by frightening the people with stories of the wanawut, a vicious man-eating monster.*

"Who has seen this wanawut?" Supnah's tone reeked of skepticism. "Who has found its hide or bones or any portion of its carcass upon the tundra? Who has seen its tracks or spoor or looked upon the living flesh of this wanawut . . . this spirit of the wind and mists that brings fear to the hearts of my people through the mouth of Navahk?" The headman's challenge was as powerful as the man.

Beside him, the boy Karana was startled and amazed. He was not certain if he had heard correctly. Had the headman actually spoken out to the magic man? Had Supnah, for the first time in his life, openly impugned his brother before the entire band?

*Yes!* It was so! The boy smiled for the first time since Supnah had insisted that he leave Torka to dwell with him and Naiapi, his third woman, as the headman's son again. He had not wanted to go, but Torka had allowed no argument from him. And although he had balked, he had actually been delighted when Navahk had glowered at him and proclaimed that the dead could not return to dwell among the living without dire consequences to all. Supnah had coldly replied that his son was alive, not dead, no thanks to his brother's mistaken portending. Then Karana had enjoyed smirking at the magic man but had not enjoyed his forced residence within Supnah's pit hut. He disliked Naiapi as much as she disliked him, although her little daughter, Pet, half smothered him with sisterly affection. She was looking at him now from across the fire, but he pretended not to notice. He wanted no part of her; she was one of only a handful of toddlers who had not been abandoned to the winter dark, because her mother, having just lost a sickly newborn, had breast milk to suckle her after the infant died. He had told her that she was not his sister, but Supnah had insisted that, although they had been born out of different mothers, they were nevertheless of his blood, and as he cherished them, so must they cherish each other.

Sullenly, Karana had kept his thought to himself. *If you cherished me, how could you have sent any of us? No matter what Navahk said, you were headman and did not have to listen. In starving times Torka found enough food to feed his people and took in a strange band's child. We were hungry, but we survived. And now Karana is Torka's son forever. Karana will never be Supnah's son again.*

The boy sighed. He had loved Supnah once and been proud of the bold hunter. Yet there was now a bittersweet emptiness within his heart where filial love should have been. There was no way to tell the headman that he was, in fact, Navahk's spawn. When Karana had returned to his people, Navahk, for reasons the boy still could not fully understand, had sought him out and smiled maliciously as he had burned him with that unwelcome truth. It both revolted and shamed him.

Yet now, as he stared at the magic man in the flickering shadows of red and black and gold, he realized that he had always sensed the truth—even in those long-ago days of his childhood, when others would remark upon his resemblance to his father's brother. The similarity did not end there. He would amaze himself, as well as the people of his band, by knowing when the weather would turn, when the game would come, and where it would be found. He had often felt the magic man watching him, measuring him out of sharp, resentful eyes. His mother had warned him to keep his portending to himself and to be wary of Navahk. He was a dangerous, ugly man, she had warned. But Karana had been baffled because Navahk was even more beautiful than his mother, and she was the headman's woman, envied by all the females of the band.

A lump formed at the back of the boy's throat. His mother had perished the winter he had been abandoned. Her reasons for distrusting the magic man had died with her, and Karana was certain that if he were to tell Supnah the truth about his parentage, the headman would never believe him. Since the death of their parents, Supnah had been like a father to his much younger brother. To speak against Navahk to the headman had always been like shouting into the north wind at the height of a gale.

So it was that now Karana stared at Supnah, then at Navahk, incredulous. The headman's words struck the magic man like a well-placed spear, actually making him stagger. Supnah had never challenged Navahk, not even when the magic man had told the headman to abandon his own son.

A dark, intense warning sparked within Karana each time his eyes met his father's. He chafed each time the headman drew him close and called him son. *Torka is my father now. Torka will always be my father!* he wanted to shout. Loyalty and love made them father and son, not blood; blood was a thin, red thing that dried and blew away on the wind.

Karana knew that all too well, for he had watched the other children slowly starve and freeze to death, one by one, crying for mothers and fathers who never came. He had been unable to help them, for he, too, was starving and dying—and all because Supnah had not been bold enough to challenge the spirits of the storms that spoke to him through his brother's mouth.

Karana wished he could spring to his feet and flee into the night. This was a bad camp, filled with bad people, and nothing good could come to any who stayed within it.

*Navahk plots against Torka and Karana and pursues Lonit, who has matured into a beauty. As a mob beats Torka and the boy and leaves them for dead, Navahk drugs and rapes Lonit. Using their last reserves of strength and courage, Torka's few allies manage to save the victims and take them to a new continent that has never known the footsteps of man.*

## FORBIDDEN LAND

*The thrilling third volume of mankind's courageous settling of North America, Lonit becomes Torka's woman and bears him two daughters. In this untamed wilderness, Torka's success is based upon his willingness to cast aside old beliefs. But while Lonit is in labor for the third time, all he can do is wait.*

Lonit was young and strong, and it was not within her nature to cry. She willed herself to run with wolves across the open miles of her imagination. Her blood surged, and her heart pounded fast and hard. She was no longer a woman. She *was* a wolf! She was a strong and sleek wild animal, just like the wolf that had once leaped upon her and nearly claimed her life. Her arm bore the white lightning mark of a jagged scar inflicted by the tearing fangs of that wolf. Her man wore the skin of the beast, and its paws and fangs were around his neck. But now, as she ran, she was pursued by a terrifying white lion with a great black mane, a lion that roared within her.

"Torka!" From out of her very soul, Lonit howled his name in unspeakable anguish as another contraction transformed the supple muscles of her abdomen into a single oiled, ash-blackened strap that tightened, boring in and down upon her unborn child, crushing it—no!—and forcing it from her body at last!

The baby was coming! She could feel the head burrowing deep, ripping her tender flesh, tearing her apart like a wolf trying to free itself of a trap—and failing. Never had she suffered such agony. Not at the birth of her firstborn child, Summer Moon, nor at the birth of her second daughter, Demmi.

Her eyes widened with terror. *Little ones! Will this woman ever look upon you and hold you close again?*

Beyond the winter hunting camp of her band, the wolves broke and scattered, disappearing into the far hills and the farthest reaches of her fevered mind. Her little girls ran with them, and her man followed. Only the pain remained. She tried to call out after the ones she loved— the wild wolves, her children, her man. But even as she attempted to form their names, light exploded within the little hut. Briefly she thought of the sun. She wondered if the intensified pain were its child; for with pain, always there was light, bright . . . glaring . . . blinding.

"Lonit! Come back to us!"

She did not want to come back, but Xhan and Kimm, the two midwives who supported her weight, shook her again, hard.

"The child comes!" Xhan was shouting. "You must kneel again now. You must try harder!"

Lonit was beyond trying. She was not even a woman anymore. She was a spirit, running away into the face of the rising sun with the ghosts of the caribou. Why did the women not leave her alone? The child would come or not come. Her body would allow it life or not; either way, she had no control. None.

The fingers of Xhan and Kimm curled into Lonit's

armpits. That caused a little pain, though of no importance. The contraction was building in waves as the midwives forced her to crouch and spread her knees wide.

"Push!" demanded Kimm.

Slumped in Kimm's arms, Lonit could not even try. The ebbing pain would come again. The next time, she knew it would kill her, and she would be glad.

Wallah knelt before her, shook her head, fixed Lonit with frightened eyes, and, with a sigh of regret, slapped her once, twice, and then again.

"You will *not* give up now, Lonit! The life you carry is the first to come forth in this new land. It will be a bad thing if it dies, and a worse thing if it takes you with it! Look at me, Woman of the West! You have never been lazy before! You must work *harder!*"

In a stupor of pain and exhaustion, her entire body was trembling as she crumpled forward, bent double against the agony of yet another contraction. Blood and fluid gushed again from her body, and still the child would not be born.

"Stand back and away!" Zhoonali's command was for Wallah as the old woman took the matron's place and reached out with taloned hands to part the curtain of black hair that had fallen before Lonit's face.

"This goes on too long. A woman can only take so much. You are young and strong. You have given life before, and if the forces of Creation allow it, you will give life again. But now the spirits have spoken with the voices of wolves—a very bad omen. The life in your belly must be taken now, before it *is* life."

Lonit blinked. The contraction was easing a little, just enough to give her time to focus her thoughts. The old woman's words had been spoken so softly, but with threat. She began to understand that Zhoonali was speaking of killing her unborn child.

Lonit stared at the old woman. She could see the pores in the creases at the sides of her wide, flat nose, and the painted patterns around her smoke-reddened, rheumy eyes had smudged and run together. But somewhere in that haggard, time-scarred face, the ghost of long-lost beauty lingered, and Lonit was not surprised to see genuine and deeply felt pity in the dirty, desiccated features. Zhoonali had borne many children, but only one had survived to offer comfort to her in her old age. The old woman was no stranger to pain or to death.

"No . . ." She sighed the word, moving back from the old woman and wrapping her long, slender arms protectively about the great, swollen mound of her belly. This was *her* baby! When her pains had first begun, a new star had shown itself above the western horizon. *A new star!* A tiny, glimmering, golden eye with a bright whisk of a coltish tail! It was the best of omens! The magic man, Karana, had said so.

*Karana.* Where was Karana? He should be here now, outside the hut of blood, making magic smokes, dancing magic dances, chanting magic chants for one who was as a sister to him. Had he left the encampment again, to seek the counsel of mammoths? Were Zhoonali and those loyal to her right about him? Was he too young and unreliable for the responsibilities of his position?

Lonit moaned. Within her belly, the baby moved. With or without omens or the presence of the magic man, her child lived, and Zhoonali had no right to speak of ending its life. The child would live or die according to the will of the forces of Creation. Apart from this, only its father and the magic man had the right to deny it a place within the band. This baby was Torka's child—perhaps Torka's *son*! And what man with only daughters at his fire circle would deny life to a son!

Pain was rising in her again, cresting, then crashing as Lonit felt her back and hips rent apart. It was excruciating, but she had no wish to evade it. This time when she gritted her teeth and closed her eyes, she did not think of wolves or spirits. She thought of her man. She thought of his child. *Their* child. And with a fully human cry, she bore down on the pain, pushing so hard that the world seemed to crack open all around her. She screamed until it seemed that her pain screamed back at her as she fell gratefully into darkness, into a thick, all-encompassing black lake of oblivion in which she would have drowned . . . but for the cry of a child. Her child!

"A male child!" The voice of Wallah was as full of pride as though she announced the birth of one of her own.

Relieved, Lonit managed a brief moaning tremor of a laugh. At last. She would look upon her infant and hold it to her breast! She had given birth to a son! Karana was right; the new star *had* been a good omen! Torka would be so proud!

She tried to open her eyes but failed; her lids were

too heavy. It did not matter. The long ordeal of childbirth was over. The pain was over. The midwives were cleansing her, stroking her back. Old Zhoonali was gently kneading her belly, seeking to purge it of the afterbirth.

Strange: Her abdomen still felt swollen, and she could have sworn that the baby still moved and kicked within her.

But the black lake of oblivion was closing over her again. It was warm. It was deep. It was welcoming. It was good to drift in it, listening in supreme contentment as the midwives fussed around her.

Then she heard Zhoonali sadly say, "The infant son of Torka is strong and sound. The first infant born in this new and forbidden land is more beautiful than any boy this woman has ever seen. It is a pity that this child must die."

*Lonit bears twin sons, Manaravak and Umak. Because twins are considered bad luck by Zhoonali, the elderly midwife steals Manaravak and exposes him on a cliffside to die. Before Torka can search for the infant, the wanawut, a huge, pre-Neanderthal hominid, finds the bady and takes him away to her cave.*

## WALKERS OF THE WIND

*After being raised by the wanawut for ten years, Manaravak is reunited with his family. But a deadly rivalry erupts between him and Umak over the affections of lovely Naya, who enjoys being the center of attention. Addicted to an aphrodisiac berry that causes hallucinations, the girl unwittingly worsens the competition and strife.*

Naya ran on, clasping a tiny hand across her mouth lest her laughter reveal her knowledge that she was being watched and followed by . . .

"Umak! *And* Manaravak!"

As long as the twin sons of the headman were near, no harm could come to her.

Why did they follow? For how long had they been watching her? Had they seen her dance naked beneath the sun? Had the sight of her childlike little body been so amusing that the sound she had heard was not a sneeze but an attempt to stifle their own laughter?

Without warning, the thong ties to Naya's right boot came loose, tripped her, and sent her sprawling. She lay still, unhurt, and cast a glance back over her shoulder. Yes. The twins were still within the grass now, with the dog between them. The corners of Naya's lips turned upward with satisfaction because Demmi was not with them. The twins' older sister was too big and too bold for a proper female. No doubt she was off tracking the bear with the other hunters. Summer Moon, the headman's eldest daughter, showed none of these faults, and neither did Swan, the youngest of the threesome. Demmi was Manaravak's constant shadow, and Naya half hoped that the young woman would run afoul of the great bear and never return to the People.

*Manaravak!* His name formed upon Naya's tongue, as complex and beautiful as the man to whom it belonged—a man who would be her man someday, when and *if* she ever grew up! With the berry necklace held between her teeth, she sat up, tied her moccasin thongs, and ran on toward the lake. She could see Grek and the others and hear their laughter. How cool the water looked! Naya hurried on, wondering if the brothers were still following her.

She stopped, turned, and planted her little feet wide. Yielding to laughter, she put her hands upon her hips, thrust her minuscule breasts forward, and worked her hips as though movement might cool the sudden, unfamiliar, and deliciously pleasant warmth that was throbbing within her loins.

"*Naya!*" Pure anger heated old Grek's tone as he roared out at her.

Turning, she frowned. So her grandfather had seen her at last! It was about time! On either side of him nine-year-old Tankh and eight-year-old Chuk, the bear-bodied boys whom he had sired through his much younger woman, Iana, clutched their boy-sized spears and looked up at him, amazed by the strength and resonance of his roar.

"Naya, how long have you been alone? Where are your clothes and your gathering basket, little girl? Answer!"

Below the crest of the ridge, the hunters paused as their headman dropped to one knee and laid his hand upon the earth.

There it was again—the sign of the bear, and of something else. He watched, listened, and waited, but no matter how hard he tried to define the warning within his brain, it refused to reveal itself.

"Torka? What is it?"

He raised a hand to silence the hunter Simu. A moment passed. Whatever had raised the hackles on his neck was gone. And now a real and immediate danger threatened them all: the great, plundering bear. All day he and the others had been searching for it. He rose and walked across the ridge until he knelt again, and with his left hand upon the earth and his right hand curled around the hafts of his spears, he saw that bear sign was fresh. The newly scattered scree revealed a massive imprint that lay bared to the sun, unmarred by the crossing of insect tracks or by the settling of dust. Beneath that massive print lay another—a much smaller, human imprint that turned him cold with dread.

At his back, his daughter Demmi stood beside Simu and his sons, Dak and young Nantu. Silent and motionless in the wind, the foursome awaited his word.

It came: "Here the great one slipped, fought for footing, and fell. She slid and then rose again, followed by her cubs, into the country of much grass."

"But that is where Grek has led the women and children!" Nantu's exlamation was as full of fear as it was loud.

"Silence!" Simu's reprimand withered his eleven-year-old son.

"I'm sorry," the boy said. "I did not mean to speak."

Simu, not a man well-known for patience, gave his younger son a hard shove to the shoulder. "Do you think that the headman of the People needs a boy to remind him of the whereabouts of the women and children of his band?"

Demmi came forward to kneel beside Torka. "Is there sign of Manaravak?" Her voice was tight with stress.

Torka looked into Demmi's worry-shaded dark eyes. He saw much of his beloved woman, Lonit, in the face of his daughter: the wide brow; the narrow, high-bridged nose; the round, deeply lidded eyes that were so like those of an antelope. These features Lonit had shared with all three of her girls, as well as with Umak, the firstborn of her twins. Of Torka's children only Manaravak and Sayanah, seven winters old and the son last born to Lonit, resembled the headman. Their fourth daughter had lived just long enough to be named, but Torka had looked upon her face and known that if the forces of Creation allowed her to be born into the world again, she would carry the look of her mother. A cold, fleeting mist of mourning chilled him.

Demmi leaned closer and put a strong, sun-browned hand over his own. "Father, is there sign of Manaravak?"

The mists within Torka's mind cleared. He nodded but could barely find the heart to speak as he looked into her distraught face. Demmi, even more than Lonit, had taught Manaravak to speak, live, and think as a human being when he had first returned to his people from the wild. From the moment that she had set eyes upon her long-lost younger brother, the girl had been fiercely protective and possessive of his affection. It was not unusual for them to know each other's thoughts, as though their ability to communicate transcended the bonds of flesh, as though their blood was one blood, and their spirits one spirit.

"Father, please, have you found any sign that he has come this way? One moment he was behind me; the next he was gone. It is not like Manaravak to leave my side without—"

"*Your* side?" Dak's query was pincer sharp. "He left us *all*, woman! Forgive me, Torka, but if we had needed Manaravak, where would he have been, eh? And you, Demmi, what is the matter with you? Soon Manaravak will take a woman of his own! It is about time that you stopped mothering him."

She glared at Dak coldly. "I am of the People. Manaravak is my brother. Ours is a bond of blood and heart and spirit. You . . . what are you to me? I sit at your fire only because this is a small band that needs children to assure its future, and it seems that a woman cannot make them by herself!"

"Demmi!" Torka sent her shrinking back like a scolded child. "Enough! This is no time for you and Dak to set to your endless bickering." Beneath his headband of lion skin, Torka's brow furrowed as he appraised the young hunter. Dak was as solidly put together as a well-made sledge and, like Simu, his father, every bit as useful to the band. He was an exemplary hunter and had proved to be a caring father to Kharn, the little son Demmi had born to him three long autumns before.

But although Dak was strong of arm and fleet of foot, steady of hand and disposition, at twenty he was two summers younger than Demmi and only a single summer older than the twins. Unfortunately, as far as Torka was concerned, Simu's elder son had yet to exhibit any imagination and was overly possessive and resentful of his woman's affection and concern for her brother.

"Come, Dak," Torka invited. "Kneel beside me and Demmi. Use your eyes *and* your head, man. Do you see it? The track of the man is overlaid by the imprint of the bear. Your woman has just cause for concern on Manaravak's behalf."

Dak glowered down at the ground, leaned low, then nodded solemnly. "The bear *follows* Manaravak!"

"Yes," confirmed Torka. "And Manaravak follows Umak, who follows Grek, the women, and children."

"And now we will follow them all!" blurted Nantu.

"Nantu is right," said Torka, rising and loping forward into the wind without looking back. "Come. Hurry! We have no time to lose!"

*Torka, who has always insisted that the People are One, must now divide his band to prevent his twin sons from killing each other. As Manaravak and his followers go in one direction and Umak and his adherents trek in another, Lonit and Torka walk eastward, into the face of the rising sun. Torka has passed the responsibility of leadership to his boys, and now he and his "always and forever woman" seek their destiny alone, having been the parents of countless generations of Americans.*

Unsurpassed in scope and authenticity, **The First Americans** calls forth the ice age of long ago, dramatically recreating the harsh life led by the people who lived then. To journey Beyond the Sea of Ice, through the Corridor of Storms and into the Forbidden Land, these Walkers of the Wind display a raw courage needed to survive in this primeval land. Theirs is truly an inspiring story worthy of The First Americans.

*In Volume Five of THE FIRST AMERICANS series, THE SACRED STONES, the descendants of Manaravak and Umak—gentle food gatherers of the Southwest and the buffalo hunters of the Plains—face a fierce enemy who carries the blood of the evil Navahk. Demanding human sacrifices, the People of the Watching Star introduce violence into a land of peace, to bands who have never been forced to defend themselves.*

Read all five volumes of this stirring saga, available wherever Bantam paperbacks are sold!

From the creator of WAGONS WEST

The

# HOLTS

*An American
Dynasty*

## OREGON LEGACY
An epic adventure emblazoned with the courage and passion of a legendary family—inheritors of a fighting spirit and an unconquerable dream.
❏ 28248-4  $4.50/$5.50 in Canada

## OKLAHOMA PRIDE
America's passionate pioneer family heads for new adventure on the last western frontier.
❏ 28446-0  $4.50/$5.50 in Canada

## CAROLINA COURAGE
The saga continues in a violence-torn land as hearts and minds catch fire with an indomitable spirit.
❏ 28756-7  $4.95/$5.95 in Canada

## CALIFORNIA GLORY
Passion and pride sweep a great American family into danger from an enemy outside... and desires within.
❏ 28970-5  $4.99/$5.99 in Canada

## HAWAII HERITAGE
The pioneer spirit lives on as an island is swept into bloody revolution.
❏ 29414-8  $4.99/$5.99 in Canada

## SIERRA TRIUMPH
A battle that goes beyond that of the sexes challenges the ideals of a nation and one remarkable family.
❏ 29750-3  $4.99/$5.99 in Canada